THE WORLD'S CLASSICS

SIR WALTER SCOTT

Redgauntlet

Edited by

KATHRYN SUTHERLAND

Oxford New York

OXFORD UNIVERSITY PRESS

Oxford University Press, Walton Street, Oxford OX2 6DP

Oxford New York Toronto
Delhi Bombay Calcutta Madras Karachi
Petaling Jaya Singapore Hong Kong Tokyo
Nairobi Dar es Salaam Cape Town
Melbourne Auckland

and associated companies in
Berlin Ibadan

Oxford is a trade mark of Oxford University Press

First published as a World's Classics paperback 1985
Reprinted 1990

British Library Cataloguing in Publication Data
Scott, Sir Walter, 1771–1832.
Redgauntlet.—(The World's classics)
I. Title II. Sutherland, Kathryn
823'.7[F] PR5315
ISBN 0–19–281668–3

Set by Herts Typesetting Services, Hertford
Printed in Great Britain by
BPCC Hazell Books
Aylesbury, Bucks

THE WORLD'S CLASSICS

REDGAUNTLET

WALTER SCOTT (1771–1832) was born in Edinburgh of a Border family. After attending the High School and University of Edinburgh he followed his father into the profession of the law, becoming an advocate (barrister) in 1792. In 1799 he was appointed Sheriff-Depute for the county of Selkirk, and in 1806 a Clerk of the Court of Session—appointments which he retained until the end of his life. His first major publication was a collection of ballads entitled *The Minstrelsy of the Scottish Border* (1802–3). He became famous as a poet with *The Lay of the Last Minstrel* (1805), *Marmion* (1808), and *The Lady of the Lake* (1810). In 1814 he published his first novel, *Waverley*, set during the Jacobite rising of 1745. Its success encouraged him to produce more historical novels, set in different countries and periods. Those set in Scotland, like *Redgauntlet*, have usually been regarded as his best. Scott's work was widely acclaimed in Europe and America. He spent the income from his writings on establishing a house and estate at Abbotsford, near Melrose. He was awarded a baronetcy by the Prince Regent in 1818. Partnership in the printing firm of James Ballantyne and Co. involved him in a financial crash in 1826. His last years were darkened by illness and the need to continue his output of writing to pay off the debts incurred. His *Journal* of those years is the most moving of his works. He died at Abbotsford in 1832; his biography was written by his son-in-law, John Gibson Lockhart.

KATHRYN SUTHERLAND is Lecturer in English Literature in the University of Manchester. She has published articles on Scott, Wordsworth, and Dickens.

THE WORLD'S CLASSICS

REDGAUNTLET

WALTER SCOTT (1771–1832) was born in Edinburgh of a Border family. After attending the High School and University of Edinburgh he followed his father into the profession of the law, becoming an advocate (barrister) in 1792. In 1799 he was appointed Sheriff-Depute for the county of Selkirk, and in 1806 a Clerk of the Court of Session—appointments which he retained until the end of his life. His first major publication was a collection of ballads entitled *The Minstrelsy of the Scottish Border* (1802–3). He became famous as a poet with *The Lay of the Last Minstrel* (1805), *Marmion* (1808), and *The Lady of the Lake* (1810). In 1814 he published his first novel, *Waverley*, set during the Jacobite rising of 1745. Its success encouraged him to produce more historical novels, set in different countries and periods. Those set in Scotland, like *Redgauntlet*, have usually been regarded as his best. Scott's work was widely acclaimed in Europe and America. He spent the income from his writings on establishing a house and estate at Abbotsford, near Melrose. He was awarded a baronetcy by the Prince Regent in 1818. Partnership in the printing firm of James Ballantyne and Co. involved him in a financial crash in 1826. His last years were darkened by illness and the need to maintain his output of writing to pay off the debts incurred. His *Journal* of those years is the most moving of his works. He died at Abbotsford in 1832. His biography was written by his son-in-law, John Gibson Lockhart.

KATHRYN SUTHERLAND is Lecturer in English Literature in the University of Manchester. She has published articles on Scott, Wordsworth, and Dickens.

CONTENTS

INTRODUCTION

In his first novel *Waverley* (1814) Scott immersed his fictional English hero in the actual events of the 1745–6 Jacobite rebellion, by which the young Stewart prince, Charles Edward, sought to overthrow Britain's established Hanoverian monarchy and reclaim the throne for his father James Francis, son of the banished James VII (of Scotland) and II (of England). Later, in *Rob Roy* (1817), his sixth novel, another Englishman finds himself embroiled in the events which led to the earlier Stewart uprising of 1715. In *Redgauntlet* (1824), the last of his major Scottish novels, Scott wrote his third and final study in fiction of Scotland's Jacobite past. Again a young Englishman is caught in the web of history, but this time the pattern is importantly changed: the Englishman proves to be Scottish, the unwitting descendant of a fanatical line of Jacobites, and the historical events he confronts prove to be illusory, fictional in every sense. Set in 1765, the narrative posits the return to Scotland at that time of Charles Edward and progresses slowly towards a third Jacobite rebellion. Unchronicled by any historian, both events prove fictionally abortive too, and the ageing prince departs without a weapon being drawn in his cause.

For Scott, as for his contemporary Wordsworth, the written products of the adult imagination find their origins in recollections of childhood; and Scott's own childhood in the 1770s and early 1780s was vividly informed by tales of the Stewart insurrections of the first half of the century. In a letter of 1806 he acknowledged:

> I became a valiant Jacobite at the age of ten years old; and, even since reason & reading came to my assistance, I have never quite got rid of the impression which the gallantry of Prince Charles made on my imagination. Certainly I will not renounce the idea of doing something to preserve these stories, and the memory of times and manners, which, though existing as it were yesterday, have so strangely vanished from our eyes.[1]

In the previous year he had projected and then temporarily abandoned the opening chapters of *Waverley; or, 'Tis Sixty Years Since* in which the outline of a semi-autobiographical hero is drawn. Working with new time laws, Scott reschedules history in the eventually completed novel, as the final chapter, the appropriately dislocated 'A Postscript, which should have been a Preface', suggests.

[1] *The Letters of Sir Walter Scott*, ed. H. J. C. Grierson, 1932–7, i, 343.

Here the martial adventures and 'wild and hair's-breadth 'scapes' of 1745–6, the kernel of the narrative, are made to exist coterminously with Scott's own lost youth ('the last twenty or twenty-five years of the eighteenth century'), whose guardians were those Jacobite warriors turned story-tellers. Scott, who tells his story 'for the purpose of preserving some idea of the ancient manners of which *I* [my italic] have witnessed the almost total extinction',[2] discovers in the events of an impersonal past the context for a self-confrontation which transforms him into history's chief recorder. The awareness of loss, inseparable in Scott's understanding from any evidence of historical progress, is referable to an equivalent in personal experience and, more specifically, to that sense of differentiation in the face of continuing existence which is symptomatic of the life of the individual in time. Through the 'objective correlative' of history,[3] Scott experienced with Wordsworth

> The vacancy between me and those days,
> Which yet have such self-presence in my mind
> That sometimes when I think of them I seem
> Two consciousnesses—conscious of myself,
> And of some other being.[4]

Hence Scott's Jacobite enthusiasm, a recurrent thread in the fabric of his texts, is less to be investigated as evidence of political equivocation behind a loyal Hanoverian façade than as signalling the temper of his essentially Romantic imagination. As late as 1831, the year before his death, he was contemplating a new undertaking, 'the personal history of Charles Edward',[5] and in the spring of 1832 on his visit to Naples and Rome in search of health he found more to interest him in the mausoleum of the Stewarts in St Peter's and the evidence of their lives in exile than in Italy's classical past.[6]

It is, then, imaginatively consistent that Scott should combine in *Redgauntlet* a Jacobite tale and his most autobiographical narrative to date, both relocated in time. With more accuracy than the resumed *Waverley*, *Redgauntlet* can be described as a tale of 'Sixty Years Since'. Set in the decade before Scott's birth, it focuses precisely on the summer of 1765 and more generally on Scotland's emergence in the

[2] *Waverley*, ch. LXXII.
[3] T. S. Eliot's phrase is used with different implications in David Daiches's pioneering article 'Scott's *Redgauntlet*' (1958), reprinted in *Walter Scott: Modern Judgements*, ed. D. D. Devlin, 1968, p. 148.
[4] *The Prelude* (1805 text), ii, 29–33.
[5] *The Journal of Sir Walter Scott*, ed. W. E. K. Anderson, 1972, p. 645.
[6] See J. G. Lockhart, *Memoirs of the Life of Sir Walter Scott, Bart.*, 2nd edn., 1839, x, 168.

1760s from an isolated, medieval society into a component state of a modern, commercial Britain. The distant Jacobite grumblings which threaten to reverse this process belong, as the novel's 1832 Introduction suggests, to a period more than ten years earlier again, to 1750–3, to the time of Charles's secret visit to London, of the Elibank Plot and Archibald Cameron's Highland mission,[7] while details in the portraits of the young heroes, Alan Fairford and Darsie Latimer, bring the narrative more than twenty years forward, to Scott's own days as a law student at Edinburgh University in the late 1780s and early 1790s. Occasionally awkward, the time-scheme has the overall appropriateness of linking memories of the passage into adult identity with the final dissolution of feudal values.

Following J. G. Lockhart, Scott's son-in-law and early biographer, critics have scrutinized the novel's autobiographical signs, its celebration and exorcism of its author's past:[8] the devoted but suffocating relationship of Saunders and Alan Fairford, mirroring Scott's troubled dealings with his own father; the portrait of the mysterious 'Green Mantle', a re-creation of Scott's traumatic early love affair; Darsie Latimer, identified with various of Scott's student friends, but also an aspect of Scott's own dual nature, the irresponsible romantic, a foil to the cautious good sense which Alan Fairford represents. Interesting as these connections may be, however, *Redgauntlet* is concerned with more problematic formulations of identity and of the relation between a sense of fiction and a sense of self. Restless in the uncongenial environment of business-obsessed, Presbyterian Edinburgh, haunted by his uncertain parentage and by early recollections of a very different world, Darsie Latimer sets off on a holiday jaunt which takes him to the Solway Firth, that stretch of water dividing Scotland at its south-west corner from England, to him forbidden territory. A mythic quest, sharing features of the traditional romance with others of Scott's narratives, the journey proves a passage into a border world in every sense.

Geographically placed between two countries, the immediate area on either side of the Solway is a testing ground where stable values disintegrate, a priori cognition is no longer verified, and events take on alarming new shapes. The detached curiosity and flippant historical judgements which Darsie assumes as the proper manner of the tourist in his early account of Dumfries will be startlingly transformed by the discovery that Robert Bruce's action there in 1306 for

[7] See pp. 5–8.

[8] See, for example, Lockhart, *Life of Scott*, i, 218, 249–53; *Journal*, p. 597 n. 2; and R. C. Gordon, *Under Which King? A Study of the Scottish Waverley Novels*, 1969, pp. 151–2.

Scotland's independence is a determining factor in his own identity.[9] The law, an arid subject of study which he gladly abandoned, is none the less an institution whose protection he confidently invokes. But here again Darsie is deceived. Confined by a man who has been, to his confusion, both 'protector' and 'oppressor',[10] he finds that the laws of neither England nor Scotland are enforced in this traditional no man's land. As Alan Fairford also must learn, when he attempts to use his brand-new legal qualifications to rescue his kidnapped friend, local officials like Provost Crosbie live a double existence: avowing allegiance to the established Hanoverian government, they have irreconcilable family ties with the Stewart past; and the Borderers themselves 'are a kind of amphibious deevils, neither land nor water beasts—neither English nor Scots—neither county nor stewartry'.[11]

Names on the Border are aliases, disguises, and nicknames, an index of hypocrisy and concealed and shifting identity. Edward Hugh Redgauntlet has 'no certain name',[12] and is called variously 'the Laird of the Lakes', Herries of Birrenswork, and Squire Ingoldsby. Maxwell of Summertrees is known as 'Pate-in-Peril', and Thomas Trumbull as Tam Turnpenny. The Jacobite Prince Charles Edward, the King, the Chevalier or the Pretender, depending on the speaker's political sympathies, is also the Catholic priest Father Buonaventure and the Wanderer; and Nanty Ewart, the drunken smuggler, compounds the confusion by drawing attention to the possible extension of his own name to Stewart.[13] Even Lilias Redgauntlet, eventually discovered to be Darsie Latimer's sister, seems compelled to adopt the thin and coy disguise of 'Green Mantle', while Darsie himself, centrally preoccupied with identity, is transformed on the Border into Sir Arthur Darsie Redgauntlet. Alan Fairford, who in this world of constant variation clings significantly to his own name when challenged to adopt an alias, finds it 'deconstructed' regardless of his wishes into Fairword, Fairweather, Fairbairn, Fairport, and Fairbird.[14]

Not only identity, but experience too is subject to bewildering reformulations. *Redgauntlet* is a novel which experiments richly with its own fictionality. Its undergraduate heroes parade their classical quotations and literary allusions with self-conscious and tedious

[9] Cf. pp. 29 and 338.
[10] p. 176.
[11] p. 228.
[12] p. 72. See Mary Cullinan, 'History and Language in Scott's *Redgauntlet*', *Studies in English Literature 1500–1900*, xviii, 1978, 672–3.
[13] p. 279.
[14] pp. 271, 281, and 284.

regularity. Darsie, in particular, strains the connection between the enigmatic blanks in his own story and the biographies of characters in romance, and merits Alan's accusation that he nurses 'Quixotical expectations', conceptions of himself as 'the hero of some romantic history'.[15] Like Don Quixote, Darsie misconceives reality, making his experiences reflect the literature he has read. 'All that happens to thee gets a touch of the wonderful and the sublime from thy own rich imagination', writes his exasperated friend; and he continues, 'Didst ever see what artists call a Claude Lorraine glass, which spreads its own particular hue over the whole landscape which you see through it?—thou beholdest ordinary events just through such a medium.'[16] Seeing differently from others the same event or person—more significantly, the fact that history itself is only constructed in the mediating consciousness of the individual—is one of the novel's most important statements. For Darsie when his adventures begin in earnest, books prove sadly inadequate to experience. He is, after all, a hero only like every other novel reader. The 'novel of action', argued Edwin Muir, 'externalizes with greater power than we ourselves possess our natural desire to live dangerously and yet be safe . . . It is a fantasy of desire rather than a picture of life'.[17] Once the exploits and vicissitudes of the heroes of romance threaten to become part of external reality, then fiction loses its charms for Darsie. At the same time, his life assumes the shape of the most bizarre nightmare vision, offering as normative the irrationalities of the wildest Gothic romance. It is a predicament which others of Scott's young heroes must face; and it is, of course, a persuasive image for the passage from the untransformed everyday world to the world of the imagination. To find sense in it all Darsie's only recourse is to writing: he keeps a journal during his captivity and finds in it 'a sedative' for his 'agitated thoughts and tumultuous passions'.

> A thousand vague fears, wild expectations, and indigested schemes, hurry through one's thoughts in seasons of doubt and of danger. But by arresting them as they flit across the mind, by throwing them on paper, and even by that mechanical act compelling ourselves to consider them with scrupulous and minute attention, we may perhaps escape becoming the dupes of our own excited imagination . . .[18]

This is a total reversal of all his previous conceptions. Moreover, in suggesting a link between his well-being and his journal, 'the history

[15] p. 24.
[16] p. 46.
[17] Edwin Muir, *The Structure of the Novel*, 1957 edn., p. 23.
[18] p. 219.

of the life of an unfortunate young man', as he entitles it in true eighteenth-century fashion,[19] Darsie alerts the reader to his complicity in fiction at a deeper level than ever Quixote reached. Darsie's ancestor is not, after all, that self-deluding romancer, bound against all his desires to the unenchanted world, but Richardson's Pamela Andrews, for whom writing was an act of personal deliverance from an imprisoning and horrifyingly re-formed reality.

Samuel Richardson's novel *Pamela* was published in 1740. In January 1824 Scott's critical biography of Richardson appeared prefixed to his major works in volume six of Ballantyne's Novelist's Library, and in the spring of the same year *Redgauntlet* began to take shape. The two novels have much in common. Like a large part of *Redgauntlet*, *Pamela* is a narrative in letters and journal-form, the heroine's story in her own words. Pamela is confined at the mercy of a man whose lawless behaviour is apparently sanctioned by the law and by a network of conventional relations: not only is her oppressor, Mr B, a JP and so the law's representative, but he is also a member of the gentry and she his mother's waiting-maid whom no social code will protect. Similarly, Hugh Redgauntlet may be an attainted man, but Border justice is corrupt and Darsie is his ward, legally bound to his authority. 'Under a legal pretext, I am detained in what must be a most illegal manner', writes Darsie.[20] In comparable dilemmas, both hero and heroine write in an attempt to master those experiences which threaten to master them and annihilate personal autonomy. Writing for their lives in the midst of turbulent events, they are conscious of the material requirements for the act of writing—privacy, the 'weapons' of pen, ink, and paper, the presence of a reader—those conditions which sustain the narrative illusion but which normally do not form its subject.[21]

This was Richardson's customary method as a novelist, but *Redgauntlet* is unique among Scott's fictions, which apart from *Rob Roy* and the long introductory section to *Chronicles of the Canongate* (1827), both first-person retrospective accounts, are told by an omniscient third-person narrator. The novel-in-letters was much in vogue in the second half of the eighteenth century and coincides neatly with *Redgauntlet*'s internal dating, but the form was unfashionable in the 1820s. *Redgauntlet* appeared anonymously, Scott's usual practice, in June 1824 and was given a cool reception by the reviewers and reading public. Lady Louisa Stuart, his friend and one

[19] p. 161.
[20] p. 217.
[21] Cf., for example, pp. 180–1; and *Pamela*, ed. Margaret Doody and Peter Sabor, Penguin English Library, 1980, p. 150.

of his acutest contemporary critics, wrote to Scott on 29 June with her comments on the new work:

It has taken my fancy very particularly, though . . . I could almost wonder why, for there is no story in it, no love, no hero unless Redgauntlet himself who would be such a one as the Devil in Milton . . .[22]

The absence of a basic, orderly sequence of events has been one of the main criticisms levelled against Scott's novels since the time when he became one of his own earliest critics. Defending the irregularities of his plots in the fictive context of the 'Introductory Epistle' to *The Fortunes of Nigel* (1822), Scott invoked the eighteenth-century precedents of Smollett and Le Sage who

have written rather a history of the miscellaneous adventures which befall an individual in the course of life, than the plot of a regular and connected epopeia, where every step brings us a point nearer to the final catastrophe. These great masters have been satisfied if they amused the reader upon the road, though the conclusion only arrived because the tale must have an end, just as the traveller alights at the inn because it is evening.[23]

The scant respect Scott has been awarded among a wide educated and academic readership in the twentieth century comes down to just this—the apparent formlessness of his narratives, as distinct, for example, from the intricately reworked structures of his contemporary Jane Austen. E. M. Forster and F. R. Leavis can take much of the blame for undervaluing Scott's greatest talent of story-telling for its own sake. Forster, who detested story, dismissed Scott rather wittily for that sad defect: 'Who shall tell us a story? Sir Walter Scott of course.'[24] Leavis, with more missionary zeal and a lower tolerance of fiction altogether, remarked in *The Great Tradition*:

Scott was primarily a kind of inspired folk-lorist . . . He was a great and very intelligent man; but, not having the creative writer's interest in literature, he made no serious attempt to work out his own form and break away from the bad tradition of the eighteenth-century romance.[25]

As the writings of Northrop Frye and Frank Kermode among others attest, however, an educated enjoyment of story has begun to generate a more complex framework within which to explore its peculiar authority; and Scott's novels can only benefit from this. In particular, the considered creative and critical principles lying

[22] National Library of Scotland MS 3898, fo. 244.
[23] *The Fortunes of Nigel*, 1822, I, xv.
[24] E. M. Forster. *Aspects of the Novel*, Pelican, 1962, p. 38.
[25] F. R. Leavis, *The Great Tradition*, Pelican, 1972, p. 14 n.

unassumingly behind those simple comments on Smollett and Le Sage may reach some attentive ears.

Redgauntlet takes narrative invention as its subject and firmly declines to accommodate the now traditional if restrictive critical distinction between 'story' and 'plot' by refusing to concentrate the details of its telling around some single originating structure which they can be said to illuminate or complicate. In this Scott is a true story-teller as Walter Benjamin, the Marxist critic, defines the story-teller:

> it is half the art of story-telling to keep a story free from explanation as one reproduces it . . . The most extraordinary things, marvellous things, are related with the greatest accuracy, but the psychological connection of the events is not forced on the reader. It is left up to him to interpret things the way he understands them, and thus the narrative achieves an amplitude that information lacks.[26]

When Darsie writes in his journal of 'the rage of narration' which besets him in every peril,[27] he points to the novel's essentially revisionary structure. Itself a record of history (the preparations for a third Jacobite rebellion) unfolding within a specific temporal dimension (the summer of 1765), *Redgauntlet* distinguishes the real from the illusory, its true centre of interest from its merely incidental concerns, through a progressive redescription of its materials. Moving from a novel-in-letters, to a third-person narrative, back to a form of personal correspondence, a journal, and subsequently back again to a third-person narrative, it establishes a world in which reality is a matter of differing perception and in which all its major characters have their perceptions authorized by their powers as story-tellers. Darsie's early plea to his friend to 'make up my history'[28] is replaced by his own 'history of a little adventure which befell me';[29] into that is interpolated Wandering Willie's tale of a slice of Redgauntlet history, which is in its turn adjusted in the light of Hugh Redgauntlet's account of the much earlier Alberick Redgauntlet and the medieval wars for Scotland's independence; that again is to be set against Pate-in-Peril's old soldier's tale of escape after Culloden, which is soon followed by Nanty Ewart's fragment of autobiography and by Lilias Redgauntlet's final episode of family history; and interpolated at various points is the tale of Peter Peebles's law-suit, begun, as Peebles himself emphasizes, in the

[26] Walter Benjamin, 'The Story-teller: Reflections on the Works of Nikolai Leskov', in *Illuminations*, Fontana, 1973, p. 89.

[27] p. 169.

[28] p. 17.

[29] p. 29.

year of 'the Grand Rebellion' of 1745.[30] The novel only ends, as Scott remarked of the romances of Smollett and Le Sage, because the travellers stop travelling and alight at the inn—Father Crackenthorp's inn on the English side of the Solway, to be exact. What never comes is the pre-emptive narrative which will draw together all these disparate narratives in a moment of shared illumination and verification. For the anticipated point of convergence for tales and tellers—the inception of a third Jacobite rebellion—is an event which never happens and a tale which cannot therefore be told. The novel's 'true centre' turns out to be story-telling itself—how stories are told and received. Significantly, it is a subject only understood in the withholding of the ultimate story.

The impossibility of disentangling fact from fiction, historiography from narrative technique, the belief that to recount what has passed constitutes an act akin to literary fabrication, justify the dominance of interpretation over event in *Redgauntlet*. In this respect, 'Wandering Willie's Tale' is paradigmatic. Seen by some critics as encapsulating the novel's thematic concerns and isolated from its surroundings by others, as one of the finest short stories in the language, it is about the meeting of inner and outer worlds. The tale of a tenant, Willie's grandfather Steenie Steenson, who goes to hell to claim from his landlord, Sir Robert Redgauntlet, a rent-receipt, it refuses precise classification. Neither documented history nor simply superstition, neither within the experience of its teller nor completely uncoloured by personal interest, its authority rests with a drunken man to whom it may have happened or who may have dreamed it. One critic who has examined the evidence for Scott's careful revision of the tale confirms the level of teasing discrepancy admitted to its final form:[31] was it, for example, Steenie or the old servant Hutcheon who saw the devil (or was it the monkey Major Weir that they saw) sitting (or was he capering) on Sir Robert Redgauntlet's coffin? At different points different readings are given. To move from small to large, what the novel as a whole comprises is a series of distinct but locally effective accounts of the past which are modified, even overturned, by the larger structuring principles of parallel and juxtaposition, causing each added narrative to set up corresponding reverberations in the others.

Hugh Redgauntlet's understanding of history as the working out of inevitable destiny in the lives of men is as tyrannical and narrowly hereditary as his notions of kingship; and believing in the necessary

[30] p. 198.

[31] See Mary Lascelles, 'Scott and the Art of Revision', in *Notions and Facts*, 1972, especially pp. 226–8.

accomplishment of the family curse—'that the cause which they espoused should never prosper'[32]—he reads events in its light. But Redgauntlet family history provides another reading of the curse, as 'Wandering Willie's Tale' reveals. When Sir Robert dies he is succeeded by a son, Sir John, a man of very different interests and loyalties. Sir Robert had been a Royalist soldier during the Civil War, and he remained a bloodthirsty and unrepentant survivor of the old Stewart order. His son, a smooth-talking city advocate, has made his peace with the post-Revolution settlement and subsequently plays his part in engineering the Union of 1707, by which Scotland gained participation in the English economy but lost a separate parliament and along with it the power to choose a different king from England and to pursue policies inimical to English interests. Willie comments, 'if his father could have come out of his grave, he would have brained him for it on his awn hearthstane'.[33] The detail, though extraneous to Willie's main concern, is a significant one: embedded in his supernatural narrative is discovered another tale, of a father and son on opposite sides over Scotland's independence; and it is that which will form the subject of Hugh Redgauntlet's aetiological legend of the fourteenth-century Alberick Redgauntlet.

In the struggle for the Scottish crown Alberick supports David Bruce's independent tenure while his son has thrown in his lot with the English-backed Edward Balliol. Face to face after Edward's flight from Annan, father accidentally kills son by a blow to the forehead from his horse's hoof.[34] So originates the horseshoe frown which is said to be transmitted from father to son, on to Darsie Latimer. What these highlighted moments of history suggest as the family curse, and what Hugh Redgauntlet fails to read, is that each generation of Redgauntlets will rebel against the last. Viewed in this way, Darsie's adherence to the victorious Hanoverian side has not, as his Jacobite uncle imagines,[35] broken the curse but fulfilled it. That this switching of allegiance is no longer the prelude to catastrophe derives from the spirit of comedy which dominates the novel's closing scenes and carefully restores the past to the future in which Scott is writing.[36] General Campbell's prescient remark in his role as fairy godfather—that 'Jacobite will be henceforward no

[32] p. 211.
[33] p. 106.
[34] p. 210.
[35] p. 399.
[36] There are exceptions of course: Nanty Ewart's tragic history remains untransformed. His conviction, comparable to the troubled father–son

longer a party name'[37]—promises tolerance and heralds an end to political division. The contemporary fears which Dr Dryasdust reports were rife in this forgiving atmosphere—that the young King George III 'might himself be induced to become one of the Stewarts' faction'[38]—are ultimately proved unfounded, but in the comic transformation of Scotland's cursed history *his* son plays a leading role: a nationalistic fervour which could be quickened, as it was in 1822, at the sight of a fat George IV entering Edinburgh in kilt and flesh-pink stockings suggests not tragedy but pantomime as its proper medium.

Hugh Redgauntlet's belief in a hereditary curse is the belief that in history everything recurs, and it is a view which the novel's interlinked episodic structure endorses. But the endorsement is ironic: events recur in *Redgauntlet* in a spirit dangerously close to mockery. That such is the typical course of history was to be suggested by Karl Marx in 1852 in *The Eighteenth Brumaire of Louis Bonaparte*, where he notes that those social oppositions which surface as tragic conflict in one generation will often, if repeated in a later age, become the subject of comedy. It is a critical commonplace that Scott's novels enact the confrontation and displacement of an older heroic world by the necessary laws of progress as embodied in the new.[39] That older world is glamorous, often brutal; the new is cautious, often commercial. The old hero is fiercely individual, at the centre of a last desperate activity; the modern hero is peripheral, an ineffective creature, acted upon but rarely acting. These are Scott's legacies to the later nineteenth-century novel. Darsie's search for a distinguishing self—the search which so many Victorian heroes and heroines will take up—generates the novel's most complex statement about history, one which lays claim to truth through this notion of ironic inversion.

From an early stage, the problem of Darsie's identity is linked to the wider issue of Scotland's national identity (that has been the point of the interpolated tales of family history); and both, individuality and nationhood, are interwoven in the Jacobite politics of his uncle with notions of hereditary tenure and vassalage, with absolute monarchy, and ultimately with the authority of the exiled House of

relationships in the Redgauntlet family, that he is a parricide confines him irremediably to the past, and his only release is in death.

[37] p. 398.

[38] p. 400.

[39] The classic statement of this view is Alexander Welsh, *The Hero of the Waverley Novels*, 1963. See also a more recent study, George Levine, *The Realistic Imagination*, 1981, chs. 4 and 5.

Stewart. But just as the exercise of prerogative and arbitrary power has been curbed in the monarch since the 1688–9 Revolution, so too the autonomy of the individual is discovered to be outmoded and unattainable. To emphasize the point, in the process of his transformation into Sir Arthur Darsie Redgauntlet of that Ilk, heir of an ancient and noble family, Darsie first becomes a baby and then a woman. Captured during the raid on Joshua Geddes's fishing station, tied up and bundled into a cart to make the journey to England, where his uncle's legal authority over him is effective, Darsie comes near to drowning in the dangerous currents of the Solway. In a scene which repeats the details of an earlier incident, he is rescued by his mysterious captor. This time helplessness and fear rob Darsie of any vestigial heroism: 'I chattered and howled to the howling and roaring sea . . . he seized me, as if I had been a child of six months old.'[40] Once in England, his humiliation is completed when he is forced to put on female clothing as a travelling disguise:

> Darsie permitted Cristal Nixon to place over his face, and secure by a string, one of those silk masks which ladies frequently wore to preserve their complexions, when exposed to the air during long journeys on horseback. He remonstrated somewhat more vehemently against the long riding-skirt, which converted his person from the waist into the female guise, but was obliged to concede this point also.
>
> The metamorphosis was then complete . . .[41]

There are sinister aspects to Darsie's transformation: his mask is reinforced with steel and secured behind with a padlock, and his skirts have been fastened under his feet to prevent escape. Literally imprisoned in his female identity, Darsie suffers some of the tribulations of the heroine of the Gothic romance, a kind of fiction with which *Redgauntlet* has much in common. Like the realistic novel to which it is usually opposed, the Gothic romance concerns itself with life in society. But where the realistic novel espouses narrative verisimilitude in its attempt to secure and validate a commonly held view of everyday reality, in Gothic fiction 'the subjective vision *became* the crucial event . . . external reality paled before it or fused with it, but never dominated it'.[42] Preoccupied with the family as its significant social unit, the Gothic impulse runs riot in the domestic world, fascinated by those possibilities in family life which are too threatening and too little understood to be openly acknowledged in the realistic novel. Instead of charting that convergence of traditional

[40] p. 176.
[41] p. 310.
[42] Robert Kiely, *The Romantic Novel in England*, 1972, pp. 20–1.

male and female characteristics which is essential to the stability and prosperity of the family, as outlined in the realistic novels of Richardson and Jane Austen, the Gothic maximizes difference and polarizes the sexes: Gothic hero-villains are tyrannical, demonic, and monomaniacal in their energy, representing that individuality which threatens to undermine and destroy community; heroines are passive, powerless in their innocent suffering; they epitomize human helplessness in the face of seemingly random and unconnected terrors. In both cases it is the isolating, subjective nature of experience which is stressed and the accompanying abuse of family relations. It is possible to trace such a pattern in *Redgauntlet*: in the process of learning his identity, Darsie uncovers a family history which has been shaped by the early crime of a father who kills his son; he develops a romantic attachment to a woman who proves to be his sister; and he finds in his uncle and guardian a parent-figure who is both attractive and repellent, a protector and a gaoler whose final despotic act is to emasculate him.

At moments, the fascination which the ambiguous Hugh Redgauntlet exerts leads Darsie to the verge of the dark and hidden places in his own unexplored personality. One such occasion comes when, after an exchange of angry glances with his captor, Darsie catches sight of his own reflection in a mirror and is startled to see the stamp of the same horseshoe frown on both their foreheads. Recalling the incident later, he experiences 'a thrill of awe . . . not unmingled with a wild and mysterious feeling of wonder, almost amounting to pleasure'.[43] It is a moment of recognition, even complicity, between innocence and evil, victim and victor. As a psychological insight, however, it remains undeveloped.

On the whole, Darsie's need to learn about his past sits oddly with his unconcern at the details of that past. 'Indeed I hear it for the first time in my life'[44] may seem an unduly restrained response to the revelation that he is the heir to an old and rich estate; but it compares favourably with his wooden impassivity when told that his father's skull is still visible rotting over Carlisle's northern gate.[45] The fact is that Darsie's initial sense of alienation in the commercial and legal society of Edinburgh and the romantic Jacobitism of which Fairford senior early accuses him have both faded rapidly when he is faced with a distinctly different heritage and the opportunity of action in another sphere. This all makes sense as part of the novel's delineation of historical knowledge as essential to the effort to distance the past,

[43] p. 207.
[44] p. 319.
[45] pp. 338–9.

a necessity if life in the present is to be properly understood and assessed. History, Scott argues in *Redgauntlet*, needs to be confronted, not to be reactivated but to be distanced, in order to release the present. Once known, the past holds no interest for Darsie. This is only one in a series of reversals by which the novel repudiates its apparent concerns—the quest for individual identity, the possibilities for vast political upheaval and large heroic action—and returns its characters from the distorting world of subjective perception to the security of an everyday, shared reality. The process is enacted in the terms of that mocking transformation of events which, according to Marx's later analysis, characterizes the encounter of human progress with history's repetitious course.

Initially nightmarish in scope and implication, Darsie's 'metamorphosis' from male to female proves in fact to be the key to the novel's comic purpose. Arrived at Father Crackenthorp's inn, Hugh Redgauntlet hastens to secure the allegiance of the wavering band of conspirators assembled there by presenting to their number the acknowledged head of the Redgauntlet family, his nephew Darsie. As a necessary prelude, he removes Darsie's disguise, the riding-skirt and mask, trusting that 'with this feminine dress' he 'will lay aside all effeminate thoughts' and enter whole-heartedly into an enterprise which has so far drawn from him only circumspect disapproval. And he underscores his point with the injunction 'Do not blush at having worn a disguise to which kings and heroes have been reduced.'[46] The reference is specifically to Charles Edward's assumption of the clothes and identity of the Irish maidservant Betty Burke in the course of his escape after Culloden. As an exhortation to heroism it is sadly mistimed, however, and as the one certain link between past and present it is unreassuring. In 1746 female disguise may have provided the final romantic detail in the portrait of the darling prince of a heroic cause, but in 1765 it points to the essentially farcical nature of the attempt to resurrect his claim. Hugh Redgauntlet's moment of awakening to his own historical belatedness ('"Then, gentlemen," said Redgauntlet, clasping his hands together as the words burst from him, "the cause is lost for ever!"'[47]) certainly engages the compassion of narrator and reader alike; but the wider context manipulates our sympathies differently. The Prince, overshadowed by his mistress and improbably concealed inside Father Buonaventure, has become, as one critic neatly expresses it, 'a character in a bedroom farce'[48]; and the conclusion of

[46] p. 367.
[47] p. 396.
[48] R. C. Gordon, *Under Which King?*, p. 160.

the enterprise has all the ingredients of the farce's denouement, from the beskirted Darsie's fall into the arms of the gallant Alan, to the comic detentions and surprise recognitions which follow swiftly on the accommodation of all interested parties in the warren of rooms at Joe Crackenthorp's inn.

Beneath these surface extravagances lie a serious statement about society and a redefinition of heroism. Early in their correspondence, Alan Fairford rebukes Darsie for making fun of his father's undistinguished career as a volunteer in the Hanoverian army during the 1745–6 uprising. 'I tell you he has courage enough', counters Alan. Fairford senior has 'civil courage', to defend 'a righteous cause with hand and purse'. With evident foresight, Alan concludes, 'it is of little consequence to most men in this age and country, whether they ever possess military courage or no'.[49] Alan's own heroic stature derives initially from the law, and specifically from combat in the suit of Peebles versus Plainstanes. Sifting through the mass of paper which obfuscates the case, Alan's father, his valiant squire, is 'like Alpheus preceding Hercules' into the Augean stables.[50] Those differences of temperament which colour the early correspondence of the 'rational' Alan and the 'romantic' Darsie fade when Alan sets out in pursuit of his friend, 'A drop, | That in the ocean seeks another drop.'[51] The quotation from *The Comedy of Errors* draws attention not only to the difficulty of Alan's task but also to the shared identity between himself and the friend he seeks: in the Border country Alan is to display a similarly unheroic delicacy of constitution and to suffer comparable illness and confinement. But love spurs him on. Confident of that love, Darsie reacts to the news that his friend is near by quoting from Romeo's opening speech from Act V of *Romeo and Juliet*.[52] The Gothic doubling of Hugh Redgauntlet and Darsie, with its suggestion of the psychological complexities attendant upon the search for identity, only temporarily supplants the securer alliance of Darsie and Alan. 'Alan doted on his friend Darsie, even more than he loved his profession', emphasizes the narrator.[53] Romantic friendship and professional ambition in fact are inextricably linked, as the closing scenes show.

In his disavowal of that arbitrary dominance which Hugh Redgauntlet represents, Darsie shows himself to be a new kind of aristocrat, one inevitably shaped by his education in the middle-class

[49] p. 47.
[50] p. 144.
[51] p. 255.
[52] p. 196.
[53] p. 226.

world of the Fairfords. (Scott always stresses the influential role of environment in conditioning behaviour.) A man of his time in his eventual acceptance of social conformity over personal autonomy, Darsie represents a merging of upper- and middle-class interests which the tyranny of the old order has shown itself unwilling to tolerate but which, as the ambitions and preoccupations of the Fairfords and Provost Crosbie reveal, must distinguish the new age if Alan is to make his way. The merger is acted out in a comic exchange of identity which finds its source in Shakespearean romantic comedy, and which again hangs on Darsie's female disguise. Darsie has approached Lilias as a lover, but finds instead a sister, not the object of his incestuous desire (any lingering Gothicism is quickly dispelled), but, as his own female attire during the recognition scene suggests, a sister who is no less than his own self; similarly, Alan finds in Lilias the female counterpart of his friend. The transformation has been prepared long in advance, and the commercial contract is not forgotten in the romantic. As Dr Dryasdust's conclusion to the novel states, 'Miss Lilias Redgauntlet . . . intermarried with Alan Fairford, Esq. Advocate, of Clinkdollar.'[54]

Eventually in *Redgauntlet* the farce of heroic resistance is exchanged for the comedy of human progress, for a novel of social realism. Implicit in the form as Richardson developed it, according to Terry Eagleton in a recent study, is a '"feminization" of values . . . which is closely allied with the emergence of the bourgeoisie' in the eighteenth century.[55] A similar process is traceable in this, Scott's most Richardsonian novel. While Alan's alliance with the Redgauntlets in no way threatens social upheaval or the overturning of the traditional power and patronage of the landed classes, it confirms the possibilities for renewal and advancement within the Scottish social order of the later eighteenth century. Scott himself was to benefit in the 1790s from such social mobility as did exist when, like Alan, he rose beyond his father in the middle reaches of the law to the aristocratic world of the Scottish bar.

Scott's vision of the new society is not wholly optimistic; its inhabitants are not morally unblemished. Quaker Geddes's refined commercialism has its disturbing aspects, and there is an apparently gratuitous parallel drawn between the hypocrite Trumball/Turnpenny and Alan Fairford when the narrator observes that 'Fairford despised a falsehood as much as any man, unless, perhaps,

[54] p. 400.

[55] Terry Eagleton, *The Rape of Clarissa: Writing, Sexuality and Class Struggle in Samuel Richardson*, 1982, p. 14.

as Tom Turnpenny might have said, "in the way of business".'[56] The novel's mercantile motif is pervasive and, in relation to Alan and Darsie, it operates with a high degree of ambiguity, in itself a complex indicator of the sixty-year distance across which the external narrator writes. But what is never suggested is the inadequacy of 'civil courage', nor, in spite of the presence of Peter Peebles, the bankruptcy of society's dealings with men and women, the ultimate unsatisfactoriness of the rewards it has to offer. These will be left for Dickens's heroes and heroines to discover.

[56] p. 358.

NOTE ON THE TEXT

Redgauntlet germinated from a mass of material and ideas engaging Scott's imagination in late 1823. He finished *St. Ronan's Well* in late November or early December and was busy with an article on Romance for the publisher Archibald Constable's *Encyclopaedia Britannica* and a life of the novelist Samuel Richardson for Ballantyne's Novelist's Library. The projected new novel, according to Constable's partner Robert Cadell, was 'to contain the Goblins and to be called the Witch'. But this plan was evidently either abandoned or much recast,[1] and the novel Scott began in earnest at this time was entitled 'Herries'. Not until he had made considerable progress with it did he take the advice of his friend and printer James Ballantyne and change its title to *Redgauntlet*. He writes to Ballantyne in ?March 1824:

> I think your name of Redgauntlet is excellent. One fault it may have—that of inducing people to think the work is a tale of Chivalry—and disappointment is a bad thing. Otherwise the name is a great hit.[2]

As a title *Redgauntlet* represents an important adjustment: it suggests that family history, the deeds of many Redgauntlets, will take precedence over the life of one individual.

Composed in the spring and early summer of 1824, the manuscript of *Redgauntlet*, complete but for two leaves, survives bound in a volume in the National Library of Scotland (Adv. MS 19.2.29). Written on large quarto paper, in a fluent if difficult hand, it conforms to Scott's usual method of working: a main draft of the novel filling the right-hand page of each opening and the opposite left-hand page providing corrections, small additions, and substantial further thoughts. The elaborate public and private disavowals of authorship of the novels in which Scott indulged for most of his career necessitated a complicated transmission of copy to the printing-house and back again for correction. Scott's custom was to send the manuscript in batches as he wrote it to James Ballantyne, under whose direction it was transcribed at the printing-house by an amanuensis, so that Scott's hand might not be recognized there where much of his acknowledged work—articles and editions—was

[1] See H. J. C. Grierson, *Sir Walter Scott, Bart.*, 1938, pp. 230–2; and Edgar Johnson, *Sir Walter Scott: The Great Unknown*, 1970, ii, 856–7.

[2] Scott, *Letters*, viii, 203.

also printed. Subsequently, when proofs were pulled, one set was corrected by Scott and a spare proof would receive these same corrections copied by Ballantyne.[3] A complete set of first-stage page-proofs with Scott's manuscript deletions, corrections, and additions is extant, now in the Pierpont Morgan Library, New York.[4] As Gillian Dyson notes, 'Scott is one of the first authors—certainly the first novelist—whose manuscripts and proof sheets have survived in any quantity.'[5]

Redgauntlet was published anonymously in June 1824 and was subsequently included, in slightly revised form, in *Tales and Romances of the Author of Waverley*. Appearing in three formats in 1827, this was a collection of the novels from *St. Ronan's Well* to *Woodstock*, Scott's novel output for 1824–6. Later, out of the financial ruin which struck Constable, Ballantyne, and Scott himself in 1826, grew the project for a uniform edition of all the novels. Nicknamed the 'Magnum Opus', it was to have new illustrations, introductions, historical and antiquarian notes, and revised texts. This task, among others, occupied Scott from 1828 to the last year of his life (1832). He was at work on *Redgauntlet* for the Magnum Opus edition in February 1831 and the novel was published as volumes 35 and 36 in 1832.

Conceived as a money-making venture, the Magnum Opus became a novelist's manifesto, a public acknowledgement of the authorship which had been an open secret for so long, and an examination in the face of severe illness and financial pressures of the imagination's refinement of its crude materials. Of the published editions of *Redgauntlet*, it is clear that it is the first edition and the Magnum Opus edition which have the greatest textual authority, the Magnum Opus being the last edition of his novels to be corrected by Scott; but it is equally clear, as the detailed studies made by Miss Mary Lascelles and Mr G. A. M. Wood of manuscript, proofs, and first and subsequent editions show,[6] that for Scott each stage in the text's transmission was a stage in composition or re-creation. He revised at every opportunity, not consistently but in bursts and

[3] Scott describes these elaborate precautions in the 'Magnum' edition of *Waverley*, 1829, I, xx–xxi.

[4] A photocopy of the proofs is in the Bodleian Library, Oxford (Facs. d. 94/1–3).

[5] Gillian Dyson, 'The Manuscripts and Proof Sheets of Scott's Waverley Novels', *Edinburgh Bibliographical Society Transactions*, iv (part 1), 1960, 15–42.

[6] Their work, listed in my Select Bibliography under 'Textual Studies', is of great importance to the study of *Redgauntlet* and of Scott's normal method of working. I am indebted to their findings for information here.

creatively, sometimes inserting important new readings, but sometimes merely patching up earlier inaccuracies—his own errors or the consequences of the copying and printing processes. Ultimately, no one version can be said to represent Scott's novel with perfect accuracy.

The Magnum Opus served as copy-text for all reprints of Scott's novels up to 1871; it was superseded by the Centenary edition of that year and later by the Dryburgh edition of 1892–4. Both editions were prepared for the publishers A. & C. Black with the help of interleaved copies of the novels said to have been annotated by Scott and used in his preparation of the 'Magnum' edition. The authority of the interleaved set is, however, questionable: they have not been available for inspection since they were offered for private sale in New York in the 1930s.[7]

This edition of *Redgauntlet* is a reprint of the text of the 'Magnum' edition of 1832. Scott's notes to that edition, located at the foot of the page if short or at the end of the relevant chapter if long, have all been moved to the end of the novel, as have a few notes which originally appeared at the foot of the page in the first edition of 1824. Scott's notes are indicated in the text by superscript numerals. My own explanatory notes, also located at the end of the novel, are signalled in the text by asterisks. In resetting, the orthography of Scott's Latin has been regularized according to accepted modern usage, double quotation marks for a first quotation have been replaced by single ones, and the following errors have been corrected in the text, in most cases the new reading representing a return to the first edition reading:

p. 29, l. 24	trivialties/trivialities
p. 34, l. 3	Scot's close/Scot's Close
p. 70, l. 6	afternoon/after noon
p. 76, l. 6	John Scot/John Scott
p. 81, l. 36	Campbell's close-foot/Campbell's Close-foot
p. 103, l. 26	back-lilt/back-lill
p. 123, l. 21	struck up to/struck up
p. 162, l. 6	detailed/detail
p. 176, l. 18	supporting with one/supporting me with one
pp. 198–9, l. 1	like yoursell, though they are nae sae keen/like yoursell, Birrenswork. I trust ye hae gotten out your pardon, though they are nae sae keen [It is clear from a comparison with the first

[7] The set is described in *Sir Walter Scott's 'Magnum Opus'*, New York, Printed for Temple Scott, Inc., 1930.

edition that this is a necessary restoration for the sense of the passage.]

p. 221, l. 11	O whistle/Oh whistle
p. 242, l. 4	shakle-bones/shackle-bones
p. 262, ll. 6–8	availing himself of a ladder, seven feet from the ground/availing himself of a ladder, removed an old picture, which showed a door about seven feet from the ground [It is clear from a comparison with the first edition that this is a necessary restoration for the sense of the passage.]
p. 271, l. 9	Fairford/Fairword [It is clear from a comparison with the first edition that this alteration of Alan's name is intentional. It is followed in both editions by further variations on Fairford.]
p. 292, l. 8	young/younger
p. 353, l. 5	refounding/refunding

SELECT BIBLIOGRAPHY

SIR WALTER SCOTT: LETTERS, BIOGRAPHIES, ETC.

The Letters of Sir Walter Scott, ed. H. J. C. Grierson, 12 vols., 1932–7.
James C. Corson, *Notes and Index to Sir Herbert Grierson's Edition of the Letters of Sir Walter Scott*, 1979.
The Journal of Sir Walter Scott, ed. W. E. K. Anderson, 1972.
J. G. Lockhart, *Memoirs of the Life of Sir Walter Scott, Bart.*, 2nd edn., 10 vols., 1839.
John Buchan, *Sir Walter Scott*, 1932.
H. J. C. Grierson, *Sir Walter Scott, Bart.*, 1938.
Edgar Johnson, *Sir Walter Scott: The Great Unknown*, 2 vols., 1970.

EARLY CRITICISM

Thomas Carlyle, 'Sir Walter Scott' (1838), in *Critical and Miscellaneous Essays*, 1899, iv, 22–87.
James C. Corson, *A Bibliography of Sir Walter Scott*, 1797–1940, 1943.
John O. Hayden, *Scott: The Critical Heritage*, 1970.
William Hazlitt, 'Sir Walter Scott' (1824), in *The Spirit of the Age*, 1825.
James T. Hillhouse, *The Waverley Novels and their Critics*, 1936.

RECENT CRITICISM: GENERAL

For a comprehensive list of books and articles published between 1932 and 1977, see Jill Rubenstein, *Sir Walter Scott, A Reference Guide*, 1978.
A. O. J. Cockshut, *The Achievement of Walter Scott*, 1969.
Daniel Cottom, 'The Waverley Novels: Superstition and the Enchanted Reader', *English Literary History*, xlvii, 1980, 80–102.
Thomas Crawford, *Scott* (Writers and Critics Series), 1965.
David Daiches, 'Scott's Achievement as a Novelist', *Nineteenth-Century Fiction*, vi, 1952, 80–95 and 153–73 (reprinted).
Donald Davie, *The Heyday of Sir Walter Scott*, 1961.
Avrom Fleishman, *The English Historical Novel*, 1971.
Robert C. Gordon, *Under Which King? A Study of the Scottish Waverley Novels*, 1969.
Francis R. Hart, *Scott's Novels: The Plotting of Historic Survival*, 1966.
Lars Hartveit, *Dream within a Dream: A Thematic Approach to Scott's Vision of Fictional Reality*, Norwegian Studies in English, xviii, 1974.

Mary Lascelles, *The Story-Teller Retrieves the Past*, 1980.
George Levine, *The Realistic Imagination*, 1981, chs. 4 and 5.
Georg Lukács, *The Historical Novel*, 1937 (English translation by H. and S. Mitchell, 1962).
Graham McMaster, *Scott and Society*, 1981.
Susan Morgan, 'Old Heroes and a New Heroine in the Waverley Novels', *English Literary History*, l, 1983, 559–85.
Richard Waswo, 'Story as Historiography in the Waverley Novels', *English Literary History*, xlvii, 1980, 304–30.
Alexander Welsh, *The Hero of the Waverley Novels*, 1963.
A. N. Wilson, *The Laird of Abbotsford: A View of Sir Walter Scott*, 1980.

REDGAUNTLET: CRITICAL STUDIES

Janet Adam Smith, '*Redgauntlet:* The Man of Law's Tale', *Times Literary Supplement*, 23 July 1971, 863–4.
James Anderson, 'Sir Walter Scott as Historical Novelist', part iv, *Studies in Scottish Literature*, v, 1967–8, 21–7.
Mary Cullinan, 'History and Language in Scott's *Redgauntlet*', *Studies in English Literature 1500–1900*, xviii, 1978, 659–75.
David Daiches, 'Scott's *Redgauntlet*', in *From Jane Austen to Joseph Conrad. Essays Collected in Memory of James T. Hillhouse*, ed. R. C. Rathburn and Martin Steinmann Jr., 1959, pp. 46–59 (reprinted).
D. D. Devlin, 'Scott and *Redgauntlet*', *Review of English Literature*, iv, 1963, 91–103.
Joan S. Elbers, 'A Contrast of Fictional Worlds: *Redgauntlet* and *St. Ronan's Well*', *Scottish Literary Journal*, vii, 1980, 155–66.
P. D. Garside, '*Redgauntlet* and the Topography of Progress', *Southern Review*, x, 1977, 155–73.
Patricia H. Sosnoski, 'Reading *Redgauntlet*', *Scottish Literary Journal*, vii, 1980, 145–54.

REDGAUNTLET: TEXTUAL STUDIES

Mary Lascelles, 'Scott and the Art of Revision', in *Imagined Worlds, Essays . . . in Honour of John Butt*, ed. Maynard Mack and Ian Gregor, 1968, pp. 139–56 (reprinted in Mary Lascelles, *Notions and Facts*, 1972, pp. 213–29).
G. A. M. Wood, 'The Great Reviser; or the Unknown Scott', *Ariel: A Review of International English Literature*, ii, 1971, 27–43.
——, 'The Manuscripts and Proof Sheets of *Redgauntlet*', in *Scott Bicentenary Essays*, ed. Alan Bell, 1973, pp. 160–75.
——, 'Scott's continuing revision: the printed texts of *Redgauntlet*', *The Bibliotheck*, vi, 1973, 121–98.

A CHRONOLOGY OF SIR WALTER SCOTT

1771	Born in Edinburgh, son of Walter Scott, W. S., and Anne Rutherford.
1772–3	suffered from poliomyelitis which left him lame.
1779–83	attended the High School, Edinburgh.
1783–86, 1789–92	attended classes at Edinburgh University; 1786, apprenticed to his father.
1792	admitted to Faculty of Advocates.
1796	*The Chase*, and *William and Helen*, translated from Burger, issued anonymously.
1797	married Charlotte Charpentier.
1799	*Goetz of Berlichingen*, translated from Goethe; *Tales of Terror*; appointed Sheriff-Depute of Selkirkshire.
1801	contributed to M. G. Lewis's *Tales of Wonder*.
1802–3	*The Minstrelsy of the Scottish Border*.
1804	moved to Ashestiel.
1805	*The Lay of the Last Minstrel*; entered into partnership with James Ballantyne & Co., printers; started *Waverley*.
1806	appointed a Principal Clerk of Session.
1808	*Marmion*; edition of *The Works of John Dryden*; completed Joseph Strutt's *Queen-Hoo Hall*.
1810	*The Lady of the Lake*; resumed *Waverley*, but laid it aside again.
1812	moved to Abbotsford.
1813	*Rokeby*; declined offer of Poet Laureateship.
1814	*Waverley*; edition of *The Works of Jonathan Swift*.
1815	*The Lord of the Isles*; *Guy Mannering*.
1816	*The Antiquary*; *The Black Dwarf* and *Old Mortality* (*Tales of My Landlord*, 1st series).
1817	*Rob Roy*.
1818	*The Heart of Midlothian* (*Tales of My Landlord*, 2nd series); accepted Baronetcy (gazetted 1820).
1819	*The Bride of Lammermoor* and *A Legend of Montrose* (*Tales of My Landlord*, 3rd series); *Ivanhoe*.
1820	*The Monastery*; *The Abbot*; his daughter, Sophia, married J. G. Lockhart.
1821	*Kenilworth*.
1822	*The Pirate*; *The Fortunes of Nigel*; *Peveril of the Peak*.
1823	*Quentin Durward*.

1824	*St. Ronan's Well*; *Redgauntlet*.
1825	*The Betrothed* and *The Talisman* (*Tales of the Crusaders*); began *Journal*.
1826	financial collapse, caused by the bankruptcy of Archibald Constable & Co., and James Ballantyne & Co; *Woodstock*.
1827	acknowledged authorship of Waverley novels; *Life of Napoleon*.
1827–8	*Chronicles of the Canongate* (two series).
1828–31	*Tales of a Grandfather* (four series).
1829	*Anne of Geierstein*; 'Magnum' series of Waverley Novels starts to appear.
1830	*Letters on Demonology and Witchcraft*.
1831	voyage to Mediterranean in search of health.
1832	*Count Robert of Paris* and *Castle Dangerous* (*Tales of My Landlord*, 4th series); 'Magnum' *Redgauntlet*. Died at Abbotsford, 21 September.

REDGAUNTLET

A TALE OF THE EIGHTEENTH CENTURY

★

Master, go on; and I will follow thee,
To the last gasp, with truth and loyalty.

As You Like it★

INTRODUCTION

TO

REDGAUNTLET

THE Jacobite enthusiasm of the eighteenth century, particularly during the rebellion of 1745, afforded a theme, perhaps the finest that could be selected, for fictitious composition, founded upon real or probable incident. This civil war, and its remarkable events, were remembered by the existing generation without any degree of the bitterness of spirit which seldom fails to attend internal dissension. The Highlanders, who formed the principal strength of Charles Edward's army, were an ancient and high-spirited race, peculiar in their habits of war and of peace, brave to romance, and exhibiting a character turning upon points more adapted to poetry than to the prose of real life. Their Prince, young, valiant, patient of fatigue, and despising danger, heading his army on foot in the most toilsome marches, and defeating a regular force in three battles,—all these were circumstances fascinating to the imagination, and might well be supposed to seduce young and enthusiastic minds to the cause in which they were found united, although wisdom and reason frowned upon the enterprise.*

The adventurous Prince, as is well known, proved to be one of those personages who distinguish themselves during some single and extraordinarily brilliant period of their lives, like the course of a shooting star, at which men wonder, as well on account of the briefness, as the brilliancy of its splendour. A long trace of darkness overshadowed the subsequent life of a man, who, in his youth, showed himself so capable of great undertakings; and, without the painful task of tracing his course further, we may say the latter pursuits and habits of this unhappy Prince, are those painfully evincing a broken heart, which seeks refuge from its own thoughts in sordid enjoyments.

Still, however, it was long ere Charles Edward appeared to be, perhaps it was long ere he altogether became, so much degraded from his original self; as he enjoyed for a time the lustre attending the progress and termination of his enterprise. Those who thought they discerned in his subsequent conduct an insensibility to the distresses of his followers, coupled with that egotistical attention to his own interests, which has been often attributed to the Stewart Family, and which is the natural effect of the principles of divine right in which they were brought up, were now generally considered as dissatisfied and splenetic persons, who, displeased with the issue of their adventure, and finding themselves involved in the ruins of a falling cause, indulged themselves in undeserved reproaches against their leader. Indeed, such censures were by no means frequent among those of his followers, who, if what was alleged had been just, had the best right to complain. Far the greater number of those unfortunate gentlemen suffered with the most dignified patience, and were either too proud to take notice of ill treatment on the part of their Prince, or so prudent as to be aware their complaints would meet with little sympathy from the world. It may be added, that the greater part of the banished Jacobites, and those of high rank and consequence, were not much within reach of the influence of the Prince's character and conduct, whether well regulated or otherwise.*

In the meantime, that great Jacobite conspiracy, of which the insurrection of 1745–6 was but a small part, precipitated into action on the failure of a far more general scheme, was resumed and again put into motion by the Jacobites of England, whose force had never been broken, as they had prudently avoided bringing it into the field. The surprising effect which had been produced by small means, in 1745–6, animated their hopes for more important successes, when the whole nonjuring interest of Britain, identified as it then was with great part of the landed gentlemen, should come forward to finish what had been gallantly attempted by a few Highland chiefs.*

It is probable, indeed, that the Jacobites of the day were incapable of considering that the very small scale on which the effort was made, was in one great measure the cause of its unexpected success. The remarkable speed with which the insurgents marched, the singularly good discipline which they preserved, the union and unanimity which for some time animated their councils, were all in a considerable degree produced by the smallness of their numbers. Notwithstanding the discomfiture of Charles Edward, the nonjurors of the period long continued to nurse unlawful schemes, and to drink treasonable toasts, until age stole upon them. Another generation arose, who did not share the sentiments which they cherished; and at length the sparkles of disaffection, which had long smouldered, but had never been heated enough to burst into actual flame, became entirely extinguished. But in proportion as the political enthusiasm died gradually away among men of ordinary temperament, it influenced those of warm imaginations and weak understandings, and hence wild schemes were formed, as desperate as they were adventurous.

Thus a young Scotchman of rank is said to have stooped so low as to plot the surprisal of St James's palace, and the assassination of the royal family.* While these ill-digested and desperate conspiracies were agitated among the few Jacobites who still adhered with more obstinacy to their purpose, there is no question but that other plots might have been brought to an open explosion, had it not suited the policy of Sir Robert Walpole,* rather to prevent or disable the conspirators in their projects, than to promulgate the tale of danger, which might thus have been believed to be more widely diffused than was really the case.

In one instance alone this very prudential and humane line of conduct was departed from, and the event seemed to confirm the policy of the general course. Doctor Archibald Cameron,* brother of the celebrated Donald Cameron of Lochiel, attainted for the rebellion of 1745, was found by a party of soldiers lurking with a comrade in the wilds of Loch Katrine, five or six years after the battle of Culloden, and was there seized. There were circumstances in his case, so far as was made known to the public, which attracted much compassion, and gave to the judicial proceedings against him an appearance of cold-blooded revenge on the part of government; and the following argument of a zealous Jacobite in his favour was received as conclusive by Dr Johnson, and other persons who might pretend to impartiality. Dr Cameron had never borne arms, although engaged in the Rebellion, but used his medical skill for the service, indifferently, of the wounded of both parties. His return to Scotland was ascribed exclusively to family affairs. His behaviour at the bar was decent, firm, and respectful. His wife threw herself, on three different occasions, before George II. and the members of his family, was rudely repulsed from their presence, and at length placed, it was said, in the same prison with her husband, and confined with unmanly severity.

Dr Cameron was finally executed, with all the severities of the law of treason; and his death remains in popular estimation a dark blot upon the memory of George II., being almost publicly imputed to a mean and personal hatred of Donald Cameron of Lochiel, the sufferer's heroic brother.

Yet the fact was, that whether the execution of Archibald Cameron was political or otherwise, it might certainly have been justified, had the King's ministers so pleased, upon reasons of a public nature. The unfortunate sufferer had not come to the Highlands solely upon his private affairs, as was the general belief; but it was not judged prudent by the English ministry to let it be generally known that he came to enquire about a considerable sum of money which had been remitted from France to the friends of the exiled family. He had also a commission to hold intercourse with the well known M'Pherson of Cluny, chief of the clan Vourich, whom the Chevalier* had left behind at his departure from Scotland in 1746, and who remained during ten years of proscription and danger, skulking from place to place in the Highlands, and maintaining an uninterrupted correspondence between Charles and his friends. That Dr Cameron should have held a commission to assist this chief in raking together the dispersed embers of disaffection, is in itself sufficiently natural, and, considering his political principles, in no respect dishonourable to his memory. But neither ought it to be imputed to George II., that he suffered the laws to be enforced against a person taken in the act of breaking them. When he lost his hazardous game, Dr Cameron only paid the forfeit which he must have calculated upon. The ministers, however, thought it proper to leave Dr Cameron's new schemes in concealment, lest by divulging them they had indicated the channel of communication which, it is now well known, they possessed to all the plots of Charles Edward. But it was equally ill advised and ungenerous to sacrifice the character of the king to the policy of the administration. Both points might have been gained by sparing the life of Dr Cameron after conviction, and limiting his punishment to perpetual exile.

These repeated and successive Jacobite plots rose and burst like bubbles on a fountain; and one of them, at least, the Chevalier judged of importance enough to induce him to risk himself within the dangerous precincts of the British capital. This appears from Dr King's Anecdotes of his Own Times.*

'September, 1750.—I received a note from my Lady Primrose,* who desired to see me immediately. As soon as I waited on her, she led me into her dressing-room, and presented me to ——,' [the Chevalier, doubtless.] 'If I was surprised to find him there, I was still more astonished when he acquainted me with the motives which had induced him to hazard a journey to England at this juncture. The impatience of his friends who were in exile, had formed a scheme which was impracticable; but although it had been as feasible as they had represented it to him, yet no preparation had been made, nor was any thing ready to carry it into execution. He was soon convinced that he had been deceived; and, therefore, after a stay in London of five days only, he returned to the place from whence he came.' Dr King was in 1750 a keen Jacobite, as may be inferred from the visit made by him to the Prince under such circumstances, and from his being one of that unfortunate person's chosen correspondents. He, as well as other men of sense and observation, began to despair of making their fortune in the party which they had chosen. It was indeed sufficiently dangerous; for, during the short visit just described, one of Dr King's servants remarked the stranger's likeness to Prince Charles, whom he recognised from the common busts.

The occasion taken for breaking up the Stewart interest, we shall tell in Dr King's own words:—'When he (Charles Edward) was in Scotland, he had a mistress whose name was Walkinshaw,* and whose sister was at that time, and is still, housekeeper at Leicester House. Some years after he was released from his prison, and conducted out of France, he sent for this girl, who soon acquired such a dominion over him, that she was acquainted with all his schemes, and trusted with his most secret correspondence. As soon as this was known in England, all those persons of distinction who were attached to him were greatly alarmed: they imagined that this wench had been placed in his family by the English ministers; and, considering her sister's situation, they seemed to have some ground for their suspicion; wherefore, they dispatched a gentleman to Paris, where the Prince then was, who had instructions to insist that Mrs Walkinshaw should be removed to a convent for a certain term; but her gallant absolutely refused to comply with this demand; and although Mr M'Namara, the gentleman who was sent to him, who has a natural eloquence, and an excellent understanding, urged the most cogent reasons, and used all the arts of persuasion, to induce him to part with his mistress, and even proceeded so far as to assure him, according to his instructions, that an immediate interruption of all correspondence with his most powerful friends in England, and, in short, that the ruin of his interest, which was now daily increasing, would be the infallible consequence of his refusal; yet he continued inflexible, and all M'Namara's entreaties and remonstrances were ineffectual. M'Namara staid in Paris some days beyond the time prescribed him, endeavouring to reason the Prince into a better temper; but finding him obstinately persevere in his first answer, he took his leave with concern and indignation, saying, as he passed out, "What has your family done, sir, thus to draw down the vengeance of Heaven on every branch of it, through so many ages?" It is worthy of remark, that in all the conferences which M'Namara had with the Prince on this occasion, the latter declared that it was not a violent passion, or indeed any particular regard, which attached him to Mrs Walkinshaw, and that he could see her removed from him without any concern; but he would not receive directions, in respect to his private conduct, from any man alive. When M'Namara returned to London, and reported the Prince's answer to the gentlemen who had employed him, they were astonished and confounded. However, they soon resolved on the measures which they were to pursue for the future, and determined no longer to serve a man who could not be persuaded to serve himself, and chose rather to endanger the lives of his best and most faithful friends, than part with an harlot, whom, as he often declared, he neither loved not esteemed.'

From this anecdote, the general truth of which is indubitable, the principal fault of Charles Edward's temper is sufficiently obvious. It was a high sense of his own importance, and an obstinate adherence to what he had once determined on—qualities which, if he had succeeded in his bold attempt, gave the nation little room to hope that he would have been found free from the love of prerogative and desire of arbitrary power, which characterised his unhappy grandfather.* He gave a notable instance how far this was the leading feature of his character, when, for no reasonable cause that can be assigned, he placed his own single will in opposition to the necessities of France, which, in order to purchase a peace become necessary to the kingdom, was reduced to gratify Britain by prohibiting the residence of Charles within any part of the French dominions. It was in vain that France endeavoured to lessen the disgrace of this step by making the most flattering offers, in hopes to induce the Prince of himself to anticipate this disagreeable alternative, which, if seriously enforced, as it was likely to be, he had no means whatever of resisting, by leaving the kingdom as of his own free-will. Inspired, however, by the spirit of hereditary obstinacy, Charles preferred a useless resistance to a dignified submission, and by a series of idle bravadoes, laid the French court under the necessity of arresting their late ally, and sending him to close confinement in the Bastile,* from which he was afterwards sent out of the French dominions, much in the manner in which a convict is transported to the place of his destination.

In addition to these repeated instances of a rash and inflexible temper, Dr King also adds faults alleged to belong to the Prince's character, of a kind less consonant with his noble birth and high pretensions. He is said by this author to have been avaricious, or parsimonious at least, to such a degree of meanness, as to fail, even when he had ample means, in relieving the sufferers who had lost their fortune, and sacrificed their all in his ill-fated attempt.[1] We must receive, however, with some degree of jealousy what is said by Dr King on this subject, recollecting that he had left at least, if he did not desert, the standard of the unfortunate Prince, and was not therefore a person who was likely to form the fairest estimate of his virtues and faults. We must also remember, that if the exiled Prince gave little, he had but little to give, especially considering how late he nourished the scheme of another expedition to Scotland, for which he was long endeavouring to hoard money.

The case, also, of Charles Edward must be allowed to have been a difficult one. He had to satisfy numerous persons, who, having lost their all in his cause, had, with that all, seen the extinction of hopes which they accounted nearly as good as certainties; some of these were perhaps clamorous in their applications, and certainly ill pleased with their want of success. Other parts of the Chevalier's conduct may have afforded grounds for charging him with coldness to the sufferings of his devoted followers. One of these was a sentiment which has nothing in it that is generous, but it was certainly a principle in which the young Prince was trained, and which may be too probably denominated peculiar to his family, educated in all the high notions of passive obedience and non-resistance. If the unhappy Prince gave implicit faith to the professions of statesmen holding such notions, which is implied by his whole conduct, it must have led to the natural, though ungracious inference, that the services of a subject could not, to whatever degree of ruin they might bring the individual, create a debt against his sovereign. Such a person could only boast that he had done his duty; nor was he entitled to be a claimant for a greater reward than it was convenient for the Prince to bestow, or to hold his sovereign his debtor for losses which he had sustained through his loyalty. To a certain extent the Jacobite principles inevitably led to this cold and egotistical mode of reasoning on the part of the sovereign; nor, with all our natural pity for the situation of royalty in distress, do we feel entitled to affirm that Charles did not use this opiate to his feelings, on viewing the misery of his followers, while he certainly possessed, though in no great degree, the means of affording them more relief than he practised. His own history, after leaving France, is brief and melancholy. For a time he seems to have held the firm belief that Providence, which had borne him through so many hazards, still reserved him for some distant occasion, in which he should be empowered to vindicate the honours of his birth. But opportunity after opportunity slipt by unimproved, and the death of his father gave him the fatal proof that none of the principal powers of Europe were, after that event, likely to interest themselves in his quarrel. They refused to acknowledge him under the title of the King of England, and, on his part, he declined to be then recognised as the Prince of Wales.*

Family discord came to add its sting to those of disappointed ambition; and, though a humiliating circumstance, it is generally acknowledged, that Charles Edward, the adventurous, the gallant, and the handsome, the leader of a race of pristine valour, whose romantic qualities may be said to have died along with him, had, in his latter days, yielded to those humiliating habits of intoxication, in which the meanest mortals seek to drown the recollection of their disappointments and miseries. Under such circumstances, the unhappy Prince lost the friendship even of those faithful followers who had most devoted themselves to his misfortunes, and was surrounded, with some honourable exceptions, by men of a lower description, regardless of the character which he was himself no longer able to protect.

It is a fact consistent with the author's knowledge, that persons totally unentitled to, and unfitted for, such a distinction, were presented to the unfortunate Prince in moments unfit for presentation of any kind. Amid these clouds was at length extinguished the torch which once shook itself over Britain with such terrific glare, and at last sunk in its own ashes, scarce remembered and scarce noted.*

Meantime, while the life of Charles Edward was gradually wasting in disappointed solitude, the number of those who had shared his misfortunes and dangers had shrunk into a small handful of veterans, the heroes of a tale which had been told. Most Scottish readers who can count the number of sixty years, must recollect many respected acquaintances of their youth, who, as the established phrase gently worded it, had been *out in the Forty-five*. It may be said, that their political principles and plans no longer either gained proselytes or attracted terror,—those who held them had ceased to be the subjects either of fear or opposition. Jacobites were looked upon in society as men who had proved their sincerity by sacrificing their interest to their principles; and in well-regulated companies, it was held a piece of ill-breeding to injure their feelings or ridicule the compromises by which they endeavoured to keep themselves abreast of the current of the day. Such, for example, was the evasion of a gentleman of fortune in Perthshire,* who, in having the newspapers read to him, caused the King and Queen to be designated by the initial letters of K. and Q., as if, by naming the full word, he might imply an acquiescence in the usurpation of the family of Hanover. George III., having heard of this gentleman's custom in the above and other particulars, commissioned the member for Perthshire to carry his compliments to the steady Jacobite—'that is,' said the excellent old King, 'not the compliments of the King of England, but those of the Elector of Hanover, and tell him how much I respect him for the steadiness of his principles.'

Those who remember such old men, will probably agree that the progress of time, which has withdrawn all of them from the field, has removed, at the same time, a peculiar and striking feature of ancient manners. Their love of past times, their tales of bloody battles fought against romantic odds, were all dear to the imagination, and their little idolatry of locks of hair, pictures, rings, ribbons, and other memorials of the time in which they still seemed to live, was an interesting enthusiasm; and although their political principles, had they existed in the relation of fathers, might have rendered them dangerous to the existing dynasty, yet, as we now recollect them, there could not be on the earth supposed to exist persons better qualified to sustain the capacity of innocuous and respectable grandsires.*

It was while reflecting on these things that the novel of Redgauntlet was undertaken. But various circumstances in the composition induced the author to alter its purport considerably, as it passed through his hands, and to carry the action to that point of time when the Chevalier Charles Edward, though fallen into the sere and yellow leaf, was yet meditating a second attempt, which could scarcely have been more hopeless than his first; although one, to which, as we have seen, the unfortunate Prince, at least as late as seventeen hundred and fifty-three, still looked with hope and expectation.

1st April, 1832.

tion, and their little display of Jacobitical patrons, rings, snuff-boxes, and other memorials of the time to which they still seemed to look back, was as [illegible] commissions, and affecting 'their' political principles, had they existed in the relatives of Cabinet ministers, rendered them dangerous to the existing dynasty, yet as we now reflect that there could not be on the earth supposed to exist persons better qualified to sustain the capacity of innocuous and respectable grandsires.

It was while reflecting on these things that the novel of Redgauntlet was undertaken. But various circumstances in the composition induced the author to alter its purport considerably, as it passed through his hands, and to carry the action to that point of time when the Chevalier Charles Edward, though fallen into the sere and yellow leaf, was yet meditating a second attempt, which could scarcely have been more hopeless than his first, although one to which, as we have seen, the unfortunate Prince, at least as late as seventeen hundred and fifty-three, still looked with hope and expectation.

1st April 1832

REDGAUNTLET

★

LETTER I*

DARSIE LATIMER TO ALAN FAIRFORD

Dumfries

*CUR me exanimas querelis tuis?**—In plain English, Why do you deafen me with your croaking? The disconsolate tone in which you bade me farewell at Noble-House,[2] and mounted your miserable hack to return to your law drudgery, still sounds in my ears. It seemed to say, 'Happy dog! you can ramble at pleasure over hill and dale, pursue every object of curiosity that presents itself, and relinquish the chase when it loses interest; while I, your senior and your better, must, in this brilliant season, return to my narrow chamber and my musty books.'

Such was the import of the reflections with which you saddened our parting bottle of claret, and thus I must needs interpret the terms of your melancholy adieu.

And why should this be so, Alan? Why the deuce should you not be sitting precisely opposite to me at this moment, in the same comfortable George Inn; thy heels on the fender, and thy juridical brow expanding its plications as a pun rose in your fancy? Above all, why, when I fill this very glass of wine, cannot I push the bottle to you, and say, 'Fairford, you are chased!' Why, I say, should not all this be, except because Alan Fairford has not the same true sense of friendship as Darsie Latimer, and will not regard our purses as common as well as our sentiments?

I am alone in the world; my only guardian writes to me of a large fortune, which will be mine when I reach the age of twenty-five complete; my present income is, thou knowest, more than sufficient for all my wants; and yet thou—traitor as thou art to the cause of friendship—dost deprive me of the pleasure of thy society, and submittest, besides, to self-denial on thine own part, rather than my wanderings should cost me a few guineas more! Is this regard for my purse, or for thine own pride? Is it not equally absurd and unreasonable, whichever source it springs from? For myself, I tell thee, I have, and shall have, more than enough for both. This same methodical Samuel Griffiths, of Ironmonger-Lane, Guildhall, London, whose letter arrives as duly as quarter-day, has sent me, as I told thee, double allowance for this my twenty-first birthday, and an assurance, in his brief fashion, that it will be again doubled for the succeeding years, until I enter into possession of my own property. Still I am to refrain from visiting England until my twenty-fifth year expires; and it is recommended that I shall forbear all enquiries concerning my family, and so forth, for the present.

Were it not that I recollect my poor mother in her deep widow's weeds, with a countenance that never smiled but when she looked on me—and then, in such wan and woful sort, as the sun when he glances through an April cloud—were it not, I say, that her mild and matron-like form and countenance forbid such a suspicion, I might think myself the son of some Indian director,* or rich citizen, who had more wealth than grace, and a handful of hypocrisy to boot, and who was breeding up privately, and obscurely enriching, one of whose existence he had some reason to be ashamed. But, as I said before, I think on my mother, and am convinced as much as of the existence of my own soul, that no touch of shame could arise from aught in which she was implicated. Meantime, I am wealthy, and I am alone, and why does my friend scruple to share my wealth?

Are you not my only friend? and have you not acquired a right to share my wealth? Answer me that, Alan Fairford. When I was brought from the solitude of my mother's dwelling into the tumult of the Gaits' Class at the High School*—when I was mocked for my English accent—salted with snow as a Southern—rolled in the gutter for a Saxon pock-pudding,—who, with stout arguments, and stouter blows, stood forth my defender?—why, Alan Fairford. Who beat me soundly when I brought the arrogance of an only son, and of course a spoiled urchin, to the forms of the little republic?—why, Alan. And who taught me to smoke a cobbler, pin a losen, head a bicker,* and hold the bannets?[3]—Alan, once more. If I became the pride of the Yards, and the dread of the hucksters in the High-School Wynd, it was under thy patronage; and, but for thee, I had been contented with humbly passing through the Cowgate-Port, without climbing over the top of it, and had never seen the *Kittle nine-steps*[4] nearer than from Bareford's Parks.* You taught me to keep my fingers off the weak, and to clench my fist against the strong—to carry no tales out of school—to stand forth like a true man—obey the stern order of a *Pande manum*, and endure my pawmies without wincing, like one that is determined not to be the better for them. In a word, before I knew thee, I knew nothing.*

At College* it was the same. When I was incorrigibly idle, your example and encouragement roused me to mental exertion, and showed me the way to intellectual enjoyment. You made me an historian, a metaphysician, (*invita Minerva*,*)—nay, by Heaven! you had almost made an advocate of me, as well as of yourself. Yes, rather than part with you, Alan, I attended a weary season at the Scotch Law Class; a wearier at the Civil;* and with what excellent advantage, my note-book filled with caricatures of the professors and my fellow-students, is it not yet extant to testify?

'Thus far have I held on with thee untired;'*

and, to say truth, purely and solely that I might travel the same road with thee. But it will not do, Alan. By my faith, man, I could as soon think of being one of those ingenious traders who cheat little Master Jackies on the outside of the partition with tops, balls, bats, and battledores, as a member of the long-robed fraternity within, who impose on grown country gentlemen with bouncing brocards of law.[5] Now, don't you read this to your worthy father, Alan—he loves me well enough, I know, of a Saturday night; but he thinks me but idle company for any other day of the week. And here, I suspect, lies your real objection to taking a ramble with me through the southern counties in this delicious weather. I know the good gentleman has hard thoughts of me for being so unsettled as to leave Edinburgh before the Session rises;* perhaps, too, he quarrels a little—I will not say, with my want of ancestry, but with my want of connexions. He reckons me a lone thing in this world, Alan, and so in good truth I am; and it seems a reason to him why you should not attach yourself to me, that I can claim no interest in the general herd.

Do not suppose I forget what I owe him, for permitting me to shelter for four years under his roof: My obligations to him are not the less, but the greater, if he never heartily loved me. He is angry, too, that I will not, or cannot, be a lawyer, and, with reference to you, considers my disinclination that way as *pessimi exempli*, as he might say.

But he need not be afraid that a lad of your steadiness will be influenced by such a reed shaken by the winds as I am. You will go on doubting with Dirleton, and resolving those doubts with Stewart,[6] until the cramp speech[7] has been spoken *more solito* from the corner of the bench, and with covered head—until you have sworn to defend the liberties and privileges of the College of Justice*—until the black gown is hung on your shoulders, and you are free as any of the Faculty to sue or defend. Then will I step forth, Alan, and in a character which even your father will allow may be more useful to you than had I shared this splendid termination of your legal studies. In a word, if I cannot be a counsel, I am determined to be a *client*, a sort of person without whom a lawsuit would be as dull as a supposed case. Yes, I am determined to give you your first fee. One can easily, I am assured, get into a lawsuit—it is only the getting out which is sometimes found troublesome;—and, with your kind father for an agent, and you for my counsel learned in the law, and the worshipful Master Samuel Griffiths to back me, a few sessions shall not tire my patience. In short, I will make my way into Court, even if it should cost me the committing a *delict*, or at least a *quasi delict*.—You see all is not lost of what Erskine wrote, and Wallace taught.*

Thus far I have fooled it off well enough; and yet, Alan, all is not at ease within me. I am affected with a sense of loneliness, the more depressing, that it seems to me to be a solitude peculiarly my own. In a country where all the world have a circle of consanguinity, extending to sixth cousins at least, I am a solitary individual, having only one kind heart to throb in unison with my own. If I were condemned to labour for my bread, methinks I should less regard this peculiar species of deprivation. The necessary communication of master and servant would be at least a tie which would attach me to the rest of my kind—as it is, my very independence seems to enhance the peculiarity of my situation. I am in the world as a stranger in the crowded coffeehouse, where he enters, calls for what refreshments he wants, pays his bill, and is forgotten so soon as the waiter's mouth has pronounced his 'Thank ye, sir.'

I know your good father would term this *sinning my mercies*,[8] and ask how I should feel if, instead of being able to throw down my reckoning, I were obliged to deprecate the resentment of the landlord for consuming that which I could not pay for. I cannot tell how it is; but, though this very reasonable reflection comes across me, and though I do confess that four hundred a-year in possession, eight hundred in near prospect, and the L—d knows how many hundreds more in the distance, are very pretty and comfortable things, yet I would freely give one half of them to call your father *father*, though he should scold me for my idleness every hour of the day, and to call you *brother*, though a brother whose merits would throw my own so completely into the shade.

The faint, yet not improbable belief often has come across me, that your father knows something more about my birth and natural condition than he is willing to communicate; it is so unlikely that I should have been left in Edinburgh at six years old, without any other recommendation than the regular payment of my board to old M——[9] of the High School. Before that time, as I have often told you, I have but a recollection of unbounded indulgence on my mother's part, and the most tyrannical exertion of caprice on my own. I remember still how bitterly she sighed, how vainly she strove to soothe me, while, in the full energy of despotism, I roared like ten bull calves, for something which it was impossible to procure for me. She is dead, that kind, that ill-rewarded mother! I remember the long faces—the darkened room—the black hangings—the mysterious impression made upon my mind by the hearse and mourning coaches, and the difficulty which I had to reconcile all this to the disappearance of my mother. I do not think I had before this event formed any idea of death, or that I had even heard of that final consummation of all that lives. The first acquaintance which I formed with it deprived me of my only relation.

A clergyman of venerable appearance, our only visitor, was my guide and companion in a journey of considerable length; and in the charge of another elderly man, substituted in his place, I know not how or why, I completed my journey to Scotland—and this is all I recollect.

I repeat the little history now, as I have a hundred times done before, merely because I would wring some sense out of it. Turn, then, thy sharp, wire-drawing, lawyer-like ingenuity to the same task—make up my history as though thou wert shaping the blundering allegations of some blue-bonneted, hard-headed client, into a condescendence of facts and circumstances, and thou shalt be, not my Apollo—*quid tibi cum lyra*?*—but my Lord Stair.[10]* Meanwhile, I have written myself out of my melancholy and blue devils, merely by prosing about them; so I will now converse half an hour with Roan Robin in his stall—the rascal knows me already, and snickers whenever I cross the threshold of the stable.

The black which you bestrode yesterday morning, promises to be an admirable roadster, and ambled as easily with Sam and the portmanteau, as with you and your load of law-learning. Sam promises to be steady, and has hitherto been so. No long trial, you will say. He lays the blame of former inaccuracies on evil company—the people who were at the livery-stable were too seductive, I suppose—he denies he ever did the horse injustice—would rather have wanted his own dinner, he says. In this I believe him, as Roan Robin's ribs and coat show no marks of contradiction. However, as he will meet with no saints in the inns we frequent, and as oats are sometimes as speedily converted into ale as John Barleycorn himself, I shall keep a look-out after Master Sam. Stupid fellow! had he not abused my good-nature, I might have chatted to him to keep my tongue in exercise; whereas now, I must keep him at a distance.

Do you remember what Mr Fairford said to me on this subject,—it did not become my father's son to speak in that manner to Sam's father's son? I asked you what your father could possibly know of mine; and you answered, 'As much, you supposed, as he knew of Sam's—it was a proverbial expression.' This did not quite satisfy me, though I am sure I cannot tell why it should not. But I am returning to a fruitless and exhausted subject. Do not be afraid that I shall come back on this well-trodden yet pathless field of conjecture I know nothing so useless, so utterly feeble and contemptible, as the groaning forth one's helpless lamentations into the ears of our friends.

I would fain promise you that my letters shall be as entertaining, as I am determined they shall be regular and well filled. We have an advantage over the dear friends of old, every pair of them. Neither David and Jonathan, nor Orestes and Pylades, nor Damon and Pythias*—although, in the latter case particularly, a letter by post would have been very acceptable—ever corresponded together; for they probably could not write, and certainly had neither posts nor franks to speed their effusions to each other; whereas yours, which you had from the old peer, being handled gently, and opened with precaution, may be returned to me again, and serve to make us free of his Majesty's post-office,* during the whole time of my proposed tour.[11] Mercy upon us, Alan! what letters I shall have to send you, with an account of all that I can collect, of pleasant or rare, in this wildgoose jaunt of mine! All I stipulate is, that you do not communicate them to the Scots Magazine;* for though you used, in a left-handed way, to compliment me on my attainments in the lighter branches of literature, at the expense of my deficiency in the weightier matters of the law, I am not yet audacious enough to enter the portal which the learned Ruddiman* so kindly opened for the acolytes of the Muses.—*Vale, sis memor mei.*

D. L.

P.S.—Direct to the Post-Office here. I shall leave orders to forward your letters wherever I may travel.

LETTER II

ALAN FAIRFORD TO DARSIE LATIMER

NEGATUR, my dear Darsie—you have logic and law enough to understand the word of denial. I deny your conclusion. The premises I admit, namely, that when I mounted on that infernal hack, I might utter what seemed a sigh, although I deemed it lost amid the puffs and groans of the broken-winded brute, matchless in the complication of her complaints by any save she, the poor man's mare, renowned in song, that died

'A mile aboon Dundee.'[12]

But credit me, Darsie, the sigh which escaped me, concerned thee more than myself, and regarded neither the superior mettle of your cavalry, nor your greater command of the means of travelling. I could certainly have cheerfully ridden on with you for a few days; and assure yourself I would not have hesitated to tax your better-filled purse for our joint expenses. But you know my father considers every moment taken from the law as a step down hill; and I owe much to his anxiety on my account, although its effects are sometimes troublesome. For example.

I found, on my arrival at the shop in Brown's Square,* that the old gentleman had returned that very evening, impatient, it seems, of remaining a night out of the guardianship of the domestic Lares. Having this information from James, whose brow wore rather an anxious look on the occasion, I dispatched a Highland chairman* to the livery stable with my Bucephalus, and slunk, with as little noise as might be, into my own den, where I began to mumble certain half-gnawed and not half-digested doctrines of our municipal code. I was not long seated, when my father's visage was thrust, in a peering sort of way, through the half-opened door; and withdrawn, on seeing my occupation, with a half-articulated *humph!* which seemed to convey a doubt of the seriousness of my application. If it were so, I cannot condemn him; for recollection of thee occupied me so entirely during an hour's reading, that although Stair lay before me, and notwithstanding that I turned over three or four pages, the sense of his lordship's clear and perspicuous style so far escaped me, that I had the mortification to find my labour was utterly in vain.

Ere I had brought up my lee-way, James appeared with his summons to our frugal supper—radishes, cheese, and a bottle of the old ale—only two plates though—and no chair set for Mr Darsie, by the attentive James Wilkinson. Said James, with his long face, lank hair, and very long pigtail in its leathern strap, was placed, as usual, at the back of my father's chair, upright as a wooden sentinel at the door of a puppet-show. 'You may go down, James,' said my father; and exit Wilkinson.—What is to come next? thought I; for the weather is not clear on the paternal brow.

My boots encountered his first glance of displeasure, and he asked me, with a sneer, which way I had been riding. He expected me to answer, 'Nowhere,' and would then have been at me with his usual sarcasm, touching the humour of walking in shoes at twenty shillings a pair. But I answered with composure, that I had ridden out to dinner as far as Noble-House. He started, (you know his way,) as if I had said that I had dined at Jericho; and as I did not choose to seem to observe his surprise, but continued munching my radishes in tranquillity, he broke forth in ire.

'To Noble-House, sir! and what had you to do at Noble-House, sir?—Do you remember you are studying law, sir?—that your Scots law trials are coming on, sir?—that every moment of your time just now is worth hours at another time?—and have you leisure to go to Noble-House, sir?—and to throw your books behind you for so many hours?—Had it been a turn in the Meadows,* or even a game at golf—but Noble-House, sir!'

'I went so far with Darsie Latimer, sir, to see him begin his journey.'

'Darsie Latimer?' he replied in a softened tone—'Humph!—Well, I do not blame you for being kind to Darsie Latimer; but it would have done as much good if you had walked with him as far as the toll-bar, and then made your farewells—it would have saved horse-hire—and your reckoning, too, at dinner.'

'Latimer paid that, sir,' I replied, thinking to soften the matter; but I had much better have left it unspoken.

'The reckoning, sir?' replied my father. 'And did you sponge upon any man for a reckoning? Sir, no man should enter the door of a public-house without paying his lawing.'

'I admit the general rule, sir,' I replied; 'but this was a parting-cup between Darsie and me; and I should conceive it fell under the exception of *Doch an dorroch*.'

'You think yourself a wit,' said my father, with as near an approach to a smile as ever he permits to gild the solemnity of his features; 'But I reckon you did not eat your dinner standing, like the Jews at their Passover? and it was decided in a case before the town-bailies of Cupar-Angus, when Luckie Simpson's cow* had drunk up Luckie Jameson's browst of ale, while it stood in the door to cool, that there was no damage to pay, because the crummie drank without sitting down; such being the very circumstance constituting *Doch an dorroch*, which is a standing drink, for which no reckoning is paid. Ha, sir! what says your advocateship (*fieri*) to that? *Exceptio firmat regulam**—But come, fill your glass, Alan; I am not sorry ye have shown this attention to Darsie Latimer, who is a good lad, as times go; and having now lived under my roof since he left the school, why, there is really no great matter in coming under this small obligation to him.'

As I saw my father's scruples were much softened by the consciousness of his superiority in the legal argument, I took care to accept my pardon as a matter of grace, rather than of justice; and only replied, we should feel ourselves duller of an evening, now that you were absent. I will give you my father's exact words in reply, Darsie. You know him so well, that they will not offend you; and you are also aware, that there mingles with the good man's preciseness and formality, a fund of shrewd observation and practical good sense.

'It is very true,' he said; 'Darsie was a pleasant companion—but over waggish, over waggish, Alan, and somewhat scatter-brained.—By the way, Wilkinson must get our ale bottled in English pints now, for a quart bottle is too much, night after night, for you and me, without his assistance.—But Darsie, as I was saying, is an arch lad, and somewhat light in the upper story—I wish him well through the world; but he has little solidity, Alan, little solidity.'

I scorn to desert an absent friend, Darsie, so I said for you a little more than my conscience warranted: but your defection from your legal studies had driven you far to leeward in my father's good opinion.

'Unstable as water, he shall not excel,' said my father; 'or, as the Septuagint hath it, *Effusa est sicut aqua—non crescat.** He goeth to dancing-houses, and readeth novels—*sat est.*'

I endeavoured to parry these texts by observing, that the dancing-houses amounted only to one night at La Pique's ball—the novels (so far as matter of notoriety, Darsie) to an odd volume of Tom Jones.*

'But he danced from night to morning,' replied my father, 'and he read the idle trash, which the author should have been scourged for, at least twenty times over. It was never out of his hand.'

I then hinted, that in all probability your fortune was now so easy as to dispense with your prosecuting the law any farther than you had done; and therefore you might think you had some title to amuse yourself. This was the least palatable argument of all.

'If he cannot amuse himself with the law,' said my father, snappishly, 'it is the worse for him. If he needs not law to teach him to make a fortune, I am sure he needs it to teach him how to keep one; and it would better become him to be learning this, than to be scouring the country like a land-louper, going he knows not where, to see he knows not what, and giving treats at Noble-House to fools like himself,' (an angry glance at poor me.) 'Noble-House, indeed!' he repeated, with elevated voice and sneering tone, as if there were something offensive to him in the very name, though I will venture to say that any place in which you had been extravagant enough to spend five shillings, would have stood as deep in his reprobation.

Mindful of your idea, that my father knows more of your real situation than he thinks proper to mention, I thought I would hazard a fishing observation. 'I did not see,' I said, 'how the Scottish law would be useful to a young gentleman whose fortune would seem to be vested in England.'—I really thought my father would have beat me.

'D'ye mean to come round me, sir, *per ambages*, as Counsellor Pest* says? What is it to you where Darsie Latimer's fortune is vested, or whether he hath any fortune, ay or no?—And what ill would the Scottish law do to him, though he had as much of it as either Stair or Bankton,* sir? Is not the foundation of our municipal law the ancient code of the Roman Empire, devised at a time when it was so much renowned for its civil polity, sir, and wisdom? Go to your bed, sir, after your expedition to Noble-House, and see that your lamp be burning, and your book before you, ere the sun peeps. *Ars longa, vita brevis,**—were it not a sin to call the divine science of the law by the inferior name of art.'

So my lamp did burn, dear Darsie, the next morning, though the owner took the risk of a domiciliary visitation, and lay snug in bed, trusting its glimmer might, without farther enquiry, be received as sufficient evidence of his vigilance. And now, upon this the third morning after your departure, things are but little better; for though the lamp burns in my den, and Voet on the Pandects* hath his wisdom spread open before me, yet as I only use him as a reading-desk on which to scribble this sheet of nonsense to Darsie Latimer, it is probable the vicinity will be of little furtherance to my studies.

And now, methinks, I hear thee call me an affected hypocritical varlet, who, living under such a system of distrust and restraint as my father chooses to govern by, nevertheless pretends not to envy you your freedom and independence.

Latimer, I will tell you no lies. I wish my father would allow me a little more exercise of my free will, were it but that I might feel the pleasure of doing what would please him of my own accord. A little more spare time, and a little more money to enjoy it, would, besides, neither misbecome my age nor my condition; and it is, I own, provoking to see so many in the same situation winging the air at freedom, while I sit here, caged up like a cobbler's linnet, to chant the same unvaried lesson from sunrise to sunset, not to mention the listening to so many lectures against idleness, as if I enjoyed or was making use of the means of amusement! But then I cannot at heart blame either the motive or the object of this severity. For the motive, it is and can only be my father's anxious, devoted, and unremitting affection and zeal for my improvement, with a laudable sense of the honour of the profession to which he has trained me.

As we have no near relations, the tie betwixt us is of even unusual closeness, though in itself one of the strongest which nature can form. I am, and have all along been, the exclusive object of my father's anxious hopes, and his still more anxious and engrossing fears; so what title have I to complain, although now and then these fears and hopes lead him to take a troublesome and incessant charge of all my motions? Besides, I ought to recollect, and, Darsie, I do recollect, that my father, upon various important occasions, has shown that he can be indulgent as well as strict. The leaving his old apartments in the Luckenbooths* was to him like divorcing the soul from the body; yet Dr R——* did but hint that the better air of this new district was more favourable to my health, as I was then suffering under the penalties of too rapid a growth, when he exchanged his old and beloved quarters, adjacent to the very Heart of Mid-Lothian, for one of those new tenements [entire within themselves] which modern taste has so lately introduced.—Instance also the inestimable favour which he conferred on me by receiving you into his house, when you had only the unpleasant alternative of remaining, though a grown-up lad, in the society of mere boys.[13] This was a thing so contrary to all my father's ideas of seclusion, of economy, and of the safety to my morals and industry, which he wished to attain, by preserving me from the society of other young people, that, upon my word, I am always rather astonished how I should have had the impudence to make the request, than that he should have complied with it.

Then for the object of his solicitude—Do not laugh, or hold up your hands, my good Darsie; but upon my word I like the profession to which I am in the course of being educated, and am serious in prosecuting the preliminary studies. The law is my vocation—in an especial, and, I may say, in an hereditary way, my vocation; for although I have not the honour to belong to any of the great families who form in Scotland, as in France, the noblesse of the robe, and with us, at least, carry their heads as high, or rather higher, than the noblesse of the sword,—for the former consist more frequently of the 'first-born of Egypt,'*—yet my grandfather, who, I dare say, was a most excellent person, had the honour to sign a bitter protest against the Union,* in the respectable character of town-clerk to the ancient Borough of Birlthegroat; and there is some reason—shall I say to hope, or to suspect?—that he may have been a natural son of a first cousin of the then Fairford of that Ilk, who had been long numbered among the minor barons. Now my father mounted a step higher on the ladder of legal promotion, being, as you know as well as I do, an eminent and respected Writer to his Majesty's Signet;* and I myself am destined to mount a round higher still, and wear the honoured robe which is sometimes supposed, like Charity, to cover a multitude of sins. I have, therefore, no choice but to climb upwards, since we have mounted thus high, or else to fall down at the imminent risk of my neck. So that I reconcile myself to my destiny; and while you are looking from mountain peaks at distant lakes and friths, I am, *de apicibus juris*, consoling myself with visions of crimson and scarlet gowns—with the appendages of handsome cowls, well lined with salary.

You smile, Darsie, *more tuo*, and seem to say it is little worth while to cozen one's self with such vulgar dreams: yours being, on the contrary, of a high and heroic character, bearing the same resemblance to mine, that a bench, covered with purple cloth, and plentifully loaded with session papers, does to some Gothic throne, rough with Barbaric pearl and gold. But what would you have?—*Sua quemque trahit voluptas*.* And my visions of preferment, though they may be as unsubstantial at present, are nevertheless more capable of being realized, than your aspirations after the Lord knows what. What says my father's proverb? 'Look to a gown of gold, and you will at least get a sleeve of it.' Such is my pursuit; but what dost thou look to? The chance that the mystery, as you call it, which at present overclouds your birth and connexions, will clear up into something inexpressibly and inconceivably brilliant; and this without any effort or exertion of your own, but purely by the good-will of Fortune. I know the pride and naughtiness of thy heart, and sincerely do I wish that thou hadst more beatings to thank me for, than those which thou dost acknowledge so gratefully. Then had I thumped these Quixotical expectations* out of thee, and thou hadst not, as now, conceived thyself to be the hero of some romantic history, and converted, in thy vain imagination, honest Griffiths, citizen and broker, who never bestows more than the needful upon his quarterly epistles, into some wise Alcander or sage Alquife,* the mystical and magical protector of thy peerless destiny. But I know not how it was, thy skull got harder, I think, and my knuckles became softer; not to mention that at length thou didst begin to show about thee a spark of something dangerous, which I was bound to respect at least, if I did not fear it.

And while I speak of this, it is not much amiss to advise thee to correct a little this cock-a-hoop courage of thine. I fear much that, like a hot-mettled horse, it will carry the owner into some scrape, out of which he will find it difficult to extricate himself, especially if the daring spirit which bore thee thither should chance to fail thee at a pinch. Remember, Darsie, thou art not naturally courageous; on the contrary, we have long since agreed, that, quiet as I am, I have the advantage in this important particular. My courage consists, I think, in strength of nerves and constitutional indifference to danger; which, though it never pushes me on adventure, secures me in full use of my recollection, and tolerably complete self-possession, when danger actually arrives. Now, thine seems more what may be called intellectual courage; highness of spirit, and desire of distinction; impulses which render thee alive to the love of fame, and deaf to the apprehension of danger, until it forces itself suddenly upon thee. I own that whether it is from my having caught my father's apprehensions, or that I have reason to entertain doubts of my own, I often think that this wildfire chase, of romantic situation and adventure, may lead thee into some mischief; and then what would become of Alan Fairford? They might make whom they pleased Lord-Advocate, or Solicitor-General,* I should never have the heart to strive for it. All my exertions are intended to vindicate myself one day in your eyes; and I think I should not care a farthing for the embroidered silk gown, more than for an old woman's apron, unless I had hopes that thou shouldst be walking the boards* to admire, and perhaps to envy me.

That this may be the case, I prithee—beware! See not a Dulcinea* in every slipshod girl, who, with blue eyes, fair hair, a tattered plaid, and a willow-wand in her gripe, drives out the village cows to the loaning. Do not think you will meet a gallant Valentine in every English rider, or an Orson* in every Highland drover. View things as they are, and not as they may be magnified through thy teeming fancy. I have seen thee look at an old gravel pit, till thou madest out capes, and bays, and inlets, crags, and precipices, and the whole stupendous scenery of the isle of Feroe,* in what was to all ordinary eyes a mere horsepond. Besides, did I not once find thee gazing with respect at a lizard, in the attitude of one who looks upon a crocodile? Now this is, doubtless, so far a harmless exercise of your imagination, for the puddle cannot drown you, nor the Lilliputian* alligator eat you up. But it is different in society, where you cannot mistake the character of those you converse with, or suffer your fancy to exaggerate their qualities, good or bad, without exposing yourself not only to ridicule, but to great and serious inconveniencies. Keep guard, therefore, on your imagination, my dear Darsie; and let your old friend assure you, it is the point of your character most pregnant with peril to its good and generous owner. Adieu! let not the franks of the worthy peer remain unemployed; above all, *Sis memor mei*.

A. F.

LETTER III

DARSIE LATIMER TO ALAN FAIRFORD

Shepherd's Bush

I HAVE received thine absurd and most conceited epistle. It is well for thee that, Lovelace and Belford like,* we came under a convention to pardon every species of liberty which we may take with each other; since, upon my word, there are some reflections in your last, which would otherwise have obliged me to return forthwith to Edinburgh, merely to show you I was not what you took me for.

Why, what a pair of prigs hast thou made of us!—I plunging into scrapes, without having courage to get out of them—thy sagacious self, afraid to put one foot before the other, lest it should run away from its companion; and so standing still like a post, out of mere faintness and coldness of heart, while all the world were driving full speed past thee. Thou a portrait-painter!—I tell thee, Alan, I have seen a better seated on the fourth round of a ladder, and painting a bare-breeched Highlander, holding a pint-stoup as big as himself, and a booted Lowlander, in a bobwig, supporting a glass of like dimensions; the whole being designed to represent the sign of the Salutation.

How hadst thou the heart to represent thine own individual self, with all thy motions, like those of a great Dutch doll, depending on the pressure of certain springs, as duty, reflection, and the like; without the impulse of which, thou wouldst doubtless have me believe thou wouldst not budge an inch? But have I not seen Gravity out of his bed at midnight?* and must I, in plain terms, remind thee of certain mad pranks? Thou hadst ever, with the gravest sentiments in thy mouth, and the most starched reserve in thy manner, a kind of lumbering proclivity towards mischief, although with more inclination to set it a-going, than address to carry it through; and I cannot but chuckle internally, when I think of having seen my most venerable monitor, the future President of some high Scottish Court, puffing, blowing, and floundering, like a clumsy cart-horse in a bog, where his efforts to extricate himself only plunged him deeper at every awkward struggle, till some one—I myself, for example—took compassion on the moaning monster, and dragged him out by mane and tail.

As for me, my portrait is, if possible, even more scandalously caricatured. *I* fail or quail in spirit at the upcome! Where canst thou show me the least symptom of the recreant temper with which thou hast invested me, (as I trust,) merely to set off the solid and impassible dignity of thine own stupid indifference? If you ever saw me tremble, be assured that my flesh, like that of the old Spanish general,* only quaked at the dangers into which my spirit was about to lead it. Seriously, Alan, this imputed poverty of spirit is a shabby charge to bring against your friend. I have examined myself as closely as I can, being, in very truth, a little hurt at your having such hard thoughts of me, and on my life I can see no reason for them. I allow you have, perhaps, some advantage of me in the steadiness and indifference of your temper; but I should despise myself, if I were conscious of the deficiency in courage which you seem willing enough to impute to me. However, I suppose this ungracious hint proceeds from sincere anxiety for my safety; and so viewing it, I swallow it as I would do medicine from a friendly doctor, although I believed in my heart he had mistaken my complaint.

This offensive insinuation disposed of, I thank thee, Alan, for the rest of thy epistle. I thought I heard your good father pronouncing the word Noble-House, with a mixture of contempt and displeasure, as if the very name of the poor little hamlet were odious to him, or, as if you had selected, out of all Scotland, the very place at which you had no call to dine. But if he had had any particular aversion to that blameless village, and very sorry inn, is it not his own fault that I did not accept the invitation of the Laird of Glengallacher, to shoot a buck in what he emphatically calls his 'country?' Truth is, I had a strong desire to have complied with his Lairdship's invitation. To shoot a buck! Think how magnificent an idea to one who never shot any thing but hedge-sparrows, and that with a horse-pistol, purchased at a broker's stand in the Cowgate!—You, who stand upon your courage, may remember that I took the risk of firing the said pistol for the first time, while you stood at twenty yards' distance; and that, when you were persuaded it would go off without bursting, forgetting all law but that of the biggest and strongest, you possessed yourself of it exclusively for the rest of the holydays. Such a day's sport was no complete introduction to the noble art of deer-stalking, as it is practised in the Highlands; but I should not have scrupled to accept honest Glengallacher's invitation, at the risk of firing a rifle for the first time, had it not been for the outcry which your father made at my proposal, in the full ardour of his zeal for King George, the Hanover succession, and the Presbyterian faith. I wish I had stood out, since I have gained so little upon his good opinion by submission. All his impressions concerning the Highlanders are taken from the recollections of the Forty-five, when he retreated from the West-Port with his brother volunteers, each to the fortalice of his own separate dwelling, so soon as they heard the Adventurer was arrived with his clans as near them as Kirkliston. The flight of Falkirk—*parma non bene selecta*—in which I think your sire had his share with the undaunted western regiment, does not seem to have improved his taste for the company of the Highlanders;* (quære, Alan, dost thou derive the courage thou makest such boast of from an hereditary source?)—and stories of Rob Roy Macgregor, and Sergeant Alan Mhor Cameron,[14]* have served to paint them in still more sable colours to his imagination.

Now, from all I can understand, these ideas, as applied to the present state of the country, are absolutely chimerical. The Pretender* is no more remembered in the Highlands, than if the poor gentleman were gathered to his hundred and eight fathers, whose portraits adorn the ancient walls of Holyrood;* the broadswords have passed into other hands; the targets are used to cover the butter-churns; and the race has sunk, or is fast sinking, from ruffling bullies into tame cheaters. Indeed, it was partly my conviction that there is little to be seen in the north, which, arriving at your father's conclusion, though from different premises, inclined my course in this direction, where perhaps I shall see as little.

One thing, however, I *have* seen; and it was with pleasure the more indescribable, that I was debarred from treading the land which my eyes were permitted to gaze upon, like those of the dying prophet from the top of Mount Pisgah,*—I have seen, in a word, the fruitful shores of merry England; merry England! of which I boast myself a native, and on which I gaze, even while raging floods and unstable quicksands divide us, with the filial affection of a dutiful son.

Thou canst not have forgotten, Alan—for when didst thou ever forget what was interesting to thy friend?—that the same letter from my friend Griffiths, which doubled my income, and placed my motions at my own free disposal, contained a prohibitory clause, by which, reason none assigned, I was interdicted, as I respected my present safety and future fortunes, from visiting England; every other part of the British dominions, and a tour, if I pleased, on the continent, being left to my own choice.—Where is the tale, Alan, of a covered dish in the midst of a royal banquet, upon which the eyes of every guest were immediately fixed, neglecting all the dainties with which the table was loaded? This clause of banishment from England—from my native country—from the land of the brave, and the wise, and the free—affects me more than I am rejoiced by the freedom and independence assigned to me in all other respects. Thus, in seeking this extreme boundary of the country which I am forbidden to tread, I resemble the poor tethered horse, which, you may have observed, is always grazing on the very verge of the circle to which it is limited by its halter.

Do not accuse me of romance for obeying this impulse towards the South; nor suppose that, to gratify the imaginary longing of an idle curiosity, I am in any danger of risking the solid comforts of my present condition. Whoever has hitherto taken charge of my motions, has shown me, by convincing proofs, more weighty than the assurances which they have withheld, that my real advantage is their principal object. I should be, therefore, worse than a fool did I object to their authority, even when it seems somewhat capriciously exercised; for assuredly, at my age, I might—intrusted as I am with the care and management of myself in every other particular—expect that the cause of excluding me from England should be frankly and fairly stated for my own consideration and guidance. However, I will not grumble about the matter. I shall know the whole story one day, I suppose; and perhaps, as you sometimes surmise, I shall not find there is any mighty matter in it after all.

Yet one cannot help wondering—but, plague on it, if I wonder any longer, my letter will be as full of wonders as one of Katterfelto's advertisements.* I have a month's mind, instead of this damnable iteration of guesses and forebodings, to give thee the history of a little adventure which befell me yesterday; though I am sure you will, as usual, turn the opposite end of the spy-glass on my poor narrative, and reduce, *more tuo*, to the most petty trivialities, the circumstances to which thou accusest me of giving undue consequence. Hang thee, Alan, thou art as unfit a confidant for a youthful gallant with some spice of imagination, as the old taciturn secretary of Facardin of Trebizond.* Nevertheless, we must each perform our separate destinies. I am doomed to see, act, and tell:—thou, like a Dutchman, enclosed in the same Diligence with a Gascon,* to hear, and shrug thy shoulders.

Of Dumfries, the capital town of this county, I have but little to say, and will not abuse your patience by reminding you, that it is built on the gallant river Nith, and that its churchyard, the highest place of the whole town, commands an extensive and fine prospect. Neither will I take the traveller's privilege of inflicting upon you the whole history of Bruce poniarding the Red Comyn in the Church of the Dominicans at this place, and becoming a king and patriot, because he had been a church-breaker and a murderer.* The present Dumfriezers remember and justify the deed, observing, it was only a papist church—in evidence whereof, its walls have been so completely demolished, that no vestiges of them remain. They are a sturdy set of true-blue Presbyterians, these burghers of Dumfries; men after your father's own heart, zealous for the Protestant succession—the rather that many of the great families around are suspected to be of a different way of thinking, and shared, a great many of them, in the insurrection of the Fifteen, and some in the more recent business of the Forty-five. The town itself suffered in the latter era; for Lord Elcho, with a large party of the rebels, levied a severe contribution upon Dumfries, on account of the citizens having annoyed the rear of the Chevalier during his march into England.*

Many of these particulars I learned from Provost C——, who, happening to see me in the market-place, remembered that I was an intimate of your father's, and very kindly asked me to dinner. Pray tell your father that the effects of his kindness to me follow me every where. I became tired, however, of this pretty town in the course of twenty-four hours, and crept along the coast eastwards, amusing myself with looking out for objects of antiquity, and sometimes making, or attempting to make, use of my new angling-rod. By the way, old Cotton's instructions,* by which I hoped to qualify myself for one of the gentle society of anglers, are not worth a farthing for this meridian. I learned this by mere accident, after I had waited four mortal hours. I shall never forget an impudent urchin, a cowherd, about twelve years old, without either brogue or bonnet, bare-legged, and with a very indifferent pair of breeches—how the villain grinned in scorn at my landing-net, my plummet, and the gorgeous jury of flies which I had assembled to destroy all the fish in the river. I was induced at last to lend the rod to the sneering scoundrel, to see what he would make of it; and he not only half filled my basket in an hour, but literally taught me to kill two trouts with my own hand. This, and Sam having found the hay and oats, not forgetting the ale, very good at this small inn, first made me take the fancy of resting here for a day or two; and I have got my grinning blackguard of a Piscator leave to attend on me, by paying sixpence a-day for a herdboy in his stead.

A notably clean Englishwoman keeps this small house, and my bedroom is sweetened with lavender, has a clean sash-window, and the walls are, moreover, adorned with ballads of Fair Rosamond and Cruel Barbara Allan.* The woman's accent, though uncouth enough, sounds yet kindly in my ear; for I have never yet forgotten the desolate effect produced on my infant organs, when I heard on all sides your slow and broad northern pronunciation, which was to me the tone of a foreign land. I am sensible I myself have since that time acquired Scotch in perfection, and many a Scotticism withal. Still the sound of the English accentuation comes to my ears as the tones of a friend; and even when heard from the mouth of some wandering beggar, it has seldom failed to charm forth my mite. You Scotch, who are so proud of your own nationality, must make due allowance for that of other folks.

On the next morning I was about to set forth to the stream where I had commenced angler the night before, but was prevented, by a heavy shower of rain, from stirring abroad the whole forenoon; during all which time I heard my varlet of a guide as loud with his blackguard jokes in the kitchen, as a footman in the shilling gallery;—so little are modesty and innocence the inseparable companions of rusticity and seclusion.

When after dinner the day cleared, and we at length sallied out to the river side, I found myself subjected to a new trick on the part of my accomplished preceptor. Apparently, he liked fishing himself better than the trouble of instructing an awkward novice, such as I; and in hopes of exhausting my patience, and inducing me to resign the rod, as I had done on the preceding day, my friend contrived to keep me thrashing the water more than an hour with a pointless hook. I detected this trick at last, by observing the rogue grinning with delight when he saw a large trout rise and dash harmless away from the angle. I gave him a sound cuff, Alan; but the next moment was sorry, and, to make amends, yielded possession of the fishing-rod for the rest of the evening, he undertaking to bring me home a dish of trouts for my supper, in atonement for his offences.

Having thus got honourably rid of the trouble of amusing myself in a way I cared not for, I turned my steps towards the sea, or rather the Solway Frith, which here separates the two sister kingdoms, and which lay at about a mile's distance, by a pleasant walk over sandy knolls, covered with short herbage, which you call Links, and we English, Downs.

But the rest of my adventure would weary out my fingers, and must be deferred until to-morrow, when you shall hear from me by way of continuation; and, in the meanwhile, to prevent overhasty conclusions, I must just hint to you, we are but yet on the verge of the adventure which it is my purpose to communicate.

LETTER IV

THE SAME TO THE SAME

Shepherd's Bush

I MENTIONED in my last, that having abandoned my fishing-rod as an unprofitable implement, I crossed over the open downs which divided me from the margin of the Solway. When I reached the banks of the great estuary, which are here very bare and exposed, the waters had receded from the large and level space of sand, through which a stream, now feeble and fordable, found its way to the ocean. The whole was illuminated by the beams of the low and setting sun, who showed his ruddy front, like a warrior prepared for defence, over a huge battlemented and turreted wall of crimson and black clouds, which appeared like an immense Gothic fortress, into which the lord of day was descending. His setting rays glimmered bright upon the wet surface of the sands, and the numberless pools of water by which it was covered, where the inequality of the ground had occasioned their being left by the tide.

The scene was animated by the exertions of a number of horsemen, who were actually employed in hunting salmon.* Ay, Alan, lift up your hands and eyes as you will, I can give their mode of fishing no name so appropriate; for they chased the fish at full gallop, and struck them with their barbed spears, as you see hunters spearing boars in the old tapestry. The salmon, to be sure, take the thing more quietly than the boars; but they are so swift in their own element, that to pursue and strike them is the task of a good horseman, with a quick eye, a determined hand, and full command both of his horse and weapon. The shouts of the fellows as they galloped up and down in the animating exercise—their loud bursts of laughter when any of their number caught a fall—and still louder acclamations when any of the party made a capital stroke with his lance—gave so much animation to the whole scene, that I caught the enthusiasm of the sport, and ventured forward a considerable space on the sands. The feats of one horseman, in particular, called forth so repeatedly the clamorous applause of his companions, that the very banks rang again with their shouts. He was a tall man, well mounted on a strong black horse, which he caused to turn and wind like a bird in the air, carried a longer spear than the others, and wore a sort of fur cap or bonnet, with a short feather in it, which gave him on the whole rather a superior appearance to the other fishermen. He seemed to hold some sort of authority among them, and occasionally directed their motions both by voice and hand; at which times I thought his gestures were striking, and his voice uncommonly sonorous and commanding.

The riders began to make for the shore, and the interest of the scene was almost over, while I lingered on the sands, with my looks turned to the shores of England, still gilded by the sun's last rays, and, as it seemed, scarce distant a mile from me. The anxious thoughts which haunt me began to muster in my bosom, and my feet slowly and insensibly approached the river which divided me from the forbidden precincts, though without any formed intention, when my steps were arrested by the sound of a horse galloping; and as I turned, the rider (the same fisherman whom I had formerly distinguished) called out to me, in an abrupt manner, 'Soho, brother! you are too late for Bowness to-night—the tide will make presently.'

I turned my head and looked at him without answering; for, to my thinking, his sudden appearance (or rather, I should say, his unexpected approach) had, amidst the gathering shadows and lingering light, something in it which was wild and ominous.

'Are you deaf?' he added—'or are you mad?—or have you a mind for the next world?'

'I am a stranger,' I answered, 'and had no other purpose than looking on at the fishing—I am about to return to the side I came from.'

'Best make haste then,' said he. 'He that dreams on the bed of the Solway, may wake in the next world. The sky threatens a blast that will bring in the waves three feet a-breast.'*

So saying, he turned his horse and rode off, while I began to walk back towards the Scottish shore, a little alarmed at what I had heard; for the tide advances with such rapidity upon these fatal sands, that well-mounted horsemen lay aside hopes of safety, if they see its white surge advancing while they are yet at a distance from the bank.

These recollections grew more agitating, and, instead of walking deliberately, I began a race as fast as I could, feeling, or thinking I felt, each pool of salt water through which I splashed, grow deeper and deeper. At length the surface of the sand did seem considerably more intersected with pools and channels full of water—either that the tide was really beginning to influence the bed of the estuary, or, as I must own is equally probable, that I had, in the hurry and confusion of my retreat, involved myself in difficulties which I had avoided in my more deliberate advance. Either way, it was rather an unpromising state of affairs, for the sands at the same time turned softer, and my footsteps, so soon as I had passed, were instantly filled with water. I began to have odd recollections concerning the snugness of your father's parlour, and the secure footing afforded by the pavement of Brown's Square and Scot's Close, when my better genius, the tall fisherman, appeared once more close to my side, he and his sable horse looming gigantic in the now darkening twilight.

'Are you mad?' he said, in the same deep tone which had before thrilled on my ear, 'or are you weary of your life?—You will be presently amongst the quicksands.'—I professed my ignorance of the way, to which he only replied, 'There is no time for prating—get up behind me.'

He probably expected me to spring from the ground with the activity which these Borderers have, by constant practice, acquired in every thing relating to horsemanship; but as I stood irresolute, he extended his hand, and grasping mine, bid me place my foot on the toe of his boot, and thus raised me in a trice to the croupe of his horse. I was scarce securely seated, ere he shook the reins of his horse, who instantly sprung forward; but annoyed, doubtless, by the unusual burden, treated us to two or three bounds, accompanied by as many flourishes of his hind heels. The rider sat like a tower, notwithstanding that the unexpected plunging of the animal threw me forward upon him. The horse was soon compelled to submit to the discipline of the spur and bridle, and went off at a steady hand gallop; thus shortening the devious, for it was by no means a direct path, by which the rider, avoiding the loose quicksands, made for the northern bank.

My friend, perhaps I may call him my preserver,—for, to a stranger, my situation was fraught with real danger,—continued to press on at the same speedy pace, but in perfect silence, and I was under too much anxiety of mind to disturb him with any questions. At length we arrived at a part of the shore with which I was utterly unacquainted, when I alighted and began to return, in the best fashion I could, my thanks for the important service which he had just rendered me.

The stranger only replied by an impatient 'pshaw!' and was about to ride off, and leave me to my own resources, when I implored him to complete his work of kindness, by directing me to Shepherd's Bush, which was, as I informed him, my home for the present.

'To Shepherd's Bush?' he said; 'it is but three miles, but if you know not the land better than the sand, you may break your neck before you get there; for it is no road for a moping boy in a dark night; and, besides, there are the brook and the fens to cross.'

I was a little dismayed at this communication of such difficulties as my habits have not called on me to contend with. Once more the idea of thy father's fireside came across me; and I could have been well contented to have swop'd the romance of my situation, together with the glorious independence of control which I possessed at the moment, for the comforts of the chimney-corner, though I were obliged to keep my eyes chained to Erskine's Larger Institutes.*

I asked my new friend whether he could not direct me to any house of public entertainment for the night; and, supposing it probable he was himself a poor man, I added, with the conscious dignity of a well-filled pocketbook, that I could make it worth any man's while to oblige me. The fisherman making no answer, I turned away from him with as gallant an appearance of indifference as I could command, and began to take, as I thought, the path which he had pointed out to me.

His deep voice immediately sounded after me to recall me. 'Stay, young man, stay—you have mistaken the road already.—I wonder your friends send out such an inconsiderate youth, without some one wiser than himself to take care of him.'

'Perhaps they might not have done so,' said I, 'if I had any friends who cared about the matter.'

'Well, sir,' he said, 'it is not my custom to open my house to strangers, but your pinch is like to be a smart one; for, besides the risk from bad roads, fords, and broken ground, and the night, which looks both black and gloomy, there is bad company on the road sometimes—at least it has a bad name, and some have come to harm; so that I think I must for once make my rule give way to your necessity, and give you a night's lodging in my cottage.'

Why was it, Alan, that I could not help giving an involuntary shudder at receiving an invitation so seasonable in itself, and so suitable to my naturally inquisitive disposition? I easily suppressed this untimely sensation; and, as I returned thanks, and expressed my hope that I should not disarrange his family, I once more dropped a hint of my desire to make compensation for any trouble I might occasion. The man answered very coldly, 'Your presence will no doubt give me trouble, sir, but it is of a kind which your purse cannot compensate; in a word, although I am content to receive you as my guest, I am no publican to call a reckoning.'

I begged his pardon, and, at his instance, once more seated myself behind him upon the good horse, which went forth steady as before—the moon, whenever she could penetrate the clouds, throwing the huge shadow of the animal, with its double burden, on the wild and bare ground over which we passed.

Thou mayst laugh till thou lettest the letter fall if thou wilt, but it reminded me of the Magician Atlantes on his hippogriff, with a knight trussed up behind him, in the manner Ariosto has depicted that matter.* Thou art, I know, matter-of-fact enough to affect contempt of that fascinating and delicious poem; but think not that, to conform with thy bad taste, I shall forbear any suitable illustration which now or hereafter may occur to me.

On we went, the sky blackening around us, and the wind beginning to pipe such a wild and melancholy tune as best suited the hollow sounds of the advancing tide, which I could hear at a distance, like the roar of some immense monster defrauded of its prey.

At length, our course was crossed by a deep dell or dingle, such as they call in some parts of Scotland a den, and in others a cleuch, or narrow glen. It seemed, by the broken glances which the moon continued to throw upon it, to be steep, precipitous, and full of trees, which are, generally speaking, rather scarce upon these shores. The descent by which we plunged into this dell was both steep and rugged, with two or three abrupt turnings; but neither danger nor darkness impeded the motion of the black horse, who seemed rather to slide upon his haunches, than to gallop down the pass, throwing me again on the shoulders of the athletic rider, who, sustaining no inconvenience by the circumstance, continued to press the horse forward with his heel, steadily supporting him at the same time by raising his bridle-hand, until we stood in safety at the bottom of the steep—not a little to my consolation, as, friend Alan, thou mayst easily conceive.

A very short advance up the glen, the bottom of which we had attained by this ugly descent, brought us in front of two or three cottages, one of which another blink of moonshine enabled me to rate as rather better than those of the Scottish peasantry in this part of the world; for the sashes seemed glazed, and there were what are called storm-windows in the roof, giving symptoms of the magnificence of a second story. The scene around was very interesting; for the cottages, and the yards or crofts annexed to them, occupied a *haugh*, or holm, of two acres, which a brook of some consequence (to judge from its roar) had left upon one side of the little glen while finding its course close to the further bank, and which appeared to be covered and darkened with trees, while the level space beneath enjoyed such stormy smiles as the moon had that night to bestow.

I had little time for observation, for my companion's loud whistle, seconded by an equally loud halloo, speedily brought to the door of the principal cottage a man and a woman, together with two large Newfoundland dogs, the deep baying of which I had for some time heard. A yelping terrier or two, which had joined the concert, were silent at the presence of my conductor, and began to whine, jump up, and fawn upon him. The female drew back when she beheld a stranger; the man, who had a lighted lantern, advanced, and without any observation, received the horse from my host, and led him, doubtless, to stable, while I followed my conductor into the house. When we had passed the *hallan*,[15] we entered a well-sized apartment, with a clean brick floor, where a fire blazed (much to my contentment) in the ordinary projecting sort of chimney, common in Scottish houses. There were stone seats within the chimney; and ordinary utensils, mixed with fishing-spears, nets, and similar implements of sport, were hung around the walls of the place. The female who had first appeared at the door, had now retreated into a side apartment. She was presently followed by my guide, after he had silently motioned me to a seat; and their place was supplied by an elderly woman, in a grey stuff gown, with a check apron and *toy*, obviously a menial, though neater in her dress than is usual in her apparent rank—an advantage which was counterbalanced by a very forbidding aspect. But the most singular part of her attire, in this very Protestant country, was a rosary, in which the smaller beads were black oak, and those indicating the *pater-noster* of silver, with a crucifix of the same metal.

This person made preparations for supper, by spreading a clean though coarse cloth over a large oaken table, placing trenchers and salt upon it, and arranging the fire to receive a gridiron. I observed her motions in silence; for she took no sort of notice of me, and as her looks were singularly forbidding, I felt no disposition to commence conversation.

When this duenna had made all preliminary arrangements, she took from the well-filled pouch of my conductor, which he had hung up by the door, one or two salmon, or *grilses*, as the smaller sort are termed, and selecting that which seemed best, and in highest season, began to cut it into slices, and to prepare a *grillade*; the savoury smell of which affected me so powerfully, that I began sincerely to hope that no delay would intervene between the platter and the lip.

As this thought came across me, the man who had conducted the horse to the stable entered the apartment, and discovered to me a countenance yet more uninviting than that of the old crone who was performing with such dexterity the office of cook to the party. He was perhaps sixty years old; yet his brow was not much furrowed, and his jet black hair was only grizzled, not whitened, by the advance of age. All his motions spoke strength unabated; and, though rather undersized, he had very broad shoulders, was square-made, thin-flanked, and apparently combined in his frame muscular strength and activity; the last somewhat impaired perhaps by years, but the first remaining in full vigour. A hard and harsh countenance—eyes far sunk under projecting eyebrows, which were grizzled like his hair—a wide mouth, furnished from ear to ear with a range of unimpaired teeth, of uncommon whiteness, and a size and breadth which might have become the jaws of an ogre, completed this delightful portrait. He was clad like a fisherman, in jacket and trowsers of the blue cloth commonly used by seamen, and had a Dutch case-knife, like that of a Hamburgh skipper, stuck into a broad buff belt, which seemed as if it might occasionally sustain weapons of a description still less equivocally calculated for violence.

This man gave me an inquisitive, and, as I thought, a sinister look, upon entering the apartment; but without any farther notice of me, took up the office of arranging the table, which the old lady had abandoned for that of cooking the fish, and, with more address than I expected from a person of his coarse appearance, placed two chairs at the head of the table, and two stools below; accommodating each seat to a cover, beside which he placed an allowance of barley-bread, and a small jug, which he replenished with ale from a large black jack. Three of these jugs were of ordinary earthenware, but the fourth, which he placed by the right-hand cover at the upper end of the table, was a flagon of silver, and displayed armorial bearings. Beside this flagon he placed a saltcellar of silver, handsomely wrought, containing salt of exquisite whiteness, with pepper and other spices. A sliced lemon was also presented on a small silver salver. The two large water-dogs, who seemed perfectly to understand the nature of the preparations, seated themselves one on each side of the table, to be ready to receive their portion of the entertainment. I never saw finer animals, or which seemed to be more influenced by a sense of decorum, excepting that they slobbered a little as the rich scent from the chimney was wafted past their noses. The small dogs ensconced themselves beneath the table.

I am aware that I am dwelling upon trivial and ordinary circumstances, and that perhaps I may weary out your patience in doing so. But conceive me alone in this strange place, which seemed, from the universal silence, to be the very temple of Harpocrates*—remember that this is my first excursion from home—forget not that the manner in which I had been brought hither had the dignity of danger and something the air of an adventure, and that there was a mysterious incongruity in all I had hitherto witnessed; and you will not, I think, be surprised that these circumstances, though trifling, should force themselves on my notice at the time, and dwell in my memory afterwards.

That a fisher, who pursued the sport perhaps for his amusement as well as profit, should be well mounted and better lodged than the lower class of peasantry, had in it nothing surprising; but there was something about all that I saw which seemed to intimate, that I was rather in the abode of a decayed gentleman, who clung to a few of the forms and observances of former rank, than in that of a common peasant, raised above his fellows by comparative opulence.

Besides the articles of plate which I have already noticed, the old man now lighted and placed on the table a silver lamp, or *cruisie*, as the Scottish term it, filled with very pure oil, which in burning diffused an aromatic fragrance, and gave me a more perfect view of the cottage walls, which I had hitherto only seen dimly by the light of the fire. The *bink*,[16] with its usual arrangement of pewter and earthen-ware, which was most strictly and critically clean, glanced back the flame of the lamp merrily from one side of the apartment. In a recess, formed by the small bow of a latticed widow, was a large writing-desk of walnut-tree wood, curiously carved, above which arose shelves of the same, which supported a few books and papers. The opposite side of the recess contained (as far as I could discern, for it lay in shadow, and I could at any rate have seen it but imperfectly from the place where I was seated) one or two guns, together with swords, pistols, and other arms—a collection which, in a poor cottage, and in a country so peaceful, appeared singular at least, if not even somewhat suspicious.

All these observations, you may suppose, were made much sooner than I have recorded, or you (if you have not skipped) have been able to read them. They were already finished, and I was considering how I should open some communication with the mute inhabitants of the mansion, when my conductor re-entered from the side-door by which he had made his exit

He had now thrown off his rough riding-cap, and his coarse jockey-coat, and stood before me in a grey jerkin trimmed with black, which sat close to, and set off, his large and sinewy frame, and a pair of trowsers of a lighter colour, cut as close to the body as they are used by Highlandmen. His whole dress was of finer cloth than that of the old man; and his linen, so minute was my observation, clean and unsullied. His shirt was without ruffles, and tied at the collar with a black riband, which showed his strong and muscular neck rising from it, like that of an ancient Hercules. His head was small, with a large forehead, and well-formed ears. He wore neither peruke nor hair-powder; and his chestnut locks, curling close to his head, like those of an antique statue, showed not the least touch of time, though the owner must have been at least fifty. His features were high and prominent in such a degree, that one knew not whether to term them harsh or handsome. In either case, the sparkling grey eye, aquiline nose, and well-formed mouth, combined to render his physiognomy noble and expressive. An air of sadness, or severity, or of both, seemed to indicate a melancholy, and, at the same time, a haughty temper. I could not help running mentally over the ancient heroes, to whom I might assimilate the noble form and countenance before me. He was too young, and evinced too little resignation to his fate, to resemble Belisarius. Coriolanus, standing by the hearth of Tullus Aufidius, came nearer the mark; yet the gloomy and haughty look of the stranger had, perhaps, still more of Marius, seated among the ruins of Carthage.*

While I was lost in these imaginations, my host stood by the fire, gazing on me with the same attention which I paid to him, until, embarrassed by his look, I was about to break silence at all hazards. But the supper, now placed upon the table, reminded me, by its appearance, of those wants which I had almost forgotten while I was gazing on the fine form of my conductor. He spoke at length, and I almost started at the deep rich tone of his voice, though what he said was but to invite me to sit down to the table. He himself assumed the seat of honour, beside which the silver flagon was placed, and beckoned to me to sit beside him.

Thou knowest thy father's strict and excellent domestic discipline has trained me to hear the invocation of a blessing before we break the daily bread, for which we are taught to pray—I paused a moment, and, without designing to do so, I suppose my manner made him sensible of what I expected. The two domestics, or inferiors, as I should have before observed, were already seated at the bottom of the table, when my host shot a glance of a very peculiar expression towards the old man, observing, with something approaching to a sneer, 'Cristal Nixon, say grace—the gentleman expects one.'

'The foul fiend shall be clerk, and say amen, when I turn chaplain,' growled out the party addressed, in tones which might have become the condition of a dying bear; 'if the gentleman is a whig,* he may please himself with his own mummery. My faith is neither in word nor writ, but in barley bread and brown ale.'

'Mabel Moffat,' said my guide, looking at the old woman, and raising his sonorous voice, probably because she was hard of hearing, 'canst thou ask a blessing upon our victuals?'

The old woman shook her head, kissed the cross which hung from her rosary, and was silent.

'Mabel will say grace for no heretic,' said the master of the house, with the same latent sneer on his brow and in his accent.

At the same moment, the side-door already mentioned opened, and the young woman (so she proved) whom I had first seen at the door of the cottage, advanced a little way into the room, then stopped bashfully, as if she had observed that I was looking at her, and asked the master of the house, 'if he had called?'

'Not louder than to make old Mabel hear me,' he replied; 'and yet,' he added, as she turned to retire, 'it is a shame a stranger should see a house where not one of the family can or will say a grace,—do thou be our chaplain.'

The girl, who was really pretty, came forward with timid modesty, and apparently unconscious that she was doing any thing uncommon, pronounced the benediction in a silver-toned voice, and with affecting simplicity—her cheek colouring just so much as to show, that, on a less solemn occasion, she would have felt more embarrassed.

Now, if thou expectest a fine description of this young woman, Alan Fairford, in order to entitle thee to taunt me with having found a Dulcinea in the inhabitant of a fisherman's cottage on the Solway Frith, thou shalt be disappointed; for, having said she seemed very pretty, and that she was a sweet and gentle-speaking creature, I have said all concerning her that I can tell thee. She vanished when the benediction was spoken.

My host, with a muttered remark on the cold of our ride, and the keen air of the Solway Sands, to which he did not seem to wish an answer, loaded my plate from Mabel's grillade, which, with a large wooden bowl of potatoes, formed our whole meal. A sprinkling from the lemon gave a much higher zest than the usual condiment of vinegar; and I promise you that whatever I might hitherto have felt, either of curiosity or suspicion, did not prevent me from making a most excellent supper, during which little passed betwixt me and my entertainer, unless that he did the usual honours of the table with courtesy, indeed, but without even the affectation of hearty hospitality, which those in his (apparent) condition generally affect on such occasions, even when they do not actually feel it. On the contrary, his manner seemed that of a polished landlord towards an unexpected and unwelcome guest, whom, for the sake of his own credit, he receives with civility, but without either good-will or cheerfulness.

If you ask how I learned all this, I cannot tell you; nor, were I to write down at length the insignificant intercourse which took place between us, would it perhaps serve to justify these observations. It is sufficient to say, that in helping his dogs, which he did from time to time with great liberality, he seemed to discharge a duty much more pleasing to himself, than when he paid the same attention to his guest. Upon the whole, the result on my mind was as I tell it you.

When supper was over, a small case-bottle of brandy, in a curious frame of silver filigree, circulated to the guests. I had already taken a small glass of the liquor, and, when it had passed to Mabel and to Cristal, and was again returned to the upper end of the table, I could not help taking the bottle in my hand, to look more at the armorial bearings, which were chased with considerable taste on the silver framework. Encountering the eye of my entertainer, I instantly saw that my curiosity was highly distasteful; he frowned, bit his lip, and showed such uncontrollable signs of impatience, that, setting the bottle immediately down, I attempted some apology. To this he did not deign either to reply, or even to listen; and Cristal, at a signal from his master, removed the object of my curiosity, as well as the cup, upon which the same arms were engraved.

There ensued an awkward pause, which I endeavoured to break by observing, that 'I feared my intrusion upon his hospitality had put his family to some inconvenience.'

'I hope you see no appearance of it, sir,' he replied, with cold civility. 'What inconvenience a family so retired as ours may suffer from receiving an unexpected guest, is like to be trifling, in comparison of what the visitor himself sustains from want of his accustomed comforts. So far, therefore, as our connexion stands, our accounts stand clear.'

Notwithstanding this discouraging reply, I blundered on, as is usual in such cases, wishing to appear civil, and being, perhaps, in reality the very reverse. 'I was afraid,' I said, 'that my presence had banished one of the family' (looking at the side-door) 'from his table.'

'If,' he coldly replied, 'I meant the young woman whom I had seen in the apartment, he bid me observe that there was room enough at the table for her to have seated herself, and meat enough, such as it was, for her supper. I might, therefore, be assured, if she had chosen it, she would have supped with us.'

There was no dwelling on this or any other topic longer; for my entertainer, taking up the lamp, observed, that 'my wet clothes might reconcile me for the night to their custom of keeping early hours; that he was under the necessity of going abroad by peep of day to-morrow morning, and would call me up at the same time, to point out the way by which I was to return to the Shepherd's Bush.'

This left no opening for farther explanation; nor was there room for it on the usual terms of civility; for, as he neither asked my name, nor expressed the least interest concerning my condition, I—the obliged person—had no pretence to trouble him with such enquiries on my part.

He took up the lamp, and led me through the side-door into a very small room, where a bed had been hastily arranged for my accommodation, and, putting down the lamp, directed me to leave my wet clothes on the outside of the door, that they might be exposed to the fire during the night. He then left me, having muttered something which was meant to pass for good-night.

I obeyed his directions with respect to my clothes, the rather that, in despite of the spirits which I had drank, I felt my teeth begin to chatter, and received various hints from an aguish feeling, that a town-bred youth, like myself, could not at once rush into all the hardihood of country sports with impunity. But my bed, though coarse and hard, was dry and clean; and I soon was so little occupied with my heats and tremors, as to listen with interest to a heavy foot which seemed to be that of my landlord, traversing the boards (there was no ceiling, as you may believe) which roofed my apartment. Light glancing through these rude planks, became visible as soon as my lamp was extinguished; and as the noise of the slow, solemn, and regular step continued, and I could distinguish that the person turned and returned as he reached the end of the apartment, it seemed clear to me that the walker was engaged in no domestic occupation, but merely pacing to and fro for his own pleasure. 'An odd amusement this,' I thought, 'for one who had been engaged at least a part of the preceding day in violent exercise, and who talked of rising by the peep of dawn on the ensuing morning.'

Meantime I heard the storm, which had been brewing during the evening, begin to descend with a vengeance; sounds, as of distant thunder, (the noise of the more distant waves, doubtless, on the shore,) mingled with the roaring of the neighbouring torrent, and with the crashing, groaning, and even screaming of the trees in the glen, whose boughs were tormented by the gale. Within the house, windows clattered, and doors clapped, and the walls, though sufficiently substantial for a building of the kind, seemed to me to totter in the tempest.

But still the heavy steps perambulating the apartment over my head, were distinctly heard amid the roar and fury of the elements. I thought more than once I even heard a groan; but I frankly own, that, placed in this unusual situation, my fancy may have misled me. I was tempted several times to call aloud, and ask whether the turmoil around us did not threaten danger to the building which we inhabited; but when I thought of the secluded and unsocial master of the dwelling, who seemed to avoid human society, and to remain unperturbed amid the elemental war, it seemed that to speak to him at that moment, would have been to address the spirit of the tempest himself, since no other being, I thought, could have remained calm and tranquil while winds and waters were thus raging around.

In process of time, fatigue prevailed over anxiety and curiosity. The storm abated, or my senses became deadened to its terrors, and I fell asleep ere yet the mysterious paces of my host had ceased to shake the flooring over my head.

It might have been expected that the novelty of my situation, although it did not prevent my slumbers, would have at least diminished their profoundness, and shortened their duration. It proved otherwise, however; for I never slept more soundly in my life, and only awoke when, at morning dawn, my landlord shook me by the shoulder, and dispelled some dream, of which, fortunately for you, I have no recollection, otherwise you would have been favoured with it, in hopes you might have proved a second Daniel* upon the occasion.

'You sleep sound'—said his full deep voice; 'ere five years have rolled over your head, your slumbers will be lighter—unless ere then you are wrapped in the sleep which is never broken.'

'How!' said I, starting up in the bed; 'do you know any thing of me—of my prospects—of my views in life?'

'Nothing,' he answered, with a grim smile; 'but it is evident you are entering upon the world young, inexperienced, and full of hopes, and I do but prophesy to you what I would to any one in your condition.—But come; there lie your clothes—a brown crust and a draught of milk wait you, if you choose to break your fast; but you must make haste.'

'I must first,' I said, 'take the freedom to spend a few minutes alone, before beginning the ordinary works of the day.'

'Oh!—humph!—I cry your devotions pardon,' he replied, and left the apartment.

Alan, there is something terrible about this man.

I joined him, as I had promised, in the kitchen where we had supped over night, where I found the articles which he had offered me for breakfast, without butter or any other addition.

He walked up and down while I partook of the bread and milk; and the slow measured weighty step seemed identified with those which I had heard last night. His pace, from its funereal slowness, seemed to keep time with some current of internal passion, dark, slow, and unchanged.—'We run and leap by the side of a lively and bubbling brook,' thought I, internally, 'as if we would run a race with it; but beside waters deep, slow, and lonely, our pace is sullen and silent as their course. What thoughts may be now corresponding with that furrowed brow, and bearing time with that heavy step!'

'If you have finished,' said he, looking up to me with a glance of impatience, as he observed that I ate no longer, but remained with my eyes fixed upon him, 'I wait to show you the way.'

We went out together, no individual of the family having been visible excepting my landlord. I was disappointed of the opportunity which I watched for of giving some gratuity to the domestics, as they seemed to be. As for offering any recompense to the Master of the Household, it seemed to me impossible to have attempted it.

What would I have given for a share of thy composure, who

wouldst have thrust half-a-crown into a man's hand whose necessities seemed to crave it, conscious that you did right in making the proffer, and not caring sixpence whether you hurt the feelings of him whom you meant to serve! I saw thee once give a penny to a man with a long beard, who, from the dignity of his exterior, might have represented Solon.* I had not thy courage, and therefore I made no tender to my mysterious host, although, notwithstanding his display of silver utensils, all around the house bespoke narrow circumstances, if not actual poverty.

We left the place together. But I hear thee murmur thy very new and appropriate ejaculation, *Ohe, jam satis!*—The rest for another time. Perhaps I may delay farther communication till I learn how my favours are valued.

LETTER V

ALAN FAIRFORD TO DARSIE LATIMER

I HAVE thy two last epistles, my dear Darsie, and, expecting the third, have been in no hurry to answer them. Do not think my silence ought to be ascribed to my failing to take interest in them, for, truly, they excel (though the task was difficult) thy usual excellings. Since the moon-calf who earliest discovered the Pandemonium of Milton* in an expiring wood-fire—since the first ingenious urchin who blew bubbles out of soap and water, thou, my best of friends, hast the highest knack at making histories out of nothing. Wert thou to plant the bean in the nursery-tale,* thou wouldst make out, so soon as it began to germinate, that the castle of the giant was about to elevate its battlements on the top of it. All that happens to thee gets a touch of the wonderful and the sublime from thy own rich imagination. Didst ever see what artists call a Claude Lorraine glass,* which spreads its own particular hue over the whole landscape which you see through it?—thou beholdest ordinary events just through such a medium.

I have looked carefully at the facts of thy last long letter, and they are just such as might have befallen any little truant of the High School, who had got down to Leith Sands,* gone beyond the *prawn-dub*, wet his hose and shoon, and, finally, had been carried home, in compassion, by some high-kilted fishwife, cursing all the while the trouble which the brat occasioned her.

I admire the figure which thou must have made, clinging for dear life behind the old fellow's back—thy jaws chattering with fear, thy muscles cramped with anxiety. Thy execrable supper of broiled salmon, which was enough to insure the nightmare's regular visits for a twelvemonth, may be termed a real affliction; but as for the storm of Thursday last, (such, I observe, was the date,) it roared, whistled, howled, and bellowed, as fearfully amongst the old chimney-heads in the Candlemaker-row, as it could on the Solway shore, for the very wind of it—*teste me per totam noctem vigilante.** And then in the morning again, when—Lord help you—in your sentimental delicacy you bid the poor man adieu, without even tendering him half-a-crown for supper and lodging!

You laugh at me for giving a penny (to be accurate, though, thou shouldst have said sixpence) to an old fellow, whom thou, in thy high flight, wouldst have sent home supperless, because he was like Solon or Belisarius. But you forget that the affront descended like a benediction into the pouch of the old gaberlunzie, who overflowed in blessings upon the generous donor—Long ere he would have thanked thee, Darsie, for thy barren veneration of his beard and his bearing. Then you laugh at my good father's retreat from Falkirk, just as if it were not time for a man to trudge when three or four mountain knaves, with naked claymores, and heels as light as their fingers, were scampering after him, crying *furinish*. You remember what he said himself when the Laird of Bucklivat told him that *furinish* signified 'stay a while.' 'What the devil,' he said, surprised out of his Presbyterian correctness by the unreasonableness of such a request under the circumstances, 'would the scoundrels have had me stop to have my head cut off?'

Imagine such a train at your own heels, Darsie, and ask yourself whether you would not exert your legs as fast as you did in flying from the Solway tide. And yet you impeach my father's courage! I tell you he has courage enough to do what is right, and to spurn what is wrong—courage enough to defend a righteous cause with hand and purse, and to take the part of the poor man against his oppressor, without fear of the consequences to himself. This is civil courage, Darsie; and it is of little consequence to most men in this age and country, whether they ever possess military courage or no.

Do not think I am angry with you, though I thus attempt to rectify your opinions on my father's account. I am well aware that, upon the whole, he is scarce regarded with more respect by me than by thee. And while I am in a serious humour, which it is difficult to preserve with one who is perpetually tempting me to laugh at him, pray, dearest Darsie, let not thy ardour for adventure carry thee into more such scrapes as that of the Solway Sands. The rest of the story is a mere imagination; but that stormy evening might have proved, as the clown says to Lear, a 'naughty night to swim in.'*

As for the rest, if you can work mysterious and romantic heroes out of old crossgrained fishermen, why, I for one will reap some amusement by the metamorphosis. Yet hold! even there, there is some need of caution. This same female chaplain—thou sayest so little of her, and so much of every one else, that it excites some doubt in my mind. *Very pretty* she is, it seems—and that is all thy discretion informs me of. There are cases in which silence implies other things than consent. Wert thou ashamed or afraid, Darsie, to trust thyself with the praises of the very pretty grace-sayer?—As I live, thou blushest! Why, do I not know thee an inveterate Squire of Dames?* and have I not been in thy confidence? An elegant elbow, displayed when the rest of the figure was muffled in a cardinal, or a neat well-turned ankle and instep, seen by chance as its owner tripped up the Old Assembly Close,[17] turned thy brain for eight days. Thou wert once caught, if I remember rightly, with a single glance of a single matchless eye, which, when the fair owner withdrew her veil, proved to be single in the literal sense of the word. And, besides, were you not another time enamoured of a voice—a mere voice, that mingled in the psalmody at the Old Greyfriars' Church*—until you discovered the proprietor of that dulcet organ to be Miss Dolly MacIzzard, who is both 'back and breast,' as our saying goes?

All these things considered, and contrasted with thy artful silence on the subject of this grace-saying Nereid of thine, I must beg thee to be more explicit upon that subject in thy next, unless thou wouldst have me form the conclusion that thou thinkest more of her than thou carest to talk of.

You will not expect much news from this quarter, as you know the monotony of my life, and are aware it must at present be devoted to uninterrupted study. You have said a thousand times, that I am only qualified to make my way by dint of plodding, and therefore plod I must.

My father seems to be more impatient of your absence than he was after your first departure. He is sensible, I believe, that our solitary meals want the light which your gay humour was wont to throw over them, and feels melancholy, as men do when the light of the sun is no longer upon the landscape. If it is thus with him, thou mayst imagine it is much more so with me, and canst conceive how heartily I wish that thy frolic were ended, and thou once more our inmate.

I resume my pen, after a few hours' interval, to say that an incident has occurred, on which you will yourself be building a hundred castles in the air, and which even I, jealous as I am of such baseless fabrics, cannot but own affords ground for singular conjecture.

My father has of late taken me frequently along with him when he attends the Courts, in his anxiety to see me properly initiated into the practical forms of business. I own I feel something on his account and my own from this over-anxiety, which, I dare say, renders us both ridiculous. But what signifies my repugnance! my father drags me up to his counsel learned in the law,—'Are you quite ready to come on to-day, Mr Crossbite?—This is my son, designed for the bar—I take the liberty to bring him with me to-day to the consultation, merely that he may see how these things are managed.'

Mr Crossbite smiles and bows, as a lawyer smiles on the solicitor who employs him, and I dare say, thrusts his tongue into his cheek, and whispers into the first great wig that passes him, 'What the d—l does old Fairford mean by letting loose his whelp on me?'

As I stood beside them, too much vexed at the childish part I was made to play to derive much information from the valuable arguments of Mr Crossbite, I observed a rather elderly man, who stood with his eyes firmly bent on my father, as if he only waited an end of the business in which he was engaged, to address him. There was something, I thought, in the gentleman's appearance, which commanded attention. Yet his dress was not in the present taste, and though it had once been magnificent, was now antiquated and unfashionable. His coat was of branched velvet, with a satin lining, a waistcoat of violet-coloured silk, much embroidered; his breeches the same stuff as the coat. He wore square-toed shoes, with foretops, as they are called; and his silk stockings were rolled up over his knee, as you may have seen in pictures, and here and there on some of those originals who seem to pique themselves on dressing after the mode of Methuselah. A *chapeau bras* and sword necessarily completed his equipment, which, though out of date, showed that it belonged to a man of distinction.

The instant Mr Crossbite had ended what he had to say, this gentleman walked up to my father, with, 'Your servant, Mr Fairford—it is long since you and I met.'

My father, whose politeness, you know, is exact and formal, bowed, and hemmed, and was confused, and at length professed that the distance since they had met was so great, that though he remembered the face perfectly, the name, he was sorry to say, had—really—somehow—escaped his memory.

'Have you forgot Herries of Birrenswork?' said the gentleman, and my father bowed even more profoundly than before; though I think his reception of his old friend seemed to lose some of the respectful civility which he bestowed on him while his name was yet unknown. It now seemed to be something like the lip-courtesy which the heart would have denied had ceremony permitted.

My father, however, again bowed low, and hoped he saw him well.

'So well, my good Mr Fairford, that I come hither determined to renew my acquaintance with one or two old friends, and with you in the first place.—I halt at my old resting-place—you must dine with me to-day at Paterson's, at the head of the Horse Wynd*—it is near your new fashionable dwelling, and I have business with you.'

My father excused himself respectfully, and not without embarrassment—'he was particularly engaged at home.'

'Then I will dine with you, man,' said Mr Herries of Birrenswork; 'the few minutes you can spare me after dinner will suffice for my business; and I will not prevent you a moment from minding your own—I am no bottle-man.'

You have often remarked that my father, though a scrupulous observer of the rites of hospitality, seems to exercise them rather as a duty than as a pleasure; indeed, but for a conscientious wish to feed the hungry and receive the stranger, his doors would open to guests much seldomer than is the case. I never saw so strong an example of this peculiarity, (which I should otherwise have said is caricatured in your description,) as in his mode of homologating the self-given invitation of Mr Herries. The embarrassed brow, and the attempt at a smile which accompanied his 'We will expect the honour of seeing you in Brown Square at three o'clock,' could not deceive any one, and did not impose upon the old Laird. It was with a look of scorn that he replied, 'I will relieve you then till that hour, Mr Fairford;' and his whole manner seemed to say, 'It is my pleasure to dine with you, and I care not whether I am welcome or no.'

When he turned away, I asked my father who he was.

'An unfortunate gentleman,' was the reply.

'He looks pretty well on his misfortunes,' replied I. 'I should not have suspected that so gay an outside was lacking a dinner.'

'Who told you that he does?' replied my father; 'he is *omni suspicione major*, so far as worldly circumstances are concerned—It is to be hoped he makes a good use of them; though, if he does, it will be for the first time in his life.'

'He has then been an irregular liver?' insinuated I.

My father replied by that famous brocard with which he silences all unacceptable queries, turning in the slightest degree upon the failings of our neighbours,—'If we mend our own faults, Alan, we shall all of us have enough to do, without sitting in judgment upon other folks.'

Here I was again at fault; but rallying once more, I observed, he had the air of a man of high rank and family.

'He is well entitled,' said my father, 'representing Herries of Birrenswork; a branch of that great and once powerful family of Herries, the elder branch whereof merged in the house of Nithesdale at the death of Lord Robin the Philosopher, Anno Domini sixteen hundred and sixty-seven.'

'Has he still,' said I, 'his patrimonial estate of Birrenswork?'

'No,' replied my father; 'so far back as his father's time, it was a mere designation—the property being forfeited by Herbert Herries following his kinsman the Earl of Derwentwater, to the Preston affair in 1715.* But they keep up the designation, thinking, doubtless, that their claims may be revived in more favourable times for Jacobites and for Popery; and folks who in no way partake of their fantastic capriccios, do yet allow it to pass unchallenged, *ex comitate*, if not *ex misericordia*.—But were he the Pope and the Pretender both, we must get some dinner ready for him, since he has thought fit to offer himself. So hasten home, my lad, and tell Hannah, Cook Epps, and James Wilkinson, to do their best; and do thou look out a pint or two of Maxwell's best—it is in the fifth bin—there are the keys of the wine-cellar.—Do not leave them in the lock—you know poor James's failing, though he is an honest creature under all other temptations—and I have but two bottles of the old brandy left—we must keep it for medicine, Alan.'

Away went I—made my preparations—the hour of dinner came, and so did Mr Herries of Birrenswork.

If I had thy power of imagination and description, Darsie, I could make out a fine, dark, mysterious, Rembrandt-looking portrait* of this same stranger, which should be as far superior to thy fisherman, as a shirt of chain-mail is to a herring-net. I can assure you there is some matter for description about him; but knowing my own imperfections, I can only say, I thought him eminently disagreeable and ill-bred.—No, *ill-bred* is not the proper word; on the contrary, he appeared to know the rules of good-breeding perfectly, and only to think that the rank of the company did not require that he should attend to them—a view of the matter infinitely more offensive than if his behaviour had been that of uneducated and proper rudeness. While my father said grace, the Laird did all but whistle aloud; and when I, at my father's desire, returned thanks, he used his toothpick, as if he had waited that moment for its exercise.

So much for Kirk—with King, matters went even worse. My father, thou knowest, is particularly full of deference to his guests; and in the present case, he seemed more than usually desirous to escape every cause of dispute. He so far compromised his loyalty, as to announce merely 'The King,' as his first toast after dinner, instead of the emphatic 'King George,' which is his usual formula. Our guest made a motion with his glass, so as to pass it over the water-decanter which stood beside him, and added, 'Over the water.'*

My father coloured, but would not seem to hear this. Much more there was of careless and disrespectful in the stranger's manner and tone of conversation; so that though I know my father's prejudices in favour of rank and birth, and though I am aware his otherwise masculine understanding has never entirely shaken off the slavish awe of the great, which in his earlier days they had so many modes of commanding, still I could hardly excuse him for enduring so much insolence—such it seemed to be—as this self-invited guest was disposed to offer to him at his own table.

One can endure a traveller in the same carriage, if he treads upon your toes by accident, or even through negligence; but it is very different when, knowing that they are rather of a tender description, he continues to pound away at them with his hoofs. In my poor opinion—and I am a man of peace—you can, in that case, hardly avoid a declaration of war.

I believe my father read my thoughts in my eye; for, pulling out his watch, he said, 'Half past four, Alan—you should be in your own room by this time—Birrenswork will excuse you.'

Our visitor nodded carelessly, and I had no longer any pretence to remain. But as I left the room I heard this Magnate of Nithesdale distinctly mention the name of Latimer. I lingered; but at length a direct hint from my father obliged me to withdraw; and when, an hour afterwards, I was summoned to partake of a cup of tea, our guest had departed. He had business that evening in the High Street, and could not spare time even to drink tea. I could not help saying, I considered his departure as a relief from incivility. 'What business has he to upbraid us,' I said, 'with the change of our dwelling from a more inconvenient to a better quarter of the town? What was it to him if we chose to imitate some of the conveniences or luxuries of an English dwelling-house, instead of living piled up above each other in flats? Have his patrician birth and aristocratic fortunes given him any right to censure those who dispose of the fruits of their own industry, according to their own pleasure?'

My father took a long pinch of snuff, and replied, 'Very well, Alan; very well indeed. I wish Mr Crossbite or Counsellor Pest had heard you; they must have acknowledged that you have a talent for forensic elocution; and it may not be amiss to try a little declamation at home now and then, to gather audacity and keep yourself in breath. But touching the subject of this paraffle of words, it's not worth a pinch of tobacco. D'ye think that I care for Mr Herries of Birrenswork more than any other gentleman who comes here about business, although I do not care to go tilting at his throat, because he speaks like a grey goose as he is? But to say no more about him, I want to have Darsie Latimer's present direction; for it is possible I may have to write the lad a line with my own hand—and yet I do not well know—but give me the direction at all events.'

I did so, and if you have heard from my father accordingly, you know more, probably, about the subject of this letter than I who write it. But if you have not, then shall I have discharged a friend's duty, in letting you know that there certainly is something afloat between this disagreeable Laird and my father, in which you are considerably interested.

Adieu! and although I have given thee a subject for waking dreams, beware of building a castle too heavy for the foundation; which, in the present instance, is barely the word Latimer occurring in a conversation betwixt a gentleman of Dumfriesshire and a W.S. of Edinburgh—*Cetera prorsus ignoro.*

LETTER VI

DARSIE LATIMER TO ALAN FAIRFORD

[In continuation of Letters III and IV]

I TOLD thee I walked out into the open air with my grave and stern landlord. I could now see more perfectly than on the preceding night the secluded glen, in which stood the two or three cottages which appeared to be the abode of him and his family.

It was so narrow, in proportion to its depth, that no ray of the morning sun was likely to reach it till it should rise high in the horizon. Looking up the dell, you saw a brawling brook issuing in foamy haste from a covert of underwood, like a racehorse impatient to arrive at the goal; and, if you gazed yet more earnestly, you might observe part of a high waterfall glimmering through the foliage, and giving occasion, doubtless, to the precipitate speed of the brook. Lower down, the stream became more placid, and opened into a quiet piece of water, which afforded a rude haven to two or three fishermen's boats, then lying high and dry on the sand, the tide being out. Two or three miserable huts could be seen beside this little haven, inhabited probably by the owners of the boats, but inferior in every respect to the establishment of mine host, though that was miserable enough.

I had but a minute or two to make these observations, yet during that space my companion showed symptoms of impatience, and more than once shouted, 'Cristal——Cristal Nixon,' until the old man of the preceding evening appeared at the door of one of the neighbouring cottages or outhouses, leading the strong black horse which I before commemorated, ready bridled and saddled. My conductor made Cristal a sign with his finger, and, turning from the cottage door, led the way up the steep path or ravine which connected the sequestered dell with the open country.

Had I been perfectly aware of the character of the road down which I had been hurried with so much impetuosity on the preceding evening, I greatly question if I should have ventured the descent; for it deserved no better name than the channel of a torrent, now in a good measure filled with water that dashed in foam and fury into the dell, being swelled with the rains of the preceding night. I ascended this ugly path with some difficulty, although on foot, and felt dizzy when I observed, from such traces as the rains had not obliterated, that the horse seemed almost to have slid down it upon his haunches the evening before.

My host threw himself on his horse's back, without placing a foot in the stirrup—passed me in the perilous ascent, against which he pressed his steed as if the animal had had the footing of a wild cat. The water and mud splashed from his heels in his reckless course, and a few bounds placed him on the top of the bank, where I presently joined him, and found the horse and rider standing still as a statue; the former panting and expanding his broad nostrils to the morning wind, the latter motionless, with his eye fixed on the first beams of the rising sun, which already began to peer above the eastern horizon, and gild the distant mountains of Cumberland and Liddesdale.

He seemed in a reverie, from which he started at my approach, and putting his horse in motion, led the way at a leisurely pace, through a broken and sandy road, which traversed a waste, level, and uncultivated tract of downs, intermixed with morass, much like that in the neighbourhood of my quarters at Shepherd's Bush. Indeed the whole open ground of this district, where it approaches the sea, has, except in a few favoured spots, the same uniform and dreary character.

Advancing about a hundred yards from the brink of the glen, we gained a still more extensive command of this desolate prospect, which seemed even more dreary, as contrasted with the opposite shores of Cumberland, crossed and intersected by ten thousand lines of trees growing in hedge-rows, shaded with groves and woods of considerable extent, and animated by hamlets and villas, from which thin clouds of smoke already gave sign of human life and human industry.

My conductor had extended his arm, and was pointing the road to Shepherd's Bush, when the step of a horse was heard approaching us. He looked sharply around, and having observed who was approaching, proceeded in his instructions to me, planting himself at the same time in the very middle of the path, which, at the place where we halted, had a slough on the one side, and a sandbank on the other.

I observed that the rider who approached us slackened his horse's pace from a slow trot to a walk, as if desirous to suffer us to proceed, or at least to avoid passing us at a spot where the difficulty of doing so must have brought us very close to each other. You know my old failing, Alan, and that I am always willing to attend to any thing in preference to the individual who has for the time possession of the conversation.

Agreeably to this amiable propensity, I was internally speculating concerning the cause of the rider keeping aloof from us, when my companion, elevating his deep voice so suddenly and so sternly, as at once to recall my wandering thoughts, exclaimed, 'In the name of the devil, young man, do you think that others have no better use for their time than you have, that you oblige me to repeat the same thing to you three times over?—Do you see, I say, yonder thing at a mile's distance, that looks like a finger-post, or rather like a gallows?—I would it had a dreaming fool hanging upon it, as an example to all meditative moon-calves!—Yon gibbet-looking pole will guide you to the bridge, where you must pass the large brook; then proceed straight forwards, till several roads divide at a cairn.—Plague on thee, thou art wandering again!'

It is indeed quite true, that at this moment the horseman approached us, and my attention was again called to him as I made way to let him pass. His whole exterior at once showed that he belonged to the Society of Friends, or, as the world and the world's law call them, Quakers. A strong and useful iron-grey galloway showed, by its sleek and good condition, that the merciful man was merciful to his beast. His accoutrements were in the usual unostentatious, but clean and serviceable order, which characterises these sectaries. His long surtout of dark-grey superfine cloth descended down to the middle of his leg, and was buttoned up to his chin, to defend him against the morning air. As usual, his ample beaver hung down without button or loop, and shaded a comely and placid countenance, the gravity of which appeared to contain some seasoning of humour, and had nothing in common with the pinched puritanical air affected by devotees in general. The brow was open and free from wrinkles, whether of age or hypocrisy. The eye was clear, calm, and considerate, yet appeared to be disturbed by apprehension, not to say fear, as, pronouncing the usual salutation of 'I wish thee a good morrow, friend,' he indicated, by turning his palfrey close to one side of the path, a wish to glide past us with as little trouble as possible—just as a traveller would choose to pass a mastiff of whose peaceable intentions he is by no means confident.

But my friend, not meaning, perhaps, that he should get off so easily, put his horse quite across the path, so that, without plunging into the slough, or scrambling up the bank, the Quaker could not have passed him. Neither of these was an experiment without hazard greater than the passenger seemed willing to incur. He halted, therefore, as if waiting till my companion should make way for him; and, as they sat fronting each other, I could not help thinking that they might have formed no bad emblem of Peace and War; for although my conductor was unarmed, yet the whole of his manner, his stern look, and his upright seat on horseback, were entirely those of a soldier in undress. He accosted the Quaker in these words,—'So ho! friend Joshua—thou art early to the road this morning. Has the spirit moved thee and thy righteous brethren to act with some honesty, and pull down yonder tide-nets that keep the fish from coming up the river?'

'Surely, friend, not so,' answered Joshua, firmly, but good-humouredly at the same time; 'thou canst not expect that our own hands should pull down what our own purses established. Thou killest the fish with spear, line, and coble-net; and we, with snares and with nets, which work by the ebb and the flow of the tide. Each doth what seems best in his eyes to secure a share of the blessing which Providence hath bestowed on the river, and that within his own bounds. I prithee seek no quarrel against us, for thou shalt have no wrong at our hand.'

'Be assured I will take none at the hand of any man, whether his hat be cocked or broad-brimmed,' answered the fisherman. 'I tell you in fair terms, Joshua Geddes, that you and your partners are using unlawful craft* to destroy the fish in the Solway by stake-nets and wears; and that we, who fish fairly, and like men, as our fathers did, have daily and yearly less sport and less profit. Do not think gravity or hypocrisy can carry it off as you have done. The world knows you, and we know you. You will destroy the salmon which make the livelihood of fifty poor families, and then wipe your mouth, and go to make a speech at Meeting. But do not hope it will last thus. I give you fair warning, we will be upon you one morning soon, when we will not leave a stake standing in the pools of the Solway; and down the tide they shall every one go, and well if we do not send a lessee along with them.'

'Friend,' replied Joshua, with a constrained smile, 'but that I know thou dost not mean as thou say'st, I would tell thee we are under the protection of this country's laws; nor do we the less trust to obtain their protection, that our principles permit us not, by any act of violent resistance, to protect ourselves.'

'All villainous cant and cowardice,' exclaimed the fisherman, 'and assumed merely as a cloak to your hypocritical avarice.'

'Nay, say not cowardice, my friend,' answered the Quaker, 'since thou knowest there may be as much courage in enduring as in acting; and I will be judged by this youth, or by any one else, whether there is not more cowardice—even in the opinion of that world whose thoughts are the breath in thy nostrils—in the armed oppressor, who doth injury, than in the defenceless and patient sufferer, who endureth it with constancy.'

'I will change no more words with you on the subject,' said the fisherman, who, as if something moved at the last argument which Mr Geddes had used, now made room for him to pass forward on his journey.—'Do not forget, however,' he added, 'that you have had fair warning, nor suppose that we will accept of fair words in apology for foul play. These nets of yours are unlawful—they spoil our fishings—and we will have them down at all risks and hazards. I am a man of my word, friend Joshua.'

'I trust thou art,' said the Quaker; 'but thou art the rather bound to be cautious in rashly affirming what thou wilt never execute. For I tell thee, friend, that though there is as great a difference between thee and one of our people, as there is between a lion and a sheep, yet I know and believe thou hast so much of the lion in thee, that thou wouldst scarce employ thy strength and thy rage upon that which professeth no means of resistance. Report says so much good of thee, at least, if it says little more.'

'Time will try,' answered the fisherman; 'and hark thee, Joshua, before we part I will put thee in the way of doing one good deed, which, credit me, is better than twenty moral speeches. Here is a stranger youth, whom heaven has so scantily gifted with brains, that he will bewilder himself in the Sands, as he did last night, unless thou wilt kindly show him the way to Shepherd's Bush; for I have been in vain endeavouring to make him comprehend the road thither—Hast thou so much charity under thy simplicity, Quaker, as to do this good turn?'

'Nay, it is thou, friend,' answered Joshua, 'that dost lack charity, to suppose any one unwilling to do so simple a kindness.'

'Thou art right—I should have remembered it can cost thee nothing.—Young gentleman, this pious pattern of primitive simplicity will teach thee the right way to the Shepherd's Bush—ay, and will himself shear thee like a sheep, if you come to buying and selling with him.'

He then abruptly asked me, how long I intended to remain at Shepherd's Bush.

I replied I was at present uncertain—as long, probably, as I could amuse myself in the neighbourhood.

'You are fond of sport?' he added, in the same tone of brief enquiry.

I answered in the affirmative, but added, I was totally inexperienced.

'Perhaps if you reside here for some days,' he said, 'we may meet again, and I may have the chance of giving you a lesson.'

Ere I could express either thanks or assent, he turned short round with a wave of his hand, by way of adieu, and rode back to the verge of the dell from which we had emerged together; and as he remained standing upon the banks, I could long hear his voice while he shouted down to those within its recesses.

Meanwhile the Quaker and I proceeded on our journey for some time in silence; he restraining his soberminded steed to a pace which might have suited a much less active walker than myself, and looking on me from time to time with an expression of curiosity, mingled with benignity. For my part, I cared not to speak first. It happened I had never before been in company with one of this particular sect, and, afraid that in addressing him I might unwittingly infringe upon some of their prejudices or peculiarities, I patiently remained silent. At length he asked me, whether I had been long in the service of the Laird, as men called him.

I repeated the words 'in his service?' with such an accent of surprise, as induced him to say, 'Nay, but, friend, I mean no offence; perhaps I should have said in his society—an inmate, I mean, in his house?'

'I am totally unknown to the person from whom we have just parted,' said I, 'and our connexion is only temporary—He had the charity to give me his guidance from the Sands, and a night's harbourage from the tempest. So our acquaintance began, and there it is likely to end; for you may observe that our friend is by no means apt to encourage familiarity.'

'So little so,' answered my companion, 'that thy case is, I think, the first in which I ever heard of his receiving any one into his house; that is, if thou hast really spent the night there.'

'Why should you doubt it?' replied I; 'there is no motive I can have to deceive you, nor is the object worth it.'

'Be not angry with me,' said the Quaker; 'but thou knowest that thine own people do not, as we humbly endeavour to do, confine themselves within the simplicity of truth, but employ the language of falsehood, not only for profit, but for compliment, and sometimes for mere diversion. I have heard various stories of my neighbour; of most of which I only believe a small part, and even then they are difficult to reconcile with each other. But this being the first time I ever heard of his receiving a stranger within his dwelling, made me express some doubts. I pray thee let them not offend thee.'

'He does not,' said I, 'appear to possess in much abundance the means of exercising hospitality, and so may be excused from offering it in ordinary cases.'

'That is to say, friend,' replied Joshua, 'thou hast supped ill, and perhaps breakfasted worse. Now my small tenement, called Mount Sharon, is nearer to us by two miles than thine inn; and although going thither may prolong thy walk, as taking thee off the straighter road to Shepherd's Bush, yet methinks exercise will suit thy youthful limbs, as well as a good plain meal thy youthful appetite. What say'st thou, my young acquaintance?'

'If it puts you not to inconvenience,' I replied; for the invitation was cordially given, and my bread and milk had been hastily swallowed, and in small quantity.

'Nay,' said Joshua, 'use not the language of compliment with those who renounce it. Had this poor courtesy been very inconvenient, perhaps I had not offered it.'

'I accept the invitation then,' said I, 'in the same good spirit in which you give it.'

The Quaker smiled, reached me his hand, I shook it, and we travelled on in great cordiality with each other. The fact is, I was much entertained by contrasting in my own mind, the open manner of the kind-hearted Joshua Geddes, with the abrupt, dark, and lofty demeanour of my entertainer on the preceding evening. Both were blunt and unceremonious; but the plainness of the Quaker had the character of devotional simplicity, and was mingled with the more real kindness, as if honest Joshua was desirous of atoning, by his sincerity, for the lack of external courtesy. On the contrary, the manners of the fisherman were those of one to whom the rules of good behaviour might be familiar, but who, either from pride or misanthropy, scorned to observe them. Still I thought of him with interest and curiosity, notwithstanding so much about him that was repulsive; and I promised myself, in the course of my conversation with the Quaker, to learn all that he knew on the subject. He turned the conversation, however, into a different channel, and enquired into my own condition of life, and views in visiting this remote frontier.

I only thought it necessary to mention my name, and add, that I had been educated to the law, but finding myself possessed of some independence, I had of late permitted myself some relaxation, and was residing at Shepherd's Bush to enjoy the pleasure of angling.

'I do thee no harm, young man,' said my new friend, 'in wishing thee a better employment for thy grave hours, and a more humane amusement (if amusement thou must have) for those of a lighter character.'

'You are severe, sir,' I replied. 'I heard you but a moment since refer yourself to the protection of the laws of the country—if there be laws, there must be lawyers to explain, and judges to administer them.'

Joshua smiled, and pointed to the sheep which were grazing on the downs over which we were travelling.—'Were a wolf,' he said, 'to come even now upon yonder flocks, they would crowd for protection, doubtless, around the shepherd and his dogs; yet they are bitten and harassed daily by the one, shorn, and finally killed and eaten by the other. But I say not this to shock you; for, though laws and lawyers are evils, yet they are necessary evils in this probationary state of society, till man shall learn to render unto his fellows that which is their due, according to the light of his own conscience, and through no other compulsion. Meanwhile, I have known many righteous men who have followed thy intended profession in honesty and uprightness of walk. The greater their merit, who walk erect in a path which so many find slippery.'

'And angling,'—said I, 'you object to that also as an amusement, you who, if I understood rightly what passed between you and my late landlord, are yourself a proprietor of fisheries?'

'Not a proprietor,' he replied, 'I am only, in copartnery with others, a tacksman or lessee of some valuable salmon-fisheries a little down the coast. But mistake me not. The evil of angling, with which I class all sports, as they are called, which have the sufferings of animals for their end and object, does not consist in the mere catching and killing those animals with which the bounty of Providence hath stocked the earth for the good of man, but in making their protracted agony a principle of delight and enjoyment. I do indeed cause these fisheries to be conducted for the necessary taking, killing, and selling the fish; and, in the same way, were I a farmer, I should send my lambs to market. But I should as soon think of contriving myself a sport and amusement out of the trade of the butcher as out of that of the fisher.'

We argued this point no farther; for though I thought his arguments a little too high-strained, yet as my mind acquitted me of having taken delight in aught but the theory of field-sports, I did not think myself called upon stubbornly to advocate a practice which had afforded me so little pleasure.

We had by this time arrived at the remains of an old finger-post, which my host had formerly pointed out as a landmark. Here, a ruinous wooden bridge, supported by long posts resembling crutches, served me to get across the water, while my new friend sought a ford a good way higher up, for the stream was considerably swelled.

As I paused for his rejoining me, I observed an angler at a little distance pouching trout after trout, as fast almost as he could cast his line; and I own, in spite of Joshua's lecture on humanity, I could not but envy his adroitness and success,—so natural is the love of sport to our minds, or so easily are we taught to assimilate success in field-sports with ideas of pleasure, and with the praise due to address and agility. I soon recognised in the successful angler little Benjie, who had been my guide and tutor in that gentle art, as you have learned from my former letters. I called—I whistled—the rascal recognised me, and, starting like a guilty thing, seemed hesitating whether to approach or to run away; and when he determined on the former, it was to assail me with a loud, clamorous, and exaggerated report of the anxiety of all at the Shepherd's Bush for my personal safety; how my landlady had wept, how Sam and the ostler had not the heart to go to bed, but sat up all night drinking—and how he himself had been up long before daybreak to go in quest of me.

'And you were switching the water, I suppose,' said I, 'to discover my dead body?'

This observation produced a long 'Na—a—a' of acknowledged detection; but, with his natural impudence, and confidence in my good-nature, he immediately added, 'that he thought I would like a fresh trout or twa for breakfast, and the water being in such rare trim for the saumon raun,[18] he couldna help taking a cast.'

While we were engaged in this discussion, the honest Quaker returned to the farther end of the wooden bridge to tell me he could not venture to cross the brook in its present state, but would be under the necessity to ride round by the stone bridge, which was a mile and a half higher up than his own house. He was about to give me directions how to proceed without him, and enquire for his sister, when I suggested to him, that if he pleased to trust his horse to little Benjie, the boy might carry him round by the bridge, while we walked the shorter and more pleasant road.

Joshua shook his head, for he was well acquainted with Benjie, who, he said, was the naughtiest varlet in the whole neighbourhood. Nevertheless, rather than part company, he agreed to put the pony under his charge for a short season, with many injunctions that he should not attempt to mount, but lead the pony (even Solomon) by the bridle, under the assurances of sixpence in case of proper demeanour, and penalty that if he transgressed the orders given him, 'verily he should be scourged.'

Promises cost Benjie nothing, and he showered them out whole-sale; till the Quaker at length yielded up the bridle to him, repeating his charges, and enforcing them by holding up his forefinger. On my part, I called to Benjie to leave the fish he had taken at Mount Sharon, making, at the same time, an apologetic countenance to my new friend, not being quite aware whether the compliment would be agreeable to such a condemner of field-sports.

He understood me at once, and reminded me of the practical distinction betwixt catching the animals as an object of cruel and wanton sport, and eating them as lawful and gratifying articles of food after they were killed. On the latter point he had no scruples; but, on the contrary, assured me, that this brook contained the real red trout, so highly esteemed by all connoisseurs, and that, when eaten within an hour of their being caught, they had a peculiar firmness of substance and delicacy of flavour, which rendered them an agreeable addition to a morning meal, especially when earned, like ours, by early rising, and an hour or two's wholesome exercise.

But to thy alarm be it spoken, Alan, we did not come so far as the frying of our fish without farther adventure. So it is only to spare thy patience, and mine own eyes, that I pull up for the present, and send thee the rest of my story in a subsequent letter.

LETTER VII

THE SAME TO THE SAME

[In continuation]

LITTLE BENJIE, with the pony, having been sent off on the left side of the brook, the Quaker and I sauntered on, like the cavalry and infantry of the same army occupying the opposite banks of a river, and observing the same line of march. But, while my worthy companion was assuring me of a pleasant greensward walk to his mansion, little Benjie, who had been charged to keep in sight, chose to deviate from the path assigned him, and, turning to the right, led his charge, Solomon, out of our vision.

'The villain means to mount him!' cried Joshua, with more vivacity than was consistent with his profession of passive endurance.

I endeavoured to appease his apprehensions, as he pushed on, wiping his brow with vexation, assuring him, that if the boy did mount, he would, for his own sake, ride gently.

'You do not know him,' said Joshua, rejecting all consolation; '*he* do any thing gently!—no, he will gallop Solomon—he will misuse the sober patience of the poor animal who has borne me so long! Yes, I was given over to my own devices when I ever let him touch the bridle, for such a little miscreant there never was before him in this country!'

He then proceeded to expatiate on every sort of rustic enormity of which he accused Benjie. He had been suspected of snaring partridges—was detected by Joshua himself in liming singing birds—stood fully charged with having worried several cats, by aid of a lurcher which attended him, and which was as lean, and ragged, and mischievous, as his master. Finally, Benjie stood accused of having stolen a duck, to hunt it with the said lurcher, which was as dexterous on water as on land. I chimed in with my friend, in order to avoid giving him farther irritation, and declared, I should be disposed, from my own experience, to give up Benjie as one of Satan's imps. Joshua Geddes began to censure the phrase as too much exaggerated, and otherwise unbecoming the mouth of a reflecting person; and, just as I was apologizing for it, as being a term of common parlance, we heard certain sounds on the opposite side of the brook, which seemed to indicate that Solomon and Benjie were at issue together. The sand-hills behind which Benjie seemed to take his course, had concealed from us, as doubtless he meant they should, his ascent into the forbidden saddle, and, putting Solomon to his mettle, which he was seldom called upon to exert, they had cantered away together in great amity, till they came near to the ford from which the palfrey's legitimate owner had already turned back.

Here a contest of opinions took place between the horse and his rider. The latter, according to his instructions, attempted to direct Solomon towards the distant bridge of stone; but Solomon opined that the ford was the shortest way to his own stable. The point was sharply contested, and we heard Benjie gee-hupping, tchek-tcheking, and, above all, flogging in great style; while Solomon, who, docile in his general habits, was now stirred beyond his patience, made a great trampling and recalcitration; and it was their joint noise which we heard, without being able to see, though Joshua might too well guess, the cause of it.

Alarmed at these indications, the Quaker began to shout out, 'Benjie—thou varlet!—Solomon—thou fool!' when the couple presented themselves in full drive, Solomon having now decidedly obtained the better of the conflict, and bringing his unwilling rider in high career down to the ford. Never was there anger changed so fast into humane fear, as that of my good companion. 'The varlet will be drowned!' he exclaimed—'a widow's son!—her only son!—and drowned!—let me go'——And he struggled with me stoutly as I hung upon him, to prevent him from plunging into the ford.

I had no fear whatever for Benjie; for the blackguard vermin, though he could not manage the refractory horse, stuck on his seat like a monkey. Solomon and Benjie scrambled through the ford with little inconvenience, and resumed their gallop on the other side.

It was impossible to guess whether on this last occasion Benjie was running off with Solomon, or Solomon with Benjie; but, judging from character and motives, I rather suspected the former. I could not help laughing as the rascal passed me, grinning betwixt terror and delight, perched on the very pommel of the saddle, and holding with extended arms by bridle and mane; while Solomon, the bit secured between his teeth, and his head bored down betwixt his fore-legs, passed his master in this unwonted guise as hard as he could pelt.

'The mischievous bastard!' exclaimed the Quaker, terrified out of his usual moderation of speech—'the doomed gallows-bird!—he will break Solomon's wind to a certainty.'

I prayed him to be comforted—assured him a brushing gallop would do his favourite no harm—and reminded him of the censure he had bestowed on me a minute before, for applying a harsh epithet to the boy.

But Joshua was not without his answer;—'Friend youth,' he said, 'thou didst speak of the lad's soul, which thou didst affirm belonged to the enemy, and of that thou couldst say nothing of thine own knowledge; on the contrary, I did but speak of his outward man, which will assuredly be suspended by a cord, if he mendeth not his manners. Men say that, young as he is, he is one of the Laird's gang.'

'Of the Laird's gang!' said I, repeating the words in surprise—'Do you mean the person with whom I slept last night?—I heard you call him the Laird—Is he at the head of a gang?'

'Nay, I meant not precisely a gang,' said the Quaker, who appeared in his haste to have spoken more than he intended—'a company, or party, I should have said; but thus it is, friend Latimer, with the wisest men, when they permit themselves to be perturbed with passion, and speak as in a fever, or as with the tongue of the foolish and the forward. And although thou hast been hasty to mark my infirmity, yet I grieve not that thou hast been a witness to it, seeing that the stumbles of the wise may be no less a caution to youth and inexperience than is the fall of the foolish.'

This was a sort of acknowledgment of what I had already begun to suspect—that my new friend's real goodness of disposition, joined to the acquired quietism of his religious sect, had been unable entirely to check the effervescence of a temper naturally warm and hasty.

Upon the present occasion, as if sensible he had displayed a greater degree of emotion than became his character, Joshua avoided farther allusion to Benjie and Solomon, and proceeded to solicit my attention to the natural objects around us, which increased in beauty and interest, as, still conducted by the meanders of the brook, we left the common behind us, and entered a more cultivated and enclosed country, where arable and pasture ground was agreeably varied with groves and hedges. Descending now almost close to the stream, our course lay through a little gate, into a pathway, kept with great neatness, the sides of which were decorated with trees and flowering shrubs of the hardier species; until, ascending by a gentle slope, we issued from the grove, and stood almost at once in front of a low but very neat building, of an irregular form; and my guide, shaking me cordially by the hand, made me welcome to Mount Sharon.

The wood through which we had approached this little mansion was thrown around it both on the north and north-west, but, breaking off into different directions, was intersected by a few fields, well watered and sheltered. The house fronted to the south-east, and from thence the pleasure-ground, or, I should rather say, the gardens, sloped down to the water. I afterwards understood that the father of the present proprietor had a considerable taste for horticulture, which had been inherited by his son, and had formed these gardens, which, with their shaven turf, pleached alleys, wildernesses,* and exotic trees and shrubs, greatly excelled any thing of the kind which had been attempted in the neighbourhood.

If there was a little vanity in the complacent smile with which Joshua Geddes saw me gaze with delight on a scene so different from the naked waste we had that day traversed in company, it might surely be permitted to one, who, cultivating and improving the beauties of nature, had found therein, as he said, bodily health and a pleasing relaxation for the mind. At the bottom of the extended gardens the brook wheeled round in a wide semicircle, and was itself their boundary. The opposite side was no part of Joshua's domain, but the brook was there skirted by a precipitous rock of limestone, which seemed a barrier of Nature's own erecting around his little Eden of beauty, comfort, and peace.

'But I must not let thee forget,' said the kind Quaker, 'amidst thy admiration of these beauties of our little inheritance, that thy breakfast has been a light one.'

So saying, Joshua conducted me to a small sashed door, opening under a porch amply mantled by honeysuckle and clematis, into a parlour, of moderate size; the furniture of which, in plainness and excessive cleanliness, bore the characteristic marks of the sect to which the owner belonged.

Thy father's Hannah is generally allowed to be an exception to all Scottish housekeepers, and stands unparalleled for cleanliness among the women of Auld Reekie;* but the cleanliness of Hannah is sluttishness, compared to the scrupulous purifications of these people, who seem to carry into the minor decencies of life that conscientious rigour which they affect in their morals.

The parlour would have been gloomy, for the windows were small and the ceiling low; but the present proprietor had rendered it more cheerful by opening one end into a small conservatory, roofed with glass, and divided from the parlour by a partition of the same. I have never before seen this very pleasing manner of uniting the comforts of an apartment with the beauties of a garden, and I wonder it is not more practised by the great. Something of the kind is hinted at in a paper of the Spectator.*

As I walked towards the conservatory to view it more closely, the parlour chimney engaged my attention. It was a pile of massive stone, entirely out of proportion to the size of the apartment. On the front had once been an armorial scutcheon; for the hammer, or chisel, which had been employed to deface the shield and crest, had left uninjured the scroll beneath, which bore the pious motto, '*Trust in God*.' Black-letter, you know, was my early passion, and the tombstones in the Greyfriars' Churchyard* early yielded up to my knowledge as a decipherer what little they could tell of the forgotten dead.

Joshua Geddes paused when he saw my eye fixed on this relic of antiquity. 'Thou canst read it?' he said.

I repeated the motto, and added, there seemed vestiges of a date.

'It should be 1537,' said he; 'for so long ago, at the least computation, did my ancestors, in the blinded times of Papistry,* possess these lands, and in that year did they build their house.'

'It is an ancient descent,' said I, looking with respect upon the monument. 'I am sorry the arms have been defaced.'

It was perhaps impossible for my friend, Quaker as he was, to seem altogether void of respect for the pedigree which he began to recount to me, disclaiming all the while the vanity usually connected with the subject; in short, with the air of mingled melancholy, regret, and conscious dignity, with which Jack Fawkes used to tell us, at College, of his ancestor's unfortunate connexion with the Gunpowder-Plot.*

'Vanity of vanities, saith the preacher,'*—thus harangued Joshua Geddes of Mount Sharon;—'if we ourselves are nothing in the sight of Heaven, how much less than nothing must be our derivation from rotten bones and mouldering dust, whose immortal spirits have long since gone to their private account! Yes, friend Latimer, my ancestors were renowned among the ravenous and bloodthirsty men who then dwelt in this vexed country; and so much were they famed for successful freebooting, robbery, and bloodshed, that they are said to have been called Geddes, as likening them to the fish called a Jack, Pike, or Luce, and in our country tongue, a *Ged*—a goodly distinction truly for Christian men! Yet did they paint this shark of the fresh waters upon their shields, and these profane priests of a wicked idolatry, the empty boasters called heralds, who make engraven images of fishes, fowls, and fourfooted beasts, that men may fall down and worship them, assigned the Ged for the device and escutcheon of my fathers, and hewed it over their chimneys, and placed it above their tombs; and the men were elated in mind, and became yet more Ged-like, slaying, leading into captivity, and dividing the spoil, until the place where they dwelt obtained the name of Sharing-Knowe, from the booty which was there divided amongst them and their accomplices. But a better judgment was given to my father's father, Philip Geddes, who, after trying to light his candle at some of the vain wildfires then held aloft at different meetings and steeple-houses, at length obtained a spark from the lamp of the blessed George Fox, who came into Scotland spreading light among darkness, as he himself hath written, as plentifully as fly the sparkles from the hoof of the horse which gallops swiftly along the stony road.'*—Here the good Quaker interrupted himself with, 'And that is very true, I must go speedily to see after the condition of Solomon.'

A Quaker servant here entered the room with a tray, and inclining his head towards his master, but not after the manner of one who bows, said composedly, 'Thou art welcome home, friend Joshua, we expected thee not so early; but what hath befallen Solomon thy horse?'

'What hath befallen him, indeed!' said my friend; 'hath he not been returned hither by the child whom they call Benjie?'

'He hath,' said his domestic, 'but it was after a strange fashion; for he came hither at a swift and furious pace, and flung the child Benjie from his back, upon the heap of dung which is in the stable-yard.'

'I am glad of it,' said Joshua, hastily,—'glad of it, with all my heart and spirit!—But stay, he is the child of the widow—hath the boy any hurt?'

'Not so,' answered the servant, 'for he rose and fled swiftly.'

Joshua muttered something about a scourge, and then enquired after Solomon's present condition.

'He seetheth like a steaming caldron,' answered the servant; 'and Bauldie, the lad, walketh him about the yard with a halter, lest he take cold.'

Mr Geddes hastened to the stable-yard to view personally the condition of his favourite, and I followed, to offer my counsel as a jockey—Don't laugh, Alan; sure I have jockeyship enough to assist a Quaker—in this unpleasing predicament.

The lad who was leading the horse seemed to be no Quaker, though his intercourse with the family had given him a touch of their prim sobriety of look and manner. He assured Joshua that his horse had received no injury, and I even hinted that the exercise would be of service to him. Solomon himself neighed towards his master, and rubbed his head against the good Quaker's shoulder, as if to assure him of his being quite well; so that Joshua returned in comfort to his parlour, where breakfast was now about to be displayed.

I have since learned that the affection of Joshua for his pony is considered as inordinate by some of his own sect; and that he has been much blamed for permitting it to be called by the name of Solomon, or any other name whatever; but he has gained so much respect and influence among them that they overlook these foibles.

I learned from him (whilst the old servant, Jehoiachim, entering and re-entering, seemed to make no end of the materials which he brought in for breakfast) that his grandfather Philip, the convert of George Fox, had suffered much from the persecution to which these harmless devotees were subjected on all sides during that intolerant period, and much of their family estate had been dilapidated. But better days dawned on Joshua's father, who, connecting himself by marriage with a wealthy family of Quakers in Lancashire, engaged successfully in various branches of commerce, and redeemed the remnants of the property, changing its name in sense, without much alteration of sound, from the Border appellation of Sharing-Knowe, to the evangelical appellation of Mount Sharon.*

This Philip Geddes, as I before hinted, had imbibed the taste for horticulture and the pursuits of the florist, which are not uncommon among the peaceful sect he belongs to. He had destroyed the remnants of the old peel-house, substituting the modern mansion in its place; and while he reserved the hearth of his ancestors, in memory of their hospitality, as also the pious motto which they had chanced to assume, he failed not to obliterate the worldly and military emblems displayed upon the shield and helmet, together with all their blazonry.

In a few minutes after Mr Geddes had concluded the account of himself and his family, his sister Rachel, the only surviving member of it, entered the room. Her appearance is remarkably pleasing, and although her age is certainly thirty at least, she still retains the shape and motion of an earlier period. The absence of every thing like fashion or ornament was, as usual, atoned for by the most perfect neatness and cleanliness of her dress; and her simple close cap was particularly suited to eyes which had the softness and simplicity of the dove's. Her features were also extremely agreeable, but had suffered a little through the ravages of that professed enemy to beauty, the small-pox; a disadvantage which was in part counter-balanced by a well-formed mouth, teeth like pearls, and a pleasing sobriety of smile, that seemed to wish good here and hereafter to every one she spoke to. You cannot make any of your vile inferences here, Alan, for I have given a full-length picture of Rachel Geddes; so that you cannot say in this case, as in the letter I have just received, that she was passed over as a subject on which I feared to dilate. More of this anon.

Well, we settled to our breakfast after a blessing, or rather an extempore prayer, which Joshua made upon the occasion, and which the spirit moved him to prolong rather more than I felt altogether agreeable. Then, Alan, there was such a dispatching of the good things of the morning, as you have not witnessed since you have seen Darsie Latimer at breakfast. Tea and chocolate, eggs, ham, and pastry, not forgetting the broiled fish, disappeared with a celerity which seemed to astonish the good-humoured Quakers, who kept loading my plate with supplies, as if desirous of seeing whether they could by any possibility tire me out. One hint, however, I received, which put me in mind where I was. Miss Geddes had offered me some sweet-cake, which, at the moment, I declined; but presently afterwards, seeing it within my reach, I naturally enough helped myself to a slice, and had just deposited it beside my plate, when Joshua, mine host, not with the authoritative air of Sancho's doctor, Tirtea Fuera,* but in a very calm and quiet manner, lifted it away and replaced it on the dish, observing only, 'Thou didst refuse it before, friend Latimer.'

These good folks, Alan, make no allowance for what your father calls the Aberdeen-man's privilege* of 'taking his word again;' or what the wise call second thoughts.

Bating this slight hint, that I was among a precise generation, there was nothing in my reception that was peculiar—unless, indeed, I were to notice the solicitous and uniform kindness with which all the attentions of my new friends were seasoned, as if they were anxious to assure me that the neglect of worldly compliments interdicted by their sect, only served to render their hospitality more sincere. At length my hunger was satisfied, and the worthy Quaker, who, with looks of great good-nature, had watched my progress, thus addressed his sister:—

'This young man, Rachel, hath last night sojourned in the tents of our neighbour, whom men call the Laird. I am sorry I had not met him the evening before, for our neighbour's hospitality is too unfrequently exercised to be well prepared with the means of welcome.'

'Nay, but, Joshua,' said Rachel, 'if our neighbour hath done a kindness, thou shouldst not grudge him the opportunity; and if our young friend hath fared ill for a night, he will the better relish what Providence may send him of better provisions.'

'And that he may do so at leisure,' said Joshua, 'we will pray him, Rachel, to tarry a day or twain with us: he is young, and is but now entering upon the world, and our habitation may, if he will, be like a resting-place, from which he may look abroad upon the pilgrimage which he must make, and the path which he has to travel.—What sayest thou, friend Latimer? We constrain not our friends to our ways, and thou art, I think, too wise to quarrel with us for following our own fashions; and if we should even give thee a word of advice, thou wilt not, I think, be angry, so that it is spoken in season.'

You know, Alan, how easily I am determined by any thing resembling cordiality—and so, though a little afraid of the formality of my host and hostess, I accepted their invitation, provided I could get some messenger to send to Shepherd's Bush for my servant and portmanteau.

'Why, truly, friend,' said Joshua, 'thine outward frame would be improved by cleaner garments; but I will do thine errand myself to the Widow Gregson's house of reception, and send thy lad hither with thy clothes. Meanwhile, Rachel will show thee these little gardens, and then will put thee in some way of spending thy time usefully, till our meal calls us together at the second hour after noon. I bid thee farewell for the present, having some space to walk, seeing I must leave the animal Solomon to his refreshing rest.'

With these words, Mr Joshua Geddes withdrew. Some ladies we have known would have felt, or at least affected, reserve or embarrassment, at being left to do the honours of the grounds to—(it will be out, Alan)—a smart young fellow—an entire stranger. She went out for a few minutes, and returned in her plain cloak and bonnet, with her beaver-gloves, prepared to act as my guide, with as much simplicity as if she had been to wait upon thy father. So forth I sallied with my fair Quaker.

If the house at Mount Sharon be merely a plain and convenient dwelling, of moderate size, and small pretensions, the gardens and offices, though not extensive, might rival an earl's in point of care and expense. Rachel carried me first to her own favourite resort, a poultry-yard, stocked with a variety of domestic fowls, of the more rare as well as the more ordinary kinds, furnished with every accommodation which may suit their various habits. A rivulet which spread into a pond for the convenience of the aquatic birds, trickled over gravel as it passed through the yards dedicated to the land poultry, which were thus amply supplied with the means they use for digestion.

All these creatures seemed to recognise the presence of their mistress, and some especial favourites hastened to her feet, and continued to follow her as far as their limits permitted. She pointed out their peculiarities and qualities, with the discrimination of one who had made natural history her study; and I own I never looked on barn-door fowls with so much interest before—at least until they were boiled or roasted. I could not help asking the trying question, how she could order the execution of any of the creatures of which she seemed so careful.

'It was painful,' she said, 'but it was according to the law of their being. They must die; but they knew not when death was approaching; and in making them comfortable while they lived, we contributed to their happiness as much as the conditions of their existence permitted to us.'

I am not quite of her mind, Alan. I do not believe either pigs or poultry would admit that the chief end of their being was to be killed and eaten. However, I did not press the argument, from which my

Quaker seemed rather desirous to escape; for, conducting me to the greenhouse, which was extensive, and filled with the choicest plants, she pointed out an aviary which occupied the farther end, where, she said, she employed herself with attending the inhabitants, without being disturbed with any painful recollections concerning their future destination.

I will not trouble you with any account of the various hothouses and gardens, and their contents. No small sum of money must have been expended in erecting and maintaining them in the exquisite degree of good order which they exhibited. The family, I understood, were connected with that of the celebrated Millar,* and had imbibed his taste for flowers and for horticulture. But instead of murdering botanical names, I will rather conduct you to the *policy*, or pleasure-garden, which the taste of Joshua or his father had extended on the banks betwixt the house and river. This also, in contradistinction to the prevailing simplicity, was ornamented in an unusual degree. There were various compartments, the connexion of which was well managed, and although the whole ground did not exceed five or six acres, it was so much varied as to seem four times larger. The space contained close alleys and open walks; a very pretty artificial waterfall; a fountain also, consisting of a considerable jet-d'eau, whose streams glittered in the sunbeams, and exhibited a continual rainbow. There was a cabinet of verdure, as the French call it, to cool the summer heat, and there was a terrace sheltered from the north-east by a noble holly hedge, with all its glittering spears, where you might have the full advantage of the sun in the clear frosty days of winter.

I know that you, Alan, will condemn all this as bad and antiquated; for, ever since Dodsley has described the Leasowes, and talked of Brown's imitations of nature, and Horace Walpole's late Essay on Gardening, you are all for simple nature—condemn walking up and down stairs in the open air, and declare for wood and wilderness. But *ne quid nimis*. I would not deface a scene of natural grandeur or beauty, by the introduction of crowded artificial decorations; yet such may, I think, be very interesting, where the situation, in its natural state, otherwise has no particular charms.*

So that when I have a country-house, (who can say how soon?) you may look for grottoes, and cascades, and fountains; nay, if you vex me by contradiction, perhaps I may go the length of a temple—so provoke me not, for you see of what enormities I am capable.

At any rate, Alan, had you condemned as artificial the rest of Friend Geddes's grounds, there is a willow walk by the very verge of the stream, so sad, so solemn, and so silent, that it must have commanded your admiration. The brook, restrained at the ultimate boundary of the grounds by a natural dam-dike or ledge of rocks, seemed, even in its present swoln state, scarcely to glide along; and the pale willow-trees, dropping their long branches into the stream, gathered around them little coronals of the foam that floated down from the more rapid stream above. The high rock, which formed the opposite bank of the brook, was seen dimly through the branches, and its pale and splintered front, garlanded with long streamers of briers and other creeping plants, seemed a barrier between the quiet path which we trode, and the toiling and bustling world beyond. The path itself, following the sweep of the stream, made a very gentle curve; enough, however, served by its inflection completely to hide the end of the walk, until you arrived at it. A deep and sullen sound, which increased as you proceeded, prepared you for this termination, which was indeed only a plain root-seat, from which you looked on a fall of about six or seven feet, where the brook flung itself over the ledge of natural rock I have already mentioned, which there crossed its course.

The quiet and twilight seclusion of this walk rendered it a fit scene for confidential communing; and having nothing more interesting to say to my fair Quaker, I took the liberty of questioning her about the Laird; for you are, or ought to be, aware, that next to discussing the affairs of the heart, the fair sex are most interested in those of their neighbours.

I did not conceal either my curiosity, or the check which it had received from Joshua, and I saw that my companion answered with embarrassment. 'I must not speak otherwise than truly,' she said; 'and therefore I tell thee, that my brother dislikes, and that I fear, the man of whom thou hast asked me. Perhaps we are both wrong—but he is a man of violence, and hath great influence over many, who, following the trade of sailors and fishermen, become as rude as the elements with which they contend. He hath no certain name among them, which is not unusual, their rude fashion being to distinguish each other by nicknames; and they have called him the Laird of the Lakes, (not remembering there should be no one called Lord, save one only,*) in idle derision; the pools of salt water left by the tide among the sands being called the Lakes of Solway.'

'Has he no other revenue than he derives from these sands?' I asked.

'That I cannot answer,' replied Rachel; 'men say that he wants not money, though he lives like an ordinary fisherman, and that he imparts freely of his means to the poor around him. They intimate that he is a man of consequence, once deeply engaged in the unhappy affair of the rebellion, and even still too much in danger from the government to assume his own name. He is often absent from his cottage at Broken-burn-cliffs, for weeks and months.'

'I should have thought,' said I, 'that the government would scarce, at this time of day, be likely to proceed against any one even of the most obnoxious rebels. Many years have passed away'——

'It is true,' she replied; 'yet such persons may understand that their being connived at depends on their living in obscurity. But indeed there can nothing certain be known among these rude people. The truth is not in them*—most of them participate in the unlawful trade betwixt these parts and the neighbouring shore of England; and they are familiar with every species of falsehood and deceit.'

'It is a pity,' I remarked, 'that your brother should have neighbours of such a description, especially as I understand he is at some variance with them.'

'Where, when, and about what matter?' answered Miss Geddes, with an eager and timorous anxiety, which made me regret having touched on the subject.

I told her, in a way as little alarming as I could devise, the purport of what had passed betwixt this Laird of the Lakes and her brother, at their morning's interview.

'You affright me much,' answered she; 'it is this very circumstance which has scared me in the watches of the night. When my brother Joshua withdrew from an active share in the commercial concerns of my father, being satisfied with the portion of worldly substance which he already possessed, there were one or two undertakings in which he retained an interest, either because his withdrawing might have been prejudicial to friends, or because he wished to retain some mode of occupying his time. Amongst the more important of these, is a fishing station on the coast, where, by certain improved modes of erecting snares, opening at the advance of the tide, and shutting at the reflux, many more fish are taken than can be destroyed by those who, like the men of Broken-burn, use only the boat-net and spear, or fishing-rod. They complain of these tide-nets, as men call them, as an innovation, and pretend to a right to remove and destroy them by the strong hand. I fear me, this man of violence, whom they call the Laird, will execute these his threats, which cannot be without both loss and danger to my brother.'

'Mr Geddes,' said I, 'ought to apply to the civil magistrate; there are soldiers at Dumfries who would be detached for his protection.'

'Thou speakest, friend Latimer,' answered the lady, 'as one who is still in the gall of bitterness and bond of iniquity. God forbid that we should endeavour to preserve nets of flax and stakes of wood, or the Mammon of gain* which they procure for us, by the hands of men of war, and at the risk of spilling human blood!'

'I respect your scruples,' I replied; 'but since such is your way of thinking, your brother ought to avert the danger by compromise or submission.'

'Perhaps it would be best,' answered Rachel; 'but what can *I* say? Even in the best-trained temper there may remain some leaven of the old Adam; and I know not whether it is this or a better spirit that maketh my brother Joshua determine, that though he will not resist force by force, neither will he yield up his right to mere threats, or encourage wrong to others by yielding to menaces. His partners, he says, confide in his steadiness; and that he must not disappoint them by yielding up their right for the fear of the threats of man, whose breath is in his nostrils.'

This observation convinced me that the spirit of the old sharers of the spoil was not utterly departed even from the bosom of the peaceful Quaker; and I could not help confessing internally that Joshua had the right, when he averred that there was as much courage in sufferance as in exertion.

As we approached the further end of the willow walk, the sullen and continuous sound of the dashing waters became still more and more audible, and at length rendered it difficult for us to communicate with each other. The conversation dropped, but apparently my companion continued to dwell upon the apprehensions which it had excited. At the bottom of the walk, we obtained a view of the cascade, where the swoln brook flung itself in foam and tumult over the natural barrier of rock, which seemed in vain to attempt to bar its course. I gazed with delight, and, turning to express my sentiments to my companion, I observed that she had folded her hands in an attitude of sorrowful resignation, which showed her thoughts were far from the scene which lay before her. When she saw that her abstraction was observed, she resumed her former placidity of manner; and having given me sufficient time to admire this termination of our sober and secluded walk, proposed that we should return to the house through her brother's farm. 'Even we Quakers, as we are called, have our little pride,' she said; 'and my brother Joshua would not forgive me, were I not to show thee the fields which he taketh delight to cultivate, after the newest and best fashion; for which, I promise thee, he hath received much praise from good judges, as well as some ridicule from those who think it folly to improve on the customs of our ancestors.'

As she spoke, she opened a low door, leading through a moss and ivy-covered wall, the boundary of the pleasure-ground, into the open fields; through which we moved by a convenient path, leading, with good taste and simplicity, by stile and hedge-row, through pasturage, and arable, and woodland; so that, in all ordinary weather, the good man might, without even soiling his shoes, perform his perambulation round the farm. There were seats also, on which to rest; and though not adorned with inscriptions, nor quite so frequent in occurrence as those mentioned in the account of the Leasowes,* their situation was always chosen with respect to some distant prospect to be commanded, or some home-view to be enjoyed.

But what struck me most in Joshua's domain, was the quantity and the tameness of the game.* The hen partridge scarce abandoned the roost at the foot of the hedge where she had assembled her covey, though the path went close beside her; and the hare, remaining on her form, gazed at us as we passed, with her full dark eye, or, rising lazily and hopping to a little distance, stood erect to look at us with more curiosity than apprehension. I observed to Miss Geddes the extreme tameness of these timid and shy animals, and she informed me that their confidence arose from protection in the summer, and relief during the winter.

'They are pets,' she said, 'of my brother, who considers them as the better entitled to this kindness that they are a race persecuted by the world in general. He denieth himself,' she said, 'even the company of a dog, that these creatures may here at least enjoy undisturbed security. Yet this harmless or humane propensity, or humour, hath given offence,' she added, 'to our dangerous neighbour.'

She explained this, by telling me that my host of the preceding night was remarkable for his attachment to field sports, which he pursued without much regard to the wishes of the individuals over whose property he followed them. The undefined mixture of respect and fear with which he was generally regarded, induced most of the neighbouring landholders to connive at what they would perhaps in another have punished as a trespass; but Joshua Geddes would not permit the intrusion of any one upon his premises, and as he had before offended several country neighbours, who, because he would neither shoot himself nor permit others to do so, compared him to the dog in the manger, so he now aggravated the displeasure which the Laird of the Lakes had already conceived against him, by positively debarring him from pursuing his sport over his grounds—'So that,' said Rachel Geddes, 'I sometimes wish our lot had been cast elsewhere than in these pleasant borders, where, if we had less of beauty around us, we might have had a neighbourhood of peace and good-will.'

We at length returned to the house, where Miss Geddes showed me a small study, containing a little collection of books, in two separate presses.

'These,' said she, pointing to the smaller press, 'will, if thou bestowest thy leisure upon them, do thee good; and these,' pointing to the other and larger cabinet, 'can, I believe, do thee little harm. Some of our people do indeed hold, that every writer who is not with us is against us; but brother Joshua is mitigated in his opinions, and correspondeth with our friend John Scott of Amwell,* who hath himself constructed verses well approved of even in the world.—I wish thee many good thoughts till our family meet at the hour of dinner.'

Left alone, I tried both collections; the first consisted entirely of religious and controversial tracts, and the latter formed a small selection of history, and of moral writers, both in prose and verse.

Neither collection promising much amusement, thou hast, in these close pages, the fruits of my tediousness; and truly, I think, writing history (one's self being the subject) is as amusing as reading that of foreign countries, at any time.

Sam, still more drunk than sober, arrived in due time with my portmanteau, and enabled me to put my dress into order, better befitting this temple of cleanliness and decorum, where (to conclude) I believe I shall be a sojourner for more days than one.[19]

P.S.—I have noted your adventure, as you home-bred youths may perhaps term it, concerning the visit of your doughty Laird. We travellers hold such an incident of no great consequence, though it may serve to embellish the uniform life of Brown's Square. But art thou not ashamed to attempt to interest one who is seeing the world at large, and studying human nature on a large scale, by so bald a narrative? Why, what does it amount to, after all, but that a Tory Laird dined with a Whig Lawyer?* no very uncommon matter, especially as you state Mr Herries to have lost the estate, though retaining the designation. The Laird behaves with haughtiness and impertinence—nothing out of character in that: Is *not* kicked down stairs, as he ought to have been, were Alan Fairford half the man that he would wish his friends to think him.—Ay, but then, as the young lawyer, instead of showing his friend the door, chose to make use of it himself, he overheard the Laird aforesaid ask the old lawyer concerning Darsie Latimer—no doubt earnestly enquiring after the handsome, accomplished inmate of his family, who has so lately made Themis his bow, and declined the honour of following her farther. You laugh at me for my air-drawn castles; but confess, have they not surer footing, in general, than two words spoken by such a man as Herries? And yet—and yet—I would rally the matter off, Alan; but in dark nights, even the glow-worm becomes an object of lustre, and to one plunged in my uncertainty and ignorance, the slightest gleam that promises intelligence, is interesting. My life is like the subterranean river in the Peak of Derby, visible only where it crosses the celebrated cavern.* I am here, and this much I know; but where I have sprung from, or whither my course of life is like to tend, who shall tell me? Your father, too, seemed interested and alarmed, and talked of writing; would to Heaven he may!—I send daily to the post-town for letters.

LETTER VIII

ALAN FAIRFORD TO DARSIE LATIMER

THOU mayst clap thy wings and crow as thou pleasest. You go in search of adventures, but adventures come to me unsought for; and oh! in what a pleasing shape came mine, since it arrived in the form of a client—and a fair client to boot! What think you of that, Darsie, you who are such a sworn squire of dames? Will this not match my adventures with thine, that hunt salmon on horseback, and will it not, besides, eclipse the history of a whole tribe of Broadbrims?—But I must proceed methodically.

When I returned to-day from the College, I was surprised to see a broad grin distending the adust countenance of the faithful James Wilkinson, which, as the circumstance seldom happens above once a-year, was matter of some surprise. Moreover, he had a knowing glance with his eye, which I should have as soon expected from a dumb-waiter—an article of furniture to which James, in his usual state, may be happily assimilated. 'What the devil is the matter, James?'

'The devil may be in the matter, for aught I ken,' said James, with another provoking grin; 'for here has been a woman calling for you, Maister Alan.'

'A woman calling for me?' said I in surprise; for you know well, that excepting old Aunt Peggy, who comes to dinner of a Sunday, and the still older Lady Bedrooket, who calls ten times a-year for the quarterly payment of her jointure of four hundred merks, a female scarce approaches our threshold, as my father visits all his female clients at their own lodgings. James protested, however, that there had been a lady calling, and for me. 'As bonny a lass as I have seen,' added James, 'since I was in the Fusileers, and kept company with Peg Baxter.' Thou knowest all James's gay recollections go back to the period of his military service, the years he has spent in ours having probably been dull enough.

'Did the lady leave no name nor place of address?'

'No,' replied James; 'but she asked when you wad be at hame, and I appointed her for twelve o'clock, when the house wad be quiet, and your father at the Bank.'

'For shame, James! how can you think my father's being at home or abroad could be of consequence?—The lady is of course a decent person?'

'I'se uphaud her that, sir—she is nane of your—*whew*'—[Here James supplied a blank with a low whistle]—'but I didna ken—my maister makes an unco wark if a woman comes here.'

I passed into my own room, not ill-pleased that my father was absent, notwithstanding I had thought it proper to rebuke James for having so contrived it. I disarranged my books, to give them the appearance of a graceful confusion on the table, and laying my foils (useless since your departure) across the mantelpiece, that the lady might see I was *tam Marte quam Mercurio*—I endeavoured to dispose my dress so as to resemble an elegant morning dishabille—gave my hair the general shade of powder which marks the gentleman*—laid my watch and seals on the table, to hint that I understood the value of time;—and when I had made all these arrangements—of which I am a little ashamed when I think of them—I had nothing better to do than to watch the dial-plate till the index pointed to noon. Five minutes elapsed, which I allowed for variation of clocks—five minutes more rendered me anxious and doubtful—and five minutes more would have made me impatient.

Laugh as thou wilt; but remember, Darsie, I was a lawyer, expecting his first client—a young man, how strictly bred up I need not remind you, expecting a private interview with a young and beautiful woman. But ere the third term of five minutes had elapsed, the door-bell was heard to tinkle low and modestly, as if touched by some timid hand.

James Wilkinson, swift in nothing, is, as thou knowest, peculiarly slow in answering the door-bell; and I reckoned on five minutes good, ere his solemn step should have ascended the stair. Time enough, thought I, for a peep through the blinds, and was hastening to the window accordingly. But I reckoned without my host; for James, who had his own curiosity as well as I, was lying *perdu* in the lobby, ready to open at the first tinkle; and there was, 'This way, ma'am—Yes, ma'am—The lady, Mr Alan,' before I could get to the chair in which I proposed to be discovered, seated in all legal dignity. The consciousness of being half caught in the act of peeping, joined to that native air of awkward bashfulness of which I am told the law will soon free me, kept me standing on the floor in some confusion; while the lady, disconcerted on her part, remained on the threshold of the room. James Wilkinson, who had his senses most about him, and was perhaps willing to prolong his stay in the apartment, busied himself in setting a chair for the lady, and recalled me to my good breeding by the hint. I invited her to take possession of it, and bid James withdraw.

My visitor was undeniably a lady, and probably considerably above the ordinary rank—very modest, too, judging from the mixture of grace and timidity with which she moved, and at my entreaty sat down. Her dress was, I should suppose, both handsome and fashionable; but it was much concealed by a walking-cloak of green silk, fancifully embroidered; in which, though heavy for the season, her person was enveloped, and which, moreover, was furnished with a hood.

The devil take that hood, Darsie! for I was just able to distinguish that, pulled as it was over the face, it concealed from me, as I was convinced, one of the prettiest countenances I have seen, and which, from a sense of embarrassment, seemed to be crimsoned with a deep blush. I could see her complexion was beautiful—her chin finely turned—her lips coral—and her teeth rivals to ivory. But further the deponent sayeth not; for a clasp of gold, ornamented with a sapphire, closed the envious mantle under the incognita's throat, and the cursed hood concealed entirely the upper part of the face.

I ought to have spoke first, that is certain; but ere I could get my phrases well arranged, the young lady, rendered desperate, I suppose, by my hesitation, opened the conversation herself.

'I fear I am an intruder, sir—I expected to meet an elderly gentleman.'

This brought me to myself. 'My father, madam, perhaps. But you enquired for Alan Fairford—my father's name is Alexander.'

'It is Mr Alan Fairford, undoubtedly, with whom I wished to speak,' she said, with greater confusion; 'but I was told that he was advanced in life.'

'Some mistake, madam, I presume, betwixt my father and myself—our Christian names have the same initials, though the terminations are different,—I—I—I would esteem it a most fortunate mistake if I could have the honour of supplying my father's place in any thing that could be of service to you.'

'You are very obliging, sir.' A pause, during which she seemed undetermined whether to rise or sit still.

'I am just about to be called to the bar, madam,' said I, in hopes to remove her scruples to open her case to me; 'and if my advice or opinion could be of the slightest use, although I cannot presume to say that they are much to be depended upon, yet'——

The lady arose. 'I am truly sensible of your kindness, sir; and I have no doubt of your talents. I will be very plain with you—it *is* you whom I came to visit; although, now that we have met, I find it will be much better that I should commit my communication to writing.'

'I hope, madam, you will not be so cruel—so tantalizing, I would say. Consider, you are my first client—your business my first consultation—do not do me the displeasure of withdrawing your confidence because I am a few years younger than you seem to have expected—My attention shall make amends for my want of experience.'

'I have no doubt of either,' said the lady, in a grave tone, calculated to restrain the air of gallantry with which I had endeavoured to address her. 'But when you have received my letter, you will find good reasons assigned why a written communication will best suit my purpose. I wish you, sir, a good morning.' And she left the apartment, her poor baffled counsel scraping, and bowing, and apologizing for any thing that might have been disagreeable to her, although the front of my offence seems to be my having been discovered to be younger than my father.

The door was opened—out she went—walked along the pavement, turned down the close, and put the sun, I believe, into her pocket when she disappeared, so suddenly did dulness and darkness sink down on the square, when she was no longer visible. I stood for a moment as if I had been senseless, not recollecting what a fund of entertainment I must have supplied to our watchful friends on the other side of the green. Then it darted on my mind that I might dog her, and ascertain at least who or what she was. Off I set—ran down the close where she was no longer to be seen, and demanded of one of the dyer's lads whether he had seen a lady go down the close, or had observed which way she turned.

'A leddy!'—said the dyer, staring at me with his rainbow countenance. 'Mr Alan, what takes you out, rinning like daft, without your hat?'

'The devil take my hat!' answered I, running back, however, in quest of it; snatched it up, and again sallied forth. But as I reached the head of the close once more, I had sense enough to recollect that all pursuit would be now in vain. Besides, I saw my friend, the journeyman dyer, in close confabulation with a pea-green personage of his own profession, and was conscious, like Scrub, that they talked of me, because they laughed consumedly.* I had no mind, by a second sudden appearance, to confirm the report that Advocate Fairford was 'gaen daft,' which had probably spread from Campbell's Close-foot to the Mealmarket Stairs; and so slunk back within my own hole again.

My first employment was to remove all traces of that elegant and fanciful disposition of my effects, from which I had hoped for so much credit; for I was now ashamed and angry at having thought an instant upon the mode of receiving a visit which had commenced so agreeably, but terminated in a manner so unsatisfactory. I put my folios in their places—threw the foils into the dressing-closet—tormenting myself all the while with the fruitless doubt, whether I had missed an opportunity or escaped a stratagem, or whether the young person had been really startled, as she seemed to intimate, by the extreme youth of her intended legal adviser. The mirror was not unnaturally called in to aid; and that cabinet-counsellor pronounced me rather short, thick-set, with a cast of features fitter, I trust, for the bar than the ball—not handsome enough for blushing virgins to pine for my sake, or even to invent sham cases to bring them to my chambers—yet not ugly enough, either, to scare those away who came on real business—dark, to be sure, but *nigri sunt hyacinthi*—there are pretty things to be said in favour of that complexion.

At length—as common sense will get the better in all cases, when a man will but give it fair play—I began to stand convicted in my own mind, as an ass before the interview, for having expected too much—an ass during the interview, for having failed to extract the lady's real purpose—and an especial ass, now that it was over, for thinking so much about it. But I can think of nothing else, and therefore I am determined to think of this to some good purpose.

You remember Murtough O'Hara's defence of the Catholic doctrine of confession; because, 'by his soul, his sins were always a great burden to his mind, till he had told them to the priest; and once confessed, he never thought more about them.' I have tried his receipt, therefore; and having poured my secret mortification into thy trusty ear, I will think no more about this maid of the mist,

'Who, with no face, as 'twere, outfaced me.'*

—— Four o'clock.

Plague on her green mantle, she can be nothing better than a fairy; she keeps possession of my head yet! All during dinner-time I was terribly absent; but, luckily, my father gave the whole credit of my reverie to the abstract nature of the doctrine, *Vinco vincentem, ergo vinco te*;* upon which brocard of law the Professor this morning lectured. So I got an early dismissal to my own crib, and here am I studying, in one sense, *vincere vincentem*, to get the better of the silly passion of curiosity—I think—I think it amounts to nothing else—which has taken such possession of my imagination, and is perpetually worrying me with the question—will she write or no? She will not—she will not! So says Reason, and adds, Why should she take the trouble to enter into correspondence with one, who, instead of a bold, alert, prompt gallant, proved a chicken-hearted boy, and left her the whole awkwardness of explanation, which he should have met half-way? But then, says Fancy, she *will* write, for she was not a bit that sort of person whom you, Mr Reason, in your wisdom, take her to be. She was disconcerted enough, without my adding to her distress by any impudent conduct on my part. And she will write, for——

By Heaven, she HAS written, Darsie, and with a vengeance!—Here is her letter, thrown into the kitchen by a cadie, too faithful to be bribed, either by money or whisky, to say more than that he received it, with sixpence, from an ordinary-looking woman, as he was plying on his station near the Cross.

'FOR ALAN FAIRFORD, ESQUIRE, BARRISTER.

'SIR,

'Excuse my mistake of to-day. I had accidentally learned that Mr Darsie Latimer had an intimate friend and associate in a Mr A. Fairford. When I enquired for such a person, he was pointed out to me at the Cross, (as I think the Exchange of your city is called,) in the character of a respectable elderly man—your father, as I now understand. On enquiry at Brown's Square, where I understood he resided, I used the full name of Alan, which naturally occasioned you the trouble of this day's visit. Upon further enquiry, I am led to believe that you are likely to be the person most active in the matter to which I am now about to direct your attention; and I regret much that circumstances, arising out of my own particular situation, prevent my communicating to you personally what I now apprize you of in this manner.

'Your friend, Mr Darsie Latimer, is in a situation of considerable danger. You are doubtless aware, that he has been cautioned not to trust himself in England—Now, if he has not absolutely transgressed this friendly injunction, he has at least approached as nearly to the menaced danger as he could do, consistently with the letter of the prohibition. He has chosen his abode in a neighbourhood very perilous to him; and it is only by a speedy return to Edinburgh, or at least by a removal to some more remote part of Scotland, that he can escape the machinations of those whose enmity he has to fear. I must speak in mystery, but my words are not the less certain; and, I believe, you know enough of your friend's fortunes to be aware, that I could not write this much without being even more intimate with them than you are.

'If he cannot, or will not, take the advice here given, it is my opinion that you should join him, if possible, without delay, and urge, by your personal presence and entreaty, the arguments which may prove ineffectual in writing. One word more, and I implore of your candour to take it as it is meant. No one supposes that Mr

Fairford's zeal in his friend's service, needs to be quickened by mercenary motives. But report says that Mr Alan Fairford not having yet entered on his professional career, may, in such a case as this, want the means, though he cannot want the inclination, to act with promptitude. The enclosed note, Mr Alan Fairford must be pleased to consider as his first professional emolument; and she who sends it hopes it will be the omen of unbounded success, though the fee comes from a hand so unknown as that of

'GREEN MANTLE.'

A bank note of L.20 was the enclosure, and the whole incident left me speechless with astonishment. I am not able to read over the beginning of my own letter, which forms the introduction to this extraordinary communication. I only know that, though mixed with a quantity of foolery, (God knows, very much different from my present feelings,) it gives an account sufficiently accurate, of the mysterious person from whom this letter comes, and that I have neither time nor patience to separate the absurd commentary from the text, which it is so necessary you should know.

Combine this warning, so strangely conveyed, with the caution impressed on you by your London correspondent, Griffiths, against your visiting England—with the character of your Laird of the Solway Lakes—with the lawless habits of the people on that frontier country, where warrants are not easily executed, owing to the jealousy entertained by either country of the legal interference of the other; remember, that even Sir John Fielding* said to my father, that he could never trace a rogue beyond the Briggend of Dumfries—think that the distinctions of Whig and Tory, Papist and Protestant, still keep that country in a loose and comparatively lawless state—think of all this, my dearest Darsie, and remember that, while at this Mount Sharon of yours, you are residing with a family actually menaced with forcible interference, and who, while their obstinacy provokes violence, are by principle bound to abstain from resistance.

Nay, let me tell you, professionally, that the legality of the mode of fishing practised by your friend Joshua, is greatly doubted by our best lawyers; and that, if the stake-nets be considered as actually an unlawful obstruction raised in the channel of the estuary, an assembly of persons who shall proceed, *via facti*, to pull down and destroy them, would not, in the eye of the law, be esteemed guilty of a riot.* So, by remaining where you are, you are likely to be engaged in a quarrel with which you have nothing to do, and thus to enable your enemies, whoever these may be, to execute, amid the confusion of a general hubbub, whatever designs they may have against your personal safety. Black-fishers, poachers, and smugglers, are a sort of gentry that will not be much checked, either by your Quaker's texts, or by your chivalry. If you are Don Quixote enough to lay lance in rest, in defence of those of the stake-net, and of the sad-coloured garment,* I pronounce you but a lost knight; for, as I said before, I doubt if these potent redressers of wrongs, the justices and constables, will hold themselves warranted to interfere. In a word, return, my dear Amadis;* the adventure of the Solway-nets is not reserved for your worship. Come back, and I will be your faithful Sancho Panza* upon a more hopeful quest. We will beat about together, in search of this Urganda,* the Unknown She of the Green Mantle, who can read this, the riddle of thy fate, better than wise Eppie of Buckhaven,[20] or Cassandra herself.

I would fain trifle, Darsie; for in debating with you, jests will sometimes go farther than arguments; but I am sick at heart, and cannot keep the ball up. If you have a moment's regard for the friendship we have so often vowed to each other, let my wishes for once prevail over your own venturous and romantic temper. I am quite serious in thinking, that the information communicated to my father by this Mr Herries, and the admonitory letter of the young lady, bear upon each other; and that, were you here, you might learn something from one or other, or from both, that might throw light on your birth and parentage. You will not, surely, prefer an idle whim to the prospect which is thus held out to you?

I would, agreeably to the hint I have received in the young lady's letter, (for I am confident that such is her condition,) have ere now been with you to urge these things, instead of pouring them out upon paper. But you know that the day for my trial is appointed; I have already gone through the form of being introduced to the examinators, and have gotten my titles assigned me. All this should not keep me at home, but my father would view any irregularity upon this occasion as a mortal blow to the hopes which he has cherished most fondly during his life; viz. my being called to the bar with some credit. For my own part, I know there is no great difficulty in passing these formal examinations, else how have some of our acquaintance got through them? But, to my father, these formalities compose an august and serious solemnity, to which he has long looked forward, and my absenting myself at this moment would wellnigh drive him distracted. Yet I shall go altogether distracted myself, if I have not an instant assurance from you that you are hastening hither—Meanwhile I have desired Hannah to get your little crib into the best order possible. I cannot learn that my father has yet written to you; nor has he spoken more of his communication with Birrenswork; but when I let him have some inkling of the dangers you are at present incurring, I know my request that you will return immediately, will have his cordial support.

Another reason yet—I must give a dinner, as usual, upon my admission, to our friends; and my father, laying aside all his usual considerations of economy, has desired it may be in the best style possible. Come hither then, dear Darsie! or, I protest to you, I shall send examination, admission-dinner, and guests, to the devil, and come, in person, to fetch you with a vengeance. Thine, in much anxiety,

A. F.

LETTER IX

ALEXANDER FAIRFORD, W.S., TO MR DARSIE LATIMER

DEAR MR DARSIE,

HAVING been your *factor loco tutoris*, or rather, I ought to say, in correctness, (since I acted without warrant from the Court,) your *negotiorum gestor*; that connexion occasions my present writing. And although having rendered an account of my intromissions, which have been regularly approved of, not only by yourself, (whom I could not prevail upon to look at more than the docket and sum total,) but also by the worthy Mr Samuel Griffiths of London, being the hand through whom the remittances were made, I may, in some sense, be considered as to you *functus officio*; yet, to speak facetiously, I trust you will not hold me accountable as a vicious intromitter, should I still consider myself as occasionally interested in your welfare. My motives for writing, at this time, are twofold.

I have met with a Mr Herries of Birrenswork, a gentleman of very ancient descent, but who hath in time past been in difficulties, nor do I know if his affairs are yet well redd. Birrenswork says, that he believes he was very familiar with your father, whom he states to have been called Ralph Latimer of Langcote-Hall, in Westmoreland; and he mentioned family affairs, which it may be of the highest importance to you to be acquainted with; but as he seemed to decline communicating them to me, I could not civilly urge him thereanent. Thus much I know, that Mr Herries had his own share in the late desperate and unhappy matter of 1745, and was in trouble about it, although that is probably now over. Moreover, although he did not profess the Popish religion openly, he had an eye that way. And both of these are reasons why I have hesitated to recommend him to a youth who maybe hath not altogether so well founded his opinions concerning Kirk and State, that they might not be changed by some sudden wind of doctrine. For I have observed ye, Master Darsie, to be rather tinctured with the old leaven of prelacy*—this under your leave; and although God forbid that you should be in any manner disaffected to the Protestant Hanoverian line, yet ye have ever loved to hear the blawing, bleezing stories which the Hieland gentlemen tell of those troublous times, which, if it were their will, they had better pretermit, as tending rather to shame than to honour. It is come to me also by a side-wind, as I may say, that you have been neighbouring more than was needful among some of the pestilent sect of Quakers—a people who own neither priest, nor king, nor civil magistrate, nor the fabric of our law,* and will not depone either *in civilibus* or *criminalibus*, be the loss to the lieges what it may. Anent which heresies, it were good ye read 'the Snake in the Grass,' or 'the Foot out of the Snare,'* being both well-approved tracts touching these doctrines.

Now, Mr Darsie, ye are to judge for yourself whether ye can safely to your soul's weal remain longer among these Papists and Quakers,—these defections on the right hand, and fallings away on the left; and truly if you can confidently resist these evil examples of doctrine, I think ye may as well tarry in the bounds where ye are, until you see Mr Herries of Birrenswork, who does assuredly know more of your matters than I thought had been communicated to any man in Scotland. I would fain have precognosced him myself on these affairs, but found him unwilling to speak out, as I have partly intimated before.

To call a new cause—I have the pleasure to tell you, that Alan has passed his private Scots Law examinations with good approbation—a great relief to my mind; especially as worthy Mr Pest told me in my ear there was no fear of the 'callant,' as he familiarly called him, which gives me great heart. His public trials, which are nothing in comparison save a mere form, are to take place, by order of the Honourable Dean of Faculty, on Wednesday first; and on Friday he puts on the gown, and gives a bit chack of dinner to his friends and acquaintances, as is, you know, the custom. Your company will be wished for there, Master Darsie, by more than him, which I regret to think is impossible to have, as well by your engagements, as that our cousin, Peter Fairford, comes from the west on purpose, and we have no place to offer him but your chamber in the wall. And, to be plain with you, after my use and wont, Master Darsie, it may be as well that Alan and you do not meet till he is hefted as it were to his new calling. You are a pleasant gentleman, and full of daffing, which may well become you, as you have enough (as I understand) to uphold your merry humour. If you regard the matter wisely, you would perchance consider that a man of substance should have a douce and staid demeanour; yet you are so far from growing grave and considerate with the increase of your annual income, that the richer you become, the merrier I think you grow. But this must be at your own pleasure, so far as you are concerned. Alan, however, (overpassing my small savings,) has the world to win; and louping and laughing, as you and he were wont to do, would soon make the powder flee out of his wig, and the pence out of his pocket. Nevertheless, I trust you will meet when you return from your rambles; for there is a time, as the wise man sayeth, for gathering, and a time for casting away;* it is always the part of a man of sense to take the gathering time first. I remain, dear sir, your well-wishing friend, and obedient to command,

ALEXANDER FAIRFORD.

P.S.—Alan's Thesis is upon the title *De periculo et commodo rei venditae,** and is a very pretty piece of Latinity.— Ross-House, in our neighbourhood, is nearly finished, and is thought to excel Duff-House* in ornature.

LETTER X

DARSIE LATIMER TO ALAN FAIRFORD

THE plot thickens, Alan. I have your letter, and also one from your father. The last makes it impossible for me to comply with the kind request which the former urges. No—I cannot be with you, Alan; and that, for the best of all reasons—I cannot and ought not to counteract your father's anxious wishes. I do not take it unkind of him that he desires my absence. It is natural that he should wish for his son, what his son so well deserves—the advantage of a wiser and steadier companion than I seem to him. And yet I am sure I have often laboured hard enough to acquire that decency of demeanour which can no more be suspected of breaking bounds, than an owl of catching a butterfly.

But it was in vain that I have knitted my brows till I had the headach, in order to acquire the reputation of a grave, solid, and well-judging youth. Your father always has discovered, or thought that he discovered, a harebrained eccentricity lying folded among the wrinkles of my forehead, which rendered me a perilous associate for the future counsellor and ultimate judge. Well, Corporal Nym's philosophy must be my comfort—'Things must be as they may.'*—I cannot come to your father's house, where he wishes not to see me; and as to your coming hither,—by all that is dear to me, I vow that if you are guilty of such a piece of reckless folly—not to say undutiful cruelty, considering your father's thoughts and wishes—I will never speak to you again as long as I live! I am perfectly serious. And besides, your father, while he in a manner prohibits me from returning to Edinburgh, gives me the strongest reasons for continuing a little while longer in this country, by holding out the hope that I may receive from your old friend, Mr Herries of Birrenswork, some particulars concerning my origin, with which that ancient recusant seems to be acquainted.

That gentleman mentioned the name of a family in Westmoreland, with which he supposes me connected. My enquiries here after such a family have been ineffectual, for the borderers, on either side, know little of each other. But I shall doubtless find some English person of whom to make enquiries, since the confounded fetterlock clapped on my movements by old Griffiths, prevents me repairing to England in person. At least, the prospect of obtaining some information is greater here than elsewhere; it will be an apology for my making a longer stay in this neighbourhood, a line of conduct which seems to have your father's sanction, whose opinion must be sounder than that of your wandering damoiselle.

If the road were paved with dangers which leads to such a discovery, I cannot for a moment hesitate to tread it. But in fact there is no peril in the case. If the Tritons of the Solway shall proceed to pull down honest Joshua's tide-nets, I am neither Quixote enough in disposition, nor Goliath enough in person, to attempt their protection. I have no idea of attempting to prop a falling house, by putting my shoulders against it. And indeed Joshua gave me a hint, that the company which he belongs to, injured in the way threatened, (some of them being men who thought after the fashion of the world,) would pursue the rioters at law, and recover damages, in which probably his own ideas of non-resistance will not prevent his participating. Therefore the whole affair will take its course as law will, as I only mean to interfere when it may be necessary to direct the course of the plaintiffs to thy chambers; and I request they may find thee intimate with all the Scottish statutes concerning salmon-fisheries, from the *Lex Aquarum*,* downward.

As for the Lady of the Mantle, I will lay a wager that the sun so bedazzled thine eyes on that memorable morning, that every thing thou didst look upon seemed green; and notwithstanding James Wilkinson's experience in the Fusileers, as well as his negative whistle, I will venture to hold a crown that she is but a what-shall-call-'um after all. Let not even the gold persuade you to the contrary. She may make a shift to cause you to disgorge that, and (immense spoil!) a session's fees to boot, if you look not all the sharper about you. Or if it should be otherwise, and if indeed there lurk some mystery under this visitation, credit me, it is one which thou canst not penetrate, nor can I as yet even attempt to explain it; since, if I prove mistaken, and mistaken I may easily be, I would be fain to creep into Phalaris's bull,* were it standing before me ready heated, rather than be roasted with thy raillery. Do not tax me with want of confidence; for the instant I can throw any light on the matter thou shalt have it; but while I am only blundering about in the dark, I do not choose to call wise folks to see me, perchance, break my nose against a post. So if you marvel at this,

'E'en marvel on till time makes all things plain.'*

In the meantime, kind Alan, let me proceed in my diurnal.

On the third or fourth day after my arrival at Mount Sharon, Time, that bald sexton to whom I have just referred you, did certainly limp more heavily along with me than he had done at first. The quaint morality of Joshua, and Huguenot simplicity* of his sister, began to lose much of their raciness with their novelty, and my mode of life, by dint of being very quiet, began to feel abominably dull. It was, as thou say'st, as if the Quakers had put the sun in their pockets—all around was soft and mild, and even pleasant; but there was, in the whole routine, a uniformity, a want of interest, a helpless and hopeless languor, which rendered life insipid. No doubt, my worthy host and hostess felt none of this void, this want of excitation, which was becoming oppressive to their guest. They had their little round of occupations, charities, and pleasures; Rachel had her poultry-yard and conservatory, and Joshua his garden. Besides this, they enjoyed, doubtless, their devotional meditations; and, on the whole, time glided softly and imperceptibly on with them, though to me, who long for stream and cataract, it seemed absolutely to stand still. I meditated returning to Shepherd's Bush, and began to think, with some hankering, after little Benjie and the rod. The imp has ventured hither, and hovers about to catch a peep of me now and then; I suppose the little sharper is angling for a few more sixpences. But this would have been, in Joshua's eyes, a return of the washed sow to wallowing in the mire,* and I resolved, while I remained his guest, to spare him so violent a shock to his prejudices. The next point was, to shorten the time of my proposed stay; but, alas! that I felt to be equally impossible. I had named a week; and however rashly my promise had been pledged, it must be held sacred, even according to the letter, from which the Friends permit no deviation.

All these considerations wrought me up to a kind of impatience yesterday evening; so that I snatched up my hat, and prepared for a sally beyond the cultivated farm and ornamented grounds of Mount Sharon, just as if I were desirous to escape from the realms of art, into those of free and unconstrained nature.

I was scarcely more delighted when I first entered this peaceful demesne, than I now was—such is the instability and inconsistency of human nature!—when I escaped from it to the open downs, which had formerly seemed so waste and dreary. The air I breathed felt purer and more bracing. The clouds, riding high upon a summer breeze, drove, in gay succession, over my head, now obscuring the sun, now letting its rays stream in transient flashes upon various parts of the landscape, and especially upon the broad mirror of the distant Frith of Solway.

I advanced on the scene with the light step of a liberated captive; and, like John Bunyan's Pilgrim, could have found in my heart to sing as I went on my way.* It seemed as if my gaiety had accumulated while suppressed, and that I was, in my present joyous mood, entitled to expend the savings of the previous week. But just as I was about to uplift a merry stave, I heard, to my joyful surprise, the voices of three or more choristers, singing, with considerable success, the lively old catch,

> 'For all our men were very very merry,
> And all our men were drinking:
> There were two men of mine,
> Three men of thine,
> And three that belong'd to old Sir Thom o' Lyne;
> As they went to the ferry, they were very very merry,
> And all our men were drinking.'[21]

As the chorus ended, there followed a loud and hearty laugh by way of cheers. Attracted by sounds which were so congenial to my present feelings, I made towards the spot from which they came,—cautiously however, for the downs, as had been repeatedly hinted to me, had no good name; and the attraction of the music, without rivalling that of the Syrens* in melody, might have been followed by similarly inconvenient consequences to an incautious amateur.

I crept on, therefore, trusting that the sinuosities of the ground, broken as it was into knolls and sand-pits, would permit me to obtain a sight of the musicians before I should be observed by them. As I advanced, the old ditty was again raised. The voices seemed those of a man and two boys; they were rough, but kept good time, and were managed with too much skill to belong to the ordinary country people.

> 'Jack look'd at the sun, and cried, Fire, fire, fire;
> Jem stabled his keffel in Birkendale mire;
> Tom startled a calf, and halloo'd for a stag;
> Will mounted a gate-post instead of his nag:
> For all our men were very very merry,
> And all our men were drinking;
> There were two men of mine,
> Three men of thine,
> And three that belong'd to old Sir Thom o' Lyne;
> As they went to the ferry they were very very merry,
> For all our men were drinking.'

The voices, as they mixed in their several parts, and ran through them, untwisting and again entwining all the links of the merry old catch, seemed to have a little touch of the bacchanalian spirit which they celebrated, and showed plainly that the musicians were engaged in the same joyous revel as the *menyie* of old Sir Thom o' Lyne. At length I came within sight of them, three in number, where they sat cosily niched into what you might call a *bunker*, a little sand-pit, dry and snug, and surrounded by its banks, and a screen of whins in full bloom.

The only one of the trio whom I recognised as a personal acquaintance was the notorious little Benjie, who, having just finished his stave, was cramming a huge luncheon of pie-crust into his mouth with one hand, while in the other he held a foaming tankard, his eyes dancing with all the glee of a forbidden revel; and his features, which have at all times a mischievous archness of expression, confessing the full sweetness of stolen waters, and bread eaten in secret.*

There was no mistaking the profession of the male and female, who were partners with Benjie in these merry doings. The man's long loose-bodied great-coat, (wrap-rascal as the vulgar term it,) the fiddle-case, with its straps, which lay beside him, and a small knapsack which might contain his few necessaries; a clear grey eye; features which, in contending with many a storm, had not lost a wild and careless expression of glee, animated at present, when he was exercising for his own pleasure the arts which he usually practised for bread,—all announced one of those peripatetic followers of Orpheus, whom the vulgar call a strolling fiddler. Gazing more attentively, I easily discovered that though the poor musician's eyes were open, their sense was shut, and that the ecstasy with which he turned them up to Heaven, only derived its apparent expression from his own internal emotions, but received no assistance from the visible objects around. Beside him sat his female companion, in a man's hat, a blue coat, which seemed also to have been an article of male apparel, and a red petticoat. She was cleaner, in person and in clothes, than such itinerants generally are; and, having been in her day a strapping *bona roba*, she did not even yet neglect some attention to her appearance; wore a large amber necklace, and silver ear-rings, and had her plaid fastened across her breast with a brooch of the same metal.

The man also looked clean, notwithstanding the meanness of his attire, and had a decent silk handkerchief well knotted about his throat, under which peeped a clean owrelay. His beard, also, instead of displaying a grizzly stubble, unmowed for several days, flowed in thick and comely abundance over the breast, to the length of six inches, and mingled with his hair, which was but beginning to exhibit a touch of age. To sum up his appearance, the loose garment which I have described, was secured around him by a large old-fashioned belt, with brass studs, in which hung a dirk, with a knife and fork, its usual accompaniments. Altogether, there was something more wild and adventurous-looking about the man, than I could have expected to see in an ordinary modern crowder; and the bow which he now and then drew across the violin, to direct his little choir, was decidedly that of no ordinary performer.

You must understand, that many of these observations were the fruits of after remark; for I had scarce approached so near as to get a distinct view of the party, when my friend Benjie's lurching attendant, which he calls by the appropriate name of Hemp, began to cock his tail and ears, and, sensible of my presence, flew, barking like a fury, to the place where I had meant to lie concealed till I heard another song. I was obliged, however, to jump on my feet, and intimidate Hemp, who would otherwise have bit me, by two sound kicks on the ribs, which sent him howling back to his master.

Little Benjie seemed somewhat dismayed at my appearance; but, calculating on my placability, and remembering, perhaps, that the ill-used Solomon was no palfrey of mine, he speedily affected great glee, and almost in one breath assured the itinerants that I was 'a grand gentleman, and had plenty of money, and was very kind to poor folk;' and informed me that this was 'Willie Steenson—Wandering Willie—the best fiddler that ever kittled thairm with horse-hair.'

The woman rose and curtsied; and Wandering Willie sanctioned his own praises with a nod, and the ejaculation, 'All is true that the little boy says.'

I asked him if he was of this country.

'*This* country!' replied the blind man—'I am of every country in broad Scotland, and a wee bit of England to the boot. But yet I am, in some sense, of this country; for I was born within hearing of the roar of Solway. Will I give your honour a touch of the auld bread-winner?'

He preluded as he spoke, in a manner which really excited my curiosity; and then taking the old tune of Galashiels for his theme, he graced it with a number of wild, complicated, and beautiful variations; during which, it was wonderful to observe how his sightless face was lighted up under the conscious pride and heartfelt delight in the exercise of his own very considerable powers.

'What think you of that, now, for threescore and twa?'

I expressed my surprise and pleasure.

'A rant, man—an auld rant,' said Willie; 'naething like the music ye hae in your ball-houses and your playhouses in Edinbro'; but it's weel aneugh anes in a way at a dike-side.—Here's another—it's no a Scots tune, but it passes for ane—Oswald made it himsell, I reckon—he has cheated mony ane, but he canna cheat Wandering Willie.'

He then played your favourite air of Roslin Castle,* with a number of beautiful variations, some of which I am certain were almost extempore.

'You have another fiddle there, my friend,' said I—'Have you a comrade?' But Willie's ears were deaf, or his attention was still busied with the tune.

The female replied in his stead, 'O ay, sir—troth we have a partner—a gangrel body like oursells. No but my hinny might have been better if he had liked; for mony a bein nook in mony a braw house has been offered to my hinny Willie, if he wad but just bide still and play to the gentles.'

'Whisht, woman! whisht!' said the blind man, angrily, shaking his locks; 'dinna deave the gentleman wi' your havers. Stay in a house and play to the gentles!—strike up when my leddy pleases, and lay down the bow when my lord bids! Na, na, that's nae life for Willie.—Look out, Maggie—peer out, woman, and see if ye can see Robin coming.—Deil be in him! he has got to the lea-side of some smuggler's punch-bowl, and he wunna budge the night, I doubt.'

'That is your consort's instrument' said I—'Will you give me leave to try my skill?' I slipped at the same time a shilling into the woman's hand.

'I dinna ken whether I dare trust Robin's fiddle to ye,' said Willie, bluntly. His wife gave him a twitch. 'Hout awa, Maggie,' he said, in contempt of the hint; 'though the gentleman may hae gien ye siller, he may have nae bow-hand for a' that, and I'll no trust Robin's fiddle wi' an ignoramus.—But that's no sae muckle amiss,' he added, as I began to touch the instrument; 'I am thinking ye have some skill o' the craft.'

To confirm him in this favourable opinion, I began to execute such a complicated flourish as I thought must have turned Crowdero* into a pillar of stone with envy and wonder. I scaled the top of the finger-board, to dive at once to the bottom—skipped with flying fingers, like Timotheus,* from shift to shift—struck arpeggios and harmonic tones, but without exciting any of the astonishment which I had expected.

Willie indeed listened to me with considerable attention; but I was no sooner finished, than he immediately mimicked on his own instrument the fantastic complication of tones which I had produced, and made so whimsical a parody of my performance, that, although somewhat angry, I could not help laughing heartily, in which I was joined by Benjie, whose reverence for me held him under no restraint; while the poor dame, fearful, doubtless, of my taking offence at this familiarity, seemed divided betwixt her conjugal reverence for her Willie, and her desire to give him a hint for his guidance.

At length the old man stopped of his own accord, and, as if he had sufficiently rebuked me by his mimicry, he said, 'But for a' that, ye will play very weel wi' a little practice and some gude teaching. But ye maun learn to put the heart into it, man—to put the heart into it.'

I played an air in simpler taste, and received more decided approbation.

'That's something like it, man. Od, ye are a clever birkie!'

The woman touched his coat again. 'The gentleman is a gentleman, Willie—ye maunna speak that gate to him, hinny.'

'The deevil I maunna!' said Willie; 'and what for maunna I?—If he was ten gentles, he canna draw a bow like me, can he?'

'Indeed I cannot, my honest friend,' said I; 'and if you will go with me to a house hard by, I would be glad to have a night with you.'

Here I looked round, and observed Benjie smothering a laugh, which I was sure had mischief in it. I seized him suddenly by the ear, and made him confess that he was laughing at the thoughts of the reception which a fiddler was likely to get from the Quakers at Mount Sharon. I chucked him from me, not sorry that his mirth had reminded me in time of what I had for the moment forgotten; and invited the itinerant to go with me to Shepherd's Bush, from which I proposed to send word to Mr Geddes that I should not return home that evening. But the minstrel declined this invitation also. He was engaged for the night, he said, to a dance in the neighbourhood, and vented a round execration on the laziness or drunkenness of his comrade, who had not appeared at the place of rendezvous.

'I will go with you instead of him,' said I, in a sudden whim; 'and I will give you a crown to introduce me as your comrade.'

'*You* gang instead of Rob the Rambler! My certie, freend, ye are no blate!' answered Wandering Willie, in a tone which announced death to my frolic.

But Maggie, whom the offer of the crown had not escaped, began to open on that scent with a maundering sort of lecture. 'O Willie! hinny Willie, whan will ye learn to be wise? There's a crown to be win for naething but saying ae man's name instead of anither. And, wae's me! I hae just a shilling of this gentleman's gieing, and a bodle of my ain; and ye wunna bend your will sae muckle as to take up the siller that's flung at your feet! Ye will die the death of a cadger's powney in a wreath of drift! and what can I do better than lie doun and die wi' you? for ye winna let me win siller to keep either you or mysell leevin.'

'Haud your nonsense tongue, woman,' said Willie, but less

absolutely than before. 'Is he a real gentleman, or ane of the player-men?'

'I'se uphaud him a real gentleman,' said the woman.

'I'se uphaud ye ken little of the matter,' said Willie; 'let us see haud of your hand, neebor, gin ye like.'

I gave him my hand. He said to himself, 'Ay, ay, here are fingers that have seen canny service.' Then running his hand over my hair, my face, and my dress, he went on with his soliloquy; 'Ay, ay, muisted hair, braid-claith o' the best, and seenteen hundred linen on his back, at the least o' it.—And how do you think, my braw birkie, that ye are to pass for a tramping fiddler?'

'My dress is plain,' said I,—indeed I had chosen my most ordinary suit, out of compliment to my Quaker friends,—'and I can easily pass for a young farmer out upon a frolic. Come, I will double the crown I promised you.'

'Damn your crowns!' said the disinterested man of music. 'I would like to have a round wi' you, that's certain;—but a farmer, and with a hand that never held pleugh-stilt or pettle, that will never do. Ye may pass for a trades-lad from Dumfries, or a student upon the ramble, or the like o' that.—But hark ye, lad; if ye expect to be ranting amang the queans o' lasses where ye are gaun, ye will come by the waur, I can tell ye; for the fishers are wild chaps, and will bide nae taunts.'

I promised to be civil and cautious; and, to smooth the good woman, I slipped the promised piece into her hand. The acute organs of the blind man detected this little manœuvre.

'Are ye at it again wi' the siller, ye jaud? I'll be sworn ye wad rather hear ae twalpenny clink against another, than have a spring from Rory Dall,[22*] if he was coming alive again, anes errand. Gang doun the gate to Lucky Gregson's and get the things ye want, and bide there till ele'en hours in the morn; and if ye see Robin, send him on to me.'

'Am I no gaun to the ploy, then?' said Maggie, in a disappointed tone.

'And what for should ye?' said her lord and master; 'to dance a' night, I'se warrant, and no to be fit to walk your tae's-length the morn, and we have ten Scots miles afore us? Na, na. Stable the steed, and pit your wife to bed, when there's night wark to do.'

'Aweel, aweel, Willie hinnie, ye ken best; but O, take an unco care o' yoursell, and mind ye hae nae the blessing o' sight.'

'Your tongue gars me whiles tire of the blessing of hearing, woman,' replied Willie, in answer to this tender exhortation.

But I now put in for my interest. 'Hollo, good folks, remember that I am to send the boy to Mount Sharon, and if you go to the

Shepherd's Bush, honest woman, how the deuce am I to guide the blind man where he is going? I know little or nothing of the country.'

'An ye ken mickle less of my hinnie, sir,' replied Maggie, 'that think he needs ony guiding; he's the best guide himsell, that ye'll find between Criffell and Carlisle. Horse-road and footpath, parish-road and kirk-road, high-road and cross-road, he kens ilka foot of ground in Nithsdale.'

'Ay, ye might have said in braid Scotland, gudewife,' added the fiddler. 'But gang your ways, Maggie, that's the first wise word ye hae spoke the day. I wish it was dark night, and rain, and wind, for the gentleman's sake, that I might show him there is whiles when ane had better want een than have them; for I am as true a guide by darkness as by daylight.'

Internally as well pleased that my companion was not put to give me this last proof of his skill, I wrote a note with a pencil, desiring Samuel to bring my horses at midnight, when I thought my frolic would be wellnigh over, to the place to which the bearer should direct him, and I sent little Benjie with an apology to the worthy Quakers.

As we parted in different directions, the good woman said, 'Oh, sir, if ye wad but ask Willie to tell ye ane of his tales to shorten the gate! He can speak like ony minister frae the pu'pit, and he might have been a minister himsell, but'——

'Had your tongue, ye fule!' said Willie,—'But stay, Meg—gie me a kiss, we maunna part in anger, neither.'—And thus our society separated.[23]★

LETTER XI

THE SAME TO THE SAME

YOU are now to conceive us proceeding in our different directions across the bare downs. Yonder flies little Benjie to the northward, with Hemp scampering at his heels, both running as if for dear life, so long as the rogue is within sight of his employer, and certain to take the walk very easy, so soon as he is out of ken. Stepping westward, you see Maggie's tall form and high-crowned hat, relieved by the fluttering of her plaid upon the left shoulder, darkening as the distance diminishes her size, and as the level sunbeams begin to sink upon the sea. She is taking her quiet journey to the Shepherd's Bush.

Then, stoutly striding over the lea, you have a full view of Darsie Latimer, with his new acquaintance, Wandering Willie, who, bating that he touched the ground now and then with his staff, not in a doubtful groping manner, but with the confident air of an experienced pilot, heaving the lead when he has the soundings by heart, walks as firmly and boldly as if he possessed the eyes of Argus.* There they go, each with his violin slung at his back, but one of them at least totally ignorant whither their course is directed.

And wherefore did you enter so keenly into such a mad frolic? says my wise counsellor—Why, I think, upon the whole, that as a sense of loneliness, and a longing for that kindness which is interchanged in society, led me to take up my temporary residence at Mount Sharon, the monotony of my life there, the quiet simplicity of the conversation of the Geddeses, and the uniformity of their amusements and employments, wearied out my impatient temper, and prepared me for the first escapade which chance might throw in my way.

What would I have given that I could have procured that solemn grave visage of thine, to dignify this joke, as it has done full many a one of thine own! Thou hast so happy a knack of doing the most foolish things in the wisest manner, that thou mightst pass thy extravagancies for rational actions, even in the eyes of prudence herself.

From the direction which my guide observed, I began to suspect that the dell at Brokenburn was our probable destination; and it became important to me to consider whether I could, with propriety, or even perfect safety, intrude myself again upon the hospitality of my former host. I therefore asked Willie, whether we were bound for the Laird's, as folk called him.

'Do ye ken the Laird?' said Willie, interrupting a sonata of Corelli, of which he had whistled several bars with great precision.

'I know the Laird a little,' said I; 'and therefore, I was doubting whether I ought to go to his town in disguise.'

'And I should doubt, not a little only, but a great deal, before I took ye there, my chap,' said Wandering Willie; 'for I am thinking it wad be worth little less than broken banes baith to you and me. Na, na, chap, we are no ganging to the Laird's, but to a blithe birling at the Brokenburn-foot, where there will be mony a braw lad and lass; and maybe there may be some of the Laird's folk, for he never comes to sic splores himsell. He is all for fowling-piece and salmon spear, now that pike and musket are out of the question.'

'He has been a soldier, then?' said I.

'I'se warrant him a soger,' answered Willie; 'but take my advice, and speer as little about him as he does about you. Best to let sleeping dogs lie. Better say naething about the Laird, my man, and tell me instead, what sort of a chap ye are, that are sae ready to cleik in with an auld gaberlunzie fiddler? Maggie says ye're gentle, but a shilling maks a' the difference that Maggie kens, between a gentle and a semple, and your crowns wad mak ye a prince of the blood in her een. But I am ane that kens full weel that ye may wear good claithes, and have a saft hand, and yet that may come of idleness as weel as gentrice.'

I told him my name, with the same addition I had formerly given to Mr Joshua Geddes; that I was a law-student, tired of my studies, and rambling about for exercise and amusement.

'And are ye in the wont of drawing up wi' a' the gangrel bodies that ye meet on the high-road, or find cowering in a sand-bunker upon the links?' demanded Willie.

'Oh no; only with honest folks like yourself, Willie,' was my reply.

'Honest folks like me!—How do ye ken whether I am honest, or what I am?—I may be the deevil himsell for what ye ken; for he has power to come disguised like an angel of light; and besides, he is a prime fiddler. He played a sonata to Corelli,* ye ken.'

There was something odd in this speech, and the tone in which it was said. It seemed as if my companion was not always in his constant mind, or that he was willing to try if he could frighten me. I laughed at the extravagance of his language, however, and asked him in reply, if he was fool enough to believe that the foul fiend would play so silly a masquerade.

'Ye ken little about it—little about it,' said the old man, shaking his head and beard, and knitting his brows—'I could tell ye something about that.'

What his wife mentioned of his being a tale-teller, as well as a musician, now occurred to me; and as you know I like tales of superstition, I begged to have a specimen of his talent as we went along.

'It is very true,' said the blind man, 'that when I am tired of scraping thairm or singing ballants, I whiles make a tale serve the turn among the country bodies; and I have some fearsome anes, that make the auld carlines shake on the settle, and the bits o' bairns skirl on their minnies out frae their beds. But this that I am gaun to tell you was a thing that befell in our ain house in my father's time—that is, my father was then a hafflins callant; and I tell it to you, that it may be a lesson to you, that are but a young, thoughtless chap, wha ye draw up wi' on a lonely road; for muckle was the dool and care that came o't to my gudesire.'

He commenced his tale accordingly, in a distinct narrative tone of voice, which he raised and depressed with considerable skill; at times sinking almost into a whisper, and turning his clear but sightless eyeballs upon my face, as if it had been possible for him to witness the impression which his narrative made upon my features. I will not spare you a syllable of it, although it be of the longest; so I make a dash——and begin

Wandering Willie's Tale*

YE maun have heard of Sir Robert Redgauntlet of that Ilk, who lived in these parts before the dear years. The country will lang mind him; and our fathers used to draw breath thick if ever they heard him named. He was out wi' the Hielandmen in Montrose's time; and again he was in the hills wi' Glencairn in the saxteen hundred and fifty-twa;* and sae when King Charles the Second came in, wha was in sic favour as the Laird of Redgauntlet? He was knighted at Lonon court, wi' the King's ain sword; and being a redhot prelatist, he came down here, rampauging like a lion, with commissions of lieutenancy, (and of lunacy,* for what I ken,) to put down a' the Whigs and Covenanters* in the country. Wild wark they made of it; for the Whigs were as dour as the Cavaliers were fierce, and it was which should first tire the other. Redgauntlet was aye for the strong hand; and his name is kend as wide in the country as Claverhouse's or Tam Dalyell's.* Glen, nor dargle, nor mountain, nor cave, could hide the puir hill-folk* when Redgauntlet was out with bugle and bloodhound after them, as if they had been sae mony deer. And troth when they fand them, they didna mak muckle mair ceremony than a Hielandman wi' a roebuck—It was just, 'Will ye tak the test?'*—if not, 'Make ready—present—fire!'—and there lay the recusant.

Far and wide was Sir Robert hated and feared. Men thought he had a direct compact with Satan*—that he was proof against steel—and that bullets happed aff his buff-coat like hailstanes from a hearth—that he had a mear that would turn a hare on the side of Carrifra-gawns[24]—and muckle to the same purpose, of whilk mair anon. The best blessing they wared on him was, 'Deil scowp wi' Redgauntlet!' He wasna a bad maister to his ain folk though, and was weel aneugh liked by his tenants; and as for the lackies and troopers that raid out wi' him to the persecutions, as the Whigs caa'd those killing times,* they wad hae drunken themsells blind to his health at ony time.

Now you are to ken that my gudesire lived on Redgauntlet's grund—they ca' the place Primrose-Knowe. We had lived on the grund, and under the Redgauntlets, since the riding days, and lang before. It was a pleasant bit; and I think the air is callerer and fresher there than ony where else in the country. It's a' deserted now; and I sat on the broken door-cheek three days since, and was glad I couldna see the plight the place was in; but that's a' wide o' the mark. There dwelt my gudesire, Steenie Steenson, a rambling, rattling chiel he had been in his young days, and could play weel on the pipes; he was famous at 'Hoopers and Girders'—a' Cumberland couldna touch him at 'Jockie Lattin'*—and he had the finest finger for the back-lill between Berwick and Carlisle. The like o' Steenie wasna the sort that they made Whigs o'. And so he became a Tory, as they ca' it, which we now ca' Jacobites,* just out of a kind of needcessity, that he might belang to some side or other. He had nae ill-will to the Whig bodies, and liked little to see the blude rin, though, being obliged to follow Sir Robert in hunting and hosting, watching and warding,* he saw muckle mischief, and maybe did some, that he couldna avoid.

Now Steenie was a kind of favourite with his master, and kend a' the folks about the castle, and was often sent for to play the pipes when they were at their merriment. Auld Dougal MacCallum, the butler, that had followed Sir Robert through gude and ill, thick and thin, pool and stream, was specially fond of the pipes, and aye gae my gudesire his gude word wi' the Laird; for Dougal could turn his master round his finger.

Weel, round came the Revolution,* and it had like to have broken the hearts baith of Dougal and his master. But the change was not a'thegether sae great as they feared, and other folk thought for. The Whigs made an unco crawing what they wad do with their auld enemies, and in special wi' Sir Robert Redgauntlet. But there were ower mony great folks dipped in the same doings, to mak a spick and span new warld. So parliament passed it a' ower easy; and Sir Robert, bating that he was held to hunting foxes instead of Covenanters, remained just the man he was. He revel was as loud, and his hall as weel lighted, as ever it had been, though maybe he lacked the fines of the non-conformists,* that used to come to stock his larder and cellar; for it is certain he began to be keener about the rents than his tenants used to find him before, and they behoved to be prompt to the rent-day, or else the Laird wasna pleased. And he was sic an awsome body, that naebody cared to anger him; for the oaths he swore, and the rage that he used to get into, and the looks that he put on, made men sometimes think him a devil incarnate.[25]

Weel, my gudesire was nae manager—no that he was a very great misguider—but he hadna the saving gift, and he got twa terms' rent in arrear. He got the first brash at Whitsunday put ower wi' fair word and piping; but when Martinmas came, there was a summons from the grund-officer to come wi' the rent on a day preceese, or else Steenie behoved to flit. Sair wark he had to get the siller; but he was weel-freended, and at last he got the haill scraped thegither—a thousand merks—the maist of it was from a neighbour they caa'd Laurie Lapraik—a sly tod. Laurie had walth o' gear—could hunt wi' the hound and rin wi' the hare—and be Whig or Tory, saunt or sinner, as the wind stood. He was a professor in this Revolution warld, but he liked an orra sough of this warld; and a tune on the pipes weel aneugh at a bytime, and abune a', he thought he had gude security for the siller he lent my gudesire ower the stocking at Primrose-Knowe.

Away trots my gudesire to Redgauntlet Castle, wi' a heavy purse and a light heart, glad to be out of the Laird's danger. Weel, the first thing he learned at the Castle was, that Sir Robert had fretted himself into a fit of the gout, because he did not appear before twelve o'clock. It wasna a'thegether for sake of the money, Dougal thought; but because he didna like to part wi' my gudesire aff the grund. Dougal was glad to see Steenie, and brought him into the great oak parlour, and there sat the Laird his leesome lane, excepting that he had beside him a great, ill-favoured jackanape, that was a special pet of his; a cankered beast it was, and mony an ill-natured trick it played—ill to please it was, and easily angered—ran about the haill castle, chattering and yowling, and pinching and biting folk, especially before ill weather, or disturbances in the state. Sir Robert caa'd it Major Weir,* after the warlock that was burnt;[26] and few folk liked either the name or the conditions of the creature—they thought there was something in it by ordinar—and my gudesire was not just easy in his mind when the door shut on him, and he saw himself in the room wi' naebody but the Laird, Dougal MacCallum, and the Major, a thing that hadna chanced to him before.

Sir Robert sat, or, I should say, lay, in a great armed chair, wi' his grand velvet gown, and his feet on a cradle; for he had baith gout and gravel, and his face looked as gash and ghastly as Satan's. Major Weir sat opposite to him, in a red laced coat, and the Laird's wig on his head; and aye as Sir Robert girned wi' pain, the jackanape girned too, like a sheep's-head between a pair of tangs*—an ill-faured, fearsome couple they were. The Laird's buff-coat was hung on a pin behind him, and his broadsword and his pistols within reach; for he keepit up the auld fashion of having the weapons ready, and a horse saddled day and night, just as he used to do when he was able to loup on horseback, and away after ony of the hill-folk he could get speerings of. Some said it was for fear of the Whigs taking vengeance, but I judge it was just his auld custom—he wasna gien to fear ony thing. The rental-book, wi' its black cover and brass clasps, was lying beside him; and a book of sculduddry sangs was put betwixt the leaves, to keep it open at the place where it bore evidence against the Goodman of Primrose-Knowe, as behind the hand with his mails and duties. Sir Robert gave my gudesire a look, as if he would have withered his heart in his bosom. Ye maun ken he had a way of bending his brows, that men saw the visible mark of a horse-shoe in his forehead, deep-dinted, as if it had been stamped there.

'Are ye come light-handed, ye son of a toom whistle?' said Sir Robert. 'Zounds! if you are'——

My gudesire, with as gude a countenance as he could put on, made a leg, and placed the bag of money on the table wi' a dash, like a man that does something clever. The Laird drew it to him hastily—'Is it all here, Steenie, man?'

'Your honour will find it right,' said my gudesire.

'Here, Dougal,' said the Laird, 'gie Steenie a tass of brandy down stairs, till I count the siller and write the receipt.'

But they werena weel out of the room, when Sir Robert gied a yelloch that garr'd the Castle rock! Back ran Dougal—in flew the livery-men—yell on yell gied the Laird, ilk ane mair awfu' than the ither. My gudesire knew not whether to stand or flee, but he ventured back into the parlour, where a' was gaun hirdy-girdie—naebody to say 'come in,' or 'gae out.' Terribly the Laird roared for cauld water to his feet, and wine to cool his throat; and hell, hell, hell, and its flames, was aye the word in his mouth. They brought him water, and when they plunged his swoln feet into the tub, he cried out it was burning; and folk say that it *did* bubble and sparkle like a seething caldron. He flung the cup at Dougal's head, and said he had given him blood instead of burgundy;* and, sure aneugh, the lass washed clotted blood aff the carpet the neist day. The jackanape they caa'd Major Weir, it jibbered and cried as if it was mocking its master; my gudesire's head was like to turn—he forgot baith siller and receipt, and down stairs he banged; but as he ran, the shrieks came faint and fainter; there was a deep-drawn shivering groan, and word gaed through the Castle, that the Laird was dead.

Weel, away came my gudesire, wi' his finger in his mouth, and his best hope was, that Dougal had seen the money-bag, and heard the Laird speak of writing the receipt. The young Laird, now Sir John, came from Edinburgh, to see things put to rights. Sir John and his father never gree'd weel. Sir John had been bred an advocate, and afterwards sat in the last Scots Parliament and voted for the Union,* having gotten, it was thought, a rug of the compensations—if his father could have come out of his grave, he would have brained him for it on his awn hearthstane. Some thought it was easier counting with the auld rough Knight than the fair-spoken young ane—but mair of that anon.

Dougal MacCallum, poor body, neither grat nor graned, but gaed about the house looking like a corpse, but directing, as was his duty, a' the order of the grand funeral. Now, Dougal looked aye waur and waur when night was coming, and was aye the last to gang to his bed, whilk was in a little round just opposite the chamber of dais, whilk his master occupied while he was living, and where he now lay in state, as they caa'd it, weel-a-day! The night before the funeral, Dougal could keep his awn counsel nae langer; he came doun with his proud spirit, and fairly asked auld Hutcheon to sit in his room with him for an hour. When they were in the round, Dougal took ae tass of brandy to himsell, and gave another to Hutcheon, and wished him all health and lang life, and said that, for himsell, he wasna lang for this world; for that, every night since Sir Robert's death, his silver call had sounded from the state chamber, just as it used to do at nights in his lifetime, to call Dougal to help to turn him in his bed. Dougal said, that being alone with the dead on that floor of the tower, (for naebody cared to wake Sir Robert Redgauntlet like another corpse,) he had never daured to answer the call, but that now his conscience checked him for neglecting his duty; for, 'though death breaks service,' said MacCallum, 'it shall never break my service to Sir Robert; and I will answer his next whistle, so be you will stand by me, Hutcheon.'

Hutcheon had nae will to the wark, but he had stood by Dougal in battle and broil, and he wad not fail him at this pinch; so down the carles sat ower a stoup of brandy, and Hutcheon, who was something of a clerk, would have read a chapter of the Bible; but

Dougal would hear naething but a blaud of Davie Lindsay,* whilk was the waur preparation.

When midnight came, and the house was quiet as the grave, sure aneugh the silver whistle sounded as sharp and shrill as if Sir Robert was blowing it, and up gat the twa auld serving-men, and tottered into the room where the dead man lay. Hutcheon saw aneugh at the first glance; for there were torches in the room, which showed him the foul fiend in his ain shape, sitting on the Laird's coffin! Over he cowped as if he had been dead. He could not tell how lang he lay in a trance at the door, but when he gathered himself, he cried on his neighbour, and getting nae answer, raised the house, when Dougal was found lying dead within twa steps of the bed where his master's coffin was placed. As for the whistle, it was gaen anes and aye; but mony a time was it heard at the top of the house on the bartizan, and amang the auld chimneys and turrets, where the howlets have their nests. Sir John hushed the matter up, and the funeral passed over without mair bogle-wark.

But when a' was ower, and the Laird was beginning to settle his affairs, every tenant was called up for his arrears, and my gudesire for the full sum that stood against him in the rental-book. Weel, away he trots to the Castle, to tell his story, and there he is introduced to Sir John, sitting in his father's chair, in deep mourning, with weepers and hanging cravat, and a small walking rapier by his side, instead of the auld broadsword that had a hundred-weight of steel about it, what with blade, chape, and basket-hilt. I have heard their communing so often tauld ower, that I almost think I was there mysell, though I couldna be born at the time. (In fact, Alan, my companion mimicked, with a good deal of humour, the flattering, conciliating tone of the tenant's address, and the hypocritical melancholy of the Laird's reply. His grandfather, he said, had, while he spoke, his eye fixed on the rental-book, as if it were a mastiff-dog that he was afraid would spring up and bite him.)

'I wuss ye joy, sir, of the head seat, and the white loaf, and the braid lairdship. Your father was a kind man to friends and followers; muckle grace to you, Sir John, to fill his shoon—his boots, I suld say, for he seldom wore shoon, unless it were muils when he had the gout.'

'Ay, Steenie,' quoth the Laird, sighing deeply, and putting his napkin to his een, 'his was a sudden call, and he will be missed in the country; no time to set his house in order—weel prepared Godward, no doubt, which is the root of the matter—but left us behind a tangled hesp to wind, Steenie.—Hem! hem! We maun go to business, Steenie; much to do, and little time to do it in.'

Here he opened the fatal volume. I have heard of a thing they call

Doomsday-book—I am clear it has been a rental of back-ganging tenants.

'Stephen,' said Sir John, still in the same soft, sleekit tone of voice—'Stephen Stevenson, or Steenson, ye are down here for a year's rent behind the hand—due at last term.'

Stephen. 'Please your honour, Sir John, I paid it to your father.'

Sir John. 'Ye took a receipt then, doubtless, Stephen; and can produce it?'

Stephen. 'Indeed I hadna time, an it like your honour; for nae sooner had I set doun the siller, and just as his honour Sir Robert, that's gaen, drew it till him to count it, and write out the receipt, he was ta'en wi' the pains that removed him.'

'That was unlucky,' said Sir John, after a pause. 'But ye maybe paid it in the presence of somebody. I want but a *talis qualis* evidence, Stephen. I would go ower strictly to work with no poor man.'

Stephen. 'Troth, Sir John, there was naebody in the room but Dougal MacCallum, the butler. But, as your honour kens, he has e'en followed his auld master.'

'Very unlucky again, Stephen,' said Sir John, without altering his voice a single note. 'The man to whom ye paid the money is dead—and the man who witnessed the payment is dead too—and the siller, which should have been to the fore, is neither seen nor heard tell of in the repositories. How am I to believe a' this?'

Stephen. 'I dinna ken, your honour; but there is a bit memorandum note of the very coins; for, God help me! I had to borrow out of twenty purses; and I am sure that ilka man there set down will take his grit oath for what purpose I borrowed the money.'

Sir John. 'I have little doubt ye *borrowed* the money, Steenie. It is the *payment* to my father that I want to have some proof of.'

Stephen. 'The siller maun be about the house, Sir John. And since your honour never got it, and his honour that was canna have ta'en it wi' him, maybe some of the family may have seen it.'

Sir John. 'We will examine the servants, Stephen; that is but reasonable.'

But lackey and lass, and page and groom, all denied stoutly that they had ever seen such a bag of money as my gudesire described. What was waur, he had unluckily not mentioned to any living soul of them his purpose of paying his rent. Ae quean had noticed something under his arm, but she took it for the pipes.

Sir John Redgauntlet ordered the servants out of the room, and then said to my gudesire, 'Now, Steenie, ye see you have fair play; and, as I have little doubt ye ken better where to find the siller than ony other body, I beg, in fair terms, and for your own sake, that you will end this fasherie; for, Stephen, ye maun pay or flit.'

'The Lord forgie your opinion,' said Stephen, driven almost to his wit's end—'I am an honest man.'

'So am I, Stephen,' said his honour; 'and so are all the folks in the house, I hope. But if there be a knave amongst us, it must be he that tells the story he cannot prove.' He paused, and then added, mair sternly, 'If I understand your trick, sir, you want to take advantage of some malicious reports concerning things in this family, and particularly respecting my father's sudden death, thereby to cheat me out of the money, and perhaps take away my character, by insinuating that I have received the rent I am demanding.—Where do you suppose this money to be?—I insist upon knowing.'

My gudesire saw every thing look sae muckle against him that he grew nearly desperate—however, he shifted from one foot to another, looked to every corner of the room, and made no answer.

'Speak out, sirrah,' said the Laird, assuming a look of his father's, a very particular ane, which he had when he was angry—it seemed as if the wrinkles of his frown made that selfsame fearful shape of a horse's shoe in the middle of his brow;—'Speak out, sir! I *will* know your thoughts;—do you suppose that I have this money?'

'Far be it frae me to say so,' said Stephen.

'Do you charge any of my people with having taken it?'

'I wad be laith to charge them that may be innocent,' said my gudesire; 'and if there be any one that is guilty, I have nae proof.'

'Somewhere the money must be, if there is a word of truth in your story,' said Sir John; 'I ask where you think it is—and demand a correct answer?'

'In hell, if you *will* have my thoughts of it,' said my gudesire, driven to extremity,—'in hell! with your father, his jackanape, and his silver whistle.'

Down the stairs he ran, (for the parlour was nae place for him after such a word,) and he heard the Laird swearing blood and wounds behind him, as fast as ever did Sir Robert, and roaring for the bailie and the baron-officer.

Away rode my gudesire to his chief creditor, (him they caa'd Laurie Lapraik,) to try if he could make ony thing out of him; but when he tauld his story, he got but the warst word in his wame—thief, beggar, and dyvour, were the saftest terms; and to the boot of these hard terms, Laurie brought up the auld story of his dipping his hand in the blood of God's saunts, just as if a tenant could have helped riding with the Laird, and that a laird like Sir Robert Redgauntlet. My gudesire was, by this time, far beyond the bounds of patience, and while he and Laurie were at deil speed the liars, he was wanchancie aneugh to abuse Lapraik's doctrine as weel as the man, and said things that garr'd folk's flesh grue that heard them;—he wasna just himsell, and he had lived wi' a wild set in his day.

At last they parted, and my gudesire was to ride hame through the wood of Pitmurkie, that is a' fou of black firs, as they say.—I ken the wood, but the firs may be black or white for what I can tell.—At the entry of the wood there is a wild common, and on the edge of the common, a little lonely change-house, that was keepit then by an ostler-wife, they suld hae caa'd her* Tibbie Faw, and there puir Steenie cried for a mutchkin of brandy, for he had had no refreshment the haill day. Tibbie was earnest wi' him to take a bite of meat, but he couldna think o't, nor would he take his foot out of the stirrup, and took off the brandy wholely at twa draughts, and named a toast at each:—the first was, the memory of Sir Robert Redgauntlet, and might he never lie quiet in his grave till he had righted his poor bond-tenant; and the second was, a health to Man's Enemy, if he would but get him back the pock of siller, or tell him what came o't, for he saw the haill world was like to regard him as a thief and a cheat, and he took that waur than even the ruin of his house and hauld.

On he rode, little caring where. It was a dark night turned, and the trees made it yet darker, and he let the beast take its ain road through the wood; when, all of a sudden, from tired and wearied that it was before, the nag began to spring, and flee, and stend, that my gudesire could hardly keep the saddle—Upon the whilk, a horseman, suddenly riding up beside him, said, 'That's a mettle beast of yours, freend; will you sell him?'—So saying, he touched the horse's neck with his riding-wand, and it fell into its auld heigh-ho of a stumbling trot. 'But his spunk's soon out of him, I think,' continued the stranger, 'and that is like mony a man's courage, that thinks he wad do great things till he come to the proof.'

My gudesire scarce listened to this, but spurred his horse, with 'Gude e'en to you, freend.'

But it's like the stranger was ane that doesna lightly yield his point; for, ride as Steenie liked, he was aye beside him at the selfsame pace. At last my gudesire, Steenie Steenson, grew half angry; and, to say the truth, half feared.

'What is it that ye want with me, freend?' he said. 'If ye be a robber, I have nae money; if ye be a leal man, wanting company, I have nae heart to mirth or speaking; and if ye want to ken the road, I scarce ken it mysell.'

'If you will tell me your grief,' said the stranger, 'I am one that, though I have been sair miscaa'd in the world, am the only hand for helping my freends.'

So my gudesire, to ease his ain heart, mair than from any hope of help, told him the story from beginning to end.

'It's a hard pinch,' said the stranger; 'but I think I can help you.'

'If you could lend the money, sir, and take a lang day—I ken nae other help on earth,' said my gudesire.

'But there may be some under the earth,' said the stranger. 'Come, I'll be frank wi' you; I could lend you the money on bond, but you would maybe scruple my terms. Now, I can tell you, that your auld Laird is disturbed in his grave by your curses, and the wailing of your family, and if ye daur venture to go to see him, he will give you the receipt.'

My gudesire's hair stood on end at this proposal, but he thought his companion might be some humorsome chield that was trying to frighten him, and might end with lending him the money. Besides, he was bauld wi' brandy, and desperate wi' distress; and he said, he had courage to go to the gate of hell, and a step farther, for that receipt.—The stranger laughed.

Weel, they rode on through the thickest of the wood, when, all of a sudden, the horse stopped at the door of a great house; and, but that he knew the place was ten miles off, my father would have thought he was at Redgauntlet Castle. They rode into the outer court-yard, through the muckle faulding yetts, and aneath the auld portcullis; and the whole front of the house was lighted, and there were pipes and fiddles, and as much dancing and deray within as used to be in Sir Robert's house at Pace and Yule, and such high seasons. They lap off, and my gudesire, as seemed to him, fastened his horse to the very ring he had tied him to that morning, when he gaed to wait on the young Sir John.

'God!' said my gudesire, 'if Sir Robert's death be but a dream!'

He knocked at the ha' door just as he was wont, and his auld acquaintance, Dougal MacCallum,—just after his wont, too,—came to open the door, and said, 'Piper Steenie, are ye there, lad? Sir Robert has been crying for you.'

My gudesire was like a man in a dream—he looked for the stranger, but he was gane for the time. At last he just tried to say, 'Ha! Dougal Driveower, are ye living? I thought ye had been dead.'

'Never fash yoursell wi' me,' said Dougal, 'but look to yoursell; and see ye tak naething frae onybody here, neither meat, drink, or siller, except just the receipt that is your ain.'

So saying, he led the way out through halls and trances that were weel kend to my gudesire, and into the auld oak parlour; and there was as much singing of profane sangs, and birling of red wine, and speaking blasphemy and sculduddry, as had ever been in Redgauntlet Castle when it was at the blithest.

But, Lord take us in keeping! what a set of ghastly revellers they were that sat round that table!—My gudesire kend mony that had long before gane to their place, for often had he piped to the most part in the hall of Redgauntlet. There was the fierce Middleton, and the dissolute Rothes, and the crafty Lauderdale; and Dalyell, with his bald head and a beard to his girdle; and Earlshall, with Cameron's blude on his hand; and wild Bonshaw, that tied blessed Mr Cargill's limbs till the blude sprung; and Dumbarton Douglas, the twice-turned traitor baith to country and king. There was the Bluidy Advocate MacKenyie, who, for his worldly wit and wisdom, had been to the rest as a god. And there was Claverhouse, as beautiful as when he lived, with his long, dark, curled locks, streaming down over his laced buff-coat, and his left hand always on his right spule-blade, to hide the wound that the silver bullet had made.[27] He sat apart from them all, and looked at them with a melancholy, haughty countenance; while the rest hallooed, and sung, and laughed, that the room rang. But their smiles were fearfully contorted from time to time; and their laughter passed into such wild sounds, as made my gudesire's very nails grow blue, and chilled the marrow in his banes.

They that waited at the table were just the wicked serving-men and troopers, that had done their work and cruel bidding on earth. There was the Lang Lad of the Nethertown, that helped to take Argyle; and the Bishop's summoner, that they called the Deil's Rattle-bag; and the wicked guardsmen, in their laced coats; and the savage Highland Amorites, that shed blood like water; and many a proud serving-man, haughty of heart and bloody of hand, cringing to the rich, and making them wickeder than they would be; grinding the poor to powder, when the rich had broken them to fragments. And mony, mony mair were coming and ganging, a' as busy in their vocation as if they had been alive.*

Sir Robert Redgauntlet, in the midst of a' this fearful riot, cried, wi' a voice like thunder, on Steenie Piper, to come to the board-head where he was sitting; his legs stretched out before him, and swathed up with flannel, with his holster pistols aside him, while the great broadsword rested against his chair, just as my gudesire had seen him the last time upon earth—the very cushion for the jackanape was close to him, but the creature itsell was not there—it wasna its hour, it's likely; for he heard them say as he came forward, 'Is not the Major come yet?' And another answered, 'The jackanape will be here betimes the morn.' And when my gudesire came forward, Sir Robert, or his ghaist, or the deevil in his likeness, said, 'Weel, piper, hae ye settled wi' my son for the year's rent?'

With much ado my father gat breath to say, that Sir John would not settle without his honour's receipt.

'Ye shall hae that for a tune of the pipes, Steenie,' said the appearance of Sir Robert—'Play us up, "Weel hoddled, Luckie."'

Now this was a tune my gudesire learned frae a warlock, that heard it when they were worshipping Satan at their meetings; and my gudesire had sometimes played it at the ranting suppers in Redgauntlet Castle, but never very willingly; and now he grew cauld at the very name of it, and said, for excuse, he hadna his pipes wi' him.

'MacCallum, ye limb of Beelzebub,' said the fearfu' Sir Robert, 'bring Steenie the pipes that I am keeping for him!'

MacCallum brought a pair of pipes might have served the piper of Donald of the Isles.* But he gave my gudesire a nudge as he offered them; and looking secretly and closely, Steenie saw that the chanter was of steel, and heated to a white heat; so he had fair warning not to trust his fingers with it. So he excused himself again, and said, he was faint and frightened, and had not wind aneugh to fill the bag.

'Then ye maun eat and drink, Steenie,' said the figure; 'for we do little else here; and it's ill speaking between a fou man and a fasting.'

Now these were the very words that the bloody Earl of Douglas said to keep the King's messenger in hand, while he cut the head off MacLellan of Bombie, at the Threave Castle;[28]* and that put Steenie mair and mair on his guard. So he spoke up like a man, and said he came neither to eat, or drink, or make minstrelsy; but simply for his ain—to ken what was come o' the money he had paid, and to get a discharge for it; and he was so stout-hearted by this time, that he charged Sir Robert for conscience-sake—(he had no power to say the holy name)—and as he hoped for peace and rest, to spread no snares for him, but just to give him his ain.

The appearance gnashed its teeth and laughed, but it took from a large pocketbook the receipt, and handed it to Steenie. 'There is your receipt, ye pitiful cur; and for the money, my dog-whelp of a son may go look for it in the Cat's Cradle.'

My gudesire uttered mony thanks, and was about to retire, when Sir Robert roared aloud, 'Stop though, thou sack-doudling son of a whore! I am not done with thee. HERE we do nothing for nothing; and you must return on this very day twelvemonth, to pay your master the homage that you owe me for my protection.'

My father's tongue was loosed of a suddenty, and he said aloud, 'I refer mysell to God's pleasure, and not to yours.'

He had no sooner uttered the word than all was dark around him; and he sunk on the earth with such a sudden shock, that he lost both breath and sense.

How lang Steenie lay there, he could not tell; but when he came to himsell, he was lying in the auld kirkyard of Redgauntlet parochine, just at the door of the family aisle, and the scutcheon of the auld knight, Sir Robert, hanging over his head. There was a deep morning fog on grass and gravestane around him, and his horse was feeding quietly beside the minister's twa cows. Steenie would have thought the whole was a dream, but he had the receipt in his hand, fairly written and signed by the auld Laird; only the last letters of his name were a little disorderly, written like one seized with sudden pain.

Sorely troubled in his mind, he left that dreary place, rode through the mist to Redgauntlet Castle, and with much ado he got speech of the Laird.

'Well, you dyvour bankrupt,' was the first word, 'have you brought me my rent?'

'No,' answered my gudesire, 'I have not; but I have brought your honour Sir Robert's receipt for it.'

'How, sirrah?—Sir Robert's receipt!—You told me he had not given you one.'

'Will your honour please to see if that bit line is right?'

Sir John looked at every line, and at every letter, with much attention; and at last, at the date, which my gudesire had not observed,—'*From my appointed place*,' he read, '*this twenty-fifth of November*.'—'What!—That is yesterday!—Villain, thou must have gone to hell for this!'

'I got it from your honour's father—whether he be in heaven or hell, I know not,' said Steenie.

'I will delate you for a warlock to the Privy Council!' said Sir John. 'I will send you to your master, the devil, with the help of a tar-barrel and a torch!'

'I intend to delate mysell to the Presbytery,'* said Steenie, 'and tell them all I have seen last night, whilk are things fitter for them to judge of than a borrel man like me.'

Sir John paused, composed himsell, and desired to hear the full history; and my gudesire told it him from point to point, as I have told it you—word for word, neither more nor less.

Sir John was silent again for a long time, and at last he said, very composedly, 'Steenie, this story of yours concerns the honour of many a noble family besides mine; and if it be a leasing-making, to keep yourself out of my danger, the least you can expect is to have a redhot iron driven through your tongue, and that will be as bad as scauding your fingers with a redhot chanter. But yet it may be true, Steenie; and if the money cast up, I shall not know what to think of it.—But where shall we find the Cat's Cradle? There are cats enough about the old house, but I think they kitten without the ceremony of bed or cradle.'

'We were best ask Hutcheon,' said my gudesire; 'he kens a' the odd corners about as weel as—another serving-man that is now gane, and that I wad not like to name.'

Aweel, Hutcheon, when he was asked, told them, that a ruinous turret, lang disused, next to the clock-house, only accessible by a ladder, for the opening was on the outside, and far above the battlements, was called of old the Cat's Cradle.

'There will I go immediately,' said Sir John; and he took (with what purpose, Heaven kens) one of his father's pistols from the hall-table, where they had lain since the night he died, and hastened to the battlements.

It was a dangerous place to climb, for the ladder was auld and frail, and wanted ane or twa rounds. However, up got Sir John, and entered at the turret door, where his body stopped the only little light that was in the bit turret. Something flees at him wi' a vengeance, maist dang him back ower—bang gaed the knight's pistol, and Hutcheon, that held the ladder, and my gudesire that stood beside him, hears a loud skelloch. A minute after, Sir John flings the body of the jackanape down to them, and cries that the siller is fund, and that they should come up and help him. And there was the bag of siller sure aneugh, and mony orra things besides, that had been missing for mony a day. And Sir John, when he had riped the turret weel, led my gudesire into the dining-parlour, and took him by the hand, and spoke kindly to him, and said he was sorry he should have doubted his word, and that he would hereafter be a good master to him, to make amends.

'And now, Steenie,' said Sir John, 'although this vision of yours tends, on the whole, to my father's credit, as an honest man, that he should, even after his death, desire to see justice done to a poor man like you, yet you are sensible that ill-dispositioned men might make bad constructions upon it, concerning his soul's health. So, I think, we had better lay the haill dirdum on that ill-deedie creature, Major Weir, and say naething about your dream in the wood of Pitmurkie. You had taken ower muckle brandy to be very certain about ony thing; and, Steenie, this receipt,' (his hand shook while he held it out,)—'its but a queer kind of document, and we will do best, I think, to put it quietly in the fire.'

'Od, but for as queer as it is, it's a' the voucher I have for my rent,' said my gudesire, who was afraid, it may be, of losing the benefit of Sir Robert's discharge.

'I will bear the contents to your credit in the rental-book, and give you a discharge under my own hand,' said Sir John, 'and that on the spot. And, Steenie, if you can hold your tongue about this matter, you shall sit, from this term downward, at an easier rent.'

'Mony thanks to your honour,' said Steenie, who saw easily in what corner the wind was; 'doubtless I will be conformable to all your honour's commands; only I would willingly speak wi' some powerful minister on the subject, for I do not like the sort of soumons of appointment whilk your honour's father'——

'Do not call the phantom my father!' said Sir John, interrupting him.

'Weel, then, the thing that was so like him,'—said my gudesire; 'he spoke of my coming back to him this time twelvemonth, and it's a weight on my conscience.'

'Aweel, then,' said Sir John, 'if you be so much distressed in mind, you may speak to our minister of the parish; he is a douce man, regards the honour of our family, and the mair that he may look for some patronage from me.'

Wi' that my gudesire readily agreed that the receipt should be burnt, and the Laird threw it into the chimney with his ain hand. Burn it would not for them, though; but away it flew up the lum, wi' a lang train of sparks at its tail, and a hissing noise like a squib.

My gudesire gaed down to the manse, and the minister, when he had heard the story, said, it was his real opinion, that though my gudesire had gaen very far in tampering with dangerous matters, yet, as he had refused the devil's arles, (for such was the offer of meat and drink,) and had refused to do homage by piping at his bidding, he hoped, that if he held a circumspect walk hereafter, Satan could take little advantage by what was come and gane. And, indeed, my gudesire, of his ain accord, lang forswore baith the pipes and the brandy—it was not even till the year was out, and the fatal day passed, that he would so much as take the fiddle, or drink usquebaugh or tippenny.

Sir John made up his story about the jackanape as he liked himsell; and some believe till this day there was no more in the matter than the filching nature of the brute. Indeed, ye'll no hinder some to threap, that it was nane o' the Auld Enemy that Dougal and my gudesire saw in the Laird's room, but only that wanchancy creature, the Major, capering on the coffin; and that as to the blawing on the Laird's whistle that was heard after he was dead, the filthy brute could do that as weel as the Laird himsell, if no better. But Heaven kens the truth, whilk first came out by the minister's wife, after Sir John and her ain gudeman were baith in the moulds. And then, my gudesire, wha was failed in his limbs, but not in his judgment or memory—at least nothing to speak of—was obliged to tell the real narrative to his freends, for the credit of his good name. He might else have been charged for a warlock.[29]

THE shades of evening were growing thicker around us as my conductor finished his long narrative with this moral—'Ye see, birkie, it is nae chancy thing to tak a stranger traveller for a guide, when ye are in an uncouth land.'

'I should not have made that inference,' said I. 'Your grandfather's adventure was fortunate for himself, whom it saved from ruin and distress; and fortunate for his landlord also, whom it prevented from committing a gross act of injustice.'

'Ay, but they had baith to sup the sauce o't sooner or later,' said Wandering Willie—'What was fristed wasna forgiven. Sir John died before he was much over threescore; and it was just like of a moment's illness. And for my gudesire, though he departed in fulness of years, yet there was my father, a yauld man of forty-five, fell down betwixt the stilts of his pleugh, and raise never again, and left nae bairn but me, a puir sightless, fatherless, motherless creature, could neither work nor want. Things gaed weel aneugh at first; for Sir Redwald Redgauntlet, the only son of Sir John, and the oye of auld Sir Robert, and, waes me! the last of the honourable house, took the farm off our hands, and brought me into his household to have care of me. He liked music, and I had the best teachers baith England and Scotland could gie me. Mony a merry year was I wi' him; but waes me! he gaed out with other pretty men in the forty-five*—I'll say nae mair about it—My head never settled weel since I lost him; and if I say another word about it, deil a bar will I have the heart to play the night.—Look out, my gentle chap,' he resumed in a different tone, 'ye should see the lights in Brokenburn Glen by this time.'

LETTER XII

THE SAME TO THE SAME

Tam Luter was their minstrel meet,
  Gude Lord as he could lance,
He played sae shrill and sang sae sweet,
  Till Towsie took a trance.
Auld Lightfoot there he did forleet,
  And counterfeited France;
He used himself as man discreet,
  And took up Morrice danse
                Sae loud,
  At Christ's Kirk on the Green that day.

KING JAMES I*

I CONTINUE to scribble at length, though the subject may seem somewhat deficient in interest. Let the grace of the narrative, therefore, and the concern we take in each other's matters, make amends for its tenuity. We fools of fancy, who suffer ourselves, like Malvolio,* to be cheated with our own visions, have, nevertheless, this advantage over the wise ones of the earth, that we have our whole stock of enjoyments under our own command, and can dish for ourselves an intellectual banquet with most moderate assistance from external objects. It is, to be sure, something like the feast which the Barmecide served up to Alnaschar;* and we cannot be expected to get fat upon such diet. But then, neither is there repletion nor nausea, which often succeed the grosser and more material revel. On the whole, I still pray, with the Ode to Castle Building—*

'Give me thy hope which sickens not the heart;
  Give me thy wealth which has no wings to fly;
Give me the bliss thy visions can impart;
  Thy friendship give me, warm in poverty!'

And so, despite thy solemn smile and sapient shake of the head, I will go on picking such interest as I can out of my trivial adventures, even though that interest should be the creation of my own fancy; nor will I cease to inflict on thy devoted eyes the labour of perusing the scrolls in which I shall record my narrative.

My last broke off as we were on the point of descending into the glen at Brokenburn, by the dangerous track which I had first travelled *en croupe*, behind a furious horseman, and was now again to brave under the precarious guidance of a blind man.

It was now getting dark; but this was no inconvenience to my guide, who moved on, as formerly, with instinctive security of step, so that we soon reached the bottom, and I could see lights twinkling in the cottage which had been my place of refuge on a former occasion. It was not thither, however, that our course was directed. We left the habitation of the Laird to the left, and turning down the brook, soon approached the small hamlet which had been erected at the mouth of the stream, probably on account of the convenience which it afforded as a harbour to the fishing-boats. A large low cottage, full in our front, seemed highly illuminated; for the light not only glanced from every window and aperture in its frail walls, but was even visible from rents and fractures in the roof, composed of tarred shingles, repaired in part by thatch and *divot*.

While these appearances engaged my attention, that of my companion was attracted by a regular succession of sounds, like a bouncing on the floor, mixed with a very faint noise of music, which Willie's acute organs at once recognised and accounted for, while to me it was almost inaudible. The old man struck the earth with his staff in a violent passion. 'The whoreson fisher rabble! They have brought another violer upon my walk! They are such smuggling blackguards, that they must run in their very music; but I'll sort them waur than ony gauger in the country.—Stay—hark—it's no a fiddle neither—it's the pipe and tabor bastard, Simon of Sowport, frae the Nicol Forest; but I'll pipe and tabor him!—Let me hae ance my left hand on his cravat, and ye shall see what my right will do. Come away, chap—come away, gentle chap—nae time to be picking and waling your steps.' And on he passed with long and determined strides, dragging me along with him.

I was not quite easy in his company; for, now that his minstrel pride was hurt, the man had changed from the quiet, decorous, I might almost say respectable person, which he seemed while he told his tale, into the appearance of a fierce, brawling, dissolute stroller. So that when he entered the large hut, where a great number of fishers, with their wives and daughters, were engaged in eating, drinking, and dancing, I was somewhat afraid that the impatient violence of my companion might procure us an indifferent reception.

But the universal shout of welcome with which Wandering Willie was received—the hearty congratulation—the repeated 'Here's t'ye, Willie!'—'Whare hae ye been, ye blind deevil?' and the call upon him to pledge them—above all, the speed with which the obnoxious pipe and tabor were put to silence, gave the old man such effectual assurance of undiminished popularity and importance, as at once put his jealousy to rest, and changed his tone of offended dignity, into one better fitted to receive such cordial greetings. Young men and women crowded round, to tell how much they were afraid some mischance had detained him, and how two or three young fellows had set out in quest of him.

'It was nae mischance, praised be Heaven,' said Willie, 'but the absence of the lazy loon Rob the Rambler, my comrade, that didna come to meet me on the Links; but I hae gotten a braw consort in his stead, worth a dozen of him, the unhanged blackguard.'

'And wha is't tou's gotten, Wullie, lad?' said half a score of voices, while all eyes were turned on your humble servant, who kept the best countenance he could, though not quite easy at becoming the centre to which all eyes were pointed.

'I ken him by his hemmed cravat,' said one fellow; 'it's Gil Hobson, the souple tailor frae Burgh.—Ye are welcome to Scotland, ye prick-the-clout loon,' he said, thrusting forth a paw much the colour of a badger's back, and of most portentous dimensions.

'Gil Hobson? Gil whoreson!' exclaimed Wandering Willie; 'it's a gentle chap that I judge to be an apprentice wi' auld Joshua Geddes, to the quaker-trade.'

'What trade be's that, man?' said he of the badger-coloured fist.

'Canting and lying,'—said Willie, which produced a thundering laugh; 'but I am teaching the callant a better trade, and that is feasting and fiddling.'

Willie's conduct in thus announcing something like my real character, was contrary to compact; and yet I was rather glad he did so, for the consequence of putting a trick upon these rude and ferocious men, might, in case of discovery, have been dangerous to us both, and I was at the same time delivered from the painful effort to support a fictitious character. The good company, except perhaps one or two of the young women, whose looks expressed some desire for better acquaintance, gave themselves no farther trouble about me; but, while the seniors resumed their places near an immense bowl, or rather reeking caldron of brandy-punch, the younger arranged themselves on the floor, and called loudly on Willie to strike up.

With a brief caution to me, to 'mind my credit, for fishers have ears, though fish have none,' Willie led off in capital style, and I followed, certainly not so as to disgrace my companion, who, every now and then, gave me a nod of approbation. The dances were, of course, the Scottish jigs, and reels, and 'twasome dances,' with a strathspey or hornpipe for interlude; and the want of grace, on the part of the performers, was amply supplied by truth of ear, vigour and decision of step, and the agility proper to the northern performers. My own spirits rose with the mirth around me, and with old Willie's admirable execution, and frequent 'weel dune, gentle chap, yet!'—and, to confess the truth, I felt a great deal more pleasure in this rustic revel, than I have done at the more formal balls and concerts in your famed city, to which I have sometimes made my way. Perhaps this was, because I was a person of more importance to the presiding matron of Brokenburn-foot, than I had the means of rendering myself to the far-famed Miss Nickie Murray, the patroness of your Edinburgh assemblies.* The person I mean was a buxom dame of about thirty, her fingers loaded with many a silver ring, and three or four of gold; her ankles liberally displayed from under her numerous blue, white, and scarlet short petticoats, and attired in hose of the finest and whitest lamb's-wool, which arose from shoes of Spanish cordwain, fastened with silver buckles. She took the lead in my favour, and declared, 'that the brave young gentleman should not weary himself to death wi' playing, but take the floor for a dance or twa.'

'And what's to come of me, Dame Martin?' said Willie.

'Come o' thee?' said the dame; 'mischanter on the auld beard o' ye! ye could play for twenty hours on end, and tire out the haill country-side wi' dancing before ye laid down your bow, saving for a by-drink or the like o' that.'

'In troth, dame,' answered Willie, 'ye are nae sae far wrang; sae if my comrade is to take his dance, ye maun gie me my drink, and then bob it away like Madge of Middlebie.'

The drink was soon brought; but while Willie was partaking of it, a party entered the hut, which arrested my attention at once, and intercepted the intended gallantry with which I had proposed to present my hand to the fresh-coloured, well-made, white-ankled Thetis, who had obtained me manumission from my musical task. This was nothing less than the sudden appearance of the old woman whom the Laird had termed Mabel; Cristal Nixon, his male attendant; and the young person who had said grace to us when I supped with him.

This young person—Alan, thou art in thy way a bit of a conjurer—this young person whom I *did not* describe, and whom you, for that very reason, suspected was not an indifferent object to me—is, I am sorry to say it, in very fact not so much so as in prudence she ought. I will not use the name of *love* on this occasion; for I have applied it too often to transient whims and fancies to escape your satire, should I venture to apply it now. For it is a phrase, I must confess, which I have used—a romancer would say, profaned—a little too often, considering how few years have passed over my head. But seriously, the fair chaplain of Brokenburn has been often in my head when she had no business there; and if this can give thee any clew for explaining my motives in lingering about the country, and assuming the character of Willie's companion, why, hang thee, thou art welcome to make use of it—a permission for which thou need'st not thank me much, as thou wouldst not have failed to assume it, whether it were given or no.

Such being my feelings, conceive how they must have been excited, when, like a beam upon a cloud, I saw this uncommonly beautiful girl enter the apartment in which they were dancing; not, however, with the air of an equal, but that of a superior, come to grace with her presence the festival of her dependants. The old man and woman attended, with looks as sinister as hers were lovely, like two of the worst winter months waiting upon the bright-eyed May.

When she entered—wonder if thou wilt—she wore *a green mantle*, such as thou hast described as the garb of thy fair client, and confirmed what I had partly guessed from thy personal description, that my chaplain and thy visitor were the same person. There was an alteration on her brow the instant she recognised me. She gave her cloak to her female attendant, and, after a momentary hesitation, as if uncertain whether to advance or retire, she walked into the room with dignity and composure, all making way, the men unbonneting, and the women curtsying respectfully, as she assumed a chair which was reverently placed for her accommodation, apart from others.

There was then a pause, until the bustling mistress of the ceremonies, with awkward, but kindly courtesy, offered the young lady a glass of wine, which was at first declined, and at length only thus far accepted, that, bowing round to the festive company, the fair visitor wished them all health and mirth, and, just touching the brim with her lip, replaced it on the salver. There was another pause; and I did not immediately recollect, confused as I was by this unexpected apparition, that it belonged to me to break it. At length a murmur was heard around me, being expected to exhibit,—nay, to lead down the dance,—in consequence of the previous conversation.

'Deil's in the fiddler lad,' was muttered from more quarters than one—'saw folk ever sic a thing as a shamefaced fiddler before?'

At length a venerable Triton, seconding his remonstrances with a hearty thump on my shoulder, cried out, 'To the floor—to the floor, and let us see how ye can fling—the lasses are a' waiting.'

Up I jumped, sprung from the elevated station which constituted our orchestra, and, arranging my ideas as rapidly as I could, advanced to the head of the room, and, instead of offering my hand to the white-footed Thetis aforesaid, I venturously made the same proposal to her of the Green Mantle.

The nymph's lovely eyes seemed to open with astonishment at the audacity of this offer; and, from the murmurs I heard around me, I also understood that it surprised, and perhaps offended, the bystanders. But after the first moment's emotion, she wreathed her neck, and drawing herself haughtily up, like one who was willing to show that she was sensible of the full extent of her own condescension, extended her hand towards me, like a princess gracing a squire of low degree.

There is affectation in all this, thought I to myself, if the Green Mantle has borne true evidence—for young ladies do not make visits, or write letters to counsel learned in the law, to interfere in the motions of those whom they hold as cheap as this nymph seems to do me; and if I am cheated by a resemblance of cloaks, still I am interested to show myself, in some degree, worthy of the favour she has granted with so much state and reserve.—The dance to be performed was the old Scots Jigg, in which you are aware I used to play no sorry figure at La Pique's, when thy clumsy movements used to be rebuked by raps over the knuckles with that great professor's fiddlestick. The choice of the tune was left to my comrade Willie, who, having finished his drink, feloniously struck up the well-known and popular measure,

> 'Merrily danced the Quaker's wife,
> And merrily danced the Quaker.'*

An astounding laugh arose at my expense, and I should have been annihilated, but that the smile which mantled on the lip of my partner, had a different expression from that of ridicule, and seemed to say, 'Do not take this to heart.' And I did not, Alan. My partner danced admirably, and I like one who was determined, if outshone, which I could not help, not to be altogether thrown into the shade.

I assure you our performance, as well as Willie's music, deserved more polished spectators and auditors; but we could not then have been greeted with such enthusiastic shouts of applause as attended while I handed my partner to her seat, and took my place by her side, as one who had a right to offer the attentions usual on such an occasion. She was visibly embarrassed, but I was determined not to observe her confusion, and to avail myself of the opportunity of learning whether this beautiful creature's mind was worthy of the casket in which Nature had lodged it.

Nevertheless, however courageously I formed this resolution, you cannot but too well guess the difficulties I must needs have felt in carrying it into execution; since want of habitual intercourse with the charmers of the other sex has rendered me a sheepish cur, only one grain less awkward than thyself. Then she was so very beautiful, and assumed an air of so much dignity, that I was like to fall under the fatal error of supposing she should only be addressed with something very clever; and in the hasty racking which my brains underwent in this persuasion, not a single idea occurred that common sense did not reject as fustian on the one hand, or weary, flat, and stale triticism on the other. I felt as if my understanding were no longer my own, but was alternately under the dominion of Aldiborontiphoscophornio, and that of his facetious friend Rigdum-Funnidos.* How did I envy at that moment our friend Jack Oliver, who produces with such happy complacence his fardel of small talk, and who, as he never doubts his own powers of affording amusement, passes them current with every pretty woman he approaches, and fills up the intervals of chat by his complete acquaintance with the exercise of the fan, the *flaçon*, and the other duties of the *Cavaliere Serviente.** Some of these I attempted, but I suppose it was awkwardly; at least the Lady Greenmantle received them as a princess accepts the homage of a clown.

Meantime the floor remained empty, and as the mirth of the good meeting was somewhat checked, I ventured, as a dernier resort, to propose a minuet. She thanked me, and told me haughtily enough, 'she was here to encourage the harmless pleasures of these good folks, but was not disposed to make an exhibition of her own indifferent dancing for their amusement.'

She paused a moment, as if she expected me to suggest something; and as I remained silent and rebuked, she bowed her head more graciously, and said, 'Not to affront you, however, a country-dance, if you please.'

What an ass was I, Alan, not to have anticipated her wishes! Should I not have observed that the ill-favoured couple, Mabel and Cristal, had placed themselves on each side of her seat, like the supporters of the royal arms? the man, thick, short, shaggy, and hirsute, as the lion; the female, skin-dried, tight-laced, long, lean, and hungry-faced, like the unicorn. I ought to have recollected, that under the close inspection of two such watchful salvages, our communication, while in repose, could not have been easy; that the period of dancing a minuet was not the very choicest time for conversation; but that the noise, the exercise, and the mazy confusion of a country-dance, where the inexperienced performers were every now and then running against each other, and compelling the other couples to stand still for a minute at a time, besides the more regular repose afforded by the intervals of the dance itself, gave the best possible openings for a word or two spoken in season, and without being liable to observation.

We had but just led down, when an opportunity of the kind

occurred, and my partner said, with great gentleness and modesty, 'It is not perhaps very proper in me to acknowledge an acquaintance that is not claimed; but I believe I speak to Mr Darsie Latimer?'

'Darsie Latimer was indeed the person that had now the honour and happiness'——

I would have gone on in the false gallop of compliment, but she cut me short. 'And why,' she said, 'is Mr Latimer here, and in disguise, or at least assuming an office unworthy of a man of education?—I beg pardon,' she continued,—'I would not give you pain, but surely making an associate of a person of that description'——

She looked towards my friend Willie, and was silent. I felt heartily ashamed of myself, and hastened to say it was an idle frolic, which want of occupation had suggested, and which I could not regret, since it had procured me the pleasure I at present enjoyed.

Without seeming to notice my compliment, she took the next opportunity to say, 'Will Mr Latimer permit a stranger who wishes him well to ask, whether it is right that, at his active age, he should be in so far void of occupation, as to be ready to adopt low society for the sake of idle amusement?'

'You are severe, madam,' I answered; 'but I cannot think myself degraded by mixing with any society where I meet'——

Here I stopped short, conscious that I was giving my answer an unhandsome turn. The *argumentum ad hominem*, the last to which a polite man has recourse, may, however, be justified by circumstances, but seldom or never the *argumentum ad feminam*.

She filled up the blank herself which I had left. 'Where you meet *me*, I suppose you would say? But the case is different. I am, from my unhappy fate, obliged to move by the will of others, and to be in places which I would by my own will gladly avoid. Besides, I am, except for these few minutes, no participator of the revels—a spectator only, and attended by my servants. Your situation is different—you are here by choice, the partaker and minister of the pleasures of a class below you in education, birth, and fortunes.—If I speak harshly, Mr Latimer,' she added, with much sweetness of manner, 'I mean kindly.'

I was confounded by her speech, 'severe in youthful wisdom;'* all of *naïve* or lively, suitable to such a dialogue, vanished from my recollection, and I answered, with gravity like her own, 'I am, indeed, better educated than these poor people; but you, madam, whose kind admonition I am grateful for, must know more of my condition than I do myself—I dare not say I am their superior in birth, since I know nothing of my own, or in fortunes, over which hangs an impenetrable cloud.'

'And why should your ignorance on these points drive you into low society and idle habits?' answered my female monitor. 'Is it manly to wait till fortune cast her beams upon you, when by exertion of your own energy you might distinguish yourself?—Do not the pursuits of learning lie open to you—of manly ambition—of war?—But no—not of war, that has already cost you too dear.'

'I will be what you wish me to be,' I replied with eagerness—'You have but to choose my path, and you shall see if I do not pursue it with energy, were it only because you command me.'

'Not because I command you,' said the maiden, 'but because reason, common sense, manhood, and, in one word, regard for your own safety, give the same counsel.'

'At least permit me to reply, that reason and sense never assumed a fairer form—of persuasion,' I hastily added; for she turned from me—nor did she give me another opportunity of continuing what I had to say till the next pause of the dance, when, determined to bring our dialogue to a point, I said, 'You mentioned manhood also, madam, and, in the same breath, personal danger. My ideas of manhood suggest that it is cowardice to retreat before dangers of a doubtful character. You, who appear to know so much of my fortunes that I might call you my guardian angel, tell me what these dangers are, that I may judge whether manhood calls on me to face or to fly them.'

She was evidently perplexed by this appeal.

'You make me pay dearly for acting as your humane adviser,' she replied at last: 'I acknowledge an interest in your fate, and yet I dare not tell you whence it arises; neither am I at liberty to say why, or from whom, you are in danger; but it is not less true that danger is near and imminent. Ask me no more, but, for your own sake, begone from this country. Elsewhere you are safe—here you do but invite your fate.'

'But, am I doomed to bid thus farewell to almost the only human being who has showed an interest in my welfare?—Do not say so—say that we shall meet again, and the hope shall be the leading star to regulate my course!'

'It is more than probable,' she said—'much more than probable, that we may never meet again. The help which I now render you is all that may be in my power; it is such as I should render to a blind man whom I might observe approaching the verge of a precipice; it ought to excite no surprise, and requires no gratitude.'

So saying, she again turned from me, nor did she address me until the dance was on the point of ending, when she said, 'Do not attempt to speak to, or approach me again in the course of the night;

leave the company as soon as you can, but not abruptly, and God be with you.'

I handed her to her seat, and did not quit the fair palm I held, without expressing my feelings by a gentle pressure. She coloured slightly, and withdrew her hand, but not angrily. Seeing the eyes of Cristal and Mabel sternly fixed on me, I bowed deeply, and withdrew from her; my heart saddening, and my eyes becoming dim in spite of me, as the shifting crowd hid us from each other.

It was my intention to have crept back to my comrade Willie, and resumed my bow with such spirit as I might, although at the moment I would have given half my income for an instant's solitude. But my retreat was cut off by Dame Martin, with the frankness—if it is not an inconsistent phrase—of rustic coquetry, that goes straight up to the point.

'Ay, lad, ye seem unca sune weary, to dance sae lightly? Better the nag that ambles a' the day, than him that makes a brattle for a mile, and then's dune wi' the road.'

This was a fair challenge, and I could not decline accepting it. Besides, I could see Dame Martin was queen of the revels; and so many were the rude and singular figures about me, that I was by no means certain whether I might not need some protection. I seized on her willing hand, and we took our places in the dance, where, if I did not acquit myself with all the accuracy of step and movement which I had before attempted, I at least came up to the expectations of my partner, who said, and almost swore, 'I was prime at it;' while, stimulated to her utmost exertions, she herself frisked like a kid, snapped her fingers like castanets, whooped like a Bacchanal, and bounded from the floor like a tennis-ball,—ay, till the colour of her garters was no particular mystery. She made the less secret of this, perhaps, that they were sky-blue, and fringed with silver.

The time has been that this would have been special fun; or rather, last night was the only time I can recollect these four years when it would *not* have been so; yet, at this moment, I cannot tell you how I longed to be rid of Dame Martin. I almost wished she would sprain one of those 'many-twinkling' ankles, which served her so alertly; and when, in the midst of her exuberant caprioling, I saw my former partner leaving the apartment, and with eyes, as I thought, turning towards me, this unwillingness to carry on the dance increased to such a point, that I was almost about to feign a sprain or a dislocation myself, in order to put an end to the performance. But there were around me scores of old women, all of whom looked as if they might have some sovereign recipe for such an accident; and, remembering Gil Blas and his pretended disorder in the robbers' cavern,* I thought it as wise to play Dame Martin fair, and dance till she thought proper to dismiss me. What I did I resolved to do strenuously, and in the latter part of the exhibition, I cut and sprang from the floor as high and as perpendicularly as Dame Martin herself; and received, I promise you, thunders of applause, for the common people always prefer exertion and agility to grace. At length Dame Martin could dance no more, and, rejoicing at my release, I led her to a seat, and took the privilege of a partner to attend her.

'Hegh, sirs,' exclaimed Dame Martin, 'I am sair forfoughen! Troth, callant, I think ye hae been amaist the death o' me.'

I could only atone for the alleged offence by fetching her some refreshment, of which she readily partook.

'I have been lucky in my partners,' I said, 'first that pretty young lady, and then you, Mrs Martin.'

'Hout wi' your fleeching,' said Dame Martin. 'Gae wa—gae wa, lad; dinna blaw in folk's lugs that gate; me and Miss Lilias even'd thegither! Na, na, lad—od, she is maybe four or five years younger than the like o' me,—by and attour her gentle havings.'

'She is the Laird's daughter?' said I, in as careless a tone of enquiry as I could assume.

'His daughter, man? Na, na, only his niece—and sib aneugh to him, I think.'

'Ay, indeed,' I replied; 'I thought she had borne his name?'

'She bears her ain name, and that's Lilias.'

'And has she no other name?' asked I.

'What needs she another till she gets a gudeman?' answered my Thetis, a little miffed perhaps—to use the women's phrase—that I turned the conversation upon my former partner, rather than addressed it to herself.

There was a short pause, which was interrupted by Dame Martin observing, 'They are standing up again.'

'True,' said I, having no mind to renew my late violent *capriole*, 'and I must go help old Willie.'

Ere I could extricate myself, I heard poor Thetis address herself to a sort of Mer-man in a jacket of seaman's blue, and a pair of trowsers, (whose hand, by the way, she had rejected at an earlier part of the evening,) and intimate that she was now disposed to take a trip.

'Trip away then, dearie,' said the vindictive man of the waters, without offering his hand; 'there,' pointing to the floor, 'is a roomy berth for you.'

Certain I had made one enemy, and perhaps two, I hastened to my original seat beside Willie, and began to handle my bow. But I could see that my conduct had made an unfavourable impression; the words, 'flory conceited chap,'—'hafflins gentle,' and at length, the still more alarming epithet of 'spy,' began to be buzzed about, and I was heartily glad when the apparition of Sam's visage at the door, who was already possessed of and draining a can of punch, gave me assurance that my means of retreat were at hand. I intimated as much to Willie, who probably had heard more of the murmurs of the company than I had, for he whispered, 'Ay, ay—awa wi' ye—ower lang here—slide out canny—dinna let them see ye are on the tramp.'

I slipped half-a-guinea into the old man's hand, who answered, 'Truts! pruts! nonsense! but I'se no refuse, trusting ye can afford it.—Awa wi' ye—and if ony body stops ye, cry on me.'

I glided, by his advice, along the room as if looking for a partner, joined Sam, whom I disengaged with some difficulty from his can, and we left the cottage together in a manner to attract the least possible observation. The horses were tied in a neighbouring shed, and as the moon was up and I was now familiar with the road, broken and complicated as it is, we soon reached the Shepherd's Bush, where the old landlady was sitting up waiting for us, under some anxiety of mind, to account for which she did not hesitate to tell me that some folks had gone to Brokenburn from her house, or neighbouring towns, that did not come so safe back again. 'Wandering Willie,' she said, 'was doubtless a kind of protection.'

Here Willie's wife, who was smoking in the chimney corner, took up the praises of her 'hinnie,' as she called him, and endeavoured to awaken my generosity afresh, by describing the dangers from which, as she was pleased to allege, her husband's countenance had assuredly been the means of preserving me. I was not, however, to be fooled out of more money at this time, and went to bed in haste, full of various cogitations.

I have since spent a couple of days betwixt Mount Sharon and this place, and betwixt reading, writing to thee this momentous history, forming plans for seeing the lovely Lilias, and—partly, I think, for the sake of contradiction—angling a little in spite of Joshua's scruples—though I am rather liking the amusement better as I begin to have some success in it.

And now, my dearest Alan, you are in full possession of my secret—let me as frankly into the recesses of your bosom. How do you feel towards this fair ignis fatuus, this lily of the desert? Tell me honestly; for however the recollection of her may haunt my own mind, my love for Alan Fairford surpasses the love of woman. I know, too, that when you *do* love, it will be to

'Love once and love no more.'

A deep-consuming passion, once kindled in a breast so steady as yours, would never be extinguished but with life. I am of another and more volatile temper, and though I shall open your next with a trembling hand, and uncertain heart, yet let it bring a frank confession that this fair unknown has made a deeper impression on your gravity than you reckoned for, and you will see I can tear the arrow from my own wound, barb and all. In the meantime, though I have formed schemes once more to see her, I will, you may rely on it, take no step for putting them into practice. I have refrained from this hitherto, and I give you my word of honour, I shall continue to do so; yet why should you need any further assurance from one who is so entirely yours as

D. L.

P.S.—I shall be on thorns till I receive your answer. I read, and re-read your letter, and cannot for my soul discover what your real sentiments are. Sometimes I think you write of her as one in jest—and sometimes I think that cannot be. Put me at ease as soon as possible.

LETTER XIII

ALAN FAIRFORD TO DARSIE LATIMER

I WRITE on the instant, as you direct; and in a tragi-comic humour, for I have a tear in my eye, and a smile on my cheek. Dearest Darsie, sure never a being but yourself could be so generous—sure never a being but yourself could be so absurd! I remember when you were a boy you wished to make your fine new whip a present to old aunt Peggy, merely because she admired it; and now, with like unreflecting and unappropriate liberality, you would resign your beloved to a smoke-dried young sophister, who cares not one of the hairs which it is his occupation to split, for all the daughters of Eve. *I* in love with your Lilias—your greenmantle—your unknown enchantress!—why I scarce saw her for five minutes, and even then only the tip of her chin was distinctly visible. She was well made, and the tip of her chin was of a most promising cast for the rest of the face; but, Heaven save you! she came upon business! and for a lawyer to fall in love with a pretty client on a single consultation, would be as wise as if he became enamoured of a particularly bright sunbeam which chanced for a moment to gild his bar-wig. I give you my word I am heart-whole; and, moreover, I assure you, that before I suffer a woman to sit near my heart's core, I must see her full face, without mask or mantle, ay, and know a good deal of her mind into the bargain. So never fret yourself on my account, my kind and generous Darsie; but, for your own sake, have a care, and let not an idle attachment, so lightly taken up, lead you into serious danger.

On this subject I feel so apprehensive, that now when I am decorated with the honours of the gown, I should have abandoned my career at the very starting to come to you, but for my father having contrived to clog my heels with fetters of a professional nature. I will tell you the matter at length, for it is comical enough; and why should not you list to my juridical adventures, as well as I to those of your fiddling knight-errantry?

It was after dinner, and I was considering how I might best introduce to my father the private resolution I had formed to set off for Dumfries-shire, or whether I had not better run away at once, and plead my excuse by letter, when, assuming the peculiar look with which he communicates any of his intentions respecting me, that he suspects may not be altogether acceptable, 'Alan,' he said, 'ye now wear a gown—ye have opened shop, as we would say of a more mechanical profession; and, doubtless, ye think the floor of the courts is strewed with guineas, and that ye have only to stoop down to gather them?'

'I hope I am sensible, sir,' I replied, 'that I have some knowledge and practice to acquire, and must stoop for that in the first place.'

'It is well said,' answered my father; and, always afraid to give too much encouragement, added, 'Very well said, if it be well acted up to—Stoop to get knowledge and practice is the very word. Ye know very well, Alan, that in the other faculty who study the *Ars medendi*, before the young doctor gets to the bedsides of palaces, he must, as they call it, walk the hospitals; and cure Lazarus of his sores, before he be admitted to prescribe for Dives,* when he has gout or indigestion'——

'I am aware, sir, that'——

'Whisht—do not interrupt the court—Well—also the chirurgeons have an useful practice, by which they put their apprentices and *tyrones* to work upon senseless dead bodies, to which, as they can do no good, so they certainly can do as little harm; while at the same time the *tyro*, or apprentice, gains experience, and becomes fit to whip off a leg or arm from a living subject, as cleanly as ye would slice an onion.'

'I believe I guess your meaning, sir,' answered I; 'and were it not for a very particular engagement'——

'Do not speak to me of engagements; but whisht—there is a good lad—and do not interrupt the court.'

My father, you know, is apt—be it said with all filial duty—to be a little prolix in his harangues. I had nothing for it but to lean back and listen.

'Maybe you think, Alan, because I have, doubtless, the management of some actions in dependence, whilk my worthy clients have intrusted me with, that I may think of airting them your way *instanter*; and so setting you up in practice, so far as my small business or influence may go; and, doubtless, Alan, that is a day whilk I hope may come round. But then, before I give, as the proverb hath it, "My own fish-guts to my own sea-maws,"* I must, for the sake of my own character, be very sure that my sea-maw can pick them to some purpose. What say ye?'

'I am so far,' answered I, 'from wishing to get early into practice, sir, that I would willingly bestow a few days'——

'In farther study, ye would say, Alan. But that is not the way either—ye must walk the hospitals—ye must cure Lazarus—ye must cut and carve on a departed subject, to show your skill.'

'I am sure,' I replied, 'I will undertake the cause of any poor man with pleasure, and bestow as much pains upon it as if it were a duke's; but for the next two or three days'——

'They must be devoted to close study, Alan—very close study indeed; for ye must stand primed for a hearing, *in presentia Dominorum*, upon Tuesday next.'

'I, sir!' I replied in astonishment—'I have not opened my mouth in the Outer-House yet!'

'Never mind the Court of the Gentiles, man,' said my father; 'we will have you into the Sanctuary at once—over shoes, over boots.'

'But, sir, I should really spoil any cause thrust on me so hastily.'

'Ye cannot spoil it, Alan,' said my father, rubbing his hands with much complacency; 'that is the very cream of the business, man—it is just, as I said before, a subject upon whilk all the *tyrones* have been trying their whittles for fifteen years; and as there have been about ten or a dozen agents concerned, and each took his own way, the case is come to that pass, that Stair or Arniston* could not mend it; and I do not think even you, Alan, can do it much harm—ye may get credit by it, but ye can lose none.'

'And pray what is the name of my happy client, sir?' said I, ungraciously enough, I believe.

'It is a well-known name in the Parliament-House,'* replied my father. 'To say the truth, I expect him every moment; it is Peter Peebles.'[30] *

'Peter Peebles!' exclaimed I, in astonishment; 'he is an insane beggar—as poor as Job, and as mad as a March hare!'

'He has been pleaing in the court for fifteen years,' said my father, in a tone of commiseration, which seemed to acknowledge that this fact was enough to account for the poor man's condition both in mind and circumstances.

'Besides, sir,' I added, 'he is on the Poor's Roll;* and you know there are advocates regularly appointed to manage those cases; and for me to presume to interfere'——

'Whisht, Alan!—never interrupt the court—all *that* is managed for ye like a tee'd ball;' (my father sometimes draws his similes from his once favourite game of golf;)—'you must know, Alan, that Peter's cause was to have been opened by young Dumtoustie—ye may ken the lad, a son of Dumtoustie of that ilk, member of Parliament for the county of——, and a nephew of the Laird's younger brother, worthy Lord Bladderskate, whilk ye are aware sounds as like being akin to a peatship[31] and a sheriffdom, as a sieve is sib to a riddle.* Now, Saunders Drudgeit, my lord's clerk, came to me this morning in the House, like ane bereft of his wits; for it seems that young Dumtoustie is ane of the Poor's Lawyers, and Peter Peebles's process had been remitted to him of course. But so soon as the harebrained goose saw the pokes,[32] (as, indeed, Alan, they are none of the least,) he took fright, called for his nag, lap on, and away to the country is he gone; and so, said Saunders, my lord is at his wit's end wi' vexation and shame, to see his nevoy break off the course at the very starting. "I'll tell you, Saunders," said I, "were I my lord, and a friend or kinsman of mine should leave the town while the court was sitting, that kinsman, or be he what he liked, should never darken my door again." And then, Alan, I thought to turn the ball our own way; and I said that you were a gey sharp birkie, just off the irons, and if it would oblige my lord, and so forth, you would open Peter's cause on Tuesday, and make some handsome apology for the necessary absence of your learned friend, and the loss which your client and the court had sustained, and so forth. Saunders lap at the proposition, like a cock at a grossart; for, he said, the only chance was to get a new hand, that did not ken the charge he was taking upon him; for there was not a lad of two Sessions' standing that was not dead-sick of Peter Peebles and his cause; and he advised me to break the matter gently to you at the first; but I told him you were a good bairn, Alan, and had no will and pleasure in these matters but mine.'

What could I say, Darsie, in answer to this arrangement, so very well meant—so very vexatious at the same time?—To imitate the defection and flight of young Dumtoustie, was at once to destroy my father's hopes of me for ever; nay, such is the keenness with which he regards all connected with his profession, it might have been a step to breaking his heart. I was obliged, therefore, to bow in sad acquiescence, when my father called to James Wilkinson to bring the two bits of pokes he would find on his table.

Exit James, and presently re-enters, bending under the load of two huge leathern bags, full of papers to the brim, and labelled on the greasy backs with the magic impress of the clerks of court, and the title, *Peebles against Plainstanes*. This huge mass was deposited on the table, and my father, with no ordinary glee in his countenance, began to draw out the various bundles of papers, secured by none of your red tape or whipcord, but stout, substantial casts of tarred rope, such as might have held small craft at their moorings.

I made a last and desperate effort to get rid of the impending job. 'I am really afraid, sir, that this case seems so much complicated, and there is so little time to prepare, that we had better move the Court to supersede it till next Session.'

'How, sir?—how, Alan?' said my father—'Would you approbate and reprobate, sir?—You have accepted the poor man's cause, and if you have not his fee in your pocket, it is because he has none to give you; and now would you approbate and reprobate in the same breath of your mouth?—Think of your oath of office, Alan, and your duty to your father, my dear boy.'

Once more, what could I say?—I saw, from my father's hurried and alarmed manner, that nothing could vex him so much as failing in the point he had determined to carry, and once more intimated my readiness to do my best, under every disadvantage.

'Well, well, my boy,' said my father, 'the Lord will make your days long in the land, for the honour you have given to your father's grey hairs.* You may find wiser advisers, Alan, but none that can wish you better.'

My father, you know, does not usually give way to expressions of affection, and they are interesting in proportion to their rarity. My eyes began to fill at seeing his glisten; and my delight at having given him such sensible gratification would have been unmixed, but for the thoughts of you. These out of the question, I could have grappled with the bags, had they been as large as corn-sacks. But, to turn what was grave into farce, the door opened, and Wilkinson ushered in Peter Peebles.

You must have seen this original, Darsie, who, like others in the same predicament, continues to haunt the courts of justice, where he has made shipwreck of time, means, and understanding. Such insane paupers have sometimes seemed to me to resemble wrecks lying upon the shoals on the Goodwin Sands, or in Yarmouth Roads, warning other vessels to keep aloof from the banks on which they have been lost; or rather such ruined clients are like scarecrows and potatoe-bogles, distributed through the courts to scare away fools from the scene of litigation.

The identical Peter wears a huge great-coat, threadbare and patched itself, yet carefully so disposed and secured by what buttons remain, and many supplementary pins, as to conceal the still more infirm state of his under garments. The shoes and stockings of a ploughman were, however, seen to meet at his knees, with a pair of brownish, blackish breeches; a rusty-coloured handkerchief, that has been black in its day, surrounded his throat, and was an apology for linen. His hair, half grey, half black, escaped in elf-locks around a huge wig, made of tow, as it seemed to me, and so much shrunk, that it stood up on the very top of his head; above which he plants, when covered, an immense cocked hat, which, like the chieftain's banner in an ancient battle, may be seen any sederunt day betwixt nine and ten, high towering above all the fluctuating and changeful scene in the Outer-House, where his eccentricities often make him the centre of a group of petulant and teasing boys, who exercise upon him every art of ingenious torture. His countenance, originally that of a portly, comely burgess, is now emaciated with poverty and anxiety, and rendered wild by an insane lightness about the eyes; a withered and blighted skin and complexion; features begrimed with snuff, charged with the self-importance peculiar to insanity; and a habit of perpetually speaking to himself. Such was my unfortunate client; and I must allow, Darsie, that my profession had need to do a great deal of good, if, as is much to be feared, it brings many individuals to such a pass.

After we had been, with a good deal of form, presented to each other, at which time I easily saw by my father's manner that he was desirous of supporting Peter's character in my eyes, as much as circumstances would permit, 'Alan,' he said, 'this is the gentleman who has agreed to accept of you as his counsel, in place of young Dumtoustie.'

'Entirely out of favour to my old acquaintance your father,' said Peter, with a benign and patronising countenance, 'out of respect to your father, and my old intimacy with Lord Bladderskate. Otherwise, by the *Regiam Majestatem!* I would have presented a petition and complaint against Daniel Dumtoustie, Advocate, by name and surname—I would, by all the practiques!—I know the forms of process; and I am not to be trifled with.'

My father here interrupted my client, and reminded him that there was a good deal of business to do, as he proposed to give the young counsel an outline of the state of the conjoined process, with a view to letting him into the merits of the cause, disencumbered from the points of form. 'I have made a short abbreviate, Mr Peebles,' said he; 'having sat up late last night, and employed much of this morning in wading through these papers, to save Alan some trouble, and I am now about to state the result.'

'I will state it myself,' said Peter, breaking in without reverence upon his solicitor.

'No, by no means,' said my father; 'I am your agent for the time.'

'Mine eleventh in number,' said Peter; 'I have a new one every year; I wish I could get a new coat as regularly.'

'Your agent for the time,' resumed my father; 'and you, who are acquainted with the forms, know that the client states the cause to the agent—the agent to the counsel'——

'The counsel to the Lord Ordinary,' continued Peter, once set a-going, like the peal of an alarm clock, 'the Ordinary to the Inner-House, the President to the Bench.* It is just like the rope to the man, the man to the axe, the axe to the ox, the ox to the water, the water to the fire'——*

'Hush, for Heaven's sake, Mr Peebles,' said my father, cutting his recitation short; 'time wears on—we must get to business—you must not interrupt the court, you know.—Hem, hem! From this abbreviate it appears'——

'Before you begin,' said Peter Peebles, 'I'll thank you to order me a morsel of bread and cheese, or some cauld meat, or broth, or the like alimentary* provision; I was so anxious to see your son, that I could not eat a mouthful of dinner.'

Heartily glad, I believe, to have so good a chance of stopping his client's mouth effectually, my father ordered some cold meat; to which James Wilkinson, for the honour of the house, was about to add the brandy bottle, which remained on the sideboard, but, at a wink from my father, supplied its place with small beer. Peter charged the provisions with the rapacity of a famished lion; and so well did the diversion engage him, that though, while my father stated the case, he looked at him repeatedly, as if he meant to interrupt his statement, yet he always found more agreeable employment for his mouth, and returned to the cold beef with an avidity which convinced me he had not had such an opportunity for many a day of satiating his appetite. Omitting much formal phraseology, and many legal details, I will endeavour to give you, in exchange for your fiddler's tale, the history of a litigant, or rather, the history of his lawsuit.

'Peter Peebles and Paul Plainstanes,' said my father, 'entered into partnership, in the year——, as mercers and linendrapers, in the Luckenbooths,* and carried on a great line of business to mutual advantage. But the learned counsel needeth not to be told, *societas est mater discordiarum*, partnership oft makes pleaship. The company being dissolved by mutual consent, in the year ——, the affairs had to be wound up, and after certain attempts to settle the matter extrajudicially, it was at last brought into the Court, and has branched out into several distinct processes, most of whilk have been conjoined by the Ordinary. It is to the state of these processes that counsel's attention is particularly directed. There is the original action of Peebles *v.* Plainstanes, convening him for payment of L.3000, less or more, as alleged balance due by Plainstanes. 2dly, There is a counter action, in which Plainstanes is pursuer and Peebles defender, for L.2500, less or more, being balance alleged *per contra*, to be due by Peebles. 3dly, Mr Peebles's seventh agent advised an action of Compt and Reckoning at his instance, wherein what balance should prove due on either side might be fairly struck and ascertained. 4thly, To meet the hypothetical case, that Peebles might be found liable in a balance to Plainstanes, Mr Wildgoose, Mr Peebles's eighth agent, recommended a Multiplepoinding, to bring all parties concerned into the field.'

My brain was like to turn at this account of lawsuit within lawsuit, like a nest of chip-boxes, with all of which I was expected to make myself acquainted.

'I understand,' I said, 'that Mr Peebles claims a sum of money from Plainstanes—how then can he be his debtor? and if not his debtor, how can he bring a Multiplepoinding, the very summons of which sets forth, that the pursuer does owe certain monies, which he is desirous to pay by warrant of a judge?'[33]

'Ye know little of the matter, I doubt, friend,' said Mr Peebles; 'a Multiplepoinding is the safest *remedium juris* in the whole form of process. I have known it conjoined with a declarator of marriage.*—Your beef is excellent,' he said to my father, who in vain endeavoured to resume his legal disquisition; 'but something highly powdered—and the twopenny is undeniable; but it is small swipes—small swipes—more of hop than malt—with your leave I'll try your black bottle.'

My father started to help him with his own hand, and in due measure; but, infinitely to my amusement, Peter got possession of the bottle by the neck, and my father's ideas of hospitality were far too scrupulous to permit his attempting, by any direct means, to redeem it; so that Peter returned to the table triumphant, with his prey in his clutch.

'Better have a wine-glass, Mr Peebles,' said my father, in an admonitory tone, 'you will find it pretty strong.'

'If the kirk is ower muckle, we can sing mass in the quire,'* said Peter, helping himself in the goblet out of which he had been drinking the small beer. 'What is it, usquebaugh?—BRANDY, as I am an honest man! I had almost forgotten the name and taste of brandy.—Mr Fairford elder, your good health,' (a mouthful of brandy)—'Mr Alan Fairford, wishing you well through your arduous undertaking,' (another go-down of the comfortable liquor.) 'And now, though you have given a tolerable breviate of this great lawsuit, of whilk every body has heard something that has walked the boards in the Outer-House, (here's to ye again, by way of interim decreet,) yet ye have omitted to speak a word of the arrestments.'

'I was just coming to that point, Mr Peebles.'

'Or of the action of suspension of the charge on the bill.'

'I was just coming to that.'

'Or the advocation of the Sheriff-Court process.'*

'I was just coming to it.'

'As Tweed comes to Melrose,* I think,' said the litigant; and then filling his goblet about a quarter full of brandy, as if in absence of mind, 'Oh, Mr Alan Fairford, ye are a lucky man to buckle to such a cause as mine at the very outset! it is like a specimen of all causes, man. By the Regiam, there is not a *remedium juris* in the practiques but ye'll find a spice o't. Here's to your getting weel through with it—Pshut—I am drinking naked spirits, I think. But if the heathen be ower strong, we'll christen him with the brewer,' (here he added a little small beer to his beverage, paused, rolled his eyes, winked, and proceeded,)—'Mr Fairford—the action of assault and battery, Mr Fairford, when I compelled the villain Plainstanes to pull my nose within two steps of King Charles's statue, in the Parliament Close—there I had him in a hose-net. Never man could tell me how to shape that process—no counsel that ever selled wind could condescend and say whether it were best to proceed by way of petition and complaint, *ad vindictam publicam*, with consent of his Majesty's advocate, or by action on the statute for battery, *pendente lite*, whilk would be the winning my plea at once, and so getting a back-door out of Court.*—By the Regiam, that beef and brandy is unco het at my heart—I maun try the ale again,' (sipped a little beer); 'and the ale's but cauld, I maun e'en put in the rest of the brandy.'

He was as good as his word, and proceeded in so loud and animated a style of elocution, thumping the table, drinking and snuffing alternately, that my father, abandoning all attempts to interrupt him, sat silent and ashamed, suffering and anxious for the conclusion of the scene.

'And then to come back to my pet process of all—my battery and assault process, when I had the good luck to provoke him to pull my nose at the very threshold of the Court, whilk was the very thing I wanted—Mr Pest, ye ken him, Daddie Fairford? Old Pest was for making it out *hamesucken*, for he said the Court might be said—said—ugh!—to be my dwelling-place. I dwell mair there than ony gate else, and the essence of hamesucken is to strike a man in his dwelling-place—mind that, young advocate—and so there's hope Plainstanes may be hanged,* as many has for a less matter; for, my Lords,—will Pest say to the Justiciary bodies,—my Lords, the Parliament House is Peebles's place of dwelling, says he—being *commune forum*, and *commune forum est commune domicilium*—Lass, fetch another glass of whisky, and score it—time to gae hame—by the practiques, I cannot find the jug—yet there's twa of them, I think. By the Regiam, Fairford—Daddie Fairford—lend us twal pennies to buy sneeshing, mine is done—Macer, call another cause.'

The box fell from his hands, and his body would at the same time have fallen from the chair, had I not supported him.

'This is intolerable,' said my father—'Call a chairman, James Wilkinson, to carry this degraded, worthless, drunken beast home.'

When Peter Peebles was removed from this memorable consultation, under the care of an able-bodied Celt,* my father hastily bundled up the papers, as a showman, whose exhibition has miscarried, hastes to remove his booth. 'Here are my memoranda, Alan,' he said, in a hurried way; 'look them carefully over—

compare them with the processes, and turn it in your head before Tuesday. Many a good speech has been made for a beast of a client; and hark ye, lad, hark ye—I never intended to cheat you of your fee when all was done, though I would have liked to have heard the speech first; but there is nothing like corning the horse before the journey. Here are five goud guineas in a silk purse—of your poor mother's netting, Alan—she would have been a blithe woman to have seen her young son with a gown on his back—but no more of that—be a good boy, and to the work like a tiger.'

I did set to work, Darsie; for who could resist such motives? With my father's assistance, I have mastered the details, confused as they are; and on Tuesday, I shall plead as well for Peter Peebles, as I could for a duke. Indeed, I feel my head so clear on the subject, as to be able to write this long letter to you; into which, however, Peter and his lawsuit have insinuated themselves so far, as to show you how much they at present occupy my thoughts. Once more, be careful of yourself, and mindful of me, who am ever thine, while

ALAN FAIRFORD.

From circumstances, to be hereafter mentioned, it was long ere this letter reached the person to whom it was addressed.*

CHAPTER I

NARRATIVE

THE advantage of laying before the reader, in the words of the actors themselves, the adventures which we must otherwise have narrated in our own, has given great popularity to the publication of epistolary correspondence, as practised by various great authors, and by ourselves in the preceding chapters. Nevertheless, a genuine correspondence of this kind (and Heaven forbid it should be in any respect sophisticated by interpolations of our own!) can seldom be found to contain all in which it is necessary to instruct the reader for his full comprehension of the story. Also it must often happen that various prolixities and redundancies occur in the course of an interchange of letters, which must hang as a dead weight on the progress of the narrative. To avoid this dilemma, some biographers have used the letters of the personages concerned, or liberal extracts from them, to describe particular incidents, or express the sentiments which they entertained; while they connect them occasionally with such portions of narrative, as may serve to carry on the thread of the story.*

It is thus that the adventurous travellers who explore the summit of Mont Blanc, now move on through the crumbling snow-drift so slowly, that their progress is almost imperceptible, and anon abridge their journey by springing over the intervening chasms which cross their path, with the assistance of their pilgrim-staves. Or, to make a briefer simile, the course of story-telling which we have for the present adopted, resembles the original discipline of the dragoons, who were trained to serve either on foot or horseback, as the emergencies of the service required. With this explanation, we shall proceed to narrate some circumstances which Alan Fairford did not, and could not, write to his correspondent.

Our reader, we trust, has formed somewhat approaching to a distinct idea of the principal characters who have appeared before him during our narrative; but in case our good opinion of his sagacity has been exaggerated, and in order to satisfy such as are addicted to the laudable practice of *skipping*, (with whom we have at times a strong fellow-feeling,) the following particulars may not be superfluous.

Mr Saunders Fairford, as he was usually called, was a man of business of the old school, moderate in his charges, economical and even niggardly in his expenditure, strictly honest in conducting his own affairs, and those of his clients, but taught by long experience to be wary and suspicious in observing the motions of others. Punctual as the clock of Saint Giles tolled nine, the neat dapper form of the little hale old gentleman was seen at the threshold of the Court hall, or at farthest, at the head of the Back Stairs, trimly dressed in a complete suit of snuff-coloured brown, with stockings of silk or woollen, as suited the weather; a bobwig, and a small cocked hat; shoes blacked as Warren would have blacked them; silver shoe-buckles, and a gold stock-buckle. A nosegay in summer, and a sprig of holly in winter, completed his well-known dress and appearance. His manners corresponded with his attire, for they were scrupulously civil, and not a little formal. He was an elder of the kirk, and, of course, zealous for King George and the government even to slaying, as he had showed by taking up arms in their cause. But then, as he had clients and connexions of business among families of opposite political tenets, he was particularly cautious to use all the conventional phrases which the civility of the time had devised, as an admissible mode of language betwixt the two parties. Thus he spoke sometimes of the Chevalier, but never either of the Prince, which would have been sacrificing his own principles, or of the Pretender, which would have been offensive to those of others. Again, he usually designated the Rebellion as the *affair* of 1745, and spoke of any one engaged in it as a person who had been *out* at a certain period.[34] So that, on the whole, Mr Fairford was a man much liked and respected on all sides, though his friends would not have been sorry if he had given a dinner more frequently, as his little cellar contained some choice old wine, of which, on such rare occasions, he was no niggard.*

The whole pleasure of this good old-fashioned man of method, besides that which he really felt in the discharge of his daily business, was the hope to see his son Alan, the only fruit of a union which death early dissolved, attain what in the father's eyes was the proudest of all distinctions—the rank and fame of a well-employed lawyer.

Every profession has its peculiar honours, and Mr Fairford's mind was constructed upon so limited and exclusive a plan, that he valued nothing, save the objects of ambition which his own presented. He would have shuddered at Alan's acquiring the renown of a hero, and laughed with scorn at the equally barren laurels of literature; it was by the path of the law alone that he was desirous to see him rise to eminence, and the probabilities of success or disappointment were the thoughts of his father by day, and his dream by night.

The disposition of Alan Fairford, as well as his talents, were such as to encourage his father's expectations. He had acuteness of intellect, joined to habits of long and patient study, improved no doubt by the discipline of his father's house; to which, generally speaking, he conformed with the utmost docility, expressing no wish for greater or more frequent relaxation than consisted with his father's anxious and severe restrictions. When he did indulge in any juvenile frolics, his father had the candour to lay the whole blame upon his more mercurial companion, Darsie Latimer.

This youth, as the reader must be aware, had been received as an inmate into the family of Mr Fairford, senior, at a time when some of the delicacy of constitution which had abridged the life of his consort, began to show itself in the son, and when the father was, of course, peculiarly disposed to indulge his slightest wish. That the young Englishman was able to pay a considerable board, was a matter of no importance to Mr Fairford; it was enough that his presence seemed to make his son cheerful and happy. He was compelled to allow that 'Darsie was a fine lad, though unsettled,' and he would have had some difficulty in getting rid of him, and the apprehensions which his levities excited, had it not been for the voluntary excursion which gave rise to the preceding correspondence, and in which Mr Fairford secretly rejoiced, as affording the means of separating Alan from his gay companion, at least until he should have assumed, and become accustomed to, the duties of his dry and laborious profession.

But the absence of Darsie was far from promoting the end which the elder Mr Fairford had expected and desired. The young men were united by the closest bonds of intimacy; and the more so, that neither of them sought nor desired to admit any others into their society. Alan Fairford was averse to general company, from a disposition naturally reserved, and Darsie Latimer from a painful sense of his own unknown origin, peculiarly afflicting in a country where high and low are professed genealogists. The young men were all in all to each other; it is no wonder, therefore, that their separation was painful, and that its effects upon Alan Fairford, joined to the anxiety occasioned by the tenor of his friend's letters, greatly exceeded what the senior had anticipated. The young man went through his usual duties, his studies, and the examinations to which he was subjected, but with nothing like the zeal and assiduity which he had formerly displayed; and his anxious and observant father saw but too plainly that his heart was with his absent comrade.

A philosopher would have given way to this tide of feeling, in hopes to have diminished its excess, and permitted the youths to have been some time together, that their intimacy might have been broken off by degrees; but Mr Fairford only saw the more direct mode of continued restraint, which, however, he was desirous of veiling under some plausible pretext. In the anxiety which he felt on this occasion, he had held communication with an old acquaintance, Peter Drudgeit,* with whom the reader is partly acquainted. 'Alan,' he said, 'was ance wud, and aye waur; and he was expecting every moment when he would start off in a wildgoose-chase after the callant Latimer; Will Sampson, the horse-hirer in Candlemaker Row,* had given him a hint that Alan had been looking for a good hack, to go to the country for a few days. And then to oppose him downright—he could not but think on the way his poor mother was removed—Would to Heaven he was yoked to some tight piece of business, no matter whether well or ill paid, but some job that would hamshackle him at least until the Courts rose, if it were but for decency's sake.'

Peter Drudgeit sympathized, for Peter had a son, who, reason or none, would needs exchange the torn and inky fustian sleeves for the blue jacket and white lapelle;* and he suggested, as the reader knows, the engaging our friend Alan in the matter of Poor Peter Peebles, just opened by the desertion of young Dumtoustie, whose defection would be at the same time concealed; and this, Drudgeit said, 'would be felling two dogs with one stone.'

With these explanations, the reader will hold a man of the elder Fairford's sense and experience free from the hazardous and impatient curiosity with which boys fling a puppy into a deep pond, merely to see if the creature can swim. However confident in his son's talents, which were really considerable, he would have been very sorry to have involved him in the duty of pleading a complicated and difficult case, upon his very first appearance at the bar, had he not resorted to it as an effectual way to prevent the young man from taking a step, which his habits of thinking represented as a most fatal one at his outset of life.

Betwixt two evils, Mr Fairford chose that which was in his own apprehension the least; and, like a brave officer sending forth his son to battle, rather chose he should die upon the breach, than desert the conflict with dishonour. Neither did he leave him to his own unassisted energies. Like Alpheus preceding Hercules, he himself encountered the Augean mass* of Peter Peebles's law-matters. It was to the old man a labour of love to place in a clear and undistorted view the real merits of this case, which the carelessness and blunders of Peter's former solicitors had converted into a huge chaotic mass of unintelligible technicality; and such was his skill and industry, that he was able, after the severe toil of two or three days, to present to the consideration of the young counsel the principal facts of the case, in a light equally simple and comprehensible. With the assistance of a solicitor so affectionate and indefatigable, Alan Fairford was enabled, when the day of trial arrived, to walk towards the Court, attended by his anxious yet encouraging parent, with some degree of confidence that he would lose no reputation upon this arduous occasion.

They were met at the door of the Court by Poor Peter Peebles, in his usual plenitude of wig and celsitude of hat. He seized on the young pleader like a lion on his prey. 'How is a' wi' you, Mr Alan—how is a' wi' you, man?—The awfu' day is come at last—a day that will be lang minded in this house. Poor Peter Peebles against Plainstanes—conjoined processes—Hearing in presence—stands for the Short Roll for this day—I have not been able to sleep for a week for thinking of it, and, I dare to say, neither has the Lord President himsell—for such a cause!! But your father garr'd me tak a wee drap ower muckle of his pint bottle the other night; it's no right to mix brandy wi' business, Mr Fairford. I would have been the waur o' liquor if I would have drank as muckle as you twa would have had me. But there's a time for a' things, and if ye will dine with me after the case is heard, or, whilk is the same, or maybe better, *I'll* gang my ways hame wi' *you*, and I winna object to a cheerfu' glass, within the bounds of moderation.'

Old Fairford shrugged his shoulders and hurried past the client, saw his son wrapt in the sable bombazine, which, in his eyes, was more venerable than an archbishop's lawn, and could not help fondly patting his shoulder, and whispering to him to take courage, and show he was worthy to wear it. The party entered the Outer Hall of the Court, once the place of meeting of the ancient Scottish Parliament,* and which corresponds to the use of Westminster Hall in England, serving as a vestibule to the Inner-House, as it is termed, and a place of dominion to certain sedentary personages called Lords Ordinary.

The earlier part of the morning was spent by old Fairford in reiterating his instructions to Alan, and in running from one person to another, from whom he thought he could still glean some grains of information, either concerning the point at issue, or collateral cases. Meantime Poor Peter Peebles, whose shallow brain was altogether unable to bear the importance of the moment, kept as close to his young counsel as shadow to substance, affected now to speak loud, now to whisper in his ear, now to deck his ghastly countenance with wreathed smiles, now to cloud it with a shade of deep and solemn importance, and anon to contort it with the sneer of scorn and derision. These moods of the client's mind were accompanied with singular 'mopings and mowings,' fantastic gestures, which the man of rags and litigation deemed appropriate to his changes of countenance. Now he brandished his arm aloft, now thrust his fist straight out, as if to knock his opponent down. Now he laid his open palm on his bosom, and now flinging it abroad, he gallantly snapped his fingers in the air.

These demonstrations, and the obvious shame and embarrassment of Alan Fairford, did not escape the observation of the juvenile idlers in the hall. They did not, indeed, approach Peter with their usual familiarity, from some feeling of deference towards Fairford, though many accused him of conceit in presuming to undertake at this early stage of his practice a case of considerable difficulty. But Alan, notwithstanding this forbearance, was not the less sensible that he and his companion were the subjects of many a passing jest, and many a shout of laughter, with which that region at all times abounds.

At length the young counsel's patience gave way, and as it threatened to carry his presence of mind and recollection along with it, Alan frankly told his father, that unless he was relieved from the infliction of his client's personal presence and instructions, he must necessarily throw up his brief, and decline pleading the case.

'Hush, hush, my dear Alan,' said the old gentleman, almost at his own wit's end upon hearing this dilemma; 'dinna mind the silly ne'er-do-weel; we cannot keep the man from hearing his own cause, though he be not quite right in the head.'

'On my life, sir,' answered Alan, 'I shall be unable to go on, he drives every thing out of my remembrance; and if I attempt to speak seriously of the injuries he has sustained, and the condition he is reduced to, how can I expect but that the very appearance of such an absurd scarecrow will turn it all into ridicule?'

'There is something in that,' said Saunders Fairford, glancing a look at Poor Peter, and then cautiously inserting his forefinger under his bobwig, in order to rub his temple and aid his invention; 'he is no figure for the fore-bar to see without laughing; but how to get rid of him? To speak sense, or any thing like it, is the last thing he will listen to.—Stay, ay—Alan, my darling, hae patience; I'll get him off on the instant, like a gowff ba'.'

So saying, he hastened to his ally, Peter Drudgeit, who, on seeing him with marks of haste in his gait, and care upon his countenance, clapped his pen behind his ear, with 'What's the stir now, Mr Saunders?—Is there aught wrang?'

'Here's a dollar, man,' said Mr Saunders; 'now, or never, Peter, do me a good turn. Yonder's your namesake, Peter Peebles, will drive the swine through our bonny hanks of yarn;[35] get him over to John's Coffee-house, man—gie him his meridian—keep him there, drunk or sober, till the hearing is ower.'

'Eneugh said,' quoth Peter Drudgeit, no way displeased with his own share in the service required,—'We'se do your bidding.'

Accordingly, the scribe was presently seen whispering in the ear of Peter Peebles, whose responses came forth in the following broken form:—

'Leave the Court for ae minute on this great day of judgment?—not I, by the Reg——Eh! what? Brandy, did ye say—French Brandy?—couldna ye fetch a stoup to the bar under your coat, man?—Impossible? Na, if it's clean impossible, and if we have an hour good till they get through the single bills and the summar-roll,* I carena if I cross the close wi' you; I am sure I need something to keep my heart up this awful day; but I'll no stay above an instant—not above a minute of time—nor drink aboon a single gill.'

In a few minutes afterwards, the two Peters were seen moving through the Parliament Close, (which newfangled affectation has termed a Square,) the triumphant Drudgeit leading captive the passive Peebles, whose legs conducted him towards the dram-shop, while his reverted eyes were fixed upon the Court. They dived into the Cimmerian abysses* of John's Coffee-house,[36] formerly the favourite rendezvous of the classical and genial Doctor Pitcairn,* and were for the present seen no more.

Relieved from his tormentor, Alan Fairford had time to rally his recollections, which, in the irritation of his spirits, had nearly escaped him, and to prepare himself for a task, the successful discharge or failure in which must, he was aware, have the deepest influence upon his fortunes. He had pride, was not without a consciousness of talent, and the sense of his father's feelings upon the subject impelled him to the utmost exertion. Above all, he had that sort of self-command which is essential to success in every arduous undertaking, and he was constitutionally free from that feverish irritability, by which those whose over-active imaginations exaggerate difficulties, render themselves incapable of encountering such when they arrive.

Having collected all the scattered and broken associations which were necessary, Alan's thoughts reverted to Dumfries-shire, and the precarious situation in which he feared his beloved friend had placed himself; and once and again he consulted his watch, eager to have his present task commenced and ended, that he might hasten to Darsie's assistance. The hour and moment at length arrived. The Macer shouted, with all his well-remembered brazen strength of lungs, 'Poor Peter Peebles *versus* Plainstanes, *per* Dumtoustie *et* Tough:—Maister Da-a-niel Dumtoustie!' Dumtoustie answered not the summons, which, deep and swelling as it was, could not reach across the Queensferry; but our Maister Alan Fairford appeared in his place.

The Court was very much crowded; for much amusement had been received on former occasions when Peter had volunteered his own oratory, and had been completely successful in routing the gravity of the whole procedure, and putting to silence, not indeed the counsel of the opposite party, but his own.

Both bench and audience seemed considerably surprised at the juvenile appearance of the young man who appeared in the room of Dumtoustie, for the purpose of opening this complicated and long depending process, and the common herd were disappointed at the absence of Peter the client, the Punchinello* of the expected entertainment. The Judges looked with a very favourable countenance on our friend Alan, most of them being acquainted, more or less, with so old a practitioner as his father, and all, or almost all, affording, from civility, the same fair play to the first pleading of a counsel, which the House of Commons yields to the maiden speech of one of its members.

Lord Bladderskate was an exception to this general expression of benevolence. He scowled upon Alan from beneath his large, shaggy, grey eyebrows, just as if the young lawyer had been usurping his nephew's honours, instead of covering his disgrace; and, from feelings which did his lordship little honour, he privately hoped the young man would not succeed in the cause which his kinsman had abandoned.

Even Lord Bladderskate, however, was, in spite of himself, pleased with the judicious and modest tone in which Alan began his address to the Court, apologizing for his own presumption, and excusing it by the sudden illness of his learned brother, for whom the labour of opening a cause of some difficulty and importance had been much more worthily designed. He spoke of himself as he really was, and of young Dumtoustie as what he ought to have been, taking care not to dwell on either topic a moment longer than was necessary. The old Judge's looks became benign; his family pride was propitiated, and, pleased equally with the modesty and civility of the young man whom he had thought forward and officious, he relaxed the scorn of his features into an expression of profound attention; the highest compliment, and the greatest encouragement, which a judge can render to the counsel addressing him.

Having succeeded in securing the favourable attention of the Court, the young lawyer, using the lights which his father's experience and knowledge of business had afforded him, proceeded with an address and clearness, unexpected from one of his years, to remove from the case itself those complicated formalities with which it had been loaded, as a surgeon strips from a wound the dressings which have been hastily wrapped round it, in order to proceed to his cure *secundum artem*. Developed of the cumbrous and complicated technicalities of litigation, with which the perverse obstinacy of the client, the inconsiderate haste or ignorance of his agents, and the evasions of a subtle adversary, had invested the process, the cause of Poor Peter Peebles, standing upon its simple merits, was no bad subject for the declamation of a young counsel, nor did our friend Alan fail to avail himself of its strong points.

He exhibited his client as a simple-hearted, honest, well-meaning man, who, during a copartnership of twelve years, had gradually become impoverished, while his partner, (his former clerk,) having no funds but his share of the same business, into which he had been admitted without any advance of stock, had become gradually more and more wealthy.

'Their association,' said Alan, and the little flight was received with some applause, 'resembled the ancient story of the fruit which was carved with a knife poisoned on one side of the blade only,* so that the individual to whom the envenomed portion was served, drew decay and death from what afforded savour and sustenance to the consumer of the other moiety.' He then plunged boldly into the *mare magnum* of accompts between the parties; he pursued each false statement from the waste-book to the day-book, from the day-book to the bill-book, from the bill-book to the ledger; placed the artful interpolations and insertions of the fallacious Plainstanes in array against each other, and against the fact; and, availing himself to the utmost of his father's previous labours, and his own knowledge of accompts, in which he had been sedulously trained, he laid before the Court a clear and intelligible statement of the affairs of the copartnery, showing, with precision, that a large balance must, at the dissolution, have been due to his client, sufficient to have enabled him to have carried on business on his own account, and thus to have retained his situation in society, as an independent and industrious tradesman. 'But, instead of this justice being voluntarily rendered by the former clerk to his former master,—by the party obliged to his benefactor,—by one honest man to another,—his wretched client had been compelled to follow his quondam clerk, his present debtor, from Court to Court; had found his just claims met with well-invented but unfounded counter-claims; had seen his party shift his character of pursuer or defender, as often as Harlequin* effects his transformations, till, in a chase so varied and so long, the unhappy litigant had lost substance, reputation, and almost the use of reason itself, and came before their Lordships an object of thoughtless derision to the unreflecting, of compassion to the better-hearted, and of awful meditation to every one, who considered that, in a country where excellent laws were administered by upright and incorruptible judges, a man might pursue an almost indisputable claim through all the mazes of litigation; lose fortune, reputation, and reason itself in the chase, and at length come before the Supreme Court of his country in the wretched condition of his unhappy client, a victim to protracted justice, and to that hope delayed which sickens the heart.'*

The force of this appeal to feeling made as much impression on the Bench, as had been previously effected by the clearness of Alan's argument. The absurd form of Peter himself, with his tow-wig, was fortunately not present to excite any ludicrous emotion, and the pause that took place when the young lawyer had concluded his speech, was followed by a murmur of approbation, which the ears of his father drank in as the sweetest sounds that had ever entered them. Many a hand of gratulation was thrust out to his grasp, trembling as it was with anxiety, and finally with delight; his voice faltering, as he replied, 'Ay, ay, I kend Alan was the lad to make a spoon or spoil a horn.'[37]

The counsel on the other side arose, an old practitioner, who had noted too closely the impression made by Alan's pleading, not to fear the consequences of an immediate decision. He paid the highest compliments to his very young brother—'the Benjamin, as he would presume to call him, of the learned Faculty—said the alleged hardships of Mr Peebles were compensated, by his being placed in a situation where the benevolence of their Lordships had assigned him gratuitously such assistance as he might not otherwise have obtained at a high price—and allowed his young brother had put many things in such a new point of view, that, although he was quite certain of his ability to refute them, he was honestly desirous of having a few hours to arrange his answer, in order to be able to follow Mr Fairford from point to point. He had further to observe, there was one point of the case to which his brother, whose attention had been otherwise so wonderfully comprehensive, had not given the consideration which he expected; it was founded on the interpretation of certain correspondence which had passed betwixt the parties, soon after the dissolution of the copartnery.'

The Court having heard Mr Tough, readily allowed him two days for preparing himself, hinting, at the same time, that he might find his task difficult, and affording the young counsel, with high encomiums upon the mode in which he had acquitted himself, the choice of speaking, either now or at next calling of the cause, upon the point which Plainstanes's lawyer had adverted to.

Alan modestly apologized for what in fact had been an omission very pardonable in so complicated a case, and professed himself instantly ready to go through that correspondence, and prove that it was in form and substance exactly applicable to the view of the case he had submitted to their lordships. He applied to his father, who sat behind him, to hand him, from time to time, the letters, in the order in which he meant to read and comment upon them.

Old Counsellor Tough had probably formed an ingenious enough scheme to blunt the effect of the young lawyer's reasoning, by thus obliging him to follow up a process of reasoning, clear and complete in itself, by a hasty and extemporary appendix. If so, he seemed likely to be disappointed; for Alan was well prepared on this, as on other parts of the cause, and recommenced his pleading with a degree of animation and spirit, which added force even to what he had formerly stated, and might perhaps have occasioned the old gentleman to regret his having again called him up; when his father, as he handed him the letters, put one into his hand which produced a singular effect on the pleader.

At the first glance, he saw that the paper had no reference to the affairs of Peter Peebles; but the first glance also showed him, what, even at that time, and in that presence, he could not help reading; and which, being read, seemed totally to disconcert his ideas. He stopped short in his harangue—gazed on the paper with a look of surprise and horror—uttered an exclamation, and, flinging down the brief which he had in his hand, hurried out of Court without returning a single word of answer to the various questions, 'what was the matter?'—'Was he taken unwell?'—'Should not a chair be called?' &c. &c. &c.

The elder Mr Fairford, who remained seated, and looking as senseless as if he had been made of stone, was at length recalled to himself by the anxious enquiries of the judges and the counsel after his son's health. He then rose with an air, in which was mingled the deep habitual reverence in which he held the Court, with some internal cause of agitation, and with difficulty mentioned something of a mistake—a piece of bad news—Alan, he hoped, would be well enough to-morrow. But unable to proceed farther, he clasped his hands together, exclaiming, 'My son! my son!' and left the court hastily, as if in pursuit of him.

'What's the matter with the auld bitch next?'[38] said an acute metaphysical judge,* though somewhat coarse in his manners, aside to his brethren. 'This is a daft cause, Bladderskate—first, it drives the poor man mad that aught it—then your nevoy goes daft with fright, and flies the pit—then this smart young hopeful is aff the hooks with too hard study, I fancy—and now auld Saunders Fairford is as lunatic as the best of them. What say ye till't, ye bitch?'

'Nothing, my lord,' answered Bladderskate, much too formal to admire the levities in which his philosophical brother sometimes indulged—'I say nothing, but pray to Heaven to keep our own wits.'

'Amen, amen,' answered his learned brother; 'for some of us have but few to spare.'

The Court then arose, and the audience departed, greatly wondering at the talent displayed by Alan Fairford, at his first appearance, in a case so difficult and so complicated, and assigning an hundred conjectural causes, each different from the others, for the singular interruption which had clouded his day of success. The worst of the whole was, that six agents, who had each come to the separate resolution of thrusting a retaining fee into Alan's hand as he left the court, shook their heads as they returned the money into their leathern pouches, and said, 'that the lad was clever, but they would like to see more of him before they engaged him in the way of business—they did not like his lowping away like a flea in a blanket.'

CHAPTER II

HAD our friend Alexander Fairford known the consequences of his son's abrupt retreat from the Court, which are mentioned in the end of the last chapter, it might have accomplished the prediction of the lively old judge, and driven him utterly distracted. As it was, he was miserable enough. His son had risen ten degrees higher in his estimation than ever, by his display of juridical talents, which seemed to assure him that the applause of the judges and professors of the law, which, in his estimation, was worth that of all mankind besides, authorized to the fullest extent the advantageous estimate which even his parental partiality had been induced to form of Alan's powers. On the other hand, he felt that he was himself a little humbled, from a disguise which he had practised towards this son of his hopes and wishes.

The truth was, that on the morning of this eventful day, Mr Alexander Fairford had received from his correspondent and friend, Provost Crosbie of Dumfries, a letter of the following tenor:—

'DEAR SIR,

'YOUR respected favour of 25th ultimo, per favour of Mr Darsie Latimer, reached me in safety, and I showed to the young gentleman such attentions as he was pleased to accept of. The object of my present writing is twofold. First, the council are of opinion that you should now begin to stir in the thirlage cause; and they think they will be able, from evidence *noviter repertum*, to enable you to amend your condescendence upon the use and wont of the burgh, touching the *grana invecta et illata*. So you will please consider yourself as authorized to speak to Mr Pest, and lay before him the papers which you will receive by the coach. The council think that a fee of two guineas may be sufficient on this occasion, as Mr Pest had three for drawing the original condescendence.

'I take the opportunity of adding, that there has been a great riot among the Solway fishermen, who have destroyed, in a masterful manner, the stake-nets set up near the mouth of this river; and have besides attacked the house of Quaker Geddes, one of the principal partners of the Tide-net Fishing Company, and done a great deal of damage. Am sorry to add, young Master Latimer was in the fray, and has not since been heard of. Murder is spoke of, but that may be a word of course. As the young gentleman has behaved rather oddly while in these parts, as in declining to dine with me more than once, and going about the country with strolling fiddlers and such-like, I rather hope that his present absence is only occasioned by a frolic;

but as his servant has been making enquiries of me respecting his master, I thought it best to acquaint you in course of post. I have only to add, that our sheriff has taken a precognition, and committed one or two of the rioters. If I can be useful in this matter, either by advertising for Mr Latimer as missing, publishing a reward, or otherwise, I will obey your respected instructions, being your most obedient to command,

'WILLIAM CROSBIE.'

When Mr Fairford received this letter, and had read it to an end, his first idea was to communicate it to his son, that an express might be instantly dispatched, or a King's messenger sent with proper authority to search after his late guest.

The habits of the fishers were rude, as he well knew, though not absolutely sanguinary or ferocious; and there had been instances of their transporting persons who had interfered in their smuggling trade to the Isle of Man, and elsewhere, and keeping them under restraint for many weeks. On this account Mr Fairford was naturally led to feel anxiety concerning the fate of his late inmate; and, at a less interesting moment, would certainly have set out himself, or licensed his son to go in pursuit of his friend.

But, alas! he was both a father and an agent. In the one capacity, he looked on his son as dearer to him than all the world besides; in the other, the lawsuit which he conducted was to him like an infant to its nurse, and the case of Poor Peter Peebles against Plainstanes was, he saw, adjourned, perhaps *sine die*, should this document reach the hands of his son. The mutual and enthusiastical affection betwixt the young men was well known to him; and he concluded, that if the precarious state of Latimer were made known to Alan Fairford, it would render him not only unwilling, but totally unfit, to discharge the duty of the day, to which the old gentleman attached such ideas of importance.

On mature reflection, therefore, he resolved, though not without some feelings of compunction, to delay communicating to his son the disagreeable intelligence which he had received, until the business of the day should be ended. The delay, he persuaded himself, could be of little consequence to Darsie Latimer, whose folly, he dared to say, had led him into some scrape which would meet an appropriate punishment, in some accidental restraint, which would be thus prolonged for only a few hours longer. Besides, he would have time to speak to the Sheriff of the county—perhaps to the King's Advocate*—and set about the matter in a regular manner, or, as he termed it, as summing up the duties of a solicitor, to *agé as accords*.[39]

The scheme, as we have seen, was partially successful, and was only ultimately defeated, as he confessed to himself with shame, by his own very unbusiness-like mistake of shuffling the Provost's letter, in the hurry and anxiety of the morning, among some papers belonging to Peter Peebles's affairs, and then handing it to his son, without observing the blunder. He used to protest, even till the day of his death, that he never had been guilty of such an inaccuracy as giving a paper out of his hand without looking at the docketing, except on that unhappy occasion, when, of all others, he had such particular reason to regret his negligence.

Disturbed by these reflections, the old gentleman had, for the first time in his life, some disinclination, arising from shame and vexation, to face his own son; so that to protract for a little the meeting which he feared would be a painful one, he went to wait upon the Sheriff-depute, who he found had set off for Dumfries, in great haste, to superintend in person the investigation which had been set on foot by his Substitute. This gentleman's clerk could say little on the subject of the riot, excepting that it had been serious, much damage done to property, and some personal violence offered to individuals; but, as far as he had yet heard, no lives lost on the spot.

Mr Fairford was compelled to return home with this intelligence; and on enquiring at James Wilkinson where his son was, received for answer, that 'Maister Alan was in his own room, and very busy.'

'We must have our explanation over,' said Saunders Fairford to himself. 'Better a finger off, as aye wagging;'* and going to the door of his son's apartment he knocked at first gently—then more loudly—but received no answer. Somewhat alarmed at this silence, he opened the door of the chamber—it was empty—clothes lay mixed in confusion with the law-books and papers, as if the inmate had been engaged in hastily packing for a journey. As Mr Fairford looked around in alarm, his eye was arrested by a sealed letter lying upon his son's writing-table, and addressed to himself. It contained the following words:—

'MY DEAREST FATHER,

'YOU will not, I trust, be surprised, nor perhaps very much displeased, to learn that I am now on my way to Dumfries-shire, to learn, by my own personal investigation, the present state of my dear friend, and afford him such relief as may be in my power, and which, I trust, will be effectual. I do not presume to reflect upon you, dearest sir, for concealing from me information of so much consequence to my peace of mind and happiness; but I hope your having done so will be, if not an excuse, at least some mitigation of my present offence, in taking a step of consequence without consulting your pleasure; and, I must further own, under circumstances which perhaps might lead to your disapprobation of my purpose. I can only say, in further apology, that if any thing unhappy, which Heaven forbid! shall have occurred to the person who, next to yourself, is dearest to me in this world, I shall have on my heart, as a subject of eternal regret, that being in a certain degree warned of his danger, and furnished with the means of obviating it, I did not instantly hasten to his assistance, but preferred giving my attention to the business of this unlucky morning. No view of personal distinction, nothing, indeed, short of your earnest and often expressed wishes, could have detained me in town till this day; and having made this sacrifice to filial duty, I trust you will hold me excused, if I now obey the calls of friendship and humanity. Do not be in the least anxious on my account; I shall know, I trust, how to conduct myself with due caution in any emergence which may occur, otherwise my legal studies for so many years have been to little purpose. I am fully provided with money, and also with arms, in case of need; but you may rely on my prudence in avoiding all occasions of using the latter, short of the last necessity. God Almighty bless you, my dearest father! and grant that you may forgive the first, and, I trust, the last act approaching towards premeditated disobedience, of which I either have now, or shall hereafter have, to accuse myself. I remain, till death, your dutiful and affectionate son,

'ALAN FAIRFORD.

'P.S.—I shall write with the utmost regularity, acquainting you with my motions, and requesting your advice. I trust my stay will be very short, and I think it possible that I may bring back Darsie along with me.'

The paper dropped from the old man's hand when he was thus assured of the misfortune which he apprehended. His first idea was to get a post-chaise and pursue the fugitive; but he recollected, that, upon the very rare occasions when Alan had shown himself indocile to the *patria potestas*, his natural ease and gentleness of disposition seemed hardened into obstinacy, and that now, entitled, as arrived at the years of majority, and a member of the learned Faculty, to direct his own motions, there was great doubt, whether, in the event of his overtaking his son, he might be able to prevail upon him to return back. In such a risk of failure, he thought it wiser to desist from his purpose, especially as even his success in such a pursuit would give a ridiculous *éclat* to the whole affair, which could not be otherwise than prejudicial to his son's rising character.

Bitter, however, were Saunders Fairford's reflections, as, again picking up the fatal scroll, he threw himself into his son's leathern easy-chair, and bestowed upon it a disjointed commentary. 'Bring back Darsie? little doubt of that—the bad shilling is sure enough to come back again. I wish Darsie no worse ill than that he were carried where the silly fool Alan should never see him again. It was an ill hour that he darkened my doors in, for, ever since that, Alan has given up his ain old-fashioned mother-wit, for the t'other's capernoited maggots and nonsense.—Provided with money? you must have more than I know of, then, my friend, for I trow I kept you pretty short for your own good.—Can he have gotten more fees? or, does he think five guineas has neither beginning nor end?—Arms! What would he do with arms, or what would any man do with them that is not a regular soldier under government, or else a thief-taker? I have had enough of arms, I trow, although I carried them for King George and the government. But this is a worse strait than Falkirk-field* yet!—God guide us, we are poor inconsistent creatures! To think the lad should have made so able an appearance, and then bolted off this gate, after a glaiket ne'er-do-weel, like a hound upon a false scent!—Las-a-day! it's a sore thing to see a stunkard cow kick down the pail when it's reaming fou.—But, after all, it's an ill bird that defiles its ain nest. I must cover up the scandal as well as I can.—What's the matter now, James?'

'A message, sir,' said James Wilkinson, 'from my Lord President; and he hopes Mr Alan is not seriously indisposed.'

'From the Lord President? the Lord preserve us!—I'll send an answer this instant; bid the lad sit down, and ask him to drink, James.—Let me see,' continued he, taking a sheet of gilt paper, 'how we are to draw our answers.'

Ere his pen had touched the paper, James was in the room again.

'What now, James?'

'Lord Bladderskate's lad is come to ask how Mr Alan is, as he left the Court'——

'Ay, ay, ay,' answered Saunders, bitterly; 'he has e'en made a moonlight flitting, like my lord's ain nevoy.'

'Shall I say sae, sir?' said James, who, as an old soldier, was literal in all things touching the service.

'The devil! no, no!—Bid the lad sit down and taste our ale. I will write his lordship an answer.'

Once more the gilt paper was resumed, and once more the door was opened by James.

'Lord —— sends his servitor to ask after Mr Alan.'

'Oh, the deevil take their civility!' said poor Saunders. 'Set him down to drink too—I will write to his lordship.'

'The lads will bide your pleasure, sir, as lang as I keep the bicker fou; but this ringing is like to wear out the bell, I think; there are they at it again.'

He answered the fresh summons accordingly, and came back to inform Mr Fairford, that the Dean of Faculty was below, enquiring for Mr Alan.—'Will I set him down to drink, too?' said James.

'Will you be an idiot, sir?' said Mr Fairford, 'Show Mr Dean into the parlour.'

In going slowly down stairs, step by step, the perplexed man of business had time enough to reflect, that if it be possible to put a fair gloss upon a true story, the verity always serves the purpose better than any substitute which ingenuity can devise. He therefore told his learned visitor, that although his son had been incommoded by the heat of the court, and the long train of hard study, by day and night, preceding his exertions, yet he had fortunately so far recovered, as to be in condition to obey upon the instant a sudden summons which had called him to the country, on a matter of life and death.

'It should be a serious matter indeed that takes my young friend away at this moment,' said the good-natured Dean. 'I wish he had staid to finish his pleading, and put down old Tough. Without compliment, Mr Fairford, it was as fine a first appearance as I ever heard. I should be sorry your son did not follow it up in a reply. Nothing like striking while the iron is hot.'

Mr Saunders Fairford made a bitter grimace as he acquiesced in an opinion which was indeed decidedly his own; but he thought it most prudent to reply, 'that the affair which rendered his son Alan's presence in the country absolutely necessary, regarded the affairs of a young gentleman of great fortune, who was a particular friend of Alan's, and who never took any material step in his affairs, without consulting his counsel learned in the law.'

'Well, well, Mr Fairford, you know best,' answered the learned Dean; 'if there be death or marriage in the case, a will or a wedding is to be preferred to all other business. I am happy Mr Alan is so much recovered as to be able for travel, and wish you a very good morning.'

Having thus taken his ground to the Dean of Faculty, Mr Fairford hastily wrote cards in answer to the enquiry of the three judges, accounting for Alan's absence in the same manner. These, being properly sealed and addressed, he delivered to James, with directions to dismiss the parti-coloured gentry, who, in the meanwhile, had consumed a gallon of twopenny ale, while discussing points of law, and addressing each other by their masters' titles.[40]

The exertion which these matters demanded, and the interest which so many persons of legal distinction appeared to have taken in his son, greatly relieved the oppressed spirit of Saunders Fairford, who continued to talk mysteriously of the very important business which had interfered with his son's attendance during the brief remainder of the session. He endeavoured to lay the same unction to his own heart; but here the application was less fortunate, for his conscience told him, that no end, however important, which could be achieved in Darsie Latimer's affairs, could be balanced against the reputation which Alan was like to forfeit, by deserting the cause of Poor Peter Peebles.

In the meanwhile, although the haze which surrounded the cause, or causes, of that unfortunate litigant had been for a time dispelled by Alan's eloquence, like a fog by the thunder of artillery, yet it seemed once more to settle down upon the mass of litigation, thick as the palpable darkness of Egypt,* at the very sound of Mr Tough's voice, who on the second day after Alan's departure, was heard in answer to the opening counsel. Deep-mouthed, long-breathed, and pertinacious, taking a pinch of snuff betwixt every sentence, which otherwise seemed interminable—the veteran pleader prosed over all the themes which had been treated so luminously by Fairford; he quietly and imperceptibly replaced all the rubbish which the other had cleared away; and succeeded in restoring the veil of obscurity and unintelligibility which had for many years darkened the case of Peebles against Plainstanes; and the matter was once more hung up by a remit to an accountant, with instruction to report before answer.* So different a result from that which the public had been led to expect from Alan's speech, gave rise to various speculations.

The client himself opined that it was entirely owing, first, to his own absence during the first day's pleading, being, as he said, deboshed with brandy, usquebaugh, and other strong waters, at John's Coffee-house, *per ambages* of Peter Drudgeit, employed to that effect by and through the device, counsel, and covyne of Saunders Fairford, his agent, or pretended agent. Secondly, by the flight and voluntary desertion of the younger Fairford, the advocate; on account of which he served both father and son with a petition and complaint against them, for malversation in office. So that the apparent and most probable issue of this cause seemed to menace the melancholy Mr Saunders Fairford with additional subject for plague and mortification; which was the more galling, as his conscience told him that the case was really given away, and that a very brief resumption of the former argument, with reference to the necessary authorities and points of evidence, would have enabled Alan, by the mere breath, as it were, of his mouth, to blow away the various cobwebs with which Mr Tough had again invested the proceedings. But it went, he said, just like a decreet in absence, and was lost for want of a contradictor.

In the meantime, nearly a week passed over without Mr Fairford hearing a word directly from his son. He learned, indeed, by a letter from Mr Crosbie, that the young counsellor had safely reached Dumfries, but had left that town upon some ulterior researches, the purpose of which he had not communicated. The old man, thus left to suspense, and to mortifying recollections, deprived also of the domestic society to which he had been habituated, began to suffer in body as well as in mind. He had formed the determination of setting out in person for Dumfries-shire, when, after having been dogged, peevish, and snappish to his clerks and domestics, to an unusual and almost intolerable degree, the acrimonious humours settled in a hissing-hot fit of the gout, which is a well-known tamer of the most froward spirits, and under whose discipline we shall, for the present, leave him, as the continuation of this history assumes, with the next division, a form somewhat different from direct narrative and epistolary correspondence, though partaking of the character of both.

CHAPTER III

JOURNAL OF DARSIE LATIMER

[The following Address is written on the inside of the envelope which contained the Journal]

INTO what hands soever these leaves may fall, they will instruct him, during a certain time at least, in the history of the life of an unfortunate young man, who, in the heart of a free country, and without any crime being laid to his charge, has been, and is, subjected to a course of unlawful and violent restraint. He who opens this letter, is therefore conjured to apply to the nearest magistrate, and, following such indications as the papers may afford, to exert himself for the relief of one, who, while he possesses every claim to assistance which oppressed innocence can give, has, at the same time, both the inclination and the means of being grateful to his deliverers. Or, if the person obtaining these letters shall want courage or means to effect the writer's release, he is, in that case, conjured, by every duty of a man to his fellow-mortals, and of a Christian towards one who professes the same holy faith, to take the earliest measures for conveying them with speed and safety to the hands of Alan Fairford, Esq., Advocate, residing in the family of his father, Alexander Fairford, Esq., Writer to the Signet, Brown's Square, Edinburgh. He may be assured of a liberal reward, besides the consciousness of having discharged a real duty to humanity.

MY DEAREST ALAN,

FEELING as warmly towards you in doubt and in distress, as I ever did in the brightest days of our intimacy, it is to you whom I address a history which may perhaps fall into very different hands. A portion of my former spirit descends to my pen, when I write your name, and indulging the happy thought that you may be my deliverer from my present uncomfortable and alarming situation, as you have been my guide and counsellor on every former occasion, I will subdue the dejection which would otherwise overwhelm me. Therefore, as, Heaven knows, I have time enough to write, I will endeavour to pour my thoughts out, as fully and freely as of old, though probably without the same gay and happy levity.

If the papers should reach other hands than yours, still I will not regret this exposure of my feelings; for, allowing for an ample share of the folly incidental to youth and inexperience, I fear not that I have much to be ashamed of in my narrative; nay, I even hope, that the open simplicity and frankness with which I am about to relate every singular and distressing circumstance, may prepossess even a stranger in my favour; and that, amid the multitude of seemingly trivial circumstances which I detail at length, a clew may be found to effect my liberation.

Another chance certainly remains—the Journal, as I may call it, may never reach the hands, either of the dear friend to whom it is addressed, or those of an indifferent stranger, but may become the prey of the persons by whom I am at present treated as a prisoner. Let it be so—they will learn from it little but what they already know; that, as a man, and an Englishman, my soul revolts at the usage which I have received; that I am determined to essay every possible means to obtain my freedom; that captivity has not broken my spirit, and that, although they may doubtless complete their oppression by murder, I am still willing to bequeath my cause to the justice of my country. Undeterred, therefore, by the probability that my papers may be torn from me, and subjected to the inspection of one in particular, who, causelessly my enemy already, may be yet farther incensed at me for recording the history of my wrongs, I proceed to resume the history of events which have befallen me since the conclusion of my last letter to my dear Alan Fairford, dated, if I mistake not, on the 5th day of this still current month of August.

Upon the night preceding the date of that letter, I had been present, for the purpose of an idle frolic, at a dancing party at the village of Brokenburn, about six miles from Dumfries; many persons must have seen me there, should the fact appear of importance sufficient to require investigation. I danced, played on the violin, and took part in the festivity, till about midnight, when my servant, Samuel Owen, brought me my horses, and I rode back to a small inn called Shepherd's Bush, kept by Mrs Gregson, which had been occasionally my residence for about a fortnight past. I spent the earlier part of the forenoon in writing a letter which I have already mentioned, to you, my dear Alan, and which, I think, you must have received in safety. Why did I not follow your advice, so often given me? Why did I linger in the neighbourhood of a danger, of which a kind voice had warned me? These are now unavailing questions. I was blinded by a fatality, and remained fluttering like a moth around the candle, until I have been scorched to some purpose.

The greater part of the day had passed, and time hung heavy on my hands. I ought, perhaps, to blush at recollecting what has been often objected to me by the dear friend to whom this letter is addressed, viz. the facility with which I have, in moments of indolence, suffered my motions to be directed by any person who chanced to be near me, instead of taking the labour of thinking or deciding for myself. I had employed for some time, as a sort of guide and errand-boy, a lad named Benjamin, the son of one widow Coltherd, who lives near the Shepherd's Bush, and I cannot but remember that, upon several occasions, I had of late suffered him to possess more influence over my motions, than at all became the difference of our age and condition. At present he exerted himself to persuade me that it was the finest possible sport to see the fish taken out from the nets placed in the Solway at the reflux of the tide, and urged my going thither this evening so much, that, looking back on the whole circumstances, I cannot but think he had some especial motive for his conduct. These particulars I have mentioned, that if these papers fall into friendly hands, the boy may be sought after and submitted to examination.

His eloquence being unable to persuade me that I should take any pleasure in seeing the fruitless struggles of the fish when left in the nets and deserted by the tide, he artfully suggested, that Mr and Miss Geddes, a respectable Quaker family well known in the neighbourhood, and with whom I had contracted habits of intimacy, would possibly be offended if I did not make them an early visit. Both, he said, had been particularly enquiring the reasons of my leaving their house rather suddenly on the previous day. I resolved, therefore, to walk up to Mount Sharon and make my apologies; and I agreed to permit the boy to attend upon me, and wait my return from the house, that I might fish on my way homeward to Shepherd's Bush, for which amusement, he assured me, I would find the evening most favourable. I mention this minute circumstance, because I strongly suspect that this boy had a presentiment how the evening was to terminate with me, and entertained the selfish though childish wish of securing to himself an angling-rod which he had often admired, as a part of my spoils. I may do the boy wrong, but I had before remarked in him the peculiar art of pursuing the trifling objects of cupidity proper to his age, with the systematic address of much riper years.

When we had commenced our walk, I upbraided him with the coolness of the evening, considering the season, the easterly wind, and other circumstances, unfavourable for angling. He persisted in his own story, and made a few casts, as if to convince me of my error, but caught no fish; and, indeed, as I am now convinced, was much more intent on watching my motions, than on taking any. When I ridiculed him once more on his fruitless endeavours, he answered with a sneering smile, that 'the trouts would not rise, because there was thunder in the air;' an intimation which, in one sense, I have found too true.

I arrived at Mount Sharon; was received by my friends there with their wonted kindness; and after being a little rallied on my having suddenly left them on the preceding evening, I agreed to make atonement by staying all night, and dismissed the lad who attended with my fishing-rod, to carry that information to Shepherd's Bush. It may be doubted whether he went thither, or in a different direction.

Betwixt eight and nine o'clock, when it began to become dark, we walked on the terrace to enjoy the appearance of the firmament, glittering with ten million of stars; to which a slight touch of early frost gave tenfold lustre. As we gazed on this splendid scene, Miss Geddes, I think, was the first to point out to our admiration a shooting or falling star, which, she said, drew a long train after it. Looking to the part of the heavens which she pointed out, I distinctly observed two successive sky-rockets arise, and burst in the sky.

'These meteors,' said Mr Geddes, in answer to his sister's observation, 'are not formed in heaven, nor do they bode any good to the dwellers upon earth.'

As he spoke, I looked to another quarter of the sky, and a rocket, as if a signal in answer to those which had already appeared, rose high from the earth, and burst apparently among the stars.

Mr Geddes seemed very thoughtful for some minutes, and then said to his sister, 'Rachel, though it waxes late, I must go down to the fishing station, and pass the night in the overseer's room there.'

'Nay, then,' replied the lady, 'I am but too well assured that the sons of Belial* are menacing these nets and devices. Joshua, art thou a man of peace, and wilt thou willingly and wittingly thrust thyself, where thou mayst be tempted by the old man Adam within thee, to enter into debate and strife?'

'I am a man of peace, Rachel,' answered Mr Geddes, 'even to the utmost extent which our friends can demand of humanity; and neither have I ever used, nor, with the help of God, will I at any future time employ, the arm of flesh to repel or to revenge injuries. But if I can, by mild reasons and firm conduct, save those rude men from committing a crime, and the property belonging to myself and others from sustaining damage, surely I do but the duty of a man and a Christian.'

With these words, he ordered his horse instantly; and his sister ceasing to argue with him, folded her arms upon her bosom, and looked up to heaven with a resigned and yet sorrowful countenance.

These particulars may appear trivial; but it is better, in my present condition, to exert my faculties in recollecting the past, and in recording it, than waste them in vain and anxious anticipations of the future.

It would have been scarcely proper in me to remain in the house, from which the master was thus suddenly summoned away; and I therefore begged permission to attend him to the fishing station, assuring his sister that I would be a guarantee for his safety.

The proposal seemed to give much pleasure to Miss Geddes. 'Let it be so, brother,' she said; 'and let the young man have the desire of his heart, that there may be a faithful witness to stand by thee in the hour of need, and to report how it shall fare with thee.'

'No, Rachel,' said the worthy man, 'thou art to blame in this, that, to quiet thy apprehensions on my account, thou shouldst thrust into danger—if danger it shall prove to be—this youth, our guest; for whom, doubtless, in case of mishap, as many hearts will ache as may be afflicted on our account.'

'Nay, my good friend,' said I, taking Mr Geddes's hand, 'I am not so happy as you suppose me. Were my span to be concluded this evening, few would so much as know that such a being had existed for twenty years on the face of the earth; and of these few, only one would sincerely regret me. Do not, therefore, refuse me the privilege of attending you; and of showing, by so trifling an act of kindness, that if I have few friends, I am at least desirous to serve them.'

'Thou hast a kind heart, I warrant thee,' said Joshua Geddes, returning the pressure of my hand. 'Rachel, the young man shall go with me. Why should he not face danger, in order to do justice and preserve peace? There is that within me,' he added, looking upwards, and with a passing enthusiasm which I had not before observed, and the absence of which perhaps rather belonged to the sect than to his own personal character—'I say, I have that within which assures me, that though the ungodly may rage even like the storm of the ocean, they shall not have freedom to prevail against us.'

Having spoken thus, Mr Geddes appointed a pony to be saddled for my use; and having taken a basket with some provisions, and a servant to carry back the horses, for which there was no accommodation at the fishing station, we set off about nine o'clock at night, and after three quarters of an hour's riding, arrived at our place of destination.

The station consists, or then consisted, of huts for four or five fishermen, a cooperage and sheds, and a better sort of cottage, at which the superintendent resided. We gave our horses to the servant, to be carried back to Mount Sharon; my companion expressing himself humanely anxious for their safety—and knocked at the door of the house. At first we only heard a barking of dogs; but these animals became quiet on snuffing beneath the door, and acknowledging the presence of friends. A hoarse voice then demanded, in rather unfriendly accents, who we were, and what we wanted; and it was not until Joshua named himself, and called upon his superintendent to open, that the latter appeared at the door of the hut, attended by three large dogs of the Newfoundland breed. He had a flambeau in his hand, and two large heavy ship-pistols stuck into his belt. He was a stout, elderly man, who had been a sailor, as I learned, during the earlier part of his life, and was now much confided in by the Fishing Company, whose concerns he directed under the orders of Mr Geddes.

'Thou didst not expect me to-night, friend Davies?' said my friend to the old man, who was arranging seats for us by the fire.

'No, Master Geddes,' answered he, 'I did not expect you, nor, to speak the truth, did I wish for you either.'

'These are plain terms, John Davies,' answered Mr Geddes.

'Ay, ay, sir, I know your worship loves no holyday speeches.'

'Thou dost guess, I suppose, what brings us here so late, John Davies?' said Mr Geddes.

'I do suppose, sir,' answered the superintendent, 'that it was because these d—d smuggling wreckers on the coast are showing their lights to gather their forces, as they did the night before they broke down the dam-dike and wears up the country; but if that same be the case, I wish once more you had staid away, for your worship carries no fighting tackle aboard, I think; and there will be work for such ere morning, your worship.'

'Worship is due to Heaven only,* John Davies,' said Geddes. 'I have often desired thee to desist from using that phrase to me.'

'I won't, then,' said John; 'no offence meant: But how the devil can a man stand picking his words, when he is just going to come to blows?'

'I hope not, John Davies,' said Joshua Geddes. 'Call in the rest of the men, that I may give them their instructions.'

'I may cry till doomsday, Master Geddes, ere a soul answers—the cowardly lubbers have all made sail—the cooper, and all the rest of them, so soon as they heard the enemy were at sea. They have all taken to the long-boat, and left the ship among the breakers, except little Phil and myself—they have, by ——!'

'Swear not at all,* John Davies—thou art an honest man; and I believe, without an oath, that thy comrades love their own bones better than my goods and chattels. And so thou hast no assistance but little Phil against a hundred men or two?'

'Why, there are the dogs, your honour knows, Neptune and Thetis—and the puppy may do something; and then though your worship—I beg pardon—though your honour be no great fighter, this young gentleman may bear a hand.'

'Ay, and I see you are provided with arms,' said Mr Geddes; 'let me see them.'

'Ay, ay, sir; here be a pair of buffers will bite as well as bark—these will make sure of two rogues at least. It would be a shame to strike without firing a shot.—Take care, your honour, they are double-shotted.'

'Ay, John Davies, I will take care of them,' throwing the pistols into a tub of water beside him; 'and I wish I could render the whole generation of them useless at the same moment.'

A deep shade of displeasure passed over John Davies's weather-beaten countenance. 'Belike your honour is going to take the command yourself, then?' he said, after a pause. 'Why, I can be of little use now; and since your worship, or your honour, or whatever you are, means to strike quietly, I believe you will do it better without me than with me, for I am like enough to make mischief, I admit; but I'll never leave my post without orders.'

'Then you have mine, John Davies, to go to Mount Sharon directly, and take the boy Phil with you. Where is he?'

'He is on the outlook for these scums of the earth,' answered Davies; 'but it is to no purpose to know when they come, if we are not to stand to our weapons.'

'We will use none but those of sense and reason, John.'

'And you may just as well cast chaff against the wind, as speak sense and reason to the like of them.'

'Well, well, be it so,' said Joshua; 'and now, John Davies, I know thou art what the world calls a brave fellow, and I have ever found thee an honest one. And now I command you to go to Mount Sharon, and let Phil lie on the bank-side—see the poor boy hath a sea-cloak, though—and watch what happens here, and let him bring you the news; and if any violence shall be offered to the property there, I trust to your fidelity to carry my sister to Dumfries, to the house of our friends the Corsacks, and inform the civil authorities of what mischief hath befallen.'

The old seaman paused a moment. 'It is hard lines for me,' he said, 'to leave your honour in tribulation; and yet, staying here, I am only like to make bad worse; and your honour's sister, Miss Rachel, must be looked to, that's certain; for if the rogues once get their hand to mischief, they will come to Mount Sharon after they have wasted and destroyed this here snug little roadstead, where I thought to ride at anchor for life.'

'Right, right, John Davies,' said Joshua Geddes; 'and best call the dogs with you.'

'Ay, ay, sir,' said the veteran, 'for they are something of my mind, and would not keep quiet if they saw mischief doing; so maybe they might come to mischief, poor dumb creatures. So God bless your honour—I mean your worship—I cannot bring my mouth to say fare you well.—Here, Neptune, Thetis! come, dogs, come.'

So saying, and with a very crestfallen countenance, John Davies left the hut.

'Now there goes one of the best and most faithful creatures that ever was born,' said Mr Geddes, as the superintendent shut the door of the cottage. 'Nature made him with a heart that would not have suffered him to harm a fly; but thou seest, friend Latimer, that as men arm their bull-dogs with spiked collars, and their game-cocks with steel spurs, to aid them in fight, so they corrupt, by education, the best and mildest natures, until fortitude and spirit become stubbornness and ferocity. Believe me, friend Latimer, I would as soon expose my faithful household dog to a vain combat with a herd of wolves, as yon trusty creature to the violence of the enraged multitude. But I need say little on this subject to thee, friend Latimer, who, I doubt not, art trained to believe that courage is displayed and honour attained, not by doing and suffering, as becomes a man, that which fate calls us to suffer, and justice commands us to do, but because thou art ready to retort violence for violence, and considerest the lightest insult as a sufficient cause for the spilling of blood, nay, the taking of life.—But, leaving these points of controversy to a more fit season, let us see what our basket of provision contains; for in truth, friend Latimer, I am one of those whom neither fear nor anxiety deprive of their ordinary appetite.'

We found the means of good cheer accordingly, which Mr Geddes seemed to enjoy as much as if it had been eaten in a situation of perfect safety; nay, his conversation appeared to be rather more gay than on ordinary occasions. After eating our supper we left the hut together, and walked for a few minutes on the banks of the sea. It was high water, and the ebb had not yet commenced. The moon shone broad and bright upon the placid face of the Solway Frith, and showed a slight ripple upon the stakes, the tops of which were just visible above the waves, and on the dark-coloured buoys which marked the upper edge of the enclosure of nets. At a much greater distance,—for the estuary is here very wide,—the line of the English coast was seen on the verge of the water, resembling one of those fog-banks on which mariners are said to gaze, uncertain whether it be land or atmospherical delusion.

'We shall be undisturbed for some hours,' said Mr Geddes; 'they will not come down upon us till the state of the tide permits them to destroy the tide-nets. Is it not strange to think that human passions will so soon transform such a tranquil scene as this, into one of devastation and confusion?'

It was indeed a scene of exquisite stillness; so much so, that the restless waves of the Solway seemed, if not absolutely to sleep, at least to slumber;—on the shore no night-bird was heard—the cock had not sung his first matins, and we ourselves walked more lightly than by day, as if to suit the sound of our own paces to the serene tranquillity around us. At length, the plaintive cry of a dog broke the silence, and on our return to the cottage, we found that the younger of the three animals which had gone along with John Davies, unaccustomed, perhaps, to distant journeys, and the duty of following to heel, had strayed from the party, and, unable to rejoin them, had wandered back to the place of its birth.

'Another feeble addition to our feeble garrison,' said Mr Geddes, as he caressed the dog, and admitted it into the cottage. 'Poor thing! as thou art incapable of doing any mischief, I hope thou wilt sustain none. At least thou mayst do us the good service of a sentinel, and permit us to enjoy a quiet repose, under the certainty that thou wilt alarm us when the enemy is at hand.'

There were two beds in the superintendent's room, upon which we threw ourselves. Mr Geddes, with his happy equanimity of temper, was asleep in the first five minutes. I lay for some time in doubtful and anxious thoughts, watching the fire and the motions of the restless dog, which, disturbed probably at the absence of John Davies, wandered from the hearth to the door and back again, then came to the bedside, and licked my hands and face, and at length, experiencing no repulse to its advances, established itself at my feet, and went to sleep, an example which I soon afterwards followed.

The rage of narration, my dear Alan—for I will never relinquish the hope that what I am writing may one day reach your hands—has not forsaken me even in my confinement, and the extensive though unimportant details into which I have been hurried, render it necessary that I commence another sheet. Fortunately, my pigmy characters comprehend a great many words within a small space of paper.

CHAPTER IV

DARSIE LATIMER'S JOURNAL, IN CONTINUATION

THE morning was dawning, and Mr Geddes and I myself were still sleeping soundly, when the alarm was given by my canine bedfellow, who first growled deeply at intervals, and at length bore more decided testimony to the approach of some enemy. I opened the door of the cottage, and perceived, at the distance of about two hundred yards, a small but close column of men, which I would have taken for a dark hedge, but that I could perceive it was advancing rapidly and in silence.

The dog flew towards them, but instantly ran howling back to me, having probably been chastised by a stick or a stone. Uncertain as to the plan of tactics or of treaty which Mr Geddes might think proper to adopt, I was about to retire into the cottage, when he suddenly joined me at the door, and, slipping his arm through mine, said, 'Let us go to meet them manfully; we have done nothing to be ashamed of.—Friends,' he said, raising his voice as we approached them, 'who and what are you, and with what purpose are you here on my property?'

A loud cheer was the answer returned, and a brace of fiddlers who occupied the front of the march immediately struck up the insulting air, the words of which begin,

> 'Merrily danced the Quaker's wife,
> And merrily danced the Quaker.'

Even at that moment of alarm, I think I recognised the tones of the blind fiddler, known by the name of Wandering Willie, from his itinerant habits. They continued to advance swiftly and in great order, in their front

> 'The fiery fiddlers playing martial airs;'

when, coming close up, they surrounded us by a single movement, and there was a universal cry, 'Whoop, Quaker—whoop, Quaker! Here have we them both, the wet Quaker and the dry one.'

'Hang up the wet Quaker to dry, and wet the dry one with a ducking,' answered another voice.

'Where is the sea-otter, John Davies, that destroyed more fish than any sealch upon Ailsay Craig?' exclaimed a third voice. 'I have an old crow to pluck with him, and a pock to put the feathers in.'

We stood perfectly passive; for, to have attempted resistance against more than a hundred men, armed with guns, fish-spears, iron-crows, spades, and bludgeons, would have been an act of utter insanity. Mr Geddes, with his strong sonorous voice, answered the question about the superintendent in a manner, the manly indifference of which compelled them to attend to him.

'John Davies,' he said, 'will, I trust, soon be at Dumfries'——

'To fetch down redcoats and dragoons against us, you canting old villain!'

A blow was, at the same time, levelled at my friend, which I parried by interposing the stick I had in my hand. I was instantly struck down, and have a faint recollection of hearing some crying, 'Kill the young spy!' and others, as I thought, interposing on my behalf. But a second blow on the head, received in the scuffle, soon deprived me of sense and consciousness, and threw me into a state of insensibility, from which I did not recover immediately. When I did come to myself, I was lying on the bed from which I had just risen before the fray, and my poor companion, the Newfoundland puppy, its courage entirely cowed by the tumult of the riot, had crept as close to me as it could, and lay trembling and whining, as if under the most dreadful terror. I doubted at first whether I had not dreamed of the tumult, until, as I attempted to rise, a feeling of pain and dizziness assured me that the injury I had sustained was but too real. I gathered together my senses—listened—and heard at a distance the shouts of the rioters, busy, doubtless, in their work of devastation. I made a second effort to rise, or at least to turn myself, for I lay with my face to the wall of the cottage, but I found that my limbs were secured, and my motions effectually prevented—not indeed by cords, but by linen or cloth bandages swathed around my ankles, and securing my arms to my sides. Aware of my utterly captive condition, I groaned betwixt bodily pain and mental distress.

A voice by my bedside whispered, in a whining tone, 'Whisht a-ye, hinnie—whisht, a-ye; haud your tongue, like a gude bairn—ye have cost us dear aneugh already. My hinnie's clean gane now.'

Knowing, as I thought, the phraseology of the wife of the itinerant musician, I asked her where her husband was, and whether he had been hurt.

'Broken,' answered the dame, 'all broken to pieces; fit for nought but to be made spunks of—the best blood that was in Scotland.'

'Broken?—blood?—is your husband wounded; has there been bloodshed—broken limbs?'

'Broken limbs?—I wish,' answered the beldam, 'that my hinnie had broken the best bane in his body, before he had broken his fiddle, that was the best blood in Scotland—it was a cremony, for aught that I ken.'

'Pshaw—only his fiddle?' said I.

'I dinna ken what waur your honour could have wished him to do, unless he had broken his neck; and this is muckle the same to my hinnie Willie and me. Chaw, indeed! It is easy to say *chaw*, but wha is to gie us ony thing to chaw?—the breadwinner's gane, and we may e'en sit down and starve.'

'No, no,' I said, 'I will pay you for twenty such fiddles.'

'Twenty such! is that a' ye ken about it? the country hadna the like o't. But if your honour were to pay us, as nae doubt wad be to your credit here and hereafter, where are ye to get the siller?'

'I have enough of money,' said I, attempting to reach my hand towards my side-pocket; 'unloose these bandages, and I will pay you on the spot.'

This hint appeared to move her, and she was approaching the bedside, as I hoped, to liberate me from my bonds, when a nearer and more desperate shout was heard, as if the rioters were close by the hut.

'I daurna—I daurna,' said the poor woman, 'they would murder me and my hinnie Willie baith, and they have misguided us aneugh already;—but if there is any thing worldly I could do for your honour, leave out loosing ye?'

What she said recalled me to my bodily suffering. Agitation, and the effects of the usage I had received, had produced a burning thirst. I asked for a drink of water.

'Heaven Almighty forbid that Epps Ainslie should gie ony sick gentleman cauld well-water, and him in a fever. Na, na, hinnie, let me alane, I'll do better for ye than the like of that.'

'Give me what you will,' I replied; 'let it but be liquid and cool.'

The woman gave me a large horn accordingly, filled with spirits and water, which, without minute enquiry concerning the nature of its contents, I drained at a draught. Either the spirits taken in such a manner, acted more suddenly than usual on my brain, or else there was some drug mixed with the beverage. I remember little after drinking it off, only that the appearance of things around me became indistinct; that the woman's form seemed to multiply itself, and to flit in various figures around me, bearing the same lineaments as she herself did. I remember also that the discordant noises and cries of those without the cottage seemed to die away in a hum like that with which a nurse hushes her babe. At length I fell into a deep sound sleep, or rather, a state of absolute insensibility.

I have reason to think this species of trance lasted for many hours; indeed, for the whole subsequent day and part of the night. It was not uniformly so profound, for my recollection of it is chequered with many dreams, all of a painful nature, but too faint and too indistinct to be remembered. At length the moment of waking came, and my sensations were horrible.

A deep sound, which, in the confusion of my senses, I identified with the cries of the rioters, was the first thing of which I was sensible; next, I became conscious that I was carried violently forward in some conveyance, with an unequal motion, which gave me much pain. My position was horizontal, and when I attempted to stretch my hands in order to find some mode of securing myself against this species of suffering, I found I was bound as before, and the horrible reality rushed on my mind, that I was in the hands of those who had lately committed a great outrage on property, and were now about to kidnap, if not to murder me. I opened my eyes, it was to no purpose—all around me was dark, for a day had passed over during my captivity. A dispiriting sickness oppressed my head—my heart seemed on fire, while my feet and hands were chilled and benumbed with want of circulation. It was with the utmost difficulty that I at length, and gradually, recovered in a sufficient degree the power of observing external sounds and circumstances; and when I did so, they presented nothing consolatory.

Groping with my hands, as far as the bandages would permit, and receiving the assistance of some occasional glances of the moonlight, I became aware that the carriage in which I was transported was one of the light carts of the country, called *tumblers*, and that a little attention had been paid to my accommodation, as I was laid upon some sacks covered with matting, and filled with straw. Without these, my condition would have been still more intolerable, for the vehicle, sinking now on one side, and now on the other, sometimes sticking absolutely fast, and requiring the utmost exertions of the animal which drew it to put it once more in motion, was subjected to jolts in all directions, which were very severe. At other times it rolled silently and smoothly over what seemed to be wet sand; and, as I heard the distant roar of the tide, I had little doubt that we were engaged in passing the formidable estuary which divides the two kingdoms.

There seemed to be at least five or six people about the cart, some on foot, others on horseback; the former lent assistance whenever it was in danger of upsetting, or sticking fast in the quicksand; the others rode before and acted as guides, often changing the direction of the vehicle as the precarious state of the passage required.

I addressed myself to the men around the cart, and endeavoured to move their compassion. I had harmed, I said, no one, and for no action in my life had deserved such cruel treatment. I had no concern whatever in the fishing station which had incurred their displeasure, and my acquaintance with Mr Geddes was of a very late date. Lastly, and as my strongest argument, I endeavoured to excite their fears, by informing them that my rank in life would not permit me to be either murdered or secreted with impunity; and to interest their avarice, by the promises I made them of reward, if they would effect my deliverance. I only received a scornful laugh in reply to my threats; my promises might have done more, for the fellows were whispering together as if in hesitation, and I began to reiterate and increase my offers, when the voice of one of the horsemen, who had suddenly come up, enjoined silence to the men on foot, and, approaching the side of the cart, said to me, with a strong and determined voice, 'Young man, there is no personal harm designed to you. If you remain silent and quiet, you may reckon on good treatment; but if you endeavour to tamper with these men in the execution of their duty, I will take such measures for silencing you, as you shall remember the longest day you have to live.'

I thought I knew the voice which uttered these threats; but, in such a situation, my perceptions could not be supposed to be perfectly accurate. I was contented to reply, 'Whoever you are that speak to me, I entreat the benefit of the meanest prisoner, who is not to be subjected legally to greater hardship than is necessary for the restraint of his person. I entreat that these bonds, which hurt me so cruelly, may be slackened at least, if not removed altogether.'

'I will slacken the belts,' said the former speaker; 'nay, I will altogether remove them, and allow you to pursue your journey in a more convenient manner, provided you will give me your word of honour that you will not attempt an escape.'

'*Never!*' I answered, with an energy of which despair alone could have rendered me capable—'I will *never* submit to loss of freedom a moment longer than I am subjected to it by force.'

'Enough,' he replied; 'the sentiment is natural; but do not on your side complain that I, who am carrying on an important undertaking, use the only means in my power for ensuring its success.'

I entreated to know what it was designed to do with me; but my conductor, in a voice of menacing authority, desired me to be silent on my peril; and my strength and spirits were too much exhausted to permit my continuing a dialogue so singular, even if I could have promised myself any good result by doing so.

It is proper here to add, that, from my recollections at the time, and from what has since taken place, I have the strongest possible belief that the man with whom I held this expostulation, was the singular person residing at Brokenburn, in Dumfries-shire, and called by the fishers of that hamlet, the Laird of the Solway Lochs. The cause for his inveterate persecution I cannot pretend even to guess at.

In the meantime, the cart was dragged heavily and wearily on, until the nearer roar of the advancing tide excited the apprehension of another danger. I could not mistake the sound, which I had heard upon another occasion, when it was only the speed of a fleet horse which saved me from perishing in the quicksands. Thou, my dear Alan, canst not but remember the former circumstances; and now, wonderful contrast! the very man, to the best of my belief, who then saved me from peril, was the leader of the lawless band who had deprived me of my liberty. I conjectured that the danger grew imminent; for I heard some words and circumstances which made me aware that a rider hastily fastened his own horse to the shafts of the cart, in order to assist the exhausted animal which drew it, and the vehicle was now pulled forward at a faster pace, which the horses were urged to maintain by blows and curses. The men, however, were inhabitants of the neighbourhood; and I had strong personal reason to believe, that one of them, at least, was intimately acquainted with all the depths and shallows of the perilous paths in which we were engaged. But they were in imminent danger themselves; and if so, as from the whispering and exertions to push on with the cart, was much to be apprehended, there was little doubt that I should be left behind as a useless encumbrance, and that while I was in a condition which rendered every chance of escape impracticable. These were awful apprehensions; but it pleased Providence to increase them to a point which my brain was scarcely able to endure.

As we approached very near to a black line, which, dimly visible as it was, I could make out to be the shore, we heard two or three sounds, which appeared to be the report of fire-arms. Immediately all was bustle among our party to get forward. Presently a fellow galloped up to us, crying out, 'Ware hawk! ware hawk! the land-sharks are out from Burgh, and Allonby Tom will lose his cargo if you do not bear a hand.'

Most of my company seemed to make hastily for the shore on receiving this intelligence. A driver was left with the cart; but at length, when, after repeated and hair-breadth escapes, it actually stuck fast in a slough or quicksand, the fellow with an oath cut the harness, and, as I presume, departed with the horses, whose feet I heard splashing over the wet sand, and through the shallows, as he galloped off.

The dropping sound of fire-arms was still continued, but lost almost entirely in the thunder of the advancing surge. By a desperate effort I raised myself in the cart, and attained a sitting posture, which served only to show me the extent of my danger. There lay my native land—my own England—the land where I was born, and to which my wishes, since my earliest age, had turned with all the prejudices of national feeling—there it lay, within a furlong of the place where I yet was; that furlong which an infant would have raced over in a minute, was yet a barrier effectual to divide me for ever from England and from life. I soon not only heard the roar of this dreadful torrent, but saw, by the fitful moonlight, the foamy crests of the devouring waves, as they advanced with the speed and fury of a pack of hungry wolves.

The consciousness that the slightest ray of hope, or power of struggling, was not left me, quite overcame the constancy which I had hitherto maintained. My eyes began to swim—my head grew giddy and mad with fear—I chattered and howled to the howling and roaring sea. One or two great waves already reached the cart, when the conductor of the party whom I have mentioned so often, was, as if by magic, at my side. He sprang from his horse into the vehicle, cut the ligatures which restrained me, and bade me get up and mount in the fiend's name.

Seeing I was incapable of obeying, he seized me, as if I had been a child of six months old, threw me across the horse, sprung on behind, supporting me with one hand, while he directed the animal with the other. In my helpless and painful posture, I was unconscious of the degree of danger which we incurred; but I believe at one time the horse was swimming, or nearly so; and that it was with difficulty that my stern and powerful assistant kept my head above water. I remember particularly the shock which I felt when the animal, endeavouring to gain the bank, reared, and very nearly fell back on his burden. The time during which I continued in this dreadful condition did not probably exceed two or three minutes, yet so strongly were they marked with horror and agony, that they seem to my recollection a much more considerable space of time.

When I had been thus snatched from destruction, I had only power to say to my protector,—or oppressor,—for he merited either name at my hand, 'You do not, then, design to murder me?'

He laughed as he replied, but it was a sort of laughter which I scarce desire to hear again,—'Else you think I had let the waves do their work? But remember, the shepherd saves his sheep from the torrent—is it to preserve its life?—Be silent, however, with questions or entreaties. What I mean to do, thou canst no more discover or prevent, than a man, with his bare palm, can scoop dry the Solway.'

I was too much exhausted to continue the argument; and, still numbed and torpid in all my limbs, permitted myself without reluctance to be placed on a horse brought for the purpose. My formidable conductor rode on the one side, and another person on the other, keeping me upright in the saddle. In this manner we travelled forward at a considerable rate, and by by-roads, with which my attendant seemed as familiar as with the perilous passages of the Solway.

At length, after stumbling through a labyrinth of dark and deep lanes, and crossing more than one rough and barren heath, we found ourselves on the edge of a high-road, where a chaise and four awaited, as it appeared, our arrival. To my great relief, we now changed our mode of conveyance; for my dizziness and headach had returned in so strong a degree, that I should otherwise have been totally unable to keep my seat on horseback, even with the support which I received.

My doubted and dangerous companion signed to me to enter the carriage—the man who had ridden on the left side of my horse stepped in after me, and, drawing up the blinds of the vehicle, gave the signal for instant departure.

I had obtained a glimpse of the countenance of my new companion, as by the aid of a dark lantern the drivers opened the carriage door, and I was wellnigh persuaded that I recognised in him the domestic of the leader of this party, whom I had seen at his house in Brokenburn on a former occasion. To ascertain the truth of my suspicion, I asked him whether his name was not Cristal Nixon.

'What is other folk's names to you,' he replied, gruffly, 'who cannot tell your own father and mother?'

'You know them, perhaps?' I exclaimed eagerly. 'You know them! and with that secret is connected the treatment which I am now receiving? It must be so, for in my life have I never injured any one. Tell me the cause of my misfortunes, or rather, help me to my liberty, and I will reward you richly.'

'Ay, ay,' replied my keeper; 'but what use to give you liberty, who know nothing how to use it like a gentleman, but spend your time with Quakers and fiddlers, and such-like raff? If I was your—hem, hem, hem!'

Here Cristal stopped short, just on the point, as it appeared, when some information was likely to escape him. I urged him once more to be my friend, and promised him all the stock of money which I had about me, and it was not inconsiderable, if he would assist in my escape.

He listened, as if to a proposition which had some interest, and replied, but in a voice rather softer than before, 'Ay, but men do not catch old birds with chaff, my master. Where have you got the rhino you are so flush of?'

'I will give you earnest directly, and that in bank-notes,' said I; but, thrusting my hand into my side-pocket, I found my pocket-book was gone. I would have persuaded myself that it was only the numbness of my hands which prevented my finding it; but Cristal

Nixon, who bears in his countenance that cynicism which is especially entertained with human misery, no longer suppressed his laughter.

'Oh, ho! my young master,' he said; 'we have taken good enough care you have not kept the means of bribing poor folk's fidelity. What, man, they have souls as well as other people, and to make them break trust is a deadly sin. And as for me, young gentleman, if you would fill Saint Mary's Kirk with gold, Cristal Nixon would mind it no more than so many chucky-stones.'

I would have persisted, were it but in hopes of his letting drop that which it concerned me to know, but he cut off further communication, by desiring me to lean back in the corner and go to sleep.

'Thou art cockbrained enough already,' he added, 'and we shall have thy young pate addled entirely, if you do not take some natural rest.'

I did indeed require repose, if not slumber; the draught which I had taken continued to operate, and satisfied in my own mind that no attempt on my life was designed, the fear of instant death no longer combated the torpor which crept over me—I slept, and slept soundly, but still without refreshment.

When I awoke, I found myself extremely indisposed; images of the past, and anticipations of the future, floated confusedly through my brain. I perceived, however, that my situation was changed, greatly for the better. I was in a good bed, with the curtains drawn round it; I heard the lowered voice and cautious step of attendants, who seemed to respect my repose; it appeared as if I was in the hands either of friends, or of such as meant me no personal harm.

I can give but an indistinct account of two or three broken and feverish days which succeeded, but if they were chequered with dreams and visions of terror, other and more agreeable objects were also sometimes presented. Alan Fairford will understand me when I say, I am convinced I saw G. M. during this interval of oblivion. I had medical attendance, and was bled more than once. I also remember a painful operation performed on my head, where I had received a severe blow on the night of the riot. My hair was cut short, and the bone of the skull examined, to discover if the cranium had received any injury.

On seeing the physician, it would have been natural to have appealed to him on the subject of my confinement, and I remember more than once attempting to do so. But the fever lay like a spell upon my tongue, and when I would have implored the doctor's assistance, I rambled from the subject, and spoke I know not what—nonsense. Some power, which I was unable to resist, seemed to impel me into a different course of conversation from what I intended, and though conscious, in some degree, of the failure, I could not mend it; and resolved, therefore, to be patient, until my capacity of steady thought and expression was restored to me with my ordinary health, which had sustained a severe shock from the vicissitudes to which I had been exposed.[41]

CHAPTER V

DARSIE LATIMER'S JOURNAL, IN CONTINUATION

TWO or three days, perhaps more, perhaps less, had been spent in bed, where I was carefully attended, and treated, I believe, with as much judgment as the case required, and I was at length allowed to quit my bed, though not the chamber. I was now more able to make some observation on the place of my confinement.

The room, in appearance and furniture, resembled the best apartment in a farmer's house; and the window, two stories high, looked into a backyard, or court, filled with poultry. There were the usual domestic offices about this yard. I could distinguish the brewhouse and the barn, and I heard, from a more remote building, the lowing of the cattle and other rural sounds, announcing a large and well-stocked farm. These were sights and sounds qualified to dispel any apprehension of immediate violence. Yet the building seemed ancient and strong, a part of the roof was battlemented, and the walls were of great thickness; lastly, I observed with some unpleasant sensations, that the windows of my chamber had been lately secured with iron stanchions, and that the servants who brought me victuals, or visited my apartment to render other menial offices, always locked the door when they retired.

The comfort and cleanliness of my chamber were of true English growth, and such as I had rarely seen on the other side of the Tweed; the very old wainscot, which composed the floor and the panelling of the room, was scrubbed with a degree of labour which the Scottish housewife rarely bestows on her most costly furniture.

The whole apartments appropriated to my use consisted of the bedroom, a small parlour adjacent, within which was a still smaller closet, having a narrow window, which seemed anciently to have been used as a shot-hole, admitting, indeed, a very moderate portion of light and air, but without its being possible to see any thing from it except the blue sky, and that only by mounting on a chair. There were appearances of a separate entrance into this cabinet, besides that which communicated with the parlour, but it had been recently built up, as I discovered, by removing a piece of tapestry which covered the fresh mason-work. I found some of my clothes here, with linen and other articles, as well as my writing case, containing pen, ink, and paper, which enables me, at my leisure, (which, God knows, is undisturbed enough,) to make this record of my confinement. It may be well believed, however, that I do not trust to the security of the bureau, but carry the written sheets about my person, so that I can only be deprived of them by actual violence. I also am cautious to write in the little cabinet only, so that I can hear any person approach me through the other apartments, and have time enough to put aside my journal before they come upon me.

The servants, a stout country fellow, and a very pretty milkmaid-looking lass, by whom I am attended, seem of the true Joan and Hodge school,* thinking of little, and desiring nothing, beyond the very limited sphere of their own duties or enjoyments, and having no curiosity whatever about the affairs of others. Their behaviour to me, in particular, is, at the same time, very kind and very provoking. My table is abundantly supplied, and they seem anxious to comply with my taste in that department. But whenever I make enquiries beyond 'what's for dinner,' the brute of a lad baffles me by his *anan*, and his *dunna knaw*, and, if hard pressed, turns his back on me composedly, and leaves the room. The girl, too, pretends to be as simple as he; but an arch grin, which she cannot always suppress, seems to acknowledge that she understands perfectly well the game which she is playing, and is determined to keep me in ignorance. Both of them, and the wench in particular, treat me as they would do a spoiled child, and never directly refuse me any thing which I ask, taking care, at the same time, not to make their words good by effectually granting my request. Thus, if I desire to go out, I am promised by Dorcas that I shall walk in the park at night and see the cows milked, just as she would propose such an amusement to a child. But she takes care never to keep her word, if it is in her power to do so.

In the meantime, there has stolen on me insensibly an indifference to my freedom—a carelessness about my situation, for which I am unable to account, unless it be the consequence of weakness and loss of blood. I have read of men who, immured as I am, have surprised the world by the address with which they have successfully overcome the most formidable obstacles to their escape; and when I have heard such anecdotes, I have said to myself, that no one who is possessed only of a fragment of freestone, or a rusty nail, to grind down rivets and to pick locks, having his full leisure to employ in the task, need continue the inhabitant of a prison. Here, however, I sit, day after day, without a single effort to effect my liberation.

Yet my inactivity is not the result of despondency, but arises, in part at least, from feelings of a very different cast. My story, long a mysterious one, seems now upon the verge of some strange developement; and I feel a solemn impression that I ought to wait the course of events, to struggle against which is opposing my feeble efforts to the high will of fate. Thou, my Alan, wilt treat as timidity this passive acquiescence, which has sunk down on me like a benumbing torpor; but if thou hast remembered by what visions my couch was haunted, and dost but think of the probability that I am in the vicinity, perhaps under the same roof with G. M., thou wilt acknowledge that other feelings than pusillanimity have tended in some degree to reconcile me to my fate.

Still I own it is unmanly to submit with patience to this oppressive confinement. My heart rises against it, especially when I sit down to record my sufferings in this Journal; and I am determined, as the first step to my deliverance, to have my letters sent to the post-house.

I am disappointed. When the girl Dorcas, upon whom I had fixed for a messenger, heard me talk of sending a letter, she willingly offered her services, and received the crown which I gave her, (for my purse had not taken flight with the more valuable contents of my pocketbook,) with a smile which showed her whole set of white teeth.

But when, with the purpose of gaining some intelligence respecting my present place of abode, I asked, to which post-town she was to send or carry the letter, a stolid '*Anan*' showed me she was either ignorant of the nature of a post-office, or that, for the present, she chose to seem so.—'Simpleton!' I said, with some sharpness.

'O Lord, sir!' answered the girl, turning pale, which they always do when I show any sparks of anger,—'Don't put yourself in a passion!—I'll put the letter in the post.'

'What! and not know the name of the post-town?' said I, out of patience. 'How on earth do you propose to manage that?'

'La you there, good master. What need you frighten a poor girl that is no schollard, bating what she learned at the Charity-School of Saint Bees?'

'Is Saint Bees far from this place, Dorcas?—Do you send your letters there?' said I, in a manner as insinuating, and yet careless, as I could assume.

'Saint Bees!—La, who but a madman—begging your honour's pardon—it's a matter of twenty years since fader lived at Saint Bees, which is twenty, or forty, or I dunna know not how many miles from this part, to the West, on the coast-side; and I would not have left Saint Bees, but that fader'——

'Oh, the devil take your father!' replied I.

To which she answered, 'Nay, but thof your honour be a little how-come-so, you shouldn't damn folk's faders; and I won't stand to it, for one.'

'Oh, I beg you a thousand pardons—I wish your father no ill in the world—he was a very honest man in his way.'

'*Was* an honest man!' she exclaimed; for the Cumbrians are, it would seem, like their neighbours the Scotch, ticklish on the point of ancestry,—'He *is* a very honest man, as ever led nag with halter on head to Staneshaw-Bank Fair—Honest!—He is a horse-couper.'

'Right, right,' I replied; 'I know it—I have heard of your father—as honest as any horse-couper of them all. Why, Dorcas, I mean to buy a horse of him.'

'Ah, your honour,' sighed Dorcas, 'he is the man to serve your honour well—if ever you should get round again—or, thof you were a bit off the hooks, he would no more cheat you than'——

'Well, well, we will deal, my girl, you may depend on't. But tell me now, were I to give you a letter, what would you do to get it forward?'

'Why, put it into Squire's own bag that hangs in hall,' answered poor Dorcas. 'What else could I do? He sends it to Brampton, or to Carloisle, or where it pleases him, once a-week, and that gate.'

'Ah!' said I; 'and I suppose your sweetheart John carries it?'

'Noa—disn't now—and Jan is no sweetheart of mine, ever since he danced at his mother's feast with Kitty Rutledge, and let me sit still; that a did.'

'It was most abominable in Jan, and what I could never have thought of him,' I replied.

'O, but a did though—a let me sit still on my seat, a did.'

'Well, well, my pretty May, you will get a handsomer fellow than Jan—Jan's not the fellow for you, I see that.'

'Noa, noa,' answered the damsel; 'but he is weel aneugh for a' that, mon. But I carena a button for him; for there is the miller's son, that suitored me last Appleby Fair, when I went wi' oncle, is a gway canny lad as you will see in the sunshine.'

'Ay, a fine stout fellow—Do you think he would carry my letter to Carlisle?'

'To Carloisle! 'Twould be all his life is worth; he maun wait on clap and hopper, as they say. Odd, his father would brain him if he went to Carloisle, bating to wrestling for the belt, or sic loike. But I ha' more bachelors than him; there is the schoolmaster can write almaist as weel as tou canst, mon.'

'Then he is the very man to take charge of a letter; he knows the trouble of writing one.'

'Ay, marry does he, an tou comest to that, mon; only it takes him four hours to write as mony lines. Tan, it is a great round hand loike, that one can read easily, and not loike your honour's, that are like midge's taes. But for ganging to Carloisle, he's dead foundered, man, as cripple as Eckie's mear.'

'In the name of God,' said I, 'how is it that you propose to get my letter to the post?'

'Why, just to put it into Squire's bag loike,' reiterated Dorcas; 'he sends it by Cristal Nixon to post, as you call it, when such is his pleasure.'

Here I was then, not much edified by having obtained a list of Dorcas's bachelors; and by finding myself with respect to any information which I desired, just exactly at the point where I set out. It was of consequence to me, however, to accustom the girl to converse with me familiarly. If she did so, she could not always be on her guard, and something, I thought, might drop from her which I could turn to advantage.

'Does not the Squire usually look into his letter-bag, Dorcas?' said I, with as much indifference as I could assume.

'That a does,' said Dorcas; 'and a threw out a letter of mine to Raff Miller, because a said'——

'Well, well, I won't trouble him with mine,' said I, 'Dorcas; but, instead, I will write to himself, Dorcas. But how shall I address him?'

'Anan?' was again Dorcas's resource.

'I mean how is he called?—What is his name?'

'Sure your honour should know best,' said Dorcas.

'I know?—The devil!—You drive me beyond patience.'

'Noa, noa! donna your honour go beyond patience—donna ye now,' implored the wench. 'And for his neame, they say he has mair nor ane in Westmoreland and on the Scottish side. But he is but seldom wi' us, excepting in the cocking season; and then we just call him Squoire loike; and so do my measter and dame.'

'And is he here at present?' said I.

'Not he, not he; he is a buck-hoonting, as they tell me, somewhere up the Patterdale way; but he comes and gangs like a flap of a whirlwind, or sic loike.'

I broke off the conversation, after forcing on Dorcas a little silver to buy ribbons, with which she was so much delighted, that she exclaimed, 'God! Cristal Nixon may say his worst on thee; but thou art a civil gentleman for all him; and a quoit man wi' woman folk loike.'*

There is no sense in being too quiet with women folk, so I added a kiss with my crown piece; and I cannot help thinking, that I have secured a partisan in Dorcas. At least she blushed, and pocketed her little compliment with one hand, while, with the other, she adjusted her cherry-coloured ribbons, a little disordered by the struggle it cost me to attain the honour of a salute.

As she unlocked the door to leave the apartment, she turned back, and looking on me with a strong expression of compassion, added the remarkable words, 'La—be'st mad or no, thou'se a mettled lad, after all.'

There was something very ominous in the sound of these farewell words, which seemed to afford me a clew to the pretext under which I was detained in confinement. My demeanour was probably insane enough, while I was agitated at once by the frenzy incident to the fever, and the anxiety arising from my extraordinary situation. But is it possible they can now establish any cause for confining me, arising out of the state of my mind?

If this be really the pretext under which I am restrained from my liberty, nothing but the sedate correctness of my conduct can remove the prejudices which these circumstances may have excited in the minds of all who have approached me during my illness. I have heard—dreadful thought!—of men who, for various reasons, have been trepanned into the custody of the keepers of private madhouses, and whose brain, after years of misery, became at length unsettled, through irresistible sympathy with the wretched beings among whom they were classed. This shall not be my case, if, by strong internal resolution, it is in human nature to avoid the action of exterior and contagious sympathies.*

Meantime I sat down to compose and arrange my thoughts, for my purposed appeal to my jailer—so I must call him—whom I addressed in the following manner; having at length, and after making several copies, found language to qualify the sense of resentment which burned in the first draughts of my letter, and endeavoured to assume a tone more conciliating. I mentioned the two occasions on which he had certainly saved my life, when at the utmost peril; and I added, that whatever was the purpose of the restraint now practised on me, as I was given to understand, by his authority, it could not certainly be with any view to ultimately injuring me. He might, I said, have mistaken me for some other person; and I gave him what account I could of my situation and education, to correct such an error. I supposed it next possible, that he might think me too weak for travelling, and not capable of taking care of myself; and I begged to assure him, that I was restored to perfect health, and quite able to endure the fatigue of a journey. Lastly, I reminded him in firm though measured terms, that the restraint which I sustained was an illegal one, and highly punishable by the laws which protect the liberties of the subject. I ended by demanding, that he would take me before a magistrate; or, at least, that he would favour me with a personal interview, and explain his meaning with regard to me.

Perhaps this letter was expressed in a tone too humble for the situation of an injured man, and I am inclined to think so when I again recapitulate its tenor. But what could I do? I was in the power of one whose passions seem as violent as his means of gratifying them appear unbounded. I had reason, too, to believe [this to thee, Alan] that all his family did not approve of the violence of his conduct towards me; my object, in fine, was freedom, and who would not sacrifice much to attain it?

I had no means of addressing my letter excepting, 'For the Squire's own hand.' He could be at no great distance, for in the course of twenty-four hours I received an answer. It was addressed to Darsie Latimer, and contained these words:—'You have demanded an interview with me. You have required to be carried before a magistrate. Your first wish shall be granted—perhaps the second also. Meanwhile, be assured that you are a prisoner for the time, by competent authority, and that such authority is supported by adequate power. Beware, therefore, of struggling with a force sufficient to crush you, but abandon yourself to that train of events by which we are both swept along, and which it is impossible that either of us can resist.'

These mysterious words were without signature of any kind, and left me nothing more important to do than to prepare myself for the meeting which they promised. For that purpose I must now break off, and make sure of the manuscript,—so far as I can, in my present condition, be sure of any thing,—by concealing it within the lining of my coat, so as not to be found without strict search.

CHAPTER VI

LATIMER'S JOURNAL, IN CONTINUATION

THE important interview expected at the conclusion of my last took place sooner than I had calculated; for the very day I received the letter, and just when my dinner was finished, the Squire, or whatever he is called, entered the room so suddenly, that I almost thought I beheld an apparition. The figure of this man is peculiarly noble and stately, and his voice has that deep fulness of accent which implies unresisted authority. I had risen involuntarily as he entered; we gazed on each other for a moment in silence, which was at length broken by my visitor.

'You have desired to see me,' he said. 'I am here; if you have aught to say, let me hear it; my time is too brief to be consumed in childish dumb-show.'

'I would ask of you,' said I, 'by what authority I am detained in this place of confinement, and for what purpose?'

'I have told you already,' said he, 'that my authority is sufficient, and my power equal to it; this is all which it is necessary for you at present to know.'

'Every British subject has a right to know why he suffers restraint,' I replied; 'nor can he be deprived of liberty without a legal warrant—Show me that by which you confine me thus.'

'You shall see more,' he said; 'you shall see the magistrate by whom it is granted, and that without a moment's delay.'

This sudden proposal fluttered and alarmed me; I felt, nevertheless, that I had the right cause, and resolved to plead it boldly, although I could well have desired a little further time for preparation. He turned, however, threw open the door of the apartment, and commanded me to follow him. I felt some inclination, when I crossed the threshold of my prison-chamber, to have turned and run for it; but I knew not where to find the stairs—had reason to think the outer-doors would be secured—and, to conclude, so soon as I had quitted the room to follow the proud step of my conductor, I observed that I was dogged by Cristal Nixon, who suddenly appeared within two paces of me, and with whose great personal strength, independent of the assistance he might have received from his master, I saw no chance of contending. I therefore followed, unresistingly, and in silence, along one or two passages of much greater length than consisted with the ideas I had previously entertained of the size of the house. At length a door was flung open, and we entered a large, old-fashioned parlour, having coloured glass in the windows, oaken panelling on the wall, a huge grate, in which a large fagot or two smoked under an arched chimneypiece of stone, which bore some armorial device, whilst the walls were adorned with the usual number of heroes in armour, with large wigs instead of helmets, and ladies in sacques, smelling to nosegays.

Behind a long table, on which were several books, sat a smart underbred-looking man, wearing his own hair tied in a club, and who, from the quire of paper laid before him, and the pen which he handled at my entrance, seemed prepared to officiate as clerk. As I wish to describe these persons as accurately as possible, I may add, he wore a dark-coloured coat, corduroy breeches, and spatterdashes. At the upper end of the same table, in an ample easy-chair, covered with black leather, reposed a fat personage, about fifty years old, who either was actually a country justice, or was well selected to represent such a character. His leathern breeches were faultless in make, his jockey boots spotless in the varnish, and a handsome and flourishing pair of boot-garters, as they are called, united the one part of his garments to the other; in fine, a richly-laced scarlet waistcoat, and a purple coat, set off the neat though corpulent figure of the little man, and threw an additional bloom upon his plethoric aspect. I suppose he had dined, for it was two hours past noon, and he was amusing himself, and aiding digestion, with a pipe of tobacco. There was an air of importance in his manner which corresponded to the rural dignity of his exterior, and a habit which he had of throwing out a number of interjectional sounds, uttered with a strange variety of intonation, running from bass up to treble in a very extraordinary manner, or breaking off his sentences with a whiff of his pipe, seemed adopted to give an air of thought and mature deliberation to his opinions and decisions. Notwithstanding all this, Alan, it might be *dooted*, as our old Professor used to say, whether the Justice was any thing more than an ass. Certainly, besides a great deference for the legal opinion of his clerk, which might be quite according to the order of things, he seemed to be wonderfully under the command of his brother Squire, if squire either of them were, and indeed much more than was consistent with so much assumed consequence of his own.

'Ho—ha—ay—so—so—Hum—humph—this is the young man, I suppose—Hum—ay—seems sickly—Young gentleman, you may sit down.'

I used the permission given, for I had been much more reduced by my illness than I was aware of, and felt myself really fatigued, even by the few paces I had walked, joined to the agitation I suffered.

'And your name, young man, is—humph—ay—ha—what is it?'

'Darsie Latimer.'

'Right—ay—humph—very right. Darsie Latimer is the very thing—ha—ay—where do you come from?'

'From Scotland, sir,' I replied.

'A native of Scotland—a—humph—eh—how is it?'

'I am an Englishman by birth, sir.'

'Right—ay—yes, you are so. But pray, Mr Darsie Latimer, have you always been called by that name, or have you any other?—Nick, write down his answers, Nick.'

'As far as I remember, I never bore any other,' was my answer.

'How, no?—well I should not have thought so—Hey, neighbour, would you?'

Here he looked towards the other Squire, who had thrown himself into a chair; and, with his legs stretched out before him, and his arms folded on his bosom, seemed carelessly attending to what was going forward. He answered the appeal of the Justice by saying, that perhaps the young man's memory did not go back to a very early period.

'Ah—eh—ha—you hear the gentleman—Pray, how far may your memory be pleased to run back to?—umph?'

'Perhaps, sir, to the age of three years, or a little farther.'

'And will you presume to say, sir,' said the Squire, drawing himself suddenly erect in his seat, and exerting the strength of his powerful voice, 'that you *then* bore your present name?'

I was startled at the confidence with which this question was put, and in vain rummaged my memory for the means of replying. 'At least,' I said, 'I always remember being called Darsie; children, at that early age, seldom get more than their Christian name.'

'O, I thought so,' he replied, and again stretched himself on his seat, in the same lounging posture as before.

'So you were called Darsie in your infancy,' said the Justice; 'and hum—ay—when did you first take the name of Latimer?'

'I did not take it, sir; it was given to me.'

'I ask you,' said the lord of the mansion, but with less severity in his voice than formerly, 'whether you can remember that you were ever called Latimer, until you had that name given you in Scotland?'

'I will be candid; I cannot recollect an instance that I was so called when in England, but neither can I recollect when the name was first given me; and if any thing is to be founded on these queries and my answers, I desire my early childhood may be taken into consideration.'

'Hum—ay—yes,' said the Justice; 'all that requires consideration shall be duly considered. Young man—eh—I beg to know the name of your father and mother?'

This was galling a wound that has festered for years, and I did not endure the question so patiently as those which preceded it; but replied, 'I demand, in my turn, to know if I am before an English Justice of the Peace?'

'His worship Squire Foxley, of Foxley Hall, has been of the quorum these twenty years,' said Master Nicholas.

'Then he ought to know, or you, sir, as his clerk, should inform him,' said I, 'that I am the complainer in this case, and that my complaint ought to be heard before I am subjected to cross-examination.'

'Humph—hoy—what, ay—there is something in that, neighbour,' said the poor Justice, who, blown about by every wind of doctrine, seemed desirous to attain the sanction of his brother Squire.

'I wonder at you, Foxley,' said his firm-minded acquaintance; 'how can you render the young man justice unless you know who he is?'

'Ha—yes—egad that's true,' said Mr Justice Foxley; 'and now—looking into the matter more closely—there is, eh, upon the whole—nothing at all in what he says—so, sir, you must tell your father's name, and surname.'

'It is out of my power, sir; they are not known to me, since you must needs know so much of my private affairs.'

The Justice collected a great *afflatus* in his cheeks, which puffed them up like those of a Dutch cherub, while his eyes seemed flying out of his head, from the effort with which he retained his breath. He then blew it forth with,—'Whew!—Hoom—poof—ha!—not know your parents, youngster?—Then I must commit you for a vagrant, I warrant you. *Omne ignotum pro terribili*,* as we used to say at Appleby school; that is, every one that is not known to the Justice, is a rogue and a vagabond. Ha!—ay, you may sneer, sir; but I question if you would have known the meaning of that Latin unless I had told you.'

I acknowledged myself obliged for a new edition of the adage, and an interpretation which I could never have reached alone and unassisted. I then proceeded to state my case with greater confidence. The Justice was an ass, that was clear; but it was scarcely possible he could be so utterly ignorant as not to know what was necessary in so plain a case as mine. I therefore informed him of the riot which had been committed on the Scottish side of the Solway Frith; explained how I came to be placed in my present situation; and requested of his worship to set me at liberty. I pleaded my cause with as much earnestness as I could, casting an eye from time to time upon the opposite party, who seemed entirely indifferent to all the animation with which I accused him.

As for the Justice, when at length I had ceased, as really not knowing what more to say in a case so very plain, he replied, 'Ho—ay—ay—yes—wonderful! and so this is all the gratitude you show to this good gentleman for the great charge and trouble he hath had with respect to and concerning of you?'

'He saved my life, sir, I acknowledge, on one occasion certainly, and most probably on two; but his having done so gives him no right over my person. I am not, however, asking for any punishment or revenge; on the contrary, I am content to part friends with the gentleman, whose motives I am unwilling to suppose are bad, though his actions have been, towards me, unauthorized and violent.'

This moderation, Alan, thou wilt comprehend, was not entirely dictated by my feelings towards the individual of whom I complained; there were other reasons, in which regard for him had little share. It seemed, however, as if the mildness with which I pleaded my cause had more effect upon him than any thing I had yet said. He was moved to the point of being almost out of countenance; and took snuff repeatedly, as if to gain time to stifle some degree of emotion.

But on Justice Foxley, on whom my eloquence was particularly designed to make impression, the result was much less favourable. He consulted in a whisper with Mr Nicholas his clerk—pshawed, hemmed, and elevated his eyebrows, as if in scorn of my supplication. At length, having apparently made up his mind, he leaned back in his chair, and smoked his pipe with great energy, with a look of defiance, designed to make me aware that all my reasoning was lost on him.

At length, when I stopped, more from lack of breath than want of argument, he opened his oracular jaws, and made the following reply, interrupted by his usual interjectional ejaculations, and by long volumes of smoke:—'Hem—ay—eh—poof—And, youngster, do you think Matthew Foxley, who has been one of the quorum for these twenty years, is to be come over with such trash as would hardly cheat an apple-woman?—Poof—poof—eh! Why, man—eh—dost thou not know the charge is not a bailable matter—and that—hum—ay—the greatest man—poof—the Baron of Graystock himself, must stand committed? and yet you pretend to have been kidnapped by this gentleman, and robbed of property, and what not; and—eh—poof—you would persuade me all you want is to get away from him?—I do believe—eh—that it *is* all you want. Therefore, as you are a sort of a slip-string gentleman, and—ay—hum—a kind of idle apprentice, and something cockbrained withal, as the honest folk of the house tell me—why, you must e'en remain under custody of your guardian, till your coming of age, or my Lord Chancellor's warrant,* shall give you the management of your own affairs, which, if you can gather your brains again, you will even then not be—ay—hem—poof—in particular haste to assume.'

The time occupied by his worship's hums, and haws, and puffs of tobacco smoke, together with the slow and pompous manner in which he spoke, gave me a minute's space to collect my ideas, dispersed as they were by the extraordinary purport of this annunciation.

'I cannot conceive, sir,' I replied, 'by what singular tenure this person claims my obedience as a guardian; it is a barefaced imposture—I never in my life saw him, until I came unhappily to this country, about four weeks since.'

'Ay, sir—we—eh—know, and are aware—that—poof—you do not like to hear some folk's names; and that—eh—you understand me—there are things, and sounds, and matters, conversation about names, and such like, which put you off the hooks—which I have no humour to witness. Nevertheless, Mr Darsie—or—poof—Mr Darsie Latimer—or—poof, poof—eh—ay, Mr Darsie without the Latimer—you have acknowledged as much to-day as assures me you will best be disposed of under the honourable care of my friend here—all your confessions—besides that—poof—eh—I know him to be a most responsible person—a—hay—ay—most responsible and honourable person—Can you deny this?'

'I know nothing of him,' I repeated; 'not even his name; and I have not, as I told you, seen him in the course of my whole life, till a few weeks since.'

'Will you swear to that?' said the singular man, who seemed to await the result of this debate, secure as a rattlesnake is of the prey which has once felt its fascination. And while he said these words in a deep under-tone, he withdrew his chair a little behind that of the Justice, so as to be unseen by him or his clerk, who sat upon the same side; while he bent on me a frown so portentous, that no one who has witnessed the look can forget it during the whole of his life. The furrows of the brow above the eyes became livid and almost black, and were bent into a semicircular, or rather elliptical form, above the junction of the eyebrows. I had heard such a look described in an old tale of *diablerie*, which it was my chance to be entertained with not long since; when this deep and gloomy contortion of the frontal muscles was not unaptly described, as forming the representation of a small horseshoe.

The tale, when told, awaked a dreadful vision of infancy, which the withering and blighting look now fixed on me again forced on my recollection, but with much more vivacity. Indeed I was so much surprised, and, I must add, terrified, at the vague ideas which were awakened in my mind by this fearful sign, that I kept my eyes fixed on the face in which it was exhibited, as on a frightful vision; until, passing his handkerchief a moment across his countenance, this mysterious man relaxed at once the look which had for me something so appalling. 'The young man will no longer deny that he has seen me before,' said he to the Justice, in a tone of complacency; 'and I trust he will now be reconciled to my temporary guardianship, which may end better for him than he expects.'

'Whatever I expect,' I replied, summoning my scattered recollections together, 'I see I am neither to expect justice nor protection from this gentleman, whose office it is to render both to the lieges. For you, sir, how strangely you have wrought yourself into the fate of an unhappy young man, or what interest you can pretend in me, you yourself only can explain. That I have seen you before, is certain: for none can forget the look with which you seem to have the power of blighting those upon whom you cast it.'

The Justice seemed not very easy under this hint. 'Ho!—ay,' he said; 'it is time to be going, neighbour. I have a many miles to ride, and I care not to ride darkling in these parts.—You and I, Mr Nicholas, must be jogging.'

The Justice fumbled with his gloves, in endeavouring to draw them on hastily, and Mr Nicholas bustled to get his great-coat and whip. Their landlord endeavoured to detain them, and spoke of supper and beds. Both pouring forth many thanks for his invitation, seemed as if they would much rather not; and Mr Justice Foxley was making a score of apologies, with at least a hundred cautionary hems and eh-ehs, when the girl Dorcas burst into the room, and announced a gentleman on justice business.

'What gentleman?—and whom does he want?'

'He is cuome post on his ten toes,' said the wench; 'and on justice business to his worship loike. I'se uphald him a gentleman, for he speaks as good Latin as the schulemeaster; but, lack-a-day! he has gotten a queer mop of a wig.'

The gentleman, thus announced and described, bounced into the room. But I have already written as much as fills a sheet of my paper, and my singular embarrassments press so hard on me, that I have matter to fill another from what followed the intrusion of—my dear Alan—your crazy client—Poor Peter Peebles!*

CHAPTER VII

LATIMER'S JOURNAL, IN CONTINUATION
Sheet 2

I HAVE rarely in my life, till the last alarming days, known what it was to sustain a moment's real sorrow. What I called such, was, I am now well convinced, only the weariness of mind, which, having nothing actually present to complain of, turns upon itself, and becomes anxious about the past and the future; those periods with which human life has so little connexion, that Scripture itself hath said, 'Sufficient for the day is the evil thereof.'*

If, therefore, I have sometimes abused prosperity, by murmuring at my unknown birth and uncertain rank in society, I will make amends by bearing my present real adversity with patience and courage, and, if I can, even with gaiety. What can they—dare they, do to me?—Foxley, I am persuaded, is a real Justice of Peace, and country gentleman of estate, though (wonderful to tell!) he is an ass notwithstanding; and his functionary in the drab coat must have a shrewd guess at the consequences of being accessary to an act of murder or kidnapping. Men invite not such witnesses to deeds of darkness. I have also—Alan, I *have* hopes, arising out of the family of the oppressor himself. I am encouraged to believe that G. M. is likely again to enter on the field. More I dare not here say; nor must I drop a hint which another eye than thine might be able to construe. Enough, my feelings are lighter than they have been; and though fear and wonder are still around me, they are unable entirely to overcloud the horizon.

Even when I saw the spectral form of the old scarecrow of the Parliament-House rush into the apartment where I had undergone so singular an examination, I thought of thy connexion with him, and could almost have parodied Lear—

> 'Death!—nothing could have thus subdued nature
> To such a lowness, but his "learned lawyers."'*

He was e'en as we have seen him of yore, Alan, when, rather to keep thee company than to follow my own bent, I formerly frequented the halls of justice. The only addition to his dress, in the capacity of a traveller, was a pair of boots, that seemed as if they might have seen the field of Sheriffmoor;* so large and heavy, that, tied as they were to the creature's wearied hams with large bunches of worsted tape of various colours, they looked as if he had been dragging them along, either for a wager, or by way of penance.

Regardless of the surprised looks of the party on whom he thus intruded himself, Peter blundered into the middle of the apartment, with his head charged like a ram's in the act of butting, and saluted them thus:—

'Gude day to ye, gude day to your honours—Is't here they sell the fugie warrants?'

I observed that, on his entrance, my friend—or enemy—drew himself back, and placed himself as if he would rather avoid attracting the observation of the new-comer. I did the same myself, as far as I was able; for I thought it likely that Mr Peebles might recognise me, as indeed I was too frequently among the group of young juridical aspirants who used to amuse themselves by putting cases for Peter's solution, and playing him worse tricks; yet I was uncertain whether I had better avail myself of our acquaintance to have the advantage, such as it might be, of his evidence before the magistrate, or whether to make him, if possible, bearer of a letter which might procure me more effectual assistance. I resolved, therefore, to be guided by circumstances, and to watch carefully that nothing might escape me. I drew back as far as I could, and even reconnoitred the door and passage, to consider whether absolute escape might not be practicable. But there paraded Cristal Nixon, whose little black eyes, sharp as those of a basilisk, seemed, the instant when they encountered mine, to penetrate my purpose.

I sat down, as much out of sight of all parties as I could, and listened to the dialogue which followed—a dialogue how much more interesting to me than any I could have conceived, in which Peter Peebles was to be one of the *Dramatis Personae*!

'Is it here where ye sell the warrants?—the fugies, ye ken?' said Peter.

'Hey—eh—what!' said Justice Foxley; 'what the devil does the fellow mean?—What would you have a warrant for?'

'It is to apprehend a young lawyer that is *in meditatione fugae*; for he has ta'en my memorial and pleaded my cause, and a good fee I gave him, and as muckle brandy as he could drink that day at his father's house—he loes the brandy ower weel for sae youthful a creature.'

'And what has this drunken young dog of a lawyer done to you, that you are come to me—eh—ha? Has he robbed you? Not unlikely, if he be a lawyer—eh—Nick—ha?' said Justice Foxley.

'He has robbed me of himself, sir,' answered Peter; 'of his help, comfort, aid, maintenance, and assistance, whilk, as a counsel to a client, he is bound to yield me *ratione officii*—that is it, ye see. He has pouched my fee, and drucken a mutchkin of brandy, and now he's ower the march, and left my cause, half won half lost—as dead a heat as e'er was run ower the back-sands. Now, I was advised by some cunning laddies that are used to crack a bit law wi' me in the House, that the best thing I could do was to take heart o' grace and set out after him; so I have taken post on my ain shanks, forby a cast in a cart, or the like. I got wind of him in Dumfries, and now I have run him ower to the English side, and I want a fugie warrant against him.'

How did my heart throb at this information, dearest Alan! Thou art near me then, and I well know with what kind purpose; thou hast abandoned all to fly to my assistance; and no wonder that, knowing thy friendship and faith, thy sound sagacity and persevering disposition, 'my bosom's lord should now sit lightly on his throne;'* that gaiety should almost involuntarily hover on my pen; and that my heart should beat like that of a general, responsive to the drums of his advancing ally, without whose help the battle must have been lost.

I did not suffer myself to be startled by this joyous surprise, but continued to bend my strictest attention to what followed among this singular party. That Poor Peter Peebles had been put upon this wildgoose chase, by some of his juvenile advisers in the Parliament House, he himself had intimated; but he spoke with much confidence, and the Justice, who seemed to have some secret apprehension of being put to trouble in the matter, and, as sometimes occurs on the English frontier, a jealousy lest the superior acuteness of their northern neighbours might overreach their own simplicity, turned to his clerk with a perplexed countenance.

'Eh—oh—Nick—d—n thee—Hast thou got nothing to say? This is more Scots law, I take it, and more Scotsmen.' (Here he cast a side-glance at the owner of the mansion, and winked to his clerk.) 'I would Solway were as deep as it is wide, and we had then some chance of keeping of them out.'

Nicholas conversed an instant aside with the supplicant, and then reported;—

'The man wants a border-warrant, I think; but they are only granted for debt—now he wants one to catch a lawyer.'

'And what for no?' answered Peter Peebles, doggedly; 'what for no, I would be glad to ken? If a day-labourer refuses to work, ye'll grant a warrant to gar him do out his daurg—if a wench quean rin away from her hairst, ye'll send her back to her heuck again—if sae mickle as a collier or a salter* make a moonlight flitting, ye will cleek him by the back-spaul in a minute of time,—and yet the damage canna amount to mair than a creelfu' of coals, and a forpit or twa of saut; and here is a chield taks leg from his engagement, and damages me to the tune of sax thousand punds sterling; that is, three thousand that I should win, and three thousand mair that I am like to lose; and you that ca' yoursell a justice canna help a poor man to catch the rinaway? A bonny like justice I am like to get amang ye!'

'The fellow must be drunk,' said the clerk.

'Black-fasting from all but sin,' replied the supplicant; 'I havena had mair than a mouthful of cauld water since I passed the Border, and deil a ane of ye is like to say to me, "Dog, will ye drink?"'

The Justice seemed moved by this appeal. 'Hem—tush, man,' replied he; 'thou speak'st to us as if thou wert in presence of one of thine own beggarly justices*—get down stairs—get something to eat, man, (with permission of my friend to make so free in his house,) and a mouthful to drink, and I will warrant we get ye such justice as will please ye.'

'I winna refuse your neighbourly offer,' said Poor Peter Peebles, making his bow; 'muckle grace be wi' your honour, and wisdom to guide ye in this extraordinary cause.'

When I saw Peter Peebles about to retire from the room, I could not forbear an effort to obtain from him such evidence as might give me some credit with the Justice. I stepped forward, therefore, and, saluting him, asked him if he remembered me?

After a stare or two, and a long pinch of snuff, recollection seemed suddenly to dawn on Peter Peebles. 'Recollect ye!' he said; 'by my troth do I.—Haud him a grip, gentlemen!—constables, keep him fast! where that ill-deedy hempy is, ye are sure that Alan Fairford is not far off.—Haud him fast, Master Constable; I charge ye wi' him, for I am mista'en if he is not at the bottom of this rinaway business. He was aye getting the silly callant Alan awa wi' gigs, and horse, and the like of that, to Roslin, and Prestonpans, and a' the idle gates he could think of. He's a rinaway apprentice, that ane.'

'Mr Peebles,' I said, 'do not do me wrong. I am sure you can say no harm of me justly, but can satisfy these gentlemen, if you will, that I am a student of law in Edinburgh—Darsie Latimer by name.'

'Me satisfy! how can I satisfy the gentlemen,' answered Peter, 'that am sae far from being satisfied mysell? I ken naething about your name, and can only testify, *nihil novit in causa*.'

'A pretty witness you have brought forward in your favour,' said Mr Foxley. 'But—ha—ay—I'll ask him a question or two.—Pray, friend, will you take your oath to this youth being a runaway apprentice?'

'Sir,' said Peter, 'I will make oath to ony thing in reason; when a case comes to my oath it's a won cause: But I am in some haste to prie your worship's good cheer;' for Peter had become much more respectful in his demeanour towards the Justice, since he had heard some intimation of dinner.

'You shall have—eh—hum—ay—a bellyful, if it be possible to fill it. First let me know if this young man be really what he pretends.—Nick, make his affidavit.'

'Ou, he is just a wud harum-scarum creature, that wad never take to his studies; daft, sir, clean daft.'

'Deft!' said the Justice; 'what d'ye mean by deft—eh?'

'Just Fifish,' replied Peter; 'wowf—a wee bit by the East-Nook or sae; it's a common case—the tae half of the warld thinks the tither daft. I have met with folk in my day, that thought I was daft mysell; and, for my part, I think our Court of Session clean daft, that have had the great cause of Peebles against Plainstanes before them for this score of years, and have never been able to ding the bottom out of it yet.'

'I cannot make out a word of his cursed brogue,' said the Cumbrian justice; 'can you, neighbour—eh? What can he mean by *deft*?'

'He means *mad*,' said the party appealed to, thrown off his guard by impatience of this protracted discussion.

'Ye have it—ye have it,' said Peter; 'that is, not clean skivie, but'——

Here he stopped, and fixed his eye on the person he addressed with an air of joyful recognition.—'Ay, ay, Mr Herries of Birrenswork, is this your ainsell in blood and bane? I thought ye had been hanged at Kennington Common, or Hairiebie,* or some of these places, after the bonny ploy ye made in the forty-five.'

'I believe you are mistaken, friend,' said Herries, sternly, with whose name and designation I was thus made unexpectedly acquainted.

'The deil a bit,' answered the undaunted Peter Peebles; 'I mind ye weel, for ye lodged in my house the great year of forty-five, for a great year it was; the Grand Rebellion broke out, and my cause—the great cause—Pebbles against Plainstanes, *et per contra*—was called in the beginning of the winter Session, and would have been heard, but that there was a surcease of justice, with your plaids, and your piping, and your nonsense.'

'I tell you, fellow,' said Herries, yet more fiercely, 'you have confused me with some of the other furniture of your crazy pate.'

'Speak like a gentleman, sir,' answered Peebles; 'these are not legal phrases, Mr Herries of Birrenswork. Speak in form of law, or I sall bid ye gude-day, sir. I have nae pleasure in speaking to proud folk, though I am willing to answer ony thing in a legal way; so if you are for a crack about auld langsyne, and the splores that you and Captain Redgimlet used to breed in my house, and the girded cask of brandy that ye drank and ne'er thought of paying for it, (not that I minded it muckle in thae days, though I have felt a lack of it sinsyne,) why I will waste an hour on ye at ony time.—And where is Captain Redgimlet now? he was a wild chap, like yoursell, Birrenswork. I trust ye hae gotten out your pardon though they are nae sae keen after you poor bodies for these some years bygane; the heading and hanging is weel ower now—awful job—awful job—will ye try my sneeshing?'

He concluded his desultory speech by thrusting out his large bony paw, filled with a Scottish mull of huge dimensions, which Herries, who had been standing like one petrified by the assurance of this unexpected address, rejected with a contemptuous motion of his hand, which spilled some of the contents of the box.

'Aweel, aweel,' said Peter Peebles, totally unabashed by the repulse, 'e'en as ye like, a wilful man maun hae his way; but,' he added, stooping down, and endeavouring to gather the spilt snuff from the polished floor, 'I canna afford to lose my sneeshing for a' that ye are gumple-foisted wi' me.'

My attention had been keenly awakened, during this extraordinary and unexpected scene. I watched, with as much attention as my own agitation permitted me to command, the effect produced on the parties concerned. It was evident that our friend, Peter Peebles, had unwarily let out something which altered the sentiments of Justice Foxley and his clerk towards Mr Herries, with whom, until he was known and acknowledged under that name, they had appeared to be so intimate. They talked with each other aside, looked at a paper or two which the clerk selected from the contents of a huge black pocketbook, and seemed, under the influence of fear and uncertainty, totally at a loss what line of conduct to adopt.

Herries made a different and a far more interesting figure. However little Peter Peebles might resemble the angel Ithuriel, the appearance of Herries, his high and scornful demeanour, vexed at what seemed detection, yet fearless of the consequences, and regarding the whispering magistrate and his clerk with looks in which contempt predominated over anger or anxiety, bore, in my opinion, no slight resemblance to

——'the regal port
And faded splendour wan'—

with which the poet has invested the detected King of the Powers of the Air.*

As he glanced round, with a look which he had endeavoured to compose to haughty indifference, his eye encountered mine, and, I thought, at the first glance sunk beneath it. But he instantly rallied his natural spirit, and returned me one of those extraordinary looks, by which he could contort so strangely the wrinkles on his forehead. I started; but, angry at myself for my pusillanimity, I answered him by a look of the same kind, and, catching the reflection of my countenance in a large antique mirror which stood before me, I started again at the real or imaginary resemblance which my countenance, at that moment, bore to that of Herries. Surely my fate is somehow strangely interwoven with that of this mysterious individual. I had no time at present to speculate upon the subject, for the subsequent conversation demanded all my attention.

The Justice addressed Herries, after a pause of about five minutes, in which all parties seemed at some loss how to proceed. He spoke with embarrassment, and his faltering voice, and the long intervals which divided his sentences, seemed to indicate fear of him whom he addressed.

'Neighbour,' he said, 'I could not have thought this; or, if *I*—eh—*did* think—in a corner of my own mind as it were—that you, I say—that you might have unluckily engaged in—eh—the matter of the forty-five—there was still time to have forgot all that.'

'And is it so singular that a man should have been out in the forty-five?' said Herries, with contemptuous composure;—'your father, I think, Mr Foxley, was out with Derwentwater in the fifteen.'*

'And lost half of his estate,' answered Foxley, with more rapidity than usual; 'and was very near—hem—being hanged into the boot. But this is—another guess job—for—eh—fifteen is not forty-five; and my father had a remission,* and you, I take it, have none.'

'Perhaps I have,' said Herries, indifferently; 'or, if I have not, I am but in the case of half a dozen others whom government do not think worth looking after at this time of day, so they give no offence or disturbance.'

'But you have given both, sir,' said Nicholas Faggot, the clerk, who, having some petty provincial situation, as I have since understood, deemed himself bound to be zealous for government. 'Mr Justice Foxley cannot be answerable for letting you pass free, now your name and surname have been spoken plainly out. There are warrants out against you from the Secretary of State's office.'*

'A proper allegation, Mr Attorney! that, at the distance of so many years, the Secretary of State should trouble himself about the unfortunate relics of a ruined cause!' answered Mr Herries.

'But if it be so,' said the clerk, who seemed to assume more confidence upon the composure of Herries's demeanour; 'and if cause has been given by the conduct of a gentleman himself, who hath been, it is alleged, raking up old matters, and mixing them with new subjects of disaffection—I say, if it be so, I should advise the party, in his wisdom, to surrender himself quietly into the lawful custody of the next Justice of Peace—Mr Foxley, suppose—where, and by whom, the matter should be regularly enquired into. I am only putting a case,' he added, watching with apprehension the effect which his words were likely to produce upon the party to whom they were addressed.

'And were I to receive such advice,' said Herries, with the same composure as before—'putting the case, as you say, Mr Faggot—I should request to see the warrant which countenanced such a scandalous proceeding.'

Mr Nicholas, by way of answer, placed in his hand a paper, and seemed anxiously to expect the consequences which were to ensue. Mr Herries looked it over with the same equanimity as before, and then continued, 'And were such a scrawl as this presented to me in my own house, I would throw it into the chimney, and Mr Faggot upon the top of it.'

Accordingly, seconding the word with the action, he flung the warrant into the fire with one hand, and fixed the other, with a stern and irresistible gripe, on the breast of the attorney, who, totally unable to contend with him, in either personal strength or mental energy, trembled like a chicken in the raven's clutch. He got off, however, for the fright; for Herries, having probably made him fully sensible of the strength of his grasp, released him, with a scornful laugh.

'Deforcement—spulzie—stouthrief—masterful rescue!' exclaimed Peter Peebles, scandalized at the resistance offered to the law in the person of Nicholas Faggot. But his shrill exclamations were drowned in the thundering voice of Herries, who, calling upon Cristal Nixon, ordered him to take the bawling fool down stairs, fill his belly, and then give him a guinea, and thrust him out of doors. Under such injunctions, Peter easily suffered himself to be withdrawn from the scene.

Herries then turned to the Justice, whose visage, wholly abandoned by the rubicund hue which so lately beamed upon it, hung out the same pale livery as that of his dismayed clerk. 'Old friend and acquaintance,' he said, 'you came here at my request, on a friendly errand, to convince this silly young man of the right which I have over his person for the present. I trust you do not intend to make your visit the pretext of disquieting me about other matters? All the world knows that I have been living at large, in these northern counties, for some months, not to say years, and might have been apprehended at any time, had the necessities of the state required, or my own behaviour deserved it. But no English magistrate has been ungenerous enough to trouble a gentleman under misfortune, on account of political opinions and disputes, which have been long ended by the success of the reigning powers. I trust, my good friend, you will not endanger yourself, by taking any other view of the subject than you have done ever since we were acquainted?'

The Justice answered with more readiness, as well as more spirit than usual, 'Neighbour Ingoldsby—what you say—is—eh—in some sort true; and when you were coming and going at markets, horse-races, and cock-fights, fairs, hunts, and such like—it was—eh—neither my business nor my wish to dispel—I say—to enquire into and dispel the mysteries which hung about you; for while you were a good companion in the field, and over a bottle now and then—I did not—eh—think it necessary to ask—into your private affairs. And if I thought you were—ahem—somewhat unfortunate in former undertakings, and enterprises, and connexions, which might cause you to live unsettledly and more private, I could have—eh—very little pleasure—to aggravate your case by interfering, or requiring explanations, which are often more easily asked than given. But when there are warrants and witnesses to names—and those names, christian and surname, belong to—eh—an attainted person—charged—I trust falsely—with—ahem—taking advantage of modern broils and heart-burnings to renew our civil disturbances, the case is altered; and I must—ahem—do my duty.'

The Justice got on his feet as he concluded this speech, and looked as bold as he could. I drew close beside him and his clerk, Mr Faggot, thinking the moment favourable for my own liberation, and intimated to Mr Foxley my determination to stand by him. But Mr Herries only laughed at the menacing posture which we assumed. 'My good neighbour,' said he, 'you talk of a witness—Is yon crazy beggar a fit witness in an affair of this nature?'

'But you do not deny that you are Mr Herries of Birrenswork, mentioned in the Secretary of State's warrant?' said Mr Foxley.

'How can I deny or own any thing about it?' said Herries, with a sneer. 'There is no such warrant in existence now; its ashes, like the poor traitor whose doom it threatened, have been dispersed to the four winds of heaven. There is now no warrant in the world.'

'But you will not deny,' said the Justice, 'that you were the person named in it; and that—eh—your own act destroyed it?'

'I will neither deny my name nor my actions, Justice,' replied Mr Herries, 'when called upon by competent authority to avow or defend them. But I will resist all impertinent attempts either to intrude into my private motives, or to control my person. I am quite well prepared to do so; and I trust that you, my good neighbour and brother sportsman, in your expostulation, and my friend Mr Nicholas Faggot here, in his humble advice and petition that I should surrender myself, will consider yourselves as having amply discharged your duty to King George and Government.'

The cold and ironical tone in which he made this declaration; the look and attitude, so nobly expressive of absolute confidence in his own superior strength and energy, seemed to complete the indecision which had already shown itself on the side of those whom he addressed.

The Justice looked to the Clerk—the Clerk to the Justice; the former *ha'd*, *eh'd*, without bringing forth an articulate syllable; the latter only said, 'As the warrant is destroyed, Mr Justice, I presume you do not mean to proceed with the arrest?'

'Hum—ay—why no—Nicholas—it would not be quite advisable—and as the Forty-five was an old affair—and—hem—as my friend here will, I hope, see his error—that is, if he has not seen it already—and renounce the Pope, the Devil, and the Pretender—I mean no harm, neighbour—I think we—as we have no *posse*, or constables, or the like—should order our horses—and, in one word, look the matter over.'

'Judiciously resolved,' said the person whom this decision affected; 'but before you go, I trust you will drink and be friends?'

'Why,' said the Justice, rubbing his brow, 'our business has been—hem—rather a thirsty one.'

'Cristal Nixon,' said Mr Herries, 'let us have a cool tankard instantly, large enough to quench the thirst of the whole commission.'

While Cristal was absent on this genial errand, there was a pause, of which I endeavoured to avail myself, by bringing back the discourse to my own concerns. 'Sir,' I said to Justice Foxley, 'I have no direct business with your late discussion with Mr Herries, only just thus far—You leave me, a loyal subject of King George, an unwilling prisoner in the hands of a person whom you have reason to believe unfriendly to the King's cause. I humbly submit that this is contrary to your duty as a magistrate, and that you ought to make Mr Herries aware of the illegality of his proceedings, and take steps for my rescue, either upon the spot, or, at least, as soon as possible after you have left this case'——

'Young man,' said Mr Justice Foxley, 'I would have you remember you are under the power, the lawful power—ahem—of your guardian.'

'He calls himself so, indeed,' I replied; 'but he has shown no evidence to establish so absurd a claim; and if he had, his circumstances, as an attainted traitor excepted from pardon, would void such a right, if it existed. I do therefore desire you, Mr Justice, and you, his clerk, to consider my situation, and afford me relief at your peril.'

'Here is a young fellow now,' said the Justice, with much embarrassed looks, 'thinks that I carry the whole statute law of England in my head, and a *posse comitatus* to execute them in my pocket! Why, what good would my interference do?—but—hum—eh—I will speak to your guardian in your favour.'

He took Mr Herries aside, and seemed indeed to urge something upon him with much earnestness; and perhaps such a species of intercession was all which, in the circumstances, I was entitled to expect from him.

They often looked at me as they spoke together; and as Cristal Nixon entered with a huge four-pottle tankard, filled with the beverage his master had demanded, Herries turned away from Mr Foxley somewhat impatiently, saying with emphasis, 'I give you my word of honour, that you have not the slightest reason to apprehend any thing on his account.' He then took up the tankard, and saying aloud in Gaelic, '*Slaint an Rey*,'[42] just tasted the liquor, and handed the tankard to Justice Foxley, who, to avoid the dilemma of pledging him to what might be the Pretender's health, drank to Mr Herries's own, with much pointed solemnity, but in a draught far less moderate.

The clerk imitated the example of his principal, and I was fain to follow their example, for anxiety and fear are at least as thirsty as sorrow is said to be. In a word, we exhausted the composition of ale, sherry, lemon-juice, nutmeg, and other good things, stranded upon the silver bottom of the tankard, the huge toast, as well as the roasted orange, which had whilome floated jollily upon the brim, and rendered legible Dr Byrom's celebrated lines* engraved thereon—

> 'God bless the King!—God bless the Faith's defender!
> God bless—No harm in blessing the Pretender.
> Who that Pretender is, and who that King,—
> God bless us all!—is quite another thing.'

I had time enough to study this effusion of the Jacobite muse, while the Justice was engaged in the somewhat tedious ceremony of taking leave. That of Mr Faggot was less ceremonious; but I suspect something besides empty compliment passed betwixt him and Mr Herries; for I remarked that the latter slipped a piece of paper into the hand of the former, which might perhaps be a little atonement for the rashness with which he had burnt the warrant, and imposed no gentle hand on the respectable minion of the law by whom it was exhibited; and I observed that he made this propitiation in such a manner as to be secret from the worthy clerk's principal.

When this was arranged, the party took leave of each other, with much formality on the part of Squire Foxley, amongst whose adieus the following phrase was chiefly remarkable:—'I presume you do not intend to stay long in these parts?'

'Not for the present, Justice, you may be sure; there are good reasons to the contrary. But I have no doubt of arranging my affairs, so that we shall speedily have sport together again.'

He went to wait upon the Justice to the court-yard; and, as he did so, commanded Cristal Nixon to see that I returned into my apartment. Knowing it would be to no purpose to resist or tamper with that stubborn functionary, I obeyed in silence, and was once more a prisoner in my former quarters.

CHAPTER VIII

LATIMER'S JOURNAL IN CONTINUATION

I SPENT more than an hour, after returning to the apartment which I may call my prison, in reducing to writing the singular circumstances which I had just witnessed. Methought I could now form some guess at the character of Mr Herries, upon whose name and situation the late scene had thrown considerable light;—one of those fanatical Jacobites, doubtless, whose arms, not twenty years since, had shaken the British throne, and some of whom, though their party daily diminished in numbers, energy, and power, retained still an inclination to renew the attempt they had found so desperate. He was indeed perfectly different from the sort of zealous Jacobites whom it had been my luck hitherto to meet with. Old ladies of family over their hyson, and grey-haired lairds over their punch, I had often heard utter a little harmless treason; while the former remembered having led down a dance with the Chevalier, and the latter recounted the feats they had performed at Preston, Clifton, and Falkirk.*

The disaffection of such persons was too unimportant to excite the attention of government. I had heard, however, that there still existed partisans of the Stewart family, of a more daring and dangerous description; men who, furnished with gold from Rome, moved, secretly and in disguise, through the various classes of society, and endeavoured to keep alive the expiring zeal of their party.

I had no difficulty in assigning an important post among this class of persons, whose agency and exertion are only doubted by those who look on the surface of things, to this Mr Herries, whose mental energies, as well as his personal strength and activity, seemed to qualify him well to act so dangerous a part; and I knew that, all along the Western Border, both in England and Scotland, there are so many Nonjurors, that such a person may reside there with absolute safety, unless it becomes, in a very especial degree, the object of the government to secure his person; and which purpose, even then, might be disappointed by early intelligence, or, as in the case of Mr Foxley, by the unwillingness of provincial magistrates to interfere in what is now considered an invidious pursuit of the unfortunate.

There have, however, been rumours lately, as if the present state of the nation, or at least of some discontented provinces, agitated by a variety of causes, but particularly by the unpopularity of the present administration, may seem to this species of agitators a favourable period for recommencing their intrigues; while, on the other hand, government may not, at such a crisis, be inclined to look upon them with the contempt which a few years ago would have been their most appropriate punishment.*

That men should be found rash enough to throw away their services and lives in a desperate cause, is nothing new in history, which abounds with instances of similar devotion—that Mr Herries is such an enthusiast, is no less evident; but all this explains not his conduct towards *me*. Had he sought to make me a proselyte to his ruined cause, violence and compulsion were arguments very unlikely to prevail with any generous spirit. But even if such were his object, of what use to him could be the acquisition of a single reluctant partisan, who could bring only his own person to support any quarrel which he might adopt? He had claimed over me the rights of a guardian; he had more than hinted that I was in a state of mind which could not dispense with the authority of such a person. Was this man, so sternly desperate in his purpose,—he who seemed willing to take on his own shoulders the entire support of a cause which had been ruinous to thousands,—was he the person that had the power of deciding on my fate? Was it from him those dangers flowed, to secure me against which I had been educated under such circumstances of secrecy and precaution?

And if this was so, of what nature was the claim which he asserted?—Was it that of propinquity?—And did I share the blood, perhaps the features, of this singular being?—Strange as it may seem, a thrill of awe, which shot across my mind at that instant, was not unmingled with a wild and mysterious feeling of wonder, almost amounting to pleasure. I remembered the reflection of my own face in the mirror, at one striking moment during the singular interview of the day, and I hastened to the outward apartment to consult a glass which hung there, whether it were possible for my countenance to be again contorted into the peculiar frown which so much resembled the terrific look of Herries. But I folded my brows in vain into a thousand complicated wrinkles, and I was obliged to conclude, either that the supposed mark on my brow was altogether imaginary, or that it could not be called forth by voluntary effort; or, in fine, what seemed most likely, that it was such a resemblance as the imagination traces in the embers of a wood fire, or among the varied veins of marble, distinct at one time, and obscure or invisible at another, according as the combination of lines strikes the eye, or impresses the fancy.

While I was moulding my visage like a mad player, the door suddenly opened, and the girl of the house entered. Angry and ashamed at being detected in my singular occupation, I turned round sharply, and, I suppose, chance produced the change on my features which I had been in vain labouring to call forth.

The girl started back, with her 'Don't ye look so now—don't ye, for love's sake—you be as like the ould Squoire as—But here a comes,' said she, huddling away out of the room; 'and if you want a third, there is none but ould Harry, as I know of, that can match ye for a brent broo!'

As the girl muttered this exclamation, and hastened out of the room, Herries entered. He stopped on observing that I had looked again to the mirror; anxious to trace the look by which the wench had undoubtedly been terrified. He seemed to guess what was passing in my mind, for, as I turned towards him, he observed, 'Doubt not that it is stamped on your forehead—the fatal mark of our race; though it is not now so apparent as it will become when age and sorrow, and the traces of stormy passions, and of bitter penitence, shall have drawn their furrows on your brow.'

'Mysterious man,' I replied, 'I know not of what you speak; your language is as dark as your purposes.'

'Sit down, then,' he said, 'and listen; thus far, at least, must the veil of which you complain be raised. When withdrawn, it will only display guilt and sorrow—guilt, followed by strange penalty, and sorrow, which Providence has entailed upon the posterity of the mourners.'

He paused a moment, and commenced his narrative, which he told with the air of one, who, remote as the events were which he recited, took still the deepest interest in them. The tone of his voice, which I have already described as rich and powerful, aided by its inflections the effects of his story, which I will endeavour to write down, as nearly as possible, in the very words which he used.

'It was not of late years that the English nation learned, that their best chance of conquering their independent neighbours must be by introducing amongst them division and civil war. You need not be reminded of the state of thraldom to which Scotland was reduced by the unhappy wars betwixt the domestic factions of Bruce and Baliol; nor how, after Scotland had been emancipated from a foreign yoke, by the conduct and valour of the immortal Bruce, the whole fruits of the triumphs of Bannockburn were lost in the dreadful defeats of Dupplin and Halidon; and Edward Baliol, the minion and feudatory of his namesake of England, seemed, for a brief season, in safe and uncontested possession of the throne, so lately occupied by the greatest general and wisest prince in Europe. But the experience of Bruce had not died with him. There were many who had shared his martial labours, and all remembered the successful efforts by which, under circumstances as disadvantageous as those of his son, he had achieved the liberation of Scotland.*

'The usurper, Edward Baliol, was feasting with a few of his favourite retainers in the Castle of Annan, when he was suddenly surprised by a chosen band of insurgent patriots. Their chiefs were, Douglas, Randolph, the young Earl of Moray, and Sir Simon Fraser;* and their success was so complete, that Baliol was obliged to fly for his life, scarcely clothed, and on a horse which there was no leisure to saddle. It was of importance to seize his person, if possible, and his flight was closely pursued by a valiant knight of Norman descent, whose family had been long settled in the marches of Dumfries-shire. Their Norman appellation was Fitz-Aldin, but this knight, from the great slaughter which he had made of the Southron, and the reluctance which he had shown to admit them to quarter during the former wars of that bloody period, had acquired the name of Redgauntlet, which he transmitted to his posterity'——

'Redgauntlet!' I involuntarily repeated.

'Yes, Redgauntlet,' said my alleged guardian, looking at me keenly; 'does that name recall any associations to your mind?'

'No,' I replied, 'except that I lately heard it given to the hero of a supernatural legend.'

'There are many such current concerning the family,' he answered; and then proceeded in his narrative.

'Alberick Redgauntlet, the first of his house so termed, was, as may be supposed from his name, of a stern and implacable disposition, which had been rendered more so by family discord. An only son, now a youth of eighteen, shared so much the haughty spirit of his father, that he became impatient of domestic control, resisted paternal authority, and finally fled from his father's house, renounced his political opinions, and awakened his mortal displeasure by joining the adherents of Baliol. It was said that his father cursed in his wrath his degenerate offspring, and swore that, if they met, he should perish by his hand. Meantime, circumstances seemed to promise atonement for this great deprivation. The lady of Alberick Redgauntlet was again, after many years, in a situation which afforded her husband the hope of a more dutiful heir.

'But the delicacy and deep interest of his wife's condition did not prevent Alberick from engaging in the undertaking of Douglas and Moray. He had been the most forward in the attack of the castle, and was now foremost in the pursuit of Baliol, eagerly engaged in dispersing or cutting down the few daring followers who endeavoured to protect the usurper in his flight.

'As these were successively routed or slain, the formidable Redgauntlet, the mortal enemy of the House of Baliol, was within two lances' length of the fugitive Edward Baliol, in a narrow pass, when a youth, one of the last who attended the usurper in his flight, threw himself between them, received the shock of the pursuer, and was unhorsed and overthrown. The helmet rolled from his head, and the beams of the sun, then rising over the Solway, showed Redgauntlet the features of his disobedient son, in the livery, and wearing the cognizance, of the usurper.

'Redgauntlet beheld his son lying before his horse's feet; but he also saw Baliol, the usurper of the Scottish crown, still, as it seemed, within his grasp, and separated from him only by the prostrate body of his overthrown adherent. Without pausing to enquire whether young Edward was wounded, he dashed his spurs into his horse, meaning to leap over him, but was unhappily frustrated in his purpose. The steed made indeed a bound forward, but was unable to clear the body of the youth, and with its hind foot struck him in the forehead, as he was in the act of rising. The blow was mortal. It is needless to add, that the pursuit was checked, and Baliol escaped.

'Redgauntlet, ferocious as he is described, was yet overwhelmed with the thoughts of the crime he had committed. When he returned to his castle, it was to encounter new domestic sorrows. His wife had been prematurely seized with the pangs of labour, upon hearing the dreadful catastrophe which had taken place. The birth of an infant boy cost her her life. Redgauntlet sat by her corpse for more than twenty-four hours without changing either feature or posture, so far as his terrified domestics could observe. The Abbot of Dundrennan* preached consolation to him in vain. Douglas, who came to visit in his affliction a patriot of such distinguished zeal, was more successful in rousing his attention. He caused the trumpets to sound an English point of war in the court-yard, and Redgauntlet at once sprung to his arms, and seemed restored to the recollection, which had been lost in the extent of his misery.

'From that moment, whatever he might feel inwardly, he gave way to no outward emotion. Douglas caused his infant to be brought; but even the iron-hearted soldiers were struck with horror to observe, that, by the mysterious law of nature, the cause of his mother's death, and the evidence of his father's guilt, was stamped on the innocent face of the babe, whose brow was distinctly marked by the miniature resemblance of a horseshoe. Redgauntlet himself pointed it out to Douglas, saying, with a ghastly smile, 'It should have been bloody.'

'Moved, as he was, to compassion for his brother-in-arms, and steeled against all softer feelings by the habits of civil war, Douglas shuddered at this sight, and displayed a desire to leave the house which was doomed to be the scene of such horrors. As his parting advice, he exhorted Alberick Redgauntlet to make a pilgrimage to

Saint Ninian's of Whiteherne,* then esteemed a shrine of great sanctity; and departed with a precipitation, which might have aggravated, had that been possible, the forlorn state of his unhappy friend. But that seems to have been incapable of admitting any addition. Sir Alberick caused the bodies of his slaughtered son and the mother to be laid side by side in the ancient chapel of his house, after he had used the skill of a celebrated surgeon of that time to embalm them; and it was said, that for many weeks he spent some hours nightly in the vault where they reposed.

'At length he undertook the proposed pilgrimage to Whiteherne, where he confessed himself for the first time since his misfortune, and was shrived by an aged monk, who afterwards died in the odour of sanctity. It is said, that it was then foretold to the Redgauntlet, that on account of his unshaken patriotism, his family should continue to be powerful amid the changes of future times; but that, in detestation of his unrelenting cruelty to his own issue, Heaven had decreed that the valour of his race should always be fruitless, and that the cause which they espoused should never prosper.

'Submitting to such penance as was there imposed, Sir Alberick went, it is thought, on a pilgrimage either to Rome, or to the Holy Sepulchre itself. He was universally considered as dead; and it was not till thirteen years afterwards, that, in the great battle of Durham,* fought between David Bruce and Queen Philippa of England, a knight, bearing a horseshoe for his crest, appeared in the van of the Scottish army, distinguishing himself by his reckless and desperate valour; who being at length overpowered and slain, was finally discovered to be the brave and unhappy Sir Alberick Redgauntlet.'

'And has the fatal sign,' said I, when Herries had ended his narrative, 'descended on all the posterity of this unhappy house?'

'It has been so handed down from antiquity, and is still believed,' said Herries. 'But perhaps there is, in the popular evidence, something of that fancy which creates what it sees. Certainly, as other families have peculiarities by which they are distinguished, this of Redgauntlet is marked in most individuals by a singular indenture of the forehead, supposed to be derived from the son of Alberick, their ancestor, and brother to the unfortunate Edward, who had perished in so piteous a manner. It is certain there seems to have been a fate upon the House of Redgauntlet, which has been on the losing side in almost all the civil broils which have divided the kingdom of Scotland, from David Bruce's days, till the late valiant and unsuccessful attempt of the Chevalier Charles Edward.'

He concluded with a deep sigh, as one whom the subject had involved in a train of painful reflections.

'And am I then,' I exclaimed, 'descended from this unhappy

race?—Do you too belong to it?—And if so, why do I sustain restraint and hard usage at the hands of a relation?'

'Enquire no farther for the present,' he said. 'The line of conduct which I am pursuing towards you, is dictated not by choice, but by necessity. You were withdrawn from the bosom of your family, and the care of your legal guardian, by the timidity and ignorance of a doting mother, who was incapable of estimating the arguments or feelings of those who prefer honour and principle to fortune, and even to life. The young hawk, accustomed only to the fostering care of its dam, must be tamed by darkness and sleeplessness, ere it is trusted on the wing for the purposes of the falconer.'

I was appalled at this declaration, which seemed to threaten a long continuance, and a dangerous termination, of my captivity. I deemed it best, however, to show some spirit, and at the same time to mingle a tone of conciliation. 'Mr Herries,' I said, '(if I call you rightly by that name,) let us speak upon this matter without the tone of mystery and fear in which you seem inclined to envelope it. I have been long, alas! deprived of the care of that affectionate mother to whom you allude—long under the charge of strangers—and compelled to form my own resolutions upon the reasoning of my own mind. Misfortune—early deprivation—has given me the privilege of acting for myself; and constraint shall not deprive me of an Englishman's best privilege.'

'The true cant of the day,' said Herries, in a tone of scorn. 'The privilege of free action belongs to no mortal—we are tied down by the fetters of duty—our moral path is limited by the regulations of honour—our most indifferent actions are but meshes of the web of destiny by which we are all surrounded.'

He paced the room rapidly, and proceeded in a tone of enthusiasm which, joined to some other parts of his conduct, seems to intimate an over-excited imagination, were it not contradicted by the general tenor of his speech and conduct.

'Nothing,' he said, in an earnest yet melancholy voice—'nothing is the work of chance—nothing is the consequence of free-will—the liberty of which the Englishman boasts, gives as little real freedom to its owner, as the despotism of an Eastern Sultan permits to his slave. The usurper, William of Nassau, went forth to hunt, and thought, doubtless, that it was by an act of his own royal pleasure that the horse of his murdered victim was prepared for his kingly sport. But Heaven had other views; and before the sun was high, a stumble of that very animal over an obstacle so inconsiderable as a mole-hillock, cost the haughty rider his life and his usurped crown. Do you think an inclination of the rein could have avoided that trifling impediment?—I tell you, it crossed his way as inevitably as all the long chain of Caucasus could have done. Yes, young man, in doing and suffering, we play but the part allotted by Destiny, the manager of this strange drama, stand bound to act no more than is prescribed, to say no more than is set down for us; and yet we mouth about free-will, and freedom of thought and action, as if Richard must not die, or Richmond conquer,* exactly where the Author has decreed it shall be so!'

He continued to pace the room after this speech, with folded arms and downcast looks; and the sound of his steps and tone of his voice brought to my remembrance, that I had heard this singular person, when I met him on a former occasion, uttering such soliloquies in his solitary chamber. I observed, that, like other Jacobites, in his inveteracy against the memory of King William, he had adopted the party opinion, that the monarch, on the day he had his fatal accident, rode upon a horse once the property of the unfortunate Sir John Friend, executed for High Treason in 1696.*

It was not my business to aggravate, but, if possible, rather to soothe him in whose power I was so singularly placed. When I conceived that the keenness of his feelings had in some degree subsided, I answered him as follows:—'I will not—indeed I feel myself incompetent to argue a question of such metaphysical subtlety, as that which involves the limits betwixt free-will and predestination. Let us hope we may live honestly and die hopefully, without being obliged to form a decided opinion upon a point so far beyond our comprehension.'

'Wisely resolved,' he interrupted, with a sneer—'there came a note from some Geneva sermon.'

'But,' I proceeded, 'I call your attention to the fact, that I, as well as you, am acted upon by impulses, the result either of my own free-will, or the consequences of the part which is assigned to me by destiny. These may be—nay, at present they are—in direct contradiction to those by which you are actuated; and how shall we decide which shall have precedence?—*You* perhaps feel yourself destined to act as my jailer. I feel myself, on the contrary, destined to attempt and effect my escape. One of us must be wrong, but who can say which errs till the event has decided betwixt us?'

'I shall feel myself destined to have recourse to severe modes of restraint,' said he, in the same tone of half jest, half earnest, which I had used.

'In that case,' I answered, 'it will be my destiny to attempt every thing for my freedom.'

'And it may be mine, young man,' he replied, in a deep and stern tone, 'to take care that you should rather die than attain your purpose.'

This was speaking out indeed, and I did not allow him to go unanswered. 'You threaten me in vain,' said I; 'the laws of my country will protect me; or whom they cannot protect, they will avenge.'

I spoke this firmly, and he seemed for a moment silenced; and the scorn with which he at last answered me, had something of affectation in it.

'The laws!' he said; 'and what, stripling, do you know of the laws of your country?—Could you learn jurisprudence under a base-born blotter of parchment, such as Saunders Fairford; or from the empty pedantic coxcomb, his son, who now, forsooth, writes himself advocate?—When Scotland was herself, and had her own King and Legislature,* such plebeian cubs, instead of being called to the bar of her Supreme Courts, would scarce have been admitted to the honour of bearing a sheepskin process-bag.'

Alan, I could not bear this, but answered indignantly, that he knew not the worth and honour from which he was detracting.

'I know as much of these Fairfords as I do of you,' he replied.

'As much,' said I, 'and as little; for you can neither estimate their real worth nor mine. I know you saw them when last in Edinburgh.'

'Ha!' he exclaimed, and turned on me an inquisitive look.

'It is true,' said I; 'you cannot deny it; and having thus shown you that I know something of your motions, let me warn you I have modes of communication with which you are not acquainted. Oblige me not to use them to your prejudice.'

'Prejudice *me*!' he replied. 'Young man, I smile at, and forgive your folly. Nay, I will tell you that of which you are not aware, namely, that it was from letters received from these Fairfords that I first suspected, what the result of my visit to them confirmed, that you were the person whom I had sought for years.'

'If you learned this,' said I, 'from the papers which were about my person on the night when I was under the necessity of becoming your guest at Brokenburn, I do not envy your indifference to the means of acquiring information. It was dishonourable to'——

'Peace, young man,' said Herries, more calmly than I might have expected; 'the word dishonour must not be mentioned as in conjunction with my name. Your pocketbook was in the pocket of your coat, and did not escape the curiosity of another, though it would have been sacred from mine. My servant, Cristal Nixon, brought me the intelligence after you were gone. I was displeased with the manner in which he had acquired his information; but it was not the less my duty to ascertain its truth, and for that purpose I went to Edinburgh. I was in hopes to persuade Mr Fairford to have entered into my views; but I found him too much prejudiced to permit me to trust him. He is a wretched, yet a timid slave of the present government, under which our unhappy country is dishonourably enthralled; and it would have been altogether unfit and unsafe to have intrusted him with the secret either of the right which I possess to direct your actions, or of the manner in which I purpose to exercise it.'

I was determined to take advantage of his communicative humour, and obtain, if possible, more light upon his purpose. He seemed most accessible to being piqued on the point of honour, and I resolved to avail myself, but with caution, of his sensibility upon that topic. 'You say,' I replied, 'that you are not friendly to indirect practices, and disapprove of the means by which your domestic obtained information of my name and quality—Is it honourable to avail yourself of that knowledge which is dishonourably obtained?'

'It is boldly asked,' he replied; 'but, within certain necessary limits, I dislike not boldness of expostulation. You have, in this short conference, displayed more character and energy than I was prepared to expect. You will, I trust, resemble a forest plant, which has indeed, by some accident, been brought up in the greenhouse, and thus rendered delicate and effeminate, but which regains its native firmness and tenacity, when exposed for a season to the winter air. I will answer your question plainly. In business, as in war, spies and informers are necessary evils, which all good men detest; but which yet all prudent men must use, unless they mean to fight and act blindfold. But nothing can justify the use of falsehood and treachery in our own person.'

'You said to the elder Mr Fairford,' continued I, with the same boldness, which I began to find was my best game, 'that I was the son of Ralph Latimer of Langcote-Hall?—How do you reconcile this with your late assertion that my name is not Latimer?'

He coloured as he replied, 'The doting old fool lied; or perhaps mistook my meaning. I said, that gentleman *might* be your father. To say truth, I wished you to visit England, your native country; because, when you might do so, my rights over you would revive.'

This speech fully led me to understand a caution which had been often impressed upon me, that if I regarded my safety, I should not cross the southern Border; and I cursed my own folly, which kept me fluttering like a moth around the candle, until I was betrayed into the calamity with which I had dallied. 'What are those rights,' I said, 'which you claim over me?—To what end do you propose to turn them?'

'To a weighty one, you may be certain,' answered Mr Herries; 'but I do not, at present, mean to communicate to you either its nature or extent. You may judge of its importance, when, in order entirely to possess myself of your person, I condescended to mix myself with the fellows who destroyed the fishing station of yon wretched Quaker. That I held him in contempt, and was displeased at the greedy devices with which he ruined a manly sport, is true enough; but, unless as it favoured my designs on you, he might have, for me, maintained his stake-nets till Solway should cease to ebb and flow.'

'Alas!' I said, 'it doubles my regret to have been the unwilling cause of misfortune to an honest and friendly man.'

'Do not grieve for that,' said Herries; 'honest Joshua is one of those who, by dint of long prayers, can possess themselves of widows' houses—he will quickly repair his losses. When he sustains any mishap, he and the other canters set it down as a debt against Heaven, and, by way of set-off, practise rogueries without compunction, till they make the balance even, or incline it to the winning side. Enough of this for the present.—I must immediately shift my quarters; for although I do not fear the over-zeal of Mr Justice Foxley or his clerk will lead them to any extreme measure, yet that mad scoundrel's unhappy recognition of me may make it more serious for them to connive at me, and I must not put their patience to an over severe trial. You must prepare to attend me, either as a captive or a companion; if as the latter, you must give your parole of honour to attempt no escape. Should you be so ill advised as to break your word once pledged, be assured that I will blow your brains out, without a moment's scruple.'

'I am ignorant of your plans and purposes,' I replied, 'and cannot but hold them dangerous. I do not mean to aggravate my present situation by any unavailing resistance to the superior force which detains me; but I will not renounce the right of asserting my natural freedom should a favourable opportunity occur. I will, therefore, rather be your prisoner than your confederate.'

'That is spoken fairly,' he said; 'and yet not without the canny caution of one brought up in the Gude Town of Edinburgh. On my part, I will impose no unnecessary hardship upon you; but, on the contrary, your journey shall be made as easy as is consistent with your being kept safely. Do you feel strong enough to ride on horseback as yet, or would you prefer a carriage? The former mode of travelling is best adapted to the country through which we are to travel, but you are at liberty to choose between them.'

I said, 'I felt my strength gradually returning, and that I should much prefer travelling on horseback. A carriage,' I added, 'is so close'——

'And so easily guarded,' replied Herries, with a look as if he would have penetrated my very thoughts,—'that, doubtless, you think horseback better calculated for an escape.'

'My thoughts are my own,' I answered; 'and though you keep my person prisoner, these are beyond your control.'

'O, I can read the book,' he said, 'without opening the leaves. But I would recommend to you to make no rash attempt, and it will be my care to see that you have no power to make any that is likely to be effectual. Linen, and all other necessaries for one in your circumstances, are amply provided. Cristal Nixon will act as your valet,—I should rather, perhaps, say, your *femme de chambre*. Your travelling dress you may perhaps consider as singular; but it is such as the circumstances require; and, if you object to use the articles prepared for your use, your mode of journeying will be as personally unpleasant as that which conducted you hither.—Adieu—We now know each other better than we did—it will not be my fault if the consequences of farther intimacy be not a more favourable mutual opinion.'

He then left me, with a civil good-night, to my own reflections, and only turned back to say, that we should proceed on our journey at daybreak next morning, at farthest; perhaps earlier, he said; but complimented me by supposing that, as I was a sportsman, I must always be ready for a sudden start.

We are then at issue, this singular man and myself. His personal views are to a certain point explained. He has chosen an antiquated and desperate line of politics, and he claims, from some pretended tie of guardianship, or relationship, which he does not deign to explain, but which he seems to have been able to pass current on a silly country Justice and his knavish clerk, a right to direct and to control my motions. The danger which awaited me in England, and which I might have escaped had I remained in Scotland, was doubtless occasioned by the authority of this man. But what my poor mother might fear for me as a child—what my English friend, Samuel Griffiths, endeavoured to guard against during my youth and nonage, is now, it seems, come upon me; and, under a legal pretext, I am detained in what must be a most illegal manner, by a person, too, whose own political immunities have been forfeited by his conduct. It matters not—my mind is made up—neither persuasion nor threats shall force me into the desperate designs which this man meditates. Whether I am of the trifling consequence which my life hitherto seems to intimate, or whether I have (as would appear from my adversary's conduct) such importance, by birth or fortune, as may make me a desirable acquisition to a political faction, my resolution is taken in either case. Those who read this Journal, if it shall be perused by impartial eyes, shall judge of me truly; and if they consider me as a fool in encountering danger unnecessarily, they shall have no reason to believe me a coward or a turncoat, when I find myself engaged in it. I have been bred in sentiments of attachment to the family on the throne, and in these sentiments I will live and die. I have, indeed, some idea that Mr Herries has already discovered that I am made of different and more unmalleable metal than he had at first believed. There were letters from my dear Alan Fairford, giving a ludicrous account of my instability of temper, in the same pocketbook, which, according to the admission of my pretended guardian, fell under the investigation of his domestic, during the night I passed at Brokenburn, where, as I now recollect, my wet clothes, with the contents of my pockets, were, with the thoughtlessness of a young traveller, committed too rashly to the care of a strange servant. And my kind friend and hospitable landlord, Mr Alexander Fairford, may also, and with justice, have spoken of my levities to this man. But he shall find he has made a false estimate upon these plausible grounds, since——

But I must break off for the present.

CHAPTER IX

LATIMER'S JOURNAL, IN CONTINUATION

THERE is at length a halt—at length I have gained so much privacy as to enable me to continue my Journal. It has become a sort of task of duty to me, without the discharge of which I do not feel that the business of the day is performed. True, no friendly eye may ever look upon these labours, which have amused the solitary hours of an unhappy prisoner. Yet, in the meanwhile, the exercise of the pen seems to act as a sedative upon my own agitated thoughts and tumultuous passions. I never lay it down but I rise stronger in resolution, more ardent in hope. A thousand vague fears, wild expectations, and indigested schemes, hurry through one's thoughts in seasons of doubt and of danger. But by arresting them as they flit across the mind, by throwing them on paper, and even by that mechanical act compelling ourselves to consider them with scrupulous and minute attention, we may perhaps escape becoming the dupes of our own excited imagination; just as a young horse is cured of the vice of starting, by being made to stand still and look for some time without any interruption at the cause of its terror.

There remains but one risk, which is that of discovery. But, besides the small characters in which my residence in Mr Fairford's house enabled me to excel, for the purpose of transferring as many scroll sheets as possible to a huge sheet of stamped paper, I have, as I have elsewhere intimated, had hitherto the comfortable reflection, that if the record of my misfortunes should fall into the hands of him by whom they are caused, they would, without harming any one, show him the real character and disposition of the person who has become his prisoner—perhaps his victim. Now, however, that other names, and other characters, are to be mingled with the register of my own sentiments, I must take additional care of these papers, and keep them in such a manner that, in case of the least hazard of detection, I may be able to destroy them at a moment's notice. I shall not soon or easily forget the lesson I have been taught, by the prying disposition which Cristal Nixon, this man's agent and confederate, manifested at Brokenburn, and which proved the original cause of my sufferings.

My laying aside the last sheet of my Journal hastily, was occasioned by the unwonted sound of a violin, in the farm-yard beneath my windows. It will not appear surprising to those who have made music their study, that, after listening to a few notes, I became at once assured that the musician was no other than the itinerant, formerly mentioned as present at the destruction of Joshua Geddes's stake-nets, the superior delicacy and force of whose execution would enable me to swear to his bow amongst a whole orchestra. I had the less reason to doubt his identity, because he played twice over the beautiful Scottish air called Wandering Willie;* and I could not help concluding that he did so for the purpose of intimating his own presence, since what the French call the *nom de guerre* of the performer was described by the tune.

Hope will catch at the most feeble twig for support in extremity. I knew this man, though deprived of sight, to be bold, ingenious, and perfectly capable of acting as a guide. I believed I had won his good-will, by having, in a frolic, assumed the character of his partner; and I remembered that, in a wild, wandering, and disorderly course of life, men, as they become loosened from the ordinary bonds of civil society, hold those of comradeship more closely sacred; so that honour is sometimes found among thieves, and faith and attachment in such as the law has termed vagrants. The history of Richard Cœur de Lion and his minstrel, Blondel,* rushed, at the same time, on my mind, though I could not even then suppress a smile at the dignity of the example, when applied to a blind fiddler and myself. Still there was something in all this to awaken a hope, that if I could open a correspondence with this poor violer, he might be useful in extricating me from my present situation.

His profession furnished me with some hope that this desired communication might be attained; since it is well known that, in Scotland, where there is so much national music, the words and airs of which are generally known, there is a kind of free-masonry amongst performers, by which they can, by the mere choice of a tune, express a great deal to the hearers. Personal allusions are often made in this manner, with much point and pleasantry; and nothing is more usual at public festivals, than that the air played to accompany a particular health or toast, is made the vehicle of compliment, of wit, and sometimes of satire.[43]

While these things passed through my mind rapidly, I heard my friend beneath recommence, for the third time, the air from which his own name had been probably adopted, when he was interrupted by his rustic auditors.

'If thou canst play no other spring but that, mon, ho hadst best put up ho's pipes and be jogging. Squoire will be back anon, or Master Nixon, and we'll see who will pay poiper then.'

Oho, thought I, if I have no sharper ears than those of my friends Jan and Dorcas to encounter, I may venture an experiment upon them; and, as most expressive of my state of captivity, I sung two or three lines of the 137th Psalm—

'By Babel's streams we sat and wept.'

The country people listened with attention, and when I ceased, I heard them whisper together in tones of commiseration, 'Lack-a-day, poor soul! so pretty a man to be beside his wits!'

'An he be that gate,' said Wandering Willie, in a tone calculated to reach my ears, 'I ken naething will raise his spirits like a spring.' And he struck up with great vigour and spirit, the lively Scottish air, the words of which instantly occurred to me,—

'Oh whistle and I'll come t'ye, my lad,
Oh whistle and I'll come t'ye, my lad;
Though father and mother and a' should gae mad,
Oh whistle and I'll come t'ye, my lad.'*

I soon heard a clattering noise of feet in the court-yard, which I concluded to be Jan and Dorcas dancing a jig in their Cumberland wooden clogs. Under cover of this din, I endeavoured to answer Willie's signal by whistling, as loud as I could,

'Come back again and loe me
When a' the lave are gane.'

He instantly threw the dancers out, by changing his air to

'There's my thumb, I'll ne'er beguile thee.'*

I no longer doubted that a communication betwixt us was happily established, and that, if I had an opportunity of speaking to the poor musician, I should find him willing to take my letter to the post, to invoke the assistance of some active magistrate, or of the commanding-officer of Carlisle Castle, or, in short, to do whatever else I could point out, in the compass of his power, to contribute to my liberation. But to obtain speech of him, I must have run the risk of alarming the suspicions of Dorcas, if not of her yet more stupid Corydon. My ally's blindness prevented his receiving any communication by signs from the window—even if I could have ventured to make them, consistently with prudence—so that, notwithstanding the mode of intercourse we had adopted was both circuitous and peculiarly liable to misapprehension, I saw nothing I could do better than to continue it, trusting my own and my correspondent's acuteness, in applying to the airs the meaning they were intended to convey. I thought of singing the words themselves of some significant song, but feared I might, by doing so, attract suspicion. I endeavoured, therefore, to intimate my speedy departure from my present place of residence, by whistling the well-known air with which festive parties in Scotland usually conclude the dance.—

> 'Good-night and joy be wi' ye a',
> For here nae langer maun I stay;
> There's neither friend nor foe of mine
> But wishes that I were away.'*

It appeared that Willie's powers of intelligence were much more active than mine, and that, like a deaf person, accustomed to be spoken to by signs, he comprehended, from the very first notes, the whole meaning I intended to convey; and he accompanied me in the air with his violin, in such a manner as at once to show he understood my meaning, and to prevent my whistling from being attended to.

His reply was almost immediate, and was conveyed in the old martial air of 'Hey, Johnnie lad, cock up your beaver.' I ran over the words, and fixed on the following stanza, as most applicable to my circumstances:—

> 'Cock up your beaver, and cock it fu' sprush,
> We'll over the Border and give them a brush;
> There's somebody there we'll teach better behaviour—
> Hey, Johnnie lad, cock up your beaver.'*

If these sounds alluded, as I hope they do, to any chance of assistance from my Scottish friends, I may indeed consider that a door is open to hope and freedom. I immediately replied with,

> 'My heart's in the Highlands, my heart is not here;
> My heart's in the Highlands, a-chasing the deer;
> A-chasing the wild deer, and following the roe;
> My heart's in the Highlands wherever I go.
>
> 'Farewell to the Highlands! farewell to the North!
> The birthplace of valour, the cradle of worth;
> Wherever I wander, wherever I rove,
> The hills of the Highlands for ever I love.'*

Willie instantly played, with a degree of spirit which might have awakened hope in Despair herself, if Despair could be supposed to understand Scotch music, the fine old Jacobite air,

> 'For a' that, and a' that,
> And twice as much as a' that.'*

I next endeavoured to intimate my wish to send notice of my condition to my friends; and, despairing to find an air sufficiently expressive of my purpose, I ventured to sing a verse, which, in various forms, occurs so frequently in old ballads—

'Whare will I get a bonny boy
That will win hose and shoon;
That will gae down to Durisdeer,
And bid my merry-men come?'*

He drowned the latter part of the verse by playing, with much emphasis,

'Kind Robin loes me.'*

Of this, though I ran over the verses of the song in my mind, I could make nothing; and before I could contrive any mode of intimating my uncertainty, a cry arose in the court-yard that Cristal Nixon was coming. My faithful Willie was obliged to retreat; but not before he had half played, half hummed, by way of farewell,

'Leave thee—leave thee, lad—
I'll never leave thee;
The stars shall gae withershins
Ere I will leave thee.'*

I am thus, I think, secure of one trusty adherent in my misfortunes; and, however whimsical it may be to rely much on a man of his idle profession and deprived of sight withal, it is deeply impressed on my mind, that his services may be both useful and necessary. There is another quarter from which I look for succour, and which I have indicated to thee, Alan, in more than one passage of my Journal. Twice, at the early hour of daybreak, I have seen the individual alluded to in the court of the farm, and twice she made signs of recognition in answer to the gestures by which I endeavoured to make her comprehend my situation; but on both occasions, she pressed her finger on her lips, as expressive of silence and secrecy.

The manner in which G. M. entered upon the scene for the first time, seems to assure me of her good-will, so far as her power may reach; and I have many reasons to believe it is considerable. Yet she seemed hurried and frightened during the very transitory moments of our interview, and I think was, upon the last occasion, startled by the entrance of some one into the farm-yard, just as she was on the point of addressing me. You must not ask whether I am an early riser, since such objects are only to be seen at daybreak; and although I have never again seen her, yet I have reason to think she is not distant. It was but three nights ago, that, worn out by the uniformity of my confinement, I had manifested more symptoms of despondence than I had before exhibited, which I conceive may have attracted the attention of the domestics, through whom the circumstance might transpire. On the next morning, the following lines lay on my table; but how conveyed there, I cannot tell. The hand in which they are written is a beautiful Italian manuscript:—

'As lords their labourers' hire delay,
  Fate quits our toil with hopes to come,
Which, if far short of present pay,
  Still owns a debt and names a sum.

'Quit not the pledge, frail sufferer, then,
  Although a distant date be given;
Despair is treason towards man,
  And blasphemy to Heaven.'

That these lines are written with the friendly purpose of inducing me to keep up my spirits, I cannot doubt; and I trust the manner in which I shall conduct myself may show that the pledge is accepted.

The dress is arrived in which it seems to be my self-elected guardian's pleasure that I shall travel; and what does it prove to be?—A skirt, or upper-petticoat of camlet, like those worn by country ladies of moderate rank when on horseback, with such a riding-mask as they frequently use on journeys to preserve their eyes and complexion from the sun and dust, and sometimes, it is suspected, to enable them to play off a little coquetry. From the gayer mode of employing the mask, however, I suspect I shall be precluded; for instead of being only pasteboard, covered with black velvet, I observe with anxiety that mine is thickened with a plate of steel, which, like Quixote's visor,* serves to render it more strong and durable.

This apparatus, together with a steel clasp for securing the mask behind me with a padlock, gave me fearful recollections of the unfortunate being, who, never being permitted to lay aside such a visor, acquired the well-known historical epithet of the Man in the Iron Mask.* I hesitated a moment whether I should so far submit to the acts of oppression designed against me as to assume this disguise, which was, of course, contrived to aid their purposes. But then I remembered Mr Herries's threat, that I should be kept close prisoner in a carriage, unless I assumed the dress which should be appointed for me; and I considered the comparative degree of freedom which I might purchase by wearing the mask and female dress, as easily and advantageously purchased. Here, therefore, I must pause for the present, and await what the morning may bring forth.

[To carry on the story from the documents before us, we think it proper here to drop the Journal of the captive Darsie Latimer, and adopt, instead, a narrative of the proceedings of Alan Fairford in pursuit of his friend, which forms another series in this history.]

CHAPTER X

NARRATIVE OF ALAN FAIRFORD

THE reader ought, by this time, to have formed some idea of the character of Alan Fairford. He had a warmth of heart which the study of the law and of the world could not chill, and talents which they had rendered unusually acute. Deprived of the personal patronage enjoyed by most of his contemporaries, who assumed the gown under the protection of their aristocratic alliances and descents, he early saw that he should have that to achieve for himself which fell to them as a right of birth. He laboured hard in silence and solitude, and his labours were crowned with success. But Alan doted on his friend Darsie, even more than he loved his profession, and, as we have seen, threw every thing aside when he thought Latimer in danger; forgetting fame and fortune, and hazarding even the serious displeasure of his father, to rescue him whom he loved with an elder brother's affection. Darsie, though his parts were more quick and brilliant than those of his friend, seemed always to the latter a being under his peculiar charge, whom he was called upon to cherish and protect, in cases where the youth's own experience was unequal to the exigency; and now, when the fate of Latimer seemed worse than doubtful, and Alan's whole prudence and energy were to be exerted in his behalf, an adventure which might have seemed perilous to most youths of his age, had no terrors for him. He was well acquainted with the laws of his country, and knew how to appeal to them; and, besides his professional confidence, his natural disposition was steady, sedate, persevering, and undaunted. With these requisites he undertook a quest which, at that time, was not unattended with actual danger, and had much in it to appal a more timid disposition.

Fairford's first enquiry concerning his friend was of the chief magistrate of Dumfries, Provost Crosbie, who had sent the information of Darsie's disappearance. On his first application, he thought he discerned in the honest dignitary a desire to get rid of the subject. The Provost spoke of the riot at the fishing station as an 'outbreak among those lawless loons the fishermen, which concerned the Sheriff,' he said, 'more than us poor Town-Council bodies, that have enough to do to keep peace within burgh, amongst such a set of commoners as the town are plagued with.'

'But this is not all, Provost Crosbie,' said Mr Alan Fairford; 'a young gentleman of rank and fortune has disappeared amongst their hands—you know him. My father gave him a letter to you—Mr Darsie Latimer.'

'Lack-a-day, yes! lack-a-day, yes!' said the Provost; 'Mr Darsie Latimer—he dined at my house—I hope he is well?'

'I hope so too,' said Alan, rather indignantly; 'but I desire more certainty on that point. You yourself wrote my father that he had disappeared.'

'Troth, yes, and that is true,' said the Provost. 'But did he not go back to his friends in Scotland? it was not natural to think he would stay here.'

'Not unless he is under restraint,' said Fairford, surprised at the coolness with which the Provost seemed to take up the matter.

'Rely on it, sir,' said Mr Crosbie, 'that if he has not returned to his friends in Scotland, he must have gone to his friends in England.'

'I will rely on no such thing,' said Alan; 'if there is law or justice in Scotland, I will have the thing cleared to the very bottom.'

'Reasonable, reasonable,' said the Provost, 'so far as is possible; but you know I have no power beyond the ports of the burgh.'

'But you are in the commission besides, Mr Crosbie; a Justice of Peace for the county.'

'True, very true—that is,' said the cautious magistrate, 'I will not say but my name may stand on the list, but I cannot remember that I have ever qualified.'[44]

'Why, in that case,' said young Fairford, 'there are ill-natured people might doubt your attachment to the Protestant line, Mr Crosbie.'

'God forbid, Mr Fairford! I who have done and suffered in the Forty-five! I reckon the Highlandmen did me damage to the amount of L.100 Scots, forby all they ate and drank—no, no, sir, I stand beyond challenge: but as for plaguing myself with county business, let them that aught the mare shoe the mare. The Commissioners of Supply* would see my back broken before they would help me in the burgh's work, and all the world kens the difference of the weight between public business in burgh and landward. What are their riots to me? have we not riots enough of our own?—But I must be getting ready, for the council meets this forenoon. I am blithe to see your father's son on the causeway of our ancient burgh, Mr Alan Fairford. Were you a twelvemonth aulder, we would make a burgess of you, man. I hope you will come and dine with me before you go away. What think you of to-day at two o'clock—just a roasted chucky and a drappit egg?'

Alan Fairford resolved that his friend's hospitality should not, as it seemed the inviter intended, put a stop to his queries. 'I must delay you for a moment,' he said, 'Mr Crosbie; this is a serious affair; a young gentleman of high hopes, my own dearest friend, is missing—you cannot think it will be passed over slightly, if a man of your high character and known zeal for the government, do not make some active enquiry. Mr Crosbie, you are my father's friend, and I respect you as such—but to others it will have a bad appearance.'

The withers of the Provost were not unwrung;* he paced the room in much tribulation, repeating, 'But what can I do, Mr Fairford? I warrant your friend casts up again—he will come back again, like the ill shilling—he is not the sort of gear that tynes—a hellicat boy, running through the country with a blind fiddler, and playing the fiddle to a parcel of blackguards, who can tell where the like of him may have scampered to?'

'There are persons apprehended, and in the jail of the town, as I understand from the Sheriff-Substitute,' said Mr Fairford; 'you must call them before you, and enquire what they know of this young gentleman.'

'Ay, ay—the Sheriff-Depute* did commit some poor creatures, I believe—wretched, ignorant fishermen bodies, that had been quarrelling with Quaker Geddes and his stake-nets, whilk, under favour of your gown be it spoken, Mr Fairford, are not over and above lawful, and the Town-Clerk thinks they may be lawfully removed *via facti*—but that is by the by. But, sir, the creatures were a' dismissed for want of evidence; the Quaker would not swear to them, and what could the Sheriff and me do but just let them loose? Come awa, cheer up, Master Alan, and take a walk till dinner-time—I must really go to the council.'

'Stop a moment, Provost,' said Alan; 'I lodge a complaint before you, as a magistrate, and you will find it serious to slight it over. You must have these men apprehended again.'

'Ay, ay—easy said; but catch them that can,' answered the Provost; 'they are ower the March by this time, or by the point of Cairn.—Lord help ye! they are a kind of amphibious deevils, neither land nor water beasts—neither English nor Scots—neither county nor stewartry, as we say—they are dispersed like so much quicksilver. You may as well try to whistle a sealgh out of the Solway, as to get hold of one of them till all the fray is over.'

'Mr Crosbie, this will not do,' answered the young counsellor; 'there is a person of more importance than such wretches as you describe concerned in this unhappy business—I must name to you a certain Mr Herries.'

He kept his eye on the Provost as he uttered the name, which he did rather at a venture, and from the connexion which that gentleman, and his real or supposed niece, seemed to have with the fate of Darsie Latimer, than from any distinct cause of suspicion which he entertained. He thought the Provost seemed embarrassed, though he showed much desire to assume an appearance of indifference, in which he partly succeeded.

'Herries!' he said—'What Herries?—There are many of that name—not so many as formerly, for the old stocks are wearing out; but there is Herries of Heathgill, and Herries of Auchintulloch, and Herries'——

'To save you farther trouble, this person's designation is Herries of Birrenswork.'

'Of Birrenswork?' said Mr Crosbie; 'I have you now, Mr Alan. Could you not as well have said, the Laird of Redgauntlet?'

Fairford was too wary to testify any surprise at this identification of names, however unexpected. 'I thought,' said he, 'he was more generally known by the name of Herries. I have seen and been in company with him under that name, I am sure.'

'O ay; in Edinburgh, belike. You know Redgauntlet was unfortunate a great while ago, and though he was maybe not deeper in the mire than other folk, yet, for some reason or other, he did not get so easily out.'

'He was attainted, I understand; and has no remission,' said Fairford.

The cautious Provost only nodded, and said, 'You may guess, therefore, why it is so convenient he should hold his mother's name, which is also partly his own, when he is about Edinburgh. To bear his proper name might be accounted a kind of flying in the face of government, ye understand. But he has been long connived at—the story is an old story—and the gentleman has many excellent qualities, and is of a very ancient and honourable house—has cousins among the great folk—counts kin with the Advocate* and with the Sheriff—hawks, you know, Mr Alan, will not pike out hawks' een—he is widely connected—*my* wife is a fourth cousin of Redgauntlet's.'

*Hinc illae lachrymae!** thought Alan Fairford to himself; but the hint presently determined him to proceed by soft means, and with caution. 'I beg you to understand,' said Fairford, 'that in the investigation which I am about to make, I design no harm to Mr Herries, or Redgauntlet—call him what you will. All I wish is, to ascertain the safety of my friend. I know that he was rather foolish in once going upon a mere frolic, in disguise, to the neighbourhood of this same gentleman's house. In his circumstances, Mr Redgauntlet may have misinterpreted the motives, and considered Darsie Latimer as a spy. His influence, I believe, is great, among the disorderly people you spoke of but now?'

The Provost answered with another sagacious shake of his head, that would have done honour to Lord Burleigh in the Critic.*

'Well, then,' continued Fairford, 'is it not possible that, in the mistaken belief that Mr Latimer was a spy, he may, upon such suspicion, have caused him to be carried off and confined somewhere?—Such things are done at elections, and on occasions less pressing than when men think their lives are in danger from an informer.'

'Mr Fairford,' said the Provost, very earnestly, 'I scarce think such a mistake possible; or if, by any extraordinary chance, it should have taken place, Redgauntlet, whom I cannot but know well, being, as I have said, my wife's first cousin, (fourth cousin, I should say,) is altogether incapable of doing any thing harsh to the young gentleman—he might send him ower to Ailsay for a night or two, or maybe land him on the north coast of Ireland, or in Islay, or some of the Hebrides; but depend upon it, he is incapable of harming a hair of his head.'

'I am determined not to trust to that, Provost,' answered Fairford, firmly; 'and I am a good deal surprised at your way of talking so lightly of such an aggression on the liberty of the subject. You are to consider, and Mr Herries or Mr Redgauntlet's friends would do very well also to consider, how it will sound in the ears of an English Secretary of State, that an attainted traitor (for such is this gentleman) has not only ventured to take up his abode in this realm—against the King of which he has been in arms—but is suspected of having proceeded, by open force and violence, against the person of one of the lieges, a young man, who is neither without friends nor property to secure his being righted.'

The Provost looked at the young counsellor with a face in which distrust, alarm, and vexation, seemed mingled. 'A fashious job,' he said at last, 'a fashious job; and it will be dangerous meddling with it. I should like ill to see your father's son turn informer against an unfortunate gentleman.'

'Neither do I mean it,' answered Alan, 'provided that unfortunate gentleman and his friends give me a quiet opportunity of securing *my* friend's safety. If I could speak with Mr Redgauntlet, and hear his own explanation, I should probably be satisfied. If I am forced to denounce him to government, it will be in his new capacity of a kidnapper. I may not be able, nor is it my business, to prevent his being recognised in his former character of an attainted person, excepted from the general pardon.'

'Master Fairford,' said the Provost, 'would ye ruin the poor innocent gentleman on an idle suspicion?'

'Say no more of it, Mr Crosbie; my line of conduct is determined—unless that suspicion is removed.'

'Weel, sir,' said the Provost, 'since so it be, and since you say that you do not seek to harm Redgauntlet personally, I'll ask a man to dine with us to-day that kens as much about his matters as most folk. You must think, Mr Alan Fairford, though Redgauntlet be my wife's near relative, and though, doubtless, I wish him weel, yet I am not the person who is like to be intrusted with his incomings and outgoings. I am not a man for that—I keep the kirk, and I abhor Popery—I have stood up for the House of Hanover, and for liberty and property—I carried arms, sir, against the Pretender, when three of the Highlandmen's baggage-carts were stopped at Ecclefechan;* and I had an especial loss of a hundred pounds'——

'Scots,' interrupted Fairford. 'You forget you told me all this before.'

'Scots or English, it was too much for me to lose,'* said the Provost; 'so you see I am not a person to pack or peel with Jacobites, and such unfreemen as poor Redgauntlet.'

'Granted, granted, Mr Crosbie; and what then?' said Alan Fairford.

'Why, then, it follows, that if I am to help you at this pinch, it cannot be by and through my ain personal knowledge, but through some fitting agent or third person.'

'Granted again,' said Fairford. 'And pray who may this third person be?'

'Wha but Pate Maxwell of Summertrees—him they call Pate-in-Peril.'

'An old forty-five man, of course?' said Fairford.

'Ye may swear that,' replied the Provost—'as black a Jacobite as the auld leaven can make him; but a sonsy, merry companion, that none of us think it worth while to break wi' for all his brags and his clavers. You would have thought, if he had had but his own way at Derby, he would have marched Charlie Stewart through between Wade and the Duke,* as a thread goes through the needle's ee, and seated him in Saint James's before you could have said haud your hand. But though he is a windy body when he gets on his auld-warld stories, he has mair gumption in him than most people—knows business, Mr Alan, being bred to the law; but never took the gown, because of the oaths,* which kept more folk out then than they do now—the more's the pity.'

'What! are you sorry, Provost, that Jacobitism is upon the decline?' said Fairford.

'No, no,' answered the Provost—'I am only sorry for folks losing the tenderness of conscience which they used to have. I have a son breeding to the bar, Mr Fairford; and, no doubt, considering my services and sufferings, I might have looked for some bit postie to him; but if the muckle tikes come in—I mean a' these Maxwells, and Johnstones, and great lairds, that the oaths used to keep out lang syne—the bits o' messan dogies, like my son, and maybe like your father's son, Mr Alan, will be sair put to the wall.'

'But to return to the subject, Mr Crosbie,' said Fairford, 'do you really think it likely that this Mr Maxwell will be of service in this matter?'

'It's very like he may be, for he is the tongue of the trump to the whole squad of them,' said the Provost; 'and Redgauntlet, though he will not stick at times to call him a fool, takes more of his counsel than any man's else that I am aware of. If Pate can bring him to a communing, the business is done. He's a sharp chield, Pate-in-Peril.'

'Pate-in-Peril!' repeated Alan; 'a very singular name.'

'Ay, and it was in as queer a way he got it; but I'll say naething about that,' said the Provost, 'for fear of forestalling his market; for ye are sure to hear it once at least, however oftener, before the punch-bowl gives place to the tea-pot.—And now, fare ye weel; for there is the council-bell clinking in earnest; and if I am not there before it jows in, Bailie Laurie will be trying some of his manœuvres.'

The Provost, repeating his expectation of seeing Mr Fairford at two o'clock, at length effected his escape from the young counsellor, and left him at a considerable loss how to proceed. The Sheriff, it seems, had returned to Edinburgh, and he feared to find the visible repugnance of the Provost to interfere with this Laird of Birrenswork, or Redgauntlet, much stronger amongst the country gentlemen, many of whom were Catholics as well as Jacobites, and most others unwilling to quarrel with kinsmen and friends, by prosecuting with severity political offences which had almost run a prescription.

To collect all the information in his power, and not to have recourse to the higher authorities until he could give all the light of which the case was capable, seemed the wiser proceeding in a choice of difficulties. He had some conversation with the Procurator-Fiscal, who, as well as the Provost, was an old correspondent of his father. Alan expressed to that officer a purpose of visiting Brokenburn, but was assured by him, that it would be a step attended with much danger to his own person, and altogether fruitless; that the individuals who had been ringleaders in the riot were long since safely sheltered in their various lurking-holes in the Isle of Man, Cumberland, and elsewhere; and that those who might remain would undoubtedly commit violence on any who visited their settlement with the purpose of enquiring into the late disturbances.

There were not the same objections to his hastening to Mount Sharon, where he expected to find the latest news of his friend; and there was time enough to do so, before the hour appointed for the Provost's dinner. Upon the road, he congratulated himself on having obtained one point of almost certain information. The person who had in a manner forced himself upon his father's hospitality, and had appeared desirous to induce Darsie Latimer to visit England, against whom, too, a sort of warning had been received from an individual connected with and residing in his own family, proved to be a promoter of the disturbance in which Darsie had disappeared.

What could be the cause of such an attempt on the liberty of an inoffensive and amiable man? It was impossible it could be merely owing to Redgauntlet's mistaking Darsie for a spy; for though that was the solution which Fairford had offered to the Provost, he well knew that, in point of fact, he himself had been warned by his singular visitor of some danger to which his friend was exposed, before such suspicion could have been entertained; and the injunctions received by Latimer from his guardian, or him who acted as such, Mr Griffiths of London, pointed to the same thing. He was rather glad, however, that he had not let Provost Crosbie into his secret, farther than was absolutely necessary; since it was plain that the connexion of his wife with the suspected party was likely to affect his impartiality as a magistrate.

When Alan Fairford arrived at Mount Sharon, Rachel Geddes hastened to meet him, almost before the servant could open the door. She drew back in disappointment when she beheld a stranger, and said, to excuse her precipitation, that 'she had thought it was her brother Joshua returned from Cumberland.'

'Mr Geddes is then absent from home?' said Fairford, much disappointed in his turn.

'He hath been gone since yesterday, friend,' answered Rachel, once more composed to the quietude which characterises her sect, but her pale cheek and red eye giving contradiction to her assumed equanimity.

'I am,' said Fairford, hastily, 'the particular friend of a young man not unknown to you, Miss Geddes—the friend of Darsie Latimer—and am come hither in the utmost anxiety, having understood from Provost Crosbie, that he had disappeared in the night when a destructive attack was made upon the fishing-station of Mr Geddes.'

'Thou dost afflict me, friend, by thy enquiries,' said Rachel, more affected than before; 'for although the youth was like those of the worldly generation, wise in his own conceit, and lightly to be moved by the breath of vanity, yet Joshua loved him, and his heart clave to him as if he had been his own son. And when he himself escaped from the sons of Belial, which was not until they had tired themselves with reviling, and with idle reproach, and the jests of the scoffer, Joshua, my brother, returned to them once and again, to give ransom for the youth called Darsie Latimer, with offers of money and with promise of remission, but they would not hearken to him. Also, he went before the Head Judge, whom men call the Sheriff, and would have told him of the youth's peril; but he would in no way hearken to him unless he would swear unto the truth of his words, which thing he might not do without sin, seeing it is written, Swear not at all—also, that our conversation shall be yea or nay. Therefore, Joshua returned to me disconsolate, and said, "Sister Rachel, this youth hath run into peril for my sake; assuredly I shall not be guiltless if a hair of his head be harmed, seeing I have sinned in permitting him to go with me to the fishing-station when such evil was to be feared. Therefore, I will take my horse, even Solomon, and ride swiftly into Cumberland, and I will make myself friends with Mammon of Unrighteousness, among the magistrates of the Gentiles, and among their mighty men; and it shall come to pass that Darsie Latimer shall be delivered, even if it were at the expense of half my substance." And I said, "Nay, my brother, go not, for they will but scoff at and revile thee; but hire with thy silver one of the scribes, who are eager as hunters in pursuing their prey, and he shall free Darsie Latimer from the men of violence by his cunning, and thy soul shall be guiltless of evil towards the lad." But he answered and said, "I will not be controlled in this matter." And he is gone forth, and hath not returned, and I fear me that he may never return; for though he be peaceful, as becometh one who holds all violence as offence against his own soul, yet neither the floods of water, nor the fear of the snare, nor the drawn sword of the adversary brandished in the path, will overcome his purpose. Wherefore the Solway may swallow him up, or the sword of the enemy may devour him—nevertheless, my hope is better in Him who directeth all things, and ruleth over the waves of the sea, and overruleth the devices of the wicked, and who can redeem us even as a bird from the fowler's net.'*

This was all that Fairford could learn from Miss Geddes; but he heard with pleasure, that the good Quaker, her brother, had many friends among those of his own profession in Cumberland, and without exposing himself to so much danger as his sister seemed to apprehend, he trusted he might be able to discover some traces of Darsie Latimer. He himself rode back to Dumfries, having left with Miss Geddes his direction in that place, and an earnest request that she would forward thither whatever information she might obtain from her brother.

On Fairford's return to Dumfries, he employed the brief interval which remained before dinner-time, in writing an account of what had befallen Latimer, and of the present uncertainty of his condition, to Mr Samuel Griffiths, through whose hands the remittances for his friend's service had been regularly made, desiring he would instantly acquaint him with such parts of his history as might direct him in the search which he was about to institute through the border counties, and which he pledged himself not to give up until he had obtained news of his friend, alive or dead. The young lawyer's mind felt easier when he had dispatched this letter. He could not conceive any reason why his friend's life should be aimed at; he knew Darsie had done nothing by which his liberty could be legally affected; and although, even of late years, there had been singular histories of men, and women also, who had been trepanned, and concealed in solitudes and distant islands, in order to serve some temporary purpose, such violences had been chiefly practised by the rich on the poor, and by the strong on the feeble; whereas, in the present case, this Mr Herries, or Redgauntlet, being amenable, for more reasons than one, to the censure of the law, must be the weakest in any struggle in which it could be appealed to. It is true that his friendly anxiety whispered, that the very cause which rendered this oppressor less formidable, might make him more desperate. Still, recalling his language, so strikingly that of the gentleman, and even of the man of honour, Alan Fairford concluded, that though, in his feudal pride, Redgauntlet might venture on the deeds of violence exercised by the aristocracy in other times, he could not be capable of any action of deliberate atrocity. And in these convictions he went to dine with Provost Crosbie, with a heart more at ease than might have been expected.[45]

CHAPTER XI

NARRATIVE OF ALAN FAIRFORD, CONTINUED

FIVE minutes had elapsed after the town-clock struck two, before Alan Fairford, who had made a small detour to put his letter into the post-house, reached the mansion of Mr Provost Crosbie, and was at once greeted by the voice of that civic dignitary, and the rural dignitary his visitor, as by the voices of men impatient for their dinner.

'Come away, Mr Fairford—the Edinburgh time is later than ours,' said the Provost.

And, 'Come away, young gentleman,' said the Laird; 'I remember your father weel, at the Cross, thirty years ago—I reckon you are as late in Edinburgh as at London, four o'clock hours—eh?'

'Not quite so degenerate,' replied Fairford; 'but certainly many Edinburgh people are so ill-advised as to postpone their dinner till three, that they may have full time to answer their London correspondents.'

'London correspondents!' said Mr Maxwell; 'and pray, what the devil have the people of Auld Reekie to do with London correspondents?'[46]

'The tradesmen must have their goods,' said Fairford.

'Can they not buy our own Scottish manufactures, and pick their customers' pockets in a more patriotic manner?'

'Then the ladies must have fashions,' said Fairford.

'Can they not busk the plaid over their heads, as their mothers did? A tartan screen, and once a-year a new cockernony from Paris, should serve a Countess. But ye have not many of them left, I think—Mareschal, Airley, Winton, Wemyss, Balmerino, all passed and gone—ay, ay, the countesses and ladies of quality will scarce take up too much of your ball-room floor with their quality hoops now-a-days.'

'There is no want of crowding, however, sir,' said Fairford; 'they begin to talk of a new Assembly-Room.'

'A new Assembly-Room!' said the old Jacobite Laird—'Umph—I mind quartering three hundred men in the old Assembly-Room[47]—But come, come—I'll ask no more questions—the answers all smell of new lords new lands,* and do but spoil my appetite, which were a pity, since here comes Mrs Crosbie to say our mutton's ready.'

It was even so. Mrs Crosbie had been absent, like Eve, 'on hospitable cares intent,'* a duty which she did not conceive herself exempted from, either by the dignity of her husband's rank in the municipality, or the splendour of her Brussels silk gown, or even by the more highly prized lustre of her birth; for she was born a Maxwell, and allied, as her husband often informed his friends, to several of the first families in the county. She had been handsome, and was still a portly good-looking woman of her years; and though her peep into the kitchen had somewhat heightened her complexion, it was no more than a modest touch of rouge might have done.

The Provost was certainly proud of his lady, nay, some said he was afraid of her; for, of the females of the Redgauntlet family there went a rumour, that, ally where they would, there was a grey mare as surely in the stables of their husbands, as there is a white horse in Wouvermans' pictures.* The good dame, too, was supposed to have brought a spice of politics into Mr Crosbie's household along with her; and the Provost's enemies at the Council-table of the burgh used to observe, that he uttered there many a bold harangue against the Pretender, and in favour of King George and government, of which he dared not have pronounced a syllable in his own bedchamber; and that, in fact, his wife's predominating influence had now and then occasioned his acting, or forbearing to act, in a manner very different from his general professions of zeal for Revolution principles. If this was in any respect true, it was certain, on the other hand, that Mrs Crosbie, in all external points, seemed to acknowledge the 'lawful sway and right supremacy'* of the head of the house, and if she did not in truth reverence her husband, she at least seemed to do so.

This stately dame received Mr Maxwell (a cousin of course) with cordiality, and Fairford with civility; answering, at the same time, with respect, to the magisterial complaints of the Provost, that dinner was just coming up. 'But since you changed poor Peter MacAlpin, that used to take care of the town-clock, my dear, it has never gone well a single day.'

'Peter MacAlpin, my dear,' said the Provost, 'made himself too busy for a person in office, and drunk healths and so forth, which it became no man to drink or to pledge, far less one that is in point of office a servant of the public. I understand that he lost the music-bells in Edinburgh, for playing "Ower the water to Charlie," upon the tenth of June.* He is a black sheep, and deserves no encouragement.'

'Not a bad tune, though, after all,' said Summertrees; and, turning to the window, he half hummed, half whistled the air in question, then sang the last verse aloud:

'Oh I loe weel my Charlie's name,
Though some there be that abhor him;

But oh to see the deil gang hame
Wi' a' the Whigs before him!
Over the water, and over the sea,
And over the water to Charlie;
Come weal, come woe, we'll gather and go,
And live or die with Charlie.'

Mrs Crosbie smiled furtively on the Laird, wearing an aspect at the same time of deep submission; while the Provost, not choosing to hear his visitor's ditty, took a turn through the room, in unquestioned dignity and independence of authority.

'Aweel, aweel, my dear,' said the lady, with a quiet smile of submission, 'ye ken these matters best, and you will do your pleasure—they are far above my hand—only, I doubt if ever the town-clock will go right, or your meals be got up so regular as I should wish, till Peter MacAlpin gets his office back again. The body's auld, and can neither work nor want, but he is the only hand to set a clock.'

It may be noticed in passing, that, notwithstanding this prediction, which, probably, the fair Cassandra had the full means of accomplishing, it was not till the second council-day thereafter that the misdemeanours of the Jacobite clock-keeper were passed over, and he was once more restored to his occupation of fixing the town's time, and the Provost's dinner-hour.

Upon the present occasion the dinner passed pleasantly away. Summertrees talked and jested with the easy indifference of a man who holds himself superior to his company. He was indeed an important person, as was testified by his portly appearance; his hat laced with *point d'Espagne*; his coat and waistcoat once richly embroidered, though now almost threadbare; the splendour of his solitaire, and laced ruffles, though the first was sorely creased, and the other sullied; not to forget the length of his silver-hilted rapier. His wit, or rather humour, bordered on the sarcastic, and intimated a discontented man; and although he showed no displeasure when the Provost attempted a repartee, yet it seemed that he permitted it upon mere sufferance, as a fencing-master, engaged with a pupil, will sometimes permit the tyro to hit him, solely by way of encouragement. The Laird's own jests, in the meanwhile, were eminently successful, not only with the Provost and his lady, but with the red-cheeked and red-ribboned servant-maid who waited at table, and who could scarce perform her duty with propriety, so effectual were the explosions of Summertrees. Alan Fairford alone was unmoved among all this mirth; which was the less wonderful, that, besides the important subject which occupied his thoughts, most of the Laird's good things consisted in sly allusions to little parochial or family incidents, with which the Edinburgh visitor was totally unacquainted; so that the laughter of the party sounded in his ear like the idle crackling of thorns under the pot,* with this difference, that they did not accompany or second any such useful operation as the boiling thereof.

Fairford was glad when the cloth was withdrawn; and when Provost Crosbie (not without some points of advice from his lady, touching the precise mixture of the ingredients) had accomplished the compounding of a noble bowl of punch, at which the old Jacobite's eyes seemed to glisten, the glasses were pushed round it, filled, and withdrawn each by its owner, when the Provost emphatically named the toast, 'The King,' with an important look to Fairford, which seemed to say, You can have no doubt whom I mean, and therefore there is no occasion to particularize the individual.

Summertrees repeated the toast with a sly wink to the lady, while Fairford drank his glass in silence.

'Well, young advocate,' said the landed proprietor, 'I am glad to see there is some shame, if there is little honesty, left in the Faculty. Some of your black-gowns, now-a-days, have as little of the one as of the other.'

'At least, sir,' replied Mr Fairford, 'I am so much of a lawyer as not willingly to enter into disputes which I am not retained to support—it would be but throwing away both time and argument.'

'Come, come,' said the lady, 'we will have no argument in this house about Whig or Tory—the Provost kens what he maun *say*, and I ken what he should *think*; and for a' that has come and gane yet, there may be a time coming when honest men may say what they think, whether they be Provosts or not.'

'D'ye hear that, Provost?' said Summertrees; 'your wife's a witch, man; you should nail a horseshoe on your chamber-door*—Ha, ha, ha!'

This sally did not take quite so well as former efforts of the Laird's wit. The lady drew up, and the Provost said, half aside, 'The sooth bourd is nae bourd.[48] You will find the horseshoe hissing hot, Summertrees.'

'You can speak from experience, doubtless, Provost,' answered the Laird; 'but I crave pardon—I need not tell Mrs Crosbie that I have all respect for the auld and honourable House of Redgauntlet.'

'And good reason ye have, that are sae sib to them,' quoth the lady, 'and kend weel baith them that are here, and them that are gane.'

'In troth, and ye may say sae, madam,' answered the Laird; 'for poor Harry Redgauntlet that suffered at Carlisle, was hand and glove with me; and yet we parted on short leave-taking.'

'Ay, Summertrees,' said the Provost; 'that was when you played Cheat-the-woodie, and gat the by-name of Pate-in-Peril. I wish you would tell the story to my young friend here. He likes weel to hear of a sharp trick, as most lawyers do.'

'I wonder at your want of circumspection, Provost,' said the Laird,—much after the manner of a singer, when declining to sing the song that is quivering upon his tongue's very end. 'Ye should mind there are some auld stories that cannot be ripped up again with entire safety to all concerned. *Tace* is Latin for a candle.'*

'I hope,' said the lady, 'you are not afraid of any thing being said out of this house to your prejudice, Summertrees? I have heard the story before; but the oftener I hear it, the more wonderful I think it.'

'Yes, madam; but it has been now a wonder of more than nine days, and it is time it should be ended,' answered Maxwell.

Fairford now thought it civil to say, 'that he had often heard of Mr Maxwell's wonderful escape, and that nothing could be more agreeable to him than to hear the right version of it.'

But Summertrees was obdurate, and refused to take up the time of the company with such 'auld warld nonsense.'

'Weel, weel,' said the Provost, 'a wilful man maun hae his way.—What do your folk in the county think about the disturbances that are beginning to spunk out in the colonies?'

'Excellent, sir, excellent. When things come to the worst they will mend; and to the worst they are coming.—But as to that nonsense ploy of mine, if ye insist on hearing the particulars,'—said the Laird, who began to be sensible that the period of telling his story gracefully was gliding fast away.

'Nay,' said the Provost, 'it was not for myself, but this young gentleman.'

'Aweel, what for should I not pleasure the young gentleman?—I'll just drink the honest folk at hame and abroad, and deil ane else. And then—but you have heard it before, Mrs Crosbie?'

'Not so often as to think it tiresome, I assure ye,' said the lady; and without further preliminaries, the Laird addressed Alan Fairford.

'Ye have heard of a year they call the *forty-five*, young gentleman; when the Southrons' heads made their last acquaintance with Scottish claymores? There was a set of rampauging chields in the country then that they called rebels—I never could find out what for—Some men should have been wi' them that never came, Provost—Skye and the Bush aboon Traquair* for that, ye ken—Weel, the job was settled at last. Cloured crowns were plenty, and raxed necks came into fashion. I dinna mind very weel what I was doing, swaggering about the country with dirk and pistol at my belt for five or six months, or thereaway; but I had a weary waking out of a wild dream. Then did I find myself on foot in a misty morning, with my hand, just for fear of going astray, linked into a handcuff, as they call it, with poor Harry Redgauntlet's fastened into the other; and there we were, trudging along, with about a score more that had thrust their horns ower deep in the bog, just like ourselves, and a sergeant's guard of redcoats, with twa file of dragoons, to keep all quiet, and give us heart to the road. Now, if this mode of travelling was not very pleasant, the object did not particularly recommend it; for you understand, young man, that they did not trust these poor rebel bodies to be tried by juries of their ain kindly countrymen, though ane would have thought they would have found Whigs enough in Scotland to hang us all; but they behoved to trounce us away to be tried at Carlisle, where the folk had been so frightened,* that had you brought a whole Highland clan at once into the court, they would have put their hands upon their een, and cried, "hang them a'," just to be quit of them.'

'Ay, ay,' said the Provost, 'that was a snell law, I grant ye.'

'Snell!' said his wife, 'snell! I wish they that passed it had the jury I would recommend them to!'

'I suppose the young lawyer thinks it all very right,' said Summertrees, looking at Fairford—'an *old* lawyer might have thought otherwise. However, the cudgel was to be found to beat the dog, and they chose a heavy one. Well, I kept my spirits better than my companion, poor fellow; for I had the luck to have neither wife nor child to think about, and Harry Redgauntlet had both one and t'other.—You have seen Harry, Mrs Crosbie?'

'In troth have I,' said she, with the sigh which we give to early recollections, of which the object is no more. 'He was not so tall as his brother, and a gentler lad every way. After he married the great English fortune, folk called him less of a Scotchman than Edward.'

'Folk lee'd, then,' said Summertrees; 'poor Harry was none of your bold-speaking, ranting reivars, that talk about what they did yesterday, or what they will do to-morrow: it was when something was to do at the moment that you should have looked at Harry Redgauntlet. I saw him at Culloden, when all was lost, doing more than twenty of these bleezing braggarts, till the very soldiers that took him, cried not to hurt him—for all somebody's orders,* Provost—for he was the bravest fellow of them all. Weel, as I went by the side of Harry, and felt him raise my hand up in the mist of the morning, as if he wished to wipe his eye—for he had not that freedom without my leave—my very heart was like to break for him, poor fellow. In the meanwhile, I had been trying and trying to make my hand as fine as a lady's, to see if I could slip it out of my iron wristband. You may think,' he said, laying his broad bony hand on the table, 'I had work enough with such a shoulder-of-mutton fist; but if you observe, the shackle-bones are of the largest, and so they were obliged to keep the handcuff wide; at length I got my hand slipped out, and slipped in again: and poor Harry was sae deep in his ain thoughts, I could not make him sensible what I was doing.'

'Why not?' said Alan Fairford, for whom the tale began to have some interest.

'Because there was an unchancy beast of a dragoon riding close beside us on the other side; and if I had let him into my confidence as well as Harry, it would not have been long before a pistol-ball slapped through my bonnet.—Well, I had little for it but to do the best I could for myself; and, by my conscience, it was time, when the gallows was staring me in the face. We were to halt for breakfast at Moffat. Well did I know the moors we were marching over, having hunted and hawked on every acre of ground in very different times. So I waited, you see, till I was on the edge of Errickstane brae—Ye ken the place they call the Marquis's Beef-stand, because the Annandale loons used to put their stolen cattle in there?'

Fairford intimated his ignorance.

'Ye must have seen it as ye cam this way; it looks as if four hills were laying their heads together, to shut out daylight from the dark hollow space between them. A d—d deep, black, blackguard-looking abyss of a hole it is, and goes straight down from the road-side, as perpendicular as it can do, to be a heathery brae. At the bottom, there is a small bit of a brook, that you would think could hardly find its way out from the hills that are so closely jammed round it.'

'A bad pass indeed,' said Alan.

'You may say that,' continued the Laird. 'Bad as it was, sir, it was my only chance; and though my very flesh creeped when I thought what a rumble I was going to get, yet I kept my heart up all the same. And so just when we came on the edge of this Beef-stand of the Johnstones, I slipped out my hand from the handcuff, cried to Harry Gauntlet, "Follow me!" —whisked under the belly of the dragoon horse—flung my plaid round me with the speed of lightning—threw myself on my side, for there was no keeping by feet, and down the brae hurled I, over heather and fern, and blackberries, like a barrel down Chalmers's Close, in Auld Reekie. G—, sir, I never could help laughing when I think how the scoundrel redcoats must have been bumbazed; for the mist being, as I said, thick, they had little notion, I take it, that they were on the verge of such a dilemma. I was half way down—for rowing is faster wark than rinning—ere they could get at their arms; and then it was flash, flash, flash—rap, rap, rap—from the edge of the road; but my head was too jumbled to think any thing either of that or the hard knocks I got among the stones. I kept my senses thegither, whilk has been thought wonderful by all that ever saw the place; and I helped myself with my hands as gallantly as I could, and to the bottom I came. There I lay for half a moment; but the thoughts of a gallows is worth all the salts and scent-bottles in the world, for bringing a man to himself. Up I sprung, like a four-year-auld colt. All the hills were spinning round with me, like so many great big humming-tops. But there was nae time to think of that neither; more especially as the mist had risen a little with the firing. I could see the villains, like sae mony craws on the edge of the brae; and I reckon that they saw me; for some of the loons were beginning to crawl down the hill, but liker auld wives in their red-cloaks, coming frae a field-preaching, than such a souple lad as I was. Accordingly, they soon began to stop and load their pieces. Good-e'en to you, gentlemen, thought I, if that is to be the gate of it. If you have any further word with me, you maun come as far as Carriefraw-gauns. And so off I set, and never buck went faster ower the braes than I did; and I never stopped till I had put three waters, reasonably deep, as the season was rainy, half-a-dozen mountains, and a few thousand acres of the worst moss and ling in Scotland, betwixt me and my friends the redcoats.'

'It was that job which got you the name of Pate-in-Peril,' said the Provost, filling the glasses, and exclaiming with great emphasis, while his guest, much animated with the recollections which the exploit excited, looked round with an air of triumph for sympathy and applause,—'Here is to your good health; and may you never put your neck in such a venture again.'[49]

'Humph!—I do not know,' answered Summertrees. 'I am not like to be tempted with another opportunity[50]—Yet who knows?' And then he made a deep pause.

'May I ask what became of your friend, sir?' said Alan Fairford.

'Ah, poor Harry!' said Summertrees. 'I'll tell you what, sir, it takes time to make up one's mind to such a venture, as my friend the Provost calls it; and I was told by Neil Maclean,—who was next file to us, but had the luck to escape the gallows by some slight-of-hand trick or other,—that, upon my breaking off, poor Harry stood like one motionless, although all our brethren in captivity made as much tumult as they could, to distract the attention of the soldiers. And run he did at last; but he did not know the ground, and either from confusion, or because he judged the descent altogether perpendicular, he fled up the hill to the left, instead of going down at once, and so was easily pursued and taken. If he had followed my example, he would have found enough among the shepherds to hide him, and feed him, as they did me, on bearmeal scones and braxy mutton,[51] till better days came round again.'

'He suffered then for his share in the insurrection?' said Alan.

'You may swear that,' said Summertrees. 'His blood was too red to be spared when that sort of paint was in request. He suffered, sir, as you call it—that is, he was murdered in cold blood, with many a pretty fellow besides.—Well, we may have our day next—what is fristed is not forgiven—they think us all dead and buried—but'—— Here he filled his glass, and muttering some indistinct denunciations, drank it off, and assumed his usual manner, which had been a little disturbed towards the end of the narrative.

'What became of Mr Redgauntlet's child?' said Fairford.

'*Mister* Redgauntlet!—He was Sir Henry Redgauntlet, as his son, if the child now lives, will be Sir Arthur—I called him Harry from intimacy, and Redgauntlet, as the chief of his name—His proper style was Sir Henry Redgauntlet.'

'His son, therefore, is dead?' said Alan Fairford. 'It is a pity so brave a line should draw to a close.'

'He has left a brother,' said Summertrees, 'Edward Hugh Redgauntlet, who has now the representation of the family. And well it is; for though he be unfortunate in many respects, he will keep up the honour of the house better than a boy bred up amongst these bitter Whigs, the relations of his elder brother Sir Henry's lady. Then they are on no good terms with the Redgauntlet line—bitter Whigs they are, in every sense. It was a runaway match betwixt Sir Henry and his lady. Poor thing, they would not allow her to see him when in confinement—they had even the meanness to leave him without pecuniary assistance; and as all his own property was seized upon and plundered, he would have wanted common necessaries, but for the attachment of a fellow who was a famous fiddler—a blind man—I have seen him with Sir Henry myself, both before the affair broke out and while it was going on. I have heard that he fiddled in the streets of Carlisle, and carried what money he got to his master, while he was confined in the castle.'

'I do not believe a word of it,' said Mrs Crosbie, kindling with indignation. 'A Redgauntlet would have died twenty times before he had touched a fiddler's wages.'

'Hout fye—hout fye—all nonsense and pride,' said the Laird of Summertrees. 'Scornful dogs will eat dirty puddings, cousin Crosbie—ye little ken what some of your friends were obliged to do yon time for a sowp of brose, or a bit of bannock.—G—d, I carried a cutler's wheel for several weeks, partly for need, and partly for disguise—there I went bizz—bizz—whizz—zizz, at every auld wife's door; and if ever you want your shears sharpened, Mrs Crosbie, I am the lad to do it for you, if my wheel was but in order.'

'You must ask my leave first,' said the Provost; 'for I have been told you had some queer fashions of taking a kiss instead of a penny, if you liked your customer.'

'Come, come, Provost,' said the lady, rising, 'if the maut gets abune the meal with you, it is time for me to take myself away—And you will come to my room, gentlemen, when you want a cup of tea.'

Alan Fairford was not sorry for the lady's departure. She seemed too much alive to the honour of the house of Redgauntlet, though only a fourth cousin, not to be alarmed by the enquiries which he proposed to make after the whereabout of its present head. Strange confused suspicions arose in his mind, from his imperfect recollection of the tale of Wandering Willie, and the idea forced itself upon him, that his friend Darsie Latimer might be the son of the unfortunate Sir Henry. But before indulging in such speculations, the point was, to discover what had actually become of him. If he were in the hands of his uncle, might there not exist some rivalry in fortune, or rank, which might induce so stern a man as Redgauntlet to use unfair measures towards a youth whom he would find himself unable to mould to his purpose? He considered these points in silence, during several revolutions of the glasses as they wheeled in galaxy round the bowl, waiting until the Provost, agreeably to his own proposal, should mention the subject, for which he had expressly introduced him to Mr Maxwell of Summertrees.

Apparently the Provost had forgot his promise, or at least was in no great haste to fulfil it. He debated with great earnestness upon the stamp act, which was then impending over the American colonies,* and upon other political subjects of the day, but said not a word of Redgauntlet. Alan soon saw that the investigation he meditated must advance, if at all, on his own special motion, and determined to proceed accordingly.

Acting upon this resolution, he took the first opportunity afforded by a pause in the discussion of colonial politics, to say, 'I must remind you, Provost Crosbie, of your kind promise to procure some intelligence upon the subject I am so anxious about.'

'Gadso!' said the Provost, after a moment's hesitation, 'it is very true.—Mr Maxwell, we wish to consult you on a piece of important business. You must know—indeed I think you must have heard, that the fishermen at Brokenburn, and higher up the Solway, have made a raid upon Quaker Geddes's stake-nets, and levelled all with the sands.'

'In troth I heard it, Provost, and I was glad to hear the scoundrels had so much pluck left, as to right themselves against a fashion which would make the upper heritors a sort of clocking-hens, to hatch the fish that folk below them were to catch and eat.'

'Well, sir,' said Alan, 'that is not the present point. But a young friend of mine was with Mr Geddes at the time this violent procedure took place, and he has not since been heard of. Now, our friend, the Provost, thinks that you may be able to advise'——

Here he was interrupted by the Provost and Summertrees speaking out both at once, the first endeavouring to disclaim all interest in the question, and the last to evade giving an answer.

'Me think!' said the Provost; 'I never thought twice about it, Mr Fairford; it was neither fish, nor flesh, nor salt herring of mine.'

'And I able to advise!' said Mr Maxwell of Summertrees; 'what the devil can I advise you to do, excepting to send the bellman through the town to cry your lost sheep, as they do spaniel dogs or stray ponies?'

'With your pardon,' said Alan, calmly, but resolutely, 'I must ask a more serious answer.'

'Why, Mr Advocate,' answered Summertrees, 'I thought it was your business to give advice to the lieges, and not to take it from poor stupid country gentlemen.'

'If not exactly advice, it is sometimes our duty to ask questions, Mr Maxwell.'

'Ay, sir, when you have your bag-wig and your gown on, we must allow you the usual privilege of both gown and petticoat, to ask what questions you please. But when you are out of your canonicals the case is altered. How come you, sir, to suppose that I have any business with this riotous proceeding, or should know more than you do what happened there? The question proceeds on an uncivil supposition.'

'I will explain,' said Alan, determined to give Mr Maxwell no opportunity of breaking off the conversation. 'You are an intimate of Mr Redgauntlet—he is accused of having been engaged in this affray, and of having placed under forcible restraint the person of my friend, Darsie Latimer, a young man of property and consequence, whose fate I am here for the express purpose of investigating. This is the plain state of the case; and all parties concerned,—your friend, in particular,—will have reason to be thankful for the temperate manner in which it is my purpose to conduct the matter, if I am treated with proportionate frankness.'

'You have misunderstood me,' said Maxwell, with a tone changed to more composure; 'I told you I was the friend of the late Sir Henry Redgauntlet, who was executed, in 1745, at Hairibie, near Carlisle, but I know no one who at present bears the name of Redgauntlet.'

'You know Mr Herries of Birrenswork,' said Alan, smiling, 'to whom the name of Redgauntlet belongs?'

Maxwell darted a keen reproachful look towards the Provost, but instantly smoothed his brow, and changed his tone to that of confidence and candour.

'You must not be angry, Mr Fairford, that the poor persecuted nonjurors are a little upon the *qui vive* when such clever young men as you are making enquiries after us. I myself now, though I am quite out of the scrape, and may cock my hat at the Cross as I best like, sunshine or moonshine, have been yet so much accustomed to walk with the lap of my cloak cast over my face, that, faith, if a redcoat walk suddenly up to me, I wish for my wheel and whetstone again for a moment. Now Redgauntlet, poor fellow, is far worse off—he is, you may have heard, still under the lash of the law,—the mark of the beast is still on his forehead, poor gentleman,—and that makes us cautious—very cautious—which I am sure there is no occasion to be towards you, as no one of your appearance and manners would wish to trepan a gentleman under misfortune.'

'On the contrary, sir,' said Fairford, 'I wish to afford Mr Redgauntlet's friends an opportunity to get him out of the scrape, by procuring the instant liberation of my friend Darsie Latimer. I will engage, that if he has sustained no greater bodily harm than a short confinement, the matter may be passed over quietly, without enquiry; but to attain this end, so desirable for the man who has committed a great and recent infraction of the laws, which he had before grievously offended, very speedy reparation of the wrong must be rendered.'

Maxwell seemed lost in reflection, and exchanged a glance or two, not of the most comfortable or congratulatory kind, with his host the Provost. Fairford rose and walked about the room, to allow them an opportunity of conversing together; for he was in hopes that the impression he had visibly made upon Summertrees was likely to ripen into something favourable to his purpose. They took the opportunity, and engaged in whispers to each other, eagerly and reproachfully on the part of the Laird, while the Provost answered in an embarrassed and apologetical tone. Some broken words of the conversation reached Fairford, whose presence they seemed to forget, as he stood at the bottom of the room, apparently intent upon examining the figures upon a fine Indian screen, a present to the Provost from his brother, captain of a vessel in the Company's service.* What he overheard made it evident that his errand, and the obstinacy with which he pursued it, occasioned altercation between the whisperers.

Maxwell at length let out the words, 'A good fright; and so send him home with his tail scalded, like a dog that has come a privateering on strange premises.'

The Provost's negative was strongly interposed—'Not to be thought of'—'making bad worse'—'my situation'—'my utility'—'you cannot conceive how obstinate—just like his father.'

They then whispered more closely, and at length the Provost raised his drooping crest, and spoke in a cheerful tone. 'Come, sit down to your glass, Mr Fairford; we have laid our heads thegither, and you shall see it will not be our fault if you are not quite pleased, and Mr Darsie Latimer let loose to take his fiddle under his neck again. But Summertrees thinks it will require you to put yourself into some bodily risk, which maybe you may not be so keen of.'

'Gentlemen,' said Fairford, 'I will not certainly shun any risk by which my object may be accomplished; but I bind it on your consciences—on yours, Mr Maxwell, as a man of honour and a gentleman; and on yours, Provost, as a magistrate and a loyal subject, that you do not mislead me in this matter.'

'Nay, as for me,' said Summertrees, 'I will tell you the truth at once, and fairly own that I can certainly find you the means of seeing Redgauntlet, poor man; and that I will do, if you require it, and conjure him also to treat you as your errand requires; but poor Redgauntlet is much changed—indeed, to say truth, his temper never was the best in the world; however, I will warrant you from any very great danger.'

'I will warrant myself from such,' said Fairford, 'by carrying a proper force with me.'

'Indeed,' said Summertrees, 'you will do no such thing; for, in the first place, do you think that we will deliver up the poor fellow into the hands of the Philistines, when, on the contrary, my only reason for furnishing you with the clew I am to put into your hands, is to settle the matter amicably on all sides? And secondly, his intelligence is so good, that were you coming near him with soldiers, or constables, or the like, I shall answer for it, you will never lay salt on his tail.'

Fairford mused for a moment. He considered, that to gain sight of this man, and knowledge of his friend's condition, were advantages to be purchased at every personal risk; and he saw plainly, that were he to take the course most safe for himself, and call in the assistance of the law, it was clear he would either be deprived of the intelligence necessary to guide him, or that Redgauntlet would be apprized of his danger, and might probably leave the country, carrying his captive along with him. He therefore repeated, 'I put myself on your honour, Mr Maxwell; and I will go alone to visit your friend. I have little doubt I shall find him amenable to reason;

and that I shall receive from him a satisfactory account of Mr Latimer.'

'I have little doubt that you will,' said Mr Maxwell of Summertrees; 'but still I think it will be only in the long run, and after having sustained some delay and inconvenience. My warrandice goes no farther.'

'I will take it as it is given,' said Alan Fairford. 'But let me ask, would it not be better, since you value your friend's safety so highly, and surely would not willingly compromise mine, that the Provost or you should go with me to this man, if he is within any reasonable distance, and try to make him hear reason?'

'Me!—I will not go my foot's length,' said the Provost; 'and that, Mr Alan, you may be well assured of. Mr Redgauntlet is my wife's fourth cousin, that is undeniable; but were he the last of her kin and mine both, it would ill befit my office to be communing with rebels.'

'Ay, or drinking with nonjurors,' said Maxwell, filling his glass. 'I would as soon expect to have met Claverhouse at a field-preaching.* And as for myself, Mr Fairford, I cannot go, for just the opposite reason. It would be *infra dig.* in the Provost of this most flourishing and loyal town to associate with Redgauntlet; and for me, it would be *noscitur a socio.* There would be post to London, with the tidings that two such Jacobites as Redgauntlet and I had met on a braeside—the Habeas Corpus* would be suspended—fame would sound a charge from Carlisle to the Land's-End— and who knows but the very wind of the rumour might blow my estate from between my fingers, and my body over Errickstane-brae again? No, no; bide a gliff—I will go into the Provost's closet, and write a letter to Redgauntlet, and direct you how to deliver it.'

'There is pen and ink in the office,' said the Provost, pointing to the door of an inner apartment, in which he had his walnut-tree desk, and east-country cabinet.

'A pen that can write, I hope?' said the old Laird.

'It can write and spell baith,—in right hands,' answered the Provost, as the Laird retired and shut the door behind him.

CHAPTER XII

NARRATIVE OF ALAN FAIRFORD, CONTINUED

THE room was no sooner deprived of Mr Maxwell of Summertrees's presence, than the Provost looked very warily above, beneath, and around the apartment, hitched his chair towards that of his remaining guest, and began to speak in a whisper which could not have startled 'the smallest mouse that creeps on floor.'*

'Mr Fairford,' said he, 'you are a good lad; and, what is more, you are my auld friend your father's son. Your father has been agent for this burgh for years, and has a good deal to say with the council; so there have been a sort of obligations between him and me; it may have been now on this side and now on that; but obligations there have been. I am but a plain man, Mr Fairford; but I hope you understand me?'

'I believe you mean me well, Provost; and I am sure,' replied Fairford, 'you can never better show your kindness than on this occasion.'

'That's it—that's the very point I would be at, Mr Alan,' replied the Provost; 'besides, I am, as becomes well my situation, a stanch friend to Kirk and King, meaning this present establishment in church and state; and so, as I was saying, you may command my best—advice.'

'I hope for your assistance and co-operation also,' said the youth.

'Certainly, certainly,' said the wary magistrate. 'Well, now, you see one may love the Kirk, and yet not ride on the rigging of it;* and one may love the King, and yet not be cramming him eternally down the throat of the unhappy folk that may chance to like another King better. I have friends and connexions among them, Mr Fairford, as your father may have clients—they are flesh and blood like ourselves, these poor Jacobite bodies—sons of Adam and Eve, after all; and therefore—I hope you understand me?—I am a plain-spoken man.'

'I am afraid I do *not* quite understand you,' said Fairford; 'and if you have any thing to say to me in private, my dear Provost, you had better come quickly out with it, for the Laird of Summertrees must finish his letter in a minute or two.'

'Not a bit, man—Pate is a lang-headed fellow, but his pen does not clear the paper as his greyhound does the Tinwald-furs. I gave him a wipe about that, if you noticed; I can say any thing to Pate-in-Peril—Indeed, he is my wife's near kinsman.'

'But your advice, Provost,' said Alan, who perceived that, like a shy horse, the worthy magistrate always started off from his own purpose just when he seemed approaching to it.

'Weel, you shall have it in plain terms, for I am a plain man.—Ye see, we will suppose that any friend like yourself were in the deepest hole of the Nith, and making a sprattle for your life. Now, you see, such being the case, I have little chance of helping you, being a fat, short-armed man, and no swimmer, and what would be the use of my jumping in after you?'—

'I understand you, I think,' said Alan Fairford. 'You think that Darsie Latimer is in danger of his life.'

'Me!—I think nothing about it, Mr Alan; but if he were, as I trust he is not, he is nae drap's blood akin to you, Mr Alan.'

'But here your friend, Summertrees,' said the young lawyer, 'offers me a letter to this Redgauntlet of yours—What say you to that?'

'Me!' ejaculated the Provost, 'me, Mr Alan? I say neither buff nor stye to it—But ye dinna ken what it is to look a Redgauntlet in the face;—better try my wife, who is but a fourth cousin, before ye venture on the Laird himself—just say something about the Revolution, and see what a look she can gie you.'

'I shall leave you to stand all the shots from that battery, Provost,' replied Fairford. 'But speak out like a man—Do you think Summertrees means fairly by me?'

'Fairly—he is just coming—fairly? I am a plain man, Mr Fairford —but ye said *Fairly?*'

'I do so,' replied Alan, 'and it is of importance to me to know, and to you to tell me if such is the case; for if you do not, you may be an accomplice to murder before the fact, and that under circumstances which may bring it near to murder under trust.'*

'Murder!—who spoke of murder?' said the Provost; 'no danger of that, Mr Alan—only, if I were you—to speak my plain mind'—Here he approached his mouth to the ear of the young lawyer, and, after another acute pang of travail, was safely delivered of his advice in the following abrupt words:—'Take a keek into Pate's letter before ye deliver it.'

Fairford started, looked the Provost hard in the face, and was silent; while Mr Crosbie, with the self-approbation of one who has at length brought himself to the discharge of a great duty, at the expense of a considerable sacrifice, nodded and winked to Alan, as if enforcing his advice; and then swallowing a large glass of punch, concluded, with the sigh of a man released from a heavy burden, 'I am a plain man, Mr Fairford.'

'A plain man?' said Maxwell, who entered the room at that

moment, with the letter in his hand,—'Provost, I never heard you make use of the word, but when you had some sly turn of your own to work out.'

The Provost looked silly enough, and the Laird of Summertrees directed a keen and suspicious glance upon Alan Fairford, who sustained it with professional intrepidity.—There was a moment's pause.

'I was trying,' said the Provost, 'to dissuade our young friend from his wildgoose expedition.'

'And I,' said Fairford, 'am determined to go through with it. Trusting myself to you, Mr Maxwell, I conceive that I rely, as I before said, on the word of a gentleman.'

'I will warrant you,' said Maxwell, 'from all serious consequences—some inconveniences you must look to suffer.'

'To these I shall be resigned,' said Fairford, 'and stand prepared to run my risk.'

'Well then,' said Summertrees, 'you must go'——

'I will leave you to yourselves, gentlemen,' said the Provost, rising; 'when you have done with your crack, you will find me at my wife's tea-table.'

'And a more accomplished old woman never drank cat-lap,' said Maxwell, as he shut the door; 'the last word has him, speak it who will—and yet because he is a whilly-whaw body, and has a plausible tongue of his own, and is well enough connected, and especially because nobody could ever find out whether he is Whig or Tory, this is the third time they have made him Provost!—But to the matter in hand. This letter, Mr Fairford,' putting a sealed one into his hand, 'is addressed, you observe, to Mr H—— of B——, and contains your credentials for that gentleman, who is also known by his family name of Redgauntlet, but less frequently addressed by it, because it is mentioned something invidiously in a certain act of Parliament.* I have little doubt he will assure you of your friend's safety, and in a short time place him at freedom—that is, supposing him under present restraint. But the point is, to discover where he is—and, before you are made acquainted with this necessary part of the business, you must give me your assurance of honour that you will acquaint no one, either by word or letter, with the expedition which you now propose to yourself.'

'How, sir?' answered Alan; 'can you expect that I will not take the precaution of informing some person of the route I am about to take, that in case of accident it may be known where I am, and with what purpose I have gone thither?'

'And can you expect,' answered Maxwell, in the same tone, 'that I am to place my friend's safety, not merely in your hands, but in those of any person you may choose to confide in, and who may use the knowledge to his destruction?—Na—ṇa—I have pledged my word for your safety, and you must give me yours to be private in the matter—giff-gaff—you know.'

Alan Fairford could not help thinking that this obligation to secrecy gave a new and suspicious colouring to the whole transaction; but, considering that his friend's release might depend upon his accepting the condition, he gave it in the terms proposed, and with the resolution of abiding by it.

'And now, sir,' he said, 'whither am I to proceed with this letter? Is Mr Herries at Brokenburn?'

'He is not: I do not think he will come thither again, until the business of the stake-nets be hushed up, nor would I advise him to do so—the Quakers, with all their demureness, can bear malice as long as other folk; and though I have not the prudence of Mr Provost, who refuses to ken where his friends are concealed during adversity, lest, perchance, he should be asked to contribute to their relief, yet I do not think it necessary or prudent to enquire into Redgauntlet's wanderings, poor man, but wish to remain at perfect freedom to answer, if asked at, that I ken nothing of the matter. You must, then, go to old Tom Trumbull's, at Annan—Tam Turnpenny, as they call him,—and he is sure either to know where Redgauntlet is himself, or to find some one who can give a shrewd guess. But you must attend that old Turnpenny will answer no question on such a subject without you give him the pass-word, which at present you must do, by asking him the age of the moon; if he answers, "Not light enough to land a cargo," you are to answer, "Then plague on Aberdeen Almanacks," and upon that he will hold free intercourse with you.—And now, I would advise you to lose no time, for the parole is often changed—and take care of yourself among these moonlight lads, for laws and lawyers do not stand very high in their favour.'

'I will set out this instant,' said the young barrister; 'I will but bid the Provost and Mrs Crosbie farewell, and then get on horseback so soon as the hostler of the George Inn can saddle him;—as for the smugglers, I am neither gauger nor supervisor, and, like the man who met the devil, if they have nothing to say to me, I have nothing to say to them.'

'You are a mettled young man,' said Summertrees, evidently with increasing good-will, on observing an alertness and contempt of danger, which perhaps he did not expect from Alan's appearance and profession,—'a very mettled young fellow indeed! and it is almost a pity'——Here he stopped short.

'What is a pity?' said Fairford.

'It is almost a pity that I cannot go with you myself, or at least send a trusty guide.'

They walked together to the bedchamber of Mrs Crosbie, for it was in that asylum that the ladies of the period dispensed their tea, when the parlour was occupied by the punch-bowl.

'You have been good bairns to-night, gentlemen,' said Mrs Crosbie: 'I am afraid, Summertrees, that the Provost has given you a bad browst; you are not used to quit the lee-side of the punchbowl in such a hurry. I say nothing to you, Mr Fairford, for you are too young a man yet for stoup and bicker; but I hope you will not tell the Edinburgh fine folk that the Provost has scrimped you of your cogie, as the sang says?'*

'I am much obliged for the Provost's kindness, and yours, madam,' replied Alan; 'but the truth is, I have still a long ride before me this evening, and the sooner I am on horseback the better.'

'This evening?' said the Provost, anxiously; 'had you not better take daylight with you to-morrow morning?'

'Mr Fairford will ride as well in the cool of the evening,' said Summertrees, taking the word out of Alan's mouth.

The Provost said no more, nor did his wife ask any questions, nor testify any surprise at the suddenness of their guest's departure.

Having drank tea, Alan Fairford took leave with the usual ceremony. The Laird of Summertrees seemed studious to prevent any further communication between him and the Provost, and remained lounging on the landing-place of the stair while they made their adieus—heard the Provost ask if Alan proposed a speedy return, and the latter reply, that his stay was uncertain, and witnessed the parting shake of the hand, which, with a pressure more warm than usual, and a tremulous, 'God bless and prosper you!' Mr Crosbie bestowed on his young friend. Maxwell even strolled with Fairford as far as the George, although resisting all his attempts at further enquiry into the affairs of Redgauntlet, and referring him to Tom Trumbull, alias Turnpenny, for the particulars which he might find it necessary to enquire into.

At length Alan's hack was produced; an animal long in neck, and high in bone, accoutred with a pair of saddle-bags containing the rider's travelling wardrobe. Proudly surmounting his small stock of necessaries, and no way ashamed of a mode of travelling which a modern Mr Silvertongue would consider as the last of degradations, Alan Fairford took leave of the old Jacobite, Pate-in-Peril, and set forward on the road to the royal burgh of Annan.* His reflections during his ride were none of the most pleasant. He could not disguise from himself that he was venturing rather too rashly into the power of outlawed and desperate persons; for with such only, a man in the situation of Redgauntlet could be supposed to associate. There were other grounds for apprehension. Several marks of intelligence betwixt Mrs Crosbie and the Laird of Summertrees had not escaped Alan's acute observation; and it was plain that the Provost's inclinations towards him, which he believed to be sincere and good, were not firm enough to withstand the influence of this league between his wife and friend. The Provost's adieus, like Macbeth's amen,* had stuck in his throat, and seemed to intimate that he apprehended more than he dared give utterance to.

Laying all these matters together, Alan thought, with no little anxiety, on the celebrated lines of Shakspeare,

> —'A drop,
> That in the ocean seeks another drop,' &c.*

But pertinacity was a strong feature in the young lawyer's character. He was, and always had been, totally unlike the 'horse hot at hand,'* who tires before noon through his own over eager exertions in the beginning of the day. On the contrary, his first efforts seemed frequently inadequate to accomplishing his purpose, whatever that for the time might be; and it was only as the difficulties of the task increased, that his mind seemed to acquire the energy necessary to combat and subdue them. If, therefore, he went anxiously forward upon his uncertain and perilous expedition, the reader must acquit him of all idea, even in a passing thought, of the possibility of abandoning his search, and resigning Darsie Latimer to his destiny.

A couple of hours riding brought him to the little town of Annan, situated on the shores of the Solway, between eight and nine o'clock. The sun had set, but the day was not yet ended; and when he had alighted and seen his horse properly cared for at the principal inn of the place, he was readily directed to Mr Maxwell's friend, old Tom Trumbull, with whom every body seemed well acquainted. He endeavoured to fish out from the lad that acted as a guide, something of this man's situation and profession; but the general expressions of 'a very decent man'—'a very honest body'—'weel to pass in the world,' and such like, were all that could be extracted from him; and while Fairford was following up the investigation with closer interrogatories, the lad put an end to them by knocking at the door of Mr Trumbull, whose decent dwelling was a little distance from the town, and considerably nearer to the sea. It was one of a little row of houses running down to the waterside, and having gardens and other accommodations behind. There was heard within the uplifting of a Scottish psalm; and the boy saying, 'They are at exercise, sir,' gave intimation they might not be admitted till prayers were over.

When, however, Fairford repeated the summons with the end of his whip, the singing ceased, and Mr Trumbull himself, with his psalm-book in his hand, kept open by the insertion of his forefinger between the leaves, came to demand the meaning of this unseasonable interruption.

Nothing could be more different than his whole appearance seemed to be from the confidant of a desperate man, and the associate of outlaws in their unlawful enterprises. He was a tall, thin, bony figure, with white hair combed straight down on each side of his face, and an iron-grey hue of complexion; where the lines, or rather, as Quin said of Macklin,* the cordage, of his countenance were so sternly adapted to a devotional and even ascetic expression, that they left no room for any indication of reckless daring, or sly dissimulation. In short, Trumbull appeared a perfect specimen of the rigid old Covenanter, who said only what he thought right, acted on no other principle but that of duty, and, if he committed errors, did so under the full impression that he was serving God rather than man.

'Do you want me, sir?' he said to Fairford, whose guide had slunk to the rear, as if to escape the rebuke of the severe old man,—'We were engaged, and it is the Saturday night.'

Alan Fairford's preconceptions were so much deranged by this man's appearance and manner, that he stood for a moment bewildered, and would as soon have thought of giving a cant password to a clergyman descending from the pulpit, as to the respectable father of a family just interrupted in his prayers for and with the objects of his care. Hastily concluding Mr Maxwell had passed some idle jest on him, or rather that he had mistaken the person to whom he was directed, he asked if he spoke to Mr Trumbull.

'To Thomas Trumbull,' answered the old man—'What may be your business, sir?' And he glanced his eye to the book he held in his hand, with a sigh like that of a saint desirous of dissolution.

'Do you know Mr Maxwell of Summertrees?' said Fairford.

'I have heard of such a gentleman in the country-side, but have no acquaintance with him,' answered Mr Trumbull; 'he is, as I have heard, a Papist; for the whore that sitteth on the seven hills* ceaseth not yet to pour forth the cup of her abomination on these parts.'

'Yet he directed me hither, my good friend,' said Alan. 'Is there another of your name in this town of Annan?'

'None,' replied Mr Trumbull, 'since my worthy father was removed; he was indeed a shining light.—I wish you good-even, sir.'

'Stay one single instant,' said Fairford; 'this is a matter of life and death.'

'Not more than the casting the burden of our sins where they should be laid,' said Thomas Trumbull, about to shut the door in the enquirer's face.

'Do you know,' said Alan Fairford, 'the Laird of Redgauntlet?'

'Now Heaven defend me from treason and rebellion!' exclaimed Trumbull. 'Young gentleman, you are importunate. I live here among my own people, and do not consort with Jacobites and mass-mongers.'

He seemed about to shut the door, but did *not* shut it, a circumstance which did not escape Alan's notice.

'Mr Redgauntlet is sometimes,' he said, 'called Herries of Birrenswork; perhaps you may know him under that name.'

'Friend, you are uncivil,' answered Mr Trumbull; 'honest men have enough to do to keep one name undefiled. I ken nothing about those who have two. Good-even to you, friend.'

He was now about to slam the door in his visitor's face without further ceremony, when Alan, who had observed symptoms that the name of Redgauntlet did not seem altogether so indifferent to him as he pretended, arrested his purpose by saying, in a low voice, 'At least you can tell me what age the moon is?'

The old man started, as if from a trance, and, before answering, surveyed the querist with a keen penetrating glance, which seemed to say, 'Are you really in possession of this key to my confidence, or do you speak from mere accident?'

To this keen look of scrutiny, Fairford replied by a smile of intelligence.

The iron muscles of the old man's face did not, however, relax, as he dropped, in a careless manner, the countersign, 'Not light enough to land a cargo.'

'Then plague of all Aberdeen Almanacks!'

'And plague of all fools that waste time,' said Thomas Trumbull. 'Could you not have said as much at first?—And standing wasting time, and encouraging lookers-on, in the open street too? Come in by—in by.'

He drew his visitor into the dark entrance of the house, and shut the door carefully; then putting his head into an apartment which the murmurs within announced to be filled with the family, he said aloud, 'A work of necessity and mercy—Malachi, take the book—you will sing six double verses of the hundred and nineteen—and you may lecture out of the Lamentations. And, Malachi,'—this he said in an under tone,—'see you give them a screed of doctrine that will last them till I come back; or else these inconsiderate lads will be out of the house, and away to the publics, wasting their precious time, and, it may be, putting themselves in the way of missing the morning tide.'

An inarticulate answer from within intimated Malachi's acquiescence in the commands imposed; and Mr Trumbull, shutting the door, muttered something about fast bind, fast find,* turned the key, and put it into his pocket; and then bidding his visitor have a care of his steps, and make no noise, he led him through the house, and out at a back-door, into a little garden. Here a plaited alley conducted them, without the possibility of their being seen by any neighbour, to a door in the garden-wall, which being opened, proved to be a private entrance into a three-stalled stable; in one of which was a horse, that whinnied on their entrance. 'Hush, hush!' cried the old man, and presently seconded his exhortations to silence by throwing a handful of corn into the manger, and the horse soon converted his acknowledgement of their presence into the usual sound of munching and grinding his provender.

As the light was now failing fast, the old man, with much more alertness than might have been expected from the rigidity of his figure, closed the window-shutters in an instant, produced phosphorus and matches, and lighted a stable-lantern, which he placed on the corn bin, and then addressed Fairford. 'We are private here, young man; and as some time has been wasted already, you will be so kind as to tell me what is your errand. Is it about the way of business, or the other job?'

'My business with you, Mr Trumbull, is to request you will find me the means of delivering this letter, from Mr Maxwell of Summertrees to the Laird of Redgauntlet.'

'Humph—fashious job!—Pate Maxwell will still be the auld man—always Pate-in-Peril—Craig-in-Peril, for what I know. Let me see the letter from him.'

He examined it with much care, turning it up and down, and looking at the seal very attentively. 'All's right, I see; it has the private mark for haste and speed. I bless my Maker that I am no great man, or great man's fellow; and so I think no more of these passages than just to help them forward in the way of business. You are an utter stranger in these parts, I warrant?'

Fairford answered in the affirmative.

'Ay—I never saw them make a wiser choice—I must call some one to direct you what to do—Stay, we must go to him, I believe. You are well recommended to me, friend, and doubtless trusty; otherwise you may see more than I would like to show, or am in the use of showing in the common line of business.'

Saying this, he placed his lantern on the ground, beside the post of one of the empty stalls, drew up a small spring-bolt which secured it to the floor, and then forcing the post to one side, discovered a small trap-door. 'Follow me,' he said, and dived into the subterranean descent to which this secret aperture gave access.

Fairford plunged after him, not without apprehensions of more kinds than one, but still resolved to prosecute the adventure.

The descent, which was not above six feet, led to a very narrow passage, which seemed to have been constructed for the precise purpose of excluding every one who chanced to be an inch more in girth than was his conductor. A small vaulted room, of about eight feet square, received them at the end of this lane. Here Mr Trumbull left Fairford alone, and returned for an instant, as he said, to shut his concealed trapdoor.

Fairford liked not his departure, as it left him in utter darkness; besides that his breathing was much affected by a strong and stifling smell of spirits, and other articles of a savour more powerful than agreeable to the lungs. He was very glad, therefore, when he heard the returning steps of Mr Trumbull, who, when once more by his side, opened a strong though narrow door in the wall, and conveyed Fairford into an immense magazine of spirit-casks, and other articles of contraband trade.

There was a small light at the end of this range of well-stocked subterranean vaults, which, upon a low whistle, began to flicker and move towards them. An undefined figure, holding a dark lantern, with the light averted, approached them, whom Mr Trumbull thus addressed:—'Why were you not at worship, Job; and this Saturday at e'en?'

'Swanston was loading the Jenny, sir; and I stayed to serve out the article.'

'True—a work of necessity, and in the way of business. Does the Jumping Jenny sail this tide?'

'Ay, ay, sir; she sails for'—

'I did not ask you *where* she sailed for, Job,' said the old gentleman, interrupting him. 'I thank my Maker, I know nothing of their incomings or outgoings. I sell my article fairly and in the ordinary way of business; and I wash my hands of every thing else. But what I wished to know is, whether the gentleman called the Laird of the Solway Lakes is on the other side of the Border even now?'

'Ay, ay,' said Job, 'the Laird is something in my own line, you know—a little contraband or so. There is a statute for him—But no matter; he took the sands after the splore at the Quaker's fish-traps yonder; for he has a leal heart the Laird, and is always true to the country-side. But avast—is all snug here?'

So saying, he suddenly turned on Alan Fairford the light side of the lantern he carried, who, by the transient gleam which it threw in passing on the man who bore it, saw a huge figure, upwards of six feet high, with a rough hairy cap on his head, and a set of features corresponding to his bulky frame. He thought also he observed pistols at his belt.

'I will answer for this gentleman,' said Mr Trumbull; 'he must be brought to speech of the Laird.'

'That will be kittle steering,' said the subordinate personage; 'for I understood that the Laird and his folk were no sooner on the other side than the land-sharks were on them, and some mounted lobsters from Carlisle; and so they were obliged to split and squander. There are new brooms out to sweep the country of them they say; for the brush was a hard one; and they say there was a lad drowned;—he was not one of the Laird's gang, so there was the less matter.'

'Peace! prithee, peace, Job Rutledge,' said honest, pacific Mr Trumbull. 'I wish thou couldst remember, man, that I desire to know nothing of your roars and splores, your brooms and brushes. I dwell here among my own people; and I sell my commodity to him who comes in the way of business; and so wash my hands of all consequences, as becomes a quiet subject and an honest man. I never take payment, save in ready money.'

'Ay, ay,' muttered he with the lantern, 'your worship, Mr Trumbull, understands that in the way of business.'

'Well, I hope you will one day know, Job,' answered Mr Trumbull,—'the comfort of a conscience void of offence, and that fears neither gauger nor collector, neither excise nor customs. The business is to pass this gentleman to Cumberland upon earnest business, and to procure him speech with the Laird of the Solway Lakes—I suppose that can be done? Now I think Nanty Ewart, if he sails with the brig this morning tide, is the man to set him forward.'

'Ay, ay, truly is he,' said Job; 'never man knew the Border, dale and fell, pasture and ploughland, better than Nanty; and he can always bring him to the Laird, too, if you are sure the gentleman's right. But indeed that's his own look-out; for were he the best man in Scotland, and the chairman of the d—d Board to boot, and had fifty men at his back, he were as well not visit the Laird for any thing but good. As for Nanty, he is word and blow, a d—d deal fiercer than Cristie Nixon that they keep such a din about. I have seen them both tried, by ——.'

Fairford now found himself called upon to say something; yet his feelings, upon finding himself thus completely in the power of a canting hypocrite, and of his retainer, who had so much the air of a determined ruffian, joined to the strong and abominable fume which they snuffed up with indifference, while it almost deprived him of respiration, combined to render utterance difficult. He stated, however, that he had no evil intentions towards the Laird, as they called him, but was only the bearer of a letter to him on particular business, from Mr Maxwell of Summertrees.

'Ay, ay,' said Job, 'that may be well enough; and if Mr Trumbull is satisfied that the scrive is right, why, we will give you a cast in the Jumping Jenny this tide, and Nanty Ewart will put you on a way of finding the Laird, I warrant you.'

'I may for the present return, I presume, to the inn where I have left my horse?' said Fairford.

'With pardon,' replied Mr Trumbull, 'you have been ower far ben with us for that; but Job will take you to a place where you may sleep rough till he calls you. I will bring you what little baggage you can need—for those who go on such errands must not be dainty. I will myself see after your horse, for a merciful man is merciful to his beast*—a matter too often forgotten in our way of business.'

'Why, Master Trumbull,' replied Job, 'you know that when we are chased, it's no time to shorten sail, and so the boys do ride whip and spur'—— He stopped in his speech, observing the old man had vanished through the door by which he had entered—'That's always the way with old Turnpenny,' he said to Fairford; 'he cares for nothing of the trade but the profit—now, d—me, if I don't think the fun of it is better worth while. But come along, my fine chap; I must stow you away in safety until it is time to go aboard.'

CHAPTER XIII

NARRATIVE OF ALAN FAIRFORD, CONTINUED

FAIRFORD followed his gruff guide among a labyrinth of barrels and puncheons, on which he had more than once like to have broken his nose, and from thence into what, by the glimpse of the passing lantern upon a desk and writing materials, seemed to be a small office for the dispatch of business. Here there appeared no exit; but the smuggler, or smuggler's ally, availing himself of a ladder, removed an old picture, which showed a door about seven feet from the ground, and Fairford, still following Job, was involved in another tortuous and dark passage, which involuntarily reminded him of Peter Peebles's lawsuit. At the end of this labyrinth, when he had little guess where he had been conducted, and was, according to the French phrase, totally *desorienté*, Job suddenly set down the lantern, and availing himself of the flame to light two candles which stood on the table, asked if Alan would choose any thing to eat, recommending, at all events, a slug of brandy to keep out the night air. Fairford declined both, but enquired after his baggage.

'The old master will take care of that himself,' said Job Rutledge; and drawing back in the direction in which he had entered, he vanished from the further end of the apartment, by a mode which the candles, still shedding an imperfect light, gave Alan no means of ascertaining. Thus the adventurous young lawyer was left alone in the apartment to which he had been conducted by so singular a passage.

In this condition, it was Alan's first employment to survey, with some accuracy, the place where he was; and accordingly, having trimmed the lights, he walked slowly round the apartment, examining its appearance and dimensions. It seemed to be such a small dining-parlour as is usually found in the house of the better class of artisans, shopkeepers, and such persons, having a recess at the upper end, and the usual furniture of an ordinary description. He found a door, which he endeavoured to open, but it was locked on the outside. A corresponding door on the same side of the apartment admitted him into a closet, upon the front shelves of which were punch-bowls, glasses, tea-cups, and the like, while on one side was hung a horseman's great-coat of the coarsest materials, with two great horse-pistols peeping out of the pocket, and on the floor stood a pair of well-spattered jack-boots, the usual equipment of the time, at least for long journeys.

Not greatly liking the contents of the closet, Alan Fairford shut the door, and resumed his scrutiny round the walls of the apartment, in order to discover the mode of Job Rutledge's retreat. The secret passage was, however, too artificially concealed, and the young lawyer had nothing better to do than to meditate on the singularity of his present situation. He had long known that the excise laws had occasioned an active contraband trade betwixt Scotland and England, which then, as now, existed, and will continue to exist, until the utter abolition of the wretched system which establishes an inequality of duties betwixt the different parts of the same kingdom; a system, be it said in passing, mightily resembling the conduct of a pugilist, who should tie up one arm that he might fight the better with the other. But Fairford was unprepared for the expensive and regular establishments by which the illicit traffic was carried on, and could not have conceived that the capital employed in it should have been adequate to the erection of these extensive buildings, with all their contrivances for secrecy of communication. He was musing on these circumstances, not without some anxiety for the progress of his own journey, when suddenly, as he lifted his eyes, he discovered old Mr Trumbull at the upper end of the apartment, bearing in one hand a small bundle, in the other his dark lantern, the light of which, as he advanced, he directed full upon Fairford's countenance.

Though such an apparition was exactly what he expected, yet he did not see the grim, stern old man present himself thus suddenly without emotion; especially when he recollected, what to a youth of his pious education was peculiarly shocking, that the grizzled hypocrite was probably that instant arisen from his knees to Heaven, for the purpose of engaging in the mysterious transactions of a desperate and illegal trade.

The old man, accustomed to judge with ready sharpness of the physiognomy of those with whom he had business, did not fail to remark something like agitation in Fairford's demeanour. 'Have ye taken the rue?' said he. 'Will ye take the sheaf from the mare, and give up the venture?'

'Never!' said Fairford, firmly, stimulated at once by his natural spirit, and the recollection of his friend; 'never, while I have life and strength to follow it out!'

'I have brought you,' said Trumbull, 'a clean shirt and some stockings, which is all the baggage you can conveniently carry, and I will cause one of the lads lend you a horseman's coat, for it is ill sailing or riding without one; and, touching your valise, it will be as safe in my poor house, were it full of the gold of Ophir,* as if it were in the depth of the mine.'

'I have no doubt of it,' said Fairford.

'And now,' said Trumbull, again, 'I pray you to tell me by what name I am to name you to Nanty [which is Antony] Ewart?'

'By the name of Alan Fairford,' answered the young lawyer.

'But that,' said Mr Trumbull, in reply, 'is your own proper name and surname.'

'And what other should I give?' said the young man; 'do you think I have any occasion for an alias? And, besides, Mr Trumbull,' added Alan, thinking a little raillery might intimate confidence of spirit, 'you blessed yourself, but a little while since, that you had no acquaintance with those who defiled their names so far as to be obliged to change them.'

'True, very true,' said Mr Trumbull; 'nevertheless, young man, my grey hairs stand unreproved in this matter; for, in my line of business, when I sit under my vine and my fig-tree,* exchanging the strong waters of the north for the gold which is the price thereof, I have, I thank Heaven, no disguises to keep with any man, and wear my own name of Thomas Trumbull, without any chance that the same may be polluted. Whereas, thou, who art to journey in miry ways, and amongst a strange people, mayst do well to have two names, as thou hast two shirts, the one to keep the other clean.'

Here he emitted a chuckling grunt, which lasted for two vibrations of the pendulum exactly, and was the only approach towards laughter in which old Turnpenny, as he was nicknamed, was ever known to indulge.

'You are witty, Mr Trumbull,' said Fairford; 'but jests are no arguments—I shall keep my own name.'

'At your own pleasure,' said the merchant; 'there is but one name which,'* &c. &c. &c.

We will not follow the hypocrite through the impious cant which he added, in order to close the subject.

Alan followed him, in silent abhorrence, to the recess in which the beaufet was placed, and which was so artificially made as to conceal another of those traps with which the whole building abounded. This concealment admitted them to the same winding passage by which the young lawyer had been brought thither. The path which they now took amid these mazes, differed from the direction in which he had been guided by Rutledge. It led upwards, and terminated beneath a garret window. Trumbull opened it, and with more agility than his age promised, clambered out upon the leads. If Fairford's journey had been hitherto in a stifled and subterranean atmosphere, it was now open, lofty, and airy enough; for he had to follow his guide over leads and slates, which the old smuggler traversed with the dexterity of a cat. It is true his course was facilitated by knowing exactly where certain stepping-places and holdfasts were placed, of which Fairford could not so readily avail himself; but, after a difficult and somewhat perilous progress along the roofs of two or three houses, they at length descended by a skylight into a garret room, and from thence by the stairs into a public-house; for such it appeared by the ringing of bells, whistling for waiters and attendance, bawling of 'House, house, here!' chorus of sea songs, and the like noises.

Having descended to the second story, and entered a room there, in which there was a light, old Mr Trumbull rung the bell of the apartment thrice, with an interval betwixt each, during which, he told deliberately the number twenty. Immediately after the third ringing the landlord appeared, with stealthy step, and an appearance of mystery on his buxom visage. He greeted Mr Trumbull, who was his landlord as it proved, with great respect, and expressed some surprise at seeing him so late, as he termed it, 'on Saturday at e'en.'

'And I, Robin Hastie,' said the landlord to the tenant, 'am more surprised than pleased, to hear sae muckle din in your house, Robie, so near the honourable Sabbath; and I must mind you, that it is contravening the terms of your tack, whilk stipulate, that you should shut your public on Saturday at nine o'clock, at latest.'

'Yes, sir,' said Robin Hastie, no way alarmed at the gravity of the rebuke, 'but you must take tent that I have admitted naebody but you, Mr Trumbull, (who, by the way, admitted yoursell,) since nine o'clock; for the most of the folk have been here for several hours about the lading, and so on, of the brig. It is not full tide yet, and I cannot put the men out into the street. If I did, they would go to some other public, and their souls would be nane the better, and my purse muckle the waur; for how am I to pay the rent, if I do not sell the liquor?'

'Nay, then,' said Thomas Trumbull, 'if it is a work of necessity, and in the honest independent way of business, no doubt there is balm in Gilead.* But prithee, Robin, wilt thou see if Nanty Ewart be, as is most likely, amongst these unhappy topers; and if so, let him step this way cannily, and speak to me and this young gentleman. And it's dry talking, Robin—you must minister to us a bowl of punch—ye ken my gage.'

'From a mutchkin to a gallon, I ken your honour's taste, Mr Thomas Trumbull,' said mine host; 'and ye shall hang me over the sign-post if there be a drap mair lemon or a curn less sugar than just suits you. There are three of you—you will be for the auld Scots peremptory pint-stoup[52] for the success of the voyage?'

'Better pray for it than drink for it, Robin,' said Mr Trumbull. 'Yours is a dangerous trade, Robin; it hurts mony a ane—baith host and guest. But ye will get the blue bowl, Robin—the blue bowl—that will sloken all their drouth, and prevent the sinful repetition of whipping for an eke of a Saturday at e'en. Ay, Robin, it is a pity of

Nanty Ewart—Nanty likes the turning up of his little finger unco weel, and we maunna stint him, Robin, so as we leave him sense to steer by.'

'Nanty Ewart could steer through the Pentland Frith though he were as drunk as the Baltic Ocean,' said Robin Hastie; and instantly tripping down stairs, he speedily returned with the materials for what he called his *browst*, which consisted of two English quarts of spirits, in a huge blue bowl, with all the ingredients for punch, in the same formidable proportion. At the same time he introduced Mr Antony or Nanty Ewart, whose person, although he was a good deal flustered with liquor, was different from what Fairford expected. His dress was what is emphatically termed the shabby genteel—a frock with tarnished lace—a small cocked-hat, ornamented in a similar way—a scarlet waistcoat, with faded embroidery, breeches of the same, with silver knee-bands, and he wore a smart hanger and a pair of pistols in a sullied sword-belt.

'Here I come, patron,' he said, shaking hands with Mr Trumbull. 'Well, I see you have got some grog aboard.'

'It is not my custom, Mr Ewart,' said the old gentleman, 'as you well know, to become a chamberer or carouser thus late on Saturday at e'en; but I wanted to recommend to your attention a young friend of ours, that is going upon a something particular journey, with a letter to our friend the Laird, from Pate-in-Peril, as they call him.'

'Ay—indeed?—he must be in high trust for so young a gentleman. —I wish you joy, sir,' bowing to Fairford. 'By'r lady, as Shakspeare says, you are bringing up a neck to a fair end.*—Come, patron, we will drink to Mr What-shall-call-um—What is his name?—Did you tell me?—And have I forgot it already?'

'Mr Alan Fairford,' said Trumbull.

'Ay, Mr Alan Fairford—a good name for a fair trader—Mr Alan Fairford; and may he be long withheld from the topmost round of ambition, which I take to be the highest round of a certain ladder.'

While he spoke, he seized the punch ladle, and began to fill the glasses. But Mr Trumbull arrested his hand, until he had, as he expressed himself, sanctified the liquor by a long grace; during the pronunciation of which, he shut indeed his eyes, but his nostrils became dilated, as if he were snuffing up the fragrant beverage with peculiar complacency.

When the grace was at length over, the three friends sat down to their beverage, and invited Alan Fairford to partake. Anxious about his situation, and disgusted as he was with his company, he craved, and with difficulty obtained permission, under the allegation of being fatigued, heated, and the like, to stretch himself on a couch which was in the apartment, and attempted at least to procure some rest before high water, when the vessel was to sail.

He was at length permitted to use his freedom, and stretched himself on the couch, having his eyes for some time fixed on the jovial party he had left, and straining his ears to catch if possible a little of their conversation. This he soon found was to no purpose; for what did actually reach his ears was disguised so completely by the use of cant words, and the thieves-Latin called slang, that even when he caught the words, he found himself as far as ever from the sense of their conversation. At length he fell asleep.

It was after Alan had slumbered for three or four hours, that he was wakened by voices bidding him rise up and prepare to be jogging. He started up accordingly, and found himself in presence of the same party of boon companions, who had just dispatched their huge bowl of punch. To Alan's surprise, the liquor had made but little innovation on the brains of men, who were accustomed to drink at all hours, and in the most inordinate quantities. The landlord indeed spoke a little thick, and the texts of Mr Thomas Trumbull stumbled on his tongue; but Nanty was one of those topers, who, becoming early what *bon vivants* term flustered, remain whole nights and days at the same point of intoxication; and, in fact, as they are seldom entirely sober, can be as rarely seen absolutely drunk. Indeed, Fairford, had he not known how Ewart had been engaged whilst he himself was asleep, would almost have sworn when he awoke, that the man was more sober than when he first entered the room.

He was confirmed in this opinion when they descended below, where two or three sailors and ruffian-looking fellows awaited their commands. Ewart took the whole direction upon himself, gave his orders with briefness and precision, and looked to their being executed with the silence and celerity which that peculiar crisis required. All were now dismissed for the brig, which lay, as Fairford was given to understand, a little farther down the river, which is navigable for vessels of light burden, till almost within a mile of the town.

When they issued from the inn, the landlord bid them good-by. Old Trumbull walked a little way with them, but the air had probably considerable effect on the state of his brain; for, after reminding Alan Fairford that the next day was the honourable Sabbath, he became extremely excursive in an attempt to exhort him to keep it holy.* At length, being perhaps sensible that he was becoming unintelligible, he thrust a volume into Fairford's hand—hiccupping at the same time—'Good book—good book—fine hymn-book—fit for the honourable Sabbath, whilk awaits us to-morrow morning.'—Here the iron tongue of time told five* from the town steeple of Annan, to the further confusion of Mr Trumbull's already disordered ideas. 'Ay? is Sunday come and gone already?—

Heaven be praised! Only it is a marvel the afternoon is sae dark for the time of the year—Sabbath has slipped ower quietly, but we have reason to bless oursells it has not been altogether misemployed. I heard little of the preaching—a cauld moralist, I doubt, served that out—but, eh—the prayer—I mind it as if I had said the words mysell.'—Here he repeated one or two petitions, which were probably a part of his family devotions, before he was summoned forth to what he called the way of business. 'I never remember a Sabbath pass so cannily off in my life.'—Then he recollected himself a little, and said to Alan, 'You may read that book, Mr Fairford, to-morrow, all the same, though it be Monday; for, you see, it was Saturday when we were thegether, and now it's Sunday, and it's dark night—so the Sabbath has slipped clean away through our fingers, like water through a sieve, which abideth not; and we have to begin again to-morrow morning, in the weariful, base, mean, earthly employments, whilk are unworthy of an immortal spirit—always excepting the way of business.'

Three of the fellows were now returning to the town, and, at Ewart's command, they cut short the patriarch's exhortation, by leading him back to his own residence. The rest of the party then proceeded to the brig, which only waited their arrival to get under weigh and drop down the river. Nanty Ewart betook himself to steering the brig, and the very touch of the helm seemed to dispel the remaining influence of the liquor which he had drunk, since, through a troublesome and intricate channel, he was able to direct the course of his little vessel with the most perfect accuracy and safety.

Alan Fairford, for some time, availed himself of the clearness of the summer morning to gaze on the dimly seen shores betwixt which they glided, becoming less and less distinct as they receded from each other, until at length, having adjusted his little bundle by way of pillow, and wrapt around him the great-coat with which old Trumbull had equipped him, he stretched himself on the deck, to try to recover the slumber out of which he had been awakened. Sleep had scarce begun to settle on his eyes, ere he found something stirring about his person. With ready presence of mind he recollected his situation, and resolved to show no alarm until the purpose of this became obvious; but he was soon relieved from his anxiety, by finding it was only the result of Nanty's attention to his comfort, who was wrapping around him, as softly as he could, a great boat-cloak, in order to defend him from the morning air.

'Thou art but a cockerel,' he muttered, 'but 'twere pity thou wert knocked off the perch before seeing a little more of the sweet and sour of this world—though, faith, if thou hast the usual luck of it, the best way were to leave thee to the chance of a seasoning fever.'

These words, and the awkward courtesy with which the skipper of the little brig tucked the sea-coat round Fairford, gave him a confidence of safety which he had not yet thoroughly possessed. He stretched himself in more security on the hard planks, and was speedily asleep, though his slumbers were feverish and unrefreshing.

It has been elsewhere intimated that Alan Fairford inherited from his mother a delicate constitution, with a tendency to consumption; and, being an only child, with such a cause for apprehension, care, to the verge of effeminacy, was taken to preserve him from damp beds, wet feet, and those various emergencies, to which the Caledonian boys of much higher birth, but more active habits, are generally accustomed. In man, the spirit sustains the constitutional weakness, as in the winged tribes the feathers bear aloft the body. But there is a bound to these supporting qualities; and as the pinions of the bird must at length grow weary, so the *vis animi* of the human struggler becomes broken down by continued fatigue.

When the voyager was awakened by the light of the sun now riding high in Heaven, he found himself under the influence of an almost intolerable headach, with heat, thirst, shootings across the back and loins, and other symptoms intimating violent cold, accompanied with fever. The manner in which he had passed the preceding day and night, though perhaps it might have been of little consequence to most young men, was to him, delicate in constitution and nurture, attended with bad and even perilous consequences. He felt this was the case, yet would fain have combated the symptoms of indisposition, which, indeed, he imputed chiefly to sea-sickness. He sat up on deck, and looked on the scene around, as the little vessel, having borne down the Solway Frith, was beginning, with a favourable northerly breeze, to bear away to the southward, crossing the entrance of the Wampool river, and preparing to double the most northerly point of Cumberland.

But Fairford felt annoyed with deadly sickness, as well as by pain of a distressing and oppressive character; and neither Criffel, rising in majesty on the one hand, nor the distant yet more picturesque outline of Skiddaw and Glaramara upon the other, could attract his attention in the manner in which it was usually fixed by beautiful scenery, and especially that which had in it something new as well as striking. Yet it was not in Alan Fairford's nature to give way to despondence, even when seconded by pain. He had recourse, in the first place, to his pocket; but instead of the little Sallust he had brought with him, that the perusal of a favourite classical author might help to pass away a heavy hour, he pulled out the supposed hymn-book with which he had been presented a few hours before, by that temperate and scrupulous person, Mr Thomas Trumbull, *alias* Turnpenny. The volume was bound in sable, and its exterior might have become a psalter. But what was Alan's astonishment to read on the titlepage the following words:—'Merry Thoughts for Merry Men; or, Mother Midnight's Miscellany for the small Hours;'* and, turning over the leaves, he was disgusted with profligate tales, and more profligate songs, ornamented with figures corresponding in infamy with the letterpress.

'Good God!' he thought, 'and did this hoary reprobate summon his family together, and, with such a disgraceful pledge of infamy in his bosom, venture to approach the throne of his Creator? It must be so; the book is bound after the manner of those dedicated to devotional subjects, and doubtless, the wretch, in his intoxication, confounded the books he carried with him, as he did the days of the week.'—Seized with the disgust with which the young and generous usually regard the vices of advanced life, Alan, having turned the leaves of the book over in hasty disdain, flung it from him, as far as he could, into the sea. He then had recourse to the Sallust, which he had at first sought for in vain. As he opened the book, Nanty Ewart, who had been looking over his shoulder, made his own opinion heard.

'I think now, brother, if you are so much scandalized at a little piece of sculduddery, which, after all, does nobody any harm, you had better have given it to me than have flung it into the Solway.'

'I hope, sir,' answered Fairford, civilly, 'you are in the habit of reading better books.'

'Faith,' answered Nanty, 'with help of a little Geneva text, I could read my Sallust as well as you can;' and snatching the book from Alan's hand, he began to read, in the Scottish accent:—'"*Igitur ex divitiis juventutem luxuria atque avaritia cum superbia invasere: rapere, consumere; sua parvi pendere, aliena cupere; pudorem, amicitiam, pudicitiam, divina atque humana promiscua, nihil pensi neque moderati habere.*"[53]—There is a slap in the face now, for an honest fellow that has been buccaniering! Never could keep a groat of what he got, or hold his fingers from what belonged to another, said you? Fie, fie, friend Crispus,* thy morals are as crabbed and austere as thy style—the one has as little mercy as the other has grace. By my soul, it is unhandsome to make personal reflections on an old acquaintance, who seeks a little civil intercourse with you after nigh twenty years' separation. On my soul, Master Sallust deserves to float on the Solway better than Mother Midnight herself.'

'Perhaps, in some respects, he may merit better usage at our hands,' said Alan; 'for if he has described vice plainly, it seems to have been for the purpose of rendering it generally abhorred.'

'Well,' said the seaman, 'I have heard of the Sortes Virgilianae,* and I dare say the Sortes Sallustianae are as true every tittle. I have consulted honest Crispus on my own account, and have had a cuff for my pains. But now see, I open the book on your behalf, and behold what occurs first to my eye!—Lo you there—"*Catilina . . . omnium flagitiosorum atque facinorosorum circum se habebat.*" And then again—"*Etiam si quis a culpa vacuus in amicitiam ejus inciderat, quotidiano usu par similisque ceteris efficiebatur.*"[54] That is what I call plain speaking on the part of the old Roman, Mr Fairword. By the way, that is a capital name for a lawyer.'

'Lawyer as I am,' said Fairford, 'I do not understand your innuendo.'

'Nay, then,' said Ewart, 'I can try it another way, as well as the hypocritical old rascal Turnpenny himself could do. I would have you to know that I am well acquainted with my Bible-book, as well as with my friend Sallust.' He then, in a snuffling and canting tone, began to repeat the Scripture text—'"*David therefore departed thence, and went to the cave of Adullam. And every one that was in distress, and every one that was in debt, and every one that was discontented, gathered themselves together unto him, and he became a captain over them.*"* What think you of that?' he said, suddenly changing his manner. 'Have I touched you now, sir?'

'You are as far off as ever,' replied Fairford.

'What the devil! and you a repeating frigate between Summertrees and the Laird! Tell that to the marines—the sailors won't believe it.* But you are right to be cautious, since you can't say who are right, who not.—But you look ill; it's but the cold morning air—Will you have a can of flip, or a jorum of hot rumbo?—or will you splice the main-brace'—(showing a spirit-flask)—'Will you have a quid—or a pipe—or a cigar?—a pinch of snuff, at least, to clear your brains and sharpen your apprehension?'

Fairford rejected all these friendly propositions.

'Why, then,' continued Ewart, 'if you will do nothing for the free trade, I must patronise it myself.'

So saying, he took a large glass of brandy.

'A hair of the dog that bit me,' he continued,—'of the dog that will worry me one day soon; and yet, and be d—d to me for an idiot, I must always have him at my throat. But, says the old catch'—Here he sung, and sung well—

> '"Let's drink—let's drink—while life we have;
> We'll find but cold drinking, cold drinking in the grave."*

All this,' he continued, 'is no charm against the headach. I wish I had any thing that could do you good.—Faith, and we have tea and coffee aboard! I'll open a chest or a bag, and let you have some in an instant. You are at the age to like such cat-lap better than better stuff.'

Fairford thanked him, and accepted his offer of tea.

Nanty Ewart was soon heard calling about, 'Break open yon chest—take out your capful, you bastard of a powder-monkey; we may want it again.—No sugar?—all used up for grog, say you?—knock another loaf to pieces, can't ye?—and get the kettle boiling, ye hell's baby, in no time at all!'

By dint of these energetic proceedings, he was in a short time able to return to the place where his passenger lay sick and exhausted, with a cup, or rather a canful, of tea; for every thing was on a large scale on board of the Jumping Jenny. Alan drank it eagerly, and with so much appearance of being refreshed, that Nanty Ewart swore he would have some too, and only laced it, as his phrase went, with a single glass of brandy.[55]*

CHAPTER XIV

NARRATIVE OF ALAN FAIRFORD, CONTINUED

WE left Alan Fairford on the deck of the little smuggling brig, in that disconsolate situation, when sickness and nausea attack a heated and fevered frame, and an anxious mind. His share of sea-sickness, however, was not so great as to engross his sensations entirely, or altogether to divert his attention from what was passing around. If he could not delight in the swiftness and agility with which the 'little frigate' walked the waves, or amuse himself by noticing the beauty of the sea-views around him, where the distant Skiddaw raised his brow, as if in defiance of the clouded eminence of Criffel, which lorded it over the Scottish side of the estuary, he had spirits and composure enough to pay particular attention to the master of the vessel, on whose character his own safety in all probability was dependent.

Nanty Ewart had now given the helm to one of his people, a bald-pated, grizzled old fellow, whose whole life had been spent in evading the revenue laws, with now and then the relaxation of a few months' imprisonment, for deforcing officers, resisting seizures, and the like offences.

Nanty himself sat down by Fairford, helped him to his tea, with such other refreshments as he could think of, and seemed in his way sincerely desirous to make his situation as comfortable as things admitted. Fairford had thus an opportunity to study his countenance and manners more closely.

It was plain, Ewart, though a good seaman, had not been bred upon that element. He was a reasonably good scholar, and seemed fond of showing it, by recurring to the subject of Sallust and Juvenal;* while, on the other hand, sea-phrases seldom chequered his conversation. He had been in person what is called a smart little man; but the tropical sun had burnt his originally fair complexion to a dusty red; and the bile which was diffused through his system, had stained it with a yellowish black—what ought to have been the white part of his eyes, in particular, had a hue as deep as the topaz. He was very thin, or rather emaciated, and his countenance, though still indicating alertness and activity, showed a constitution exhausted with excessive use of his favourite stimulus.

'I see you look at me hard,' said he to Fairford. 'Had you been an officer of the d—d customs, my terriers' backs would have been up.' He opened his breast, and showed Alan a pair of pistols disposed between his waistcoat and jacket, placing his finger at the same time upon the cock of one of them. 'But come, you are an honest fellow, though you're a close one. I dare say you think me a queer customer; but I can tell you, they that see the ship leave harbour, know little of the seas she is to sail through. My father, honest old gentleman, never would have thought to see me master of the Jumping Jenny.'

Fairford said, it seemed very clear indeed that Mr Ewart's education was far superior to the line he at present occupied.

'O, Criffel to Solway Moss!' said the other. 'Why, man, I should have been an expounder of the word, with a wig like a snow-wreath, and a stipend like—like—like a hundred pounds a-year, I suppose. I can spend thrice as much as that, though, being such as I am.' Here he sung a scrap of an old Northumbrian ditty, mimicking the burr of the natives of that county:—

'Willy Foster's gone to sea,
Siller buckles at his knee,
He'll come back and marry me—
Canny Willy Foster.'*

'I have no doubt,' said Fairford, 'your present occupation is more lucrative; but I should have thought the church might have been more'——

He stopped, recollecting that it was not his business to say any thing disagreeable.

'More respectable, you mean, I suppose?' said Ewart, with a sneer, and squirting the tobacco-juice through his front teeth; then was silent for a moment, and proceeded in a tone of candour which some internal touch of conscience dictated. 'And so it would, Mr Fairford—and happier, too, by a thousand degrees—though I have had my pleasures too. But there was my father, (God bless the old man!) a true chip of the old Presbyterian block, walked his parish like a captain on the quarterdeck, and was always ready to do good to rich and poor—Off went the laird's hat to the minister, as fast as the poor man's bonnet. When the eye saw him—Pshaw! what have I to do with that now?—Yes, he was, as Virgil hath it, "*Vir sapientia et pietate gravis*."* But he might have been the wiser man, had he kept me at home, when he sent me at nineteen to study Divinity at the head of the highest stair in the Covenant-Close.* It was a cursed mistake in the old gentleman. What though Mrs Cantrips of Kittlebasket* (for she wrote herself no less) was our cousin five times removed, and took me on that account to board and lodging, at six shillings, instead of seven shillings a-week? it was a d—d bad saving, as the case proved. Yet her very dignity might have kept me in order; for she never read a chapter excepting out of a Cambridge Bible, printed by Daniel,* and bound in embroidered velvet. I think

I see it at this moment! And on Sundays, when we had a quart of twopenny ale, instead of buttermilk, to our porridge, it was always served up in a silver posset-dish. Also she used silver-mounted spectacles, whereas even my father's were cased in mere horn. These things had their impression at first, but we get used to grandeur by degrees. Well, sir!—Gad, I can scarce get on with my story—it sticks in my throat—must take a trifle to wash it down.—Well, this dame had a daughter—Jess Cantrips, a black-eyed, bouncing wench—and, as the devil would have it, there was the d—d five-story stair—her foot was never from it, whether I went out or came home from the Divinity Hall. I would have eschewed her, sir—I would, on my soul; for I was as innocent a lad as ever came from Lammermuir; but there was no possibility of escape, retreat, or flight, unless I could have got a pair of wings, or made use of a ladder seven stories high, to scale the window of my attic. It signifies little talking—you may suppose how all this was to end—I would have married the girl, and taken my chance—I would, by Heaven! for she was a pretty girl, and a good girl, till she and I met; but you know the old song, "Kirk would not let us be."* A gentleman, in my case, would have settled the matter with the Kirk-treasurer for a small sum of money; but the poor stibbler, the penniless dominie, having married his cousin of Kittlebasket, must next have proclaimed her frailty to the whole parish, by mounting the throne of Presbyterian penance,* and proving, as Othello says, "his love a whore,"* in face of the whole congregation.

'In this extremity I dared not stay where I was, and so thought to go home to my father. But first I got Jack Hadaway, a lad from the same parish, and who lived in the same infernal stair, to make some enquiries how the old gentleman had taken the matter. I soon, by way of answer, learned, to the great increase of my comfortable reflections, that the good old man made as much clamour, as if such a thing as a man's eating his wedding dinner without saying grace had never happened since Adam's time. He did nothing for six days but cry out, "Ichabod, Ichabod, the glory is departed from my house!"* and on the seventh he preached a sermon, in which he enlarged on this incident as illustrative of one of the great occasions for humiliation, and causes of national defection. I hope the course he took comforted himself—I am sure it made me ashamed to show my nose at home. So I went down to Leith, and, exchanging my hoddin grey coat of my mother's spinning for such a jacket as this, I entered my name at the rendezvous as an able-bodied landsman, and sailed with the tender round to Plymouth, where they were fitting out a squadron for the West Indies. There I was put aboard the Fearnought, Captain Daredevil—among whose crew I soon learned to fear Satan, (the terror of my early youth,) as little as the toughest Jack on board. I had some qualms at first, but I took the remedy' (tapping the case-bottle) 'which I recommended to you, being as good for sickness of the soul as for sickness of the stomach—What, you won't?—very well, I must, then—here is to ye.'

'You would, I am afraid, find your education of little use in your new condition?' said Fairford.

'Pardon me, sir,' resumed the Captain of the Jumping Jenny; 'my handful of Latin, and small pinch of Greek, were as useless as old junk, to be sure; but my reading, writing, and accompting, stood me in good stead, and brought me forward. I might have been school-master—ay, and master, in time; but that valiant liquor, rum, made a conquest of me rather too often, and so, make what sail I could, I always went to leeward. We were four years broiling in that blasted climate, and I came back at last with a little prize-money.—I always had thoughts of putting things to rights in the Covenant-Close, and reconciling myself to my father. I found out Jack Hadaway, who was *Tuptowing* away with a dozen of wretched boys, and a fine string of stories he had ready to regale my ears withal. My father had lectured on what he called "my falling away," for seven Sabbaths, when, just as his parishioners began to hope that the course was at an end, he was found dead in his bed on the eighth Sunday morning. Jack Hadaway assured me, that if I wished to atone for my errors, by undergoing the fate of the first martyr, I had only to go to my native village, where the very stones of the street would rise up against me as my father's murderer. Here was a pretty item—well, my tongue clove to my mouth for an hour, and was only able at last to utter the name of Mrs Cantrips. O, this was a new theme for my Job's comforter. My sudden departure—my father's no less sudden death—had prevented the payment of the arrears of my board and lodging—the landlord was a haberdasher, with a heart as rotten as the muslin wares he dealt in. Without respect to her age, or gentle kin, my Lady Kittlebasket was ejected from her airy habitation—her porridge-pot, silver posset-dish, silver-mounted spectacles, and Daniel's Cambridge Bible, sold, at the Cross of Edinburgh, to the cadie who would bid highest for them, and she herself driven to the workhouse, where she got in with difficulty, but was easily enough lifted out, at the end of the month, as dead as her friends could desire. Merry tidings this to me, who had been the d—d' (he paused a moment) '*origo mali*—Gad, I think my confession would sound better in Latin than in English!

'But the best jest was behind—I had just power to stammer out something about Jess—by my faith he *had* an answer! I had taught Jess one trade, and, like a prudent girl, she had found out another for herself; unluckily, they were both contraband, and Jess Cantrips, daughter of the Lady Kittlebasket, had the honour to be transported to the plantations, for street-walking and pocket-picking, about six months before I touched shore.'

He changed the bitter tone of affected pleasantry into an attempt to laugh; then drew his swarthy hand across his swarthy eyes, and said in a more natural accent, 'Poor Jess!'

There was a pause—until Fairford, pitying the poor man's state of mind, and believing he saw something in him that, but for early error and subsequent profligacy, might have been excellent and noble, helped on the conversation by asking, in a tone of commiseration, how he had been able to endure such a load of calamity.

'Why, very well,' answered the seaman; 'exceedingly well—like a tight ship in a brisk gale.—Let me recollect.—I remember thanking Jack, very composedly, for the interesting and agreeable communication; I then pulled out my canvass pouch, with my hoard of moidores, and taking out two pieces, I bid Jack keep the rest till I came back, as I was for a cruise about Auld Reekie. The poor devil looked anxiously, but I shook him by the hand and ran down stairs, in such confusion of mind, that, notwithstanding what I had heard, I expected to meet Jess at every turning.

'It was market-day, and the usual number of rogues and fools were assembled at the Cross. I observed every body looked strange on me, and I thought some laughed. I fancy I had been making queer faces enough, and perhaps talking to myself. When I saw myself used in this manner, I held out my clenched fists straight before me, stooped my head, and, like a ram when he makes his race, darted off right down the street, scattering groups of weatherbeaten lairds and periwigged burgesses, and bearing down all before me. I heard the cry of "Seize the madman!" echoed, in Celtic sounds, from the City Guard, with "Ceaze ta matman!"*—but pursuit and opposition were in vain. I pursued my career; the smell of the sea, I suppose, led me to Leith, where, soon after, I found myself walking very quietly, on the shore, admiring the tough round and sound cordage of the vessels, and thinking how a loop, with a man at the end of one of them, would look, by way of tassel.

'I was opposite to the rendezvous, formerly my place of refuge—in I bolted—found one or two old acquaintances, made half-a-dozen new ones—drank for two days—was put aboard the tender—off to Portsmouth—then landed at the Haslaar hospital* in a fine hissing-hot fever. Never mind—I got better—nothing can kill me—the West Indies were my lot again, for since I did not go where I deserved in the next world, I had something as like such quarters as can be had in this—black devils for inhabitants—flames and earthquakes, and so forth, for your element. Well, brother, something or other I did or said—I can't tell what—How the devil should I when I was as drunk as David's sow,* you know?—But I was punished, my lad—made to kiss the wench that never speaks but when she scolds, and that's the gunner's daughter, comrade. Yes, the minister's son of—no matter where—has the cat's scratch on his back! This roused me—and when we were ashore with the boat, I gave three inches of the dirk, after a stout tussle, to the fellow I blamed most, and so took the bush for it. There were plenty of wild lads then along shore—and, I don't care who knows—I went on the account,* look you—sailed under the black flag and marrow-bones—was a good friend to the sea, and an enemy to all that sailed on it.'

Fairford, though uneasy in his mind at finding himself, a lawyer, so close to a character so lawless, thought it best, nevertheless, to put a good face on the matter, and asked Mr Ewart, with as much unconcern as he could assume, 'whether he was fortunate as a rover?'

'No, no—d—n it, no,' replied Nanty; 'the devil a crumb of butter was ever churned that would stick upon my bread. There was no order among us—he that was captain to-day, was swabber to-morrow; and as for plunder—they say old Avery,* and one or two close hunks, made money; but in my time, all went as it came: and reason good, for if a fellow had saved five dollars, his throat would have been cut in his hammock—And then it was a cruel, bloody work—Pah—we'll say no more about it. I broke with them at last, for what they did on board of a bit of a snow—no matter what it was—bad enough, since it frightened me—I took French leave, and came in upon the proclamation, so I am free of all that business. And here I sit, the skipper of the Jumping Jenny—a nutshell of a thing, but goes through the water like a dolphin. If it were not for yon hypocritical scoundrel at Annan, who has the best end of the profit, and takes none of the risk, I should be well enough—as well as I want to be. Here is no lack of my best friend,'—touching his case-bottle;—'but, to tell you a secret, he and I have got so used to each other, I begin to think he is like a professed joker, that makes your sides sore with laughing, if you see him but now and then; but if you take up house with him, he can only make your head stupid. But I warrant the old fellow is doing the best he can for me, after all.'

'And what may that be?' said Fairford.

'He is KILLING me,' replied Nanty Ewart; 'and I am only sorry he is so long about it.'

So saying he jumped on his feet, and tripping up and down the deck, gave his orders with his usual clearness and decision, notwithstanding the considerable quantity of spirits which he had contrived to swallow while recounting his history.

Although far from feeling well, Fairford endeavoured to rouse himself and walk to the head of the brig, to enjoy the beautiful prospect, as well as to take some note of the course which the vessel held. To his great surprise, instead of standing across to the opposite shore from which she had departed, the brig was going down the Frith, and apparently steering into the Irish sea. He called to Nanty Ewart, and expressed his surprise at the course they were pursuing, and asked why they did not stand straight across the Frith for some port in Cumberland.

'Why, this is what I call a reasonable question, now,' answered Nanty; 'as if a ship could go as straight to its port, as a horse to the stable, or a free-trader could sail the Solway as securely as a King's cutter! Why, I'll tell ye, brother—if I do not see a smoke on Bowness, that is the village upon the headland yonder, I must stand out to sea for twenty-four hours at least, for we must keep the weathergage if there are hawks abroad.'

'And if you do see the signal of safety, Master Ewart, what is to be done then?'

'Why then, and in that case, I must keep off till night, and then run you, with the kegs and the rest of the lumber, ashore at Skinburness.'

'And then I am to meet with this same Laird whom I have the letter for?' continued Fairford.

'That,' said Ewart, 'is thereafter as it may be: the ship has its course—the fair-trader has his port—but it is not so easy to say where the Laird may be found. But he will be within twenty miles of us, off or on—and it will be my business to guide you to him.'

Fairford could not withstand the passing impulse of terror which crossed him, when thus reminded that he was so absolutely in the power of a man, who, by his own account, had been a pirate, and who was at present, in all probability, an outlaw as well as a contraband trader. Nanty Ewart guessed the cause of his involuntary shuddering.

'What the devil should I gain,' he said, 'by passing so poor a card as you are?—Have I not had ace of trumps in my hand, and did I not play it fairly?—Ay, I say the Jumping Jenny can run in other ware as well as kegs. Put *sigma* and *tau* to *Ewart*,* and see how that will spell—D'ye take me now?'

'No indeed,' said Fairford; 'I am utterly ignorant of what you allude to.'

'Now, by Jove!' said Nanty Ewart, 'thou art either the deepest or the shallowest fellow I ever met with—or you are not right after all. I wonder where Summertrees could pick up such a tender along-shore. Will you let me see his letter?'

Fairford did not hesitate to gratify his wish, which, he was aware, he could not easily resist. The master of the Jumping Jenny looked at the direction very attentively, then turned the letter to and fro, and examined each flourish of the pen, as if he were judging of a piece of ornamented manuscript; then handed it back to Fairford, without a single word of remark.

'Am I right now?' said the young lawyer.

'Why, for that matter,' answered Nanty, 'the letter is right, sure enough; but whether *you* are right or not, is your own business, rather than mine.'—And, striking upon a flint with the back of a knife, he kindled a cigar as thick as his finger, and began to smoke away with great perseverance.

Alan Fairford continued to regard him with a melancholy feeling divided betwixt the interest he took in the unhappy man, and a not unnatural apprehension for the issue of his own adventure.

Ewart, notwithstanding the stupifying nature of his pastime, seemed to guess what was working in his passenger's mind; for, after they had remained some time engaged in silently observing each other, he suddenly dashed his cigar on the deck, and said to him, 'Well then, if you are sorry for me, I am sorry for you. D—n me, if I have cared a button for man or mother's son, since two years since, when I had another peep of Jack Hadaway. The fellow was got as fat as a Norway whale—married to a great Dutch-built quean that had brought him six children. I believe he did not know me, and thought I was come to rob his house; however, I made up a poor face, and told him who I was. Poor Jack would have given me shelter and clothes, and began to tell me of the moidores that were in bank, when I wanted them. Egad, he changed his note when I told him what my life had been, and only wanted to pay me my cash and get rid of me. I never saw so terrified a visage. I burst out a-laughing in his face, told him it was all a humbug, and that the moidores were all his own, henceforth and for ever, and so ran off. I caused one of our people send him a bag of tea and a keg of brandy, before I left—poor Jack! I think you are the second person these ten years, that has cared a tobacco-stopper for Nanty Ewart.'

'Perhaps, Mr Ewart,' said Fairford, 'you live chiefly with men too deeply interested for their own immediate safety, to think much upon the distress of others?'

'And with whom do you yourself consort, I pray?' replied Nanty, smartly. 'Why with plotters, that can make no plot to better purpose than their own hanging; and incendiaries, that are snapping the flint upon wet tinder. You'll as soon raise the dead as raise the Highlands—you'll as soon get a grunt from a dead sow as any comfort from Wales or Cheshire. You think because the pot is boiling, that no scum but yours can come uppermost—I know better, by ——. All these rackets and riots that you think are trending your way, have no relation at all to your interest; and the best way to make the whole kingdom friends again at once, would be the alarm of such an undertaking as these mad old fellows are trying to launch into.'

'I really am not in such secrets as you seem to allude to,' said Fairford; and, determined at the same time to avail himself as far as possible of Nanty's communicative disposition, he added, with a smile, 'And if I were, I should not hold it prudent to make them much the subject of conversation. But I am sure, so sensible men as Summertrees and the Laird may correspond together without offence to the state.'

'I take you, friend—I take you,' said Nanty Ewart, upon whom, at length, the liquor and tobacco-smoke began to make considerable innovation. 'As to what gentlemen may or may not correspond about, why we may pretermit the question, as the old Professor used to say at the Hall; and as to Summertrees, I will say nothing, knowing him to be an old fox. But I say that this fellow the Laird is a firebrand in the country; that he is stirring up all the honest fellows who should be drinking their brandy quietly, by telling them stories about their ancestors and the forty-five; and that he is trying to turn all waters into his own mill-dam, and to set his sails to all winds. And because the London people are roaring about for some pinches of their own,* he thinks to win them to his turn with a wet finger. And he gets encouragement from some, because they want a spell of money from him; and from others, because they fought for the cause once, and are ashamed to go back; and others, because they have nothing to lose; and others, because they are discontented fools. But if he has brought you, or any one, I say not whom, into this scrape, with the hope of doing any good, he's a d—d decoy-duck, and that's all I can say for him; and you are geese, which is worse than being decoy-ducks, or lame-ducks either. And so here is to the prosperity of King George the Third, and the true Presbyterian religion, and confusion to the Pope, the Devil, and the Pretender!—I'll tell you what, Mr Fairbairn, I am but tenth owner of this bit of a craft, the Jumping Jenny—but tenth owner—and must sail her by my owners' directions. But if I were whole owner, I would not have the brig be made a ferry-boat for your jacobitical, old-fashioned Popish riff-raff, Mr Fairport—I would not, by my soul; they should walk the plank, by the gods, as I have seen better men do when I sailed under the What-d'ye-callum colours. But being contraband goods, and on board my vessel, and I with my sailing orders in my hand, why, I am to forward them as directed—I say, John Roberts, keep her up a bit with the helm.—And so, Mr Fairweather, what I do is—as the d—d villain Turnpenny says—all in the way of business.'

He had been speaking with difficulty for the last five minutes, and now at length dropped on the deck, fairly silenced by the quantity of spirits which he had swallowed, but without having shown any glimpse of the gaiety, or even of the extravagance, of intoxication.

The old sailor stepped forward and flung a sea-cloak over the slumberer's shoulders, and added, looking at Fairford, 'Pity of him he should have this fault; for without it, he would have been as clever a fellow as ever trode a plank with ox leather.'

'And what are we to do now?' said Fairford.

'Stand off and on, to be sure, till we see the signal, and then obey orders.'

So saying, the old man turned to his duty, and left the passenger to amuse himself with his own meditations. Presently afterward a light column of smoke was seen rising from the little headland.

'I can tell you what we are to do now, master,' said the sailor. 'We'll stand out to sea, and then run in again with the evening tide, and make Skinburness; or, if there's not light, we can run into the Wampool river, and put you ashore about Kirkbride or Leaths, with the long-boat.'

Fairford, unwell before, felt this destination condemned him to an agony of many hours, which his disordered stomach and aching head were ill able to endure. There was no remedy, however, but patience, and the recollection that he was suffering in the cause of friendship. As the sun rose high, he became worse; his sense of smell appeared to acquire a morbid degree of acuteness, for the mere purpose of inhaling and distinguishing all the various odours with which he was surrounded, from that of pitch, to all the complicated smells of the hold. His heart, too, throbbed under the heat, and he felt as if in full progress towards a high fever.

The seamen, who were civil and attentive, considering their calling, observed his distress, and one contrived to make an awning out of an old sail, while another compounded some lemonade, the only liquor which their passenger could be prevailed upon to touch. After drinking it off, he obtained, but could not be said to enjoy, a few hours of troubled slumber.

CHAPTER XV

NARRATIVE OF ALAN FAIRFORD, CONTINUED

ALAN FAIRFORD's spirit was more ready to encounter labour than his frame was adequate to support it. In spite of his exertions, when he awoke, after five or six hours' slumber, he found that he was so much disabled by dizziness in his head, and pains in his limbs, that he could not raise himself without assistance. He heard with some pleasure that they were now running right for the Wampool river, and that he would be put on shore in a very short time. The vessel accordingly lay to, and presently showed a weft in her ensign, which was hastily answered by signals from on shore. Men and horses were seen to come down the broken path which leads to the shore; the latter all properly tackled for carrying their loading. Twenty fishing barks were pushed afloat at once, and crowded round the brig with much clamour, laughter, cursing, and jesting. Amidst all this apparent confusion there was the essential regularity. Nanty Ewart again walked his quarterdeck as if he had never tasted spirits in his life, issued the necessary orders with precision, and saw them executed with punctuality. In half an hour the loading of the brig was in a great measure disposed in the boats; in a quarter of an hour more, it was landed on the beach, and another interval of about the same duration was sufficient to distribute it on the various strings of packhorses which waited for that purpose, and which instantly dispersed, each on its own proper adventure. More mystery was observed in loading the ship's boat with a quantity of small barrels, which seemed to contain ammunition. This was not done until the commercial customers had been dismissed; and it was not until this was performed that Ewart proposed to Alan, as he lay stunned with pain and noise, to accompany him ashore.

It was with difficulty that Fairford could get over the side of the vessel, and he could not seat himself on the stern of the boat without assistance from the captain and his people. Nanty Ewart, who saw nothing in this worse than an ordinary fit of sea-sickness, applied the usual topics of consolation. He assured his passenger that he would be quite well by and by, when he had been half an hour on terra firma, and that he hoped to drink a can and smoke a pipe with him at Father Crackenthorp's, for all that he felt a little out of the way for riding the wooden horse.

'Who is Father Crackenthorp?' said Fairford, though scarcely able to articulate the question.

'As honest a fellow as is of a thousand,' answered Nanty. 'Ah, how much good brandy he and I have made little of in our day! By my soul, Mr Fairbird, he is the prince of skinkers, and the father of the free trade—not a stingy hypocritical devil like old Turnpenny Skinflint, that drinks drunk on other folk's cost, and thinks it sin when he has to pay for it—but a real hearty old cock;—the sharks have been at and about him this many a day, but Father Crackenthorp knows how to trim his sails—never a warrant but he hears of it before the ink's dry. He is *bonus socius* with headborough and constable. The King's Exchequer could not bribe a man to inform against him. If any such rascal were to cast up, why, he would miss his ears next morning, or be sent to seek them in the Solway. He is a statesman,[56] though he keeps a public; but, indeed, that is only for convenience, and to excuse his having cellarage and folk about him; his wife's a canny woman—and his daughter Doll too. Gad, you'll be in port there till you get round again; and I'll keep my word with you, and bring you to speech of the Laird. Gad, the only trouble I shall have is to get you out of the house; for Doll is a rare wench, and my dame a funny old one, and Father Crackenthorp the rarest companion! He'll drink you a bottle of rum or brandy without starting, but never wet his lips with that nasty Scottish stuff that the canting old scoundrel Turnpenny has brought into fashion. He is a gentleman, every inch of him, old Crackenthorp; in his own way, that is; and besides, he has a share in the Jumping Jenny, and many a moonlight outfit besides. He can give Doll a pretty penny, if he likes the tight fellow that would turn in with her for life.'

In the midst of this prolonged panegyric on Father Crackenthorp, the boat touched the beach, the rowers backed their oars to keep her afloat, whilst the other fellows jumped into the surf, and, with the most rapid dexterity, began to hand the barrels ashore.

'Up with them higher on the beach, my hearties,' exclaimed Nanty Ewart—'High and dry—high and dry—this gear will not stand wetting. Now, out with our spare hand here—high and dry with him too. What's that?—the galloping of horse! Oh, I hear the jingle of the packsaddles—they are our own folk.'

By this time all the boat's load was ashore, consisting of the little barrels; and the boat's crew, standing to their arms, ranged themselves in front, waiting the advance of the horses which came clattering along the beach. A man, overgrown with corpulence, who might be distinguished in the moonlight, panting with his own exertions, appeared at the head of the cavalcade, which consisted of horses linked together, and accommodated with packsaddles, and chains for securing the kegs, which made a dreadful clattering.

'How now, Father Crackenthorp?' said Ewart—'Why this hurry

with your horses?—We mean to stay a night with you, and taste your old brandy, and my dame's home-brewed. The signal is up, man, and all is right.'

'All is wrong, Captain Nanty,' cried the man to whom he spoke; 'and you are the lad that is like to find it so, unless you bundle off—there are new brooms bought at Carlisle yesterday to sweep the country of you and the like of you—so you were better be jogging inland.'

'How many rogues are the officers?—If not more than ten, I will make fight.'

'The devil you will!' answered Crackenthorp. 'You were better not, for they have the bloody-backed dragoons from Carlisle with them.'

'Nay, then,' said Nanty, 'we must make sail.—Come, Master Fairlord, you must mount and ride.—He does not hear me—he has fainted, I believe—What the devil shall I do?—Father Crackenthorp, I must leave this young fellow with you till the gale blows out—hark ye—goes between the Laird and the t'other old one; he can neither ride nor walk—I must send him up to you.'

'Send him up to the gallows!' said Crackenthorp; 'there is Quartermaster Thwacker, with twenty men, up yonder; an he had not some kindness for Doll, I had never got hither for a start—but you must get off, or they will be here to seek us, for his orders are woundy particular; and these kegs contain worse than whisky—a hanging matter, I take it.'

'I wish they were at the bottom of Wampool river, with them they belong to,' said Nanty Ewart. 'But they are part of cargo; and what to do with the poor young fellow'——

'Why, many a better fellow has roughed it on the grass, with a cloak o'er him,' said Crackenthorp. 'If he hath a fever, nothing is so cooling as the night air.'

'Yes, he would be cold enough in the morning, no doubt; but it's a kind heart, and shall not cool so soon, if I can help it,' answered the Captain of the Jumping Jenny.

'Well, Captain, an ye will risk your own neck for another man's, why not take him to the old girls at Fairladies?'

'What, the Miss Arthurets!—The Papist jades! But never mind; it will do—I have known them take in a whole sloop's crew that were stranded on the sands.'

'You may run some risk, though, by turning up to Fairladies; for I tell you they are all up through the country.'

'Never mind—I may chance to put some of them down again,' said Nanty, cheerfully.—'Come, lads, bustle to your tackle. Are you all loaded?'

'Ay, ay, Captain; we will be ready in a jiffy,' answered the gang.

'D—n your captains!—Have you a mind to have me hanged if I am taken?—All's hail-fellow, here.'

'A sup at parting,' said Father Crackenthorp, extending a flask to Nanty Ewart.

'Not the twentieth part of a drop', said Nanty. 'No Dutch courage for me—my heart is always high enough when there's a chance of fighting; besides, if I live drunk, I should like to die sober.—Here, old Jephson—you are the best-natured brute amongst them—get the lad between us on a quiet horse, and we will keep him upright, I warrant.'

As they raised Fairford from the ground, he groaned heavily, and asked faintly where they were taking him to.

'To a place where you will be as snug and quiet as a mouse in his hole,' said Nanty, 'if so be that we can get you there safely.—Good by, Father Crackenthorp—poison the quartermaster, if you can.'

The loaded horses then sprang forward at a hard trot, following each other in a line, and every second horse being mounted by a stout fellow in a smock-frock, which served to conceal the arms with which most of these desperate men were provided. Ewart followed in the rear of the line, and, with the occasional assistance of old Jephson, kept his young charge erect in the saddle. He groaned heavily from time to time; and Ewart, more moved with compassion for his situation than might have been expected from his own habits, endeavoured to amuse him and comfort him, by some account of the place to which they were conveying him—his words of consolation being, however, frequently interrupted by the necessity of calling to his people, and many of them being lost amongst the rattling of the barrels, and clinking of the tackle and small chains by which they are secured on such occasions.

'And you see, brother, you will be in safe quarters at Fairladies—good old scrambling house—good old maids enough, if they were not Papists.—Hollo, you Jack Lowther; keep the line, can't ye, and shut your rattle-trap, you broth of a——! And so, being of a good family, and having enough, the old lasses have turned a kind of saints, and nuns, and so forth. The place they live in was some sort of nun-shop long ago, as they have them still in Flanders;* so folk call them the Vestals of Fairladies—that may be or may not be; and I care not whether it be or no.—Blinkinsop, hold your tongue, and be d—d!—And so, betwixt great alms and good dinners, they are well thought of by rich and poor, and their trucking with Papists is looked over. There are plenty of priests, and stout young scholars, and such like, about the house—it's a hive of them—More shame that government send dragoons out after a few honest fellows that bring the old women of England a drop of brandy, and let these ragamuffins smuggle in as much papistry and—Hark!—was that a whistle?—No, it's only a plover. You, Jem Collier, keep a look-out a-head—we'll meet them at the High Whins, or Brotthole bottom, or nowhere. Go a furlong a-head, I say, and look sharp.—These Miss Arthurets feed the hungry, and clothe the naked, and such like acts—which my poor father used to say were filthy rags,* but he dressed himself out with as many of them as most folk.—D—n that stumbling horse! Father Crackenthorp should be d—d himself for putting an honest fellow's neck in such jeopardy.'

Thus, and with much more to the same purpose, Nanty ran on, increasing, by his well-intended annoyance, the agony of Alan Fairford, who, tormented by racking pain along the back and loins, which made the rough trot of the horse torture to him, had his aching head still further rended and split by the hoarse voice of the sailor, close to his ear. Perfectly passive, however, he did not even essay to give any answer; and indeed his own bodily distress was now so great and engrossing, that to think of his situation was impossible, even if he could have mended it by doing so.

Their course was inland; but in what direction, Alan had no means of ascertaining. They passed at first over heaths and sandy downs; they crossed more than one brook, or *beck*, as they are called in that country—some of them of considerable depth—and at length reached a cultivated country, divided, according to the English fashion of agriculture, into very small fields or closes, by high banks, overgrown with underwood, and surmounted by hedge-row trees, amongst which winded a number of impracticable and complicated lanes, where the boughs projecting from the embankments on each side, intercepted the light of the moon, and endangered the safety of the horsemen. But through this labyrinth the experience of the guides conducted them without a blunder, and without even the slackening of their pace. In many places, however, it was impossible for three men to ride abreast; and therefore the burden of supporting Alan Fairford fell alternately to old Jephson, and to Nanty; and it was with much difficulty that they could keep him upright in his saddle.

At length when his powers of sufferance were quite worn out, and he was about to implore them to leave him to his fate in the first cottage or shed—or under a haystack or a hedge—or anywhere, so he was left at ease, Collier, who rode a-head, passed back the word that they were at the avenue to Fairladies—'Was he to turn up?'

Committing the charge of Fairford to Jephson, Nanty dashed up to the head of the troop, and gave his orders.—'Who knows the house best?'

'Sam Skelton's a Catholic,' said Lowther.

'A d—d bad religion,' said Nanty, of whose Presbyterian education, a hatred of Popery seemed to be the only remnant. 'But I am glad there is one amongst us, any how.—You, Sam, being a Papist, know Fairladies, and the old maidens, I dare say; so do you fall out of the line, and wait here with me; and do you, Collier, carry on to Walinford bottom, then turn down the beck till you come to the old mill, and Goodman Grist the Miller, or old Peel-the-Causeway, will tell you where to stow; but I will be up with you before that.'

The string of loaded horses then struck forward at their former pace, while Nanty, with Sam Skelton, waited by the road-side till the rear came up, when Jephson and Fairford joined them, and, to the great relief of the latter, they began to proceed at an easier pace than formerly, suffering the gang to precede them, till the clatter and clang attending their progress began to die away in the distance. They had not proceeded a pistol-shot from the place where they parted, when a short turning brought them in front of an old mouldering gateway, whose heavy pinnacles were decorated in the style of the seventeenth century, with clumsy architectural ornaments; several of which had fallen down from decay, and lay scattered about, no further care having been taken than just to remove them out of the direct approach to the avenue. The great stone pillars, glimmering white in the moonlight, had some fanciful resemblance to supernatural apparitions, and the air of neglect all around, gave an uncomfortable idea of the habitation to those who passed its avenue.

'There used to be no gate here,' said Skelton, finding their way unexpectedly stopped.

'But there is a gate now, and a porter too,' said a rough voice from within. 'Who be you, and what do you want at this time of night?'

'We want to come to speech of the ladies—of the Miss Arthurets,' said Nanty; 'and to ask lodging for a sick man.'

'There is no speech to be had of the Miss Arthurets at this time of night, and you may carry your sick man to the doctor,' answered the fellow from within, gruffly; 'for as sure as there is savour in salt, and scent in rosemary, you will get no entrance—put your pipes up and be jogging on.'

'Why, Dick Gardener,' said Skelton, 'be thou then turned porter?'

'What, do you know who I am?' said the domestic sharply.

'I know you, by your by-word,' answered the other; 'What, have you forgot little Sam Skelton, and the brock in the barrel?'

'No, I have not forgotten you,' answered the acquaintance of Sam Skelton; 'but my orders are peremptory to let no one up the avenue this night, and therefore'——

'But we are armed, and will not be kept back,' said Nanty. 'Hark ye, fellow, were it not better for you to take a guinea and let us in, than to have us break the door first, and thy pate afterwards? for I won't see my comrade die at your door—be assured of that.'

'Why, I dunna know,' said the fellow; 'but what cattle were those that rode by in such hurry?'

'Why, some of our folk from Bowness, Stoniecultrum, and thereby,' answered Skelton; 'Jack Lowther, and old Jephson, and broad Will Lamplugh, and such like.'

'Well,' said Dick Gardener, 'as sure as there is savour in salt, and scent in rosemary, I thought it had been the troopers from Carlisle and Wigton, and the sound brought my heart to my mouth.'

'Had thought thou wouldst have known the clatter of a cask from the clash of a broadsword, as well as e'er a quaffer in Cumberland,' answered Skelton.

'Come, brother, less of your jaw, and more of your legs, if you please,' said Nanty; 'every moment we stay is a moment lost. Go to the ladies, and tell them that Nanty Ewart, of the Jumping Jenny, has brought a young gentleman, charged with letters from Scotland, to a certain gentleman of consequence in Cumberland—that the soldiers are out, and the gentleman is very ill, and if he is not received at Fairladies, he must be left either to die at the gate, or to be taken, with all his papers about him, by the redcoats.'

Away ran Dick Gardener with this message; and, in a few minutes, lights were seen to flit about, which convinced Fairford, who was now, in consequence of the halt, a little restored to self-possession, that they were traversing the front of a tolerably large mansion-house.

'What if thy friend, Dick Gardener, comes not back again?' said Jephson to Skelton.

'Why, then,' said the person addressed, 'I shall owe him just such a licking as thou, old Jephson, hadst from Dan Cooke, and will pay as duly and truly as he did.'

The old man was about to make an angry reply, when his doubts were silenced by the return of Dick Gardener, who announced that Miss Arthuret was coming herself as far as the gateway to speak with them.

Nanty Ewart cursed, in a low tone, the suspicion of old maids and the churlish scruples of Catholics, that made so many obstacles to helping a fellow-creature, and wished Miss Arthuret a hearty rheumatism or toothach as the reward of her excursion; but the lady presently appeared, to cut short farther grumbling. She was attended by a waiting-maid with a lantern, by means of which she examined the party on the outside, as closely as the imperfect light, and the spars of the newly-erected gate, would permit.

'I am sorry we have disturbed you so late, Madam Arthuret,' said Nanty; 'but the case is this'——

'Holy Virgin,' said she, 'why do you speak so loud? Pray, are you not the Captain of the Sainte Genevieve?'

'Why, ay, ma'am,' answered Ewart, 'they call the brig so at Dunkirk, sure enough; but along shore here, they call her the Jumping Jenny.'

'You brought over the holy Father Buonaventure, did you not?'

'Ay, ay, madam, I have brought over enough of them black cattle,' answered Nanty.

'Fie! fie! friend,' said Miss Arthuret; 'it is a pity that the saints should commit these good men to a heretic's care.'

'Why, no more they would, ma'am,' answered Nanty, 'could they find a Papish lubber that knew the coast as I do; then I am trusty as steel to owners, and always look after cargo—live lumber, or dead flesh, or spirits, all is one to me; and your Catholics have such d—d large hoods, with pardon, ma'am, that they can sometimes hide two faces under them. But here is a gentleman dying, with letters about him from the Laird of Summertrees to the Laird of the Lochs, as they call him, along Solway, and every minute he lies here is a nail in his coffin.'

'Saint Mary! what shall we do?' said Miss Arthuret; 'we must admit him, I think, at all risks.—You, Richard Gardener, help one of these men to carry the gentleman up to the Place; and you, Selby, see him lodged at the end of the long gallery.—You are a heretic, Captain, but I think you are trusty, and I know you have been trusted—but if you are imposing on me'——

'Not I, madam—never attempt to impose on ladies of your experience—my practice that way has been all among the young ones.—Come, cheerly, Mr Fairford—you will be taken good care of—try to walk.'

Alan did so; and, refreshed by his halt, declared himself able to walk to the house with the sole assistance of the gardener.

'Why, that's hearty. Thank thee, Dick, for lending him thine arm,'—and Nanty slipped into his hand the guinea he had promised. —'Farewell then, Mr Fairford, and farewell, Madam Arthuret, for I have been too long here.'

So saying, he and his two companions threw themselves on horseback, and went off at a gallop. Yet, even above the clatter of their hoofs did the incorrigible Nanty hollow out the old ballad—

> 'A lovely lass to a friar came,
> To confession a-morning early;—
> "In what, my dear, are you to blame?
> Come tell me most sincerely?"
> "Alas! my fault I dare not name—
> But my lad he loved me dearly."'*

'Holy Virgin!' exclaimed Miss Seraphina, as the unhallowed sounds reached her ears; 'what profane heathens be these men, and what frights and pinches we be put to among them! The saints be good to us, what a night has this been!—the like never seen at Fairladies.—Help me to make fast the gate, Richard, and thou shalt come down again to wait on it, lest there come more unwelcome visitors—Not that you are unwelcome, young gentleman, for it is sufficient that you need such assistance as we can give you, to make you welcome to Fairladies—only, another time would have done as well—but, hem! I dare say it is all for the best. The avenue is none of the smoothest, sir, look to your feet. Richard Gardener should have had it mown and levelled, but he was obliged to go on a pilgrimage to Saint Winifred's Well, in Wales.'—(Here Dick gave a short dry cough, which, as if he had found it betrayed some internal feeling a little at variance with what the lady said, he converted into a muttered *Sancta Winifreda, ora pro nobis.** Miss Arthuret, meantime, proceeded)—'We never interfere with our servants' vows or penances, Master Fairford—I know a very worthy father of your name, perhaps a relation—I say, we never interfere with our servants' vows. Our Lady forbid they should not know some difference between our service and a heretic's.—Take care, sir, you will fall if you have not a care. Alas! by night and day there are many stumbling-blocks in our paths!'

With more talk to the same purpose, all of which tended to show a charitable, and somewhat silly woman, with a strong inclination to her superstitious devotion, Miss Arthuret entertained her new guest, as, stumbling at every obstacle which the devotion of his guide, Richard, had left in the path, he at last, by ascending some stone steps decorated on the side with griffins, or some such heraldic anomalies, attained a terrace extending in front of the Place of Fairladies; an old-fashioned gentleman's house of some consequence, with its range of notched gable-ends and narrow windows, relieved by here and there an old turret about the size of a pepper-box. The door was locked, during the brief absence of the mistress; a dim light glimmered through the sashed door of the hall, which opened beneath a huge stone porch, loaded with jessamine and other creepers. All the windows were dark as pitch.

Mrs Arthuret tapped at the door. 'Sister, sister Angelica!'

'Who is there?' was answered from within; 'is it you, sister Seraphina?'

'Yes, yes, undo the door; do you not know my voice?'

'No doubt, sister,' said Angelica, undoing bolt and bar; 'but you know our charge, and the enemy is watchful to surprise us—*incedit sicut leo vorans*, saith the breviary.*—Whom have you brought here? Oh, sister, what have you done!'

'It is a young man,' said Seraphina, hastening to interrupt her sister's remonstrance, 'a relation, I believe, of our worthy Father Fairford; left at the gate by the captain of that blessed vessel the Sainte Genevieve—almost dead—and charged with dispatches to'——

She lowered her voice as she mumbled over the last words.

'Nay, then, there is no help,' said Angelica; 'but it is unlucky.'

During this dialogue between the vestals of Fairladies, Dick Gardener deposited his burden in a chair, where the younger lady, after a moment of hesitation, expressing a becoming reluctance to touch the hand of a stranger, put her finger and thumb upon Fairford's wrist, and counted his pulse.

"There is fever here, sister,' she said; 'Richard must call Ambrose, and we must send some of the febrifuge.'

Ambrose arrived presently, a plausible and respectable-looking old servant, bred in the family, and who had risen from rank to rank in the Arthuret service, till he was become half-physician, half-almoner, half-butler, and entire governor; that is, when the Father Confessor, who frequently eased him of the toils of government, chanced to be abroad. Under the direction, and with the assistance, of this venerable personage, the unlucky Alan Fairford was conveyed to a decent apartment at the end of a long gallery, and, to his inexpressible relief, consigned to a comfortable bed. He did not attempt to resist the prescription of Mr Ambrose, who not only presented him with the proposed draught, but proceeded so far as to take a considerable quantity of blood from him, by which last operation he probably did his patient much service.

CHAPTER XVI

NARRATIVE OF ALAN FAIRFORD, CONTINUED

ON the next morning, when Fairford awoke, after no very refreshing slumbers, in which were mingled many wild dreams of his father, and of Darsie Latimer,—of the damsel in the green mantle, and the vestals of Fairladies,—of drinking small beer with Nanty Ewart, and being immersed in the Solway with the Jumping Jenny,—he found himself in no condition to dispute the order of Mr Ambrose, that he should keep his bed, from which, indeed, he could not have raised himself without assistance. He became sensible that his anxiety, and his constant efforts for some days past, had been too much for his health, and that, whatever might be his impatience, he could not proceed in his undertaking until his strength was re-established.

In the meanwhile, no better quarters could have been found for an invalid. The attendants spoke under their breath, and moved only on tiptoe—nothing was done unless *par ordonnance du medecin*—Esculapius reigned paramount in the premises at Fairladies. Once a-day, the ladies came in great state to wait upon him, and enquire after his health, and it was then that Alan's natural civility, and the thankfulness which he expressed for their timely and charitable assistance, raised him considerably in their esteem. He was on the third day removed to a better apartment than that in which he had been at first accommodated. When he was permitted to drink a glass of wine, it was of the first quality; one of those curious old-fashioned cobwebbed bottles being produced on the occasion, which are only to be found in the crypts of old country seats, where they may have lurked undisturbed for more than half a century.

But however delightful a residence for an invalid, Fairladies, as its present inmate became soon aware, was not so agreeable to a convalescent. When he dragged himself to the window so soon as he could crawl from bed, behold it was closely grated, and commanded no view except of a little paved court. This was nothing remarkable, most old Border-houses having their windows so secured; but then Fairford observed, that whoever entered or left the room, always locked the door with great care and circumspection; and some proposals which he made to take a walk in the gallery, or even in the garden, were so coldly received, both by the ladies and their prime minister, Mr Ambrose, that he saw plainly such an extension of his privileges as a guest would not be permitted.

Anxious to ascertain whether this excessive hospitality would permit him his proper privilege of free-agency, he announced to this important functionary, with grateful thanks for the care with which he had been attended, his purpose to leave Fairladies next morning, requesting only, as a continuance of the favours with which he had been loaded, the loan of a horse to the next town; and, assuring Mr Ambrose that his gratitude would not be limited by such a trifle, he slipped three guineas into his hand, by way of seconding his proposal. The fingers of that worthy domestic closed as naturally upon the *honorarium*, as if a degree in the learned faculty had given him a right to clutch it; but his answer concerning Alan's proposed departure was at first evasive, and when he was pushed, it amounted to a peremptory assurance that he could not be permitted to depart to-morrow; it was as much as his life was worth, and his ladies would not authorise it.

'I know best what my own life is worth,' said Alan; 'and I do not value it in comparison to the business which requires my instant attention.'

Receiving still no satisfactory answer from Mr Ambrose, Fairford thought it best to state his resolution to the ladies themselves, in the most measured, respectful, and grateful terms; but still such as expressed a firm determination to depart on the morrow, or next day at farthest. After some attempts to induce him to stay, on the alleged score of health, which were so expressed that he was convinced they were only used to delay his departure, Fairford plainly told them that he was intrusted with dispatches of consequence to the gentleman known by the name of Herries, Redgauntlet, and the Laird of the Lochs; and that it was matter of life and death to deliver them early.

'I dare say, Sister Angelica,' said the elder Miss Arthuret, 'that the gentleman is honest; and if he is really a relation of Father Fairford, we can run no risk.'

'Jesu Maria!' exclaimed the younger. 'Oh fie, Sister Seraphina! Fie, fie!—*Vade retro*—get thee behind me!'*

'Well, well; but sister—Sister Angelica—let me speak with you in the gallery.'

So out the ladies rustled in their silks and tissues, and it was a good half hour ere they rustled in again, with importance and awe on their countenances.

'To tell you the truth, Mr Fairford, the cause of our desire to delay you is—there is a religious gentleman in this house at present'——

'A most excellent person indeed'—said the sister Angelica.

'An anointed of his Master!' echoed Seraphina.—'and we should be glad that, for conscience' sake, you would hold some discourse with him before your departure.'

'Oho!' thought Fairford, 'the murder is out—here is a design of conversion!—I must not affront the good old ladies, but I shall soon send off the priest, I think.'—He then answered aloud, 'that he should be happy to converse with any friend of theirs—that in religious matters he had the greatest respect for every modification of Christianity, though, he must say, his belief was made up to that in which he had been educated; nevertheless, if his seeing the religious person they recommended could in the least show his respect'——

'It is not quite that,' said Sister Seraphina, 'although I am sure the day is too short to hear him—Father Buonaventure, I mean—speak upon the concerns of our souls; but'——

'Come, come, sister Seraphina,' said the younger, 'it is needless to talk so much about it. His—his Eminence—I mean Father Buonaventure—will himself explain what he wants this gentleman to know.'

'His Eminence,' said Fairford, surprised—'Is this gentleman so high in the Catholic Church?—The title is given only to Cardinals, I think.'

'He is not a Cardinal as yet,' answered Seraphina; 'but I assure you, Mr Fairford, he is as high in rank as he is eminently endowed with good gifts, and'——

'Come away,' said Sister Angelica. 'Holy Virgin, how you do talk!—What has Mr Fairford to do with Father Buonaventure's rank?—Only, sir, you will remember that the Father has been always accustomed to be treated with the most profound deference;—indeed'——

'Come away, sister,' said Sister Seraphina, in her turn; 'who talks now, I pray you? Mr Fairford will know how to comport himself.'

'And we had best both leave the room,' said the younger lady, 'for here his Eminence comes.'

She lowered her voice to a whisper as she pronounced the last words; and as Fairford was about to reply, by assuring her that any friend of hers should be treated by him with all the ceremony he could expect, she imposed silence on him, by holding up her finger.

A solemn and stately step was now heard in the gallery; it might have proclaimed the approach not merely of a bishop or cardinal, but of the Sovereign Pontiff himself. Nor could the sound have been more respectfully listened to by the two ladies, had it announced that the Head of the Church was approaching in person. They drew themselves, like sentinels on duty, one on each side of the door by which the long gallery communicated with Fairford's apartment, and stood there immovable, and with countenances expressive of the deepest reverence.

The approach of Father Buonaventure was so slow, that Fairford had time to notice all this, and to marvel in his mind what wily and ambitious priest could have contrived to subject his worthy but simple-minded hostesses to such superstitious trammels. Father Buonaventure's entrance and appearance in some degree accounted for the whole.

He was a man of middle life, about forty or upwards; but either care, or fatigue, or indulgence, had brought on the appearance of premature old age, and given to his fine features a cast of seriousness or even sadness. A noble countenance, however, still remained; and though his complexion was altered, and wrinkles stamped upon his brow in many a melancholy fold, still the lofty forehead, the full and well-opened eye, and the well-formed nose, showed how handsome in better days he must have been. He was tall, but lost the advantage of his height by stooping; and the cane which he wore always in his hand, and occasionally used, as well as his slow though majestic gait, seemed to intimate that his form and limbs felt already some touch of infirmity. The colour of his hair could not be discovered, as, according to the fashion, he wore a periwig. He was handsomely, though gravely dressed in a secular habit, and had a cockade in his hat; circumstances which did not surprise Fairford, who knew that a military disguise was very often assumed by the seminary priests, whose visits to England, or residence there, subjected them to legal penalties.

As this stately person entered the apartment, the two ladies facing inward, like soldiers on their post when about to salute a superior officer, dropped on either hand of the Father a courtesy so profound, that the hoop petticoats which performed the feat seemed to sink down to the very floor, nay, through it, as if a trapdoor had opened for the descent of the dames who performed this act of reverence.

The Father seemed accustomed to such homage, profound as it was; he turned his person a little way first towards one sister, and then towards the other, while, with a gracious inclination of his person, which certainly did not amount to a bow, he acknowledged their courtesy. But he passed forward without addressing them, and seemed by doing so, to intimate that their presence in the apartment was unnecessary.

They accordingly glided out of the room, retreating backwards, with hands clasped and eyes cast upwards, as if imploring blessings on the religious man whom they venerated so highly. The door of the apartment was shut after them, but not before Fairford had perceived that there were one or two men in the gallery, and that, contrary to what he had before observed, the door, though shut, was not locked on the outside.

'Can the good souls apprehend danger from me to this god of their idolatry?' thought Fairford. But he had no time to make farther observations, for the stranger had already reached the middle of the apartment.

Fairford rose to receive him respectfully, but as he fixed his eyes on the visitor, he thought that the Father avoided his looks. His reasons for remaining incognito were cogent enough to account for this, and Fairford hastened to relieve him, by looking downwards in his turn; but when again he raised his face, he found the broad light eye of the stranger so fixed on him, that he was almost put out of countenance by the steadiness of his gaze. During this time they remained standing.

'Take your seat, sir,' said the Father; 'you have been an invalid.'

He spoke with the tone of one who desires an inferior to be seated in his presence, and his voice was full and melodious.

Fairford, somewhat surprised to find himself overawed by the airs of superiority, which could be only properly exercised towards one over whom religion gave the speaker influence, sat down at his bidding, as if moved by springs, and was at a loss how to assert the footing of equality on which he felt that they ought to stand. The stranger kept the advantage which he had obtained.

'Your name, sir, I am informed, is Fairford?' said the Father.

Alan answered by a bow.

'Called to the Scottish bar,' continued his visitor. 'There is, I believe, in the West, a family of birth and rank called Fairford of Fairford.'

Alan thought this a strange observation from a foreign ecclesiastic, as his name intimated Father Buonaventure to be; but only answered, he believed there was such a family.

'Do you count kindred with them, Mr Fairford?' continued the enquirer.

'I have not the honour to lay such a claim,' said Fairford. 'My father's industry has raised his family from a low and obscure situation—I have no hereditary claim to distinction of any kind.—May I ask the cause of these enquiries?'

'You will learn it presently,' said Father Buonaventure, who had given a dry and dissatisfied *hem* at the young man's acknowledging a plebeian descent. He then motioned to him to be silent, and proceeded with his queries.

'Although not of condition, you are, doubtless, by sentiments and education, a man of honour and a gentleman?'

'I hope so, sir,' said Alan, colouring with displeasure. 'I have not been accustomed to have it questioned.'

'Patience, young man,' said the unperturbed querist—'we are on serious business, and no idle etiquette must prevent its being discussed seriously.—You are probably aware, that you speak to a person proscribed by the severe and unjust laws of the present government?'

'I am aware of the statute 1700, chapter 3,'* said Alan, 'banishing from the realm Priests and trafficking Papists, and punishing by death, on summary conviction, any such person who being so banished may return. The English law, I believe, is equally severe. But I have no means of knowing you, sir, to be one of those persons; and I think your prudence may recommend to you to keep your own counsel.'

'It is sufficient, sir; and I have no apprehensions of disagreeable consequences from your having seen me in this house,' said the Priest.

'Assuredly no,' said Alan. 'I consider myself as indebted for my life to the Mistresses of Fairladies; and it would be a vile requital on my part to pry into or make known what I may have seen or heard under this hospitable roof. If I were to meet the Pretender himself in such a situation, he should, even at the risk of a little stretch to my loyalty, be free from any danger from my indiscretion.'

'The Pretender!' said the Priest, with some angry emphasis; but immediately softened his tone and added, 'No doubt, however, that person *is* a pretender; and some people think his pretensions are not ill founded. But before running into politics, give me leave to say, that I am surprised to find a gentleman of your opinions in habits of intimacy with Mr Maxwell of Summertrees and Mr Redgauntlet, and the medium of conducting the intercourse betwixt them.'

'Pardon me, sir,' replied Alan Fairford; 'I do not aspire to the honour of being reputed their confidant or go-between. My concern with those gentlemen is limited to one matter of business, dearly interesting to me, because it concerns the safety—perhaps the life—of my dearest friend.'

'Would you have any objections to intrust me with the cause of your journey?' said Father Buonaventure. 'My advice may be of service to you, and my influence with one or both these gentlemen is considerable.'

Fairford hesitated a moment, and hastily revolving all circumstances, concluded that he might perhaps receive some advantage from propitiating this personage; while, on the other hand, he endangered nothing by communicating to him the occasion of his journey. He, therefore, after stating shortly, that he hoped Mr

Buonaventure would render him the same confidence which he required on his part, gave a short account of Darsie Latimer—of the mystery which hung over his family—and of the disaster which had befallen him. Finally, of his own resolution to seek for his friend, and to deliver him, at the peril of his own life.

The Catholic Priest, whose manner it seemed to be to avoid all conversation which did not arise from his own express motion, made no remarks upon what he had heard, but only asked one or two abrupt questions, where Alan's narrative appeared less clear to him; then rising from his seat, he took two turns through the apartment, muttering between his teeth, with emphasis, the word 'Madman!' But apparently he was in the habit of keeping all violent emotions under restraint; for he presently addressed Fairford with the most perfect indifference.

'If,' said he, 'you thought you could do so without breach of confidence, I wish you would have the goodness to show me the letter of Mr Maxwell of Summertrees. I desire to look particularly at the address.'

Seeing no cause to decline this extension of his confidence, Alan, without hesitation, put the letter into his hand. Having turned it round as old Trumbull and Nanty Ewart had formerly done, and, like them, having examined the address with much minuteness, he asked whether he had observed these words, pointing to a pencil-writing upon the under side of the letter. Fairford answered in the negative, and, looking at the letter, read with surprise, '*Cave ne literas Bellerophontis adferres;*'* a caution which coincided so exactly with the Provost's admonition, that he would do well to inspect the letter of which he was bearer, that he was about to spring up and attempt an escape, he knew not wherefore or from whom.

'Sit still, young man' said the Father, with the same tone of authority which reigned in his whole manner, although mingled with stately courtesy. 'You are in no danger—my character shall be a pledge for your safety.—By whom do you suppose these words have been written?'

Fairford could have answered, 'by Nanty Ewart,' for he remembered seeing that person scribble something with a pencil, although he was not well enough to observe with accuracy where, or upon what. But not knowing what suspicions, or what worse consequences, the seaman's interest in his affairs might draw upon him, he judged it best to answer that he knew not the hand.

Father Buonaventure was again silent for a moment or two, which he employed in surveying the letter with the strictest attention; then stepped to the window, as if to examine the address and writing of the envelope with the assistance of a stronger light, and Alan

Fairford beheld him, with no less amazement than high displeasure, coolly and deliberately break the seal, open the letter, and peruse the contents.

'Stop, sir, hold!' he exclaimed, so soon as his astonishment permitted him to express his resentment in words: 'by what right do you dare'——

'Peace, young gentleman,' said the Father, repelling him with a wave of his hand; 'be assured I do not act without warrant—nothing can pass betwixt Mr Maxwell and Mr Redgauntlet that I am not fully entitled to know.'

'It may be so,' said Alan, extremely angry; 'but though you may be these gentlemen's father confessor, you are not mine; and in breaking the seal of a letter intrusted to my care, you have done me'——

'No injury, I assure you,' answered the unperturbed priest; 'on the contrary, it may be a service.'

'I desire no advantage at such a rate, or to be obtained in such a manner,' answered Fairford; 'restore me the letter instantly, or'——

'As you regard your own safety,' said the priest, 'forbear all injurious expressions, and all menacing gestures. I am not one who can be threatened or insulted with impunity; and there are enough within hearing to chastise any injury or affront offered to me, in case I may think it unbecoming to protect or avenge myself with my own hand.'

In saying this, the Father assumed an air of such fearlessness and calm authority, that the young lawyer, surprised and overawed, forbore, as he had intended, to snatch the letter from his hand, and confined himself to bitter complaints of the impropriety of his conduct, and of the light in which he himself must be placed to Redgauntlet, should he present him a letter with a broken seal.

'That,' said Father Buonaventure, 'shall be fully cared for. I will myself write to Redgauntlet, and enclose Maxwell's letter, provided always you continue to desire to deliver it, after perusing the contents.'

He then restored the letter to Fairford, and, observing that he hesitated to peruse it, said emphatically, 'Read it, for it concerns you.'

This recommendation, joined to what Provost Crosbie had formerly recommended, and to the warning, which he doubted not that Nanty intended to convey by his classical allusion, decided Fairford's resolution. 'If these correspondents,' he thought, 'are conspiring against my person, I have a right to counterplot them; self-preservation, as well as my friend's safety, require that I should not be too scrupulous.'

So thinking, he read the letter, which was in the following words:—

'DEAR RUGGED AND DANGEROUS,

'WILL you never cease meriting your old nickname? You have springed your dottrel, I find, and what is the consequence?—why, that there will be hue and cry after you presently. The bearer is a pert young lawyer, who has brought a formal complaint against you, which, luckily, he has preferred in a friendly court. Yet, favourable as the judge was disposed to be, it was with the utmost difficulty that cousin Jenny and I could keep him to his tackle. He begins to be timid, suspicious, and intractable, and I fear Jenny will soon bend her brows on him in vain. I know not what to advise—the lad who carries this is a good lad—active for his friend—and I have pledged my honour he shall have no personal ill-usage—Pledged my honour, remark these words, and remember I can be rugged and dangerous as well as my neighbours. But I have not ensured him against a short captivity, and as he is a stirring active fellow, I see no remedy but keeping him out of the way till this business of the good Father B—— is safely blown over, which God send it were!—Always thine, even should I be once more

'CRAIG-IN-PERIL.'

'What think you, young man, of the danger you have been about to encounter so willingly?'

'As strangely,' replied Alan Fairford, 'as of the extraordinary means which you have been at present pleased to use for the discovery of Mr Maxwell's purpose.'

'Trouble not yourself to account for my conduct,' said the Father; 'I have a warrant for what I do, and fear no responsibility. But tell me what is your present purpose.'

'I should not perhaps name it to you, whose own safety may be implicated.'

'I understand you,' answered the Father; 'you would appeal to the existing government?—That can at no rate be permitted—we will rather detain you at Fairladies by compulsion.'

'You will probably,' said Fairford, 'first weigh the risk of such a proceeding in a free country.'

'I have incurred more formidable hazard,' said the priest, smiling; 'yet I am willing to find a milder expedient. Come; let us bring the matter to a compromise.'—And he assumed a conciliating graciousness of manner, which struck Fairford as being rather too condescending for the occasion; 'I presume you will be satisfied to remain here in seclusion for a day or two longer, provided I pass my solemn word to you, that you shall meet with the person whom you seek after—meet with him in perfect safety, and, I trust, in good health, and be afterwards both at liberty to return to Scotland, or dispose of yourselves as each of you may be minded?'

'I respect the *verbum sacerdotis* as much as can reasonably be expected from a Protestant,' answered Fairford; 'but, methinks, you can scarce expect me to repose so much confidence in the word of an unknown person, as is implied in the guarantee which you offer me.'

'I am not accustomed, sir,' said the Father, in a very haughty tone, 'to have my word disputed. But,' he added, while the angry hue passed from his cheek, after a moment's reflection, 'you know me not, and ought to be excused. I will repose more confidence in your honour than you seem willing to rest upon mine; and since we are so situated that one must rely upon the other's faith, I will cause you to be set presently at liberty, and furnished with the means of delivering your letter as addressed, provided that now, knowing the contents, you think it safe for yourself to execute the commission.'

Alan Fairford paused. 'I cannot see,' he at length replied, 'how I can proceed with respect to the accomplishment of my sole purpose, which is the liberation of my friend, without appealing to the law, and obtaining the assistance of a magistrate. If I present this singular letter of Mr Maxwell, with the contents of which I have become so unexpectedly acquainted, I shall only share his captivity.'

'And if you apply to a magistrate, young man, you will bring ruin on these hospitable ladies, to whom, in all human probability, you owe your life. You cannot obtain a warrant for your purpose, without giving a clear detail of all the late scenes through which you have passed. A magistrate would oblige you to give a complete account of yourself, before arming you with his authority against a third party; and in giving such an account, the safety of these ladies will necessarily be compromised. A hundred spies have had, and still have, their eyes upon this mansion; but God will protect his own.'—He crossed himself devoutly, and then proceeded.—'You can take an hour to think of your best plan, and I will pledge myself to forward it thus far, provided it be not asking you to rely more on my word than your prudence can warrant. You shall go to Redgauntlet,—I name him plainly, to show my confidence in you,—and you shall deliver him this letter of Mr Maxwell's, with one from me, in which I will enjoin him to set your friend at liberty, or at least to make no attempts upon your own person, either by detention or otherwise. If you can trust me thus far,' he said, with a proud emphasis on the words, 'I will on my side see you depart from this place with the most perfect confidence that you will not return armed with powers to drag its inmates to destruction. You are young and inexperienced—bred to a profession also which sharpens suspicion, and gives false views of human nature. I have seen much of the world, and have known better than most men, how far mutual confidence is requisite in managing affairs of consequence.'

He spoke with an air of superiority, even of authority, by which Fairford, notwithstanding his own internal struggles, was silenced and overawed so much, that it was not till the Father had turned to leave the apartment that he found words to ask him what the consequences would be, should he decline to depart on the terms proposed.

'You must then, for the safety of all parties, remain for some days an inhabitant of Fairladies, where we have the means of detaining you, which self-preservation will in that case compel us to make use of. Your captivity will be short; for matters cannot long remain as they are—The cloud must soon rise, or it must sink upon us for ever.—*Benedicite!*'

With these words he left the apartment.

Fairford, upon his departure, felt himself much at a loss what course to pursue. His line of education, as well as his father's tenets in matters of church and state, had taught him a holy horror for Papists, and a devout belief in whatever had been said of the punic faith of Jesuits,* and of the expedients of mental reservation, by which the Catholic priests in general were supposed to evade keeping faith with heretics. Yet there was something of majesty, depressed indeed, and overclouded, but still grand and imposing, in the manner and words of Father Buonaventure, which it was difficult to reconcile with those preconceived opinions which imputed subtlety and fraud to his sect and order. Above all, Alan was aware, that if he accepted not his freedom upon the terms offered him, he was likely to be detained by force; so that, in every point of view, he was a gainer by adopting them.

A qualm, indeed, came across him, when he considered, as a lawyer, that this Father was probably, in the eye of law, a traitor; and that there was an ugly crime on the Statute Book, called Misprision of Treason.* On the other hand, whatever he might think or suspect, he could not take upon him to say that the man was a priest, whom he had never seen in the dress of his order, or in the act of celebrating mass; so that he felt himself at liberty to doubt of that, respecting which he possessed no legal proof. He therefore arrived at the conclusion, that he would do well to accept his liberty, and proceed to Redgauntlet under the guarantee of Father Buonaventure, which he scarce doubted would be sufficient to save him from personal inconvenience. Should he once obtain speech of that gentleman, he felt the same confidence as formerly, that he might be able to convince him of the rashness of his conduct, should he not consent to liberate Darsie Latimer. At all events, he should learn where his friend was, and how circumstanced.

Having thus made up his mind, Alan waited anxiously for the expiration of the hour which had been allowed him for deliberation. He was not kept on the tenter-hooks of impatience an instant longer than the appointed moment arrived, for, even as the clock struck, Ambrose appeared at the door of the gallery, and made a sign that Alan should follow him. He did so, and after passing through some of the intricate avenues common in old houses, was ushered into a small apartment, commodiously fitted up, in which he found Father Buonaventure reclining on a couch, in the attitude of a man exhausted by fatigue or indisposition. On a small table beside him, a silver embossed salver sustained a Catholic book of prayer, a small flask of medicine, a cordial, and a little tea-cup of old china. Ambrose did not enter the room—he only bowed profoundly, and closed the door with the least possible noise, so soon as Fairford had entered.

'Sit down, young man,' said the Father, with the same air of condescension which had before surprised, and rather offended Fairford. 'You have been ill, and I know too well by my own case, that indisposition requires indulgence.—Have you,' he continued, so soon as he saw him seated, 'resolved to remain, or to depart?'

'To depart,' said Alan, 'under the agreement that you will guarantee my safety with the extraordinary person who has conducted himself in such a lawless manner towards my friend, Darsie Latimer.'

'Do not judge hastily, young man,' replied the Father. 'Redgauntlet has the claims of a guardian over his ward, in respect to the young gentleman, and a right to dictate his place of residence, although he may have been injudicious in selecting the means by which he thinks to enforce his authority.'

'His situation as an attainted person abrogates such rights,' said Fairford, hastily.

'Surely,' replied the priest, smiling at the young lawyer's readiness, 'in the eye of those who acknowledge the justice of the attainder—but that do not I. However, sir, here is the guarantee—look at its contents, and do not again carry the letters of Uriah.'*

Fairford read these words:—

'GOOD FRIEND,

'We send you hither a young man desirous to know the situation of your ward, since he came under your paternal authority, and hopeful of dealing with you for having your relative put at large. This we recommend to your prudence, highly disapproving, at the same time, of any force or coercion, when such can be avoided, and wishing, therefore, that the bearer's negotiation may be successful. At all rates, however, the bearer hath our pledged word for his safety and freedom, which, therefore, you are to see strictly observed, as you value our honour and your own. We farther wish to converse with you, with as small loss of time as may be, having matters of the utmost confidence to impart. For this purpose we desire you to repair hither with all haste, and thereupon we bid you heartily farewell.

'P. B.'

'You will understand, sir,' said the Father, when he saw that Alan had perused his letter, 'that, by accepting charge of this missive, you bind yourself to try the effect of it before having recourse to any legal means, as you term them, for your friend's release.'

'There are a few ciphers added to this letter,' said Fairford, when he had perused the paper attentively,—'may I enquire what their import is?'

'They respect my own affairs,' answered the Father, briefly; 'and have no concern whatever with yours.'

'It seems to me, however,' replied Alan, 'natural to suppose'——

'Nothing must be supposed incompatible with my honour,' replied the priest, interrupting him; 'when such as I am confer favours, we expect that they shall be accepted with gratitude, or declined with thankful respect—not questioned or discussed.'

'I will accept your letter, then,' said Fairford, after a minute's consideration, 'and the thanks you expect shall be most liberally paid, if the result answer what you teach me to expect.'

'God only commands the issue,' said Father Buonaventure. 'Man uses means.—You understand, that, by accepting this commission, you engage yourself in honour to try the effect of my letter upon Mr Redgauntlet, before you have recourse to informations or legal warrants?'

'I hold myself bound, as a man of good faith and honour, to do so,' said Fairford.

'Well, I trust you,' said the Father. 'I will now tell you, that an express, dispatched by me last night, has, I hope, brought Redgauntlet to a spot many miles nearer this place, where he will not find it safe to attempt any violence on your friend, should he be rash enough to follow the advice of Mr Maxwell of Summertrees rather than my commands. We now understand each other.'

He extended his hand towards Alan, who was about to pledge his faith in the usual form by grasping it with his own, when the Father drew back hastily. Ere Alan had time to comment upon this repulse, a small side-door, covered with tapestry, was opened; the hangings were drawn aside, and a lady, as if by sudden apparition, glided into the apartment. It was neither of the Miss Arthurets, but a woman in the prime of life, and in the full-blown expansion of female beauty, tall, fair, and commanding in her aspect. Her locks, of paly gold, were taught to fall over a brow, which, with the stately glance of the large, open, blue eyes, might have become Juno herself; her neck and bosom were admirably formed, and of a dazzling whiteness. She was rather inclined to *embonpoint*, but not more than became her age, of apparently thirty years. Her step was that of a queen, but it was of Queen Vashti, not Queen Esther*—the bold and commanding, not the retiring beauty.

Father Buonaventure raised himself on the couch, angrily, as if displeased by this intrusion. 'How now, madam,' he said, with some sternness; 'why have we the honour of your company?'

'Because it is my pleasure,' answered the lady, composedly.

'Your pleasure, madam!' he repeated in the same angry tone.

'My pleasure, sir,' she continued, 'which always keeps exact pace with my duty. I had heard you were unwell—let me hope it is only business which produces this seclusion.'

'I am well,' he replied; 'perfectly well, and I thank you for your care—but we are not alone, and this young man'——

'That young man?' she said, bending her large and serious eye on Alan Fairford, as if she had been for the first time aware of his presence—'may I ask who he is?'

'Another time, madam; you shall learn his history after he is gone. His presence renders it impossible for me to explain farther.'

'After he is gone may be too late,' said the lady; 'and what is his presence to me, when your safety is at stake? He is the heretic lawyer whom those silly fools, the Arthurets, admitted into this house, at a time when they should have let their own father knock at the door in vain, though the night had been a wild one. You will not surely dismiss him?'

'Your own impatience can alone make that step perilous,' said the Father; 'I have resolved to take it—do not let your indiscreet zeal, however excellent its motive, add any unnecessary risk to the transaction.'

'Even so?' said the lady, in a tone of reproach, yet mingled with respect and apprehension. 'And thus you will still go forward, like a stag upon the hunter's snares, with undoubting confidence, after all that has happened?'

'Peace, madam,' said Father Buonaventure, rising up; 'be silent, or quit the apartment; my designs do not admit of female criticism.'

To this peremptory command the lady seemed about to make a sharp reply; but she checked herself, and pressing her lips strongly together, as if to secure the words from bursting from them which were already formed upon her tongue, she made a deep reverence, partly as it seemed in reproach, partly in respect, and left the room as suddenly as she had entered it.

The Father looked disturbed at this incident, which he seemed sensible could not but fill Fairford's imagination with an additional throng of bewildering suspicions; he bit his lip, and muttered something to himself as he walked through the apartment; then suddenly turned to his visitor with a smile of much sweetness, and a countenance in which every rougher expression was exchanged for those of courtesy and kindness.

'The visit we have been just honoured with, my young friend, has given you,' he said, 'more secrets to keep than I would have wished you burdened with. The lady is a person of condition—of rank and fortune—but nevertheless, is so circumstanced, that the mere fact of her being known to be in this country, would occasion many evils. I should wish you to observe secrecy on this subject, even to Redgauntlet or Maxwell, however much I trust them in all that concerns my own affairs.'

'I can have no occasion,' replied Fairford, 'for holding any discussion with these gentlemen, or with any others, on the circumstance which I have just witnessed—it could only have become the subject of my conversation by mere accident, and I will now take care to avoid the subject entirely.'

'You will do well, sir, and I thank you,' said the Father, throwing much dignity into the expression of obligation which he meant to convey. 'The time may perhaps come when you will learn what it is to have obliged one of my condition. As to the lady, she has the highest merit, and nothing can be said of her justly which would not redound to her praise. Nevertheless—in short, sir, we wander at present as in a morning mist—the sun will, I trust, soon rise and dispel it, when all that now seems mysterious will be fully revealed—or it will sink into rain,' he added, in a solemn tone, 'and then explanation will be of little consequence.—Adieu, sir; I wish you well.'

He made a graceful obeisance, and vanished through the same side-door by which the lady had entered; and Alan thought he heard their voices high in dispute in the adjoining apartment.

Presently afterwards, Ambrose entered, and told him that a horse and guide waited him beneath the terrace.

'The good Father Buonaventure,' added the butler, 'has been

graciously pleased to consider your situation, and desired me to enquire whether you have any occasion for a supply of money?'

'Make my respects to his reverence,' answered Fairford, 'and assure him I am provided in that particular. I beg you also to make my acknowledgments to the Miss Arthurets, and assure them that their kind hospitality, to which I probably owe my life, shall be remembered with gratitude as long as that life lasts. You yourself, Mr Ambrose, must accept of my kindest thanks for your skill and attention.'

Mid these acknowledgments they left the house, descended the terrace, and reached the spot where the gardener, Fairford's old acquaintance, waited for him, mounted upon one horse, and leading another.

Bidding adieu to Ambrose, our young lawyer mounted, and rode down the avenue, often looking back to the melancholy and neglected dwelling in which he had witnessed such strange scenes, and musing upon the character of its mysterious inmates, especially the noble and almost regal seeming priest, and the beautiful but capricious dame, who, if she was really Father Buonaventure's penitent, seemed less docile to the authority of the church, than, as Alan conceived, the Catholic discipline permitted. He could not indeed help being sensible that the whole deportment of these persons differed much from his preconceived notions of a priest and devotee. Father Buonaventure, in particular, had more natural dignity and less art and affectation in his manner, than accorded with the idea which Calvinists were taught to entertain of that wily and formidable person, a Jesuitical missionary.

While reflecting on these things, he looked back so frequently at the house, that Dick Gardener, a forward, talkative fellow, who began to tire of silence, at length said to him, 'I think you will know Fairladies when you see it again, sir?'

'I dare say I shall, Richard,' answered Fairford, good-humouredly. 'I wish I knew as well where I am to go next. But you can tell me, perhaps?'

'Your worship should know better than I,' said Dick Gardener; 'nevertheless, I have a notion you are going where all you Scotsmen should be sent, whether you will or no.'

'Not to the devil, I hope, good Dick?' said Fairford.

'Why, no. That is a road which you may travel as heretics; but as Scotsmen, I would only send you three-fourths of the way—and that is back to Scotland again—always craving your honour's pardon.'

'Does our journey lie that way?' said Fairford.

'As far as the water side,' said Richard. 'I am to carry you to old

Father Crackenthorp's, and then you are within a spit and a stride of Scotland, as the saying is. But mayhap you may think twice of going thither, for all that; for Old England is fat feeding-ground for north-country cattle.'

CHAPTER XVII

NARRATIVE OF DARSIE LATIMER

OUR history must now, as the old romancers wont to say, 'leave to tell' of the quest of Alan Fairford, and instruct our readers of the adventures which befell Darsie Latimer, left as he was in the precarious custody of his self-named tutor, the Laird of the Lochs of Solway, to whose arbitrary pleasure he found it necessary for the present to conform himself.

In consequence of this prudent resolution, and although he did not assume such a disguise without some sensations of shame and degradation, Darsie permitted Cristal Nixon to place over his face, and secure by a string, one of those silk masks which ladies frequently wore to preserve their complexions, when exposed to the air during long journeys on horseback. He remonstrated somewhat more vehemently against the long riding-skirt, which converted his person from the waist into the female guise, but was obliged to concede this point also.

The metamorphosis was then complete; for the fair reader must be informed, that in those rude times, the ladies, when they honoured the masculine dress by assuming any part of it, wore just such hats, coats, and waistcoats, as the male animals themselves made use of, and had no notion of the elegant compromise betwixt male and female attire, which has now acquired, *par excellence*, the name of a *habit*. Trolloping things our mothers must have looked, with long square-cut coats, lacking collars, and with waistcoats plentifully supplied with a length of pocket, which hung far downwards from the middle. But then they had some advantage from the splendid colours, lace, and gay embroidery, which masculine attire then exhibited; and, as happens in many similar instances, the finery of the materials made amends for the want of symmetry and grace of form in the garments themselves. But this is a digression.

In the court of the old mansion, half manor-place, half farm-house, or rather a decayed manor-house, converted into an abode for a Cumberland tenant, stood several saddled horses. Four or five of them were mounted by servants or inferior retainers, all of whom were well-armed with sword, pistol, and carabine. But two had riding furniture for the use of females—the one being accoutred with a side-saddle, the other with a pillion attached to the saddle.

Darsie's heart beat quicker within him; he easily comprehended that one of these was intended for his own use; and his hopes suggested that the other was designed for that of the fair Green-

Mantle, whom, according to his established practice, he had adopted for the queen of his affections, although his opportunities of holding communication with her had not exceeded the length of a silent supper on one occasion, and the going down a country-dance on another. This, however, was no unwonted mood of passion with Darsie Latimer, upon whom Cupid was used to triumph only in the degree of a Mahratta conqueror,* who overruns a province with the rapidity of lightning, but finds it impossible to retain it beyond a very brief space. Yet this new love was rather more serious than the scarce skinned-up wounds which his friend Fairford used to ridicule. The damsel had shown a sincere interest in his behalf; and the air of mystery with which that interest was veiled, gave her, to his lively imagination, the character of a benevolent and protecting spirit, as much as that of a beautiful female.

At former times, the romance attending his short-lived attachments had been of his own creating, and had disappeared soon as ever he approached more closely to the object with which he had invested it. On the present occasion, it really flowed from external circumstances, which might have interested less susceptible feelings, and an imagination less lively than that of Darsie Latimer, young, inexperienced, and enthusiastic as he was.

He watched, therefore, anxiously to whose service the palfrey bearing the lady's saddle was destined. But ere any female appeared to occupy it, he was himself summoned to take his seat on the pillion behind Cristal Nixon, amid the grins of his old acquaintance Jan, who helped him to horse, and the unrestrained laughter of Cicely, who displayed on the occasion a case of teeth which might have rivalled ivory.

Latimer was at an age when being an object of general ridicule even to clowns and milkmaids, was not a matter of indifference, and he longed heartily to have laid his horsewhip across Jan's shoulders. That, however, was a solacement of his feelings which was not at the moment to be thought of; and Cristal Nixon presently put an end to his unpleasant situation, by ordering the riders to go on. He himself kept the centre of the troop, two men riding before and two behind him, always, as it seemed to Darsie, having their eye upon him, to prevent any attempt to escape. He could see from time to time, when the straight line of the road, or the advantage of an ascent permitted him, that another troop of three or four riders followed them at about a quarter of a mile's distance, amongst whom he could discover the tall form of Redgauntlet, and the powerful action of his gallant black horse. He had little doubt that Green-Mantle made one of the party, though he was unable to distinguish her from the others.

In this manner they travelled from six in the morning until nearly ten of the clock, without Darsie's exchanging a word with any one; for he loathed the very idea of entering into conversation with Cristal Nixon, against whom he seemed to feel an instinctive aversion; nor was that domestic's saturnine and sullen disposition such as to have encouraged advances, had he thought of making them.

At length the party halted for the purpose of refreshment; but as they had hitherto avoided all villages and inhabited places upon their route, so they now stopped at one of those large ruinous Dutch barns, which are sometimes found in the fields, at a distance from the farm-houses to which they belong. Yet in this desolate place some preparations had been made for their reception. There were in the end of the barn, racks filled with provender for the horses, and plenty of provisions for the party were drawn from the trusses of straw, under which the baskets that contained them had been deposited. The choicest of these were selected and arranged apart by Cristal Nixon, while the men of the party threw themselves upon the rest, which he abandoned to their discretion. In a few minutes afterwards the rearward party arrived and dismounted, and Redgauntlet himself entered the barn with the green-mantled maiden by his side. He presented her to Darsie with these words:—

'It is time you two should know each other better. I promised you my confidence, Darsie, and the time is come for reposing it. But first we will have our breakfast; and then, when once more in the saddle, I will tell you that which it is necessary that you should know. Salute Lilias, Darsie.'

The command was sudden, and surprised Latimer, whose confusion was increased by the perfect ease and frankness with which Lilias offered at once her cheek and her hand, and pressing his, as she rather took it than gave her own, said very frankly, 'Dearest Darsie, how rejoiced I am that our uncle has at last permitted us to become acquainted!'

Darsie's head turned round; and it was perhaps well that Redgauntlet called on him to sit down, as even that movement served to hide his confusion. There is an old song which says—

——'when ladies are willing,
A man can but look like a fool;'*

And on the same principle Darsie Latimer's looks at this unexpected frankness of reception, would have formed an admirable vignette for illustrating the passage. 'Dearest Darsie,' and such a ready, nay, eager salute of lip and hand!—It was all very gracious, no doubt—and ought to have been received with much gratitude; but, constituted as our friend's temper was, nothing could be more inconsistent with his tone of feeling. If a hermit had proposed to him to club for a pot of beer, the illusion of his reverend sanctity could not have been dispelled more effectually than the divine qualities of Green-Mantle faded upon the ill-imagined frank-heartedness of poor Lilias. Vexed with her forwardness, and affronted at having once more cheated himself, Darsie could hardly help muttering two lines of the song we have already quoted:

> 'The fruit that must fall without shaking
> Is rather too mellow for me.'

And yet it was pity of her too—she was a very pretty young woman—his fancy had scarce overrated her in that respect—and the slight derangement of the beautiful brown locks which escaped in natural ringlets from under her riding-hat, with the bloom which exercise had brought into her cheek, made her even more than usually fascinating. Redgauntlet modified the sternness of his look when it was turned towards her, and, in addressing her, used a softer tone than his usual deep bass. Even the grim features of Cristal Nixon relaxed when he attended on her, and it was then, if ever, that his misanthropical visage expressed some sympathy with the rest of humanity.

'How can she,' thought Latimer, 'look so like an angel, yet be so mere a mortal after all?—How could so much seeming modesty have so much forwardness of manner, when she ought to have been most reserved? How can her conduct be reconciled to the grace and ease of her general deportment?'

The confusion of thoughts which occupied Darsie's imagination, gave to his looks a disordered appearance, and his inattention to the food which was placed before him, together with his silence and absence of mind, induced Lilias solicitously to enquire, whether he did not feel some return of the disorder under which he had suffered so lately. This led Mr Redgauntlet, who seemed also lost in his own contemplations, to raise his eyes, and join in the same enquiry with some appearance of interest. Latimer explained to both, that he was perfectly well.

'It is well it is so,' answered Redgauntlet; 'for we have that before us which will brook no delay from indisposition—we have not, as Hotspur says, leisure to be sick.'*

Lilias, on her part, endeavoured to prevail upon Darsie to partake of the food which she offered him, with a kindly and affectionate courtesy, corresponding to the warmth of the interest she had displayed at their meeting; but so very natural, innocent, and pure in its character, that it would have been impossible for the vainest coxcomb to have mistaken it for coquetry, or a desire of captivating a prize so valuable as his affections. Darsie, with no more than the reasonable share of self-opinion common to most youths when they approach twenty-one, knew not how to explain her conduct.

Sometimes he was tempted to think that his own merits had, even during the short intervals when they had seen each other, secured such a hold of the affections of a young person, who had probably been bred up in ignorance of the world and its forms, that she was unable to conceal her partiality. Sometimes he suspected that she acted by her guardian's order, who, aware that he, Darsie, was entitled to a considerable fortune, might have taken this bold stroke to bring about a marriage betwixt him and so near a relative.

But neither of these suppositions was applicable to the character of the parties. Miss Lilias's manners, however soft and natural, displayed in their ease and versatility considerable acquaintance with the habits of the world, and in the few words she said during the morning repast, there were mingled a shrewdness and good sense, which could scarce belong to a Miss capable of playing the silly part of a love-smitten maiden so broadly. As for Redgauntlet, with his stately bearing, his fatal frown, his eye of threat and of command, it was impossible, Darsie thought, to suspect him of a scheme having private advantage for its object;—he could as soon have imagined Cassius picking Caesar's pocket, instead of drawing his poniard on the Dictator.*

While he thus mused, unable either to eat, drink, or answer to the courtesy of Lilias, she soon ceased to speak to him, and sat silent as himself.

They had remained nearly an hour in their halting-place, when Redgauntlet said aloud, 'Look out, Cristal Nixon. If we hear nothing from Fairladies, we must continue our journey.'

Cristal went to the door, and presently returned and said to his master, in a voice as harsh as his features, 'Gilbert Gregson is coming, his horse as white with foam as if a fiend had ridden him.'

Redgauntlet threw from him the plate on which he had been eating, and hastened towards the door of the barn, which the courier at that moment entered; a smart jockey with a black velvet hunting-cap, and a broad belt drawn tight round his waist, to which was secured his express-bag. The variety of mud with which he was splashed from cap to spur, showed he had had a rough and rapid ride. He delivered a letter to Mr Redgauntlet, with an obeisance, and then retired to the end of the barn, where the other attendants were sitting or lying upon the straw, in order to get some refreshment.

Redgauntlet broke the letter open with haste, and read it with anxious and discomposed looks. On a second perusal, his displeasure seemed to increase, his brow darkened, and was distinctly marked with the fatal sign peculiar to his family and house. Darsie had never before observed his frown bear such a close resemblance to the shape which tradition assigned it.

Redgauntlet held out the open letter with one hand, and struck it with the forefinger of the other, as, in a suppressed and displeased tone, he said to Cristal Nixon, 'Countermanded—ordered northward once more!—Northward, when all our hopes lie to the south—a second Derby direction,* when we turned our back on glory, and marched in quest of ruin!'

Cristal Nixon took the letter and ran it over, then returned it to his master with the cold observation, 'a female influence predominates.'

'But it shall predominate no longer,' said Redgauntlet; 'it shall wane as ours rises in the horizon. Meanwhile, I will on before—and you, Cristal, will bring the party to the place assigned in the letter. You may now permit the young persons to have unreserved communication together; only mark that you watch the young man closely enough to prevent his escape, if he should be idiot enough to attempt it, but not approaching so close as to watch their free conversation.'

'I care nought about their conversation,' said Nixon, surlily.

'You hear my commands, Lilias,' said the Laird, turning to the young lady. 'You may use my permission and authority, to explain so much of our family matters as you yourself know. At our next meeting I will complete the task of disclosure, and I trust I shall restore one Redgauntlet more to the bosom of our ancient family. Let Latimer, as he calls himself, have a horse to himself; he must for some time retain his disguise.—My horse—my horse!'

In two minutes they heard him ride off from the door of the barn, followed at speed by two of the armed men of his party.

The commands of Cristal Nixon, in the meanwhile, put all the remainder of the party in motion, but the Laird himself was long out of sight ere they were in readiness to resume their journey. When at length they set out, Darsie was accommodated with a horse and side-saddle, instead of being obliged to resume his place on the pillion behind the detestable Nixon. He was obliged, however, to retain his riding skirt, and to reassume his mask. Yet notwithstanding this disagreeable circumstance, and although he observed that they gave him the heaviest and slowest horse of the party, and that, as a farther precaution against escape, he was closely watched on every side, yet riding in company with the pretty Lilias was an advantage which overbalanced these inconveniences.

It is true, that this society, to which that very morning he would have looked forward as a glimpse of heaven, had, now that it was thus unexpectedly indulged, something much less rapturous than he had expected.

It was in vain that, in order to avail himself of a situation so favourable for indulging his romantic disposition, he endeavoured to coax back, if I may so express myself, that delightful dream of ardent and tender passion; he felt only such a confusion of ideas at the difference between the being whom he had imagined, and her with whom he was now in contact, that it seemed to him like the effect of witchcraft. What most surprised him was, that this sudden flame should have died away so rapidly, notwithstanding that the maiden's personal beauty was even greater than he had expected—her demeanour, unless it should be deemed over kind towards himself, as graceful and becoming as he could have fancied it, even in his gayest dreams. It were judging hardly of him to suppose that the mere belief of his having attracted her affections more easily than he expected, was the cause of his ungratefully undervaluing a prize too lightly won, or that his transient passion played around his heart with the flitting radiance of a wintry sunbeam flashing against an icicle, which may brighten it for a moment, but cannot melt it. Neither of these was precisely the case, though such fickleness of disposition might also have some influence in the change.

The truth is, perhaps, that the lover's pleasure, like that of the hunter, is in the chase; and that the brightest beauty loses half its merit, as the fairest flower its perfume, when the willing hand can reach it too easily. There must be doubt—there must be danger—there must be difficulty; and if, as the poet says, the course of ardent affection never does run smooth,* it is perhaps because, without some intervening obstacle, that which is called the romantic passion of love, in its high poetical character and colouring, can hardly have an existence;—any more than there can be a current in a river, without the stream being narrowed by steep banks, or checked by opposing rocks.

Let not those, however, who enter into a union for life without those embarrassments which delight a Darsie Latimer, or a Lydia Languish,* and which are perhaps necessary to excite an enthusiastic passion in breasts more firm than theirs, augur worse of their future happiness, because their own alliance is formed under calmer auspices. Mutual esteem, an intimate knowledge of each other's character, seen, as in their case, undisguised by the mists of too partial passion—a suitable proportion of parties in rank and fortune, in taste and pursuits—are more frequently found in a marriage of reason, than in a union of romantic attachment; where the imagination, which probably created the virtues and accomplishments with which it invested the beloved object, is frequently afterwards employed in magnifying the mortifying consequences of its own delusion, and exasperating all the stings of disappointment. Those who follow the banners of Reason are like the well-disciplined battalion which, wearing a more sober uniform, and making a less dazzling show, than the light troops commanded by Imagination, enjoy more safety, and even more honour, in the conflicts of human life. All this, however, is foreign to our present purpose.

Uncertain in what manner to address her whom he had been lately so anxious to meet with, and embarrassed by a *tête-à-tête* to which his own timid inexperience gave some awkwardness, the party had proceeded more than a hundred yards before Darsie assumed courage to accost, or even to look at, his companion. Sensible, however, of the impropriety of his silence, he turned to speak to her; and observing that, although she wore her mask, there was something like disappointment and dejection in her manner, he was moved by self-reproach for his own coldness, and hastened to address her in the kindest tone he could assume.

'You must think me cruelly deficient in gratitude, Miss Lilias, that I have been thus long in your company, without thanking you for the interest which you have deigned to take in my unfortunate affairs?'

'I am glad you have at length spoken,' she said, 'though I own it is more coldly than I expected.—*Miss* Lilias! *Deign* to take interest—In whom, dear Darsie, *can* I take interest but in you? and why do you put this barrier of ceremony betwixt us, whom adverse circumstances have already separated for such a length of time?'

Darsie was again confounded at the extra candour, if we may use the term, of this frank avowal—'One must love partridge very well,' thought he, 'to accept it when thrown in one's face—if this is not plain speaking, there is no such place as downright Dunstable* in being!'

Embarrassed with these reflections, and himself of a nature fancifully, almost fastidiously, delicate, he could only in reply stammer forth an acknowledgment of his companion's goodness, and his own gratitude. She answered in a tone partly sorrowful and partly impatient, repeating, with displeased emphasis, the only distinct words he had been able to bring forth—'Goodness—gratitude!—O Darsie, should these be the phrases between you and me?—Alas! I am too sure you are displeased with me, though I cannot even guess on what account. Perhaps you think I have been too free in venturing upon my visit to your friend. But then remember it was in your behalf, and that I knew no better way to put you on your guard against the misfortunes and restraint which you have been subjected to, and are still enduring.'

'Dear lady'—said Darsie, rallying his recollection, and suspicious of some error in apprehension,—a suspicion which his mode of address seemed at once to communicate to Lilias, for she interrupted him,—

'*Lady!* dear *lady!*—For whom, or for what, in Heaven's name, do you take me, that you address me so formally?'

Had the question been asked in that enchanted hall in Fairy-land,* where all interrogations must be answered with absolute sincerity, Darsie had certainly replied, that he took her for the most frank-hearted and ultra-liberal lass that had ever lived since Mother Eve eat the pippin without paring. But as he was still on middle-earth, and free to avail himself of a little polite deceit, he barely answered, that he believed he had the honour of speaking to the niece of Mr Redgauntlet.

'Surely,' she replied; 'but were it not as easy for you to have said, to your own only sister?'

Darsie started in his saddle, as if he had received a pistol-shot.

'My sister!' he exclaimed.

'And you did *not* know it, then?' said she. 'I thought your reception of me was cold and indifferent!'

A kind and cordial embrace took place betwixt the relatives; and so light was Darsie's spirit, that he really felt himself more relieved, by getting quit of the embarrassments of the last half hour, during which he conceived himself in danger of being persecuted by the attachment of a forward girl, than disappointed by the vanishing of so many day-dreams as he had been in the habit of encouraging during the time when the green-mantled maiden was goddess of his idolatry. He had been already flung from his romantic Pegasus, and was too happy at length to find himself with bones unbroken, though with his back on the ground. He was, besides, with all his whims and follies, a generous, kind-hearted youth, and was delighted to acknowledge so beautiful and amiable a relative, and to assure her in the warmest terms of his immediate affection and future protection, so soon as they should be extricated from their present situation. Smiles and tears mingled on Lilias's cheeks, like showers and sunshine in April weather.

'Out on me,' she said, 'that I should be so childish as to cry at what makes me so sincerely happy! since, God knows, family-love is what my heart has most longed after, and to which it has been most a stranger. My uncle says that you and I, Darsie, are but half Redgauntlets, and that the metal of which our father's family was made, has been softened to effeminacy in our mother's offspring.'

'Alas!' said Darsie, 'I know so little of our family story, that I almost doubted that I belonged to the House of Redgauntlet, although the chief of the family himself intimated so much to me.'

'The Chief of the family!' said Lilias. 'You must know little of your own descent indeed, if you mean my uncle by that expression. You yourself, my dear Darsie, are the heir and representative of our ancient House, for our father was the elder brother—that brave and unhappy Sir Henry Darsie Redgauntlet, who suffered at Carlisle in the year 1746. He took the name of Darsie, in conjunction with his own, from our mother, heiress to a Cumberland family of great wealth and antiquity, of whose large estates you are the undeniable heir, although those of your father have been involved in the general doom of forfeiture. But all this must be necessarily unknown to you.'

'Indeed I hear it for the first time in my life,' answered Darsie.

'And you knew not that I was your sister?' said Lilias. 'No wonder you received me so coldly. What a strange, wild, forward young person you must have thought me—mixing myself in the fortunes of a stranger whom I had only once spoken to—corresponding with him by signs—Good Heaven! what can you have supposed me?'

'And how should I have come to the knowledge of our connexion?' said Darsie. 'You are aware I was not acquainted with it when we danced together at Brokenburn.'

'I saw that with concern, and fain I would have warned you,' answered Lilias; 'but I was closely watched, and before I could find or make an opportunity of coming to a full explanation with you on a subject so agitating, I was forced to leave the room. What I did say was, you may remember, a caution to leave the southern border, for I foresaw what has since happened. But since my uncle has had you in his power, I never doubted he had communicated to you our whole family history.'

'He has left me to learn it from you, Lilias; and assure yourself that I will hear it with more pleasure from your lips than from his. I have no reason to be pleased with his conduct towards me.'

'Of that,' said Lilias, 'you will judge better when you have heard what I have to tell you;' and she began her communication in the following manner.

CHAPTER XVIII

NARRATIVE OF DARSIE LATIMER, CONTINUED

'THE House of Redgauntlet,' said the young lady, 'has for centuries been supposed to lie under a doom, which has rendered vain their courage, their talents, their ambition, and their wisdom. Often making a figure in history, they have been ever in the situation of men striving against both wind and tide, who distinguish themselves by their desperate exertions of strength, and their persevering endurance of toil, but without being able to advance themselves upon their course, by either vigour or resolution. They pretend to trace this fatality to a legendary history, which I may tell you at a less busy moment.'

Darsie intimated, that he had already heard the tragic story of Sir Alberick Redgauntlet.

'I need only say, then,' proceeded Lilias, 'that our father and uncle felt the family doom in its full extent. They were both possessed of considerable property, which was largely increased by our father's marriage, and were both devoted to the service of the unhappy House of Stewart; but (as our mother at least supposed) family considerations might have withheld her husband from joining openly in the affair of 1745, had not the high influence which the younger brother possessed over the elder, from his more decided energy of character, hurried him along with himself into that undertaking.

'When, therefore, the enterprise came to the fatal conclusion, which bereaved our father of his life, and consigned his brother to exile, Lady Redgauntlet fled from the north of England, determined to break off all communication with her late husband's family, particularly his brother, whom she regarded as having, by their insane political enthusiasm, been the means of his untimely death; and determined that you, my brother, an infant, and that I, to whom she had just given birth, should be brought up as adherents of the present dynasty. Perhaps she was too hasty in this determination—too timidly anxious to exclude, if possible, from the knowledge of the very spot where we existed, a relation so nearly connected with us as our father's only brother. But you must make allowance for what she had suffered. See, brother,' she said, pulling her glove off, 'these five blood-specks on my arm are a mark by which mysterious Nature has impressed, on an unborn infant, a record of its father's violent death and its mother's miseries.'[57]

'You were not, then, born when my father suffered?' said Darsie.

'Alas, no!' she replied; 'nor were you a twelvemonth old. It was no wonder that my mother, after going through such scenes of agony, became irresistibly anxious for the sake of her children—of her son in particular; the more especially as the late Sir Henry, her husband, had, by a settlement of his affairs, confided the custody of the persons of her children, as well as the estates which descended to them, independently of those which fell under his forfeiture, to his brother Hugh, in whom he placed unlimited confidence.'

'But my mother had no reason to fear the operation of such a deed, conceived in favour of an attainted man,' said Darsie.

'True,' replied Lilias; 'but our uncle's attainder might have been reversed, like that of so many other persons, and our mother, who both feared and hated him, lived in continual terror that this would be the case, and that she should see the author, as she thought him, of her husband's death, come armed with legal powers, and in a capacity to use them, for the purpose of tearing her children from her protection. Besides, she feared, even in his incapacitated condition, the adventurous and pertinacious spirit of her brother-in-law, Hugh Redgauntlet, and felt assured that he would make some attempt to possess himself of the persons of the children. On the other hand, our uncle, whose proud disposition might, perhaps, have been soothed by the offer of her confidence, revolted against the distrustful and suspicious manner in which Lady Darsie Redgauntlet acted towards him. She basely abused, he said, the unhappy circumstances in which he was placed, in order to deprive him of his natural privilege of protecting and educating the infants, whom nature and law, and the will of their father, had committed to his charge, and he swore solemnly he would not submit to such an injury. Report of his threats was made to Lady Redgauntlet, and tended to increase those fears which proved but too well founded. While you and I, children at that time of two or three years old, were playing together in a walled orchard, adjacent to our mother's residence, which she had fixed somewhere in Devonshire, my uncle suddenly scaled the wall with several men, and I was snatched up and carried off to a boat which waited for them. My mother, however, flew to your rescue, and as she seized on and held you fast, my uncle could not, as he has since told me, possess himself of your person, without using unmanly violence to his brother's widow. Of this he was incapable; and, as people began to assemble upon my mother's screaming, he withdrew, after darting upon you and her one of those fearful looks, which, it is said, remain with our family, as a fatal bequest of Sir Alberick, our ancestor.'

'I have some recollection of the scuffle which you mention,' said

Darsie; 'and I think it was my uncle himself (since my uncle he is) who recalled the circumstance to my mind on a late occasion. I can now account for the guarded seclusion under which my poor mother lived—for her frequent tears, her starts of hysterical alarm, and her constant and deep melancholy. Poor lady! what a lot was hers, and what must have been her feelings when it approached to a close!'

'It was then that she adopted,' said Lilias, 'every precaution her ingenuity could suggest, to keep your very existence concealed from the person whom she feared—nay, from yourself; for she dreaded, as she is said often to have expressed herself, that the wildfire blood of Redgauntlet would urge you to unite your fortunes to those of your uncle, who was well known still to carry on political intrigues, which most other persons had considered as desperate. It was also possible that he, as well as others, might get his pardon, as government showed every year more lenity towards the remnant of the Jacobites, and then he might claim the custody of your person, as your legal guardian. Either of these events she considered as the direct road to your destruction.'

'I wonder she had not claimed the protection of Chancery for me,' said Darsie; 'or confided me to the care of some powerful friend.'

'She was on indifferent terms with her relations, on account of her marriage with our father,' said Lilias, 'and trusted more to secreting you from your uncle's attempts, than to any protection which law might afford against them. Perhaps she judged unwisely, but surely not unnaturally, for one rendered irritable by so many misfortunes and so many alarms. Samuel Griffiths, an eminent banker, and a worthy clergyman now dead, were, I believe, the only persons whom she intrusted with the execution of her last will; and my uncle believes that she made them both swear to observe profound secrecy concerning your birth and pretensions, until you should come to the age of majority, and, in the meantime, to breed you up in the most private way possible, and that which was most likely to withdraw you from my uncle's observation.'

'And I have no doubt,' said Darsie, 'that, betwixt change of name and habitation, they might have succeeded perfectly, but for the accident—lucky or unlucky, I know not which to term it—which brought me to Brokenburn, and into contact with Mr Redgauntlet. I see also why I was warned against England, for in England'——

'In England alone, if I understand rightly,' said Miss Redgauntlet, 'the claims of your uncle to the custody of your person could have been enforced, in case of his being replaced in the ordinary rights of citizenship, either by the lenity of the government or by some change in it. In Scotland, where you possess no property, I understand his authority might have been resisted, and measures taken to put you under the protection of the law.* But, pray, think it not unlucky that you have taken the step of visiting Brokenburn—I feel confident that the consequences must be ultimately fortunate, for, have they not already brought us into contact with each other?'

So saying, she held out her hand to her brother, who grasped it with a fondness of pressure very different from the manner in which they first clasped hands that morning. There was a moment's pause, while the hearts of both were overflowing with a feeling of natural affection, to which circumstances had hitherto rendered them strangers.

At length Darsie broke silence: 'I am ashamed,' he said, 'my dearest Lilias, that I have suffered you to talk so long about matters concerning myself only, while I remain ignorant of your story, and your present situation.'

'The former is none of the most interesting, nor the latter the most safe or agreeable,' answered Lilias; 'but now, my dearest brother, I shall have the inestimable support of your countenance and affection; and were I but sure that we could weather the formidable crisis which I find so close at hand, I should have little apprehensions for the future.'

'Let me know,' said Darsie, 'what our present situation is; and rely upon my utmost exertions both in your defence and my own. For what reason can my uncle desire to detain me a prisoner?—If in mere opposition to the will of my mother, she has long been no more; and I see not why he should wish, at so much trouble and risk, to interfere with the free will of one, to whom a few months will give a privilege of acting for himself, with which he will have no longer any pretence to interfere.'

'My dearest Arthur,' answered Lilias—'for that name, as well as Darsie, properly belongs to you—it is the leading feature in my uncle's character, that he has applied every energy of his powerful mind to the service of the exiled family of Stewart. The death of his brother, the dilapidation of his own fortunes, have only added to his hereditary zeal for the House of Stewart, a deep and almost personal hatred against the present reigning family. He is, in short, a political enthusiast of the most dangerous character, and proceeds in his agency with as much confidence, as if he felt himself the very Atlas, who is alone capable of supporting a sinking cause.'

'And where or how did you, my Lilias, educated, doubtless, under his auspices, learn to have a different view of such subjects?'

'By a singular chance,' replied Lilias, 'in the nunnery where my uncle placed me. Although the Abbess was a person exactly after his own heart, my education as a pensioner devolved much on an excellent old mother who had adopted the tenets of the Jansenists, with perhaps a still further tendency towards the reformed doctrines, than those of Porte-Royale.* The mysterious secrecy with which she inculcated these tenets, gave them charms to my young mind, and I embraced them the rather that they were in direct opposition to the doctrines of the Abbess, whom I hated so much for her severity, that I felt a childish delight in setting her control at defiance, and contradicting in my secret soul all that I was openly obliged to listen to with reverence. Freedom of religious opinion brings on, I suppose, freedom of political creed; for I had no sooner renounced the Pope's infallibility, than I began to question the doctrine of hereditary and indefeasible right. In short, strange as it may seem, I came out of a Parisian convent, not indeed an instructed Whig and Protestant, but with as much inclination to be so as if I had been bred up, like you, within the presbyterian sound of Saint Giles's chimes.'

'More so, perhaps,' replied Darsie; 'for the nearer the church*—the proverb is somewhat musty. But how did these liberal opinions of yours agree with the very opposite prejudices of my uncle?'

'They would have agreed like fire and water,' answered Lilias, 'had I suffered mine to become visible; but as that would have subjected me to constant reproach and upbraiding, or worse, I took great care to keep my own secret; so that occasional censures for coldness, and lack of zeal for the good cause, were the worst I had to undergo; and these were bad enough.'

'I applaud your caution,' said Darsie.

'You have reason,' replied his sister; 'but I got so terrible a specimen of my uncle's determination of character, before I had been acquainted with him for much more than a week, that it taught me at what risk I should contradict his humour. I will tell you the circumstances; for it will better teach you to appreciate the romantic and resolved nature of his character, than any thing which I could state of his rashness and enthusiasm.'

'After I had been many a long year at the convent, I was removed from thence, and placed with a meagre old Scottish lady of high rank, the daughter of an unfortunate person, whose head had in the year 1715 been placed on Temple-bar.* She subsisted on a small pension from the French Court, aided by an occasional gratuity from the Stewarts; to which the annuity paid for my board formed a desirable addition. She was not ill-tempered, nor very covetous—neither beat me nor starved me—but she was so completely trammelled by rank and prejudices, so awfully profound in genealogy, and so bitterly keen, poor lady, in British politics, that I sometimes thought it pity that the Hanoverians, who murdered, as she used to tell me, her poor dear father, had left his dear daughter in the land of the living. Delighted, therefore, was I, when my uncle made his appearance, and abruptly announced his purpose of conveying me to England. My extravagant joy at the idea of leaving Lady Rachel Rougedragon, was somewhat qualified by observing the melancholy look, lofty demeanour, and commanding tone of my near relative. He held more communication with me on the journey, however, than consisted with his taciturn demeanour in general, and seemed anxious to ascertain my tone of character, and particularly in point of courage. Now, though I am a tamed Redgauntlet, yet I have still so much of our family spirit as enables me to be as composed in danger as most of my sex; and upon two occasions in the course of our journey—a threatened attack by banditti, and the overturn of our carriage—I had the fortune so to conduct myself, as to convey to my uncle a very favourable idea of my intrepidity. Probably this encouraged him to put in execution the singular scheme which he had in agitation.

'Ere we reached London we changed our means of conveyance, and altered the route by which we approached the city, more than once; then, like a hare which doubles repeatedly at some distance from the seat she means to occupy, and at last leaps into her form from a distance as great as she can clear by a spring, we made a forced march, and landed in private and obscure lodgings in a little old street in Westminster, not far distant from the Cloisters.

'On the morning of the day on which we arrived my uncle went abroad, and did not return for some hours. Meantime I had no other amusement than to listen to the tumult of noises which succeeded each other, or reigned in confusion together, during the whole morning. Paris I had thought the most noisy capital in the world, but Paris seemed midnight silence compared to London. Cannon thundered near and at a distance—drums, trumpets, and military music of every kind, rolled, flourished, and pierced the clouds, almost without intermission. To fill up the concert, bells pealed incessantly from a hundred steeples. The acclamations of an immense multitude were heard from time to time, like the roaring of a mighty ocean, and all this without my being able to glean the least idea of what was going on, for the windows of our apartment looked upon a waste back-yard, which seemed totally deserted. My curiosity became extreme, for I was satisfied, at length, that it must be some festival of the highest order which called forth these incessant sounds.

'My uncle at length returned, and with him a man of an exterior singularly unprepossessing. I need not describe him to you, for—do not look round—he rides behind us at this moment.'

'That respectable person, Mr Cristal Nixon, I suppose?' said Darsie.

'The same,' answered Lilias; 'make no gesture that may intimate we are speaking of him.'

Darsie signified that he understood her, and she pursued her relation.

'They were both in full dress, and my uncle, taking a bundle from Nixon, said to me, "Lilias, I am come to carry you to see a grand ceremony—put on as hastily as you can the dress you will find in that parcel, and prepare to attend me." I found a female dress, splendid and elegant, but somewhat bordering upon the antique fashion. It might be that of England, I thought, and I went to my apartment full of curiosity, and dressed myself with all speed.

'My uncle surveyed me with attention—"She may pass for one of the flower-girls," he said to Nixon, who only answered with a nod.

'We left the house together, and such was their knowledge of the lanes, courts, and bypaths, that though there was the roar of a multitude in the broad streets, those which we traversed were silent and deserted; and the strollers whom we met, tired of gazing upon gayer figures, scarcely honoured us with a passing look, although, at any other time, we should, among these vulgar suburbs, have attracted a troublesome share of observation. We crossed at length a broad street, where many soldiers were on guard, while others, exhausted with previous duty, were eating, drinking, smoking, and sleeping beside their piled arms.

'"One day, Nixon," whispered my uncle, "we will make these redcoated gentry stand to their muskets more watchfully."

'"Or it will be the worse for them," answered his attendant, in a voice as unpleasant as his physiognomy.

'Unquestioned and unchallenged by any one, we crossed among the guards, and Nixon tapped thrice at a small postern door in a huge ancient building which was straight before us. It opened, and we entered without my perceiving by whom we were admitted. A few dark and narrow passages at length conveyed us into an immense Gothic hall, the magnificence of which baffles my powers of description.

'It was illuminated by ten thousand wax lights, whose splendour at first dazzled my eyes, coming as we did from these dark and secret avenues. But when my sight began to become steady, how shall I describe what I beheld! Beneath were huge ranges of tables, occupied by princes and nobles in their robes of state—high officers of the crown, wearing their dresses and badges of authority—reverend prelates and judges, the sages of the church and law, in their more sombre, yet not less awful robes—with others whose antique and striking costume announced their importance, though I could not even guess who they might be. But at length the truth burst on me at once—it was, and the murmurs around confirmed it, the Coronation

Feast.* At a table above the rest, and extending across the upper end of the hall, sat enthroned the youthful Sovereign himself, surrounded by the princes of the blood, and other dignitaries, and receiving the suit and homage of his subjects. Heralds and pursuivants, blazing in their fantastic yet splendid armorial habits, and pages of honour, gorgeously arrayed in the garb of other days, waited upon the princely banqueters. In the galleries with which this spacious hall was surrounded, shone all, and more than all, that my poor imagination could conceive, of what was brilliant in riches, or captivating in beauty. Countless rows of ladies, whose diamonds, jewels, and splendid attire, were their least powerful charms, looked down from their lofty seats on the rich scene beneath, themselves forming a show as dazzling and as beautiful as that of which they were spectators. Under these galleries, and behind the banqueting tables, were a multitude of gentlemen, dressed as if to attend a court, but whose garb, although rich enough to have adorned a royal drawingroom, could not distinguish them in such a high scene as this. Amongst these we wandered for a few minutes, undistinguished and unregarded. I saw several young persons dressed as I was, so was under no embarrassment from the singularity of my habit, and only rejoiced, as I hung on my uncle's arm, at the magical splendour of such a scene, and at his goodness for procuring me the pleasure of beholding it.

'By and by, I perceived that my uncle had acquaintances among those who were under the galleries, and seemed, like ourselves, to be mere spectators of the solemnity. They recognised each other with a single word, sometimes only with a gripe of the hand—exchanged some private signs, doubtless—and gradually formed a little group, in the centre of which we were placed.

'"Is it not a grand sight, Lilias?" said my uncle. "All the noble, and all the wise, and all the wealthy of Britain, are there assembled."

'"It is indeed," said I, "all that my mind could have fancied of regal power and splendour."

'"Girl," he whispered,—and my uncle can make his whispers as terribly emphatic as his thundering voice or his blighting look,—"all that is noble and worthy in this fair land are there assembled—but it is to bend like slaves and sycophants before the throne of a new usurper."

'I looked at him, and the dark hereditary frown of our unhappy ancestor was black upon his brow.

'"For God's sake," I whispered, "consider where we are."

'"Fear nothing," he said; "we are surrounded by friends."—As he proceeded, his strong and muscular frame shook with suppressed agitation.—"See," he said, "yonder bends Norfolk, renegade to his Catholic faith; there stoops the Bishop of————, traitor to the

Church of England; and,—shame of shames! yonder the gigantic form of Errol bows his head before the grandson of his father's murderer! But a sign shall be seen this night amongst them—*Mene, Mene, Tekel, Upharsin*, shall be read on these walls, as distinctly as the spectral handwriting made them visible on those of Belshazzar!"*

'"For God's sake," said I, dreadfully alarmed, "it is impossible you can meditate violence in such a presence!"

'"None is intended, fool," he answered, "nor can the slightest mischance happen, provided you will rally your boasted courage, and obey my directions. But do it coolly and quickly, for there are an hundred lives at stake."

'"Alas! what can I do?" I asked in the utmost terror.

'"Only be prompt to execute my bidding," said he; "it is but to lift a glove—Here, hold this in your hand—throw the train of your dress over it, be firm, composed, and ready—or, at all events, I step forward myself."

'"If there is no violence designed," I said, taking, mechanically, the iron glove he put into my hand.

'I could not conceive his meaning; but, in the excited state of mind in which I beheld him, I was convinced that disobedience on my part would lead to some wild explosion. I felt, from the emergency of the occasion, a sudden presence of mind, and resolved to do any thing that might avert violence and bloodshed. I was not long held in suspense. A loud flourish of trumpets, and the voice of heralds, were mixed with the clatter of horse's hoofs, while a champion armed at all points, like those I had read of in romances, attended by squires, pages, and the whole retinue of chivalry, pranced forward, mounted upon a barbed steed. His challenge, in defiance of all who dared impeach the title of the new sovereign, was recited aloud—once and again.

'"Rush in at the third sounding," said my uncle to me; "bring me the parader's gage, and leave mine in lieu of it."

'I could not see how this was to be done, as we were surrounded by people on all sides. But, at the third sounding of the trumpets, a lane opened as if by word of command, betwixt me and the champion, and my uncle's voice said, "Now, Lilias, NOW!"

'With a swift and yet steady step, and with a presence of mind for which I have never since been able to account, I discharged the perilous commission. I was hardly seen, I believe, as I exchanged the pledges of battle, and in an instant retired. "Nobly done, my girl!" said my uncle, at whose side I found myself, shrouded as I was before, by the interposition of the bystanders. "Cover our retreat, gentlemen," he whispered to those around him.

'Room was made for us to approach the wall, which seemed to

open, and we were again involved in the dark passages through which we had formerly passed. In a small anteroom, my uncle stopped, and hastily muffling me in a mantle which was lying there, we passed the guards—threaded the labyrinth of empty streets and courts, and reached our retired lodgings without attracting the least attention.'

'I have often heard,' said Darsie, 'that a female, supposed to be a man in disguise,—and yet, Lilias, you do not look very masculine,—had taken up the champion's gauntlet at the present King's Coronation, and left in its place a gage of battle, with a paper, offering to accept the combat, provided a fair field should be allowed for it. I have hitherto considered it as an idle tale.* I little thought how nearly I was interested in the actors of a scene so daring—How could you have courage to go through with it?'[58]

'Had I had leisure for reflection,' answered his sister, 'I should have refused, from a mixture of principle and of fear. But, like many people who do daring actions, I went on because I had not time to think of retreating. The matter was little known, and it is said the King had commanded that it should not be farther enquired into;—from prudence, as I suppose, and lenity, though my uncle chooses to ascribe the forbearance of the Elector of Hanover,* as he calls him, sometimes to pusillanimity, and sometimes to a presumptuous scorn of the faction who opposes his title.'

'And have your subsequent agencies under this frantic enthusiast,' said Darsie, 'equalled this in danger?'

'No—nor in importance,' replied Lilias; 'though I have witnessed much of the strange and desperate machinations, by which, in spite of every obstacle, and in contempt of every danger, he endeavours to awaken the courage of a broken party. I have traversed, in his company, all England and Scotland, and have visited the most extraordinary and contrasted scenes; now lodging at the castles of the proud gentry of Cheshire and Wales, where the retired aristocrats, with opinions as antiquated as their dwellings and their manners, still continue to nourish jacobitical principles; and the next week, perhaps, spent among outlawed smugglers or Highland banditti. I have known my uncle often act the part of a hero, and sometimes that of a mere vulgar conspirator, and turn himself, with the most surprising flexibility, into all sorts of shapes to attract proselytes to his cause.'

'Which, in the present day,' said Darsie, 'he finds, I presume, no easy task.'

'So difficult,' said Lilias, 'that I believe, he has, at different times, disgusted with the total falling away of some friends, and the coldness of others, been almost on the point of resigning his undertaking. How often have I known him affect an open brow and a jovial manner, joining in the games of the gentry, and even in the sports of the common people, in order to invest himself with a temporary degree of popularity; while, in fact, his heart was bursting to witness what he called the degeneracy of the times, the decay of activity among the aged, and the want of zeal in the rising generation. After the day has been passed in the hardest exercise, he has spent the night in pacing his solitary chamber, bewailing the downfall of the cause, and wishing for the bullet of Dundee, or the axe of Balmerino.'*

'A strange delusion,' said Darsie; 'and it is wonderful that it does not yield to the force of reality.'

'Ah, but,' replied Lilias, 'realities of late have seemed to flatter his hopes. The general dissatisfaction with the peace—the unpopularity of the minister, which has extended itself even to the person of his master—the various uproars which have disturbed the quiet of the metropolis,* and a general state of disgust and dissatisfaction, which seems to affect the body of the nation, have given unwonted encouragement to the expiring hopes of the Jacobites, and induced many, both at the Court of Rome, and, if it can be called so, of the Pretender, to lend a more favourable ear than they had hitherto done to the insinuations of those, who, like my uncle, hope, when hope is lost to all but themselves. Nay, I really believe that at this moment they meditate some desperate effort. My uncle has been doing all in his power, of late, to conciliate the affections of those wild communities that dwell on the Solway, over whom our family possessed a seigniorial interest before the forfeiture, and amongst whom, on the occasion of 1745, our unhappy father's interest, with his own, raised a considerable body of men. But they are no longer willing to obey his summons; and, as one apology among others, they allege your absence as their natural head and leader. This has increased his desire to obtain possession of your person, and, if he possibly can, to influence your mind, so as to obtain your authority to his proceedings.'

'That he shall never obtain,' answered Darsie; 'my principles and my prudence alike forbid such a step. Besides, it would be totally unavailing to his purpose. Whatever these people may pretend, to evade your uncle's importunities, they cannot, at this time of day, think of subjecting their necks again to the feudal yoke, which was effectually broken by the act of 1748, abolishing vassalage and hereditary jurisdictions.'*

'Ay, but that my uncle considers as the act of a usurping government,' said Lilias.

'Like enough *he* may think so,' answered her brother, 'for he is a superior, and loses his authority by the enactment. But the question is, what the vassals will think of it, who have gained their freedom from feudal slavery, and have now enjoyed that freedom for many years? However, to cut the matter short, if five hundred men would rise at the wagging of my finger, that finger should not be raised in a cause which I disapprove of, and upon that my uncle may reckon.'

'But you may temporize,' said Lilias, upon whom the idea of her uncle's displeasure made evidently a strong impression,—'you may temporize, as most of the gentry in this country do, and let the bubble burst of itself; for it is singular how few of them venture to oppose my uncle directly. I entreat you to avoid direct collision with him. To hear you, the head of the House of Redgauntlet, declare against the family of Stewart, would either break his heart, or drive him to some act of desperation.'

'Yes, but, Lilias, you forget that the consequences of such an act of complaisance might be, that the House of Redgauntlet and I might lose both our heads at one blow.'

'Alas!' said she, 'I had forgotten that danger. I have grown familiar with perilous intrigues, as the nurses in a pest-house are said to become accustomed to the air around them, till they forget even that it is noisome.'

'And yet,' said Darsie, 'if I could free myself from him without coming to an open rupture—Tell me, Lilias, do you think it possible that he can have any immediate attempt in view?'

'To confess the truth,' answered Lilias, 'I cannot doubt that he has. There has been an unusual bustle among the Jacobites of late. They have hopes, as I told you, from circumstances unconnected with their own strength. Just before you came to the country, my uncle's desire to find you out, became, if possible, more eager than ever—he talked of men to be presently brought together, and of your name and influence for raising them. At this very time, your first visit to Brokenburn took place. A suspicion arose in my uncle's mind, that you might be the youth he sought, and it was strengthened by papers and letters which the rascal Nixon did not hesitate to take from your pocket. Yet a mistake might have occasioned a fatal explosion; and my uncle therefore posted to Edinburgh to follow out the clew he had obtained, and fished enough of information from old Mr Fairford to make him certain that you were the person he sought. Meanwhile, and at the expense of some personal, and perhaps too bold exertion, I endeavoured, through your friend young Fairford, to put you on your guard.'

'Without success,' said Darsie, blushing under his mask, when he recollected how he had mistaken his sister's meaning.

'I do not wonder that my warning was fruitless,' said she; 'the thing was doomed to be. Besides, your escape would have been difficult. You were dogged the whole time you were at the Shepherd's Bush and at Mount Sharon, by a spy who scarcely ever left you.'

'The wretch little Benjie!' exclaimed Darsie. 'I will wring the monkey's neck round, the first time we meet.'

'It was he indeed who gave constant information of your motions to Cristal Nixon,' said Lilias.

'And Cristal Nixon—I owe him, too, a day's work in harvest,'* said Darsie; 'for I am mistaken if he is not the person that struck me down when I was made prisoner among the rioters.'

'Like enough; for he has a head and hand for any villainy. My uncle was very angry about it; for though the riot was made to have an opportunity of carrying you off in the confusion, as well as to put the fishermen at variance with the public law, it would have been his last thought to have injured a hair of your head. But Nixon has insinuated himself into all my uncle's secrets, and some of these are so dark and dangerous, that though there are few things he would *not* dare, I doubt if he dare quarrel with him.—And yet I know that of Cristal, would move my uncle to pass his sword through his body.'

'What is it, for Heaven's sake?' said Darsie, 'I have a particular desire for wishing to know.'

'The old brutal desperado, whose face and mind are a libel upon human nature, has had the insolence to speak to his master's niece as one whom he was at liberty to admire; and when I turned on him with the anger and contempt he merited, the wretch grumbled out something, as if he held the destiny of our family in his hand.'

'I thank you, Lilias,' said Darsie, eagerly,—'I thank you with all my heart for this communication. I have blamed myself as a Christian man for the indescribable longing I felt from the first moment I saw that rascal, to send a bullet through his head; and now you have perfectly accounted for and justified this very laudable wish. I wonder my uncle, with the powerful sense you describe him to be possessed of, does not see through such a villain.'

'I believe he knows him to be capable of much evil,' answered Lilias—'selfish, obdurate, brutal, and a man-hater. But then he conceives him to possess the qualities most requisite for a conspirator—undaunted courage, imperturbable coolness and address, and inviolable fidelity. In the last particular he may be mistaken. I have heard Nixon blamed for the manner in which our poor father was taken after Culloden.'

'Another reason for my innate aversion,' said Darsie; 'but I will be on my guard with him.'

'See, he observes us closely,' said Lilias. 'What a thing is conscience!—He knows we are now speaking of him, though he cannot have heard a word that we have said.'

It seemed as if she had guessed truly; for Cristal Nixon at that moment rode up to them, and said, with an affectation of jocularity, which sat very ill upon his sullen features, 'Come, young ladies, you have had time enough for your chat this morning, and your tongues, I think, must be tired. We are going to pass a village, and I must beg you to separate—you, Miss Lilias, to ride a little behind—and you, Mrs, or Miss, or Master, whichever you choose to be called, to be jogging a little bit before.'

Lilias checked her horse without speaking, but not until she had given her brother an expressive look, recommending caution; to which he replied by a signal, indicating that he understood and would comply with her request.

CHAPTER XIX

NARRATIVE OF DARSIE LATIMER, CONTINUED

LEFT to his solitary meditations, Darsie (for we will still term Sir Arthur Darsie Redgauntlet of that Ilk, by the name to which the reader is habituated) was surprised not only at the alteration of his own state and condition, but at the equanimity with which he felt himself disposed to view all these vicissitudes.

His fever-fit of love had departed like a morning's dream, and left nothing behind but a painful sense of shame, and a resolution to be more cautious ere he again indulged in such romantic visions. His station in society was changed from that of a wandering, unowned youth, in whom none appeared to take an interest, excepting the strangers by whom he had been educated, to the heir of a noble house, possessed of such influence and such property, that it seemed as if the progress or arrest of important political events were likely to depend upon his resolution. Even this sudden elevation, the more than fulfilment of those wishes which had haunted him ever since he was able to form a wish on the subject, was contemplated by Darsie, volatile as his disposition was, without more than a few thrills of gratified vanity.

It is true, there were circumstances in his present situation to counterbalance such high advantages. To be a prisoner in the hands of a man so determined as his uncle, was no agreeable consideration, when he was calculating how he might best dispute his pleasure, and refuse to join him in the perilous enterprise which he seemed to meditate. Outlawed and desperate himself, Darsie could not doubt that his uncle was surrounded by men capable of any thing—that he was restrained by no personal considerations—and therefore what degree of compulsion he might apply to his brother's son, or in what manner he might feel at liberty to punish his contumacy, should he disavow the Jacobite cause, must depend entirely upon the limits of his own conscience; and who was to answer for the conscience of a heated enthusiast, who considers opposition to the party he has espoused, as treason to the welfare of his country? After a short interval, Cristal Nixon was pleased to throw some light upon the subject which agitated him.

When that grim satellite rode up without ceremony close to Darsie's side, the latter felt his very flesh creep with abhorrence, so little was he able to endure his presence, since the story of Lilias had added to his instinctive hatred of the man. His voice, too, sounded like that of a screech-owl, as he said, 'So, my young cock of the north, you now know it all, and no doubt are blessing your uncle for stirring you up to such an honourable action.'

'I will acquaint my uncle with my sentiments on the subject, before I make them known to any one else,' said Darsie, scarcely prevailing on his tongue to utter even these few words in a civil manner.

'Umph,' murmured Cristal between his teeth. 'Close as wax, I see; and perhaps not quite so pliable.—But take care, my pretty youth,' he added, scornfully; 'Hugh Redgauntlet will prove a rough colt-breaker—he will neither spare whipcord nor spur-rowel, I promise you.'

'I have already said, Mr Nixon,' answered Darsie, 'that I will canvass those matters of which my sister has informed me, with my uncle himself, and with no other person.'

'Nay, but a word of friendly advice would do you no harm, young master,' replied Nixon. 'Old Redgauntlet is apter at a blow than a word—likely to bite before he barks—the true man for giving Scarborough warning,* first knock you down, then bid you stand. —So, methinks, a little kind warning as to consequences were not amiss, lest they come upon you unawares.'

'If the warning is really kind, Mr Nixon,' said the young man, 'I will hear it thankfully; and indeed, if otherwise, I must listen to it whether I will or no, since I have at present no choice of company or of conversation.'

'Nay, I have but little to say,' said Nixon, affecting to give to his sullen and dogged manner the appearance of an honest bluntness; 'I am as little apt to throw away words as any one. But here is the question—Will you join heart and hand with your uncle, or no?'

'What if I should say Ay?' said Darsie, determined, if possible, to conceal his resolution from this man.

'Why, then,' said Nixon, somewhat surprised at the readiness of his answer, 'all will go smooth, of course—you will take share in this noble undertaking, and, when it succeeds, you will exchange your open helmet for an Earl's coronet perhaps.'

'And how if it fails?' said Darsie.

'Thereafter as it may be,' said Nixon; 'they who play at bowls must meet with rubbers.'*

'Well, but suppose, then, I have some foolish tenderness for my windpipe, and that, when my uncle proposes the adventure to me, I should say No—how then, Mr Nixon?'

'Why, then, I would have you look to yourself, young master—

There are sharp laws in France against refractory pupils—*lettres de cachet* are easily come by, when such men as we are concerned with interest themselves in the matter.'

'But we are not in France,' said poor Darsie, through whose blood ran a cold shivering at the idea of a French prison.

'A fast-sailing lugger will soon bring you there though, snug stowed under hatches, like a cask of moonlight.'

'But the French are at peace with us,' said Darsie, 'and would not dare'——

'Why, who would ever hear of you?' interrupted Nixon; 'do you imagine that a foreign Court would call you up for judgment, and put the sentence of imprisonment in the *Courier de l'Europe*, as they do at the Old Bailey?—No, no, young gentleman—the gates of the Bastile, and of Mont Saint Michel, and the Castle of Vincennes, move on d—d easy hinges when they let folk in—not the least jar is heard. There are cool cells there for hot heads—as calm, and quiet, and dark, as you could wish in Bedlam*—and the dismissal comes when the carpenter brings the prisoner's coffin, and not sooner.'

'Well, Mr Nixon,' said Darsie, affecting a cheerfulness which he was far from feeling, 'mine is a hard case—a sort of hanging choice, you will allow—since I must either offend our own government here, and run the risk of my life for doing so, or be doomed to the dungeons of another country, whose laws I have never offended, since I have never trod its soil—Tell me what you would do if you were in my place.'

'I'll tell you that when I *am* there,' said Nixon, and, checking his horse, fell back to the rear of the little party.

'It is evident,' thought the young man, 'that the villain believes me completely noosed, and perhaps has the ineffable impudence to suppose that my sister must eventually succeed to the possessions which have occasioned my loss of freedom, and that his own influence over the destinies of our unhappy family may secure him possession of the heiress; but he shall perish by my hand first!—I must now be on the alert to make my escape, if possible, before I am forced on shipboard—Blind Willie will not, I think, desert me without an effort on my behalf, especially if he has learned that I am the son of his late unhappy patron.—What a change is mine! Whilst I possessed neither rank nor fortune, I lived safely and unknown, under the protection of the kind and respectable friends whose hearts Heaven had moved towards me—Now that I am the head of an honourable house, and that enterprises of the most daring character wait my decision, and retainers and vassals seem ready to rise at my beck, my safety consists chiefly in the attachment of a blind stroller!'

While he was revolving these things in his mind, and preparing himself for the interview with his uncle, which could not but be a stormy one, he saw Hugh Redgauntlet come riding slowly back to meet them, without any attendants. Cristal Nixon rode up as he approached, and, as they met, fixed on him a look of enquiry.

'The fool, Crackenthorp,' said Redgauntlet, 'has let strangers into his house. Some of his smuggling comrades, I believe; we must ride slowly, to give him time to send them packing.'

'Did you see any of your friends?' said Cristal.

'Three, and have letters from many more. They are unanimous on the subject you wot of—and the point must be conceded to them, or, far as the matter has gone, it will go no farther.'

'You will hardly bring the Father to stoop to his flock,' said Cristal, with a sneer.

'He must, and shall!' answered Redgauntlet, briefly. 'Go to the front, Cristal—I would speak with my nephew.—I trust, Sir Arthur Redgauntlet, you are satisfied with the manner in which I have discharged my duty to your sister?'

'There can be no fault found to her manners or sentiments,' answered Darsie; 'I am happy in knowing a relative so amiable.'

'I am glad of it,' answered Mr Redgauntlet. 'I am no nice judge of women's qualifications, and my life has been dedicated to one great object; so that since she left France she has had but little opportunity of improvement. I have subjected her, however, as little as possible to the inconveniences and privations of my wandering and dangerous life. From time to time she has resided for weeks and months with families of honour and respectability, and I am glad that she has, in your opinion, the manners and behaviour which become her birth.'

Darsie expressed himself perfectly satisfied, and there was a little pause, which Redgauntlet broke by solemnly addressing his nephew.

'For you, my nephew, I also hoped to have done much. The weakness and timidity of your mother sequestered you from my care, or it would have been my pride and happiness to have trained up the son of my unhappy brother in those paths of honour in which our ancestors have always trod.'

'Now comes the storm,' thought Darsie to himself, and began to collect his thoughts, as the cautious master of a vessel furls his sails, and makes his ship snug, when he discerns the approaching squall.

'My mother's conduct, in respect to me, might be misjudged,' he said, 'but it was founded on the most anxious affection.'

'Assuredly,' said his uncle, 'and I have no wish to reflect on her memory, though her mistrust has done so much injury, I will not say to me, but to the cause of my unhappy country. Her scheme was, I think, to have made you that wretched pettifogging being, which they still continue to call in derision by the once respectable name of a Scottish Advocate; one of those mongrel things, that must creep to learn the ultimate decision of his causes to the bar of a foreign Court, instead of pleading before the independent and august Parliament of his own native kingdom.'*

'I did prosecute the study of law for a year or two,' said Darsie, 'but I found I had neither taste nor talents for the science.'

'And left it with scorn, doubtless,' said Mr Redgauntlet. 'Well, I now hold up to you, my dearest nephew, a more worthy object of ambition. Look eastward—do you see a monument standing on yonder plain, near a hamlet?'

Darsie replied that he did.

'The hamlet is called Burgh-upon-sands, and yonder monument is erected to the memory of the tyrant Edward I. The just hand of Providence overtook him on that spot, as he was leading his bands to complete the subjugation of Scotland, whose civil dissensions began under his accursed policy. The glorious career of Bruce might have been stopped in its outset; the field of Bannockburn might have remained a bloodless turf, if God had not removed, in the very crisis, the crafty and bold tyrant who had so long been Scotland's scourge. Edward's grave is the cradle of our national freedom. It is within sight of that great landmark of our liberty that I have to propose to you an undertaking, second in honour and importance to none since the immortal Bruce stabbed the Red Comyn, and grasped, with his yet bloody hand, the independent crown of Scotland.'*

He paused for an answer; but Darsie, overawed by the energy of his manner, and unwilling to commit himself by a hasty explanation, remained silent.

'I will not suppose,' said Hugh Redgauntlet, after a pause, 'that you are either so dull as not to comprehend the import of my words—or so dastardly as to be dismayed by my proposal—or so utterly degenerate from the blood and sentiments of your ancestors, as not to feel my summons as the horse hears the war-trumpet.'

'I will not pretend to misunderstand you, sir,' said Darsie; 'but an enterprise directed against a dynasty now established for three reigns requires strong arguments, both in point of justice and of expediency, to recommend it to men of conscience and prudence.'

'I will not,' said Redgauntlet, while his eyes sparkled with anger,—'I will not hear you speak a word against the justice of that enterprise, for which your oppressed country calls with the voice of a parent, entreating her children for aid—or against that noble revenge which your father's blood demands from his dishonoured grave. His skull is yet standing over the Rikargate,[59] and even its bleak and mouldered jaws command you to be a man. I ask you, in the name of God, and of your country, will you draw your sword, and go with me to Carlisle, were it but to lay your father's head, now the perch of the obscene owl and carrion crow, and the scoff of every ribald clown, in consecrated earth, as befits his long ancestry?'

Darsie, unprepared to answer an appeal urged with so much passion, and not doubting a direct refusal would cost him his liberty or life, was again silent.

'I see,' said his uncle, in a more composed tone, 'that it is not deficiency of spirit, but the grovelling habits of a confined education, among the poor-spirited class you were condemned to herd with, that keeps you silent. You scarce yet believe yourself a Redgauntlet; your pulse has not yet learned the genuine throb that answers to the summons of honour and of patriotism.'

'I trust,' replied Darsie, at last, 'that I shall never be found indifferent to the call of either; but to answer them with effect—even were I convinced that they now sounded in my ear—I must see some reasonable hope of success in the desperate enterprise in which you would involve me. I look around me, and I see a settled government—an established authority—a born Briton on the throne*—the very Highland mountaineers, upon whom alone the trust of the exiled family reposed, assembled into regiments, which act under the orders of the existing dynasty.[60] France has been utterly dismayed by the tremendous lessons of the last war, and will hardly provoke another. All without and within the kingdom is adverse to encountering a hopeless struggle, and you alone, sir, seem willing to undertake a desperate enterprise.'

'And would undertake it were it ten times more desperate; and have agitated it when ten times the obstacles were interposed.—Have I forgot my brother's blood?—Can I—dare I even now repeat the Pater Noster, since my enemies and the murderers remain unforgiven?—Is there an art I have not practised—a privation to which I have not submitted, to bring on the crisis which I now behold arrived?—Have I not been a vowed and a devoted man, foregoing every comfort of social life, renouncing even the exercise of devotion unless when I might name in prayer my prince and country, submitting to every thing to make converts to this noble cause?—Have I done all this, and shall I now stop short?'—Darsie was about to interrupt him, but he pressed his hand affectionately upon his shoulder, and enjoining, or rather imploring silence,—'Peace,' he said, 'heir of my ancestors' fame—heir of all my hopes and wishes—Peace, son of my slaughtered brother! I have sought for thee, and mourned for thee, as a mother for an only child. Do not let me again lose you in the moment when you are restored to my hopes. Believe me, I distrust so much my own impatient temper, that I entreat you, as the dearest boon, do nought to awaken it at this crisis.'

Darsie was not sorry to reply, that his respect for the person of his relation would induce him to listen to all which he had to apprize him of, before he formed any definite resolution upon the weighty subjects of deliberation which he proposed to him.

'Deliberation!' repeated Redgauntlet, impatiently; 'and yet it is not ill said.—I wish there had been more warmth in thy reply, Arthur; but I must recollect were an eagle bred in a falcon's mew, and hooded like a reclaimed hawk, he could not at first gaze steadily on the sun. Listen to me, my dearest Arthur. The state of this nation no more implies prosperity, then the florid colour of a feverish patient is a symptom of health. All is false and hollow—the apparent success of Chatham's administration has plunged the country deeper in debt than all the barren acres of Canada are worth, were they as fertile as Yorkshire—the dazzling lustre of the victories of Minden and Quebec* have been dimmed by the disgrace of the hasty peace—by the war, England, at immense expense, gained nothing but honour, and that she has gratuitously resigned. Many eyes, formerly cold and indifferent, are now looking towards the line of our ancient and rightful monarchs, as the only refuge in the approaching storm—the rich are alarmed—the nobles are disgusted—the populace are inflamed—and a band of patriots, whose measures are more safe that their numbers are few, have resolved to set up King Charles's standard.'

'But the military,' said Darsie—'how can you, with a body of unarmed and disorderly insurgents, propose to encounter a regular army? The Highlanders are now totally disarmed.'*

'In a great measure, perhaps,' answered Redgauntlet; 'but the policy which raised the Highland regiments has provided for that. We have already friends in these corps; nor can we doubt for a moment what their conduct will be, when the white cockade* is once more mounted. The rest of the standing army has been greatly reduced since the peace; and we reckon confidently on our standard being joined by thousands of the disbanded troops.'

'Alas!' said Darsie, 'and is it upon such vague hopes as these, the inconstant humour of a crowd, or of a disbanded soldiery, that men of honour are invited to risk their families, their property, their life?'

'Men of honour, boy,' said Redgauntlet, his eyes glancing with impatience, 'set life, property, family, and all at stake, when that honour commands it! We are not now weaker than when seven men, landing in the wilds of Moidart, shook the throne of the usurper till it tottered—won two pitched fields, besides overrunning one kingdom and the half of another, and, but for treachery, would have achieved what their venturous successors are now to attempt in their turn.'*

'And will such an attempt be made in serious earnest?' said Darsie. Excuse me, my uncle, if I can scarce believe a fact so extraordinary.

Will there really be found men of rank and consequence sufficient to renew the adventure of 1745?'

'I will not give you my confidence by halves, Sir Arthur,' replied his uncle—'Look at that scroll—what say you to these names?—Are they not the flower of the Western shires—of Wales—of Scotland?'

'The paper contains indeed the names of many that are great and noble,' replied Darsie, after perusing it; 'but'——

'But what?' asked his uncle, impatiently; 'do you doubt the ability of those nobles and gentlemen to furnish the aid in men and money, at which they are rated?'

'Not their ability certainly,' said Darsie, 'for of that I am no competent judge;—but I see in this scroll the name of Sir Arthur Darsie Redgauntlet of that Ilk, rated at an hundred men and upwards—I certainly am ignorant how he is to redeem that pledge.'

'I will be responsible for the men,' replied Hugh Redgauntlet.

'But, my dear uncle,' added Darsie, 'I hope for your sake, that the other individuals, whose names are here written, have had more acquaintance with your plan than I have been indulged with.'

'For thee and thine I can be myself responsible,' said Redgauntlet; 'for if thou hast not the courage to head the force of thy house, the leading shall pass to other hands, and thy inheritance shall depart from thee, like vigour and verdure from a rotten branch.* For these honourable persons, a slight condition there is which they annex to their friendship—something so trifling that it is scarce worthy of mention. This boon granted to them by him who is most interested, there is no question they will take the field in the manner there stated.'

Again Darsie perused the paper, and felt himself still less inclined to believe that so many men of family and fortune were likely to embark in an enterprise so fatal. It seemed as if some rash plotter had put down at a venture the names of all whom common report tainted with Jacobitism; or if it was really the act of the individuals named, he suspected they must be aware of some mode of excusing themselves from compliance with its purport. It was impossible, he thought, that Englishmen, of large fortune, who had failed to join Charles when he broke into England at the head of a victorious army, should have the least thoughts of encouraging a descent when circumstances were so much less propitious. He therefore concluded the enterprise would fall to pieces of itself, and that his best way was, in the meantime, to remain silent, unless the actual approach of a crisis (which might, however, never arrive) should compel him to give a downright refusal to his uncle's proposition; and if, in the interim, some door for escape should be opened, he resolved within himself not to omit availing himself of it.

Hugh Redgauntlet watched his nephew's looks for some time, and then, as if arriving from some other process of reasoning at the same conclusion, he said, 'I have told you, Sir Arthur, that I do not urge your immediate accession to my proposal; indeed the consequences of a refusal would be so dreadful to yourself, so destructive to all the hopes which I have nursed, that I would not risk, by a moment's impatience, the object of my whole life. Yes, Arthur, I have been a self-denying hermit at one time—at another, the apparent associate of outlaws and desperadoes—at another, the subordinate agent of men whom I felt every way my inferiors—not for any selfish purpose of my own, no, not even to win for myself the renown of being the principal instrument in restoring my King and freeing my country. My first wish on earth is for that restoration and that freedom—my next, that my nephew, the representative of my house, and of the brother of my love, may have the advantage and the credit of all my efforts in the good cause. But,' he added, darting on Darsie one of his withering frowns, 'if Scotland and my father's House cannot stand and flourish together, then perish the very name of Redgauntlet! perish the son of my brother, with every recollection of the glories of my family, of the affections of my youth, rather than my country's cause should be injured in the tithing of a barleycorn! The spirit of Sir Alberick is alive within me at this moment,' he continued, drawing up his stately form, and sitting erect in his saddle, while he pressed his finger against his forehead; 'and if you yourself crossed my path in opposition, I swear, by the mark that darkens my brow, that a new deed should be done—a new doom should be deserved!'

He was silent, and his threats were uttered in a tone of voice so deeply resolute, that Darsie's heart sunk within him, when he reflected on the storm of passion which he must encounter, if he declined to join his uncle in a project to which prudence and principle made him equally adverse. He had scarce any hope left but in temporizing until he could make his escape, and resolved to avail himself for that purpose of the delay which his uncle seemed not unwilling to grant. The stern, gloomy look of his companion became relaxed by degrees, and presently afterwards he made a sign to Miss Redgauntlet to joint the party, and began a forced conversation on ordinary topics; in the course of which Darsie observed that his sister seemed to speak under the most cautious restraint, weighing every word before she uttered it, and always permitting her uncle to give the tone to the conversation, though of the most trifling kind. This seemed to him (such an opinion had he already entertained of his sister's good sense and firmness) the strongest proof he had yet received of his uncle's peremptory character, since he saw it observed with so much deference by a young person, whose sex might have given her privileges, and who seemed by no means deficient either in spirit or firmness.

The little cavalcade was now approaching the house of Father Crackenthorp, situated, as the reader knows, by the side of the Solway, and not far distant from a rude pier, near which lay several fishing-boats, which frequently acted in a different capacity. The house of the worthy publican was also adapted to the various occupations which he carried on, being a large scrambling assemblage of cottages attached to a house of two stories, roofed with flags of sandstone—the original mansion, to which the extension of Master Crackenthorp's trade had occasioned his making many additions. Instead of the single long watering-trough, which usually distinguishes the front of the English public-house of the second class, there were three conveniences of that kind, for the use, as the landlord used to say, of the troop-horses, when the soldiers came to search his house; while a knowing leer and a nod let you understand what species of troops he was thinking of. A huge ash-tree before the door, which had reared itself to a great size and height, in spite of the blasts from the neighbouring Solway, overshadowed, as usual, the ale-bench, as our ancestors called it, where, though it was still early in the day, several fellows, who seemed to be gentlemen's servants, were drinking beer and smoking. One or two of them wore liveries, which seemed known to Mr Redgauntlet, for he muttered between his teeth, 'Fools, fools! were they on a march to hell, they must have their rascals in livery with them, that the whole world might know who were going to be damned.'

As he thus muttered, he drew bridle before the door of the place, from which several other lounging guests began to issue, to look with indolent curiosity, as usual, upon an *arrival*.

Redgauntlet sprung from his horse, and assisted his niece to dismount; but, forgetting, perhaps, his nephew's disguise, he did not pay him the attention which his female dress demanded.

The situation of Darsie was indeed something awkward; for Cristal Nixon, out of caution perhaps to prevent escape, had muffled the extreme folds of the riding-skirt with which he was accoutred, around his ankles and under his feet, and there secured it with large corking-pins. We presume that gentlemen-cavaliers may sometimes cast their eyes to that part of the person of the fair equestrians whom they chance occasionally to escort; and if they will conceive their own feet, like Darsie's, muffled in such a labyrinth of folds and amplitude of robe, as modesty doubtless induces the fair creatures to assume upon such occasions, they will allow that, on a first attempt, they might find some awkwardness in dismounting. Darsie, at least, was in such a predicament, for, not receiving adroit assistance from the attendant of Mr Redgauntlet, he stumbled as he dismounted from the horse, and might have had a bad fall, had it not been broken by the gallant interposition of a gentleman, who probably was, on his part, a little surprised at the solid weight of the distressed fair one whom he had the honour to receive in his embrace. But what was his surprise to that of Darsie's, when the hurry of the moment, and of the accident, permitted him to see that it was his friend Alan Fairford in whose arms he found himself! A thousand apprehensions rushed on him, mingled with the full career of hope and joy, inspired by the unexpected appearance of his beloved friend, at the very crisis, it seemed, of his fate.

He was about to whisper in his ear, cautioning him at the same time to be silent; yet he hesitated for a second or two to effect his purpose, since, should Redgauntlet take the alarm from any sudden exclamation on the part of Alan, there was no saying what consequences might ensue.

Ere he could decide what was to be done, Redgauntlet, who had entered the house, returned hastily, followed by Cristal Nixon. 'I'll release you of the charge of this young lady, sir;' he said, haughtily, to Alan Fairford, whom he probably did not recognise.

'I had no desire to intrude, sir,' replied Alan; 'the lady's situation seemed to require assistance—and—but have I not the honour to speak to Mr Herries of Birrenswork?'

'You are mistaken, sir,' said Redgauntlet, turning short off, and making a sign with his hand to Cristal, who hurried Darsie, however unwillingly, into the house, whispering in his ear, 'Come, miss, let us have no making of acquaintance from the windows. Ladies of fashion must be private. Show us a room, Father Crackenthorp.'

So saying, he conducted Darsie into the house, interposing at the same time his person betwixt the supposed young lady and the stranger of whom he was suspicious, so as to make communication by signs impossible. As they entered, they heard the sound of a fiddle in the stone-floored and well-sanded kitchen, through which they were about to follow their corpulent host, and where several people seemed engaged in dancing to its strains.

'D—n thee,' said Nixon to Crackenthorp, 'would you have the lady go through all the mob of the parish?—Hast thou no more private way to our sitting-room?'

'None that is fit for my travelling,' answered the landlord, laying his hand on his portly stomach. 'I am not Tom Turnpenny, to creep like a lizard through keyholes.'

So saying, he kept moving on through the revellers in the kitchen;

and Nixon holding Darsie by his arm, as if to offer the lady support, but in all probability to frustrate any effort at escape, moved through the crowd, which presented a very motley appearance, consisting of domestic servants, country fellows, seamen, and other idlers, whom Wandering Willie was regaling with his music.

To pass another friend without intimation of his presence would have been actual pusillanimity; and just when they were passing the blind man's elevated seat, Darsie asked him, with some emphasis, whether he could not play a Scottish air?—The man's face had been the instant before devoid of all sort of expression, going through his performance like a clown through a beautiful country, too much accustomed to consider it as a task, to take any interest in the performance, and, in fact, scarce seeming to hear the noise that he was creating. In a word, he might at the time have made a companion to my friend Wilkie's inimitable blind crowder.* But with Wandering Willie this was only an occasional, and a rare fit of dulness, such as will at times creep over all the professors of the fine arts, arising either from fatigue, or contempt of the present audience, or that caprice which so often tempts painters and musicians, and great actors, in the phrase of the latter, to *walk through* their part, instead of exerting themselves with the energy which acquired their fame. But when the performer heard the voice of Darsie, his countenance became at once illuminated, and showed the complete mistake of those who suppose that the principal point of expression depends upon the eyes. With his face turned to the point from which the sound came, his upper lip a little curved, and quivering with agitation, and with a colour which surprise and pleasure had brought at once into his faded cheek, he exchanged the humdrum hornpipe which he had been sawing out with reluctant and lazy bow, for the fine Scottish air,

'You're welcome, Charlie Stewart,'*

which flew from his strings as if by inspiration, and after a breathless pause of admiration among the audience, was received with a clamour of applause, which seemed to show that the name and tendency, as well as the execution of the tune, was in the highest degree acceptable to all the party assembled.

In the meantime, Cristal Nixon, still keeping hold of Darsie, and following the landlord, forced his way with some difficulty through the crowded kitchen, and entered a small apartment on the other side of it, where they found Lilias Redgauntlet already seated. Here Nixon gave way to his suppressed resentment, and turning sternly on Crackenthorp, threatened him with his master's severest displeasure, because things were in such bad order to receive his family, when he had given such special advice that he desired to be private. But Father Crackenthorp was not a man to be browbeaten.

'Why, brother Nixon, thou art angry this morning,' he replied; 'hast risen from thy wrong side, I think. You know, as well as I, that most of this mob is of the Squire's own making—gentlemen that come with their servants, and so forth, to meet him in the way of business, as old Tom Turnpenny says—the very last that came was sent down with Dick Gardener from Fairladies.'

'But the blind scraping scoundrel yonder,' said Nixon, 'how dared you take such a rascal as that across your threshold at such a time as this?—If the Squire should dream you have a thought of peaching—I am only speaking for your good, Father Crackenthorp.'

'Why, look ye, brother Nixon,' said Crackenthorp, turning his quid with great composure, 'the Squire is a very worthy gentleman, and I'll never deny it; but I am neither his servant nor his tenant, and so he need send me none of his orders till he hears I have put on his livery. As for turning away folk from my door, I might as well plug up the ale-tap, and pull down the sign—and as for peaching, and such like, the Squire will find the folk here are as honest to the full as those he brings with him.'

'How, you impudent lump of tallow,' said Nixon, 'what do you mean by that?'

'Nothing,' said Crackenthorp, 'but that I can tour out as well as another—you understand me—keep good lights in my upper story—know a thing or two more than most folk in this country. If folk will come to my house on dangerous errands, egad they shall not find Joe Crackenthorp a cat's-paw. I'll keep myself clear, you may depend on it, and let every man answer for his own actions—that's my way—Any thing wanted, Master Nixon?'

'No—Yes—begone!' said Nixon, who seemed embarrassed with the landlord's contumacy, yet desirous to conceal the effect it produced on him.

The door was no sooner closed on Crackenthorp, than Miss Redgauntlet, addressing Nixon, commanded him to leave the room, and go to his proper place.

'How, madam?' said the fellow sullenly, yet with an air of respect, 'Would you have your uncle pistol me for disobeying his orders?'

'He may perhaps pistol you for some other reason, if you do not obey mine,' said Lilias, composedly.

'You abuse your advantage over me, madam—I really dare not go—I am on guard over this other Miss here; and if I should desert my post, my life were not worth five minutes' purchase.'

'Then know your post, sir,' said Lilias, 'and watch on the outside of the door. You have no commission to listen to our private conversation, I suppose? Begone, sir, without further speech or remonstrance, or I will tell my uncle that which you would have reason to repent he should know.'

The fellow looked at her with a singular expression of spite, mixed with deference. 'You abuse your advantages, madam,' he said, 'and act as foolishly in doing so, as I did in affording you such a hank over me. But you are a tyrant; and tyrants have commonly short reigns.'

So saying, he left the apartment.

'The wretch's unparalleled insolence,' said Lilias to her brother, 'has given me one great advantage over him. For, knowing that my uncle would shoot him with as little remorse as a woodcock, if he but guessed at his brazen-faced assurance towards me, he dares not since that time assume, so far as I am concerned, the air of insolent domination which the possession of my uncle's secrets, and the knowledge of his most secret plans, have led him to exert over others of his family.'

'In the meantime,' said Darsie, 'I am happy to see that the landlord of the house does not seem so devoted to him as I apprehended; and this aids the hope of escape which I am nourishing for you and for myself. O, Lilias! the truest of friends, Alan Fairford, is in pursuit of me, and is here at this moment. Another humble, but, I think, faithful friend, is also within these dangerous walls.'

Lilias laid her finger on her lips, and pointed to the door. Darsie took the hint, lowered his voice, and informed her in whispers of the arrival of Fairford, and that he believed he had opened a communication with Wandering Willie. She listened with the utmost interest, and had just begun to reply, when a loud noise was heard in the kitchen, caused by several contending voices, amongst which Darsie thought he could distinguish that of Alan Fairford.

Forgetting how little his own condition permitted him to become the assistant of another, Darsie flew to the door of the room, and finding it locked and bolted on the outside, rushed against it with all his force, and made the most desperate efforts to burst it open, notwithstanding the entreaties of his sister that he would compose himself, and recollect the condition in which he was placed. But the door, framed to withstand attacks from excisemen, constables, and other personages, considered as worthy to use what are called the King's keys,[61] 'and therewith to make lockfast places open and patent,' set his efforts at defiance. Meantime the noise continued without, and we are to give an account of its origin in our next chapter.

CHAPTER XX

NARRATIVE OF DARSIE LATIMER, CONTINUED

JOE CRACKENTHORP'S public-house had never, since it first reared its chimneys on the banks of the Solway, been frequented by such a miscellaneous group of visitors as had that morning become its guests. Several of them were persons whose quality seemed much superior to their dresses and modes of travelling. The servants who attended them contradicted the inferences to be drawn from the garb of their masters, and, according to the custom of the knights of the rainbow, gave many hints that they were not people to serve any but men of first-rate consequence. These gentlemen, who had come thither chiefly for the purpose of meeting with Mr Redgauntlet, seemed moody and anxious, conversed and walked together, apparently in deep conversation, and avoided any communication with the chance travellers whom accident brought that morning to the same place of resort.

As if Fate had set herself to confound the plans of the Jacobite conspirators, the number of travellers was unusually great, their appearance respectable, and they filled the public tap-room of the inn, where the political guests had already occupied most of the private apartments.

Amongst others, honest Joshua Geddes had arrived, travelling, as he said, in the sorrow of the soul, and mourning for the fate of Darsie Latimer as he would for his first-born child. He had skirted the whole coast of the Solway, besides making various trips into the interior, not shunning, on such occasions, to expose himself to the laugh of the scorner, nay, even to serious personal risk, by frequenting the haunts of smugglers, horse-jockeys, and other irregular persons, who looked on his intrusion with jealous eyes, and were apt to consider him as an exciseman in the disguise of a Quaker. All this labour and peril, however, had been undergone in vain. No search he could make obtained the least intelligence of Latimer, so that he began to fear the poor lad had been spirited abroad; for the practice of kidnapping was then not infrequent, especially on the western coasts of Britain, if indeed he had escaped a briefer and more bloody fate.

With a heavy heart, he delivered his horse, even Solomon, into the hands of the hostler, and walking into the inn, demanded from the landlord breakfast and a private room. Quakers, and such hosts as old Father Crackenthorp, are no congenial spirits; the latter looked askew over his shoulder, and replied, 'If you would have breakfast here, friend, you are like to eat it where other folk eat theirs.'

'And wherefore can I not,' said the Quaker, 'have an apartment to myself, for my money?'

'Because, Master Jonathan, you must wait till your betters be served, or else eat with your equals.'

Joshua Geddes argued the point no farther, but sitting quietly down on the seat which Crackenthorp indicated to him, and calling for a pint of ale, with some bread, butter, and Dutch cheese, began to satisfy the appetite which the morning air had rendered unusually alert.

While the honest Quaker was thus employed, another stranger entered the apartment, and sat down near to the table on which his victuals were placed. He looked repeatedly at Joshua, licked his parched and chopped lips as he saw the good Quaker masticate his bread and cheese, and sucked up his thin chops when Mr Geddes applied the tankard to his mouth, as if the discharge of these bodily functions by another had awakened his sympathies in an uncontrollable degree. At last, being apparently unable to withstand his longings, he asked, in a faltering tone, the huge landlord, who was tramping through the room in all corpulent impatience, 'whether he could have a plack-pie?'

'Never heard of such a thing, master,' said the landlord, and was about to trudge onward; when the guest, detaining him, said, in a strong Scottish tone, 'Ye will maybe have nae whey then, nor buttermilk, nor ye couldna exhibit a souter's clod?'

'Can't tell what ye are talking about, master,' said Crackenthorp.

'Then ye will have nae breakfast that will come within the compass of a shilling Scots?'

'Which is a penny sterling,' answered Crackenthorp, with a sneer. 'Why, no, Sawney, I can't say as we have—we can't afford it; but you shall have a bellyful for love, as we say in the bull-ring.'

'I shall never refuse a fair offer,' said the poverty-stricken guest; 'and I will say that for the English, if they were deils, that they are a ceeveleesed people to gentlemen that are under a cloud.'

'Gentlemen!—humph!' said Crackenthorp—'not a bluecap among them but halts upon that foot.' Then seizing on a dish which still contained a huge cantle of what had been once a princely mutton pasty, he placed it on the table before the stranger, saying, 'There, master gentleman; there is what is worth all the black pies, as you call them, that were ever made of sheep's head.'

'Sheep's head is a gude thing, for a' that,' replied the guest; but not being spoken so loud as to offend his hospitable entertainer, the interjection might pass for a private protest against the scandal thrown out against the standing dish of Caledonia.

This premised, he immediately began to transfer the mutton and pie-crust from his plate to his lips, in such huge gobbets, as if he was refreshing after a three days' fast, and laying in provisions against a whole Lent to come.

Joshua Geddes in his turn gazed on him with surprise, having never, he thought, beheld such a gaunt expression of hunger in the act of eating. 'Friend,' he said, after watching him for some minutes, 'if thou gorgest thyself in this fashion, thou wilt assuredly choke. Wilt thou not take a draught out of my cup to help down all that dry meat?'

'Troth,' said the stranger, stopping and looking at the friendly propounder, 'that's nae bad overture, as they say in the General Assembly.* I have heard waur motions than that frae wiser counsel.'

Mr Geddes ordered a quart of home-brewed to be placed before our friend Peter Peebles; for the reader must have already conceived that this unfortunate litigant was the wanderer in question.

The victim of Themis had no sooner seen the flagon than he seized it with the same energy which he had displayed in operating upon the pie—puffed off the froth with such emphasis, that some of it lighted on Mr Geddes's head—and then said, as if with a sudden recollection of what was due to civility, 'Here's to ye, friend.—What! are ye ower grand to give me an answer, or are ye dull o' hearing?'

'I prithee drink thy liquor, friend,' said the good Quaker; 'thou meanest it in civility, but we care not for these idle fashions.'

'What! ye are a Quaker, are ye?' said Peter; and without further ceremony reared the flagon to his head, from which he withdrew it not while a single drop of 'barley-broo' remained.—'That's done you and me muckle gude,' he said, sighing as he set down his pot; 'but twa mutchkins o' yill between twa folk is a drappie ower little measure. What say ye to anither pot? or shall we cry in a blithe Scots pint at ance?—The yill is no amiss.'

'Thou mayst call for what thou wilt on thine own charges, friend,' said Geddes; 'for myself, I willingly contribute to the quenching of thy natural thirst; but I fear it were no such easy matter to relieve thy acquired and artificial drouth.'

'That is to say, in plain terms, ye are for withdrawing your caution with the folk of the house? You Quaker folk are but fause comforters; but since ye have garred me drink sae muckle cauld yill—me that am no used to the like of it in the forenoon—I think ye might as weel have offered me a glass of brandy or usquabae—I'm nae nice body— I can drink ony thing that's wet and toothsome'.

'Not a drop at my cost, friend,' quoth Geddes. 'Thou art an old man, and hast, perchance, a heavy and long journey before thee. Thou art, moreover, my countryman, as I judge from thy tongue;

and I will not give thee the means of dishonouring thy grey hairs in a strange land.'

'Grey hairs, neighbour!' said Peter, with a wink to the bystanders,—whom this dialogue began to interest, and who were in hopes of seeing the Quaker played off by the crazed beggar, for such Peter Peebles appeared to be,—'Grey hairs! The Lord mend your eyesight, neighbour, that disna ken grey hairs frae a tow wig!'

This jest procured a shout of laughter, and, what was still more acceptable than dry applause, a man who stood beside called out, 'Father Crackenthorp, bring a nipperkin of brandy. I'll bestow a dram on this fellow, were it but for that very word.'

The brandy was immediately brought by a wench who acted as bar-maid; and Peter, with a grin of delight, filled a glass, quaffed it off, and then saying, 'God bless me! I was so unmannerly as not to drink to ye—I think the Quaker has smitten me wi' his ill-bred havings,'—he was about to fill another, when his hand was arrested by his new friend; who said at the same time, 'No, no, friend—fair play's a jewel—time about, if you please.' And filling a glass for himself, emptied it as gallantly as Peter could have done. 'What say you to that, friend?' he continued, addressing the Quaker.

'Nay, friend,' answered Joshua, 'it went down thy throat, not mine; and I have nothing to say about what concerns me not; but if thou art a man of humanity, thou wilt not give this poor creature the means of debauchery. Bethink thee that they will spurn him from the door, as they would do a houseless and masterless dog, and that he may die on the sands or on the common. And if he has through thy means been rendered incapable of helping himself, thou shalt not be innocent of his blood.'

'Faith, Broadbrim, I believe thou art right, and the old gentleman in the flaxen jazy shall have no more of the comforter—Besides, we have business in hand to-day, and this fellow, for as mad as he looks, may have a nose on his face after all.—Hark ye, father,—what is your name, and what brings you into such an out-of-the-way corner?'

'I am not just free to condescend on my name,' said Peter; 'and as for my business—there is a wee dribble of brandy in the stoup—it would be wrang to leave it to the lass—it is learning her bad usages.'

'Well, thou shalt have the brandy, and be d—d to thee, if thou wilt tell me what you are making here.'

'Seeking a young advocate chap that they ca' Alan Fairford, that has played me a slippery trick, an ye maun ken a' about the cause,' said Peter.

'An advocate, man!' answered the Captain of the Jumping Jenny—for it was he, and no other, who had taken compassion on Peter's drought; 'why, Lord help thee, thou art on the wrong side of the Frith to seek advocates, whom I take to be Scottish lawyers, not English.'

'English lawyers, man!' exclaimed Peter, 'the deil a lawyer's in a' England.'

'I wish from my soul it were true,' said Ewart; 'but what the devil put that in your head?'

'Lord, man, I got a grip of ane of their attorneys in Carlisle, and he tauld me that there wasna a lawyer in England, ony mair than himsell, that kend the nature of a multiplepoinding! And when I tauld him how this loopy lad, Alan Fairford, had served me, he said I might bring an action on the case—just as if the case hadna as mony actions already as one case can weel carry. By my word, it is a gude case, and muckle has it borne, in its day, of various procedure—but it's the barley-pickle breaks the naig's back, and wi' my consent it shall not hae ony mair burden laid upon it.'

'But this Alan Fairford?' said Nanty—'come—sip up the drop of brandy, man, and tell me some more about him, and whether you are seeking him for good or for harm.'

'For my ain gude, and for his harm, to be sure,' said Peter. 'Think of his having left my cause in the dead-thraw between the tyneing and the winning, and capering off into Cumberland here, after a wild loup-the-tether lad they ca' Darsie Latimer.'

'Darsie Latimer!' said Mr Geddes, hastily; 'do you know any thing of Darsie Latimer?'

'Maybe I do, and maybe I do not,' answered Peter; 'I am no free to answer every body's interrogatory, unless it is put judicially, and by form of law—specially where folk think so much of a caup of sour yill, or a thimblefu' of brandy. But as for this gentleman, that has shown himself a gentleman at breakfast, and will show himself a gentleman at the meridian, I am free to condescend upon any points in the cause that may appear to bear upon the question at issue.'

'Why, all I want to know from you, my friend, is, whether you are seeking to do this Mr Alan Fairford good or harm; because if you come to do him good, I think you could maybe get speech of him—and if to do him harm, I will take the liberty to give you a cast across the Frith, with fair warning not to come back on such an errand, lest worse come of it.'

The manner and language of Ewart were such, that Joshua Geddes resolved to keep cautious silence, till he could more plainly discover whether he was likely to aid or impede him in his researches after Darsie Latimer. He therefore determined to listen attentively to what should pass between Peter and the seaman, and to watch for an opportunity of questioning the former, so soon as he should be separated from his new acquaintance.

'I wad by no means,' said Peter Peebles, 'do any substantial harm to the poor lad Fairford, who has had mony a gowd guinea of mine, as weel as his father before him; but I wad hae him brought back to the minding of my business and his ain; and maybe I wadna insist farther in my action of damages against him, than for refunding the fees, and for some annual rent on the principal sum, due frae the day on which he should have recovered it for me, plack and bawbee, at the great advising; for, ye are aware, that is the least that I can ask *nomine damni*; and I have nae thought to break down the lad bodily a' thegither—we maun live and let live—forgie and forget.'

'The deuce take me, friend broadbrim,' said Nanty Ewart, looking to the Quaker, 'if I can make out what this old scarecrow means. If I thought it was fitting that Master Fairford should see him, why perhaps it is a matter that could be managed. Do you know any thing about the old fellow?—you seemed to take some charge of him just now.'

'No more than I should have done by any one in distress,' said Geddes, not sorry to be appealed to; 'but I will try what I can do to find out who he is, and what he is about in this country—But are we not a little too public in this open room?'

'It's well thought of,' said Nanty; and at his command the barmaid ushered the party into a side-booth, Peter attending them, in the instinctive hope that there would be more liquor drank among them before parting. They had scarce sat down in their new apartment, when the sound of a violin was heard in the room which they had just left.

'I'll awa back yonder,' said Peter, rising up again; 'yon's the sound of a fiddle, and when there is music, there's aye something ganging to eat or drink.'

'I am just going to order something here,' said the Quaker; 'but, in the meantime, have you any objection, my good friend, to tell us your name?'

'None in the world, if you are wanting to drink to me by name and surname,' answered Peebles; 'but, otherwise, I would rather evite your interrogatories.'

'Friend,' said the Quaker, 'it is not for thine own health, seeing thou hast drunk enough already—however—Here, handmaiden—bring me a gill of sherry.'

'Sherry's but shilpit drink, and a gill's a sma' measure for twa gentlemen to crack ower at their first acquaintance.—But let us see your sneaking gill of sherry,' said Poor Peter, thrusting forth his huge hand to seize on the diminutive pewter measure, which, according to the fashion of the time, contained the generous liquor freshly drawn from the butt.

'Nay, hold, friend,' said Joshua, 'thou hast not yet told me what name and surname I am to call thee by.'

'D—d sly in the Quaker,' said Nanty, apart, 'to make him pay for his liquor before he gives it him. Now, I am such a fool, that I should have let him get too drunk to open his mouth, before I thought of asking him a question.'

'My name is Peter Peebles, then,' said the litigant, rather sulkily, as one who thought his liquor too sparingly meted out to him; 'and what have you to say to that?'

'Peter Peebles?' repeated Nanty Ewart, and seemed to muse upon something which the words brought to his remembrance, while the Quaker pursued his examination.

'But I prithee, Peter Peebles, what is thy further designation?—Thou knowest, in our country, that some men are distinguished by their craft and calling, as cordwainers, fishers, weavers, or the like, and some by their titles as proprietors of land, (which savours of vanity)—Now, how may you be distinguished from others of the same name?'

'As Peter Peebles of the great plea of Poor Peter Peebles against Plainstanes, *et per contra**—if I am laird of naething else, I am aye a *dominus litis*.'

'It's but a poor lairdship, I doubt,' said Joshua.

'Pray, Mr Peebles,' said Nanty, interrupting the conversation abruptly, 'were not you once a burgess of Edinburgh?'

'*Was* I a burgess!' said Peter indignantly, 'and *am* I not a burgess even now? I have done nothing to forfeit my right, I trow—once provost and aye my lord.'

'Well, Mr Burgess, tell me farther, have you not some property in the Gude Town?' continued Ewart.

'Troth have I—that is, before my misfortunes, I had twa or three bonny bits of mailings amang the closes and wynds, forby the shop and the story abune it. But Plainstanes has put me to the causeway now. Never mind though, I will be upsides with him yet.'

'Had not you once a tenement in the Covenant Close?' again demanded Nanty.

'You have hit it, lad, though ye look not like a Covenanter,' said Peter; 'we'll drink to its memory—[Hout! the heart's at the mouth o' that ill-faur'd bit stoup already!]—it brought a rent, reckoning from the crawstep to the groundsill, that ye might ca' fourteen punds a-year, forby the laigh cellar that was let to Lucky Littleworth.'

'And do you not remember that you had a poor old lady for your tenant, Mrs Cantrips of Kittlebasket?' said Nanty, suppressing his emotion with difficulty.

'Remember! G—d, I have gude cause to remember her,' said Peter, 'for she turned a dyvour on my hands, the auld besom! and, after a' that the law could do to make me satisfied and paid, in the way of poinding and distrenzieing, and sae forth, as the law will, she ran awa to the Charity Workhouse, a matter of twenty punds Scots in my debt—it's a great shame and oppression that Charity Workhouse, taking in bankrupt dyvours that canna pay their honest creditors.'

'Methinks, friend,' said the Quaker, 'thine own rags might teach thee compassion for other people's nakedness.'

'Rags!' said Peter, taking Joshua's words literally; 'does ony wise body put on their best coat when they are travelling, and keeping company with Quakers, and such other cattle as the road affords?'

'The old lady *died*, I have heard,' said Nanty, affecting a moderation which was belied by accents that faltered with passion.

'She might live or die, for what I care,' answered Peter the Cruel;* 'what business have folk to do to live, that canna live as law will, and satisfy their just and lawful creditors?'

'And you—you that are now yourself trodden down in the very kennel, are you not sorry for what you have done? Do you not repent having occasioned the poor widow-woman's death?'

'What for should I repent?' said Peter; 'the law was on my side—a decreet of the Bailies' followed by poinding, and an act of warding—a suspension intented, and the letters found orderly proceeded.*—I followed the auld rudas through twa Courts—she cost me mair money than her lugs were worth.'

'Now, by Heaven!' said Nanty, 'I would give a thousand guineas, if I had them, to have you worth my beating! Had you said you repented, it had been between God and your conscience; but to hear you boast of your villainy—Do you think it little to have reduced the aged to famine, and the young to infamy—to have caused the death of one woman, the ruin of another, and to have driven a man to exile and despair? By Him that made me, I can scarce keep hands off you!'

'Off me?—I defy ye!' said Peter. 'I take this honest man to witness, that if ye stir the neck of my collar, I will have my action for stouthreif, spulzie, oppression, assault and battery. Here's a bra' din, indeed, about an auld wife gaun to the grave, a young limmer to the close-heads and causeway, and a sticket stibbler[62] to the sea instead of the gallows!'

'Now, by my soul,' said Nanty, 'this is too much! and since you can feel no otherwise, I will try if I cannot beat some humanity into your head and shoulders.'

He drew his hanger as he spoke, and although Joshua, who had in vain endeavoured to interrupt the dialogue, to which he foresaw a violent termination, now threw himself between Nanty and the old litigant, he could not prevent the latter from receiving two or three sound slaps over the shoulder with the flat side of the weapon.

Poor Peter Peebles, as inglorious in his extremity as he had been presumptuous in bringing it on, now ran and roared, and bolted out of the apartment and house itself, pursued by Nanty, whose passion became high in proportion to his giving way to its dictates, and by Joshua, who still interfered at every risk, calling upon Nanty to reflect on the age and miserable circumstances of the offender, and upon Poor Peter to stand and place himself under his protection. In front of the house, however, Peter Peebles found a more efficient protector than the worthy Quaker.

CHAPTER XXI

NARRATIVE OF ALAN FAIRFORD

OUR readers may recollect, that Fairford had been conducted by Dick Gardener from the House of Fairladies, to the inn of old Father Crackenthorp, in order, as he had been informed by the mysterious Father Buonaventure, that he might have the meeting which he desired with Mr Redgauntlet, to treat with him for the liberty of his friend Darsie. His guide, by the special direction of Mr Ambrose, had introduced him into the public-house by a back-door, and recommended to the landlord to accommodate him with a private apartment, and to treat him with all civility; but in other respects to keep his eye on him, and even to secure his person, if he saw any reason to suspect him to be a spy. He was not, however, subjected to any direct restraint, but was ushered into an apartment, where he was requested to await the arrival of the gentleman with whom he wished to have an interview, and who, as Crackenthorp assured him with a significant nod, would be certainly there in the course of an hour. In the meanwhile, he recommended to him, with another significant sign, to keep his apartment, 'as there were people in the house who were apt to busy themselves about other folk's matters.'

Alan Fairford complied with the recommendation, so long as he thought it reasonable; but when, among a large party riding up to the house, he discerned Redgauntlet, whom he had seen under the name of Mr Herries of Birrenswork, and whom, by his height and strength, he easily distinguished from the rest, he thought it proper to go down to the front of the house, in hopes that, by more closely reconnoitring the party, he might discover if his friend Darsie was among them.

The reader is aware that, by doing so, he had an opportunity of breaking Darsie's fall from his side-saddle, although his disguise and mask prevented his recognising his friend. It may be also recollected, that while Nixon hurried Miss Redgauntlet and her brother into the house, their uncle, somewhat chafed at an unexpected and inconvenient interruption, remained himself in parley with Fairford, who had already successively addressed him by the names of Herries and Redgauntlet; neither of which, any more than the acquaintance of the young lawyer, he seemed at the moment willing to acknowledge, though an air of haughty indifference, which he assumed, could not conceal his vexation and embarrassment.

'If we must needs be acquainted, sir,' he said at last—'for which I am unable to see any necessity, especially as I am now particularly disposed to be private—I must entreat you will tell me at once what you have to say, and permit me to attend to matters of more importance.'

'My introduction,' said Fairford, 'is contained in this letter,'—(delivering that of Maxwell.)—'I am convinced that, under whatever name it may be your pleasure for the present to be known, it is into your hands, and yours only, that it should be delivered.'

Redgauntlet turned the letter in his hand—then read the contents—then again looked upon the letter, and sternly observed, 'The seal of the letter has been broken. Was this the case, sir, when it was delivered into your hand?'

Fairford despised a falsehood as much as any man, unless, perhaps, as Tom Turnpenny might have said, 'in the way of business.' He answered readily and firmly, 'The seal was whole when the letter was delivered to me by Mr Maxwell of Summertrees.'

'And did you dare, sir, to break the seal of a letter addressed to me?' said Redgauntlet, not sorry, perhaps, to pick a quarrel upon a point foreign to the tenor of the epistle.

'I have never broken the seal of any letter committed to my charge,' said Alan; 'not from fear of those to whom such letter might be addressed, but from respect to myself.'

'That is well worded,' said Redgauntlet; 'and yet, young Mr Counsellor, I doubt whether your delicacy prevented your reading my letter, or listening to the contents as read by some other person after it was opened.'

'I certainly did hear the contents read over,' said Fairford; 'and they were such as to surprise me a good deal.'

'Now that,' said Redgauntlet, 'I hold to be pretty much the same, *in foro conscientiae*, as if you had broken the seal yourself. I shall hold myself excused from entering upon farther discourse with a messenger so faithless; and you may thank yourself if your journey has been fruitless.'

'Stay, sir,' said Fairford; 'and know that I became acquainted with the contents of the paper without my consent—I may even say against my will; for Mr Buonaventure'——

'Who?' demanded Redgauntlet, in a wild and alarmed manner—'*Whom* was it you named?'

'Father Buonaventure,' said Alan,—'a Catholic priest, as I apprehend, whom I saw at the Miss Arthurets' house, called Fairladies.'

'Miss Arthurets!—Fairladies!—A Catholic priest!—Father Buonaventure!' said Redgauntlet, repeating the words of Alan with astonishment,—'Is it possible that human rashness can reach such a point of infatuation?—Tell me the truth, I conjure you, sir—I have the deepest interest to know whether this is more than an idle legend, picked up from hearsay about the country. You are a lawyer, and know the risk incurred by the Catholic clergy, whom the discharge of their duty sends to these bloody shores.'

'I am a lawyer, certainly,' said Fairford; 'but my holding such a respectable condition in life warrants that I am neither an informer nor a spy. Here is sufficient evidence that I have seen Father Buonaventure.'

He put Buonaventure's letter into Redgauntlet's hand, and watched his looks closely while he read it. 'Double-dyed infatuation!' he muttered, with looks in which sorrow, displeasure, and anxiety were mingled. '"Save me from the indiscretion of my friends," says the Spaniard; "I can save myself from the hostility of my enemies."'*

He then read the letter attentively, and for two or three minutes was lost in thought, while some purpose of importance seemed to have gathered and sit brooding upon his countenance. He held up his finger towards his satellite, Cristal Nixon, who replied to his signal with a prompt nod; and with one or two of the attendants approached Fairford in such a manner as to make him apprehensive they were about to lay hold of him.

At this moment a noise was heard from withinside of the house, and presently rushed forth Peter Peebles, pursued by Nanty Ewart with his drawn hanger, and the worthy Quaker, who was endeavouring to prevent mischief to others, at some risk of bringing it on himself.

A wilder and yet a more absurd figure can hardly be imagined, than that of Poor Peter clattering along as fast as his huge boots would permit him, and resembling nothing so much as a flying scarecrow; while the thin emaciated form of Nanty Ewart, with the hue of death on his cheek, and the fire of vengeance glancing from his eye, formed a ghastly contrast with the ridiculous object of his pursuit.

Redgauntlet threw himself between them. 'What extravagant folly is this?' he said. 'Put up your weapon, Captain. Is this a time to indulge in drunken brawls, or is such a miserable object as that a fitting antagonist for a man of courage?'

'I beg pardon,' said the Captain, sheathing his weapon—'I was a little bit out of the way, to be sure; but to know the provocation, a man must read my heart, and that I hardly dare to do myself. But the wretch is safe from me. Heaven has done its own vengeance on us both.'

While he spoke in this manner, Peter Peebles, who had at first crept behind Redgauntlet in bodily fear, began now to reassume his spirits. Pulling his protector by the sleeve, 'Mr Herries—Mr Herries,' he whispered, eagerly, 'ye have done me mair than ae gude turn, and if ye will but do me anither at this dead pinch, I'll forgie the girded keg of brandy that you and Captain Sir Harry Redgimlet drank out yon time. Ye sall hae an ample discharge and renunciation, and, though I should see you walking at the Cross of Edinburgh, or standing at the bar of the Court of Justiciary,* no the very thumbikins themselves should bring to my memory that ever I saw you in arms yon day.'

He accompanied this promise by pulling so hard at Redgauntlet's cloak, that he at last turned round. 'Idiot! speak in a word what you want.'

'Aweel, aweel. In a word then,' said Peter Peebles, 'I have a warrant on me to apprehend that man that stands there, Alan Fairford by name, and advocate by calling. I bought it from Maister Justice Foxley's clerk, Maister Nicholas Faggot, wi' the guinea that you gied me.'

'Ha!' said Redgauntlet, 'hast thou really such a warrant? let me see it.—Look sharp that no one escape, Cristal Nixon.'

Peter produced a huge, greasy, leathern pocketbook, too dirty to permit its original colour to be visible, filled with scrolls of notes, memorials to counsel, and Heaven knows what besides. From amongst this precious mass he culled forth a paper, and placed it in the hands of Redgauntlet or Herries, as he continued to call him, saying, at the same time, 'It's a formal and binding warrant, proceeding on my affidavy made, that the said Alan Fairford, being lawfully engaged in my service, had slipped the tether and fled over the Border, and was now lurking there and thereabouts, to elude and evite the discharge of his bounden duty to me; and therefore granting warrant to constables and others, to seek for, take, and apprehend him, that he may be brought before the Honourable Justice Foxley for examination, and, if necessary, for commitment. Now, though a' this be fairly set down as I tell ye, yet where am I to get an officer to execute this warrant in sic a country as this, where swords and pistols flee out at a word's speaking, and folk care as little for the peace of King George, as the peace of Auld King Coul?*— There's that drunken skipper, and that wet Quaker, enticed me into the public this morning, and because I wadna gie them as much brandy as wad have made them blind-drunk, they baith fell on me, and were in the way of guiding me very ill.'

While Peter went on in this manner, Redgauntlet glanced his eye over the warrant, and immediately saw that it must be a trick passed by Nicholas Faggot, to cheat the poor insane wretch out of his solitary guinea. But the Justice had actually subscribed it, as he did whatever his clerk presented to him, and Redgauntlet resolved to use it for his own purposes.

Without making any direct answer, therefore, to Peter Peebles, he walked up gravely to Fairford, who had waited quietly for the termination of a scene, in which he was not a little surprised to find his client, Mr Peebles, a conspicuous actor.

'Mr Fairford,' said Redgauntlet, 'there are many reasons which might induce me to comply with the request, or rather the injunctions, of the excellent Father Buonaventure, that I should communicate with you upon the present condition of my ward, whom you know under the name of Darsie Latimer; but no man is better aware than you that the law must be obeyed, even in contradiction to our own feelings; now, this poor man has obtained a warrant for carrying you before a magistrate, and, I am afraid, there is a necessity of your yielding to it, although to the postponement of the business which you may have with me.'

'A warrant against me!' said Alan, indignantly; 'and at that poor miserable wretch's instance?—why, this is a trick, a mere and most palpable trick!'

'It may be so,' replied Redgauntlet, with great equanimity; 'doubtless you know best; only the writ appears regular, and with that respect for the law which has been,' he said, with hypocritical formality, 'a leading feature of my character through life, I cannot dispense with giving my poor aid to the support of a legal warrant. Look at it yourself, and be satisfied it is no trick of mine.'

Fairford ran over the affidavit and the warrant, and then exclaimed once more, that it was an impudent imposition, and that he would hold those who acted upon such a warrant liable in the highest damages. 'I guess at your motive, Mr Redgauntlet,' he said, 'for acquiescing in so ridiculous a proceeding. But be assured you will find that, in this country, one act of illegal violence will not be covered or atoned for by practising another. You cannot, as a man of sense and honour, pretend to say you regard this as a legal warrant.'

'I am no lawyer, sir,' said Redgauntlet; 'and pretend not to know what is or is not law—the warrant is quite formal, and that is enough for me.'

'Did ever any one hear,' said Fairford, 'of an advocate being compelled to return to his task, like a collier or a salter[63] who has deserted his master?'

'I see no reason why he should not,' said Redgauntlet, dryly, 'unless on the ground that the services of the lawyer are the most expensive and least useful of the two.'

'You cannot mean this in earnest,' said Fairford; 'you cannot really mean to avail yourself of so poor a contrivance, to evade the word pledged by your friend, your ghostly father, in my behalf. I may have been a fool for trusting it too easily, but think what you must be if you can abuse my confidence in this manner. I entreat you to reflect that this usage releases me from all promises of secrecy or connivance at what I am apt to think are very dangerous practices, and that'——

'Hark ye, Mr Fairford,' said Redgauntlet; 'I must here interrupt you for your own sake. One word of betraying what you may have seen, or what you may have suspected, and your seclusion is like to have either a very distant or a very brief termination; in either case a most undesirable one. At present, you are sure of being at liberty in a very few days—perhaps much sooner.'

'And my friend,' said Alan Fairford, 'for whose sake I have run myself into this danger, what is to become of him?—Dark and dangerous man!' he exclaimed, raising his voice, 'I will not be again cajoled by deceitful promises'——

'I give you my honour that your friend is well,' interrupted Redgauntlet; 'perhaps I may permit you to see him, if you will but submit with patience to a fate which is inevitable.'

But Alan Fairford, considering his confidence as having been abused, first by Maxwell, and next by the Priest, raised his voice, and appealed to all the King's lieges within hearing, against the violence with which he was threatened. He was instantly seized on by Nixon and two assistants, who, holding down his arms, and endeavouring to stop his mouth, were about to hurry him away.

The honest Quaker, who had kept out of Redgauntlet's presence, now came boldly forward.

'Friend,' said he, 'thou dost more than thou canst answer. Thou knowest me well, and thou art aware, that in me thou hast a deeply injured neighbour, who was dwelling beside thee in the honesty and simplicity of his heart.'

'Tush, Jonathan,' said Redgauntlet; 'talk not to me, man; it is neither the craft of a young lawyer, nor the *simplicity* of an old hypocrite, can drive me from my purpose.'

'By my faith,' said the Captain, coming forward in his turn, 'this is hardly fair, General; and I doubt,' he added, 'whether the will of my owners can make me a party to such proceedings.—Nay, never fumble with your sword-hilt, but out with it like a man, if you are for a tilting.'—He unsheathed his hanger, and continued.—'I will neither see my comrade Fairford, nor the old Quaker, abused. D—n all warrants, false or true—curse the justice—confound the constable! —and here stands little Nanty Ewart to make good what he says against gentle and simple, in spite of horseshoe or horseradish either.'

The cry of 'Down with all warrants!' was popular in the ears of the militia of the inn, and Nanty Ewart was no less so. Fishers, ostlers, seamen, smugglers, began to crowd to the spot. Crackenthorp endeavoured in vain to mediate. The attendants of Redgauntlet began to handle their firearms; but their master shouted to them to forbear, and, unsheathing his sword as quick as lightning, he rushed on Ewart in the midst of his bravade, and struck his weapon from his hand with such address and force, that it flew three yards from him. Closing with him at the same moment, he gave him a severe fall, and waved his sword over his head, to show he was absolutely at his mercy.

'There, you drunken vagabond,' he said, 'I give you your life—you are no bad fellow, if you could keep from brawling among your friends.—But we all know Nanty Ewart,' he said to the crowd around. with a forgiving laugh, which, joined to the awe his prowess had inspired, entirely confirmed their wavering allegiance.

They shouted, 'The Laird for ever!' while poor Nanty, rising from the earth, on whose lap he had been stretched so rudely, went in quest of his hanger, lifted it, wiped it, and, as he returned the weapon to the scabbard, muttered between his teeth, 'It is true they say of him, and the devil will stand his friend till his hour come; I will cross him no more.'

So saying, he slunk from the crowd, cowed and disheartened by his defeat.

'For you, Joshua Geddes,' said Redgauntlet, approaching the Quaker, who, with lifted hands and eyes, had beheld the scene of violence, 'I shall take the liberty to arrest thee for a breach of the peace, altogether unbecoming thy pretended principles; and I believe it will go hard with thee both in a Court of Justice and among thine own Society of Friends, as they call themselves, who will be but indifferently pleased to see the quiet tenor of their hypocrisy insulted by such violent proceedings.'

'*I* violent!' said Joshua; '*I* do aught unbecoming the principles of the Friends! I defy thee, man, and I charge thee, as a Christian, to forbear vexing my soul with such charges: it is grievous enough to me to have seen violences which I was unable to prevent.'

'Oh, Joshua, Joshua!' said Redgauntlet, with a sardonic smile; 'thou light of the faithful in the town of Dumfries and the places adjacent, wilt thou thus fall away from the truth? Hast thou not, before us all, attempted to rescue a man from the warrant of law? Didst thou not encourage that drunken fellow to draw his weapon—and didst thou not thyself flourish thy cudgel in the cause? Think'st thou that the oaths of the injured Peter Peebles, and the conscientious Cristal Nixon, besides those of such gentlemen as look on this strange scene, who not only put on swearing as a garment, but to whom, in Custom-House matters, oaths are literally meat and drink,—dost thou not think, I say, that these men's oaths will go farther than thy Yea and Nay in this matter?'*

'I will swear to any thing,' said Peter. 'All is fair when it comes to an oath *ad litem*.'

'You do me foul wrong', said the Quaker, undismayed by the general laugh. 'I encouraged no drawing of weapons, though I attempted to move an unjust man by some use of argument—I brandished no cudgel, although it may be that the ancient Adam struggled within me, and caused my hand to grasp mine oaken staff firmer than usual, when I saw innocence borne down with violence. —But why talk I what is true and just to thee, who hast been a man of violence from thy youth upwards? Let me rather speak to thee such language as thou canst comprehend. Deliver these young men up to me,' he said, when he had led Redgauntlet a little apart from the crowd, 'and I will not only free thee from the heavy charge of damages which thou hast incurred by thine outrage upon my property, but I will add ransom for them and for myself. What would it profit thee to do the youths wrong, by detaining them in captivity?'

'Mr Geddes,' said Redgauntlet, in a tone more respectful than he had hitherto used to the Quaker, 'your language is disinterested, and I respect the fidelity of your friendship. Perhaps we have mistaken each other's principles and motives; but if so, we have not at present time for explanation. Make yourself easy. I hope to raise your friend Darsie Latimer to a pitch of eminence which you will witness with pleasure;—nay, do not attempt to answer me. The other young man shall suffer restraint a few days, probably only a few hours,—it is not more than due for his pragmatical interference in what concerned him not. Do you, Mr Geddes, be so prudent as to take your horse and leave this place, which is growing every moment more unfit for the abode of a man of peace. You may wait the event in safety at Mount Sharon.'

'Friend,' replied Joshua, 'I cannot comply with thy advice; I will remain here, even as thy prisoner, as thou didst but now threaten, rather than leave the youth, who hath suffered by and through me and my misfortunes, in his present state of doubtful safety. Wherefore I will not mount my steed Solomon; neither will I turn his head towards Mount Sharon, until I see an end of this matter.'

'A prisoner, then, you must be,' said Redgauntlet. 'I have no time to dispute the matter farther with you.—But tell me for what you fix your eyes so attentively on yonder people of mine?'

'To speak the truth,' said the Quaker, 'I admire to behold among them a little wretch of a boy called Benjie, to whom I think Satan has given the power of transporting himself wheresoever mischief is going forward; so that it may be truly said, there is no evil in this land wherein he hath not a finger, if not a whole hand.'

The boy, who saw their eyes fixed on him as they spoke, seemed embarrassed, and rather desirous of making his escape; but at a signal from Redgauntlet he advanced, assuming the sheepish look and rustic manner with which the jackanapes covered much acuteness and roguery.

'How long have you been with the party, sirrah,' said Redgauntlet.

'Since the raid on the stake-nets,' said Benjie, with his finger in his mouth.

'And what made you follow us?'

'I dauredna stay at hame for the constables,' replied the boy.

'And what have you been doing all this time?'

'Doing, sir?—I dinna ken what ye ca' doing—I have been doing naething,' said Benjie; then seeing something in Redgauntlet's eye which was not to be trifled with, he added, 'Naething but waiting on Maister Cristal Nixon.'

'Hum!—ay—indeed?' muttered Redgauntlet. 'Must Master Nixon bring his own retinue into the field?—This must be seen to.'

He was about to pursue his enquiry, when Nixon himself came to him with looks of anxious haste. 'The Father is come,' he whispered, 'and the gentlemen are getting together in the largest room of the house, and they desire to see you. Yonder is your nephew, too, making a noise like a man in Bedlam.'

'I will look to it all instantly,' said Redgauntlet. 'Is the Father lodged as I directed?'

Cristal nodded.

'Now, then, for the final trial,' said Redgauntlet. He folded his hands—looked upwards—crossed himself—and after this act of devotion, (almost the first which any one had observed him make use of,) he commanded Nixon to keep good watch—have his horses and men ready for every emergence—look after the safe custody of the prisoners—but treat them at the same time well and civilly. And these orders given, he darted hastily into the house.

CHAPTER XXII

NARRATIVE CONTINUED

REDGAUNTLET's first course was to the chamber of his nephew. He unlocked the door, entered the apartment, and asked what he wanted, that he made so much noise.

'I want my liberty,' said Darsie, who had wrought himself up to a pitch of passion in which his uncle's wrath had lost its terrors. 'I desire my liberty, and to be assured of the safety of my beloved friend, Alan Fairford, whose voice I heard but now.'

'Your liberty shall be your own within half an hour from this period—your friend shall be also set at freedom in due time—and you yourself be permitted to have access to his place of confinement.'

'This does not satisfy me,' said Darsie; 'I must see my friend instantly; he is here, and he is here endangered on my account only—I have heard violent exclamations—the clash of swords. You will gain no point with me unless I have ocular demonstration of his safety.'

'Arthur—dearest nephew,' answered Redgauntlet, 'drive me not mad! Thine own fate—that of thy house—that of thousands—that of Britain herself, are at this moment in the scales; and you are only occupied about the safety of a poor insignificant pettifogger!'

'He has sustained injury at your hands, then?' said Darsie, fiercely. 'I know he has; but if so, not even our relationship shall protect you.'

'Peace, ungrateful and obstinate fool!' said Redgauntlet. 'Yet stay—Will you be satisfied if you see this Alan Fairford, the bundle of bombazine—this precious friend of yours—well and sound?—Will you, I say, be satisfied with seeing him in perfect safety, without attempting to speak to or converse with him?'—Darsie signified his assent. 'Take hold of my arm, then,' said Redgauntlet; 'and do you, niece Lilias, take the other; and beware, Sir Arthur, how you bear yourself.'

Darsie was compelled to acquiesce, sufficiently aware that his uncle would permit him no interview with a friend whose influence would certainly be used against his present earnest wishes, and in some measure contented with the assurance of Fairford's personal safety.

Redgauntlet led them through one or two passages, (for the house, as we have before said, was very irregular, and built at different times,) until they entered an apartment, where a man with shouldered carabine kept watch at the door, but readily turned the key for their reception. In this room they found Alan Fairford and the Quaker, apparently in deep conversation with each other. They looked up as Redgauntlet and his party entered; and Alan pulled off his hat and made a profound reverence, which the young lady, who recognised him,—though, masked as she was, he could not know her,—returned with some embarrassment, arising probably from the recollection of the bold step she had taken in visiting him.

Darsie longed to speak, but dared not. His uncle only said, 'Gentlemen, I know you are as anxious on Mr Darsie Latimer's account as he is upon yours. I am commissioned by him to inform you, that he is as well as you are—I trust you will all meet soon. Meantime, although I cannot suffer you to be at large, you shall be as well treated as is possible under your temporary confinement.'

He passed on, without pausing to hear the answers which the lawyer and the Quaker were hastening to prefer; and only waving his hand by way of adieu, made his exit, with the real and the seeming lady whom he had under his charge, through a door at the upper end of the apartment, which was fastened and guarded like that by which they entered.

Redgauntlet next led the way into a very small room; adjoining which, but divided by a partition, was one of apparently larger dimensions; for they heard the trampling of the heavy boots of the period, as if several persons were walking to and fro, and conversing in low and anxious whispers.

'Here,' said Redgauntlet to his nephew, as he disencumbered him from the riding-skirt and the mask, 'I restore you to yourself, and trust you will lay aside all effeminate thoughts with this feminine dress. Do not blush at having worn a disguise to which kings and heroes have been reduced.* It is when female craft or female cowardice find their way into a manly bosom, that he who entertains these sentiments should take eternal shame to himself for thus having resembled womankind. Follow me, while Lilias remains here. I will introduce you to those whom I hope to see associated with you in the most glorious cause that hand ever drew sword in.'

Darsie paused. 'Uncle,' he said, 'my person is in your hands; but remember, my will is my own. I will not be hurried into any resolution of importance. Remember what I have already said—what I now repeat—that I will take no step of importance but upon conviction.'

'But canst thou be convinced, thou foolish boy, without hearing and understanding the grounds on which we act?'

So saying, he took Darsie by the arm, and walked with him to the next room—a large apartment, partly filled with miscellaneous articles of commerce, chiefly connected with contraband trade; where, among bales and barrels, sat, or walked to and fro, several gentlemen, whose manners and looks seemed superior to the plain riding-dresses which they wore.

There was a grave and stern anxiety upon their countenances, when, on Redgauntlet's entrance, they drew from their separate coteries into one group around him, and saluted him with a formality, which had something in it of ominous melancholy. As Darsie looked around the circle, he thought he could discern in it few traces of that adventurous hope which urges men upon desperate enterprises; and began to believe that the conspiracy would dissolve of itself, without the necessity of his placing himself in direct opposition to so violent a character as his uncle, and incurring the hazard with which such opposition must needs be attended.

Mr Redgauntlet, however, did not, or would not, see any such marks of depression of spirit amongst his coadjutors, but met them with cheerful countenance, and a warm greeting of welcome. 'Happy to meet you here, my lord,' he said, bowing low to a slender young man. 'I trust you come with the pledges of your noble father, of B——, and all that loyal house.—Sir Richard, what news in the west? I am told you had two hundred men on foot to have joined when the fatal retreat from Derby was commenced. When the White Standard* is again displayed, it shall not be turned back so easily, either by the force of its enemies, or the falsehood of its friends.—Doctor Grumball, I bow to the representative of Oxford, the mother of learning and loyalty.—Pengwinion, you Cornish chough, has this good wind blown you north?—Ah, my brave Cambro-Britons, when was Wales last in the race of honour!'

Such and such-like compliments he dealt around, which were in general answered by silent bows; but when he saluted one of his own countrymen by the name of MacKellar, and greeted Maxwell of Summertrees by that of Pate-in-Peril, the latter replied, 'that if Pate were not a fool, he would be Pate-in-Safety;' and the former, a thin old gentleman, in tarnished embroidery, said bluntly, 'Ay, troth, Redgauntlet, I am here just like yourself; I have little to lose—they that took my land the last time, may take my life this; and that is all I care about it.'

The English gentlemen, who were still in possession of their paternal estates, looked doubtfully on each other, and there was something whispered among them of the fox which had lost his tail.

Redgauntlet hastened to address them. 'I think, my lords and gentlemen,' he said, 'that I can account for something like sadness which has crept upon an assembly gathered together for so noble a purpose. Our numbers seem, when thus assembled, too small and inconsiderable to shake the firm-seated usurpation of a half century. But do not count us by what we are in thewe and muscle, but by what our summons can do among our countrymen. In this small party are those who have power to raise battalions, and those who have wealth to pay them. And do not believe our friends who are absent are cold or indifferent to the cause. Let us once light the signal, and it will be hailed by all who retain love for the Stewart, and by all—a more numerous body—who hate the Elector. Here I have letters from'——

Sir Richard Glendale interrupted the speaker. 'We all confide, Redgauntlet, in your valour and skill—we admire your perseverance; and probably nothing short of your strenuous exertions, and the emulation awakened by your noble and disinterested conduct, could have brought so many of us, the scattered remnant of a disheartened party, to meet together once again in solemn consultation;—for I take it, gentlemen,' he said, looking round, 'this is only a consultation.'

'Nothing more,' said the young lord.

'Nothing more,' said Doctor Grumball, shaking his large academical peruke.

And 'Only a consultation,' was echoed by the others.

Redgauntlet bit his lip. 'I had hopes,' he said, 'that the discourses I have held with most of you, from time to time, had ripened into more maturity than your words imply, and that we were here to execute as well as to deliberate; and for this we stand prepared. I can raise five hundred men with my whistle.'

'Five hundred men!' said one of the Welsh squires, 'Cot bless us! and, pray you, what cood* could five hundred men do?'

'All that the priming does for the cannon, Mr Meredith,' answered Redgauntlet; 'it will enable us to seize Carlisle, and you know what our friends have engaged for in that case.'

'Yes—but,' said the young nobleman, 'you must not hurry us on too fast, Mr Redgauntlet; we are all, I believe, as sincere and truehearted in this business as you are, but we will not be driven forward blindfold. We owe caution to ourselves and our families, as well as to those whom we are empowered to represent on this occasion.'

'Who hurries you, my lord? Who is it that would drive this meeting forward blindfold? I do not understand your lordship,' said Redgauntlet.

'Nay,' said Sir Richard Glendale, 'at least do not let us fall under our old reproach of disagreeing among ourselves. What my lord means, Redgauntlet, is, that we have this morning heard it is uncertain whether you could even bring that body of men whom you count upon; your countryman, Mr MacKellar, seemed, just before you came in, to doubt whether your people would rise in any force, unless you could produce the authority of your nephew.'

'I might ask,' said Redgauntlet, 'what right MacKellar, or any one, has to doubt my being able to accomplish what I stand pledged for?—But our hopes consist in our unity.—Here stands my nephew. —Gentlemen, I present to you my kinsman, Sir Arthur Darsie Redgauntlet of that Ilk.'

'Gentlemen,' said Darsie, with a throbbing bosom, for he felt the crisis a very painful one, 'Allow me to say, that I suspend expressing my sentiments on the important subject under discussion, until I have heard those of the present meeting.'

'Proceed in your deliberations, gentlemen,' said Redgauntlet; 'I will show my nephew such reasons for acquiescing in the result, as will entirely remove any scruples which may hang around his mind.'

Dr Grumball now coughed, 'shook his ambrosial curls,'* and addressed the assembly.

'The principles of Oxford,' he said, 'are well understood, since she was the last to resign herself to the Arch-Usurper*—since she has condemned, by her sovereign authority, the blasphemous, atheistical, and anarchical tenets of Locke,* and other deluders of the public mind. Oxford will give men, money, and countenance, to the cause of the righful monarch. But we have been often deluded by foreign powers,* who have availed themselves of our zeal to stir up civil dissensions in Britain, not for the advantage of our blessed though banished monarch, but to engender disturbances by which they might profit, while we, their tools, are sure to be ruined. Oxford, therefore, will not rise, unless our Sovereign comes in person to claim our allegiance, in which case, God forbid we should refuse him our best obedience.'

'It is a very cood advice,' said Mr Meredith.

'In troth,' said Sir Richard Glendale, 'it is the very keystone of our enterprise, and the only condition upon which I myself and others could ever have dreamt of taking up arms. No insurrection which has not Charles Edward himself at its head, will ever last longer than till a single foot-company of redcoats march to disperse it.'

'This is my own opinion, and that of all my family,' said the young nobleman already mentioned; 'and I own I am somewhat surprised at being summoned to attend a dangerous rendezvous such as this, before something certain could have been stated to us on this most important preliminary point.'

'Pardon me, my lord,' said Redgauntlet; 'I have not been so unjust either to myself or my friends—I had no means of communicating to our distant confederates (without the greatest risk of discovery) what is known to some of my honourable friends. As courageous, and as resolved, as when, twenty years since, he threw himself into the wilds of Moidart, Charles Edward has instantly complied with the wishes of his faithful subjects. Charles Edward is in this country—Charles Edward is in this house!—Charles Edward waits but your present decision, to receive the homage of those who have ever called themselves his loyal liegemen. He that would now turn his coat, and change his note, must do so under the eye of his sovereign.'

There was a deep pause. Those among the conspirators whom mere habit, or a desire of preserving consistency, had engaged in the affair, now saw with terror their retreat cut off; and others, who at a distance had regarded the proposed enterprise as hopeful, trembled when the moment of actually embarking in it was thus unexpectedly and almost inevitably precipitated.

'How now, my lords and gentlemen!' said Redgauntlet; 'Is it delight and rapture that keep you thus silent? where are the eager welcomes that should be paid your rightful King, who a second time confides his person to the care of his subjects, undeterred by the hairbreadth escapes and severe privations of his former expedition? I hope there is no gentleman here that is not ready to redeem, in his prince's presence, the pledge of fidelity which he offered in his absence?'

'I, at least,' said the young nobleman, resolutely, and laying his hand on his sword, 'will not be that coward. If Charles is come to these shores, I will be the first to give him welcome, and to devote my life and fortune to his service.'

'Before Cot,' said Mr Meredith, 'I do not see that Mr Redcantlet has left us any thing else to do.'

'Stay,' said Summertrees, 'there is yet one other question. Has he brought any of those Irish rapparees* with him, who broke the neck of our last glorious affair?'

'Not a man of them,' said Redgauntlet.

'I trust,' said Dr Grumball, 'that there are no Catholic priests in his company? I would not intrude on the private conscience of my Sovereign, but, as an unworthy son of the Church of England, it is my duty to consider her security.'

'Not a Popish dog or cat is there, to bark or mew about his Majesty,' said Redgauntlet. 'Old Shaftesbury himself* could not wish a prince's person more secure from Popery—which may not be the worst religion in the world, notwithstanding.—Any more doubts, gentlemen? can no more plausible reasons be discovered for postponing the payment of our duty, and discharge of our oaths and engagements? Meantime your King waits your declaration—by my faith he hath but a frozen reception!'

'Redgauntlet,' said Sir Richard Glendale, calmly, 'your reproaches shall not goad me into any thing of which my reason disapproves. That I respect my engagement as much as you do, is evident, since I am here, ready to support it with the best blood in my veins. But has the King really come hither entirely unattended?'

'He has no man with him but young——, as aid-de-camp, and a single valet-de-chambre.'

'No *man;*—but, Redgauntlet, as you are a gentleman, has he no *woman* with him?'

Redgauntlet cast his eyes on the ground and replied, 'I am sorry to say—he has.'

The company looked at each other, and remained silent for a moment. At length Sir Richard proceeded. 'I need not repeat to you, Mr Redgauntlet, what is the well-grounded opinion of his Majesty's friends concerning that most unhappy connexion; there is but one sense and feeling amongst us upon the subject. I must conclude that our humble remonstrances were communicated by you, sir, to the King?'

'In the same strong terms in which they were couched,' replied Redgauntlet. 'I love his Majesty's cause more than I fear his displeasure.'

'But, apparently, our humble expostulation has produced no effect. This lady, who has crept into his bosom, has a sister in the Elector of Hanover's Court,* and yet we are well assured that every point of our most private communication is placed in her keeping.'

'*Varium et mutabile semper femina,*'* said Dr Grumball.

'She puts his secrets into her work-bag,' said Maxwell; 'and out they fly whenever she opens it. If I must hang, I would wish it to be in somewhat a better rope than the string of a lady's hussey.'

'Are you, too, turning dastard, Maxwell?' said Redgauntlet, in a whisper.

'Not I,' said Maxwell; 'let us fight for it, and let them win and wear us; but to be betrayed by a brimstone like that'——

'Be temperate, gentlemen,' said Redgauntlet; 'the foible of which you complain so heavily has always been that of kings and heroes; which I feel strongly confident the King will surmount, upon the humble entreaty of his best servants, and when he sees them ready to peril their all in his cause, upon the slight condition of his resigning the society of a female favourite, of whom I have seen reason to think he hath been himself for some time wearied. But let us not press upon him rashly with our well-meant zeal. He has a princely will, as becomes his princely birth, and we, gentlemen, who are royalists, should be the last to take advantage of circumstances to limit its exercise. I am as much surprised and hurt as you can be, to find that he has made her the companion of this journey, increasing every chance of treachery and detection. But do not let us insist upon a sacrifice so humiliating, while he has scarce placed a foot upon the beach of his kingdom. Let us act generously by our Sovereign; and when we have shown what we will do for him, we shall be able, with better face, to state what it is we expect him to concede.'

'Indeed, I think it is but a pity,' said MacKellar, 'when so many pretty gentlemen are got together, that they should part without the flash of a sword among them.'

'I should be of that gentleman's opinion,' said Lord ——, 'had I nothing to lose but my life; but I frankly own, that the conditions on which our family agreed to join having been, in this instance, left unfulfilled, I will not peril the whole fortunes of our house on the doubtful fidelity of an artful woman.'

'I am sorry to see your lordship,' said Redgauntlet, 'take a course, which is more likely to secure your house's wealth than to augment its honours.'

'How am I to understand your language, sir?' said the young nobleman, haughtily.

'Nay, gentlemen,' said Dr Grumball, interposing, 'do not let friends quarrel; we are all zealous for the cause—but truly, although I know the license claimed by the great in such matters, and can, I hope, make due allowance, there is, I may say, an indecorum in a prince who comes to claim the allegiance of the Church of England, arriving on such an errand with such a companion—*si non caste, caute, tamen*.'*

'I wonder how the Church of England came to be so heartily attached to his merry old namesake,'* said Redgauntlet.

Sir Richard Glendale then took up the question, as one whose authority and experience gave him right to speak with much weight. 'We have no leisure for hesitation,' he said; 'it is full time that we decide what course we are to hold. I feel as much as you, Mr Redgauntlet, the delicacy of capitulating with our Sovereign in his present condition. But I must also think of the total ruin of the cause, the confiscation and bloodshed which will take place among his adherents, and all through the infatuation with which he adheres to a woman who is the pensionary of the present minister, as she was for years Sir Robert Walpole's.* Let his Majesty send her back to the continent, and the sword on which I now lay my hand shall instantly be unsheathed, and, I trust, many hundred others at the same moment.'

The other persons present testified their unanimous acquiescence in what Sir Richard Glendale had said.

'I see you have taken your resolutions, gentlemen,' said Redgauntlet; 'unwisely, I think, because I believe that, by softer and more generous proceedings, you would have been more likely to carry a point which I think as desirable as you do. But what is to be done if Charles should refuse, with the inflexibility of his grandfather,* to comply with this request of yours? Do you mean to abandon him to his fate?'

'God forbid!' said Sir Richard, hastily; 'and God forgive you, Mr Redgauntlet, for breathing such a thought. No! I for one will, with all duty and humility, see him safe back to his vessel, and defend him with my life against whoever shall assail him. But when I have seen his sails spread, my next act will be to secure, if I can, my own safety, by retiring to my house; or, if I find our engagement, as is too probable, has taken wind, by surrendering myself to the next Justice of Peace, and giving security that hereafter I shall live quiet, and submit to the ruling powers.'

Again the rest of the persons present intimated their agreement in opinion with the speaker.

'Well, gentlemen,' said Redgauntlet, 'it is not for me to oppose the opinion of every one; and I must do you the justice to say, that the King has, in the present instance, neglected a condition of your agreement, which was laid before him in very distinct terms. The question now is, who is to acquaint him with the result of this conference? for I presume you would not wait on him in a body to make the proposal, that he should dismiss a person from his family as the price of your allegiance.'

'I think Mr Redgauntlet should make the explanation,' said Lord ——. 'As he has, doubtless, done justice to our remonstrances by communicating them to the King, no one can, with such propriety and force, state the natural and inevitable consequence of their being neglected.'

'Now, I think,' said Redgauntlet, 'that those who make the objection should state it; for I am confident the King will hardly believe, on less authority than that of the heir of the loyal House of B——, that he is the first to seek an evasion of his pledge to join him.'

'An evasion, sir!' repeated Lord ——, fiercely. 'I have borne too much from you already, and this I will not endure. Favour me with your company to the downs yonder.'

Redgauntlet laughed scornfully, and was about to follow the fiery young man, when Sir Richard again interposed. 'Are we to exhibit,' he said, 'the last symptoms of the dissolution of our party, by turning our swords against each other?—Be patient, Lord ——; in such conferences as this, much must pass unquestioned which might brook challenge elsewhere. There is a privilege of party as of parliament—men cannot, in emergency, stand upon picking phrases. —Gentlemen, if you will extend your confidence in me so far, I will wait upon his Majesty, and I hope my Lord —— and Mr Redgauntlet will accompany me. I trust the explanation of this unpleasant matter will prove entirely satisfactory, and that we shall find ourselves at liberty to render our homage to our Sovereign without reserve, when I for one will be the first to peril all in his just quarrel.'

Redgauntlet at once stepped forward. 'My lord,' he said, 'if my zeal made me say any thing in the slightest degree offensive, I wish it unsaid, and ask your pardon. A gentleman can do no more.'

'I could not have asked Mr Redgauntlet to do so much,' said the young nobleman, willingly accepting the hand which Redgauntlet offered. 'I know no man living from whom I could take so much reproof without a sense of degradation, as from himself.'

'Let me then hope, my lord, that you will go with Sir Richard and me to the presence. Your warm blood will heat our zeal—our colder resolves will temper yours.'

The young lord smiled, and shook his head. 'Alas! Mr Redgauntlet,' he said, 'I am ashamed to say, that in zeal you surpass us all. But I will not refuse this mission, provided you will permit Sir Arthur, your nephew, also to accompany us.'

'My nephew?' said Redgauntlet, and seemed to hesitate, then added, 'Most certainly.—I trust,' he said, looking at Darsie, 'he will bring to his Prince's presence such sentiments as fit the occasion.'

It seemed however to Darsie, that his uncle would rather have left him behind, had he not feared that he might in that case have been influenced by, or might perhaps himself influence, the unresolved confederates with whom he must have associated during his absence.

'I will go,' said Redgauntlet, 'and request admission.'

In a moment after he returned, and without speaking, motioned for the young nobleman to advance. He did so, followed by Sir Richard Glendale and Darsie, Redgauntlet himself bringing up the rear. A short passage and a few steps brought them to the door of the temporary presence-chamber, in which the Royal Wanderer was to receive their homage. It was the upper loft of one of those cottages which made additions to the Old Inn, poorly furnished, dusty, and in disorder; for rash as the enterprise might be considered, they had been still careful not to draw the attention of strangers by any particular attentions to the personal accommodation of the Prince. He was seated, when the deputies, as they might be termed, of his remaining adherents entered; and as he rose, and came forward and bowed in acceptance of their salutation, it was with a dignified courtesy which at once supplied whatever was deficient in external pomp, and converted the wretched garret into a saloon worthy of the occasion.

It is needless to add, that he was the same personage already introduced in the character of Father Buonaventure, by which name he was distinguished at Fairladies. His dress was not different from what he then wore, excepting that he had a loose riding-coat of camlet, under which he carried an efficient cut-and-thrust sword, instead of his walking rapier, and also a pair of pistols.

Redgauntlet presented to him successively the young Lord ——, and his kinsman, Sir Arthur Darsie Redgauntlet, who trembled as, bowing and kissing his hand, he found himself surprised into what might be construed an act of high treason, which yet he saw no safe means to avoid.

Sir Richard Glendale seemed personally known to Charles Edward, who received him with a mixture of dignity and affection, and seemed to sympathize with the tears which rushed into that gentleman's eyes as he bid his Majesty welcome to his native kingdom.

'Yes, my good Sir Richard,' said the unfortunate Prince, in a tone melancholy, yet resolved, 'Charles Edward is with his faithful friends once more—not, perhaps, with his former gay hopes which undervalued danger, but with the same determined contempt of the worst which can befall him, in claiming his own rights and those of his country.'

'I rejoice, sire—and yet, alas! I must also grieve, to see you once more on the British shores,' said Sir Richard Glendale, and stopped short—a tumult of contradictory feelings preventing his farther utterance.

'It is the call of my faithful and suffering people which alone could have induced me to take once more the sword in my hand. For my own part, Sir Richard, when I have reflected how many of my loyal and devoted friends perished by the sword and by proscription, or died indigent and neglected in a foreign land, I have often sworn that no view to my personal aggrandizement should again induce me to agitate a title which has cost my followers so dear. But since so many men of worth and honour conceive the cause of England and Scotland to be linked with that of Charles Stewart, I must follow their brave example, and, laying aside all other considerations, once more stand forward as their deliverer. I am, however, come hither upon your invitation; and as you are so completely acquainted with circumstances to which my absence must necessarily have rendered me a stranger, I must be a mere tool in the hands of my friends. I know well I never can refer myself implicitly to more loyal hearts or wiser heads, than Herries Redgauntlet, and Sir Richard Glendale. Give me your advice, then, how we are to proceed, and decide upon the fate of Charles Edward.'

Redgauntlet looked at Sir Richard, as if to say, 'Can you press an additional or unpleasant condition at a moment like this?' And the other shook his head and looked down, as if his resolution was unaltered, and yet as feeling all the delicacy of the situation.

There was a silence, which was broken by the unfortunate representative of an unhappy dynasty, with some appearance of irritation. 'This is strange, gentlemen,' he said; 'you have sent for me from the bosom of my family, to head an adventure of doubt and danger; and when I come, your own minds seem to be still irresolute. I had not expected this on the part of two such men.'

'For me, sire,' said Redgauntlet, 'the steel of my sword is not truer than the temper of my mind.'

'My Lord ——'s and mine are equally so,' said Sir Richard; 'but you had in charge, Mr Redgauntlet, to convey our request to his Majesty, coupled with certain conditions.'

'And I discharged my duty to his Majesty and to you,' said Redgauntlet.

'I looked at no condition, gentlemen,' said their King,* with dignity, 'save that which called me here to assert my rights in person. *That* I have fulfilled at no common risk. Here I stand to keep my word, and I expect of you to be true to yours.'

'There was, or should have been, something more than that in our proposal, please your Majesty,' said Sir Richard. 'There was a condition annexed to it.'

'I saw it not,' said Charles, interrupting him. 'Out of tenderness towards the noble hearts of whom I think so highly, I would neither see nor read any thing which could lessen them in my love and my esteem. Conditions can have no part betwixt Prince and subject.'

'Sire,' said Redgauntlet, kneeling on one knee, 'I see from Sir Richard's countenance he deems it my fault that your Majesty seems ignorant of what your subjects desired that I should communicate to your Majesty. For Heaven's sake! for the sake of all my past services and sufferings, leave not such a stain upon my honour! The note, Number D., of which this is a copy, referred to the painful subject to which Sir Richard again directs your attention.'

'You press upon me gentlemen,' said the Prince, colouring highly, 'recollections, which, as I hold them most alien to your character, I would willingly have banished from my memory. I did not suppose that my loyal subjects would think so poorly of me, as to use my depressed circumstances as a reason for forcing themselves into my domestic privacies, and stipulating arrangements with their

King regarding matters, in which the meanest hinds claim the privilege of thinking for themselves. In affairs of state and public policy, I will ever be guided as becomes a prince, by the advice of my wisest counsellors; in those which regard my private affections, and my domestic arrangements, I claim the same freedom of will which I allow to all my subjects, and without which a crown were less worth wearing than a beggar's bonnet.'

'May it please your Majesty,' said Sir Richard Glendale, 'I see it must be my lot to speak unwilling truths; but believe me, I do so with as much profound respect as deep regret. It is true, we have called you to head a mighty undertaking, and that your Majesty, preferring honour to safety, and the love of your country to your own ease, has condescended to become our leader. But we also pointed out as a necessary and indispensable preparatory step to the achievement of our purpose—and, I must say, as a positive condition of our engaging in it— that an individual, supposed,—I presume not to guess how truly,—to have your Majesty's more intimate confidence, and believed, I will not say on absolute proof, but upon the most pregnant suspicion, to be capable of betraying that confidence to the Elector of Hanover, should be removed from your royal household and society.'

'This is too insolent, Sir Richard!' said Charles Edward. 'Have you inveigled me into your power to bait me in this unseemly manner?—And you, Redgauntlet, why did you suffer matters to come to such a point as this, without making me more distinctly aware what insults were to be practised on me?'

'My gracious Prince,' said Redgauntlet, 'I am so far to blame in this, that I did not think so slight an impediment as that of a woman's society could have really interrupted an undertaking of this magnitude. I am a plain man, sire, and speak but bluntly; I could not have dreamt but what, within the first five minutes of this interview, either Sir Richard and his friends would have ceased to insist upon a condition so ungrateful to your Majesty, or that your Majesty would have sacrificed this unhappy attachment to the sound advice, or even to the over-anxious suspicions, of so many faithful subjects. I saw no entanglement in such a difficulty, which on either side might not have been broken through like a cobweb.'

'You were mistaken, sir,' said Charles Edward, 'entirely mistaken —as much so as you are at this moment, when you think in your heart my refusal to comply with this insolent proposition is dictated by a childish and romantic passion for an individual. I tell you, sir, I could part with that person to-morrow, without an instant's regret— that I have had thoughts of dismissing her from my court, for reasons known to myself; but that I will never betray my rights as a sovereign and a man, by taking this step to secure the favour of any one, or to purchase that allegiance, which, if you owe it to me at all, is due to me as my birthright.'

'I am sorry for this,' said Redgauntlet; 'I hope both your Majesty and Sir Richard will reconsider your resolutions, or forbear this discussion in a conjuncture so pressing. I trust your Majesty will recollect that you are on hostile ground; that our preparations cannot have so far escaped notice as to permit us now with safety to retreat from our purpose; insomuch, that it is with the deepest anxiety of heart I foresee even danger to your own royal person, unless you can generously give your subjects the satisfaction, which Sir Richard seems to think they are obstinate in demanding.'

'And deep indeed your anxiety ought to be,' said the Prince. 'Is it in these circumstances of personal danger in which you expect to overcome a resolution, which is founded on a sense of what is due to me as a man or a prince? If the axe and scaffold were ready before the windows of Whitehall, I would rather tread the same path with my great-grandfather,* than concede the slightest point in which my honour is concerned.'

He spoke these words with a determined accent, and looked around him on the company, all of whom (excepting Darsie, who saw, he thought, a fair period to a most perilous enterprise) seemed in deep anxiety and confusion. At length, Sir Richard spoke in a solemn and melancholy tone.

'If the safety,' he said, 'of poor Richard Glendale were alone concerned in this matter, I have never valued my life enough to weigh it against the slightest point of your Majesty's service. But I am only a messenger—a commissioner, who must execute my trust, and upon whom a thousand voices will cry Curse and woe, if I do it not with fidelity. All of your adherents, even Redgauntlet himself, see certain ruin to this enterprise—the greatest danger to your Majesty's person—the utter destruction of all your party and friends, if they insist not on the point, which, unfortunately, your Majesty is so unwilling to concede. I speak it with a heart full of anguish—with a tongue unable to utter my emotions—but it must be spoken—the fatal truth—that if your royal goodness cannot yield to us a boon which we hold necessary to our security and your own, your Majesty with one word disarms ten thousand men, ready to draw their swords in your behalf; or, to speak yet more plainly, you annihilate even the semblance of a royal party in Great Britain.'

'And why do you not add,' said the Prince, scornfully, 'that the men who have been ready to assume arms in my behalf, will atone for their treason to the Elector, by delivering me up to the fate for which so many proclamations have destined me? Carry my head to

St James's, gentlemen; you will do a more acceptable and a more honourable action, than, having inveigled me into a situation which places me so completely in your power, to dishonour yourselves by propositions which dishonour me.'

'My God, sire!' exclaimed Sir Richard, clasping his hands together, in impatience, 'of what great and inexpiable crime can your Majesty's ancestors have been guilty, that they have been punished by the infliction of judicial blindness on their whole generation!—Come, my Lord ——, we must to our friends.'

'By your leave, Sir Richard,' said the young nobleman, 'not till we have learned what measures can be taken for his Majesty's personal safety.'

'Care not for me, young man,' said Charles Edward; 'when I was in the society of Highland robbers and cattle-drovers, I was safer than I now hold myself among the representatives of the best blood in England.—Farewell, gentlemen—I will shift for myself.'

'This must never be,' said Redgauntlet. 'Let me that brought you to the point of danger, at least provide for your safe retreat.'

So saying, he hastily left the apartment, followed by his nephew. The Wanderer, averting his eyes from Lord —— and Sir Richard Glendale, threw himself into a seat at the upper end of the apartment, while they, in much anxiety, stood together at a distance from him, and conversed in whispers.

CHAPTER XXIII

NARRATIVE CONTINUED

WHEN Redgauntlet left the room, in haste and discomposure, the first person he met on the stair, and indeed so close by the door of the apartment that Darsie thought he must have been listening there, was his attendant Nixon.

'What the devil do you here?' he said, abruptly and sternly.

'I wait your orders,' said Nixon. 'I hope all's right?—excuse my zeal.'

'All is wrong, sir—Where is the seafaring fellow—Ewart—what do you call him?'

'Nanty Ewart, sir—I will carry your commands,' said Nixon.

'I will deliver them myself to him,' said Redgauntlet: 'call him hither.'

'But should your honour leave the presence?' said Nixon, still lingering.

''Sdeath, sir, do you prate to me?' said Redgauntlet, bending his brows. 'I, sir, transact my own business; you, I am told, act by a ragged deputy.'

Without farther answer, Nixon departed, rather disconcerted, as it seemed to Darsie.

'That dog turns insolent and lazy,' said Redgauntlet; 'but I must bear with him for a while.'

A moment after, Nixon returned with Ewart.

'Is this the smuggling fellow?' demanded Redgauntlet.

Nixon nodded.

'Is he sober now?—he was brawling anon.'

'Sober enough for business,' said Nixon.

'Well then, hark ye, Ewart—man your boat with your best hands, and have her by the pier—get your other fellows on board the brig—if you have any cargo left, throw it overboard; it shall be all paid, five times over—and be ready for a start to Wales or the Hebrides, or perhaps for Sweden or Norway.'

Ewart answered sullenly enough, 'Ay, ay, sir.'

'Go with him, Nixon,' said Redgauntlet, forcing himself to speak with some appearance of cordiality to the servant with whom he was offended; 'see he does his duty.'

Ewart left the house sullenly, followed by Nixon. The sailor was just in that species of drunken humour which made him jealous, passionate, and troublesome, without showing any other disorder than that of irritability. As he walked towards the beach he kept muttering to himself, but in such a tone that his companion lost not a word, 'Smuggling fellow—Ay, smuggler—and, start your cargo into the sea—and be ready to start for the Hebrides, or Sweden—or the devil, I suppose.—Well, and what if I said in answer—Rebel, Jacobite—traitor—I'll make you and your d—d confederates walk the plank—I have seen better men do it—half-a-score of a morning—when I was across the Line.'*

'D—d unhandsome terms those Redgauntlet used to you, brother,' said Nixon.

'Which do you mean?' said Ewart, starting, and recollecting himself. 'I have been at my old trade of thinking aloud, have I?'

'No matter,' answered Nixon, 'none but a friend heard you. You cannot have forgotten how Redgauntlet disarmed you this morning?'

'Why, I would bear no malice about that—only he is so cursedly high and saucy,' said Ewart.

'And then,' said Nixon, 'I know you for a truehearted Protestant.'

'That I am, by G—,' said Ewart. 'No, the Spaniards could never get my religion from me.'

'And a friend to King George, and the Hanover line of succession,' said Nixon, still walking and speaking very slow.

'You may swear I am, excepting in the way of business, as Turnpenny says. I like King George, but I can't afford to pay duties.'

'You are outlawed, I believe?' said Nixon.

'Am I?—faith, I believe I am,' said Ewart. 'I wish I were *inlawed* again with all my heart—But come along, we must get all ready for our peremptory gentleman, I suppose.'

'I will teach you a better trick,' said Nixon. 'There is a bloody pack of rebels yonder.'

'Ay, we all know that,' said the smuggler; 'but the snowball's melting, I think.'

'There is some one yonder, whose head is worth—thirty—thousand—pounds—of sterling money,' said Nixon, pausing between each word, as if to enforce the magnificence of the sum.

'And what of that?' said Ewart, quickly.

'Only that if, instead of lying by the pier with your men on their oars, if you will just carry your boat on board just now, and take no notice of any signal from the shore, by G—d, Nanty Ewart, I will make a man of you for life!'

'Oh, ho! then the Jacobite gentry are not so safe as they think themselves?' said Nanty.

'In an hour or two,' replied Nixon, 'they will be made safer in Carlisle Castle.'

'The devil they will!' said Ewart; 'and you have been the informer, I suppose?'

'Yes; I have been ill paid for my service among the Redgauntlets—have scarce got dog's wages—and been treated worse than ever dog was used. I have the old fox and his cubs in the same trap now, Nanty; and we'll see how a certain young lady will look then. You see I am frank with you, Nanty.'

'And I will be as frank with you,' said the smuggler. 'You are a d—d old scoundrel—traitor to the man whose bread you eat! Me help to betray poor devils, that have been so often betrayed myself!—Not if they were a hundred Popes, Devils, and Pretenders. I will back and tell them their danger—they are part of cargo—regularly invoiced—put under my charge by the owners—I'll back'——

'You are not stark mad?' said Nixon, who now saw he had miscalculated in supposing Nanty's wild ideas of honour and fidelity could be shaken even by resentment, or by his Protestant partialities. 'You shall not go back—it is all a joke.'

'I'll back to Redgauntlet, and see whether it is a joke he will laugh at.'

'My life is lost if you do,' said Nixon—'hear reason.'

They were in a clump or cluster of tall furze at the moment they were speaking, about half way between the pier and the house, but not in a direct line, from which Nixon, whose object it was to gain time, had induced Ewart to diverge insensibly.

He now saw the necessity of taking a desperate resolution. 'Hear reason,' he said; and added, as Nanty still endeavoured to pass him, 'Or else hear this!' discharging a pocket-pistol into the unfortunate man's body.

Nanty staggered, but kept his feet. 'It has cut my back-bone asunder,' he said; 'you have done me the last good office, and I will not die ungrateful.'

As he uttered the last words, he collected his remaining strength, stood firm for an instant, drew his hanger, and fetching a stroke with both hands, cut Cristal Nixon down. The blow, struck with all the energy of a desperate and dying man, exhibited a force to which Ewart's exhausted frame might have seemed inadequate;—it cleft the hat which the wretch wore, though secured by a plate of iron within the lining, bit deep into his skull, and there left a fragment of the weapon, which was broke by the fury of the blow.

One of the seamen of the lugger, who strolled up, attracted by the firing of the pistol, though, being a small one, the report was very trifling, found both the unfortunate men stark dead. Alarmed at what he saw, which he conceived to have been the consequence of some unsuccessful engagement betwixt his late commander and a revenue officer, (for Nixon chanced not to be personally known to him,) the sailor hastened back to the boat, in order to apprize his comrades of Nanty's fate, and to advise them to take off themselves and the vessel.

Meantime Redgauntlet, having, as we have seen, dispatched Nixon for the purpose of securing a retreat for the unfortunate Charles in case of extremity, returned to the apartment where he had left the Wanderer. He now found him alone.

'Sir Richard Glendale,' said the unfortunate Prince, 'with his young friend, has gone to consult their adherents now in the house. Redgauntlet, my friend, I will not blame you for the circumstances in which I find myself, though I am at once placed in danger, and rendered contemptible. But you ought to have stated to me more strongly the weight which these gentlemen attached to their insolent proposition. You should have told me that no compromise would have any effect—that they desired, not a Prince to govern them, but one, on the contrary, over whom they were to exercise restraint on all occasions, from the highest affairs of the state, down to the most intimate and closest concerns of his own privacy, which the most ordinary men desire to keep secret, and sacred from interference.'

'God knows,' said Redgauntlet, in much agitation, 'I acted for the best when I pressed your Majesty to come hither—I never thought that your Majesty, at such a crisis, would have scrupled, when a kingdom was in view, to sacrifice an attachment, which'——

'Peace, sir!' said Charles; 'it is not for you to estimate my feelings upon such a subject.'

Redgauntlet coloured high, and bowed profoundly. 'At least,' he resumed, 'I hoped that some middle way might be found, and it shall—and must—Come with me, nephew. We will to these gentlemen, and I am confident I shall bring back heart-stirring tidings.'

'I will do much to comply with them, Redgauntlet. I am loath, having again set my foot on British land, to quit it without a blow for my right. But this which they demand of me is a degradation, and compliance is impossible.'

Redgauntlet, followed by his nephew, the unwilling spectator of this extraordinary scene, left once more the apartment of the adventurous Wanderer, and was met on the top of the stairs by Joe Crackenthorp. 'Where are the other gentlemen?' he said.

'Yonder, in the west barrack,' answered Joe; 'but, Master Ingoldsby,'—that was the name by which Redgauntlet was most generally known in Cumberland,—'I wished to say to you that I must put yonder folk together in one room.'

'What folk?' said Redgauntlet, impatiently.

'Why, them prisoner stranger folk, as you bid Cristal Nixon look after. Lord love you! this is a large house enow, but we cannot have separate lock-ups for folk, as they have in Newgate or in Bedlam.

Yonder's a mad beggar, that is to be a great man when he wins a lawsuit, Lord help him!—Yonder's a Quaker and a lawyer charged with a riot; and, ecod, I must make one key and one lock keep them, for we are chokeful, and you have sent off old Nixon, that could have given one some help in this confusion. Besides, they take up every one a room, and call for noughts on earth,—excepting the old man, who calls lustily enough,—but he has not a penny to pay shot.'

'Do as thou wilt with them,' said Redgauntlet, who had listened impatiently to his statement; 'so thou dost but keep them from getting out and making some alarm in the country, I care not.'

'A Quaker and a lawyer!' said Darsie. 'This must be Fairford and Geddes.—Uncle, I must request of you'——

'Nay, nephew,' interrupted Redgauntlet, 'this is no time for asking questions. You shall yourself decide upon their fate in the course of an hour—no harm whatever is designed them.'

So saying, he hurried towards the place where the Jacobite gentlemen were holding their council, and Darsie followed him, in the hope that the obstacle which had arisen to the prosecution of their desperate adventure would prove unsurmountable, and spare him the necessity of a dangerous and violent rupture with his uncle. The discussions among them were very eager; the more daring part of the conspirators, who had little but life to lose, being desirous to proceed at all hazards; while the others, whom a sense of honour and a hesitation to disavow long-cherished principles had brought forward, were perhaps not ill satisfied to have a fair apology for declining an adventure, into which they had entered with more of reluctance than zeal.

Meanwhile Joe Crackenthorp, availing himself of the hasty permission attained from Redgauntlet, proceeded to assemble in one apartment those whose safe custody had been thought necessary; and without much considering the propriety of the matter, he selected for the common place of confinement, the room which Lilias had since her brother's departure occupied alone. It had a strong lock, and was double-hinged, which probably led to the preference assigned to it as a place of security.

Into this, Joe, with little ceremony, and a good deal of noise, introduced the Quaker and Fairford; the first descanting on the immorality, the other on the illegality, of his proceedings; and he turning a deaf ear both to the one and the other. Next he pushed in, almost in headlong fashion, the unfortunate litigant, who having made some resistance at the threshold, had received a violent thrust in consequence, and came rushing forward, like a ram in the act of charging, with such impetus, as must have carried him to the top of the room, and struck the cocked hat which sat perched on the top of his tow wig against Miss Redgauntlet's person, had not the honest Quaker interrupted his career by seizing him by the collar, and bringing him to a stand. 'Friend,' said he, with the real good-breeding which so often subsists independently of ceremonial, 'thou art no company for that young person; she is, thou seest, frightened at our being so suddenly thrust in hither; and although that be no fault of ours, yet it will become us to behave civilly towards her. Wherefore come thou with me to this window, and I will tell thee what it concerns thee to know.'

'And what for should I no speak to the leddy, friend?' said Peter, who was now about half seas over. 'I have spoke to leddies before now, man—What for should she be frightened at me?—I am nae bogle, I ween.—What are ye pooin' me that gate for?—Ye will rive my coat, and I will have a good action for having myself made *sartum atque tectum* at your expenses.'

Notwithstanding this threat, Mr Geddes, whose muscles were as strong as his judgment was sound and his temper sedate, led Poor Peter, under the sense of a control against which he could not struggle, to the farther corner of the apartment, where, placing him, whether he would or no, in a chair, he sat down beside him, and effectually prevented his annoying the young lady, upon whom he had seemed bent on conferring the delights of his society.

If Peter had immediately recognised his counsel learned in the law, it is probable that not even the benevolent efforts of the Quaker could have kept him in a state of restraint; but Fairford's back was turned towards his client, whose optics, besides being somewhat dazzled with ale and brandy, were speedily engaged in contemplating a half-crown which Joshua held between his finger and his thumb, saying, at the same time, 'Friend, thou art indigent and improvident. This will, well employed, procure thee sustentation of nature for more than a single day; and I will bestow it on thee if thou wilt sit here and keep me company; for neither thou nor I, friend, are fit company for ladies.'

'Speak for yourself, friend,' said Peter, scornfully; 'I was aye kend to be agreeable to the fair sex; and when I was in business I served the leddies wi' anither sort of decorum than Plainstanes, the d—d awkward scoundrel! It was one of the articles of dittay between us.'

'Well, but, friend,' said the Quaker, who observed that the young lady still seemed to fear Peter's intrusion, 'I wish to hear thee speak about this great lawsuit of thine, which has been matter of such celebrity.'

'Celebrity?—Ye may swear that,' said Peter, for the string was touched to which his crazy imagination always vibrated. 'And I dinna wonder that folk that judge things by their outward grandeur, should think me something worth their envying. It's very true that it is grandeur upon earth to hear ane's name thunnered out along the long-arched roof of the Outer-House,—"*Poor* Peter Peebles against Plainstanes, *et per contra;*" a' the best lawyers in the house fleeing like eagles to the prey; some because they are in the cause, and some because they want to be thought engaged (for there are tricks in other trades by selling muslins*)—to see the reporters mending their pens to take down the debate—the Lords themselves pooin' in their chairs, like folk sitting down to a gude dinner, and crying on the clerks for parts and pendicles of the process, who, puir bodies, can do little mair than cry on their closet-keepers to help them. To see a' this,' continued Peter, in a tone of sustained rapture, 'and to ken that naething will be said or dune amang a' thae grand folk, for maybe the feck of three hours, saving what concerns you and your business—O, man, nae wonder that ye judge this to be earthly glory!—And yet, neighbour, as I was saying, there be unco draw-backs—I whiles think of my bit house, where dinner, and supper, and breakfast, used to come without the crying for, just as if fairies had brought it—and the gude bed at e'en— and the needfu' penny in the pouch.—And then to see a' ane's warldly substance capering in the air in a pair of weigh-bauks, now up, now down, as the breath of judge or counsel inclines it for pursuer or defender,—troth, man, there are times I rue having ever begun the plea wark, though, maybe, when ye consider the renown and credit I have by it, ye will hardly believe what I am saying.'

'Indeed, friend,' said Joshua, with a sigh, 'I am glad thou hast found any thing in the legal contention which compensates thee for poverty and hunger; but I believe, were other human objects of ambition looked upon as closely, their advantages would be found as chimerical as those attending thy protracted litigation.'

'But never mind, friend,' said Peter, 'I'll tell you the exact state of the conjunct processes, and make you sensible that I can bring mysell round with a wet finger, now I have my finger and my thumb on this loup-the-dike loon, the lad Fairford.'

Alan Fairford was in the act of speaking to the masked lady, (for Miss Redgauntlet had retained her riding vizard,) endeavouring to assure her, as he perceived her anxiety, of such protection as he could afford, when his own name, pronounced in a loud tone, attracted his attention. He looked round, and, seeing Peter Peebles, as hastily turned to avoid his notice, in which he succeeded, so earnest was Peter upon his colloquy with one of the most respectable auditors whose attention he had ever been able to engage. And by this little motion, momentary as it was, Alan gained an unexpected advantage; for while he looked round, Miss Lilias, I could never ascertain why, took the moment to adjust her mask, and did it so awkwardly, that when her companion again turned his head, he recognised as much of her features as authorized him to address her as his fair client, and to press his offers of protection and assistance with the boldness of a former acquaintance.

Lilias Redgauntlet withdrew the mask from her crimsoned cheek. 'Mr Fairford,' she said, in a voice almost inaudible, 'you have the character of a young gentleman of sense and generosity; but we have already met in one situation which you must think singular; and I must be exposed to misconstruction, at least, for my forwardness, were it not in a cause in which my dearest affections were concerned.'

'Any interest in my beloved friend Darsie Latimer,' said Fairford, stepping a little back, and putting a marked restraint upon his former advances, 'gives me a double right to be useful to'——. He stopped short.

'To his sister, your goodness would say,' answered Lilias.

'His sister, madam!' replied Alan, in the extremity of astonishment —'Sister, I presume, in affection only?'

'No, sir; my dear brother Darsie and I are connected by the bonds of actual relationship; and I am not sorry to be the first to tell this to the friend he most values.'

Fairford's first thought was on the violent passion which Darsie had expressed towards the fair unknown. 'Good God!' he exclaimed, 'how did he bear the discovery?'

'With resignation, I hope,' said Lilias, smiling. 'A more accomplished sister he might easily have come by, but scarcely could have found one who could love him more than I do.'

'I meant—I only meant to say,' said the young counsellor, his presence of mind failing him for an instant—'that is, I meant to ask where Darsie Latimer is at this moment.'

'In this very house, and under the guardianship of his uncle, whom I believe you knew as a visitor of your father, under the name of Mr Herries of Birrenswork.'

'Let me hasten to him,' said Fairford; 'I have sought him through difficulties and dangers—I must see him instantly.'

'You forget you are a prisoner,' said the young lady.

'True—true; but I cannot be long detained—the cause alleged is too ridiculous.'

'Alas!' said Lilias, 'our fate—my brother's and mine, at least—must turn on the deliberations perhaps of less than an hour.—For you, sir, I believe and apprehend nothing but some restraint; my uncle is neither cruel nor unjust, though few will go farther in the cause which he has adopted.'

'Which is that of the Pretend—'

'For God's sake speak lower!' said Lilias, approaching her hand, as if to stop him. 'The word may cost you your life. You do not know—indeed you do not—the terrors of the situation in which we at present stand, and in which I fear you also are involved by your friendship for my brother.'

'I do not indeed know the particulars of our situation,' said Fairford; 'but, be the danger what it may, I shall not grudge my share of it for the sake of my friend; or,' he added, with more timidity, 'of my friend's sister. Let me hope,' he said, 'my dear Miss Latimer, that my presence may be of some use to you; and that it may be so, let me entreat a share of your confidence, which I am conscious I have otherwise no right to ask.'

He led her, as he spoke, towards the recess of the farther window of the room, and observing to her that, unhappily, he was particularly exposed to interruption from the mad old man whose entrance had alarmed her, he disposed of Darsie Latimer's riding-skirt, which had been left in the apartment, over the back of two chairs, forming thus a sort of screen, behind which he ensconced himself with the maiden of the green mantle; feeling at the moment, that the danger in which he was placed was almost compensated by the intelligence which permitted those feelings towards her to revive, which justice to his friend had induced him to stifle in the birth.

The relative situation of adviser and advised, of protector and protected, is so peculiarly suited to the respective condition of man and woman, that great progress towards intimacy is often made in very short space; for the circumstances call for confidence on the part of the gentleman, and forbid coyness on that of the lady, so that the usual barriers against easy intercourse are at once thrown down.

Under these circumstances, securing themselves as far as possible from observation, conversing in whispers, and seated in a corner, where they were brought into so close contact that their faces nearly touched each other, Fairford heard from Lilias Redgauntlet the history of her family, particularly of her uncle; his views upon her brother, and the agony which she felt, lest at that very moment he might succeed in engaging Darsie in some desperate scheme, fatal to his fortune, and perhaps to his life.

Alan Fairford's acute understanding instantly connected what he had heard with the circumstances he had witnessed at Fairladies. His first thought was, to attempt, at all risks, his instant escape, and procure assistance powerful enough to crush, in the very cradle, a conspiracy of such a determined character. This he did not consider as difficult; for, though the door was guarded on the outside, the window, which was not above ten feet from the ground, was open for escape, the common on which it looked was unenclosed, and profusely covered with furze. There would, he thought, be little difficulty in effecting his liberty, and in concealing his course after he had gained it.

But Lilias exclaimed against this scheme. Her uncle, she said, was a man, who, in his moments of enthusiasm, knew neither remorse nor fear. He was capable of visiting upon Darsie any injury which he might conceive Fairford had rendered him—he was her near kinsman also, and not an unkind one, and she deprecated any effort, even in her brother's favour, by which his life must be exposed to danger. Fairford himself remembered Father Buonaventure, and made little question but that he was one of the sons of the old Chevalier de Saint George; and with feelings which, although contradictory of his public duty, can hardly be much censured, his heart recoiled from being the agent by whom the last scion of such a long line of Scottish Princes should be rooted up. He then thought of obtaining an audience, if possible, of this devoted person, and explaining to him the utter hopelessness of his undertaking, which he judged it likely that the ardour of his partisans might have concealed from him. But he relinquished this design as soon as formed. He had no doubt, that any light which he could throw on the state of the country, would come too late to be serviceable to one who was always reported to have his own full share of the hereditary obstinacy which had cost his ancestors so dear, and who, in drawing the sword, must have thrown from him the scabbard.

Lilias suggested the advice which, of all others, seemed most suited to the occasion, that yielding, namely, to the circumstances of their situation, they should watch carefully when Darsie should obtain any degree of freedom, and endeavour to open a communication with him, in which case their joint flight might be effected, and without endangering the safety of any one.

Their youthful deliberation had nearly fixed in this point, when Fairford, who was listening to the low sweet whispering tones of Lilias Redgauntlet, rendered yet more interesting by some slight touch of foreign accent, was startled by a heavy hand which descended with full weight on his shoulder, while the discordant voice of Peter Peebles, who had at length broken loose from the well-meaning Quaker, exclaimed in the ear of his truant counsel—'Aha, lad! I think ye are catched—An' so ye are turned chamber-counsel, are ye?—And ye have drawn up wi' clients in scarfs and hoods? But bide a wee, billie, and see if I dinna sort ye when my petition and complaint comes to be discussed, with or without answers, under certification.'

Alan Fairford had never more difficulty in his life to subdue a first emotion, than he had to refrain from knocking down the crazy blockhead who had broke in upon him at such a moment. But the length of Peter's address gave him time, fortunately perhaps for both parties, to reflect on the extreme irregularity of such a proceeding. He stood silent, however, with vexation, while Peter went on.

'Weel, my bonnie man, I see ye are thinking shame o' yoursell, and nae great wonder. Ye maun leave this quean—the like of her is ower light company for you. I have heard honest Mr Pest say, that the gown grees ill wi' the petticoat. But come awa hame to your puir father, and I'll take care of you the haill gate, and keep you company, and deil a word we will speak about, but just the state of the conjoined processes of the great cause of Poor Peebles against Plainstanes.'

'If thou canst endure to hear as much of that suit, friend,' said the Quaker, 'as I have heard out of mere compassion for thee, I think verily thou wilt soon be at the bottom of the matter, unless it be altogether bottomless.'

Fairford shook off, rather indignantly, the large bony hand which Peter had imposed upon his shoulder, and was about to say something peevish, upon so unpleasant and insolent a mode of interruption, when the door opened, a treble voice saying to the sentinel, 'I tell you I maun be in, to see if Mr Nixon's here;' and Little Benjie thrust in his mop-head and keen black eyes. Ere he could withdraw it, Peter Peebles sprang to the door, seized on the boy by the collar, and dragged him forward into the room.

'Let me see it,' he said, 'ye ne'er-do-weel limb of Satan—I'll gar you satisfy the production, I trow—I'll hae first and second diligence against you, ye deevil's buckie!'

'What dost thou want?' said the Quaker, interfering; 'why dost thou frighten the boy, friend Peebles?'

'I gave the bastard a penny to buy me snuff,' said the pauper, 'and he has rendered no account of his intromissions; but I'll gar him as gude.'

So saying, he proceeded forcibly to rifle the pockets of Benjie's ragged jacket, of one or two snares for game, marbles, a half-bitten apple, two stolen eggs, (one of which Peter broke in the eagerness of his research,) and various other unconsidered trifles, which had not the air of being very honestly come by. The little rascal, under this discipline, bit and struggled like a fox-cub, but, like that vermin, uttered neither cry nor complaint, till a note, which Peter tore from his bosom, flew as far as Lilias Redgauntlet, and fell at her feet. It was addressed to C. N.

'It is for the villain Nixon,' she said to Alan Fairford; 'open it without scruple; that boy is his emissary; we shall now see what the miscreant is driving at.'

Little Benjie now gave up all farther struggle, and suffered Peebles to take from him, without resistance, a shilling, out of which Peter declared he would pay himself principal and interest, and account for the balance. The boy, whose attention seemed fixed on something very different, only said, 'Maister Nixon will murder me!'

Alan Fairford did not hesitate to read the little scrap of paper, on which was written, 'All is prepared—keep them in play until I come up—You may depend on your reward.—C. C.'

'Alas, my uncle—my poor uncle!' said Lilias; 'this is the result of his confidence! Methinks, to give him instant notice of his confidant's treachery, is now the best service we can render all concerned—if they break up their undertaking, as they must now do, Darsie will be at liberty.'

In the same breath, they were both at the half-opened door of the room, Fairford entreating to speak with the Father Buonaventure, and Lilias, equally vehemently, requesting a moment's interview with her uncle. While the sentinel hesitated what to do, his attention was called to a loud noise at the door, where a crowd had been assembled in consequence of the appalling cry, that the enemy were upon them, occasioned, as it afterwards proved, by some stragglers having at length discovered the dead bodies of Nanty Ewart and of Nixon.

Amid the confusion occasioned by this alarming incident, the sentinel ceased to attend to his duty; and, accepting Alan Fairford's arm, Lilias found no opposition in penetrating even to the inner apartment, where the principal persons in the enterprise, whose conclave had been disturbed by this alarming incident, were now assembled in great confusion, and had been joined by the Chevalier himself.

'Only a mutiny among these smuggling scoundrels,' said Redgauntlet.

'*Only* a mutiny, do you say?' said Sir Richard Glendale; 'and the lugger, the last hope of escape for'—he looked towards Charles,—'stands out to sea under a press of sail!'

'Do not concern yourself about me,' said the unfortunate Prince; 'this is not the worst emergency in which it has been my lot to stand; and if it were, I fear it not. Shift for yourselves, my lords and gentlemen.'

'No, never!' said the young Lord——. 'Our only hope now is in an honourable resistance.'

'Most true,' said Redgauntlet; 'let despair renew the union amongst us which accident disturbed. I give my voice for displaying the royal banner instantly, and——How now!' he concluded, sternly, as Lilias, first soliciting his attention by pulling his cloak, put into his hand the scroll, and added, it was designed for that of Nixon.

Redgauntlet read—and, dropping it on the ground, continued to stare upon the spot where it fell, with raised hands and fixed eyes. Sir Richard Glendale lifted the fatal paper, read it, and saying, 'Now all is indeed over,' handed it to Maxwell, who said aloud, 'Black Colin Campbell,* by G—d! I heard he had come post from London last night.'

As if in echo to his thoughts, the violin of the blind man was heard, playing with spirit, 'The Campbells are coming,'* a celebrated clan-march.

'The Campbells are coming in earnest,' said MacKellar; 'they are upon us with the whole battalion from Carlisle.'

There was a silence of dismay, and two or three of the company began to drop out of the room.

Lord —— spoke with the generous spirit of a young English nobleman. 'If we have been fools, do not let us be cowards. We have one here more precious than us all, and come hither on our warranty—let us save him at least.'

'True, most true,' answered Sir Richard Glendale. 'Let the King be first cared for.'

'That shall be my business,' said Redgauntlet; 'if we have but time to bring back the brig, all will be well—I will instantly dispatch a party in a fishing skiff to bring her to.'—He gave his commands to two or three of the most active among his followers.—'Let him be once on board,' he said, 'and there are enough of us to stand to arms and cover his retreat.'

'Right, right,' said Sir Richard, 'and I will look to points which can be made defensible; and the old powder-plot boys* could not have made a more desperate resistance than we shall.—Redgauntlet,' continued he, 'I see some of our friends are looking pale; but methinks your nephew has more mettle in his eye now than when we were in cold deliberation, with danger at a distance.'

'It is the way of our house,' said Redgauntlet; 'our courage ever kindles highest on the losing side. I, too, feel that the catastrophe I have brought on must not be survived by its author. Let me first,' he said, addressing Charles, 'see your Majesty's sacred person in such safety as can now be provided for it, and then'——

'You may spare all considerations concerning me, gentlemen,' again repeated Charles; 'yon mountain of Criffel shall fly as soon as I will.'

Most threw themselves at his feet with weeping and entreaty; some one or two slunk in confusion from the apartment, and were heard riding off. Unnoticed in such a scene, Darsie, his sister, and Fairford, drew together, and held each other by the hands, as those who, when a vessel is about to founder in the storm, determine to take their chance of life and death together.

Amid this scene of confusion, a gentleman, plainly dressed in a riding-habit, with a black cockade in his hat, but without any arms except a *couteau-de-chasse*, walked into the apartment without ceremony. He was a tall, thin, gentlemanly man, with a look and bearing decidedly military. He had passed through their guards, if in the confusion they now maintained any, without stop or question, and now stood, almost unarmed, among armed men, who, nevertheless, gazed on him as on the angel of destruction.

'You look coldly on me, gentlemen,' he said. 'Sir Richard Glendale—my Lord ——, we were not always such strangers. Ha, Pate-in-Peril, how is it with you? and you, too, Ingoldsby—I must not call you by any other name—why do you receive an old friend so coldly? But you guess my errand.'

'And are prepared for it, General,' said Redgauntlet; 'we are not men to be penned up like sheep for the slaughter.'

'Pshaw! you take it too seriously—let me speak but one word with you.'

'No words can shake our purpose,' said Redgauntlet, 'were your whole command, as I suppose is the case, drawn round the house.'

'I am certainly not unsupported,' said the General; 'but if you would hear me'——

'Hear *me*, sir,' said the Wanderer, stepping forward; 'I suppose I am the mark you aim at—I surrender myself willingly, to save these gentlemen's danger—let this at least avail in their favour.'

An exclamation of 'Never, never!' broke from the little body of partisans, who threw themselves round the unfortunate Prince, and would have seized or struck down Campbell, had it not been that he remained with his arms folded, and a look, rather indicating impatience because they would not hear him, than the least apprehension of violence at their hand.

At length he obtained a moment's silence. 'I do not,' he said, 'know this gentleman'—(Making a profound bow to the unfortunate Prince)—'I do not wish to know him; it is a knowledge which would suit neither of us.'

'Our ancestors, nevertheless, have been well acquainted,' said Charles, unable to suppress, even in that hour of dread and danger, the painful recollections of fallen royalty.

'In one word, General Campbell,' said Redgauntlet, 'is it to be peace or war?—You are a man of honour, and we can trust you.'

'I thank you, sir,' said the General; 'and I reply that the answer to your question rests with yourself. Come, do not be fools, gentlemen; there was perhaps no great harm meant or intended by your gathering together in this obscure corner, for a bear-bait or a cock-fight, or whatever other amusement you may have intended; but it was a little imprudent, considering how you stand with government, and it has occasioned some anxiety. Exaggerated accounts of your purpose have been laid before government by the information of a traitor in your own counsels; and I was sent down post to take the command of a sufficient number of troops, in case these calumnies should be found to have any real foundation. I have come here, of course, sufficiently supported both with cavalry and infantry, to do whatever might be necessary; but my commands are—and I am sure they agree with my inclination—to make no arrests, nay, to make no farther enquiries of any kind, if this good assembly will consider their own interest so far as to give up their immediate purpose, and return quietly home to their own houses.'

'What!—all?' exclaimed Sir Richard Glendale—'all, without exception?'

'ALL, without one single exception,' said the General; 'such are my orders. If you accept my terms, say so, and make haste; for things may happen to interfere with his Majesty's kind purposes towards you all.'

'His Majesty's kind purposes!' said the Wanderer. 'Do I hear you aright, sir?'

'I speak the King's very words, from his very lips,' replied the General. '"I will," said his Majesty, "deserve the confidence of my subjects by reposing my security in the fidelity of the millions who acknowledge my title—in the good sense and prudence of the few who continue, from the errors of education, to disown it."—His Majesty will not even believe that the most zealous Jacobites who yet remain can nourish a thought of exciting a civil war, which must be fatal to their families and themselves, besides spreading bloodshed and ruin through a peaceful land. He cannot even believe of his kinsman, that he would engage brave and generous, though mistaken men, in an attempt which must ruin all who have escaped former calamities; and he is convinced, that, did curiosity or any other motive lead that person to visit this country, he would soon see it was his wisest course to return to the continent; and his Majesty compassionates his situation too much to offer any obstacle to his doing so.'

'Is this real?' said Redgauntlet. 'Can you mean this?—Am I—are all, are any of these gentlemen at liberty, without interruption, to embark in yonder brig, which, I see, is now again approaching the shore?'

'You, sir—all—any of the gentlemen present,' said the General,—'all whom the vessel can contain, are at liberty to embark uninterrupted by me; but I advise none to go off who have not powerful reasons, unconnected with the present meeting, for this will be remembered against no one.'

'Then, gentlemen,' said Redgauntlet, clasping his hands together as the words burst from him, 'the cause is lost for ever!'

General Campbell turned away to the window, as if to avoid hearing what they said. Their consultation was but momentary; for the door of escape which thus opened was as unexpected as the exigence was threatening.

'We have your word of honour for our protection,' said Sir Richard Glendale, 'if we dissolve our meeting in obedience to your summons?'

'You have, Sir Richard,' answered the General.

'And I also have your promise,' said Redgauntlet, 'that I may go on board yonder vessel, with any friend whom I may choose to accompany me?'

'Not only that, Mr Ingoldsby—or I *will* call you Redgauntlet once more—you may stay in the offing for a tide, until you are joined by any person who may remain at Fairladies. After that, there will be a sloop of war on the station, and I need not say your condition will then become perilous.'

'Perilous it should not be, General Campbell,' said Redgauntlet, 'or more perilous to others than to us, if others thought as I do even in this extremity.'

'You forget yourself, my friend,' said the unhappy Adventurer; 'you forget that the arrival of this gentleman only puts the copestone on our already adopted resolution to abandon our bull-fight, or by whatever other wild name this headlong enterprise may be termed. I bid you farewell, unfriendly friends—I bid *you* farewell,' (bowing to the General,) 'my friendly foe—I leave this strand as I landed upon it, alone, and to return no more!'

'Not alone,' said Redgauntlet, 'while there is blood in the veins of my father's son.'

'Not alone,' said the other gentlemen present, stung with feelings which almost overpowered the better reasons under which they had acted. 'We will not disown our principles, or see your person endangered.'

'If it be only your purpose to see the gentleman to the beach,' said General Campbell, 'I will myself go with you. My presence among you, unarmed, and in your power, will be a pledge of my friendly intentions, and will overawe, should such be offered, any interruption on the part of officious persons.'

'Be it so,' said the Adventurer, with the air of a Prince to a subject; not of one who complied with the request of an enemy too powerful to be resisted.

They left the apartment—they left the house—an unauthenticated and dubious, but appalling, sensation of terror had already spread itself among the inferior retainers, who had so short time before strutted, and bustled, and thronged the doorway and the passages. A report had arisen, of which the origin could not be traced, of troops advancing towards the spot in considerable numbers; and men who, for one reason or other, were most of them amenable to the arm of power, had either shrunk into stables or corners, or fled the place entirely. There was solitude on the landscape, excepting the small party which now moved towards the rude pier, where a boat lay manned, agreeably to Redgauntlet's orders previously given.

The last heir of the Stewarts* leant on Redgauntlet's arm as they walked towards the beach; for the ground was rough, and he no longer possessed the elasticity of limb and of spirit which had, twenty years before, carried him over many a Highland hill, as light as one of their native deer. His adherents followed, looking on the ground, their feelings struggling against the dictates of their reason.

General Campbell accompanied them with an air of apparent ease and indifference, but watching, at the same time, and no doubt with some anxiety, the changing features of those who acted in this extraordinary scene.

Darsie and his sister naturally followed their uncle, whose violence they no longer feared, while his character attracted their respect; and Alan Fairford accompanied them from interest in their fate, unnoticed in a party where all were too much occupied with their own thoughts and feelings, as well as with the impending crisis, to attend to his presence.

Half way betwixt the house and the beach, they saw the bodies of Nanty Ewart and Cristal Nixon blackening in the sun.

'That was your informer?' said Redgauntlet, looking back to General Campbell, who only nodded his assent.

'Caitiff wretch!' exclaimed Redgauntlet;—'and yet the name were better bestowed on the fool who could be misled by thee.'

'That sound broadsword cut,' said the General, 'has saved us the shame of rewarding a traitor.'

They arrived at the place of embarkation. The Prince stood a moment with folded arms, and looked around him in deep silence. A paper was then slipped into his hands—he looked at it, and said, 'I find the two friends I have left at Fairladies are apprized of my destination, and propose to embark from Bowness. I presume this will not be an infringement of the conditions under which you have acted?'

'Certainly not,' answered General Campbell; 'they shall have all facility to join you.'

'I wish, then,' said Charles, 'only another companion.—Redgauntlet, the air of this country is as hostile to you as it is to me.

These gentlemen have made their peace, or rather they have done nothing to break it. But you—come you, and share my home where chance shall cast it. We shall never see these shores again; but we will talk of them, and of our disconcerted bull-fight.'

'I follow you, Sire, through life,' said Redgauntlet, 'as I would have followed you to death. Permit me one moment.'

The Prince then looked round, and seeing the abashed countenances of his other adherents bent upon the ground, he hastened to say, 'Do not think that you, gentlemen, have obliged me less because your zeal was mingled with prudence, entertained, I am sure, more on my own account, and on that of your country, than from selfish apprehensions.'

He stepped from one to another, and, amid sobs and bursting tears, received the adieus of the last remnant which had hitherto supported his lofty pretensions, and addressed them individually with accents of tenderness and affection.

The General drew a little aloof, and signed to Redgauntlet to speak with him while this scene proceeded. 'It is now all over,' he said, 'and Jacobite will be henceforward no longer a party name. When you tire of foreign parts, and wish to make your peace, let me know. Your restless zeal alone has impeded your pardon hitherto.'

'And now I shall not need it,' said Redgauntlet. 'I leave England for ever; but I am not displeased that you should hear my family adieus.—Nephew, come hither. In presence of General Campbell, I tell you, that though to breed you up in my own political opinions has been for many years my anxious wish, I am now glad that it could not be accomplished. You pass under the service of the reigning Monarch without the necessity of changing your allegiance —a change, however,' he added, looking around him, 'which sits more easy on honourable men than I could have anticipated; but some wear the badge of their loyalty on the sleeve, and others in the heart.—You will, from henceforth, be uncontrolled master of all the property of which forfeiture could not deprive your father—of all that belonged to him—excepting this, his good sword,' (laying his hand on the weapon he wore,) 'which shall never fight for the House of Hanover; and as my hand will never draw weapon more, I shall sink it forty fathoms deep in the wide ocean. Bless you, young man! If I have dealt harshly with you, forgive me. I had set my whole desires on one point,—God knows, with no selfish purpose; and I am justly punished by this final termination of my views, for having been too little scrupulous in the means by which I pursued them. Niece, farewell, and may God bless you also!'

'No, sir,' said Lilias, seizing his hand eagerly. 'You have been hitherto my protector,—you are now in sorrow, let me be your attendant and your comforter in exile!'

'I thank you, my girl, for your unmerited affection; but it cannot and must not be. The curtain here falls between us. I go to the house of another—If I leave it before I quit the earth, it shall be only for the House of God. Once more, farewell both!—The fatal doom,' he said, with a melancholy smile, 'will, I trust, now depart from the House of Redgauntlet, since its present representative has adhered to the winning side. I am convinced he will not change it, should it in turn become the losing one.'

The unfortunate Charles Edward had now given his last adieus to his downcast adherents. He made a sign with his hand to Redgauntlet, who came to assist him into the skiff. General Campbell also offered his assistance; the rest appearing too much affected by the scene which had taken place to prevent him.

'You are not sorry, General, to do me this last act of courtesy,' said the Chevalier; 'and, on my part, I thank you for it. You have taught me the principle on which men on the scaffold feel forgiveness and kindness even for their executioner.—Farewell!'

They were seated in the boat, which presently pulled off from the land. The Oxford divine broke out into a loud benediction, in terms which General Campbell was too generous to criticise at the time, or to remember afterwards;—nay, it is said that, Whig and Campbell as he was, he could not help joining in the universal Amen! which resounded from the shore.

CONCLUSION

By Dr DRYASDUST

IN A LETTER TO THE AUTHOR OF WAVERLEY*

I AM truly sorry, my worthy and much-respected sir, that my anxious researches have neither, in the form of letters, nor of diaries, or other memoranda, been able to discover more than I have hitherto transmitted, of the history of the Redgauntlet family. But I observe in an old newspaper called the Whitehall Gazette,* of which I fortunately possess a file for several years, that Sir Arthur Darsie Redgauntlet was presented to his late Majesty* at the drawingroom, by Lieut.-General Campbell—upon which the Editor observes, in the way of comment, that we were going, *remis atque velis*, into the interests of the Pretender, since a Scot had presented a Jacobite at Court. I am sorry I have not room (the frank being only uncial) for his farther observations, tending to show the apprehensions entertained by many well-instructed persons of the period, that the young King might himself be induced to become one of the Stewarts' faction,—a catastrophe from which it has pleased Heaven to preserve these kingdoms.

I perceive also, by a marriage contract in the family repositories, that Miss Lilias Redgauntlet of Redgauntlet, about eighteen months after the transactions you have commemorated, intermarried with Alan Fairford, Esq. Advocate, of Clinkdollar, who, I think, we may not unreasonably conclude to be the same person whose name occurs so frequently in the pages of your narration. In my last excursion to Edinburgh, I was fortunate enough to discover an old cadie, from whom, at the expense of a bottle of whisky, and half a pound of tobacco, I extracted the important information, that he knew Peter Peebles very well, and had drunk many a mutchkin with him in Cadie Fraser's time. He said that he lived ten years after King George's accession, in the momentary expectation of winning his cause every day in the Session time, and every hour in the day, and at last fell down dead, in what my informer called a 'Perplexity fit,' upon a proposal for a composition being made to him in the Outer-House. I have chosen to retain my informer's phrase, not being able justly to determine whether it is a corruption of the word apoplexy, as my friend Mr Oldbuck* supposes, or the name of some peculiar disorder incidental to those who have concern in the Courts of Law, as many callings and conditions of men have diseases appropriate to themselves. The same cadie also remembered Blind Willie Stevenson, who was called Wandering Willie, and who ended his days 'unco beinly, in Sir Arthur Redgauntlet's ha' neuk.' 'He had done the family some good turn,' he said, 'specially when ane of the Argyle gentlemen was coming down on a wheen of them that had the "auld leaven" about them, and wad hae taen every man of them, and nae less nor headed and hanged them. But Willie, and a friend they had, called Robin the Rambler, gae them warning, by playing tunes such as, "the Campbells are coming," and the like, whereby they got timeous warning to take the wing.' I need not point out to your acuteness, my worthy sir, that this seems to refer to some inaccurate account of the transactions in which you seem so much interested.

Respecting Redgauntlet, about whose subsequent history you are more particularly inquisitive, I have learned from an excellent person who was a priest in the Scottish Monastery of Ratisbon,* before its suppression, that he remained for two or three years in the family of the Chevalier, and only left it at last in consequence of some discords in that melancholy household. As he had hinted to General Campbell, he exchanged his residence for the cloister, and displayed in the latter part of his life a strong sense of the duties of religion, which in his earlier days he had too much neglected, being altogether engaged in political speculations and intrigues. He rose to the situation of Prior, in the house which he belonged to, and which was of a very strict order of religion. He sometimes received his countrymen, whom accident brought to Ratisbon, and curiosity induced to visit the Monastery of——. But it was remarked, that though he listened with interest and attention, when Britain, or particularly Scotland, became the subject of conversation, yet he never either introduced or prolonged the subject, never used the English language, never enquired about English affairs, and, above all, never mentioned his own family. His strict observation of the rules of his order gave him, at the time of his death, some pretensions to be chosen a saint, and the brethren of the Monastery of—— made great efforts for that effect, and brought forward some plausible proofs of miracles. But there was a circumstance which threw a doubt over the subject, and prevented the consistory from acceding to the wishes of the worthy brethren. Under his habit, and secured in a small silver box, he had worn perpetually around his neck a lock of hair, which the fathers avouched to be a relic. But the Avocato del Diablo,* in combating (as was his official duty) the pretensions of the candidate for sanctity, made it at least equally probable that the supposed relic was taken from the head of a brother of the deceased Prior, who had been executed for adherence to the Stewart family in 1745–6; and the motto, *Haud obliviscendum*, seemed to intimate a tone of mundane feeling and recollection of injuries, which made it at least doubtful whether, even in the quiet and gloom of the cloister, Father Hugo had forgotten the sufferings and injuries of the House of Redgauntlet.

SCOTT'S NOTES

SCOTT's annotations mainly date from the 'Magnum' edition of 1832, of which the present edition is a reprint. Some few notes appeared in the first edition of 1824 and are indicated here by the date of that edition placed in square brackets after the appropriate note. A few minor points seemed to require elucidation, and this also is provided in square brackets, set apart from Scott's note.

1. The reproach is thus expressed by Dr King, who brings the charge:—'But the most odious part of his character is his love of money, a vice which I do not remember to have been imputed by our historians to any of his ancestors, and is the certain index of a base and little mind. I know it may be urged in his vindication, that a Prince in exile ought to be an economist. And so he ought; but, nevertheless, his purse should be always open as long as there is any thing in it, to relieve the necessities of his friends and adherents. King Charles II., during his banishment, would have shared the last pistole in his pocket with his little family. But I have known this gentleman with two thousand louis-d'ors in his strong-box, pretend he was in great distress, and borrow money from a lady in Paris who was not in affluent circumstances. His most faithful servants, who had closely attended him in all his difficulties, were ill rewarded.'— King's *Memoirs*.
2. The first stage on the road from Edinburgh to Dumfries, *via* Moffat.
3. Break a window, head a skirmish with stones, and hold the bonnet or handkerchief, which used to divide high-school boys when fighting.
4. A pass on the very brink of the Castle-rock to the north, by which it is just possible for a goat, or a high-school boy, to turn the corner of the building where it rises from the edge of the precipice. This was so favourite a feat with the 'hell and neck boys' of the higher classes, that at one time sentinels were posted to prevent its repetition. One of the nine-steps was rendered more secure because the climber could take hold of the root of a nettle, so precarious were the means of passing this celebrated spot. The manning the Cowgate Port, especially in snow-ball time, was also a choice amusement, as it offered an inaccessible station for the boys who used these missiles to the annoyance of the passengers. The gateway is now demolished; and probably most of its garrison lie as low as the fortress. To recollect that the author himself, however naturally disqualified, was one of those juvenile dreadnoughts, is a sad reflection to one who cannot now step over a brook without assistance. [1824, revised 1832]

[Scott was 'naturally disqualified' having suffered from poliomyelitis as a baby, and this left him lame.]

5. The Hall of the Parliament House of Edinburgh was, in former days, divided into two unequal portions by a partition, the inner side of which was consecrated to the use of the Courts of Justice and the gentlemen of the law; while the outer division was occupied by the stalls of stationers, toymen, and the like, as in a modern bazaar. From the old play of the Plain Dealer, it seems such was formerly the case with Westminster-Hall. Minos has now purified his courts in both cities from all traffic but his own. [1824]
   [William Wycherley, *The Plain Dealer*, 1677]
6. 'Sir John Nisbett of Dirleton's Doubts and Questions upon the Law, especially of Scotland;' and, 'Sir James Stewart's Dirleton's Doubts and Questions on the Law of Scotland resolved and answered,' are works of authority in Scottish jurisprudence. As is generally the case, the Doubts are held more in respect than the solution.
7. Till of late years, every advocate who entered at the Scottish bar made a Latin address to the Court, faculty, and audience, in set terms, and said a few words upon a text of the civil law, to show his Latinity and jurisprudence. He also wore his hat for a minute, in order to vindicate his right of being covered before the court, which is said to have originated from the celebrated lawyer, Sir Thomas Hope, having two sons on the Bench while he himself remained at the bar. Of late this ceremony has been dispensed with, as occupying the time of the court unnecessarily. The entrant lawyer merely takes the oaths to government, and swears to maintain the rules and privileges of his order.
8. A peculiar Scottish phrase, expressive of ingratitude for the favours of Providence.
9. Probably Mathieson, the predecessor of Dr Adams, to whose memory the author and his contemporaries owe a deep debt of gratitude.
10. Celebrated as a Scottish lawyer.
11. It is well known and remembered, that when Members of Parliament enjoyed the unlimited privilege of franking by the mere writing the name on the cover, it was extended to the most extraordinary occasions. One noble lord, to express his regard for a particular regiment, franked a letter for every rank and file. It was customary also to save the covers and return them, in order that the correspondence might be carried on as long as the envelopes could hold together.
12. Alluding, as all Scotsmen know, to the humorous old song:—

    'The auld man's mare's dead,
    The puir man's mare's dead,
    The auld man's mare's dead,
    A mile aboon Dundee.'

    [By ?Patrick Birnie (*fl.* 1710)]

13. The diminutive and obscure *place* called Brown's Square, was hailed about the time of its erection as an extremely elegant improvement upon the style of designing and erecting Edinburgh residences. Each house was, in the phrase used by appraisers, 'finished within itself,' or, in the still newer phraseology, 'self-contained.' It was built about the year 1763–4; and the old part of the city being near and accessible, this square soon received many inhabitants, who ventured to remove to so moderate a distance from the High Street.
14. Of Rob Roy we have had more than enough. Alan Cameron, commonly called Sergeant Mhor, a freebooter of the same period, was equally remarkable for strength, courage, and generosity.
15. The partition which divides a Scottish cottage.
16. The frame of wooden shelves placed in a Scottish kitchen for holding plates.
17. Of old this almost deserted alley formed the most common access betwixt the High Street and the southern suburbs.
18. The bait made of salmon-row salted and preserved. In a swollen river, and about the month of October, it is a most deadly bait.
19. In explanation of this circumstance, I cannot help adding a note not very necessary for the reader, which yet I record with pleasure, from recollection of the kindness which it evinces. In early youth I resided for a considerable time in the vicinity of the beautiful village of Kelso, where my life passed in a very solitary manner. I had few acquaintances, scarce any companions, and books, which were at the time almost essential to my happiness, were difficult to come by. It was then that I was particularly indebted to the liberality and friendship of an old lady of the Society of Friends, eminent for her benevolence and charity. Her deceased husband had been a medical man of eminence, and left her, with other valuable property, a small and well-selected library. This the kind old lady permitted me to rummage at pleasure, and carry home what volumes I chose, on condition that I should take, at the same time, some of the tracts printed for encouraging and extending the doctrines of her own sect. She did not even exact any assurance that I would read these performances, being too justly afraid of involving me in a breach of promise, but was merely desirous that I should have the chance of instruction within my reach, in case whim, curiosity, or accident, might induce me to have recourse to it.
20. Well known in the Chap-Book, called the History of Buckhaven.
21. The original of this catch is to be found in Cowley's witty comedy of the Guardian, the first edition. It does not exist in the second and revised edition, called the Cutter of Coleman Street.

    'CAPTAIN BLADE. Ha, ha, boys, another catch.
    And all our men were very very merry,
    And all our men were drinking.

CUTTER. *One man of mine.*
DOGREL. *Two men of mine.*
BLADE. *Three men of mine.*
CUTTER. *And one man of mine.*
OMNES. *As we went by the way we were drunk, drunk, damnably drunk.*
And all our men were very very merry, &c.'

Such are the words, which are somewhat altered and amplified in the text. The play was acted in presence of Charles II., then Prince of Wales, in 1641. The catch in the text has been happily set to music.

22. Blind Rorie, a famous performer, according to tradition.

23. It is certain that in many cases the blind have, by constant exercise of their other organs, learned to overcome a defect which one would think incapable of being supplied. Every reader must remember the celebrated Blind Jack of Knaresborough, who lived by laying out roads.

24. A precipitous side of a mountain in Moffatdale.

25. The caution and moderation of King William III., and his principles of unlimited toleration, deprived the Cameronians of the opportunity they ardently desired, to retaliate the injuries which they had received during the reign of prelacy, and purify the land, as they called it, from the pollution of blood. They esteemed the Revolution, therefore, only a half measure, which neither comprehended the rebuilding the Kirk in its full splendour, nor the revenge of the death of the Saints on their persecutors.

26. A celebrated wizard, executed at Edinburgh for sorcery and other crimes.

27. The personages here mentioned are most of them characters of historical fame; but those less known and remembered may be found in the tract entitled, 'The Judgment and Justice of God Exemplified, or, a Brief Historical Account of some of the Wicked Lives and Miserable Deaths of some of the most remarkable Apostates and Bloody Persecutors, from the Reformation till after the Revolution.' This constitutes a sort of postscript or appendix to John Howie of Lochgoin's 'Account of the Lives of the most eminent Scots Worthies.' The author has, with considerable ingenuity, reversed his reasoning upon the inference to be drawn from the prosperity or misfortunes which befall individuals in this world, either in the course of their lives or in the hour of death. In the account of the martyrs' sufferings, such inflictions are mentioned only as trials permitted by Providence, for the better and brighter display of their faith, and constancy of principle. But when similar afflictions befell the opposite party, they are imputed to the direct vengeance of Heaven upon their impiety. If, indeed, the life of any person obnoxious to the historian's censures happened to have passed in unusual prosperity, the mere fact of its being finally concluded by death, is assumed as an undeniable token of the judgment of Heaven, and, to render the conclusion inevitable, his last scene is generally garnished with some singular circumstances. Thus the Duke of Lauderdale is said, through old

age but immense corpulence, to have become so sunk in spirits, 'that his heart was not the bigness of a walnut.'

28. The reader is referred for particulars to Pitscottie's History of Scotland.

29. I have heard in my youth some such wild tale as that placed in the mouth of the blind fiddler, of which, I think, the hero was Sir Robert Grierson of Lagg, the famous persecutor. But the belief was general throughout Scotland, that the excessive lamentation over the loss of friends disturbed the repose of the dead, and broke even the rest of the grave. There are several instances of this in tradition, but one struck me particularly, as I heard it from the lips of one who professed receiving it from those of a ghost-seer. This was a Highland lady, named Mrs C—— of B——, who probably believed firmly in the truth of an apparition, which seems to have originated in the weakness of her nerves and strength of her imagination. She had been lately left a widow by her husband, with the office of guardian to their only child. The young man added to the difficulties of his charge by an extreme propensity for a military life, which his mother was unwilling to give way to, while she found it impossible to repress it. About this time the Independent Companies, formed for the preservation of the peace of the Highlands, were in the course of being levied; and as a gentleman named Cameron, nearly connected with Mrs C——, commanded one of those companies, she was at length persuaded to compromise the matter with her son, by permitting him to enter this company in the capacity of a cadet; thus gratifying his love of a military life without the dangers of foreign service, to which no one then thought these troops were at all liable to be exposed, while even their active service at home was not likely to be attended with much danger. She readily obtained a promise from her relative that he would be particular in his attention to her son, and therefore concluded she had accommodated matters between her son's wishes and his safety in a way sufficiently attentive to both. She set off to Edinburgh to get what was awanting for his outfit, and shortly afterwards received melancholy news from the Highlands. The Independent Company into which her son was to enter had a skirmish with a party of catherans engaged in some act of spoil, and her friend the Captain being wounded, and out of the reach of medical assistance, died in consequence. This news was a thunderbolt to the poor mother, who was at once deprived of her kinsman's advice and assistance, and instructed by his fate of the unexpected danger to which her son's new calling exposed him. She remained also in great sorrow for her relative, whom she loved with sisterly affection. These conflicting causes of anxiety, together with her uncertainty whether to continue or change her son's destination, were terminated in the following manner:—

The house in which Mrs C—— resided in the old town of Edinburgh, was a flat or story of a land, accessible, as was then universal, by a common stair. The family who occupied the story beneath were her acquaintances, and she was in the habit of drinking tea with them every evening. It was accordingly about six o'clock, when, recovering herself from a deep fit of anxious reflection, she was about to leave the parlour in which she sat in order to attend this engagement. The door through which she was to pass opened, as was very common in Edinburgh, into a dark passage. In this passage, and within a yard of her when she opened the door, stood the apparition of her kinsman, the deceased officer, in his full tartans, and wearing his bonnet. Terrified at what she saw, or thought she saw, she closed the door hastily, and, sinking on her knees by a chair, prayed to be delivered from the horrors of the vision. She remained in that posture till her friends below tapped on the floor to intimate that tea was ready. Recalled to herself by the signal, she arose, and, on opening the apartment door, again was confronted by the visionary Highlander, whose bloody brow bore token, on this second appearance, to the death he had died. Unable to endure this repetition of her terrors, Mrs C—— sunk on the floor in a swoon. Her friends below, startled with the noise, came up stairs, and, alarmed at the situation in which they found her, insisted on her going to bed and taking some medicine, in order to compose what they took for a nervous attack. They had no sooner left her in quiet, than the apparition of the soldier was once more visible in the apartment. This time she took courage and said, 'In the name of God, Donald, why do you haunt one who respected and loved you when living?' To which he answered readily, in Gaelic, 'Cousin, why did you not speak sooner? My rest is disturbed by your unnecessary lamentation—your tears scald me in my shroud. I come to tell you that my untimely death ought to make no difference in your views for your son; God will raise patrons to supply my place, and he will live to the fulness of years, and die honoured and at peace.' The lady of course followed her kinsman's advice; and as she was accounted a person of strict veracity, we may conclude the first apparition an illusion of the fancy, the final one a lively dream suggested by the other two.

30. PETER PEEBLES. This unfortunate litigant (for a person named Peter Peebles actually flourished) frequented the courts of justice in Scotland about the year 1792, and the sketch of his appearance is given from recollection. The author is of opinion that he himself had at one time the honour to be counsel for Peter Peebles, whose voluminous course of litigation served as a sort of assay-pieces to most young men who were called to the bar. The scene of the consultation is entirely imaginary.

31. Formerly, a lawyer, supposed to be under the peculiar patronage of any particular judge, was invidiously termed his *peat* or *pet*. [1824]

32. Process-bags.

33. Multiplepoinding is, I believe, equivalent to what is called in England a case of Double Distress.

34. OLD-FASHIONED SCOTTISH CIVILITY.—Such were literally the points of politeness observed in general society during the author's youth, where it was by no means unusual in a company assembled by chance, to find

individuals who had borne arms on one side or other in the civil broils of 1745. Nothing, according to my recollection, could be more gentle and decorous than the respect these old enemies paid to each other's prejudices. But in this I speak generally. I have witnessed one or two explosions.

35. The simile is obvious, from the old manufacture of Scotland, when the guidwife's thrift, as the yarn wrought in the winter was called, when laid down to bleach by the burn-side, was peculiarly exposed to the inroads of the pigs, seldom well-regulated about a Scottish farm-house.

36. This small dark coffeehouse, now burnt down, was the resort of such writers and clerks belonging to the Parliament House above thirty years ago, as retained the ancient Scottish custom of a meridian, as it was called, or noontide dram of spirits. If their proceedings were watched, they might be seen to turn fidgety about the hour of noon, and exchange looks with each other from their separate desks, till at length some one of formal and dignified presence assumed the honour of leading the band, when away they went, threading the crowd like a string of wild-fowl, crossed the square or close, and following each other into the coffee-house, received in turn from the hand of the waiter, the meridian, which was placed ready at the bar. This they did, day by day: and though they did not speak to each other, they seemed to attach a certain degree of sociability to performing the ceremony in company.

37. Said of an adventurous gipsy, who resolves at all risks to convert a sheep's horn into a spoon.

38. Tradition ascribes this whimsical style of language to the ingenious and philosophical Lord Kaimes.

39. A Scots law phrase of no very determinate import, meaning, generally, to do what is fitting.

40. The Scottish Judges are distinguished by the title of lord prefixed to their own temporal designation. As the ladies of these official dignitaries do not bear any share in their husband's honours, they are distinguished only by their lords' family name. They were not always contented with this species of Salique law, which certainly is somewhat inconsistent. But their pretensions to title are said to have been long since repelled by James V., the Sovereign who founded the College of Justice. 'I,' said he, 'made the carles lords, but who the devil made the carlines ladies?'

41. RIOTOUS ATTACK UPON THE DAM-DIKE OF SIR JAMES GRAHAM OF NETHERBY. It may be here mentioned, that a violent and popular attack upon what the country people of this district considered as an invasion of their fishing right, is by no means an improbable fiction. Shortly after the close of the American war, Sir James Graham of Netherby constructed a dam-dike, or cauld, across the Esk, at a place where it flowed through his estate, though it has its origin, and the principal part of its course, in Scotland. The new barrier at Netherby was considered as an

encroachment calculated to prevent the salmon from ascending into Scotland; and the right of erecting it being an international question of law betwixt the sister kingdoms, there was no court in either competent to its decision. In this dilemma, the Scots people assembled in numbers by signal of rocket lights, and, rudely armed with fowlingpieces, fishspears, and such rustic weapons, marched to the banks of the river for the purpose of pulling down the dam-dike objected to. Sir James Graham armed many of his own people to protect his property, and had some military from Carlisle for the same purpose. A renewal of the Border wars had nearly taken place in the eighteenth century, when prudence and moderation on both sides saved much tumult, and perhaps some bloodshed. The English proprietor consented that a breach should be made in his dam-dike sufficient for the passage of the fish, and thus removed the Scottish grievance. I believe the river has since that time taken the matter into its own disposal, and entirely swept away the dam-dike in question.

42. The King's health.

43. Every one must remember instances of this festive custom, in which the adaptation of the tune to the toast was remarkably felicitous. Old Niel Gow, and his son Nathaniel, were peculiarly happy on such occasions.

44. By taking the oaths to Government.

45. Scotland, in its half civilized state, exhibited too many examples of the exertion of arbitrary force and violence, rendered easy by the dominion which lairds exerted over their tenants, and chiefs over their clans. The captivity of Lady Grange, in the desolate cliffs of Saint Kilda, is in the recollection of every one. At the supposed date of the novel also, a man of the name of Merrilees, a tanner in Leith, absconded from his country to escape his creditors; and after having slain his own mastiff dog, and put a bit of red cloth in its mouth, as if it had died in a contest with soldiers, and involved his own existence in as much mystery as possible, made his escape into Yorkshire. Here he was detected by persons sent in search of him, to whom he gave a portentous account of his having been carried off and concealed in various places. Mr Merrilees was, in short, a kind of male Elizabeth Canning, but did not trespass on the public credulity quite so long.

46. Not much in those days, for within my recollection the London post was brought north in a small mail-cart; and men are yet alive who recollect when it came down with only one single letter for Edinburgh, addressed to the manager of the British Linen Company.

47. I remember hearing this identical answer given by an old Highland gentleman of the Forty-Five, when he heard of the opening of the New Assembly-Rooms in George Street.

48. The true joke is no joke. [1824]

49. ESCAPE OF PATE-IN-PERIL. The escape of a Jacobite gentleman while on

the road to Carlisle to take his trial for his share in the affair of 1745, took place at Errickstane-brae, in the singular manner ascribed to the Laird of Summertrees in the text. The author has seen in his youth the gentleman to whom the adventure actually happened. The distance of time makes some indistinctness of recollection, but it is believed the real name was MacEwen, or MacMillan.

50. An old gentleman of the author's name was engaged in the affair of 1715, and with some difficulty was saved from the gallows, by the intercession of the Duchess of Buccleuch and Monmouth. Her Grace, who maintained a good deal of authority over her clan, sent for the object of her intercession, and warning him of the risk which he had run, and the trouble she had taken on his account, wound up her lecture by intimating, that in case of such disloyalty again, he was not to expect her interest in his favour. 'An it please your Grace,' said the stout old Tory, 'I fear I am too old to see another opportunity.'

[The 'old gentleman' here described was Scott's paternal great-grandfather.]

51. BRAXY MUTTON.—The flesh of sheep that has died of disease, not by the hand of the butcher. In pastoral countries it is used as food with little scruple.

52. The Scottish pint of liquid measure comprehends four English measures of the same denomination. The jest is well-known of my poor countryman, who, driven to extremity by the raillery of the Southern, on the small denomination of the Scottish coin, at length answered, 'Ay, ay! But the deil tak them that has the *least pint-stoup*.'

53. The translation of the passage is thus given by Sir Henry Steuart of Allanton.—'The youth, taught to look up to riches as the sovereign good, became apt pupils in the school of Luxury. Rapacity and profusion went hand in hand. Careless of their own fortunes, and eager to possess those of others, shame and remorse, modesty and moderation, every principle gave way.'—*Works of Sallust, with Original Essays*, vol. ii, p. 17. [1824]

54. After enumerating the evil qualities of Catiline's associates, the author adds, 'If it happened that any as yet uncontaminated by vice were fatally drawn into his friendship, the effects of intercourse and snares artfully spread, subdued every scruple, and early assimilated them to their conductors.'—*Ibidem*, p.19. [1824]

55. CONCEALMENTS FOR THEFT AND SMUGGLING. I am sorry to say, that the modes of concealment described in the imaginary premises of Mr Trumbull, are of a kind which have been common on the frontiers of late years. The neighbourhood of two nations having different laws, though united in government, still leads to a multitude of transgressions on the Border, and extreme difficulty in apprehending delinquents. About twenty years since, as far as my recollection serves, there was along the frontier an organized gang of coiners, forgers, smugglers, and other

malefactors, whose operations were conducted on a scale not inferior to what is here described. The chief of the party was one Richard Mendham, a carpenter, who rose to opulence, although ignorant even of the arts of reading and writing. But he had found a short road to wealth, and had taken singular measures for conducting his operations. Amongst these, he found means to build, in a suburb of Berwick called Spittal, a street of small houses, as if for the investment of property. He himself inhabited one of these; another, a species of public-house, was open to his confederates, who held secret and unsuspected communication with him by crossing the roofs of the intervening houses, and descending by a trap-stair, which admitted them into the alcove of the diningroom of Dick Mendham's private mansion. A vault, too, beneath Mendham's stable, was accessible in the manner mentioned in the novel. The post of one of the stalls turned round on a bolt being withdrawn, and gave admittance to a subterranean place of concealment for contraband and stolen goods, to a great extent. Richard Mendham, the head of this very formidable conspiracy, which involved malefactors of every kind, was tried and executed at Jedburgh, where the author was present as Sheriff of Selkirkshire. Mendham had previously been tried, but escaped by want of proof and the ingenuity of his counsel.

56. A small landed proprietor.

57. Several persons have brought down to these days the impressions which Nature had thus recorded, when they were yet babes unborn. One lady of quality, whose father was long under sentence of death, previous to the rebellion, was marked on the back of the neck by the sign of a broad axe. Another, whose kinsmen had been slain in battle, and died on the scaffold to the number of seven, bore a child spattered on the right shoulder, and down the arm, with scarlet drops, as if of blood. Many other instances might be quoted.

58. CORONATION OF GEORGE III. The particulars here given are of course entirely imaginary; that is, they have no other foundation than what might be supposed probable, had such a circumstance actually taken place. Yet a report to such an effect was long and generally current, though now having wholly lost its lingering credit; those who gave it currency, if they did not originate it, being, with the tradition itself, now mouldered in the dust. The attachment to the unfortunate house of Stewart among its adherents, continued to exist and to be fondly cherished, longer perhaps than in any similar case in any other country; and when reason was baffled, and all hope destroyed, by repeated frustration, the mere dreams of imagination were summoned in to fill up the dreary blank, left in so many hearts. Of the many reports set on foot and circulated from this cause, the tradition in question, though amongst the least authenticated, is not the least striking; and, in excuse of what may be considered as a violent infraction of probability in the foregoing chapter, the author is under the necessity of quoting it. It was always said, though with very little appearance of truth, that upon the corona-

tion of George III., when the Champion of England, Dymock, or his representative, appeared in Westminster Hall, and, in the language of chivalry, solemnly wagered his body to defend in single combat the right of the young King to the crown of these realms, at the moment when he flung down his gauntlet as the gage of battle, an unknown female stepped from the crowd and lifted the pledge, leaving another gage in room of it, with a paper expressing, that if a fair field of combat should be allowed, a champion of rank and birth would appear with equal arms to dispute the claim of King George to the British kingdoms. The story, as we have said, is probably one of the numerous fictions which were circulated to keep up the spirits of a sinking faction. The incident was, however, possible, if it could be supposed to be attended by any motive adequate to the risk, and might be imagined to occur to a person of Redgauntlet's enthusiastic character.

59. The northern gate of Carlisle was long garnished with the heads of the Scottish rebels executed in 1746.

60. The Highland regiments were first employed by the celebrated Earl of Chatham, who assumed to himself no small degree of praise for having called forth to the support of the country and the government, the valour which had been too often directed against both.

61. In common parlance, a crowbar and hatchet.

62. A student of divinity who has not been able to complete his studies on theology.

63. COLLIER AND SALTER. The persons engaged in these occupations were at this time bondsmen; and in case they left the ground of the farm to which they belonged, and as pertaining to which their services were bought or sold, they were liable to be brought back by a summary process. The existence of this species of slavery being thought irreconcilable with the spirit of liberty, colliers and salters were declared free, and put upon the same footing with other servants, by the Act 15 Geo. III. chapter 28th. They were so far from desiring or prizing the blessing conferred on them, that they esteemed the interest taken in their freedom to be a mere decree on the part of the proprietors to get rid of what they called head and harigald money, payable to them when a female of their number, by bearing a child, made an addition to the live stock of their master's property.

APPENDIX

Redgauntlet and Scottish History

1660 The restoration of Charles II (1630–85), the Stewart monarch; the fictional Robert Redgauntlet, Darsie Latimer's ancestor, is knighted in London for his services to the Royalist cause during the civil wars of the previous two decades.

1662 The reintroduction of an Episcopal liturgy into Scotland results in increasingly severe government suppression of the Covenanters (those who support the 'Covenants' to preserve the purity of the reformed Presbyterian worship), especially in the south-west, Redgauntlet's country.

1669 The Act of Supremacy passed by the Scottish Parliament accords the king supreme authority over all persons and in all causes ecclesiastical.

1681 The Test Act and Oath requires all office-holders to recognize royal supremacy in spiritual as well as temporal matters. For the Covenanters, whose Church has an invisible head in Christ, such an oath is impossible and the following years, in particular 1684–5, see their persecution by such notorious Royalists as John Graham of Claverhouse and Tam Dalyell, the associates of Sir Robert Redgauntlet on earth and in hell (Letter XI).

1685 The death of Charles II, the unsuccessful rebellion in favour of his illegitimate son the Protestant Duke of Monmouth, and the accession of Charles's brother James VII (of Scotland) and II (of England) (1633–1701), a Roman Catholic.

1688–9 James II flees from England; the Scottish Convention offer the Scottish crown to his Protestant daughter Mary and son-in-law William of Orange (1650–1702). Wandering Willie refers to these events as 'the Revolution' (Letter XI).

1690 Presbyterianism is re-established in Scotland, bringing an end to the persecution of the Covenanters.

Some time in the next decade or so, before 1707, Sir Robert Redgauntlet dies.

1702 The accession of the childless Queen Anne (1665–1714), second daughter of James II. The previous year the English Parliament, by the Act of Settlement, conveyed the succession to the English throne (and by implication to the Scottish) to the Electress Sophia of Hanover and her descendants, as the nearest Protestant heirs, should Anne remain childless. Thus the Roman Catholic son of James II is excluded and becomes known as the Pretender.

1707 The Union of the Parliaments of Scotland and England. Sir John, son of Sir Robert Redgauntlet, is active in promoting the Union, probably making financial gains thereby (Letter XI).

1712 An Act of Toleration permits Episcopal worship in Scotland, all clergy being required to forswear the Pretender, pray for Queen Anne, and take an oath of loyalty to the government.

1714 The death of Queen Anne without issue, the last Stewart monarch. The throne passes to George I (1660–1727), of the house of Brunswick, the Protestant Elector of Hanover and great-grandson of James VI and I.

1715 Supporters of the Roman Catholic line of James II (Jacobites, from the Latin *Jacobus*, meaning James) rise on behalf of his son, Anne's half-brother, James Francis (1688–1766), the Pretender. The rebellion quickly proves abortive.

The collapse of the Jacobite-tainted Tory party as an effective political force after 1715 leaves the Whigs, with the support of the new Hanoverian monarchy, to operate something like one-party government for the next half century.

1716 An Act of Forfeiture is passed on the property of attainted persons convicted of high treason for their participation in 'the Fifteen', as the first Jacobite rebellion is called. Many English and Scottish Jacobites, among them Herbert Herries, Hugh Redgauntlet's kinsman, forfeit their estates (Letter V).

1719 An Abjuration Oath is passed, penalizing Non-juring Episcopal Clergy (those refusing the terms of the 1712 Act of Toleration).

1720 The birth of Charles Edward Stewart, the Young Pretender, son of James Francis, at Rome.

1721–42 The ascendancy of Sir Robert Walpole, 1st Earl of Orford (1676–1745), Whig Prime Minister and fierce anti-Jacobite.

1727 The accession of George II (1683–1760), son of George I.

1745–6 A second Jacobite rebellion with Charles Edward Stewart, the Young Pretender, at its head. Minor successes in battle in England and Scotland, one at Falkirk where Alan Fairford's father is said to have been among the defeated Hanoverian force (Letter III), are followed by the total overthrow of the Jacobite cause at Culloden near Inverness in April 1746 and the flight of Charles Edward. It is after fighting for the Stewart prince at Culloden that Darsie Latimer's father, Sir Henry Redgauntlet, is captured by the Hanoverian army, marched to Carlisle and beheaded. This is also the occasion of the escape of Pate-in-Peril (Chapter XI).

Culloden sees the end of the Stewart hopes for a dynastic reversal and marks the beginning of a consolidation of Hanoverian, Westminster-centred power in Scotland. Walpole's disciple Henry Pelham (1696–1754) is Prime Minister for most of the period 1744–54.

1746 An Act of Attainder listing all prominent Jacobites is passed. A Disarming Act, forbidding Highlanders to carry weapons in public, imposes stiffer penalties than a similar act of 1716. The wearing of Highland dress is also banned. Further acts this year and in 1748 against Non-juring Episcopal clergy forbid them, *inter alia*, from holding services outside their own homes.

1747 The Abolition of Heritable Jurisdictions (Scotland) Act does away with the hereditary rights of landowners over their tenants, so breaking clan power.

Henry, Charles Edward's younger brother, accepts a Cardinal's hat in the Roman Catholic Church, a severe blow to the Stewart cause in Britain.

1750 Charles Edward secretly visits England, meeting Dr William King (1832 Introduction to *Redgauntlet*).

1752 An Annexing Act inalienably annexes to the Crown thirteen of the Jacobite estates forfeited after 'the Forty-five', thus giving central government in London control over a huge chain of land in the Highlands.

1752–3 A resurgence of Jacobite activity proves abortive (the Elibank Plot), and Dr Archibald Cameron, arrested in the Highlands, is the last Jacobite to be executed for his politics (1832 Introduction to *Redgauntlet*).

1756–63 The Seven Years War, in which the combined forces of Britain and Hanover face the French and later their Spanish allies in Westphalia, North America, and the Indian subcontinent. William Pitt the Elder (1708–78), supported by the Duke of Newcastle, Henry Pelham's brother, leads Britain successfully through the war from 1756–61.

1760 The accession of George III (1738–1820), grandson of George II.

1761 A Scot, John Stuart, 3rd Earl of Bute (1713–92) and favourite of George III, becomes Prime Minister.

1763 In February the Peace of Paris brings the Seven Years War to an end, leaving Britain the dominant power. The war years have seen a new generation of Scots emerging, eager for greater integration in the British state. In April Bute resigns in the face of violent opposition and anti-Scottish feeling, fuelled by John Wilkes MP and his anti-government paper the North Briton.

Domestically the 1760s and 1770s are an era of considerable optimism and prosperity in Lowland Scotland, witnessing the first stages of an ambitious architectural plan to expand Edinburgh's cramped medieval community into a spacious neo-classical city and a modern commercial centre. Brown's Square, the home of the Fairfords, south of the Old Town and built in the early 1760s, is one of the first of the modern developments (Letter II).

1763–5 George Grenville (1712–70) becomes Prime Minister on Bute's resignation and takes on the problem of Britain's post-war economic recession. He paves the way for a serious Anglo-American crisis when on 22 March 1765 the controversial Stamp Act levying stamp-duties on the American colonies is passed. Hated by George III, Grenville's ministry is dissolved in June 1765.

1765 The first Rockingham ministry is formed in July, led by the 2nd Marquis of Rockingham (1730–82).

The summer months of this year witness the adventures of Alan Fairford and Darsie Latimer and the fictitious return of Charles Edward Stewart (Chapters III and XI confirm this dating).

1766 The Stamp Act is repealed in February, but the Rockingham ministry, commanding insufficient support, is dissolved and Pitt returns to power in August, accepting a peerage as Lord Chatham.

James Craig, son of an Edinburgh merchant, wins the competition for the plan for the New Town of Edinburgh and in the following year lays the foundation-stone of the first house.

James Francis Stewart, the Old Pretender and son of James II, dies in Rome.

1771 The birth of Walter Scott in Edinburgh.

1776–83 The War of the American Revolution.

1784 The remaining forfeited estates annexed after 'the Forty-five' are returned to the representatives of the forfeited families.

1788 Charles Edward Stewart, the Young Pretender, dies in Rome without legitimate heir.

1789 The outbreak of the French Revolution.

1792 Episcopalian religious disabilities, reinforced in 1746 and 1748, are removed.

1793 France declares war on Britain.

1802 The Peace of Amiens with Napoleon's France.

1803 A renewal of the war with France.

1811 The regency of George, Prince of Wales (1762–1830), during the final illness of his father George III.

1814–15 The defeat of Napoleon and a European peace settlement.

1820 The accession of George IV.

1822 The Hanoverian George IV, complete with Highland dress, pays a state visit to Edinburgh. Scott plays a large part in the visit's organization.

1824 *Redgauntlet* is published.

EDITOR'S NOTES

FOR clarification of pertinent points of Scots law and, in particular, in my attempts to make sense of Peter Peebles's legal obfuscations, I have drawn upon the manuscript notes of the late Lord Normand (1884–1962), Lord Justice General of Scotland and President of the Court of Session. Lord Normand's study of Scott's use of the law in his novels is preserved in the National Library of Scotland (Acc. 4874, notes for *Redgauntlet* being in envelope 14), and my precise debts are recorded below, in parentheses after the relevant note. I am also much indebted to Marilyn Deegan for advice and assistance on many points.

1 *epigraph*: *As You Like It*, II, iii, 69–70.

INTRODUCTION (1832)

3 *The Jacobite enthusiasm of the eighteenth century . . . although wisdom and reason frowned upon the enterprise*: Jacobites, a name derived from the Latin word *Jacobus*, meaning 'James', were opposed to the Glorious Revolution of 1688–9, which expelled the Roman Catholic James VII and II from the thrones of Scotland and England. They showed their allegiance to this exiled senior line of the House of Stewart in two significant though unsuccessful rebellions in the first half of the eighteenth century. After the death of Queen Anne without issue in 1714, the Jacobites supported the claim of her half-brother, the Roman Catholic James Francis (1688–1766), son of James II, against the Protestant George, Elector of Hanover. In 1715 a rebellion was engineered with James Francis as its figure-head. In 1745–6 his son, Charles Edward (1720–88), led a second campaign against Britain's now established Hanoverian monarchy. Equally disastrous, it is generally accorded a more romantic place in history owing to the degree of personal initiative Prince Charles showed in its management, marching at the head of his small army from Glenfinnan in the western Highlands as far as Derby before turning back into Scotland. Victories in minor engagements at Prestonpans near Edinburgh on the outward march, and, on the march back, at Clifton near Penrith and at Falkirk in Scotland, were followed by the total defeat of the Jacobite force at Culloden near Inverness in April 1746. Apparently spectacular, Charles's progress into England never seriously unsettled George II. The English Jacobites failed to rally to the cause, and the Highland army on its six-week foray into England was only 5,500 strong, the most powerful Scottish magnates and Highland chiefs refusing to stir in the Jacobite interest. (See my historical appendix for an outline of the events and consequences of the 1745–6 rising.)

4 *an insensibility to the distresses of his followers . . . well regulated or otherwise*: Of Charles Edward's ingratitude, Andrew Lang notes: 'It must be confessed . . . that after landing in France, Charles seems to have neglected the men and women who saved his life in Scotland, at the risk of their own. . . . As long as he was among them, he was grateful, considerate, chivalrously courteous, generous out of his scanty means . . . When he had once crossed over to Morbihan, Charles became a changed man. We hear of his sumptuous costume, of a splendid service of plate which he bought; we do not hear that he remembered his Highland friends.' (*Redgauntlet*, Border Edition, 1894, i, 305.) In the immediate government reprisals of 1746, Jacobite landowners forfeited their estates and in some cases their lives. Other well-connected prisoners, exiled or escaping abroad, found service in various European armies. Those taken as common prisoners were transported for life to the North American or West Indian colonies as virtual slaves. Among the few who collected rewards for their services to Prince Charles was Donald Cameron of Lochiel, who in exile was given a French regiment to command. But against this can be set Charles's reappropriation for his personal use of funds sent to relieve the remnants of his army after Culloden. (See Bruce Lenman, *The Jacobite Risings in Britain 1689–1746*, 1980, pp. 248, 261, and 271–6.)

that great Jacobite conspiracy . . . a few Highland chiefs: Charles Edward initiated the 1745–6 Highland rising after the collapse of the planned French invasion of England in February 1744, by which Louis XV was to have restored the Stewarts to the British throne. English Jacobite sympathizers, mainly a landed Tory interest, were unhappy with government by a minority Whig regime, the servants of a foreign Hanoverian dynasty, but their support for invasion was in real terms reserved, and never after 1744 was it organized on any large scale. Nonjurors were those Scottish Episcopalians and English High Churchmen who refused to take oaths to post-Revolution sovereigns until after 1788 and therefore did not qualify for toleration or office in Church, State, or University under the Toleration Act of 1712.

5 *a young Scotchman of rank . . . assassination of the royal family*: Alexander Murray, brother to Lord Elibank, is said to have assembled in London sixty men prepared to attack St James's Palace and assassinate all the royal family. Charles consistently refused to countenance violence against individual members of the Hanoverian royal family, and Murray apparently lost his nerve. The plot (known to history as the Elibank Plot) was originally laid for November 1752 but delayed into 1753. (See David Daiches, *Charles Edward Stuart*, 1973, pp. 261–2.)

Sir Robert Walpole: 1st Earl of Orford (1676–1745), a powerful Whig leader in the first half of the eighteenth century. He took a hard line against Jacobite offenders after the 1715 rising and maintained a complex counter-espionage network in the European centres of Jacobite intelligence throughout his ministry. Scott's reference here is misleading, since

Walpole's ministry was over in 1742. His successor in office was his pupil Henry Pelham (1696–1754), and he it was who dealt with the Jacobite plots of the early 1750s.

Doctor Archibald Cameron: The last victim of the government's reprisals, Archibald Cameron (1707–53) attained the stature of a Jacobite martyr. He was arrested in the Highlands in March 1753 and hanged on 7 June. His brother, Donald Cameron of Lochiel, had been one of the main contributors to Prince Charles's success in the early stages of the rebellion, bringing with him 700 fighting men. For Samuel Johnson's reaction to Cameron's execution, see Boswell's *Life*, ed. G. Birkbeck Hill and L. F. Powell, 1964, i, 146–7. Cameron was in the Highlands in 1753 to arrange a Scottish rising in concert with a planned infiltration of London. The 'considerable sum of money' which Scott mentions was the Locharkaig treasure, 35,000 *louis d'ors* sent by Louis XV to Charles in 1746. Partly misappropriated, the money had been used by Euan Macpherson of Cluny, one of the most notorious of the uncaptured rebels, to support families left destitute by their involvement in the Stewart cause. (See Marion F. Hamilton, 'The Locharkaig Treasure', *Miscellany of the Scottish History Society*, VII, 3rd series, xxxv, 1941, 131–68.)

6 *the Chevalier*: From the three titles most often used to describe Charles Edward Stewart, Scott chooses in this 1832 introduction to *Redgauntlet* to use Prince (Charles's adherents acknowledged him Prince of Wales) and Chevalier (his father was given the title of Chevalier de St George by Louis XIV). The common Hanoverian description, the Pretender, with its connotation of false claimant, he deliberately avoids, even to the point of emending an editorial insertion in the passage quoted from King's *Anecdotes* on p. 6. (See also *The Letters of Sir Walter Scott*, ed. H. J. C. Grierson, 1932–7, iii, 302, to Margaret Clephane, on this subject of designating Charles.)

Dr King's Anecdotes of his Own Times: Dr William King (1685–1763), Principal of St Mary Hall, Oxford, and leader of the Jacobite party in that university. His *Political and Literary Anecdotes of His Own Times*, published posthumously in 1818, were written in 1761, when he was 76. His harsh character study of Charles Edward is a vindication of personal disaffection with the Jacobite cause he earlier espoused so vehemently. The relevant passages drawn upon by Scott from the *Anecdotes*, which ramble widely on many topics, are pp. 196–209.

Lady Primrose: Jacobite daughter of Peter Drelincourt, Dean of Armagh, and widow of the third Viscount Primrose.

7 *a mistress . . . Walkinshaw*: Charles's mistress was Clementina Walkinshaw (1721–1802), daughter of a Scottish Jacobite who had fought in the 1715 rising. They met in January 1746, but Clementina only joined Charles on the Continent in November 1752, the very time that information of a Jacobite conspiracy began to be leaked to the British

government. She was an obvious suspect, her elder sister Catherine being mistress of the bedchamber to the Hanoverian Princess of Wales at Leicester House. Hence the quarrel between Charles and his supporters urging him to abandon her, as outlined by King, and post-dated in the novel to 1765 (see Ch. XXII), by which time Clementina had in fact left Charles. She bore him a child, Charlotte, in 1753, his only child, and left him in 1760.

8 *the love of prerogative . . . which characterised his unhappy grandfather*: Charles's grandfather was the Roman Catholic James VII and II (1633–1701), who had fled to France after the 1688–9 Revolution, when both his crowns were offered to his daughter and son-in-law, the Protestant Mary and William of Orange. James II was a passionate and unrealistic believer in royal absolutism, and it is this trait which King and Scott and modern historians concur in highlighting as the great Stewart defect. The shadow over all the Stewarts is, of course, Charles I, Charles Edward's great-grandfather, beheaded in 1649.

confinement in the Bastile: It was a condition of the Peace of Aix-la-Chapelle (1748) that France recognize the House of Hanover and expel Charles. (By the Treaty of Utrecht in 1713, James Francis, Charles's father, had been required to leave France.) Charles was confined at the Castle of Vincennes, four miles east of Paris, not in the Bastille. Arrested at the Opéra on 11 December 1748, he was kept under guard for less than a week before being escorted to the French border.

9 *the death of his father . . . recognised as the Prince of Wales*: After his flight from Britain, James II found refuge in France, Louis XIV placing at his disposal the Chateau of Saint-Germain-en-Laye, near Paris. Here in 1701, on his death, French heralds proclaimed his thirteen-year-old son, James Francis, James VIII and III, King of Scotland, England, and Ireland. Charles felt that James's death in 1766 made him King Charles III, but by this time neither the Pope nor any European sovereign was prepared to admit his claim.

10 *scarce remembered and scarce noted*: On his expulsion from France in December 1748, Charles briefly took up residence in the papal city of Avignon. But at the end of February 1749 he was again moved on. Thereafter, until his return to Rome in 1766, he led a life of wandering and intrigue on the Continent, alienated from his father and his younger brother Henry, who had seriously jeopardized the already fragile Stewart cause by accepting a cardinalate in the Roman Catholic Church. Abandoned by his remaining powerful supporters, drinking heavily, Charles was a broken man by 1755, in his mid-thirties. From 1766 he lived mainly in Rome and Florence, officially recognized only as the Count of Albany. He married disastrously in 1772. There was no heir, and Charles died in Rome in January 1788.

a gentleman of fortune in Perthshire: Laurence Oliphant of Gask, the younger (d. 1792).

11 *innocuous and respectable grandsires*: Scott's defence of the eighteenth-century Jacobite enthusiasm as fit subject for romantic fiction derives from his own childhood memories of the 1770s and 1780s, when the Jacobite clients of his solicitor father regaled his young imagination with tales of the 1715 and 1745 risings in which they had played their parts. (See *Letters*, x, 238–9, and *Waverley* (1814), ch. LXXII.) Throughout life Scott was an eager collector of Jacobite relics: Flora Macdonald's pocket-book, Prince Charles's drinking-cup, and a fragment of oatcake belonging to a Highlander at Culloden, all found their way into his collection at his home, Abbotsford.

THE NOVEL

13 *Letter I*: As first published in 1824, the novel began here with Darsie Latimer's letter to his friend Alan Fairford. There was no historical introduction to suggest that it was to be a Jacobite tale.

Cur me exanimas querelis tuis? Literally, 'Why do you kill me with your complainings?' The line is slightly misquoted from *Odes*, II, xvii, 1, by Horace (65–8 BC).

14 *some Indian director*: a Director of the Honourable East India Company. The comment provides an insight into Darsie's nice social sense. Incorporated in 1600, the English Company was in the later eighteenth century a vastly profitable commercial organization, with returned officials, 'nabobs', forming an influential group in England and Scotland. As Darsie snobbishly implies, their wealth was often considered to outrun their taste and breeding. See, for example, Scott's Peregrine Touchwood in *St. Ronan's Well* (1824).

the Gaits' Class at the High School: Edinburgh High School, a medieval foundation, was situated in the eighteenth century in High School Yards, south-west of the Cowgate Port. According to Hugo Arnot, its reputation for Latin scholarship was excellent (*The History of Edinburgh*, 1779, p. 421). Scott was himself a pupil at the school from 1779, and Darsie Latimer and Alan Fairford self-consciously display their education in the Latin phrases which pepper their correspondence. The Gaits' Class (pronounced 'Gytes', meaning 'brats') is the youngest class.

head a bicker: See Scott's reminiscences of these traditional schoolboy battles in the 'General Preface' to *Waverley*, 1829, i, xci–xcvi.

Cowgate-Port . . . Bareford's Parks: The Cowgate Port, one of the old city gates, led east out of Edinburgh and was the meeting-place for the Cowgate, a main thoroughfare, south of and parallel to the High Street, and St Mary's Street. Bareford's Parks were the area north of the Old Town and of the North Loch where after draining the New Town began to be built in the late 1760s. Bareford's Parks roughly correspond to present-day George Street.

before I knew thee, I knew nothing: Falstaff to Prince Henry, with very different implications, *1 Henry IV*, I, ii, 90–1.

College: Edinburgh University. Building began in 1581 and the first professor was appointed in 1583. In the 1760s, when Darsie Latimer and Alan Fairford are to be imagined as students there, there were four faculties, Theology, Law, Medicine, and Arts.

invita Minerva: 'against the will of Minerva'; that is, contrary to the bent of one's genius. See Horace, *Ars Poetica*, 385.

15 *Scotch Law Class ... the Civil*: 'the Roman or Civil Law was the first object of my attention — the second, the Municipal Law of Scotland'. So Scott describes the course of his law studies at Edinburgh University from 1790 to 1792, in J. G. Lockhart, *Memoirs of the Life of Sir Walter Scott, Bart.*, 2nd edn., 1839, i, 80.

'Thus far have I held on with thee untired': adapted from *Richard III*, IV, ii, 44.

before the Session rises: For most of the eighteenth century (until 1790) the sittings of the Edinburgh law courts were from 1 June to 31 July and from 1 November to the end of February, with a short Christmas break. *Redgauntlet* is set in the summer months of 1765.

the College of Justice: in Scotland, a great forensic society, comprising all the different legal bodies.

16 *what Erskine wrote, and Wallace taught*: John Erskine (1695–1768), Professor of Scots Law at Edinburgh University (1736–65). He wrote *Principles of the Law of Scotland* (1754) and, published after the date of *Redgauntlet*'s internal events, *Institutes of the Law of Scotland* (1773). William Wallace succeeded Erskine as professor in 1765 and, according to Hugo Arnot, lectured 'upon that excellent compendious system of the law of Scotland, written by the late Mr Erskine his predecessor'. (*The History of Edinburgh*, 1779, p. 399.)

17 *quid tibi cum lyra?* 'What have you to do with poetry?' Apollo was, among his other duties, Roman god of poetry.

Lord Stair: James Dalrymple, 1st Viscount Stair (1619–95), a Lord President of the Court of Session. His *Institutions of the Law of Scotland* (1681) was an important contribution to the making of Scots law into a systematic code.

18 *David and Jonathan ... Damon and Pythias*: all proverbial examples of devoted friendship. For David and Jonathan, see 1 Samuel 18: 1–4. Orestes, son of Agamemnon, and his constant friend Pylades appear in the *Oresteia* by Aeschylus (525–*c*.456 BC). Pythias of Syracuse was only saved from execution at the last minute by the return of Damon, hence Darsie's reference to the acceptability of a letter in their trying situation.

his Majesty's post-office: The privilege of franking letters, thereby avoiding postal charges, was claimed by MPs at the establishment of a regular post office at the Restoration. But it was a system open to great abuse and an act of 1764 attempted to confine its use. The postal system in Scotland was less than efficient for a large part of the eighteenth century, with a post-boy travelling on foot between most places only once or twice a week. In the 1760s things had improved, with a system of regular stages, fresh horses, and runners. (Hugo Arnot, *The History of Edinburgh*, 1779, pp. 536–40.)

Scots Magazine: Commencing publication in 1739, it was the first substantial Scottish literary journal which did not lean heavily on London news. It ceased publication in 1826, to be resumed sporadically from 1888.

the learned Ruddiman: The Ruddimans were not, contrary to Darsie's implication, connected with the *Scots Magazine*. Thomas Ruddiman (1674–1757), an outstanding Latin scholar, a passionate Jacobite and vigorous reviver of Scottish vernacular literature, published from 1724 the *Caledonian Mercury*. It continued in his family until 1772. His nephew Walter Ruddiman (1719–81) founded in 1754 a second publishing- and printing-house, owning and issuing various journals, among them the *Edinburgh Magazine* (1757–62) and the *Weekly Magazine* (1768–83). He was the first patron and publisher of Robert Fergusson, the Edinburgh poet.

19 *Brown's Square*: Named after its builder James Brown, it was completed in 1764, a year before the events of the novel. South of the Cowgate and just within the Bristo Port with an entry into Candlemaker Row (where the western end of Chambers Street now meets George IV Bridge), Brown's Square was part of the first modern house-building project in Edinburgh with accommodation modelled on the self-contained English style as distinct from the traditional tenement dwellings of the Old Town. In the later decades of the eighteenth century, the inhabitants of Brown's Square and the neighbouring squares were among the most select and fashionable. (See Robert Chambers, *Traditions of Edinburgh*, 1825, i, 38–42.) In the opening chapters of the novel Scott is using such specific details to suggest a context of cultural and national change within which his characters must find themselves.

Highland chairman: 'All the chairmen, most of the porters and servants in Edinburgh, come from the Highlands. This affords a supply of healthy and robust people.' (Hugo Arnot, *The History of Edinburgh*, 1779, p. 337.)

20 *the Meadows*: a spacious park on the south side of Edinburgh, formed in the early 1760s out of the marsh where the former Burgh Loch had been drained.

Luckie Simpson's cow: Alexander Fairford's case of the cow which drank the ale standing and so came within the terms of the *doch an dorroch*

(Scott's spelling; Gaelic, meaning 'a stirrup-cup') seems to be a favourite tale with Scott. It is told at tedious length in Richard Franck's *Northern Memoirs, calculated for the Meridian of Scotland* (1694), edited by Scott, 1821, pp. 186–92; and the anecdote is retold in a late note to *Waverley*, 1829, ch. XI.

21 *Exceptio firmat regulam*: 'The exception proves the rule.' Columella (*fl.* AD 50). It is a phrase used in Scots law.

Effusa est sicut aqua—non crescat: Genesis 49: 4.

La Pique's ball . . . Tom Jones: The reference here and Darsie's comments later in Letter XII suggest that La Pique's was a fashionable Edinburgh dancing school. *The History of Tom Jones, a Foundling* (1749), by Henry Fielding, is in six volumes. Fairford senior's attack on dancing and novel reading establishes his old-style Presbyterianism. The first half of the eighteenth century had seen an Edinburgh society 'remarkable for stiff reserve, precise moral carriage, and a species of decorum amounting almost to moroseness.' (Robert Chambers, *Traditions of Edinburgh*, 1825, i, 20.) By the 1750s a moderate element was beginning to dominate society and Church.

22 *Counsellor Pest*: The original of this figure who is referred to at several points later in the novel was, Scott writes, Robin MacIntosh. (*Letters*, xi, 375–6 and note.) Lockhart's note suggesting that '*Pest* is a misprint for *Peat*' (*Life of Scott*, 1839, i, 251) is wrong.

Stair or Bankton: For Lord Stair, see note to p. 17(2). Andrew Macdowall, Lord Bankton (1685–1760), a Scottish lawyer and judge, was author of *An Institute of the Laws of Scotland in Civil Rights*, along the lines of Stair's *Institutions*. In it he made a comparison of English and Scots law for the benefit of lawyers in both countries. (Normand.)

Ars longa, vita brevis: Ascribed to Hippocrates (b. 460? BC), this aphorism is rendered by Chaucer as 'The lyf so short, the craft so long to lerne'. (*The Parliament of Fowls*, l. 1.)

the ancient code of the Roman Empire . . . Voet on the Pandects: The Pandects were books of Roman Civil Law commissioned by the Emperor Justinian in the sixth century, and Jan Voet, a Dutch law professor, wrote a *Compendium* (1693) on them. Scots law, like Dutch, is modelled on Roman, and it was part of a law student's basic training in eighteenth-century Scotland to study these texts.

23 *the Luckenbooths . . . adjacent to the very Heart of Mid-Lothian*: The Luckenbooths (locked booths) were a row of shops and tenements between St Giles' Cathedral and the north side of the High Street, adjacent to the Edinburgh prison, ironically named the Heart of Midlothian. Along with the prison, they were removed in 1817. The prison gave its name to an earlier Scott novel, *The Heart of Midlothian* (1818).

Dr R——: probably a passing compliment to Scott's maternal grandfather, Dr John Rutherford, professor of medicine at Edinburgh University. Concern for his children's health (Walter contracted poliomyelitis as a baby) induced Scott's father to move his family in 1774 from the crowded tenements of the Old Town to the airier, modern George's Square, close to Brown's Square. (Lockhart, *Life of Scott*, 1839, i, 108–9.)

the noblesse of the robe ... 'first-born of Egypt': 'Throughout the eighteenth century some 90 per cent of entrants to the Faculty of Advocates ... were from landed families. Any advocate rising to the top of his profession as a Senator of the College of Justice automatically joined the *noblesse de robe* with the judicial title of a Lord of Session. In control of politics, and entrenched at the top of the legal system, the landed interest could and did use its power and property to construct elaborate vertical chains of patronage and dependence tying society together under its lead.' (Bruce Lenman, *Integration, Enlightenment, and Industrialization: Scotland 1746–1832*, 1981, p. 9.) The hold that the aristocracy and gentry kept on the law at this time is the subject of a later conversation between Alan Fairford and Provost Crosbie, in Ch. X.

the Union: James VI of Scotland's accession to the English throne in 1603 produced only a personal link, for there were still two kingdoms, each with its own institutions of government. The Act of Union of 1707 was legislative and to a large extent administrative. Through it, the kingdoms of England and Scotland alike ceased to exist and were incorporated in a United Kingdom of Great Britain. Although the Union preserved the separate legal and educational systems and the Presbyterian Church of Scotland, it was felt by many Scotsmen that the settlement was prejudicial to Scotland's interests and identity, not least in that government was settled firmly in London.

24 *Writer to his Majesty's Signet*: Originally a clerk in the office of the Secretary, who kept the signet or royal seal; by the late sixteenth century he was a solicitor conducting legal proceedings before the Court of Session, the supreme civil court of Scotland. Like Alan Fairford's father, Scott's own father was a Writer to the Signet.

Sua quemque trahit voluptas: 'Everyone is drawn on by his favourite pleasure.' *Eclogues*, ii, 65, by Virgil (70–19 BC).

Quixotical expectations: expectations which are lofty and fantastical and wildly unrealistic, like those of Don Quixote, the hero of the Spanish satiric romance, *The Adventures of Don Quixote* (1605–15) by Miguel de Cervantes Saavedra (1547–1616).

some wise Alcander or sage Alquife: Alcander, son of Munichus, king of the Molossi, was an ancient Greek soothsayer. Alquife was a famous enchanter introduced into the medieval Amadis of Gaul romance cycle.

25 *Lord-Advocate, or Solicitor-General*: Lord-Advocate, the head of the Scottish legal administration, with complete discretion over prosecution

for crimes; Solicitor-General, the second law-officer in the land, with authority in the civil court.

embroidered silk gown . . . walking the boards: The official gown of the advocate is embroidered silk, and the boards are the floor of the Parliament House, Edinburgh, where advocates still meet their clients. (Normand.)

Dulcinea: Don Quixote's extravagant name for a farm girl whom he imagines to be a noble lady and his mistress. (*Don Quixote*, part I, ch. i.)

Valentine . . . Orson: Two brothers, they are the subject of an early French romance. The story appeared in English *c.*1550 and Scott owned a chapbook version of it. (See Arthur Melville Clark, *Sir Walter Scott: The Formative Years*, 1969, p. 59.)

isle of Feroe: the Faeroes. North of Scotland, they present steep and spectacular rugged cliffs to the sea.

Lilliputian: diminutive. Lilliput is an imaginary country described by Jonathan Swift in *Gulliver's Travels* (1726), inhabited by pygmies.

26 *Lovelace and Belford like*: Lovelace is the 'hero' of Samuel Richardson's *Clarissa* (1747–8), and John Belford is his friend and correspondent.

Gravity out of his bed at midnight: *1 Henry IV*, II, iv, 290.

27 *like that of the old Spanish general*: Don Quixote makes a comparable comment on his courage. (*Don Quixote*, part I, ch. xx.)

28 *his zeal for King George . . . the company of the Highlanders*: Darsie Latimer refers to two encounters of 1745–6 between the rebel army of Charles Edward Stewart and the government forces of George II. As a Presbyterian, a member of the Church re-established in Scotland after the 1688–9 Revolution, Alexander Fairford is anti-Jacobite and loyal to Britain's Hanoverian monarch. He is said to have seen service defending the western city gate during the brief and farcical resistance Edinburgh showed to Charles in September 1745. (See Robert Chambers, *Traditions of Edinburgh*, 1825, ii, 180.) Later, he shared in the government defeat under General Hawley at Falkirk (17 January 1746), probably serving as a volunteer in the Edinburgh Company. (See K. Tomasson and F. Buist, *Battles of the '45*, 1962, pp. 33–4 and 88 ff.) For *parma non bene selecta* read *Relicta non bene parmula*, 'a shield not well forsaken', Horace's account of his own flight from battle at Philippi, from *Odes*, II, vii, 10.

Rob Roy Macgregor, and Sergeant Alan Mhor Cameron: Rob Roy MacGregor (1671–1734), a cattle-dealer and notorious Highland bandit. Often arrested, his escapes are legendary. He gave his name to a novel by Scott, *Rob Roy* (1817). Sergeant Alan Mhor (Gaelic—'of great size') Cameron (d. 1753). Having served in the French army, he fought for the Jacobite cause in 1745–6 and later lived in the Highlands as a cattle-lifter and bandit. He was executed at Perth in 1753.

The Pretender: from the French *prétendant*, 'claimant', applied first to

James Francis Stewart, son of James VII and II, and subsequently to his son, Charles Edward, the Young Pretender. It was a description favoured by those unsympathetic to their claim.

his hundred and eight fathers . . . walls of Holyrood: The royal palace of Holyroodhouse at the east end of the Canongate was extensively restored by Charles II in 1671. Charles commissioned the Dutch artist Jacob de Wet to supply portraits of the Scottish Kings. He produced one hundred and eleven (three more than Darsie counted), a legendary pedigree which continues to provoke amusement in modern visitors to the palace.

Mount Pisgah: The reference is to Moses in sight of the Promised Land. (Deuteronomy 34: 1.)

29 *Katterfelto's advertisements*: Gustavus Katterfelto (d. 1799), a well-known conjurer and quack-doctor, in London 1782–4. He advertised in the newspapers under the heading 'Wonders! Wonders! Wonders!' (See William Cowper's *The Task*, 1785, iv, 86–7.) The reference to Katterfelto does not, of course, fit the novel's internal chronology: Darsie writes in 1765.

Facardin of Trebizond: an allusion to *Les Quatre Facardins* (1749), one of four *Contes* written to satirize the then fashionable stories of the marvellous by Count Anthony Hamilton (1646?–1720).

like a Dutchman . . . with a Gascon: To talk like a Gascon was to indulge in absurd bragging. The Dutchman, on the other hand, was popularly characterized as phlegmatic.

the whole history of Bruce . . . and a murderer: Robert Bruce (1274–1329) killed 'the Red Comyn' (John Comyn of Badenoch) before the high altar in the Franciscan (not Dominican) Greyfriars' church in Dumfries on 10 February 1306, for refusing to co-operate in his plan to revive the Scottish kingship in defiance of Edward I of England (1239–1307). Bruce was subsequently inaugurated as king at Scone on 25 March. The incident is referred to later in the novel, in Ch. XIX.

30 *burghers of Dumfries . . . march into England*: A small noble-born Jacobite faction survived in the south-west of Scotland, an area otherwise fiercely Whig and Presbyterian. In the 1715 rising several local aristocrats were 'out' for the exiled Stewarts, among them the Earl of Kenmure, one of only two peers ultimately beheaded for High Treason in 1716. Dumfries was a centre of extreme Whiggish sentiment, and on their march into England in November 1745 the Jacobite army had baggage looted by a harrying force from the town. On the return march in late December Charles occupied rooms in Dumfries, but mindful of the looting, David Wemyss, Lord Elcho (1721–87), the young commander of the Jacobite Life Guards, levied a considerable fine on the town: £2,000 and 1,000 pairs of shoes.

old Cotton's instructions: Part II of Izaak Walton's *The Compleat Angler* (1653) was a treatise on fly-fishing (1676) by Walton's friend Charles

Cotton. In addition, Walton is the source for what immediately follows — Scott's account of Darsie's attempts at fishing and the description of his lodgings at the Shepherd's Bush. (See *The Compleat Angler*, ed. John Buchan and John Buxton, World's Classics, 1982, pp. 64 and 105.)

Fair Rosamond and Cruel Barbara Allan: Both ballads can be found in *Reliques of Ancient English Poetry*, ed. Thomas Percy, 1765, ii, 133–45, and iii, 125–31.

32 *hunting salmon*: Salmon-spearing is described in Scott's second novel, *Guy Mannering* (1815), ch. XXVI, and in Richard Franck's *Northern Memoirs* (1694), ed. Scott, 1821, pp. 71–3 and 363, note 2 (Scott's annotation).

33 *'He that dreams . . . three feet a-breast'*: H. J. C. Grierson finds here the influence of an anecdote about the Solway Firth which Scott had received in 1801 and included with the romantic ballad 'Annan Water' in *Minstrelsy of the Scottish Border* (1802–3). (See Scott, *Letters*, i, 119–20 n.)

35 *Erskine's Larger Institutes: Institutes of the Law of Scotland* by John Erskine, standard reading when Scott was a student, but not published until 1773, too late for Darsie to benefit from. The 'Larger Institutes' are the folio edition in two volumes. (Normand.)

36 *the Magician Atlantes . . . Ariosto has depicted that matter: Orlando Furioso* (1516) by Ludovico Ariosto (1474–1533), cantos II, xxxvii, xlviii–lvi, and IV, vi, describe how the sorcerer Atlas, riding on a fabulous beast, half griffin and half winged horse, abducts wandering knights and maidens to his castle.

38 *Harpocrates*: the Greek equivalent of the Egyptian god Harpechrat. Represented with its finger in its mouth to indicate youth, the Greeks mistakenly adopted it as a symbol of silence.

40 *Belisarius . . . the ruins of Carthage*: all famous Roman soldiers who suffered tragic reversals in their fortunes. Belisarius, the greatest of Justinian's generals, accused of conspiring against the emperor's life (548), was deprived of all his property, blinded, and left a beggar. Caius Marcius Coriolanus, a patrician and soldier (fifth century BC), was banished from Rome and sought shelter at the hearth of his arch enemy Tullus Aufidius, the Volscian chief. (See Shakespeare, *Coriolanus*, I, v, 68 ff.) Caius Marius (157–86 BC), a soldier and several times consul, fell from favour and fled from his enemy Sulla to North Africa. He lived to return to Rome and again be consul, as Plutarch describes.

if the gentleman is a whig: What is implied here is that Darsie follows the Presbyterian forms of worship, as opposed to Episcopalian or Roman Catholic. The Presbyterian Church was re-established as the official Church of Scotland after the 1688–9 Revolution and adherence to it implied more than religious persuasion. For a fuller explanation of the terms Whig and Tory as used in eighteenth-century Scotland, see note to p. 76(2).

44 *a second Daniel*: Daniel had from God the gift of interpreting dreams. (Daniel 1: 17.)

45 *Solon*: (640?–558? BC) an aristocratic Athenian, famous as a poet and a statesman. He reorganized the Athenian constitution.

46 *Pandemonium of Milton*: 'the high capital | Of Satan and his peers', *Paradise Lost*, i, 756–7.

the bean in the nursery-tale: from the version of Jack and the Beanstalk recorded in Katharine M. Briggs, *A Dictionary of British Folk-Tales*, part A, 1970, i, 316.

a Claude Lorraine glass: named from the painter (1600–82). A slightly convex, dark or coloured hand-mirror, described by William Gilpin (*Picturesque Beauty*, 1792, i, 124) as giving 'the objects of nature a soft, mellow tinge, like the colouring of that master'.

Leith Sands: Two miles east of Edinburgh Old Town, Leith has been the city's seaport since medieval times. The sands are east of the town.

teste me per totam noctem vigilante: 'I can testify by being kept awake the whole night.'

47 *'naughty night to swim in'*: *King Lear*, III, iv, 113.

Squire of Dames: See Edmund Spenser, *The Faerie Queene* (1590–6), III, vii, 51: 'Call me the *Squyre of Dames*, that me beseemeth well.'

48 *Old Greyfriars' Church*: south of the Cowgate, off Candlemaker Row. Close to the Fairfords' new home in Brown's Square, Greyfriars' Church, erected 1612–20, saw the signing of the National Covenant of 1638. New Greyfriars' was added to the west end in 1721. Both were burned in 1845 and reconstructed as a single church in 1936. Scott attended Old Greyfriars' from childhood.

49 *Horse Wynd*: 'Before the erection of the South Bridge, the Horse Wynd was the best access to the City from the southern districts, and was then a place of fashionable resort.' (Robert Chambers, *Traditions of Edinburgh*, 1825, i, 189.)

50 *Herries of Birrenswork ... the Preston affair in 1715*: As Herries of Birrenswork, Redgauntlet is given a verifiable and solid Jacobite ancestry. A native of south-west Scotland, where Herries is an old Annandale name, he is related to the Scottish Roman Catholic house of Nithsdale and the English Roman Catholic Earl of Derwentwater. Both houses played leading roles in the first Jacobite rebellion of 1715. James Radcliffe, 3rd Earl of Derwentwater, commander of the southern Jacobite army overcome at Preston in Lancashire, was one of only two peers beheaded for high treason in 1716, while the Earl of Nithsdale only avoided execution at the same time by escaping from the Tower of London disguised as a woman. (Bruce Lenman, *The Jacobite Risings in Britain: 1689–1746*, 1980, p. 161.) Only when the printing of *Redgauntlet* was well advanced did Scott alter his early plan to call the novel *Herries*. (See *Letters*, viii, 203.) Herries of Birrenswork (the name appeared as Birvenswork, Boirenswork, and Birrenswork in the first edition of

1824) was itself an alteration at proof stage from Herries of Dryfesdale. Burrens and Burnswark, from which Herries's designation perhaps derives, were the sites of Roman encampments east of Dumfries.

51 *Rembrandt-looking portrait*: The pictorial method of the Dutch painter Rembrandt van Rijn (1606–69) involved refining the relationship of light to shade to register subtle emotional nuances.

'*Over the water*': a reference to the exiled Stewart claimant, James Francis, James III as his adherents called him. This was a common Jacobite toast. Common too was the gesture which Redgauntlet makes with his glass over the water-decanter. Some drinking vessels in the eighteenth century were even made with a small quantity of water under the glass for toasting the distant king in safety.

56 *unlawful craft*: The word 'craft' is used here in the precise sense of *OED*, V, 10, 'implements used in catching or killing fish'. Salmon fishing in the Solway was much regulated by acts of the Scottish Parliament. Some of this legislation was obscure, and the position was complicated because English law also applied in part. (Normand.) There were various attempts to render the law clearer, and in 1824, the year in which *Redgauntlet* was written, the legality of stake-nets was the subject of a parliamentary report. The hazard which they represented of over-fishing is considered by Scott in his 1828 review of Humphry Davy's *Salmonia, or Days of Fly-Fishing*. Further, Redgauntlet's defence of the traditional fishing economy over against Geddes's modern industry relates to the novel's central political oppositions.

65 *pleached alleys, wildernesses*: features of the old-fashioned, formal garden which was beginning to lose favour in the later eighteenth century. Pleached alleys were overarched with closely interlaced ('pleached') branches, and wildernesses were stretches of ground planted with trees and shrubs in an ornamentally wild style, often forming a maze or labyrinth. Scott seems to have revived the word 'pleached', finding it in Shakespeare (*Much Ado about Nothing*, I, ii, 8).

cleanliness among the women of Auld Reekie: Edinburgh was notorious in the eighteenth century for the squalid accommodation afforded to residents and visitors in its overcrowded tenements. Defoe provides an early impression: 'the city suffers infinite disadvantages, and lies under such scandalous inconveniences as are, by its enemies, made a subject of scorn and reproach; as if the people . . . delighted in stench and nastiness'. (Daniel Defoe, *A Tour through the Whole Island of Great Britain* (1724–6), ed. Pat Rogers, Penguin, 1971, p. 577.) Improvements were only beginning in the 1760s.

hinted at in a paper of the Spectator: I have not been able to trace any such idea in the *Spectator*, but something very similar is described in *Fragments on the Theory and Practice of Landscape Gardening* (1816) by Humphry Repton (1752–1818). It was a work known to Scott.

66 *Black-letter . . . Greyfriars' Churchyard*: Greyfriars' Churchyard, south of the Old Town, was until the end of the eighteenth century the principal Edinburgh cemetery. It contains the graves of many distinguished Scots. Black-letter or Gothic is a type-face used by printers pre-1600. Here it refers to inscriptions in stone from that time.

blinded times of Papistry: A reformed church was established in Scotland on Presbyterian lines in 1560.

the Gunpowder-Plot: See note to p. 393 (3).

Vanity of vanities, saith the preacher: Ecclesiastes 1: 2.

67 *the blessed George Fox . . . along the stony road*: George Fox (1624–90), founder of the Society of Friends (Quakers), first visited Scotland in September 1657. In a letter to Robert Barclay, written in 1675, he recalled his feelings on the occasion: 'as soon as ever my Horse set his feet upon the land of the Scottish Nation, the Infinite Sparks of life sparkled about me.' (See *The Journal of George Fox*, ed. Norman Penney, 1911, i, 454.)

68 *the persecution to which these harmless devotees were subjected . . . Mount Sharon*: Quakers were first heard of in Scotland in 1653, but the sect never gathered a strong following there. Scott's knowledge of their early persecutions, their beliefs, and manner of address came from several sources. His note 19 acknowledges the thanks he owed as a child to the elderly Kelso Quakeress who lent him books and tracts during his solitary holidays. Chief among Fox's disciples in the Borders were Walter Scott of Raeburn and John Swinton of Swinton, ancestors of Scott's on both sides of his family. Like Philip Geddes, Joshua's grandfather, they had suffered imprisonment and loss of estates in the 1660s. (See Scott's note 1 to *The Heart of Midlothian*, ed. Claire Lamont, World's Classics, 1982, pp. 509–12.) Further, Scott owned several standard works of Quaker doctrine. (See J. G. Cochrane, *A Catalogue of the Library at Abbotsford*, 1838, pp. 72 and 77–8.) As a sign of his redemption, Joshua's father changed the name of his home from Sharing-Knowe (Sharing Hill) to Mount Sharon, Sharon being the great maritime plain described in Isaiah 35: 2 and 65: 10.

69 *Sancho's doctor, Tirtea Fuera*: *Don Quixote*, part II, ch. xlvii. Scott errs slightly: the doctor's name is Pedro Recio de Aguero; his native village is Tirtea-fuera.

the Aberdeen-man's privilege: a phrase applied 'to them who deny what they have said'. (James Kelly, *A Complete Collection of Scotish Proverbs Explained and made Intelligible to the English Reader*, 1721, p. 151.)

71 *the celebrated Millar*: Philip Millar or Miller (1691–1771), gardener to the Apothecaries Company at Chelsea and author of several books for gardeners.

the policy, or pleasure-garden . . . no particular charms: The garden at Mount Sharon is, to some extent, an example of the old-fashioned, semi-formal style admired by Scott himself. The 'cabinet of verdure', popular in the reign of Charles II, is representative. According to Philip Miller, a cabinet is 'either square, circular, or in Cants, making a kind of Salon' of lattice-work. (*The Gardeners and Florists Dictionary*, 1724, i.) The 'jet d'eau', 'cabinet', and compartmented summer and winter gardens are in contrast to the more 'natural-seeming', irregular style favoured in the later eighteenth century by Robert Dodsley, whose description of the poet William Shenstone's (1714–63) garden at the Leasowes, Worcestershire, is included in his edition of Shenstone's *Works*, ii (1764). Lancelot 'Capability' Brown (1715–83), a celebrated landscape gardener, caused a stream to flow through the grounds of Blenheim Palace, Oxfordshire. Horace Walpole's (1717–97) essay 'On Modern Gardening', printed 1771, was not published until 1780; so in terms of the novel's internal dating this reference is erroneous. The artificiality of Mount Sharon, however, would have been welcomed by one enthusiast of the time on account of its valuable contrast to the dismal landscape beyond its bounds. Henry Home, Lord Kames, the famous Scottish judge, clearly influences Darsie's conclusion when he writes, 'the solitariness . . . of a waste country ought to be contrasted in forming a garden . . . *jets d'eau*, cascades, objects active, gay, and splendid. Nay such a garden should in some measure avoid imitating nature, by taking on an extraordinary appearance of regularity and art.' (*Elements of Criticism* (1762), 4th edn., 1769, i, 299.)

72 *no one called Lord, save one only*: a Quaker tenet finding justification in, for example, 1 Corinthians 8: 4–6. The language of Joshua and Rachel Geddes is steeped in biblical allusion, often little more than half quotation or paraphrase.

73 *The truth is not in them*: Cf. 1 John 1: 8.

the Mammon of gain: Cf. Luke 16: 13.

75 *account of the Leasowes*: In contrast to the old-fashioned character of the garden, Joshua Geddes's farm is a modern venture, comparable to the larger-scale projects to reclaim poor land which were undertaken in Scotland in the second half of the eighteenth century by such improvers as Lord Kames. Designed to expose the beauties of the natural landscape while ensuring the comfort of clean feet, the farm combines imaginative potential with security. As his religious beliefs would suggest, however, Geddes has not succumbed to the vogue for inscriptions, moral and classical, on benches, urns, trees, etc. to be found in Shenstone's garden at the Leasowes.

tameness of the game: For a similar description, see the *Spectator*, ed. Donald F. Bond, 1965, iv, 189–90 (No. 477).

76 *John Scott of Amwell*: (1730–83), a Quaker of Southwark who wrote *Four Elegies, descriptive and moral* (1760) and *Amwell* (1776), descriptive of his estate in Hertfordshire. In general, Quakers at this time considered novels and plays to be pernicious, and most other forms of diversion to

be at best a waste of time. (See Stephen Hobhouse, *William Law and Eighteenth-Century Quakerism*, 1927, p. 326.)

Tory Laird ... Whig Lawyer: To make a crude but workable distinction, Whigs were identified in Scotland in the first half of the eighteenth century with the party who supported the 1688–9 Revolution, with adherence to the Presbyterian form of worship and the Hanoverian succession and often with business and city interests. Tories had in religion Episcopalian, even Roman Catholic leanings, they early supported the royal prerogative against the encroachments of Parliament, and many were old landed families (though there were Whigs among the landed gentry and nobility), and there was certainly a Jacobite faction within the Tory party. The involvement of a handful of Tory leaders in the 1715 Jacobite rising effectively barred the party from office for most of the century.

77 *the subterranean river ... the celebrated cavern*: The reference is to the river which runs through Peak Cavern, near Castleton in Derbyshire. A favourite tourist spot in the eighteenth century, it is described by Daniel Defoe and earlier by Celia Fiennes (1662–1741) after her visit of 1697. (See *The Journeys of Celia Fiennes*, ed. John Hillaby, 1983, pp. 128–9.)

79 *the general shade of powder which marks the gentleman*: Gentlemen and ladies powdered their hair in the eighteenth century. Elizabeth Montagu, the bluestocking, writes to her husband in 1764: 'All the powder is combed out of my hair, all the vanities are vanished out of my head. I am meek in my Manners and humble in my apparel.' (*Mrs Montagu, 'Queen of the Blues'*, ed. Reginald Blunt, 1923, i, 100.) The fashion died out at the end of the century, hastened by Pitt's tax of 1795 on hair powder.

81 *conscious, like Scrub ... because they laughed consumedly*: Scrub, a servant to Mr Sullen in George Farquhar's *The Beaux' Stratagem*, 1707 (see act III, i).

82 *'Who, with no face, as 'twere, outfaced me'*: *The Comedy of Errors*, v, i, 245.

Vinco vincentem, ergo vinco te: 'If I defeat the one who defeated you [in competition at law], I defeat you.' The phrase is from the law relating to bankruptcy and states the rule of preference among competing creditors' claims.

84 *Sir John Fielding*: (d. 1780.) Blind apparently from birth, he was a celebrated and much feared Westminster justice, carrying on the plan for breaking up gangs of robbers introduced by his half-brother, the novelist Henry Fielding.

legality of the mode of fishing ... guilty of a riot: See the note to p. 56. What was clear about the laws controlling salmon fishing in the eighteenth century and in 1824, when the novel was written, is that they favoured no one method. As the context implies, the destruction of an illegal obstruction *via facti* ('by force') is lawful, provided excessive violence is avoided. (Normand.)

85 *Don Quixote enough . . . the sad-coloured garment*: Cervantes' absurdly chivalric hero received the sobriquet 'the Knight of the Sad Countenance' (*Don Quixote*, part I, ch. xix). Here 'those . . . of the sad-coloured garment' are Quakers, noted for their sombre and plain dress.

Amadis: Amadis of Gaul, the hero of a medieval romance in prose of the same title. Originally written in Portuguese by Vasco de Lobeira, there are subsequent versions in Spanish and French. Robert Southey, in 1803, translated and published an abridged version admired by Scott.

Sancho Panza: the commonsensical but devoted squire of Don Quixote.

Urganda: Urganda la Desconecida (the Unknown), an enchantress, the patroness and guardian of Amadis in the romances of that cycle.

87 *old leaven of prelacy*: the Episcopalian Church, disestablished in Scotland after the 1688–9 Revolution, was prelatic, governed from above by bishops, unlike the Presbyterian system which invests oversight not in individuals but in a hierarchy of courts or councils constituted from ministers and elders holding office through the choice of the congregation. Episcopalian religious disabilities were not removed until 1792.

88 *Quakers . . . the fabric of our law*: The Quaker refused to confirm his word by an oath in courts of law, relying on the scriptural injunction of Matthew 5: 33–7 and James 5: 12. Oaths, it was argued, set up a double standard of truth. (See William Penn, *A Treatise of Oaths*, 1675, introductory sections ii and ix.) Provision was made instead, as early as George I's reign, for the making of a solemn affirmation.

'the Snake in the Grass,' or 'the Foot out of the Snare': both attacks on the Quakers; the first by Charles Leslie, an Anglo-Irish Nonjuror (1650–1722), published 1696; the second by John Toldervy, Thomas Brooks, and seven others, published 1656.

there is a time . . . for casting away: Ecclesiastes 3: 5.

89 *the title De periculo et commodo rei venditae*: 'Concerning the risk and profit of things that are sold.' The term 'title' refers to the descriptive heading of each subdivision of a law-book, in this case of the Pandects (the digest of Roman law), XVIII, i, 5 f.

Ross-House . . . Duff-House: Duff House near Banff was the work of William Adam, the outstanding Scottish architect of the first half of the eighteenth century and the father of Robert Adam. William Adam's style was neo-classical and showed some influence from the baroque style of the English architect Vanbrugh. Ross House was on the south side of Edinburgh, near where the McEwan Hall now is.

90 *Corporal Nym's philosophy . . . 'Things must be as they may'*: *Henry V*, II, i, 21. This was a favourite saying with Scott. (See his *Journal*, ed. W. E. K. Anderson, 1972, pp. 175 and 596.)

91 *Lex Aquarum*: 'the law of the waters'; it is attributed to Alexander II (1198–1249) and is printed in John Skene, *Regiam Majestatem* (1609). (Normand.)

Phalaris's bull: a huge copper bull devised for burning people alive. It was invented for Phalaris, a tyrant of Sicily in the sixth century BC, by Perillos, an Athenian, who became its first victim.

'E'en marvel on till time makes all things plain': misquoted from *A Midsummer Night's Dream*, v, i, 127.

Huguenot simplicity: simplicity like that of the Huguenots, French Calvinists.

92 *a return of the washed sow to wallowing in the mire*: 2 Peter 2: 22.

like John Bunyan's Pilgrim . . . sing as I went on my way: See John Bunyan, *The Pilgrim's Progress*, part I (1678), ed. J. B. Wharey and R. Sharrock, 1960, p. 66. Since Bunyan's Pilgrim sings as a thanksgiving to God for deliverance from worldly temptations, Darsie's allusion is scarcely appropriate in context.

93 *the Syrens*: in Greek mythology, sea-nymphs whose bewitching songs lure sailors to their destruction. (Homer, *Odyssey*, xii, 39 ff.)

94 *the full sweetness . . . and bread eaten in secret*: Proverbs 9: 17.

96 *Oswald made it himsell . . . air of Roslin Castle*: James Oswald, a musician and collector of Scottish traditional tunes. The air 'Roslin Castle' can be found in his compilation *The Caledonian Pocket Companion* (1752), iv, 3.

Crowdero: the name means fiddler. Crowdero was a lame fiddler in *Hudibras* (1662–78) by Samuel Butler.

Timotheus: (447–357 BC.) A poet and musician of Miletus, he made many innovations to the lyre. Reference to the power of his playing is common. Scott seems to have in mind here Dryden's description in 'Alexander's Feast; or the Power of Music: an Ode in Honour of St Cecilia's Day' (1697), l. 22.

98 *Rory Dall*: Roderick Morison (1656–1714?), bard and harper to the Chief of Macleod at Dunvegan. He was blind, as *dall* (Gaelic) signifies.

99 *thus our society separated*: Scott's note 23 on Blind Jack of Knaresborough suggests one influence in the creation of Wandering Willie. Blind Jack, in reality a Harrogate fiddler John Metcalf, conceived an attachment to a Hanoverian army captain and loyally followed him through various dangers in the 1745–6 rising. The relationship between Sir Henry Redgauntlet, Darsie's father, and Wandering Willie is comparable (Ch. XI). A further influence is the blind Welsh harper and fiddler, William ap Prichard, as described to Scott by Joseph Train (National Library of Scotland MS 3277, fos. 42–9). The same details are also recorded in John Patterson, *Memoir of Joseph Train*, 1857, pp. 44–53.

100 *the eyes of Argus*: According to Greek fable, Argus, the herdsman whom Hera set to watch Io, had eyes all over his body. When Hermes killed him, Hera placed his eyes in the peacock's tail.

101 *He played a sonata to Corelli*: Arcangelo Corelli (1653–1713), Italian

violinist and composer. The 'Devil's Sonata' was composed not by Corelli but by Giuseppe Tartini (1692–1770).

102 *Wandering Willie's Tale*: The reputation of Sir Robert Grierson of Lag (1655?–1733) provides details, situation, and tone for Wandering Willie's tale of Sir Robert Redgauntlet. As early as 1802, Scott mentions his knowledge of 'Lag's Elegy', a chap-book lampoon on the death and subsequent reception of Grierson into hell, where, surrounded by the Royalist persecutors of the Covenanters, he is pre-eminent among the damned. (See *Letters*, i, 161; and Alexander Fergusson, *The Laird of Lag: A Life-Sketch*, 1886.) But Scott's most immediate debt for the outlines of the tale is probably to an anecdote in Joseph Train's *Strains of the Mountain Muse*, 1814, pp. 191–5. Mary Lascelles provides an excellent account of the tale, its sources and revisions in 'Scott and the Art of Revision', reprinted in *Notions and Facts*, 1972, pp. 213–29. Scott, *Tales of a Grandfather*, 2nd Series, 1829, ii, 206 ff., contains details of the characters and incidents of the post-Restoration persecutions mentioned in the tale; so too does Scott's source, Patrick Walker, *Six Saints of the Covenant*, ed. D. Hay Fleming, 2 vols., 1901. But Scott's own 1832 note on the tale (note 29) is, as so often with these late annotations, quite misleading.

out wi' the Hielandmen ... in the saxteen hundred and fifty-twa: James Graham, 5th Earl and 1st Marquis of Montrose (1612–50), at the head of a Highland and Irish army conducted a brilliant campaign for the Crown against the Covenanting forces (1644–5) until defeated in September 1645 at the battle of Philiphaugh. He was hanged in Edinburgh in May 1650. William Cunningham, 9th Earl of Glencairn (1610–64) tried to raise the Highlands for Charles II in 1652–3 after the Cromwellian occupation of Scotland.

commissions of lieutenancy, and of lunacy: The first were crown commissions, giving authority to use military force for the suppression of rebellion; the second were issued by the Lord Chancellor, appointing the commissioner to manage the affairs of a lunatic. (Normand.)

Whigs and Covenanters: The term 'Whig' was probably first used in Scotland following the 'Whiggamore Raid' on Edinburgh in 1648, when Presbyterian insurgents from the radical south-west (Redgauntlet country) marched on the capital. Gilbert Burnet derives the word from 'Whiggam', a south-west word used for driving horses on. (*History of My Own Time*, 1724, i, 43.) Only later, from about 1679, was 'Whig' applied to the party in Britain who opposed the succession of the Roman Catholic James Duke of York to the Crown, and from 1689 to the supporters of the Glorious Revolution. Covenanters were the supporters of the National Covenant of 1638 and the Solemn League and Covenant of 1643. The Covenanting army was pledged to preserve the purity of the reformed Presbyterian religion and, at one stage, to establish Presbyterianism in both England and Scotland. At the Restoration

Charles II repudiated the Covenants and in the years that followed many Presbyterians suffered persecution. (See my historical appendix.)

Claverhouse's or Tam Dalyell's: Both persecutors of the Covenanters, they are historical guarantors of Sir Robert Redgauntlet's brutality. John Graham of Claverhouse, Viscount Dundee (1648–89), was active during the reigns of Charles II and James II. After James's flight, he led a Highland army in support of the Stewart cause and defeated the troops of Mary and William of Orange at Killiecrankie in July 1689 but was killed at the moment of victory. Sir Thomas Dalyell (or Dalziel) of the Binns (1599?–1685) was Commander-in-Chief of the royal forces in Scotland, 1679–85, and notorious for the savagery of his treatment of the Covenanters.

the puir hill-folk: *c.*1670–88 the Covenanters were known as hill-folk, from their seeking refuge in the hills to worship secretly during the persecutions.

103 *'Will ye tak the test?'* The Test Act and Oath of 1681 was the main instrument used against the Presbyterians of the south-west, requiring all office-holders to accept royal supremacy in spiritual as well as temporal matters. For a Covenanter this was impossible, the Church having a divine head in Christ.

a direct compact with Satan: The details of Redgauntlet's pact are drawn from Covenanting superstitions concerning various Royalist leaders. Tam Dalyell was said to be unharmed by lead bullets 'seen hopping like hailstones from [his] buff-coat and boots', while Claverhouse's horse, a gift from the devil, once turned a hare on a precipitous slope. (Scott, *Tales of a Grandfather*, 2nd Series, 1829, ii, 277–9.)

those killing times: the years 1681–5, when the persecution of the Covenanters reached its height.

'Jockie Lattin': to be found in *The Scots Musical Museum*, ed. James Johnson, 1787–1803, v, no. 430.

a Tory . . . which we now ca' Jacobites: See note to p. 76(2).

hunting and hosting, watching and warding: The obligation to follow one's feudal superior into private or public war and the right to muster tenants to patrol and suppress disturbances were abolished in 1747 in an attempt to break the local power of landlords after the second Jacobite rebellion.

the Revolution: of 1688–9. In 1690 Presbyterianism was re-established in Scotland, bringing an end to the persecution of the Covenanters. But, as Scott's note 25 states, the extreme purists (the Cameronians) were not pleased with the compromises of the re-established Kirk and rejected the Revolution settlement.

104 *fines of the non-conformist*: Charles II had re-established Episcopacy in Scotland in 1662, and there were various exactions for nonconformity in the following years. (See my historical appendix.)

Major Weir: Major Thomas Weir (1600?–70), an officer in the Covenanting army and later head of the Edinburgh City Guard. Outwardly religious but secretly vicious, he was found guilty of adultery, incest, and bestiality, and was burned as a wizard in 1670. His sister Grizel, burned as his accomplice, was apparently the original owner of the horseshoe frown which marks the foreheads of the Redgauntlets. (See Hugo Arnot, *A Collection and Abridgment of Celebrated Criminal Trials in Scotland (1536–1784)*, 1785, pp. 359 f.; and Scott, *Letters on Demonology and Witchcraft*, 1830, pp. 329 ff.)

105 *like a sheep's-head . . . tangs*: The phrase is proverbial, as recorded in Allan Ramsay, *A Collection of Scots Proverbs*, 1737, included in Thomas Fuller, *Aphorisms of Wisdom*, 1814, p. 261.

106 *blood instead of burgundy*: Scott used a variation of this detail in his portrait of Graham of Claverhouse in *Old Mortality* (1816), ch. XXXIV, and added the note: 'The author is uncertain whether this was ever said of Claverhouse. But it was currently reported of Sir Robert Grierson of Lagg, another of the persecutors, that a cup of wine placed in his hand turned to clotted blood.' Grierson of Lag, as Scott suggests in his note 29, was the original of Sir Robert Redgauntlet.

the Union: See note to p. 23(4).

107 *Davie Lindsay*: Sir David Lindsay of the Mount (1490–1555), diplomat and poet. His poetry is mainly satirical.

110 *they suld hae caa'd her*: meaning 'I am told that she was called' — a Scots usage in indirect statements to express past time.

112 *There was the fierce Middleton . . . as if they had been alive*: John Middleton, later Earl of Middleton (1619–74), was a military commander who had changed in 1648 from the side of Parliament and the Covenanters to the Royalist cause. With Glencairn (see note to p. 102(2)) he led a Royalist uprising in 1653 and at the Restoration was made Commander-in-Chief in Scotland and Commissioner to the Scottish Parliament (1660–3). John Leslie, 7th Earl and 1st Duke of Rothes (1630–81), was Treasurer and Commissioner to the Scottish Parliament (1663) and Chancellor (1667), and a cruel persecutor of the Covenanters. John Maitland, 2nd Earl and 1st Duke of Lauderdale (1616–82), had been a leading Covenanter in the early 1640s, but from 1660–80 he was Charles II's Secretary for Scottish Affairs. Personally inclined to Presbyterianism, he attempted to destroy opposition to the Episcopal Settlement by alternate measures of conciliation and repression. He was corrupt, but inventively so, and deeply patriotic. Sir Thomas Dalyell (see note to p. 102(5)), fierce and eccentric in appearance, is described elsewhere by Scott, in *Old Mortality*, ch. XXX. Captain Andrew Bruce of Earl's Hall was commissioned jointly with Claverhouse (see note to p. 102(5)) as Sheriff-Depute in Galloway in 1679. A ruthless persecutor, he commanded the party which defeated and killed Richard Cameron, the militant extremist Covenanting preacher, at Aird's Moss, Ayrshire, in July 1680. Donald Cargill, associated in leadership with Cameron, was captured in 1681 by James

Irvine of Bonshaw and subsequently executed. Dumbarton (Thomas) Douglas was also a Covenanting minister and an associate of Cameron and Cargill. The 'Bluidy Advocate MacKenyie' was Sir George Mackenzie of Rosehaugh (1636–91), who as Lord-Advocate ruthlessly prosecuted the Covenanters. He was also a scholar, writing an *Institution of the Law of Scotland* (1684) and founding the Advocates' Library (1682), now the National Library of Scotland. John Graham of Claverhouse was superstitiously thought to be impervious to lead bullets. The tale of his death from a silver bullet is in Scott, *Tales of a Grandfather*, 2nd Series, 1829, iii, 157–9. The 'Lang Lad of the Nethertown' might be the weaver described in a note to *Tales of a Grandfather*, 1851, ii, 187. The Argyle whom he helped to capture was Archibald Campbell, 9th Earl of Argyll (usual modern spelling) (1629–85), who was in arms for the Protestant Duke of Monmouth in his unsuccessful bid for the throne in 1685. The 'Bishop's summoner, that they called the Deil's Rattle-bag' is identified by Andrew Lang (*Redgauntlet*, Border Edition, 1894, i, 309) as David Mason, a Covenanter turned Royalist informer. The 'wicked guardsmen' were the Life Guards, Charles II's crack regiment of horse, set up in 1682 with Claverhouse as Colonel. Their ruthlessness was well known. The 'savage Highland Amorites' were the so-called 'Highland Host' of 1678, some 6,000 Gaels and 3,000 Lowland militiamen, sent to repress the Covenanters of the south-west. A Covenanting poem on the Battle of Bothwell Bridge (1679), quoted in Scott's 1830 note to *Old Mortality*, ch. XXIX, contains the line, 'And all the Highland Amorites'. The Amorites are mentioned as an enemy tribe of the Israelites in the 1662 *Prayer Book*, 135: 10.

113 *Donald of the Isles*: Donald, 2nd Lord of the Isles (d. 1420), a powerful chief of the Western Isles.

Earl of Douglas . . . at the Threave Castle: MacLellan, tutor or guardian to the young Lord of Bomby, was beheaded by the Earl of Douglas in 1452, while the messenger bringing the order for his release was detained to take refreshment after his journey. Scott relates the incident in *Tales of a Grandfather*, 1828, ii, 120–3.

114 *the Privy Council . . . the Presbytery*: the Privy Council, a body of private advisers to and selected by the sovereign; the Presbytery, an organ of government in the Presbyterian Church, made up of representative ministers and elders of the parishes in an area. Both used their extensive powers to suppress witchcraft in the late seventeenth century.

117 *Sir Redwald Redgauntlet . . . the forty-five*: For inconsistencies in the generations of Redgauntlets, see Mary Lascelles, 'Scott and the Art of Revision', *Notions and Facts*, 1972, p. 226.

118 *epigraph*: *Christis Kirk on the Grene*, stanza vi, an anonymous poem, attributed to James I of Scotland, but more often to James V (1513–42).

like Malvolio: Malvolio, steward to Olivia in *Twelfth Night*. His self-delusions run riot at II, v, 23–179.

the Barmecide . . . Alnaschar: The illusory feast was prepared not for Alnaschar but for Shacabac, the barber's sixth brother. (See *Tales of the East*, ed. Henry Weber, 1812, i, 147–9.)

the Ode to Castle Building: to be found in *English Minstrelsy*, ed. Walter Scott, 1810, i, 242.

121 *Miss Nickie Murray . . . Edinburgh assemblies*: In her office as 'Lady-Directress' Miss Nicolas (Nickie) Murray, sister of the Earl of Mansfield, presided over the public dances held in the Edinburgh assembly rooms in Old Assembly Close, off the High Street, during the middle of the eighteenth century. According to Robert Chambers, she regulated the conduct of the young dancers with 'all the bland and amiable gentleness of a downright, arbitrary, feudal, and undisputed sovereignty'. (*Traditions of Edinburgh*, 1825, ii, 29–30.)

123 *'And merrily danced the Quaker'*: The traditional words can be found in *Love, Labour and Liberty: The Eighteenth-Century Scottish Lyric*, ed. Thomas Crawford, 1976, p. 15, and the tune in *The Poems and Songs of Robert Burns*, ed. James Kinsley, 1968, ii, 689. The song is, of course, a gibe at the Quaker disapproval of dancing as a device of the devil.

124 *Aldiborontiphoscophornio . . . Rigdum-Funnidos*: characters in Henry Carey's farce *Chrononhotonthologos* (1734). Scott humorously gave the names respectively to two brothers, his friends, his printer James Ballantyne and the publisher John Ballantyne.

duties of the Cavaliere Serviente: Cf. Lord George Byron, *Beppo* (1818), stanza xl, on the duties of the attentive beau.

125 *'severe in youthful wisdom'*: In Milton, *Paradise Lost*, iv, 845, the angel Zephon is described as 'Severe in youthful beauty'.

128 *Gil Blas . . . in the robbers' cavern*: Alain René Le Sage (1668–1747) published his prose romance *Les Aventures de Gil Blas de Santillane* between 1715 and 1735. The incident to which Darsie refers is in book I, ch. x.

132 *Lazarus . . . Dives*: Christ's parable of the poor man, Lazarus, and the rich man, Dives (Latin adj., 'rich'), is to be found in Luke 16: 19–31.

'My own fish-guts to my own sea-maws': a proverb meaning, 'If you have any Superfluities give them to your poor Relations, Friends, or Countrymen, rather than to others.' (James Kelly, *A Complete Collection of Scotish Proverbs*, 1721, p. 118.)

133 *Stair or Arniston*: For Lord Stair, see note to p. 17(2). Arniston is possibly Robert Dundas of Arniston (1685–1753), who was King's Advocate or Crown Prosecutor before becoming Lord President of the Court of Session. More likely, it is his son, also Robert Dundas, Lord President (appointed 1760) at the time of Alan Fairford's entry into court. (Normand.)

the Parliament-House: just south of St Giles' Cathedral. A new Parliament

House was opened in 1639, and since 1642 the Courts of Justice have met in the same building.

Peter Peebles: Scott's note 30 can be supplemented by the longer account of Peter Peebles in Robert Chambers, *Traditions of Edinburgh*, 1825, ii, 100–1.

the Poor's Roll: The Faculty of Advocates appointed six of their number to be available as counsel for the poor, and Writers to the Signet and Solicitors to the Supreme Court likewise appointed four members. This, or a comparable system, operated from the fifteenth century until the Legal Aid Act of 1949 superseded previous arrangements. Consequently, the epithet 'Poor' before Peter Peebles's name is a legal title signifying that he is on the Poor's Roll and receiving free legal assistance.

as a sieve is sib to a riddle: A riddle is a coarse-meshed sieve. The phrase is proverbial, denoting close relationship. (James Kelly, *A Complete Collection of Scottish Proverbs*, 1721, p. 31.)

135 *the Lord will make your days long ... your father's grey hairs*: a reference to the Fifth Commandment, 'Honour your father and your mother ...'. (Exodus 20: 12.)

136 *the Lord Ordinary ... the President to the Bench*: The Court of Session, the Scottish judicature, is divided into an Outer and an Inner House. In the eighteenth century, routine cases were heard in the Outer House (the old Parliament Hall) in the presence of a single judge, the Lord Ordinary. The essential feature of the Inner House was that the Bench (all fifteen judges), presided over by the Lord President, sat together to hear argument and pronounce decisions on complex cases. In the early nineteenth century this unwieldy process was made more expeditious by using the Outer House as a Court of First Instance and dividing the Inner House into two Appeal Courts.

like the rope to the man ... the water to the fire: from the Scottish folk-tale 'The Wife and her Bush of Berries', recorded in Katharine M. Briggs, *A Dictionary of British Folk-Tales*, part A, 1970, ii, 579–80.

137 *alimentary*: nutritious; perhaps here, given Peebles's characteristically legal mode of speaking, with a suggestion of the word's forensic application, referring to the fund of maintenance (aliment) which the law allowed to certain persons.

the Luckenbooths: See note to p. 23(1).

138 *Multiplepoinding ... declarator of marriage*: A means of settling competing claims on a fund, a multiplepoinding is a convenient and safe legal remedy because it brings all claimants into the field. The nearest English equivalent is not 'double distress', as Scott suggests in his note 33, but a bill of interpleader. A multiplepoinding might be conjoined with a declarator of marriage when the conflicting claims depend on determining whether a marriage took place or not. (Normand.)

If the kirk is ower muckle ... in the quire: a proverb, 'Spoken when People say something is too much, intimating that they need take no more than they have use for.' (James Kelly, *A Complete Collection of Scotish Proverbs*, 1721, pp. 314–15.)

interim decreet ... action of suspension ... Sheriff-Court process: An interim decree may be pronounced by the court when a part of a litigation can be disposed of before judgement is given on the whole matter. If a bill is protested for non-payment or non-acceptance, a charge can at once be made against the drawee. A suspension is the proper procedure for delaying this. An advocation was a mode of appeal to the Court of Session, the supreme civil court in Scotland, from the Sheriff Court (County Court) or another subordinate court. (Normand.)

As Tweed comes to Melrose: The river Tweed approaches Melrose by a slow and winding course.

139 *by way of petition and complaint ... back-door out of Court*: Peter Peebles cannot decide how to punish at law Plainstanes's 'assault' on him. He might initiate criminal proceedings against him and this would require the consent of the Lord-Advocate as public prosecutor. Alternatively, an assault upon the opposite party while the action is still in court can be penalized by the loss of the action, thus giving Peebles immediate release from the suit. (Normand.)

the essence of hamesucken ... hanged: The crime of committing a premeditated assault upon a person in his own house or dwelling-place (hamesucken) was formerly a capital offence in Scotland.

an able-bodied Celt: See note to p. 19(2).

140 *From circumstances ... to whom it was addressed*: Added at proof stage, this sentence ended the first volume in the three-volume first edition of 1824.

141 *carry on the thread of the story*: This is the case in Samuel Richardson's hugely successful novel *Pamela* (1740). Mainly in letter and journal form with some intervention from an external narrator, it was a landmark in the development of the novel and clearly influential on *Redgauntlet*. (See my introduction.)

142 *Mr Saunders Fairford ... he was no niggard*: Scott's own father, also called Walter Scott, a Writer to the Signet, is generally considered to be the original of Alexander (Saunders) Fairford. (See Lockhart, *Life of Scott*, 1839, i, 242–3 and 249–52.) St Giles' Cathedral, the principal Presbyterian church in Edinburgh, forms the north side of Parliament Square, on the south side of the High Street, the Square housing Parliament Hall (the law court of the Outer House) and the courts of the Inner House. Warren was a well-known manufacturer of blacking, his name best remembered by the modern reader from Charles Dickens's employment in Warren's blacking-factory as a child. An elder (layman with administrative office) in the Presbyterian Church, Fairford senior demonstrated his loyalty to the Hanoverian establishment in the 1745 rebellion. (See

note to p. 28(1).) Consequently, he refuses to recognize Charles Edward Stewart as Prince of Wales (his title among the Jacobites); but he is not so insensitive as to refer to him by the common title of 'Pretender', with its implication of 'false claimant'. Chevalier is a compromise, the Chevalier de St George being a title conferred on James Francis, Charles Edward's father, by Louis XIV.

144 *Peter Drudgeit*: He was Saunders Drudgeit at p. 133.

Candlemaker Row: south of the Cowgate. Brown's Square, where Alan is said to live, had an entry into Candlemaker Row.

the blue jacket and white lapelle: the uniform of officers in the Royal Navy.

Like Alpheus ... Augean mass: In the sixth of his twelve labours Hercules was set to cleanse in a single day the stables of Augeas, King of Elis. One explanation of how he did it was that he turned the course of the river Alpheus through them.

145 *the ancient Scottish Parliament*: The Scottish Parliament sat here for the last time in 1707, to debate the Union with England.

147 *single bills ... summar-roll*: All proceedings when they first come before the Inner House are enrolled under the head 'single bills'. The summar roll is a list of cases which require speedy disposal.

Cimmerian abysses: The Cimmerii were fabled to live in perpetual darkness. (Homer, *Odyssey*, xi, 14.)

Doctor Pitcairn: Archibald Pitcairn(e) (1652–1713), a noted Jacobite physician and poet, author of *The Assembly*, a play satirizing the Presbyterian Church, and of much Latin verse.

148 *Punchinello*: Adapted from the character of Pulcinella, a buffoon, in the Italian *Commedia dell' arte*, he first appeared in Britain as a puppet at the end of the seventeenth century.

149 *ancient story of the fruit ... one side of the blade only*: The tale of Snowwhite (no. 53 in the Grimm brothers' collection) contains a comparable detail. In his *Life of Artaxerxes* Plutarch (AD *c*.45–*c*.120) describes how Parysatis, mother of Artaxerxes II, murdered her son's consort by poisoning a bird in this fashion. Alan Fairford appears to conflate the two stories.

Harlequin: a character from the Italian *Commedia dell' arte*, armed with a wand supposed to make him invisible.

150 *hope delayed which sickens the heart*: Proverbs 13: 12.

Benjamin: the youngest of Jacob's twelve sons. (Genesis 35: 18.)

151 *an acute metaphysical judge*: Henry Home, Lord Kames (1696–1782). Something of an eccentric, he was appointed Lord of Session in 1752 and wrote on widely diverse subjects: the philosophy of law, religion, history, aesthetic theory, and farming.

154 *the Sheriff ... the King's Advocate*: Before 1747 the office of Sheriff in Scotland was hereditary. After 1747 all sheriffdoms were Crown

appointments. The Sheriff-depute, as he was called, was the principal executive officer of the Crown in the county (Scott was Sheriff-depute of Selkirkshire from 1799) and he appointed a Sheriff-substitute to help him with his work. In the eighteenth century the Sheriff had the duty of investigating crimes. The King's Advocate, also called the Lord-Advocate, is the Scottish Attorney-General and public prosecutor of crimes.

155 *Better a finger off, as aye wagging*: a proverb meaning, 'Better put an end to a troublesome Business, than to be always vex'd with it.' (James Kelly, *A Complete Collection of Scotish Proverbs*, 1721, p. 56.)

157 *Falkirk-field*: See note to p. 28(1).

159 *thick as the palpable darkness of Egypt*: a reference to the ninth plague sent to punish the Egyptians. (Exodus 10: 21.)

hung up by a remit . . . report before answer: The case has been referred for professional advice and recommendations to an accountant before the court is prepared to come to any decision.

164 *sons of Belial*: a common biblical phrase to describe the wicked; for example 1 Samuel 2: 12. Belial, an abstract noun meaning 'iniquity', is given personification in 2 Corinthians 6: 15.

166 *Worship is due to Heaven only*: The Quaker aversion to titles, honours, and distinctions can be traced to Exodus 20: 4–5 among other places.

Swear not at all: Matthew 5: 34.

181 *true Joan and Hodge school*: generic names for female and male rustics. (See *Love's Labour's Lost*, III, i, 207.)

184 *a quoit man wi' woman folk loike*: Scott indicates Cumbrian speech in a similar way in *Waverley* (1814), ch. LX, and in *The Heart of Midlothian* (1818), ch. XL.

185 *avoid the action of exterior and contagious sympathies*: This detail contributes to the novel's Gothic atmosphere. Such imprisonment and consequent insanity feature, for example, in Charles Maturin's Gothic romance *Melmoth the Wanderer* (1820), ch. III, a work which *Redgauntlet* echoes more than once.

190 *Omne ignotum pro terribili*: 'everything unknown is held to be dreadful', a parody of *Agricola*, 30, by Tacitus (AD *c*.55–119), *omne ignotum pro magnifico est*, 'everything unknown is held to be glorious', part of a description of Britain.

192 *Lord Chancellor's warrant*: The Lord Chancellor had a general jurisdiction over guardians to appoint or remove them, except where they derived their status from statute, that is, from appointment in a parent's will. (Normand.)

193 *Poor Peter Peebles!* In the two-volume 'Magnum' edition of 1832, the first volume ended here.

194 '*Sufficient . . . the evil thereof*': Matthew 6: 34.

'*To such a lowness, but his "learned lawyers"*': *King Lear*, III, iv, 70–1 ('To such a lowness but his unkind daughters').

Sheriffmoor: On 13 November 1715 at Sheriffmuir north of Stirling the Jacobites under the Earl of Mar encountered government forces led by the Duke of Argyll. Tactically indecisive, the battle was a strategic defeat for the Jacobites, who retreated.

196 '*my bosom's lord . . . on his throne*': *Romeo and Juliet*, v, i, 3.

a collier or a salter: Until the end of the eighteenth century (1799), colliers and salters existed in a state of slavery with no rights as British subjects. They were sold as part of the machinery of the mines in which they worked. (See Henry Cockburn, *Memorials of His Time*, 1856, pp. 76–9, and Scott's note 63 above.)

197 *thine own beggarly justices*: Scottish Justices of the Peace never assumed the importance they had in eighteenth-century England, having in Scotland only a minimal jurisdiction over oaths, licenses, and weights and measures.

198 *Kennington Common, or Hairiebie*: Kennington Common, on the south side of London, and Harraby Hill, near Carlisle, where executions of Jacobites took place after the 1745–6 rebellion.

199 *the angel Ithuriel . . . the detected King of the Powers of the Air*: The reference is to Milton, *Paradise Lost*, iv, 869–70, Satan's confrontation with Ithuriel and the other angels who guard Eden.

200 *out with Derwentwater in the fifteen*: See the note to p. 50.

lost half of his estate . . . my father had a remission: English law was applied to Scotland for all purposes in prosecuting treason by the Act 7 Anne, c. 21. One effect was that forfeiture deprived the descendants of convicted traitors of their rights to succeed to forfeited properties. By the act of forfeiture passed in 1716, after the first Jacobite rising, Justice Foxley's father lost his estate, as did Herbert Herries, Redgauntlet's kinsman (Letter V). By a similar act of 1746, the Redgauntlet estates were also forfeited (Ch. XVII). Justice Foxley's father received a remission (a pardon from the sovereign) for his part in the rebellion, but Redgauntlet has no such pardon.

warrants out against you from the Secretary of State's office: By English law, applicable in this instance in Scotland, the Secretary of State might commit a person to prison on suspicion of any treasonable offence. (Normand.)

204 *Dr Byrom's celebrated lines*: 'Extempore Verses, Intended to allay the Violence of Party-Spirit', by Dr John Byrom (1692–1763), Jacobite, shorthand specialist and writer of minor verses.

206 *Preston, Clifton, and Falkirk*: The Jacobites under Thomas Forster (1675?–

1738) and James, Earl of Derwentwater (1689–1716) occupied Preston in Lancashire in 1715. Their surrender on 14 November was the end of the rebellion in England. The Skirmish of Clifton, a few miles south of Penrith, 17 December 1745, was a minor Jacobite victory on the march back into Scotland. Across the Border, Falkirk saw the final Jacobite victory on 17 January 1746, when the government troops under General Hawley were defeated.

207 *partisans of the Stewart family . . . their most appropriate punishment*: Scott is here conflating the Jacobite agitations of 1752–3, outlined in his 1832 introduction, and the political conditions in Britain in the early 1760s. In fact, by 1765, the supposed date of the novel's action, Jacobite sympathy in Charles's birthplace Rome and elsewhere on the Continent and in Britain had dwindled to harmless proportions. However, the years 1762–6 saw a period of instability in British politics. The demagogue John Wilkes (1727–97) fiercely opposed the government of the Scottish John Stuart, 3rd Earl of Bute (1713–92) and Prime Minister from 1761–3. Bute's influence over the youthful George III made him for a time the most powerful man in Britain. The attack was mainly conducted through Wilkes's paper, the *North Briton*, no. 45 of which led to his prosecution, Bute's resignation, and popular action against the government. Wilkes continued to stimulate London radicalism and economic discontent throughout the 1760s.

209 *the liberation of Scotland*: Robert Bruce the elder and John Balliol were the chief claimants to the Scottish throne after the death of Queen Margaret in 1290. Edward I of England, assuming overlordship of Scotland, chose John Balliol as king in 1292, but in 1296 division between John and Edward led to John's defeat, abdication, and exile. There followed ten years in which Scotland struggled for independence from England, led by William Wallace (d. 1305) and latterly by Robert Bruce, grandson of Bruce the elder. In 1306 Robert Bruce declared himself king (Robert I), and in June 1314 he defeated Edward II of England at Bannockburn. After King Robert's death in 1329, the throne was again in jeopardy, the successor, his son, David II (1324–71), being a minor. Edward Balliol (1283?–1364), elder son of the exiled John, with English support, defeated the Scots at the Battle of Dupplin, near Perth, in August 1332 and assumed the crown. The Scots were again defeated at Halidon Hill, near Berwick, in July 1333, by Edward III of England, who reassumed overlordship of Scotland.

and Sir Simon Fraser: The ordering of events is inaccurate here. Edward Balliol was hunted out of Annan, Dumfriesshire, by the Scots in December 1332, before the crushing defeat at Halidon and England's reassertion of control in Scotland. The patriot chiefs at Annan were Archibald Douglas, Guardian (Regent) in David II's minority, and subsequently killed at Halidon, and John Randolph, second son of Guardian Thomas Randolph, Earl of Moray, who had died at Musselburgh in July 1332. The story of Alberick Redgauntlet's part in the episode is of course fictional. (See Scott, *Tales of a Grandfather*, 1828, ii, 13–14.)

210 *Dundrennan*: a Cistercian abbey in Kirkcudbrightshire, founded by David I of Scotland in 1142.

211 *Saint Ninian's of Whiteherne*: St Ninian (*fl.* 400?) was the first missionary to Scotland whose name is known. He is said to have founded a church at Whiteherne, now called Whithorn, in Wigtownshire. A Romanesque cathedral and priory were begun there in the twelfth century. St Ninian was at the height of his popularity in the early fourteenth century, King Robert I undertaking a pilgrimage to Whithorn in the last months of his life.

battle of Durham: the Battle of Neville's Cross, near Durham, 17 October 1346. David II of Scotland was defeated, led in triumph through London, and imprisoned in the Tower. Many of the Scottish nobility were slain or imprisoned.

213 *or Richmond conquer*: See *Richard III*, v, iii, 125–31.

Sir John Friend, executed for High Treason in 1696: Scott confuses here two adherents of the Stewarts, Sir John Friend and Sir John Fenwick. Both executed for treason, Friend in April 1696 and Fenwick in January 1697, it was Fenwick's horse that the Jacobites claimed as the horse William III rode when he met his fatal accident. There is no evidence for this and it seems to be merely a pious legend. William III died in March 1702 after breaking his collar-bone while trying out a new horse in Richmond Park.

214 *When Scotland was herself . . . Legislature*: Redgauntlet refers to the period before the Act of Union of 1707, which dissolved the Scottish parliament and centred all government in London.

220 *the beautiful Scottish air called Wandering Willie*: to be found in *The Scots Musical Museum*, ed. James Johnson, 1787–1803, i, no. 57. Robert Burns developed the well-known song 'Wandering Willie' from a model found in David Herd, *Ancient and Modern Scottish Songs*, 1776, ii, 140.

Blondel: The troubadour Blondel is said to have discovered Richard I, Cœur de Lion (1157–99), in the Castle of Durrenstein, by singing a song to which the king replied.

221 '*Oh whistle and I'll come t'ye, my lad*': The tune is in *The Scots Musical Museum*, ii, no. 106. For the traditional words and Robert Burns's adaptation of them, see *The Poems and Songs of Robert Burns*, ed. James Kinsley, 1968, ii, 700–1.

'*I'll ne'er beguile thee*': to be found in Allan Ramsay, *The Tea-Table Miscellany*, 10th edn., 1740, i, 70.

222 '*But wishes that I were away*': The tune, which commonly occurs as the last entry in song collections, is in *The Scots Musical Museum*, vi, no. 600.

For the traditional words, see *The Poems and Songs of Robert Burns*, iii, 1194–5.

'*Hey, Johnnie lad, cock up your beaver*': The tune is in *The Scots Musical Museum*, iv, no. 309. For the words, see *The Poems and Songs of Robert Burns*, ii, 604–5.

'*The hills of the Highlands for ever I love*': The tune is in *The Scots Musical Museum*, iii, no. 259. For the words, see *The Poems and Songs of Robert Burns*, ii, 527–8.

'*And twice as much as a' that*': The tune is in *The Scots Musical Museum*, iii, no. 290. For the words, see Joseph Ritson, *Scotish Songs*, 1869, ii, 441–3.

223 '*And bid my merry-men come?*': For a similar stanza, see the ballad 'Prince Robert' in *Minstrelsy of the Scottish Border, The Poetical Works of Sir Walter Scott*, 1833–4, iii, 270.

'*Kind Robin loes me*': to be found in Allan Ramsay, *The Tea-Table Miscellany*, 1740, iv, 338–9.

'*Ere I will leave thee*': to be found in Allan Ramsay, *The Tea-Table Miscellany*, 1740, i, 54–5.

224 *like Quixote's visor*: After making a visor from pasteboard, Don Quixote discovered its weakness and strengthened it inside with strips of iron. (*Don Quixote*, part I, ch. i.) Robert Chambers notes, 'It was very common for Scottish ladies of rank, even till the middle of the last century, to wear black masks, in walking abroad or airing in a carriage.' (*Traditions of Edinburgh*, 1825, ii. 267.)

the Man in the Iron Mask: Variously identified, he was a mysterious State prisoner of France, confined in the Bastille and other prisons for thirty years in the reign of Louis XIV.

227 *Commissioners of Supply*: Next in importance after Sheriff-deputes in Scottish local government, Commissioners of Supply were the main element in county administration until 1889, when county councils were set up. Among their duties, they were responsible for catching and holding criminals. Justices of the Peace had more restricted authority.

228 *The withers . . . were not unwrung*: adapted from *Hamlet*, III, ii, 249.

Sherrif-Substitute . . . Sheriff-Depute: See the note to p. 154.

stake-nets . . . lawfully removed via facti: See note to p. 84(2).

229 *the Advocate*: the Lord-Advocate, the public prosecutor of all serious crime in Scotland.

Hinc illae lachrymae! Hence [came] those tears'; Terence (*c.*190–159 BC), *Andria*, I, i, 99, and generally used. Here it indicates that Alan now knows the reason for his difficulties in interviewing Provost Crosbie.

230 *Lord Burleigh in the Critic*: *The Critic* (1781), III, i, 140–9, a play by Richard Brinsley Sheridan.

231 *Ecclefechan*: east of Dumfries. Provost Crosbie refers to the harrying of

Charles Edward's baggage wagons on the march south in November 1745. On his return north Charles exacted a fine for the damage, including the Provost's hundred pounds Scots. (See note to p. 30(1).)

Scots or English . . . too much for me to lose: The Scottish currency, though once of the same value, had become by 1700 worth only one-twelfth of the English. It was officially terminated in 1707 at the Union, but calculations on the basis of it continued until late in the eighteenth century.

Wade and the Duke: Field-Marshal George Wade (1673–1748) and William Augustus, Duke of Cumberland (1721–65), third son of George II, were the commanders of the Hanoverian army sent to quell the Jacobite rebellion of 1745–6. Charles Edward turned back north at Derby on 6 December 1745, his march to London threatened by Wade's army at his rear, Cumberland's to the west, and the Brigade of Guards ahead.

the oaths: These were the oaths of allegiance to the Hanoverian establishment and of abjuration of the Stewarts, required of office-holders and those seeking admission to the Faculty of Advocates. Even in the 1760s there were those who felt unable to take these oaths, and Provost Crosbie's own status as Juror or Nonjuror is unclear. (See p. 227.)

234 *as a bird from the fowler's net*: The Quaker Rachel Geddes's speech is permeated with biblical phrases and allusions. See, for example, Proverbs 26: 12; 1 Samuel 2: 12, Matthew 5: 34 and 37; Luke 16: 9; and Psalm 124.

236 *the answers all smell of new lords new lands*: Through this conversation between the old Jacobite and the young advocate, Scott indicates some of those changes, which in the twenty years since the 1745–6 rebellion, marked Edinburgh's transformation from a distinct, semi-feudal Scottish community to a modern, commercial British city, looking to London for its identity. A delicate social pointer in the late eighteenth century was the hour at which one ate what one called dinner: the later the hour, the more fashionable and London-influenced one was. The Fairfords dine at three (Letter V) and the Crosbie household at two. (See also *Johnson's England*, ed. A. S. Turberville, 1933, i, 344–5.) Postal communication between London and Edinburgh, unreliable in the earlier part of the century, was more efficient from 1763, with a mail-coach making the journey five times a week, taking three to four days for the one-way trip. (Hugo Arnot, *The History of Edinburgh*, 1779, pp. 538–9.) Female fashions of the 1730s and 1740s — the plaid and the huge evening hoop — alluded to by Maxwell of Summertrees, are described in Robert Chambers, *Traditions of Edinburgh*, 1825, ii, 56–60. Mareschal, Airley, Winton, Wemyss, and Balmerino were all aristocratic Scottish Jacobite families who suffered and forfeited estates in 1715 and 1745. The weekly dancing assemblies moved in 1787 from Old Assembly Close to modern rooms in George Street in the New Town.

'*on hospitable cares intent*': Milton, *Paradise Lost*, v, 332.

237 *a grey mare . . . a white horse in Wouvermans' pictures*: Philips Wouwerman(s) (1619–68), a prolific Dutch painter of genre scenes, noted for his inclusion of white horses in his compositions. The proverb, 'the grey mare is the better horse', alluded to here, means that the wife rules the husband.

'lawful sway and right supremacy': slightly misquoted from *The Taming of the Shrew*, v, ii, 110.

'Ower the water to Charlie,' . . . tenth of June: James Francis Stewart was born on 10 June 1688. 'O'er the water to Charlie' is to be found in James Hogg, *Jacobite Relics of Scotland*, 1819–20, ii, 76.

239 *crackling of thorns under the pot*: Ecclesiastes 7: 6.

nail a horseshoe on your chamber-door: held to be a protection against witches. (See John Aubrey, *Miscellanies* (1696), ch. xiii, in *Three Prose Works*, ed. John Buchanan-Brown, 1972, p. 89.)

240 *Tace is Latin for a candle*: a proverbial phrase enjoining silence and caution (*tace*, Latin, meaning 'be silent'). It is used in this way in Henry Fielding, *Amelia* (1751), book I, ch. x.

Skye and the Bush aboon Traquair: The major Skye chiefs, Macleod of Macleod and Macdonald of Sleat, refused to serve Charles Edward in 1745; so too did Charles Stewart, Earl of Traquair, who gave only cautious support. 'The Bush aboon Traquair' is the title of an old Scottish song to be found in Allan Ramsay, *The Tea-Table Miscellany*, 10th edn., 1740, i, 2–3.

241 *Carlisle, where the folk had been so frightened*: The city and castle of Carlisle surrendered to the Jacobites on 15 November 1745 and were garrisoned by a hundred of Charles Edward's men until 30 December when retaken by the Hanoverian army under the Duke of Cumberland. This fact did nothing to sway local opinion in favour of the rebels during the Jacobite trials held there the following year.

for all somebody's orders: The Jacobite army was finally defeated at Culloden, six miles east of Inverness, on 16 April 1746. Afterwards the Duke of Cumberland, commanding the victorious Hanoverian force, gave orders that no mercy be shown. For the atrocities after Culloden Cumberland earned his nickname 'Butcher'.

245 *the stamp act . . . impending over the American colonies*: part of the precise dating of the novel's main events in the mid-1760s. Disturbances, referred to earlier in Provost Crosbie's conversation (at p. 240), broke out all along the Atlantic coast from Boston to Virginia, caused by the Stamp Act of March 1765, which levied taxes in the American colonies on legal transactions, playing cards, newspapers, etc. American resistance made it impossible to enforce and the act was repealed early in 1766, but not before a Declaratory Act was passed which maintained Parliament's full sovereignty over the colonies. Disaffection in North America continued.

247 *in the Company's service*: in the service of the East India Company, formed for carrying on trade in India.

249 *Claverhouse at a field-preaching*: As an inveterate persecutor of the Covenanters, John Graham of Claverhouse would not be found worshipping at one of the open-air services they held secretly in the hills. (See note to p. 102(5).)

Habeas Corpus: an English act of 1679 requiring prisoners to be brought to speedy trial and allowing the right to be liberated on bail, except in cases of felony and treason. The act never applied to Scotland, but the name was often used inaccurately for a comparable Scottish act of 1701, the Act Anent Wrangous Imprisonment. (Normand.)

250 '*the smallest mouse that creeps on floor*': *A Midsummer Night's Dream*, v, i, 215.

one may love the Kirk . . . ride on the rigging of it: a proverb meaning, 'A Man may love a Thing, or Person, very well, and yet not shew too much Fondness.' (James Kelly, *A Complete Collection of Scotish Proverbs*, 1721, p. 37.)

251 *murder under trust*: regarded as treason and punishable by death in England and Scotland.

252 *a certain act of Parliament*: An Act of Attainder was passed in 1746 listing the more prominent Jacobites who took part in the rebellion and rendering them liable to the penalties of treason if they failed to surrender by 12 July 1746.

254 *scrimped you of your cogie, as the sang says*: The song is 'There's cauld kail in Aberdeen' and the reference is to stanza ii, to be found in *Love, Labour and Liberty: The Eighteenth-Century Scottish Lyric*, ed. Thomas Crawford, 1976, pp. 30–1.

the royal burgh of Annan: South-east of Dumfries on the Solway Firth, it was held by the Bruces in the thirteenth century and figured in the war of independence against England. Often overrun by the English, the Battle of Annan was fought here on 17 December 1332. (See note to p. 209(2).) It was made a royal burgh in 1539.

255 *like Macbeth's amen*: *Macbeth*, ii, ii, 32.

'*That in the ocean seeks another drop*': *The Comedy of Errors*, i, ii, 35–6.

'*horse hot at hand*': *Julius Caesar*, iv, ii, 23.

256 *as Quin said of Macklin*: James Quin (1693–1766), an English actor, at the head of his profession until supplanted by David Garrick. Charles Macklin (1697?–1797), an Irish actor, who excelled as Shylock.

the whore that sitteth on the seven hills: interpreted as the Roman Catholic Church and the seven hills of Rome by anti-Catholics. The whole passage is to be found in Revelation 17: 3–9.

258 *fast bind, fast find*: a common and obvious enough saying. (See *The Merchant of Venice*, II, v, 53.)

261 *a merciful man is merciful to his beast*: Proverbs 12: 10.

263 *the gold of Ophir*: In the Old Testament Ophir was the place from which the ships of King Solomon brought gold and precious stones. (1 Kings 10: 11.)

264 *when I sit under my vine and my fig-tree*: Micah 4:4.

there is but one name which: Cf. Acts 4: 12.

265 *balm in Gilead*: Jeremiah 8: 22.

266 *bringing up a neck to a fair end*: *Titus Andronicus*, IV, iv, 48.

267 *keep it holy*: Exodus 20: 8, 'Remember the sabbath day, to keep it holy', the Fourth Commandment.

the iron tongue of time told five: Cf. *A Midsummer Night's Dream*, v, i, 349.

270 *Merry Thoughts for Merry Men ... for the small Hours*: Scott owned several such collections; for example, *The Merry Thought: or the Glass-Window and Boghouse Miscellany* (printed about 1730). (See J. G. Cochrane, *A Catalogue of the Library at Abbotsford*, 1838, p. 128.)

friend Crispus: Caius Sallustius Crispus (Sallust) (86–35 BC), a Roman historian. The work which Nanty quotes from is *Catilina*, a history of the anti-Republican conspiracy of Lucius Sergius Catilina in 63 BC.

271 *the Sortes Virgilianae*: 'prophecies according to Virgil', telling one's fortune by consulting Virgil's *Aeneid*, opening it at random and relating to one's own situation the passage one first comes across. It was a custom with ancient precedents.

'*David therefore departed ... became a captain over them*': 1 Samuel 22: 1–2. Nanty Ewart compares Charles Edward Stewart to the fugitive future King David, and in his second reading from Sallust, to Catiline who had plotted against the State of Rome.

Tell that to the marines—the sailors won't believe it: a colloquialism expressive of disbelief, marines being looked down upon as inexperienced and credulous by regular sailors. (See Byron, *The Island* (1823), II, xxi, and *OED*, 4c.) A repeating frigate is a smaller vessel reproducing signals made by the admiral's ship. (*OED*, *repeat*, *v*, II, 3b.)

'*cold drinking in the grave*': from a song in *The Lovers' Progress*, III, v, by John Fletcher (1579–1625).

272 *Alan drank it eagerly ... with a single glass of brandy*: This sentence ended the second volume in the three-volume first edition of 1824.

273 *Juvenal*: Decimus Junius Juvenalis, a Roman satiric poet (AD *c*.60–130).

274 '*Canny Willy Foster*': See *The Oxford Dictionary of Nursery Rhymes*, ed. Iona and Peter Opie, 1951, pp. 90–1.

'Vir sapientia et pietate gravis': 'A man eminent in wisdom and piety'. Cf. Virgil, *Aeneid*, i, 151.

Covenant-Close: on the south side of the High Street in Edinburgh, connecting with the Cowgate.

Mrs Cantrips of Kittlebasket: 'Kittlebasket' (difficult or precarious basket) is appropriate enough as part of the impoverished widow's description, but 'Cantrips' (spells, magic, or mischief) is less obvious.

Cambridge Bible, printed by Daniel: the King James's Bible or Authorized Version of 1611, with marginal references, printed in 1637 by Thomas Buck and Roger Daniel, printers to the University of Cambridge.

275 *'Kirk would not let us be'*: 'The blythsome bridal, or Kirk wad let me be', to be found in David Herd, *The Ancient and Modern Scots Songs*, 1769, p. 114, and see James C. Dick, *The Songs of Robert Burns*, 1903, p. 458.

the throne of Presbyterian penance: The Kirk-session, the lowest court in the Presbyterian Church, consisting of the minister and elders of the parish, exercised a disciplinary function in matters of sexual misdemeanour, requiring offenders to sit on the 'stool of repentance' at the front of the church and in full view of the congregation. The payment of a fine ensured the avoidance of the penance.

proving, as Othello says, 'his love a whore': *Othello*, III, iii, 365.

'Ichabod . . . from my house': 1 Samuel 4: 21.

277 *'Ceaze ta matman'*: The Edinburgh City Guard, disbanded in the early nineteenth century, was a peace-keeping force, semi-military and with a strong Highland element. This is Scott's attempt to suggest a Gaelic speaker speaking English. (See Mairi Robinson, 'Modern Literary Scots: Fergusson and after', in *Lowland Scots*, Association for Scottish Literary Studies, Occasional Papers, 2, 1975, p. 39.)

Haslaar hospital: Haslar Naval Hospital, Hampshire.

278 *as drunk as David's sow*: The saying, said to derive from a facetious confusion between the six-legged sow and the drunken wife of David Lloyd, a Welshman, is explained in Francis Grose, *A Classical Dictionary of the Vulgar Tongue*, 1785, under 'D'.

made to kiss the wench that never speaks . . . on the account: Nanty Ewart displays his pirate's slang in this paragraph. The 'gunner's daughter' was the gun to which sailors were lashed ('married') to receive a whipping. To 'take the bush' is to become an outlaw, and to 'go on the account' is to turn pirate. (See Eric Partridge, *A Dictionary of Slang and Unconventional English*, 2 vols., 1961.)

Avery: John Avery (*fl.* 1695), a noted and successful pirate, who married a daughter of the Great Mogul, according to his biographer Charles Johnson. Scott owned at least two books on Avery, whose adventures provided material for his novel *The Pirate* (1822). (See J. G. Cochrane, *A Catalogue of the Library at Abbotsford*, 1838, p. 129.)

279 *sigma and tau to Ewart*: The letters of the Greek alphabet answering to 's' and 't' combine with 'Ewart' to make 'Stewart'. Nanty Ewart implies that his ship has brought over Charles Edward to Britain.

281 *the London people ... pinches of their own*: See the note to p. 207.

286 *some sort of nun-shop ... in Flanders*: Ewart probably refers to the Dutch and Belgian béguinages, communities of lay sisters, devoted to good works and the religious life, but under no vows.

287 *filthy rags*: Isaiah 64: 6, 'all our righteousnesses are as filthy rags'. Ewart touches here on the Roman Catholic/Protestant distinction between justification by works or by faith alone.

290 '*But my lad he loved me dearly*': from 'The Fair Penitent', Allan Ramsay, *The Tea-Table Miscellany*, 1740, i, 38.

291 *Sancta Winifreda, ora pro nobis*: 'Saint Winifred, pray for us.' A seventh-century saint, Winifred's well is at Holywell in Flintshire.

incedit sicut leo vorans, saith the breviary: '[the devil] walks about like a roaring lion, seeking whom he may devour' (1 Peter 5: 8). The breviary is the book containing the daily offices of the Roman Catholic Church.

294 *Vade retro—get thee behind me!* Matthew 16: 23.

298 *the statute* 1700, *chapter* 3: This revived old acts against Catholics and made further provision against this faith. (Normand.) Charles Edward had arrived in the Outer Hebrides in July 1745 dressed as a Catholic priest. George III's assumption that all Roman Catholics were Jacobites was a simplification, but it held a substantial truth up to 1766, the exiled King James II and later his son James Francis having authority from the Pope to nominate to the senior posts in the Catholic hierarchy in Britain and Ireland. Realizing the degree of suspicion and animosity to Catholicism in Britain and the danger which his brother's acceptance of a cardinal's hat in 1747 was to the Stewart cause, Charles had been formally accepted into the Church of England on his visit to London in 1750. But it was a belated gesture, and in later life he returned to the Church of Rome. (See Bruce Lenman, *The Jacobite Risings in Britain 1689–1746*, 1980, pp. 228–30; and David Daiches, *Charles Edward Stuart*, 1973, p. 260.) Throughout the eighteenth century, Roman Catholics in Britain were not permitted to hold office or to enter Parliament, and their disabilities were not completely removed until 1829.

299 '*Cave ne literas Bellerophontis adferres*': 'Take heed lest you carry Bellerophon's letters', letters dangerous to the bearer. In Greek mythology Anteia, wife of Proitos, king of Argos, falsely accused Bellerophon of seducing her, and as a result Proitos sent Bellerophon to his father-in-law carrying a letter requesting the bearer's death. By his bravery in various trials, however, Bellerophon survived. (Homer, *Iliad*, vi, 160 ff.)

303 *the punic faith of Jesuits*: Punic faith (Latin *fides Punica*) is faith of the kind which the Romans attributed to the Carthaginians, that is, treachery and faithlessness. (*OED*, *faith*, III, 2.) Jesuits are members of the Roman

Catholic 'Society of Jesus', an order founded by Ignatius Loyola in 1534, specifically to defend the Church against the Reformation. In French as well as English its name can be synonymous with casuistical argument and secret power. (*OED*, *Jesuit*, 1 and 2.) Particularly resented at this time, the Jesuits were expelled from France and Spain in the 1760s.

Misprision of Treason: committed by having knowledge of the treason and failing to disclose it. The act applied to both England and Scotland. An act of William III's reign attainted the pretended Prince of Wales and anyone assisting him of high treason. (Normand.)

304 *the letters of Uriah*: King David, wanting Bathsheba, wife of Uriah, for himself, gave Uriah a letter consigning him to the most dangerous place in battle, and so to his death. (2 Samuel 11: 14–15.)

306 *Juno ... Queen Vashti ... Queen Esther*: Juno was wife of Jupiter and queen of heaven in Roman mythology. The compliant and more politic Esther became wife to King Ahasuerus after Queen Vashti's imperiousness cost her the royal favour. (See Esther 1: 22 and 2: 17.)

311 *Mahratta conqueror*: one of a warlike Hindu race occupying central and south-western India. (*OED*.)

312 '*A man can but look like a fool*': Slightly misquoted from 'Answer'd by Me, lines written on behalf of Lord William Hamilton', ll. 1–2, by Lady Mary Wortley Montagu (1689–1762). Darsie quotes ll. 11–12 from the same poem a few lines later.

313 *we have not, as Hotspur says, leisure to be sick*: 1 Henry IV, IV, i, 17.

314 *Cassius ... drawing his poniard on the Dictator*: Caius Cassius Longinus was the arch-conspirator in the assassination of Julius Caesar in 44 BC, described by Plutarch and Shakespeare.

315 *Derby direction*: Having marched as far south as Derby, Charles Edward's Jacobite army turned north again on 6 December 1745, so abandoning hope of capturing London. In spite of a few minor victories later, the decision to return north marked the end of the Jacobite success.

316 *the course of ardent affection never does run smooth*: *A Midsummer Night's Dream*, I, i, 134.

Lydia Languish: a character of romantic notions in *The Rivals* (1775), by Richard Brinsley Sheridan.

317 *downright Dunstable*: 'Said to express a plain, simple, honest person, devoid of any turns or duplicity in their character. A comparison with the straightness and openness of that road.' (Francis Grose, *A Provincial Glossary, with a collection of local proverbs and popular superstitions*, 1787. The work is unpaginated with entries arranged alphabetically under the counties of England. Dunstable is in Bedfordshire.)

318 *that enchanted hall in Fairy-land*: This detail is common in Celtic mythology.

323 *In Scotland . . . the protection of the law*: The guardian of a minor in Scotland has powers of administration over his estate but not over his person. (Normand.)

324 *the Jansenists . . . Porte-Royale*: Jansenists, followers of Cornelius Jansen, Bishop of Ypres in Flanders (d. 1638), were a puritanical movement in the Roman Catholic Church, teaching the doctrines of predestination, 'original sin', and the inability for good of the natural human will. Jansen's doctrines, formulated from the teachings of St Augustine, resembled Calvinism in some respects and had strong support in the two convents of the Port-Royal in Paris and the Port-Royal-des-Champs, eight miles south-west of Versailles. Denounced as heretics during the reign of Louis XIV, Jansenists were at the centre of a prolonged conflict between Louis XV and the Parlements in the 1750s.

the nearer the church: an old proverb. See Spenser, *The Shepheardes Calender*, (1579), 'Julye', ll. 97–8, 'To Kerke the narre, from God more farre, | has bene an old sayd sawe.'

Temple-bar: the gateway closing the entrance into the City of London from the Strand (near the Temple buildings). Called the 'City Golgotha' because of the heads of traitors exposed there, it was removed in 1878.

326 *the Coronation Feast*: Lilias is in Westminster Hall, witnessing the coronation feast of the young King George III (1738–1820), on 22 September 1761. Scott's description of the scene may be compared with that of an eyewitness, Horace Walpole, in a letter to George Montagu. (*Horace Walpole's Correspondence*, ed. W. S. Lewis, 1941, ix, 386–9.)

328 *Norfolk, renegade to his Catholic faith . . . Belshazzar*: Redgauntlet combines an allusion to the supernatural warning at the feast of Belshazzar, King of Babylon, in Daniel 5: 1–5 and 24–8, with references to those specific traitors to the Jacobite cause who participated in George III's coronation. Among them is the Earl Marshal, the Duke of Norfolk, who being a Roman Catholic was disqualified to act and might be presumed sympathetic to the exiled Stewarts. He attended the coronation but the Earl of Effingham as Deputy Earl Marshal performed his office. Only those members of the Church of England who swore oaths of abjuration of the House of Stewart qualified for official clerical posts; consequently, any office-holder is a traitor in Redgauntlet's eyes. More particular is the desertion of James Boyd, 15th Earl of Errol (1726–78). Present at the coronation as High Constable of Scotland, he was the son of William Boyd, 4th Earl of Kilmarnock, who was beheaded in 1746 for his part in the Jacobite rising.

329 *an idle tale*: Scott's note 58 outlines the unlikely 'tradition' on which Lilias's acceptance of the champion's challenge is based. There was an equally romantic fiction that Charles Edward Stewart himself was present at George III's coronation and let fall a white kid-glove from the

gallery in response to the ritual challenge. (See David Daiches, *Charles Edward Stuart*, 1973, p. 270.)

Elector of Hanover: George III was the great-grandson of George I (1660–1727), Elector of Hanover, and King of England on the death of Queen Anne, the last Stewart monarch, in 1714. To the Jacobites, supporters of James Francis Stewart, Anne's half-brother, and his heirs, the Georges were usurpers, Electors of Hanover merely.

330 *the bullet of Dundee, or the axe of Balmerino*: According to a superstition among the Covenanters, John Graham of Claverhouse, Viscount Dundee, was protected by the devil from lead shot. Consequently, after his death in battle at Killiecrankie in 1689, it was said that he was struck down by a silver button used as a bullet. (See Scott's note to the 1830 edition of *Old Mortality*, ch. XVI.) Arthur Elphinstone, 6th Baron Balmerino (1688–1746), a commander in Charles Edward's army, was beheaded on 18 August 1746. He met his death with exemplary courage, taking the axe and feeling its edge before returning it to his executioner. Scott tells this story in *Tales of a Grandfather*, 3rd Series, iii, 312–15.

The general dissatisfaction with the peace ... the quiet of the metropolis: The peace treaty bringing to an end the Seven Years War was signed in February 1763. Lord Bute was its chief negotiator and it had many critics, among them William Pitt (1708–78), who had led Britain successfully through most of the war. Bute's unpopularity and the high prices and increasing unemployment that accompanied the ending of the war led to considerable anti-government agitation. But it is highly unlikely that such opposition to ministerial tyranny could have been turned, as Redgauntlet seems to have supposed, to the advantage of the Stewart cause, represented as it was by one who believed firmly in royal absolutism. (See the note to p. 207.)

the act of 1748, abolishing ... hereditary jurisdictions: An act abolishing the heritable rights of landowners over their tenants was passed in 1747, to take effect from 25 March 1748. It was a direct result of the 1745–6 Jacobite rising and proved a successful expedient in the breaking of traditional clan power.

332 *I owe him, too, a day's work in harvest*: 'spoken of one to whom I owe a good turn', used ironically here. (See James Kelly, *A Complete Collection of Scotish Proverbs*, 1721, p. 166.)

335 *Scarborough warning*: As the context implies, the phrase means no warning at all. It is variously derived from a practice said to have prevailed in Scarborough of lynching robbers summarily, and from Thomas Stafford's seizure of Scarborough Castle in 1557, before the inhabitants knew he was there. (E. C. Brewer, *The Dictionary of Phrase and Fable*, 1978, p. 1109.)

they who play at bowls must meet with rubbers: Those who enter on affairs of chance must expect to run risks.

336 *lettres de cachet ... Bedlam*: *Lettres de cachet* were originally letters under

the private seal of the French king containing orders of exile or imprisonment. The *Courier de l'Europe* is, as it sounds, a newspaper. The Old Bailey, in London, is the seat of the Central Criminal Court of England. The Bastille, the Parisian prison-fortress, was destroyed in 1789. Mont-Saint-Michel, an island fortress off the north coast of France, was used as a State prison from the Revolution until 1863. The Castle of Vincennes, four miles east of Paris, was sometimes used as a State prison. Bedlam was a London lunatic asylum, the name being a contraction of St Mary of Bethlehem.

338 *independent and august Parliament of his own native kingdom*: By the Union of 1707 between England and Scotland, Scotland lost an independent parliament and legislature. (See note to p. 23(4).) One of Charles Edward's first gestures on taking Edinburgh in September 1745 had been to abolish the unpopular Act of Union by decree, an attempt to consolidate Scottish support for his cause.

the independent crown of Scotland: Incensed by Robert Bruce's stabbing of John ('the Red') Comyn in February 1306 and seizure of the Scottish crown the following month, Edward I of England started an intensive policy of terrorizing the Scots into submission to his overlordship. Only his death at Burgh-on-Sands, a village on the English side of the Solway five miles from Carlisle, on 7 July 1307 averted what would have been a successful English invasion of Scotland, his son Edward II lacking the vigorous initiative needed to pursue the campaign at that time. When Edward II was ready to march again on Scotland, Bruce as King Robert I had consolidated his power and was able to defeat a full-scale campaign at Bannockburn in June 1314. (See note to p. 29(4) and to p. 209(1).)

339 *a born Briton on the throne*: George III, king on the death of his grandfather George II in 1760, was the first of the Hanoverian monarchs to be born in England, and he was a fiercely patriotic Briton.

340 *the apparent success of Chatham's administration . . . Minden and Quebec*: William Pitt, not created 1st Earl of Chatham until the start of his third ministry in 1766, was in office for almost all of the Seven Years War. During his first ministry (1756–7) he introduced the controversial but successful experiment of forming two new regiments drawn from the Highland clans which had rebelled against the Hanoverian dynasty only eleven years earlier. In his coalition ministry with the Duke of Newcastle (1757–62), Britain recovered from early reverses to achieve important victories over the French. At Minden, forty miles west of Hanover, in August 1759 the Anglo-Hanoverian army won a crucial European campaign, and at Quebec in the following month General James Wolfe, assisted by the Fraser Highlanders, against whom he had fought in 1745, dealt a lethal blow to French Canada. When peace was signed in 1763, Britain was the dominant European power in North America and the Indian subcontinent. (For the dissatisfaction and economic depression following on the war, see note to p. 330(2).)

Highlanders are now totally disarmed: In 1716 a Disarming Act had been passed whereby Highlanders were forbidden under penalties to carry weapons in public. The act was tightened up in 1725 to include the surrender of all weapons to the government. In 1746 a further Disarming Act was combined with the banning of Highland dress with its warlike associations. In spite of severe penalties, both were difficult measures to enforce.

white cockade: a knot of ribbon worn on the hat as a Jacobite badge. The Hanoverian cockade was black.

seven men, landing in the wilds of Moidart ... now to attempt in their turn: It was in Moidart in the West Highlands that Charles Edward landed towards the end of July 1745 with companions known in Jacobite folklore as 'the Seven Men of Moidart'—the Marquis of Tullibardine; Aeneas MacDonald, the expedition's banker; Francis Strickland, of a Westmorland family; Sir Thomas Sheridan, Charles's old tutor; George Kelly, a Non-juring clergyman; and Sir John MacDonald and John William O'Sullivan, both professional soldiers. The two pitched battles won by the Jacobite army were Prestonpans, 21 September 1745, and Falkirk, 17 January 1746. At Derby on 6 December Charles was over-ruled by his generals led by Lord George Murray and reluctantly turned back, his army of under 5,000 men menaced by a combined Hanoverian force of 30,000. The support he expected from a French invasion on the south coast, an event which the English Jacobites had made a condition of their rising, had never materialized.

341 *thy inheritance shall depart from thee, like vigour and verdure from a rotten branch*: Similar threats had been used in 1745. Simon Fraser, Lord Lovat, forced his eldest son, at heart a Whig, to lead his clansmen into the rebellion or face being cut off and sent to be a cowherd. (See Bruce Lenman, *The Jacobite Risings in Britain 1689–1746*, 1980, p. 256.)

345 *Wilkie's inimitable blind crowder*: An allusion to the genre picture 'The Blind Fiddler' (1806) by the Scottish painter Sir David Wilkie (1785–1841).

'*You're welcome, Charlie Stewart*': A Jacobite air and song, the music is reprinted in *The Poems and Songs of Robert Burns*, ed. James Kinsley, 1968, ii, 864.

350 *nae bad overture, as they say in the General Assembly*: The General Assembly is the highest governing body of the Presbyterian Church, consisting of ministers and elders. An overture is a formal motion proposing or calling for legislation. (*OED*, 4.)

354 *Poor Peter Peebles ... et per contra*: Here, as in several other places, Peebles is confused over terminology: *e contra* and not *per contra* is the appropriate phrase to indicate a counter action. (Normand.)

355 *Peter the Cruel*: possibly a reference to the fourteenth-century Pedro I of Portugal, called '*le Justicier*'.

a decreet of the Bailies' ... letters found orderly proceeded: The decision of the magistrates' court, executable only within a narrow jurisdiction, that the debtor's goods be impounded, has been followed by a warrant for the debtor's imprisonment for failure to make payment within a prescribed term and then by letters issued by the Court of Session enforcing the earlier decision in any part of Scotland. (Normand.)

359 '*Save me from the indiscretion of my friends ... of my enemies*': This is a proverb common in many languages.

360 *Court of Justiciary*: the supreme criminal court in Scotland.

Auld King Coul: according to Scottish legend, the father of the giant Fin McCoul. For the song of that name, see David Herd, *Ancient and Modern Scottish Songs*, 1776, ii, 183–5.

364 *these men's oaths ... thy Yea and Nay in this matter*: For the Quaker's refusal to take oaths, see note to p. 88(1).

367 *a disguise to which kings and heroes have been reduced*: Charles Edward Stewart had changed into women's clothing, assuming the identity of an Irish maidservant Betty Burke, in his escape from mainland Scotland after the 1745–6 rising. As late as 1766–7, the small remnant of the Scottish Jacobites referred to Charles in their correspondence as 'Cousin Peggie' or 'the young lady'. (David Daiches, *Charles Edward Stuart*, 1973, pp. 221, 226, and 274.)

368 *the White Standard*: the white and red standard of the Stewarts.

369 *Cot bless us ... what cood*: This is Scott's attempt to signalize a Welshman speaking English.

370 '*shook his ambrosial curls*': Homer, *Iliad*, i, 528–30 (Pope's translation).

Oxford ... last to resign herself to the Arch-Usurper: Traditionally a centre of Royalism supporting the concepts of divine right and passive obedience dear to the Stewart monarchs, Oxford showed its allegiance by the 1683 decrees and during the 1715 riots. But there is little evidence to suggest the University was a hotbed of Jacobitism for much of the eighteenth century, and in 1763 it had offered a loyal address to George III on the successful ending of the Seven Years War. (See W. R. Ward, *Georgian Oxford: University Politics in the Eighteenth Century*, 1958.)

anarchical tenets of Locke: John Locke (1632–1704), philosopher and political thinker. A refugee in Holland from 1683–8, he was concerned in the movement which overthrew James II. His second *Treatise on Civil Government* (1690) provided the theoretical justification for the contractual view of monarchy as a limited and revocable agreement between ruler and ruled.

deluded by foreign powers: specifically, French support for a Jacobite rising in Britain. Such support had been promised to Charles Edward by Louis XV in 1744, when a planned French invasion of England was foiled by the British navy. But serious commitment was ultimately withheld in 1745.

371 *Irish rapparees*: historically, Irish pikemen or irregular soldiers (armed with rapparees or short pikes); hence, Irish bandits (*OED*). Four of the seven who landed with Charles Edward at Moidart in 1745 were Irishmen (Thomas Sheridan, George Kelly, Sir John MacDonald, and John William O'Sullivan). They formed an inner circle about the Prince, the arrogant and incompetent O'Sullivan receiving the disastrous appointment of Quartermaster- and Adjutant-General to the Jacobite army. Deeply resented by the Scottish adherents, they thwarted Lord George Murray, Charles's best general, at every turn. After Culloden, Scottish bitterness increased when Charles fled to the Islands with his Irish followers instead of joining Murray in reforming his Highland army at Ruthven. (David Daiches, *Charles Edward Stuart*, 1973, p. 110 and *passim*.)

Old Shaftesbury himself: Anthony Ashley Cooper, 1st Earl of Shaftesbury (1621–83). He led the campaign to exclude the Roman Catholic James II from the throne, and in so doing provided the driving force behind the opposition groupings who came to be known as the Whigs.

372 *a sister in the Elector of Hanover's Court*: See the note to p. 7.

Varium et mutabile semper femina: 'Fickle and changeable always is woman', Virgil, *Aeneid*, iv, 569.

373 *si non caste, caute, tamen*: 'if not chaste, yet be prudent'.

his merry old namesake: Charles II (1630–85), Charles Edward's great-uncle, was notorious for his illicit sexual affairs.

the pensionary of the present minister ... Sir Robert Walpole's: Sir Robert Walpole, Whig Prime Minister from 1721–42, handed on his counter-espionage network in the Jacobite circles of Europe to his pupil Henry Pelham, Prime Minister from 1744–54, the final period of serious Jacobite activity. The demands of his followers that Charles abandon Clementina Walkinshaw, whom circumstances plausibly suggested to be a spy, are post-dated in the novel from 1753–4 to 1765. Clementina had, of course, left Charles in 1760. (See note to p. 5(2) and to p. 7.)

374 *inflexibility of his grandfather*: Charles's grandfather was James VII and II, a Roman Catholic and intransigent believer in absolute monarchy, deposed in the Glorious Revolution of 1688–9.

377 *their King*: Scott originally wrote 'the King', but after comment from his critic and printer, James Ballantyne, it was changed in the first edition to this more discreet phrase. James Francis Stewart died on 1 January 1766; so in the summer of 1765, the apparent date of the novel's events, Charles would still be technically Jacobite Prince of Wales.

379 *the axe and scaffold ... my great-grandfather*: Charles Edward's great-grandfather Charles I was beheaded on 30 January 1649 outside the Banqueting Hall at Whitehall.

382 *the Line*: the Equator.

387 *tricks in other trades by selling muslins*: by—besides (*Scottish National Dictionary*, *by*, 3).

393 *Black Colin Campbell*: The Campbells were a powerful Whig clan, loyal to the Hanoverian government during the Jacobite uprisings of the eighteenth century. The famous General Campbell of the time was not Colin but John Campbell (1693–1770), Major-General and Colonel of the 21st Foot and commander of troops in the west of Scotland. He succeeded as 4th Duke of Argyll in 1761. Scott's reference may be to him or may be deliberately fictitious.

'*The Campbells are coming*': The tune can be found in *The Scots Musical Museum*, ed. James Johnson, 1787–1803, iii, no. 299.

the old powder-plot boys: the Catholic Robert Catesby and his fellow conspirators in the plot to blow up the English Parliament while the King, Lords, and Commons were assembled (the Gunpowder Plot, 5 November 1605). Catesby and three others died resisting the government force sent to arrest them.

397 *The last heir of the Stewarts*: Charles Edward died in Rome on 31 January 1788, aged 67. He had no legitimate children, and his illegitimate daughter by Clementina Walkinshaw died the following year. Charles's brother, Henry, Cardinal of York, died in 1807.

400 *Dr Dryasdust . . . the Author of Waverley*: One of the complicated series of fictional disguises which Scott used to hide his identity as a novel-writer, the Revd Dr Jonas Dryasdust of York is a scholar and antiquarian. Committed to historical verisimilitude, he is introduced in the 'Dedicatory Epistle' prefixed to *Ivanhoe* (1820) and pedantically criticizes the 'Author of *Waverley*' (Scott himself) for his fictional licence in the 'Prefatory Letter' to *Peveril of the Peak* (1822).

Whitehall Gazette: I have been unable to trace a newspaper of this name which would fit Scott's dating scheme in the novel. There was the paper started by Defoe in 1718 and issued to the end of the century, the *Whitehall Evening Post*, and it was common at this time for Whitehall news to be issued as part of the *London Gazette*.

his late Majesty: Dr Dryasdust is to be imagined writing in 1824, the year of the novel's publication, when George IV, George III's son, was on the throne.

Mr Oldbuck: Jonathan Oldbuck, titular hero of Scott's third novel *The Antiquary* (1816).

401 *Scottish Monastery of Ratisbon*: the Abbey of St James, at Ratisbon in Germany. An Irish foundation, it was reconstituted after the Reformation as a monastery and college for Scottish exiles.

Avocato del Diablo: In the Roman Catholic Church when a name is suggested for canonization an *Avocato del Diablo* ('Devil's Advocate') is appointed to oppose the proposition and is expected to give reasons why it should not take place, after which the conclave makes its decision.

GLOSSARY

THE glossary comprises a full list of words in Scots, together with difficult, obsolete, or dialect words in English, place-names, legal and foreign expressions, and some other specialist terms in use throughout the novel, except where explanations in context render this unnecessary. Sources include the glossary to the 'Magnum' edition of Scott's novels (Vol. 48, 1833), the glossary to the Dryburgh edition of *Redgauntlet* (1894), the *Oxford English Dictionary*, and the *Scottish National Dictionary*.

a', all
abbreviate, an abridgement, abstract
abune, above
accompts, accounts
ad litem, *oath*, an oath admitted 'for a suit' in exceptional circumstances
adust, gloomy, melancholy
ad vindictam publicam, in the public defence
advising, the deliberation of a cause or process so as to give judgement upon it
advocate, a barrister
advocation, in Scots law, the calling of an action before itself by a superior court
ae, one
aff, off
affidavy, affidavit, a written statement, confirmed by oath, to be used as judicial evidence
afflatus, breath
afore, before
agent, a solicitor
Ailsay Craig, a rocky island in the Firth of Clyde
ain, own
ainsell, own self
airting, directing
alane, alone
Allonby, a town in Cumberland
almaist, amaist, almost
amang, among
an, if; *an it like*—if it please
anan, what did you say? eh?
ance, anes, once
ance wud and aye waur, daft once, daft always; getting madder and madder
ane, one
aneath, underneath
anent, concerning
anes and aye, from that very moment, for ever
anes errand, for that very purpose
aneugh, enough
anither, another
another guess job, another sort of job
approbate and reprobate, in Scots law, to assent to part of a deed and object against the rest—a course which the law does not admit of
argumentum ad hominem/ad feminam, an appeal to the known character, reputation, or previous admissions of one's opponent, male or female
arles, money given to bind a bargain when a servant is hired
arrestment, in Scots law, the process by which a creditor may attach money which a third party owes his debtor
Ars medendi, art of healing, medicine

aside, beside
a'thegether, a'thegither, altogether
Atlas, in classical mythology, he bore the heavens on his shoulders
attainder, a loss of civil rights through conviction for high treason; *to attaint*—to deprive of such rights by conviction
aught, to own, be chiefly concerned in; *let them that aught the mare shoe the mare*—an expression advocating responsibility for one's own concerns
auld, old
auld-warld, old-fashioned; *auld-warld stories*—tales of long-gone days
awa, away
aweel, oh well
awn, own
ay, yes
aye, always

back and breast, hump-backed and chicken-breasted
back-ganging, behindhand in paying
back-lill, the left-hand thumb-hole at the back of a bagpipe chanter
back-sands, Leith sands, two miles east of Edinburgh, used for horse-races until 1816
back-spaul, the back of the shoulder
bag-wig, an eighteenth-century wig with back hair enclosed in an ornamental bag, favoured by lawyers
bailie, a municipal officer, Scottish magistrate
bairn, a child
baith, both
ballants, ballads
banes, bones
banged, rushed impetuously
bannock, a flat round cake, of oatmeal or barley or pease-meal
barbed, (of a horse) clad in armour
bare-breeched, trouserless
barley-broo, malt beer, strong ale
barley-pickle, a grain of barley, a small particle; *it's the barley-pickle breaks the naig's back*—cf. 'it's the last straw that breaks the camel's back'
baron-officer, an estate official
bartizan, battlement
bating, excepting
bauld, bold
bawbee, a halfpenny
bear-meal, meal made from a hardier kind of barley
beaufet, a cupboard in a recess for china and glass
beaver, any hat in the making of which beaver-fur is used
Beelzebub, a god of the Philistines, a fallen angel in Milton's *Paradise Lost*, i, 79–81, and next in rank to Satan
bein, snug
belang, belong
beldam, an old woman
belike, perhaps
ben, inside; *ower far ben*—too far in, much too intimate
Benedicite, bless you (plural imperative)
be's, be'st, an old indicative form used as the subjunctive mood of 'to be', third and second person singular
besom, a contemptuous term for a woman, a slattern
bicker, a wooden bowl for holding liquor
bide, stay, endure
billie, brother, comrade
birkie, a smart fellow
birling, a carousal
Birlthegroat, toss or spend the groat (a coin)
bit, a diminutive with some non-English uses: *a pleasant bit*—a pleasant spot; quasi-adjectival in *a*

bit chack—a little snack; *bits o' bairns*—little children
black-fasting, abstaining completely from food and drink (*black* has an intensive force)
black-fishers, night poachers of salmon, especially in the prohibited season (15 August to 30 November)
black jack, a jug of waxed leather for holding ale
Bladderskate, a silly person, a babbler
blate, bashful, modest
blaud, a selection of verses
blaw, to blow; *blaw in the lugs of*—to flatter, cajole
blawing, boasting
bleezing, bragging
blude, bluidy, blood, bloody
bluecap, a Scotsman
bob, to dance up and down
bobwig, a wig in which the lower locks are turned up into short curls or bobs
bodle, a coin worth two pence Scots or one-sixth of an English penny
bogle, a ghost; *bogle-wark*—spookery; *potatoe-bogles*—scarecrows
bombazine, a twilled material of silk and worsted used in making a barrister's gown
bona roba, a showy wanton
bond-tenant, a tenant required to perform certain services to his landlord
bonnet, a flat woollen cap
bonnie, bonny, pretty, fine; *a bonny like justice*—a fine kind of justice
bonus socius *with*, on good terms with
boot, into the boot, to the boot of, in addition, over and above
border-warrant, a writ issued on one side of the English–Scottish Border for apprehension of a person on the other
borrel, common, simple
brae, a hill
braid, broad, wide; *braid-claith*—broadcloth, a fine quality black cloth
branched, (of cloth) embroidered with a figured pattern
brash, a short burst of stormy weather (used figuratively here)
brattle, a clattering noise
bravade, a swaggering display of courage
braw, bra', fine, splendid
brent broo, a high forehead
breviate, a summary, a lawyer's brief
briggend, bridge-end
Broadbrims, a nickname for Quakers, who commonly wore such hats
brocard, a principle, maxim
brock, a badger
broil, a tumult, a quarrel
brose, oatmeal over which boiling water or broth has been poured
browst, a brewing, as much as is brewed at one time
Bucephalus, 'Ox Head', Alexander the Great's favourite horse
buckie, a perverse or refractory young person; *deevil's buckie*—imp of Satan
buff, neither buff nor stye, neither one thing nor another
buffers, pistols
bumbazed, confounded
burgess, a freeman, member of a privileged class in a town
Burgh-upon-sands, a village on the English side of the Solway, five miles from Carlisle
burr, an accent in which the letter *r* is sounded roughly
busk, to dress, arrange
buxom, good-tempered
by and attour, over and above
by-drink, (in this context) a drink between tunes

by-name, a nickname
by-ordinar, extraordinary, uncommon
bytime, an interval of leisure; *at a bytime*—occasionally

ca', *caa'd*, call, called
cabinet, a small or private room; *cabinet-counsellor*—a private counsellor
cadger, a hawker
cadie, an errand-boy. Cadies provided an organized service in eighteenth-century Edinburgh
Cairn, point of, or Cairn Head, a promontory in the south-east of Wigtownshire
callant, a youth, lad
caller, fresh, crisp
cam, came
camlet, a fine cloth of wool and silk
canna, cannot
canny, quiet, cautious, shrewd; *cannily*—quietly
cantle, a fragment
capernoited, giddy, crazy
capriccios, caprices, fantastical opinions
caprioling, capering, leaping
carabine, a firearm, between a pistol and a musket
cardinal, a short cloak, originally of scarlet cloth with a hood, worn by women
carena, care not
carles, old men
carlines, old women
Carriefraw-gauns, or Carrifran Gans, the steep side of a mountain in Moffatdale, Dumfriesshire
Cassandra, daughter of Priam, King of Troy, she was a prophetess of disasters but herself fated never to be believed
cast (*in a cart*), a lift, a short ride
cast up, to turn up, appear
catch, a round for three or more voices
catherans, Highland marauders
cat-lap, slops
cat's-paw, a person used as a tool by another
cattle, used contemptuously of persons
cauld, cold
caup, a cup or wooden bowl
causeway, pavement
caution, in Scots law, security
ceeveleesed, civilized
celsitude, height, tallness
certie, my, assuredly
certification, a judicial intimation or order served on a party to a cause, requiring him to state a defence within a prescribed time
cetera prorsus ignoro, in all other respects, in short, I know nothing
chack, a snack, light meal
chamber-counsel, a lawyer who gives advice in his chambers, not in court
chancy, auspicious
change-house, a small inn
chanter, melody-pipe, with finger-holes, of a bagpipe
chape, the metal mountings on a scabbard, the scabbard itself
chapeau bras, a three-cornered hat which could be carried flat under the arm
chaw, to chew
Cheat-the-woodie, cheat-the-gallows
chield, *chiel*, a fellow, lad
chirurgeons, surgeons
chucky, a chicken, a fowl generally
chucky-stones, pebbles, used in a children's game
claithes, clothes
clap and hopper, the symbols of investiture in the property of a mill
clavers, idle talk

claymores, (Gaelic) Highland broadswords
cleek, cleik, to lay hold on, to hook; *cleik in with*—to hook on to, join company with
clew, a thread, clue
clocking-hens, brood-hens
close, an alley, passageway; *close-foot*—the end of an alley furthest from the street; *close-head*—top of or entrance to an alley
cloured crowns, broken heads
cockernony, a woman's cap with a starched crown
cock up, turn up a hat in front (in military fashion is implied)
cogie, a small wooden bowl, for holding liquor etc.
commune forum est commune domicilium, the common court is a common domicile
composition, the sum paid to a creditor in satisfaction of part of a debt from an insolvent debtor
Compt and Reckoning, action of, whereby a party could obtain an account of the transactions between himself and his opponent and payment of any balance due to him
condescend, in Scots law, to agree, to specify
condescendence, a statement of the grounds of action, with the answers of the defender, part of the written pleadings
conjoined, conjunct, consolidated; *conjoined processes*—when two or more actions at law can be tried as one
conjure, to entreat
convene, in Scots law, bring in a party as defender in an action
cordwain, Spanish leather (originally from Cordova) used for shoes; *cordwainers*—shoe-makers
corking-pins, pins of the largest size
Cornish chough, the red-legged crow, the bird of Cornwall
Corydon, a rustic, a shepherd's name in Virgil's *Eclogues*
couldna, could not
counterfeited France, counterfeited a French dance
counting with, settling accounts with
couteau-de-chasse, a hunting-knife, short sword
covyne, artifice
cowp, to overturn, tumble over
crack, to gossip; a gossip, a chat
craig, neck
crawing, crowing
crawstep, one of a set of projecting steps on the gables of old houses
creelfu', basketful
cremony, Cremona, in Italy, where the celebrated violin-makers, the Amati family, lived in the sixteenth and seventeenth centuries
Criffel, a mountain in Kirkcudbright overlooking the estuary of the Nith
Cross, the, the Mercat (Market) Cross, the centre of business in eighteenth-century Edinburgh
crowder, a fiddler
crummie, a cow, specifically one with crooked horns
curn, a grain, a particle

daffing, fooling, thoughtless fun
dais, chamber of, the best bedroom
dang, knocked over
dargle, a river valley
daur, daurna, dauredna, dare, dare not, dared not
daurg, a day's work
dead-thraw, last dying agony
de apicibus juris, from the summits of the law
deave, to deafen, to annoy someone by constant talking
deboshed, drunk, debauched

declarator, in Scots law, a form of action by which some right or status is sought to be judicially declared
decreet, an authoritative decision of a court of law
deep-mouthed, having a deep voice
deevil, deil, de'il, devil; *deil speed the liars*—a quarrel
deforcement, in Scots law, the prevention by force of an officer of the law from carrying out his duty
delate, to accuse, denounce judicially, especially before an ecclesiastical court
delict, an offence committed with criminal purpose; quasi delict— an offence suggesting culpable negligence, though there may be no grounds for a criminal prosecution
depone, to give evidence upon oath; *deponent*—one who depones
deray, disorderly revelry
dernier resort, a last resort
desorienté, having lost all bearings
developed, unwrapped, disentangled
dike, a low wall or fence of turf or stone
Diligence, a stage-coach
diligence, in Scots law, a writ of execution; *first and second (letters of) diligence*—warrants to produce witnesses, documents, etc.
ding, to knock
dinna, do not
dirdum, blame, disagreeable consequences
dirk, a short Highland dagger
disna, does not
dittay, indictment
divot, a thin, flat turf used for thatching
dollar, a five-shilling piece, so called from its resemblance in size and shape to a dollar
dominie, a schoolmaster
dominus litis, in Scots law, a master of the lawsuit, one who backs the pursuer (plaintiff) and has control of the litigation
dool, grief, suffering
door-cheek, door-post
dooted, suspected
dottrel, a small plover, so named for the ease with which it is caught; a stupid person
doubt, suspect
douce, quiet, respectable, sedate
doun, down
dour, stern, severe
drap, a drop; *drappie*—a little drop; *drappie ower little measure*—a little drop too short
drappit egg, an egg poached in the gravy made from the liver of a fowl, or in water
drawing up wi', becoming friendly with
drouth, thirst
drucken, drunk
dune, done
dyvour, a bankrupt

East-Nook, a promontory of Fifeshire; *by the East-Nook*—a little deranged
éclat, notoriety
ecod, egad, a mild oath
ee, een, eye, eyes
e'en, even
e'en, evening
eke, addition, an additional drink
ele'en, eleven
elf-locks, tangled locks of hair
embonpoint, plumpness
en croupe, on the horse's rump
eneugh, enow, enough
Errickstane brae, a steep hillside at the head of the river Annan in Dumfriesshire
Esculapius, son of Apollo and god of medicine

even'd, compared, put on a level
evite, avoid, escape
examinators, examiners
ex comitate, out of courtesy
ex misericordia, out of compassion

factor loco tutoris, an agent acting in the place of a guardian
fain, gladly
fand, found
fardel, a bundle, a parcel
fash, to trouble
fasherie, trouble
fashious, troublesome
faulding, folding
fause, false
febrifuge, a medicine to reduce fever
feck, the, the greater part
fieri, [yet] to be made
Fifish, eccentric, cranky
finger in his mouth, wi' his, looking foolish, with nothing accomplished
fish, neither fish, nor flesh, nor salt herring of mine, neither one thing nor another to me, an expression registering unconcern
flaçon, a smelling-bottle
flambeau, a lighted torch
flee, fly
fleeching, flattering, cajolery
fling, to dance energetically, as in a country dance
flip, a mixture of beer and spirit, sweetened, spiced and heated
flit, to move, depart
flory, vain, showy
forby, besides
fore-bar, the bar at which advocates plead causes of first instance
forfoughen, exhausted, puffed
forgie, forgive
forleet, forsake
forpit, a measure, a fourth of a peck
fou, full
frae, from
freend, friend
free trade, smuggling; *free-trader*—a smuggling vessel
fristed, postponed, granted time, as for payment
fu', full, very
fugie warrant, a warrant issued by a sheriff to a creditor to apprehend a debtor on sworn information that he is contemplating flight, obtainable only in Scotland
fule, a fool
functus officio, having fulfilled an office and no longer having official power to act
fund, found
furs, furrows

gaberlunzie, a professional beggar
gae, gaed, gaen, go, went, gone
gae, gave
galloway, a small, strong horse, originally bred in Galloway in Scotland
gane, gone
gang, go
gangrel, vagrant; *gangrel body*—a tramp
gar, make, cause, compel; *gar him as gude*—pay him back in his own coin
gash, dismal
gat, got
gate, way, manner, road
gauger, an exciseman
gaun, going
gear, goods, property
gentle, well born; *gentles*—gentlefolk
gentrice, good birth, good breeding
gey, pretty, very
ghaist, a ghost
gie, gied, gieing, gien, give, gave, giving, given
giff-gaff, tit for tat
gin, if
girned, grimaced

glaiket, foolish, irresponsible
Glaramara, a mountain in the west of Cumberland
gliff, a moment, an instant
goud, gowd, gold
gowff ba', a golf ball
grana invecta et illata, grain brought in and imported
graned, groaned
grat, wept
gree'd, agreed
grillade, a broiled dish
gripe, grasp
grit, great; *grit oath*—a solemn oath
grossart, a gooseberry
groundsill, lowest timber, threshold
grue, to creep (of flesh)
grund, ground, estate
grund-officer, a bailiff, one who supervises the practical administration of the lands of an estate
gude, good; *the Gude Town*—Edinburgh
gudeman, goodman, husband, tenant of a small farm, and used as a term of address
gudesire, grandfather
gudewife, wife, mistress of the house, and used as a term of address
guide, deal with, treat
gumple-foisted, in an ill humour, huffed

ha', hall; *ha' door*—the main door; *ha' neuk*—a cosy corner beside the hall fireplace
had, hold
hadna, had not
hae, haena, have, have not
hafflins, half-grown, teenage
haill, whole
hailstanes, hailstones
hairst, an engagement for harvest work
halt, limp
hame, home
hanger, a short broadsword
hank, a hold, an influence, control
happed aff, skipped off, turned from
haud, hold
Haud obliviscendum, never at all to be forgotten
haugh, low ground beside a river
hauld, habitation; *house and hauld*—house and home
havers, nonsense, idle talk
havings, behaviour, manners
headborough, the head of a frank-pledge in a borough
hefted, settled, established
hegh, an exclamation akin to a sigh
hellicat, wild, irresponsible, crazy
hempy, a rogue
heritors, landowners in a Scottish parish liable to public burdens
hesp, a length of yarn
het, hot
heuck, a reaping hook
Hielandmen, Highlanders
hinnie, hinny, honey, a term of endearment
hirdy-girdie, topsy-turvy
hoddin grey, coarse homespun cloth made from a mixture of white and black wool
hoddled, waddled
homologating, in Scots law, rendering valid or ratifying an informal deed or contract by subsequent approval of it
hooks, off the, not quite right, crazy
hose-net, a small net like a stocking; hence figuratively, a position from which it is difficult to escape
host, I reckoned without my, I failed to take account of some important possibility, as the action of another
hout, an exclamation; *hout awa*—nonsense, get away with you; *hout fye*—an expression of dissatis-

faction; *hout na*—a strong negative
howlets, owls
hunks, a miser
hyson, a species of green tea from China

ignis fatuus, a delusive guide or ideal that leads one astray
Ilk, of that, of that same, i.e. of the estate of the same name as the family
ilk, ilka, each, every
ill-deedie, mischievous
ill-faured, bad-looking, ugly
in by, inside
in civilibus, in matters of civil law
in criminalibus, in matters of criminal law
in foro conscientiae, in the court of (before) one's conscience
in meditatione fugae, contemplating flight
in presentia Dominorum, in the presence of the law lords
instanter, forthwith (originally a law term)
intent, in Scots law, to institute legal proceedings
interrogatory, in Scots law, questions put to witnesses
intromissions, in Scots law, the transactions of an agent with the money or estate of his employer; *vicious intromitter*—one who assumes the management of another's funds without authority
I'se, I shall
ither, other

jackanape(s), a tame monkey, an impudent lad
jaud, a hussy
jazy, a wig
John Barleycorn, a personification of barley, especially when in the form of malt liquor
jorum, a large drinking vessel
jows in, tolls quickly to indicate that the ringing is about to end
junk, old and useless cable or cordage (nautical)

keek, a peep, a stolen glance
keepit, kept
keffel, an old or inferior horse
ken, kend, know, known, knew
kennel, a gutter
kirk, church, especially the Presbyterian Church in Scotland
kirk-road, a path used as of old by parishioners going to church, and so constituting a right-of-way
kittle, tickle; *kittled thairm*—played the fiddle
kittle, ticklish, difficult, risky
knights of the rainbow, liveried servants
knowe, a hillock

laigh, low, below street-level
laird, a landed proprietor
laith, reluctant
Lammermuir, a rural and highland area south-east of Edinburgh
lance, to spring
land, a group of dwellings or flats under one roof and having a common entry
landlord, (sometimes) the head of a family where one is a guest
land-louper, an adventurer, a vagabond
landward, in the country (as opposed to the town)
lane, his, alone, by himself
lang, long; *take a lang day*—to give long credit on a debt
lang-headed, discerning, sagacious
lang syne, long since; *auld langsyne*—the old times
lap, leapt
Lares, guardian deities of the Roman family
lave, remainder

lawing, a bill for food and drink supplied in an inn
leal, honest
leasing-making, verbal sedition, slander
leaven, the auld leaven, traces of the unregenerate condition (1 Corinthians 5: 6,7)
leddy, a lady
lee'd, lied
leesome lane, his, absolutely by himself
leevin, alive
limmer, a prostitute
ling, heather, or (in this context) coarse grass
loaning, an open uncultivated tract of land near a farmhouse or village, where cows were pastured and milked
lobsters, contemptuous name for soldiers, on account of their red coats
loe, love
Lonon, London
loon, a rascal
loopy, crafty, shifty
louis-d'ors, French gold coins, valued from 16s. 6d. to 18s. 9d. sterling
loup, lowp, leap, spring
loup-the-dike, leap-the-wall, wayward
loup-the-tether, escape-the-tether, undisciplined
Luckie, Lucky, a familiar term of address to an old woman
lugs, ears
lum, chimney
luncheon, a large hunk of food

Macer, an usher in the Court of Session
maggots, fancies, whims
mailings, rented properties
mails and duties, rents of an estate payable under lease
mair, maist, more, most
maist, almost
maister, master
mak, make
malversation, misconduct in office
manse, a Scottish parsonage
march, border; *the March*—the English–Scottish Border
mare magnum, vast ocean
mass-mongers, Roman Catholics
masterful, in Scots law, threatening or using violence
maun, maunna, must, must not
maut, malt; *the maut gets abune the meal*—said of one who is drunk
mear, a mare
memorial, a brief
menyie, a retinue
meridian, midday, when the midday dram of spirits was taken
merk, a mark, a coin worth 13s. 4d. Scots, 13⅓d. sterling
messan dogies, little dogs
Methuselah, a patriarch said to have lived 969 years (Genesis 5: 27)
mettle, mettled, spirited
mind, remember
minnie, infantine word for mother
miscaa'd, maligned
mischanter, mishap; *mischanter on*—the devil take
misguided, ill-treated
misguider, a wasteful person
mista'en, mistaken
moidores, Portuguese gold coins, valued at 27s. sterling and formerly current in Britain
month's mind, an inclination
mony, many
moon-calf, a mooning, absent-minded person
more solito, in the usual fashion
more tuo, in your own fashion
moulds, the grave
muckle, mickle, much, great
muils, loose slippers
muisted, scented
mull, a snuff-box

multiplepoinding, in Scots law, an action brought by or in the name of one holding funds to determine which of two or more claimants has a preferential claim thereto
mutchkin, a liquid measure, one-fourth of a Scots pint, three-fourths of an imperial, though commonly held equivalent to one pint imperial

na, nae, no, not; *nae less nor*—no less than
naebody, naething, nobody, nothing
naig, a nag
nane, none
napkin, a pocket handkerchief
neebor, neighbour
needcessity, necessity
needfu', necessary
negatur, it is denied
negotiorum gestor, a manager of affairs
neist, next
Neptune, Roman sea-god
ne quid nimis, nothing in excess
Nereid, a sea-nymph, daughter of the sea-god Nereus
nevoy, nephew
Newgate, a famous London prison
Nicol Forest, a Border township in Cumberland
nigri sunt hyacinthi, there are black hyacinths
nihil novit in causa, he knew nothing about the case
nipperkin, a small measure of liquor
Nith, the river on which Dumfries stands
nom de guerre, a professional nickname
nomine damni, under the head of damages
nonage, legal minority
Nonjurors, those refusing to take oaths of allegiance to post-Revolution (1689) sovereigns and so not qualifying for office or toleration under the act of 1712
noscitur a socio, he is known by the company he keeps
noviter repertum, more recently ascertained

o', of
Od, a mild oath
Ohe, jam satis, hold, enough now (a common Latin phrase)
omni suspicione major, above all suspicion
ony, any
origo mali, the source of evil
Orpheus, in Greek mythology, a celebrated musician and singer
orra, odd, occasional
ostler-wife, female keeper of a hostelry
o't, of it
ould Harry, the devil
ower, over, too
owrelay, a cravat
oye, grandson

Pace and Yule, Easter and Christmas
pack or peel, to have underhand or clandestine relations (with anyone)
Pande manum, stretch out [your] hand
paraffle, ostentatious display
parochine, a parish
par ordonnance du medecin, by doctor's orders
patria potestas, paternal authority
pawmies, strokes with a strap or cane on the palm of the hand
peel-house, a small fortified dwelling
Pegasus, in classical mythology, a winged horse, said allusively to bear poets in their 'flights'
pendente lite, during the process of litigation

pendicles, parts and pendicles, in Scots law, adjuncts and dependencies
per ambages, in a roundabout way (a phrase still used in forensic argument)
per contra, on the contrary
perdu, concealed, lying in wait
peruke, a wig
pessimi exempli, the worst of precedents
pettle, a stick for cleaning the earth adhering to a plough
Piscator, a fisherman
pike, pick
pistole, a gold coin, approximately valued at 17s. sterling
pit, put
plack, a copper coin worth four pence Scots and one-third of an English penny; *plack and bawbee*—to the last farthing; *plack-pie*—a pie costing a plack
plaited, interlaced with branches overhead
plea, plea wark, a lawsuit; *pleaship*—litigiousness
pleugh-stilt, a plough-handle
ploy, a party, a merry-making
pock, a bag
pock-pudding, a pudding steamed in a bag, a contemptuous name applied to the English
poinding and distrenzieing, in Scots law, terms for the impounding of goods to be sold in payment of debt
point d'Espagne, Spanish lace
pooin', pulling
ports, gateways, especially in the wall of a city
posse comitatus, a sheriff's levy of citizens to enable him to execute the law
pottle, a measure containing half a gallon
powdered, cured (of meat)
powder-monkey, a boy employed on board ship to carry powder to the guns
powney, pony
practiques, in Scots law, case-law, specifically the *Practicks*, collected by Sir James Balfour (1525–83), published in 1754
prawn-dub, a small pool in which prawns could be found
preceese, precise
precognition, in Scots law, a preliminary examination of witnesses as to whether there is ground for prosecution
precognosce, to take precognition of
presently, now, at this present moment (Scots usage)
presses, shelved cupboards
pretermit, omit
prick-the-clout, prick-the-cloth, a tailor
prie, to sample by tasting
process, the proceedings in an action at law, a writ
Procurator-Fiscal, in Scotland, the public prosecutor for a shire or district
production, satisfy the, in Scots law, to produce a document when challenged to do so in court
professor, an acknowledged adherent of some religious doctrine
provost, the chief magistrate of a Scottish town, equivalent to an English mayor
pu'in, pulling
puir, poor
pund, pound; *pund Scots*—one-twelfth of a pound sterling
pu'pit, pulpit
pursuer, in Scots law, a plaintiff

quaere, enquire (sing. imperative)
quean, a lass; *wench quean, queans o' lasses*—young girl(s)

Queensferry, the passage of the Firth of Forth, where the Forth Bridge now stands
quorum, a body of Justices of the Peace

raff, rabble
raid, rode
raise, got up
rambling, wayward
rampauging, raging furiously
rant, a noisy dance tune
ranting, romping, revelling
ratione officii, by reason of his office
rattling, rollicking, wild
raxed, stretched
reaming fou, full to the brim
redd, disencumbered, settled
reekie, smoky; *Auld Reekie*—Edinburgh
Regiam Majestatem, an ancient collection of Scots laws
reivars, bandits, raiders
remedium juris, remedy at law
remis atque velis, with all possible speed
rhino, money (slang)
riding days, the period of the Border wars and raids
rin, run
riped, searched
ripped up, disclosed, reopened
round, a projecting corner-turret in a building
rowing, rolling
rudas, an old hag
rue, taken the rue, repented
ruffling, looting, swaggering
rug, a cut, a rake-off
rumbo, rum, water, and sugar

sack-doudling, bag-piping
sacques, loose gowns fashionable in the eighteenth century
sae, so
saft, soft
sair, sore, very much
sall, shall
sangs, songs
sartum atque tectum, repaired and covered
sat est, it is enough
Saunders, a shortened form of Alexander
saunt, saint
saut, salt
Sawney, an old slang name for a Scotsman, from Alexander
sax, saxteen, six, sixteen
scauding, scalding
Scots mile, almost nine furlongs
Scots pint, three pints imperial
scowp, to bound, run hither and thither; *Deil scowp wi'*—Devil take
scrive, a piece of writing, a letter
sculduddery, sculduddry, obscenity, obscene
sealch, sealgh, a seal
secundum artem, according to the recognized rules of the art
sederunt day, a day appointed for a sitting of the law court
seenteen, seventeen
sell, self
semple, one of humble rank
shackle-bones, wrists
sheaf, take the sheaf from the mare, to put off a journey
shilpit, insipid
shoon, shoes
Short Roll, the roll of cases to be heard on a named day in the Inner House
sib, related to (by blood)
sic, such
Signet, Writer to the, a member of a distinguished body of Scottish solicitors
siller, silver, money
sine die, without a day appointed, indefinitely
sinsyne, since then

Sis memor mei, keep me in mind
skelloch, a screech
Skiddaw, a mountain in Cumberland
skill, have skill o', be experienced in
skinker, one who serves out drink
skirl, to scream, squeal
skivie, deranged
sleekit, smooth, unctuous
slip-string, deserving to be hanged, rascally
sloken, to quench
sma', small
sneeshing, snuff
snell, hard, severe
snow, a small sailing-vessel
societas est mater discordiarum, partnership breeds disagreements
soger, a soldier
solitaire, a large, loose silk necktie worn by men in the eighteenth century
sonsy, good-humoured, engaging
sort, put someone in his place, rebuke
sough, a strain, tune
soumons, summons
souple, agile, supple
souter's clod, a small loaf of coarse bread
Southrons, Englishmen
sowp, a spoonful, sip
speer, enquire, ask
speerings, information, news
splore, a spree, frolic, escapade, scrape
sprattle, a struggle
spring, a lively tune
sprush, spruce
spule-blade, shoulder-blade
spulzie, in Scots law, illegal removal of another person's goods
spunk out, to break out sporadically
spunks, matches, spills
Staneshaw-Bank Fair, held on the bank of the river Eden, near Carlisle
stend, to rear on hind legs
stewartry, the territory over which the jurisdiction of a steward extended in Scotland. The office was abolished in 1747
stibbler, a clerical probationer, divinity student (applied in ridicule)
stoup, a wooden drinking vessel, a liquid measure; *pint-stoup*—a vessel containing three pints imperial
stouthreif, stouthrief, in Scots law, robbery with violence (especially in a dwelling-house)
stunkard, sullen, obstinate
suddenty, of a, all of a sudden
suld, should
summary process, in Scots law, a term applied to such procedures as dispense with the full formalities of the law
sune, soon
supersede, in Scots law, to defer
surcease, a temporary suspension
suspension, in Scots law, a postponement of the execution of a sentence pending its discussion in the Supreme Court
swipes, small, thin, weak beer
syne, since, ago

tack, a lease
tae, the, the one
ta'en, taen, taken
taes, toes; *tae's-length*—a very short distance
tak, take; *taks leg from*—runs off from
talis qualis, of some kind; talis qualis *evidence*—in Scots law, it is evidence which is not such as is strictly demanded, but which may serve where there is goodwill
tam Marte quam Mercurio, as much a soldier as a pleader
tan, then

targets, light, round Highland shields
tass, a cup
tauld, told
tent, notice, note
thae, those
thairm, a fiddle-string
thegither, together
Themis, Greek goddess of justice
thereanent, concerning the matter already mentioned (Scots legal usage)
Thetis, a sea deity, daughter of Nereus and Doris
thirlage, an obligation imposed on tenants to take their corn to a specified mill
thof, although
threap, to persist in maintaining
thumbikins, thumbscrews
tikes, big dogs
till, to
timeous, well timed, timely
Tinwald, a seat in Dumfriesshire
tippenny, twopenny, weak ale, sold at twopence a quart
tither, the, the other
tithing of a barleycorn, the smallest possible amount
tod, a fox
tongue of the trump, the vibrator in a Jew's harp; hence, an indispensable person in a group
toom, empty
tour out, to look about one, keep one's weather eye open
town, (sometimes) a house and its outbuildings
tow-wig, a wig made from unspun flax
toy, a close-fitting linen cap with flaps hanging down to the shoulders, worn by elderly and married women
trances, passages within a house
trepan, to ensnare, trap
Triton, in classical mythology, a merman, son of Neptune
trolloping, ungainly
trounce away, to whisk away, take away at a swoop
trow, believe
truts! pruts! an exclamation of impatience
Tuptowing, beating, caning; literally, conjugating the Greek verb 'tupto', I beat
tutor, a guardian
twa, two
twalpenny, a shilling Scots, a penny sterling
twasome dances, Scottish country dances, danced in couples
tyne, go astray, lose one's way; *between the tyneing and the winning*—hovering between failure and success, in a critical state

ultimo, of last month
unchancy, not to be meddled with, dangerous
unco, unca, unheard of, strange, considerable, particularly; *unco wark*—an extraordinary fuss
unfreemen, men not having certain privileges, outlaws
uphald, uphaud, maintain
upsides with, even with, revenged on
usquabae, usquebaugh, whisky

Vale, sis memor mei, farewell, keep me in mind
verbum sacerdotis, the word of a priest
via facti, by personal act, by force
violer, a fiddler
vis animi, force of spirit

wa, away
wad, wadna, would, would not
wae, woe
wake, to keep vigil over a corpse
waling, choosing
walth, plenty
wame, belly; *the warst word in his*

wame—his most virulent abuse
wanchancie, wanchancy, ill-omened, unlucky
want, to do without, as in *could neither work nor want*
warding, act of, in Scots law, a warrant for imprisonment for debt
wared, bestowed
ware hawk, beware of, look out for customs men, soldiers, etc.
wark, work, business
warld, world
warrandice, an undertaking of safe keeping
warst, worst
wasna, was not
waur, worse; *come by the waur*—come off worst
weal, well-being
wears, weirs, fences of stakes set in a river for taking fish
wee, little
weel, well
weel-freended, having good or helpful friends
weel to pass, prosperous
ween, guess, imagine
weepers, white borders stitched to the cuffs of sleeves as a sign of mourning
weft, a flag knotted and hoisted in a particular fashion as a signal
weigh-bauks, scales
werena, were not
we'se, we shall
wet finger, with a, very easily
wha, who
whan, when
whare, where
what for no, why not
wheen, a few, several
whiles, from time to time; (as noun) occasions
whilk, which
whilly-whaw, flattering, insinuating
whilome, formerly
whin, furze
whisht, be quiet, hush
whittles, knives
wi', with
wife, (sometimes) woman
win, earn, get
windy, boastful, bragging
winna, will not
wipe, a taunt, rejoinder
withershins, anticlockwise
wot, know
woundy, extremely
wowf, a little deranged
wrang, wrong
wreath of drift, a heaped up snow-drift
writer, a solicitor
wud, mad
wunna, will not
wuss, wish
wynd, a lane leading off a main street

yauld, active, healthy
yelloch, a scream, shriek
yetts, gates
yill, ale
yowling, howling